The Tiger's Time

Chronicles of a Legionary Officer:
Book One: **Stiger's Tigers**
Book Two: **The Tiger**
Book Three: **The Tiger's Fate**
Book Four: **The Tiger's Time**
Book Five: **The Tiger's Wrath** (Coming 2019)

Tales of the Seventh:
Part One: **Stiger**
Part Two: **Fort Covenant**
Part Three: **Eli** (Coming 2018)

The Karus Saga:
Book One: **Lost Legio IX**
Book Two: **Fortress of Radiance** (Coming 2018)

The Tiger's Time

Book 4

Marc Alan Edelheit

The Tiger's Time: Book 4, Chronicles of an Imperial Legionary Officer

First Edition

I wish to thank my agent, Andrea Hurst, for her invaluable support and assistance. I would also like to thank my beta readers, who suffered through several early drafts. My betas: Jon Cockes, Nicolas Weiss, Melinda Vallem, Paul Klebaur, James Doak, David Cheever, Bruce Heaven, Erin Penny, April Faas, Rodney Gigone, Brandon Purcell, Tim Adams, Paul Bersoux, Phillip Broom, David Houston, Sheldon Levy, Michael Hetts, Walker Graham, Bill Schnippert, Jan McClintock, Jonathan Parkin, Spencer Morris, Jimmy McAfee, Rusty Juban, Marshall Clowers. I would also like to take a moment to thank my loving wife who sacrificed many an evening and weekend to allow me to work on my writing.

Editing Assistance by Hannah Streetman, Audrey Mackaman, Stephanie Mesa

Cover Art by Piero Mng (Gianpiero Mangialardi)

Cover Formatting by Telemachus Press

Agented by Andrea Hurst & Associates

http://maenovels.com/

This one is for those who serve!

AUTHOR'S NOTE:

Writing *The Tiger's Time* has been an experience of both joy and pain as well as a labor of love. It is the largest book I've written to date and is more than twice as large as *The Tiger's Fate*. I've also included concept art that was done prior to writing the book.

You may wish to sign up to my newsletter to get the latest updates. You can find it on my website at:

http://maenovels.com/

Reviews keep me motivated and also help to drive sales. I make a point to read each and every one, so please continue to post them.

I hope you enjoy *The Tiger's Time* and would like to offer a sincere thank you for your purchase and support.

Best regards,

Marc Alan Edelheit, author and your tour guide to the worlds of Tannis and Istros

Excerpt from Thelius's Histories, The Mal'Zeelan Empire, Volume 3, Book 2.

The Mal'Zeelan Imperial Legion
Pre-Emperor Midisian Reformation

The imperial legion was a formation that numbered, when at full strength, 5,500 to 6,000 men. The legion was composed of heavy infantry recruited exclusively from the citizens of the empire. Slaves and non-citizens were prohibited from serving. The legion was divided into ten cohorts of 480 men, with First Cohort, being an over-strength unit, numbering around a thousand. A legion usually included a mix of engineers, surgeons, and various support staff. Legions were always accompanied by allied auxiliary formations, ranging from cavalry to various forms of light infantry. The imperial legion was commanded by a legate (general).

The basic unit of the legion was the century, numbering eighty men in strength. There were six centuries in a cohort. A centurion (basic officer) commanded the century. The centurion was supported by an optio (equivalent of a corporal) who handled minor administrative duties. Both had to be capable of reading and performing basic math.

Note: Very rarely were legions ever maintained at full strength. This was due primarily to the following reasons: retirement, death, disability, budget shortages (graft), and the slow stream of replacements.

The most famous legion was the Thirteenth, commanded by Legate …

Post-Emperor Midisian Reformation

Emperor Midiuses's reforms were focused on streamlining the legions and cutting cost through the elimination of at least half of the officer corps per legion, amongst other changes.

The basic unit of the legion became the company, numbering around two hundred men in strength. There were ten twenty-man files per company. A captain commanded the company. The captain was supported by a lieutenant, two sergeants, and a corporal per file.

CONTENTS:

CONTINENT OF ILOSTA
WORLD OF ISTROS
NORTHERN REACH
KINGDOM OF THE RIVAN
CASTOL MALLARA
ELVEN LANDS
MOGUE ZETH
FORESTS OF ABATH
INLAND SEA
EASTERN OCEAN
SERTAL ZETH
THE WILDS
BARRENS
URA STEPPE
OCCUPIED SOUTHERN PROVINCES
SENTINEL FOREST
INDEPENDENT KINGDOMS
TEWAN
NARROW SEA
CYPHAN CONFEDERACY
CARTOGRAPHER:

Part One

Prologue

Cetrite dropped the scrubbing brush into the bucket. It landed with an unsatisfying plop and rapidly sank beneath the water to join its twin, which he had tossed in moments before.

"Here, take it."

Gnarled hands shaking with age, Cetrite handed the old, battered broom to Harig. The initiate took it, glaring disdainfully. Harig was but a youthful orc, just a few years short of the rut that signaled maturity amongst their kind. And yet, even now Cetrite could read the rage and chaos of emotion that the rut brought in the initiate's eyes. With a shudder of revulsion, Cetrite recalled his own rut and was grateful that it was behind him and buried along with so many other fading memories.

"You know," Cetrite said, slowly picking up the bucket handle, his joints crying out with pain. It seemed that with each passing winter, he became less mobile. "There was a time such attitude would have seen you beaten to within an inch of your life."

"Thankfully"—Harig spat into the bucket and then bared his sharpened tusks in a bold grin—"we no longer live in such times."

Cetrite took a deep, calming breath, free hand caressing the hilt of his athame. As a lowly rudimentary priest, his sacrificial knife had never tasted blood.

"You are right, it is a shame." Cetrite removed his hand and turned to go, shuffling out of the storage room. "In my youth, I would have beaten you myself."

Harig followed and chuckled darkly, the sound echoing off the stone walls.

Cetrite moved slowly through the winding passageways of the temple. So far underground the air was pleasingly cold. It was late and there were few about. For that little mercy, Cetrite was enormously grateful. His rank amongst the priestly order was low, just above the initiate class. He was also reviled by most—if not all—of the senior priests.

"We go to perform an important task," he said, sensing Harig's impatience at their pace. "Try to show some respect."

"If you mattered, old one," Harig said, "you would not have been sent to do an initiate's job."

"That may be so," Cetrite said with a cackle that sounded, even to his ears, slightly mad. "But it makes no difference. Our task matters. That is all I need to know."

"Scrubbing the altars clean?" Harig expelled a disgusted breath. "Please. You delude yourself, old one."

Cetrite eyed Harig a moment as they walked.

"No matter how large or small the task, by simply performing it, we honor our god," Cetrite said, the feeling of belief welling up within him. "I am proud to have dedicated my life to Castor."

"You have wasted your life," Harig snorted.

"Have I?" Cetrite's tongue flicked out to his shattered right tusk. He had broken it in his youth, fighting with another male. His tongue gently caressed the broken stump that was yellowed with age. "Have I really?"

"If you hadn't, you would have risen higher than a rudimentary."

"There is more to faith than priestly rank," Cetrite countered. "More than a simple pre-rut bull can know."

"Bah," Harig said and spat again, this time on the stone floor. "There is nothing worthier. Rank is everything. It brings one power."

"Priestly rank is nothing," Cetrite said, turning a corner and stepping out into the main corridor that led to the great worship hall. "Faith to Castor is all that matters. You are a fool to think otherwise, for faith brings its own power."

Harig made to reply, but then shut his mouth with a snap as two advanced priests rounded a corner ahead, moving in their direction. As they neared, both Cetrite and Harig lowered their heads and averted their gazes. They stepped aside, pressing their backs to the walls, permitting their seniors free passage.

"You should just die, already," one of the two said, stopping to look mockingly upon Cetrite.

"Soon enough, Karf." Cetrite felt nothing but loathing for his fellow priests, this one included. "Age will likely take me before long."

"Let him be," Erog, the other advanced, said. "You are wasting your time with this old fool. As he said, time will claim him."

Cetrite spared a glance at Erog. He saw barely concealed sympathy in the other's gaze. It stoked the fire of Cetrite's hate for these priests with their pretend faith. Though middle-aged, both Erog and Karf had played the game well enough to climb the priestly ranks. Cetrite had never felt inclined to do so. In Cetrite's mind politics had nothing to do with faith, and yet these two advanced priests held the power here, not him.

"Why let him be?" Karf demanded, looking back to Erog. "He is a disgrace to the order."

"Even so," Erog said. "It is late and I wish to eat before the kitchen closes for the night."

"You think too much with your stomach," Karf said, and turned back to Cetrite with a malicious look.

Cetrite knew what was coming. He set his bucket down so as to not spill the water he had drawn from the holiest of wells, the Deep Dark. He raised his gaze to lock eyes with Karf. These encounters always ended with some form of violence. There was no avoiding it, and so he embraced what was to come.

"I promise you, Karf," Cetrite said, throwing caution to the wind. "There shall be a reckoning between us, either in this life or the next. I swear it upon my faith."

Karf's eyes widened in surprise, as did Erog's. Cetrite sensed Harig stiffening in surprise at his side. A moment later Karf's fist lashed out and connected with Cetrite's jaw, slamming the back of his head into the wall. Another powerful fist to his stomach doubled him over, driving him to his knees. Pain exploded in his side as a kick rolled him over onto his back.

"Speak to me again like that…" Karf stood over Cetrite, rage mottling the green of his face. Karf's hand went to the hilt of his athame. As an advanced, his sacrificial blade had drawn blood. "…and I will send you on to our master."

"I hope you do." Cetrite gasped with pain as he pulled himself up into a sitting position. Wiping dark green blood from his mouth, he turned his gaze back to his tormentor. "My faith is firm. When the time comes for me to cross over, my lord will welcome me." He managed a bloody grin. "Perhaps he will even send me back to deal with unfinished business."

Karf straightened and actually took a step back, eyes narrowing.

"Come on," Erog said, grabbing at Karf's shoulder. "Don't listen to the old fool."

Karf hesitated. His eyes ran over Cetrite, and there was uncertainty in them. He was clearly weighing Cetrite's words.

"Remember what I said," Karf finally said. He turned and started walking down the corridor, Erog at his side.

Cetrite watched the backs of the two advanced priests.

"I always remember," Cetrite said, struggling to his feet. There was no help from Harig.

Cetrite gingerly felt his lip, which had split. Thick dark-green blood ran down his age-wrinkled hand. He was sure there would be some bruising. He tested his jaw. Nothing seemed broken, his few remaining teeth included. The back of his head was bleeding too, but not terribly badly, he decided, after gently touching the wound. He had suffered much worse than what Karf dished out.

"Not only are you old," Harig said, letting out a sigh, "but you are stupid as well. Life would be so much simpler for you if you conformed."

Cetrite considered the initiate, hating him as much as the others. Harig played the game, too. The youth would likely rise high amongst the ranks and lead a comfortable life, pampered even. All the while, Cetrite would live out the remainder of his days in obscurity and simplicity, seeking only the honoring of his god.

"You confuse stupidity with faith and strength of will," Cetrite snarled. "These petty diversions mean little to *my* lord. He cares nothing for such insignificant games."

"Our lord," Harig corrected.

"I wonder, is he? Truly?" Cetrite reached for the handle, once again picking up the bucket. He continued down the hall, shuffling a little slower than before. Castor taught that suffering was only an affliction of the mind, and as such, he did his best to put it aside. "Pain is only transitory, for faith and obedience are all that matter."

Harig grunted at the quotation from the holy books. He spared another disdainful look and then continued along the corridor, leaving Cetrite behind. The old priest followed as best he could.

The path to their destination was long. The two passed several chapels. All were empty. It was late. Even so, not much was different during the daylight hours. Few these days bothered to honor Castor. Cetrite recalled a time when these chapels had been full of the faithful, but now... He allowed a disgusted breath to escape slowly.

Like the priesthood, the flock had turned away.

The church was out of favor with the populace. Despite that, it wanted for nothing. Castor's temples and shrines were well maintained and cared for. Dues and tithings were still paid. It was either contribute your share, which in recent years had become burdensome, or fall under a poorly sharpened sacrificial knife. Where priests had once been welcomed and honored, they were now reviled and despised.

"Things should be different."

"What was that?" Harig, ahead, turned slightly. "What are you blathering on about now?"

Cetrite did not bother to reply as they entered the main worship hall. It was a vast space. The hall was arranged in the shape of a half oval with tiered stone benches for worshippers to look down upon the great black marble statue of Castor and the three sacrificial altars arrayed before it. Massive arches supported the ceiling high above, from which darkened candle-bearing chandeliers hung down on thick iron chains. During services, these chandeliers were lit and the subterranean hall was bathed in a yellowed radiance.

A few fires burned around the base of the great statue. These shed dim light outward and up to where Cetrite and Harig had entered the hall. As expected, there was not a soul about.

In all his years, Cetrite had never seen the worship hall completely filled. It had been made to hold twenty thousand orcs. On holidays, barely a third of that number bothered to attend. Even fewer were truly faithful. Most only paid lip service. How Cetrite longed for the day when the faithful returned.

"Let's get this over with," Harig said and started down the steps toward the altars. The initiate's voice echoed harshly off of the hall's walls.

Ignoring Harig, Cetrite took a moment to savor the view. He drew in a deep breath of cool air. The altars and statue of his god never failed to touch his heart. Naked, Castor stood tall, chest bare, muscles bulging. The god's tusks were bared as if facing an enemy. Castor held forth a great sword in one hand and a lantern in the other. The sword represented the god's strength and power, the lantern the light of faith, righteousness, and wisdom.

Legend told that once the lantern had shone with holy light. Now it was simply cold, black marble carved by mortal hands. The days of miracles and priestly medicine were gone. The flock had turned away from Castor, away from hope. And the great god had turned his back upon the people.

The scripture spoke of such miracles as being commonplace during the age of wonders, but today such things existed only in one's imagination and faith. Cetrite considered, not for the first time, that he had been born in the wrong time.

Breathing out slowly, Cetrite started down after Harig. The bucket sloshed water but never spilled. Harig waited impatiently for Cetrite to make his way down to the dais. When he finally arrived, he carefully set the bucket down and looked up at the statue of his god. With knees that protested painfully, especially so after his recent beating, he knelt upon the hard stone. He waited a moment, then looked meaningfully at Harig, who gave him an irked look in return.

"Kneel and pray," Cetrite demanded, though he should not have to remind the initiate. "Honor *our* god."

Resentful, Harig knelt and bowed his head.

Though he suspected Harig would not pray, Cetrite dutifully lowered his head as well and offered up a silent but brief prayer honoring Castor. He was about to rise, when he decided to add something.

"Lend me your strength, oh great god," Cetrite said silently, closing his eyes and mouthing the words. "These are difficult times. Though many have turned away, I have remained faithful. Help your poor servant through the last of his days. Give him the strength needed to serve you humbly and faithfully until you call him into your keeping."

When Cetrite opened his eyes, he found that Harig already stood. The younger orc reached into the bucket, grabbed one of the scrubbing brushes, and approached the nearest altar. Placing a supporting hand upon the cold stone, Cetrite stood slowly. He waited a moment until the pain in his knees subsided, then picked up the bucket and approached one of the other altars, the top of which was covered with dried candle wax. Setting the bucket down, he took the remaining brush and began working away the wax. Harig had already started and was brushing in short but vigorous strokes.

Cetrite felt honored to perform this task. In the very heart of the temple, here in this holy place, he felt closer to his god than anywhere else. Cetrite paused in his brushing and glanced up at the great statue. Down the marble blade of the great sword ran blood that had long since dried. It was as if Castor had slaughtered a heathen, making way for the faithful.

Cetrite's mood darkened at the sight of the blood. He had learned that in recent years the statue had been hollowed out. Hidden from view, a priest pumped animal blood into the statue during services, which flowed liberally out of drilled holes and down the blade, where some of it splashed upon the stone floor below. It was a simple design to impress the masses and yet, in Cetrite's eyes, it was an unworthy trick.

Cetrite bent his head and continued cleaning the altar. It was hard work and his hand began to ache terribly. Still, he kept at it, for a little suffering was nothing compared to the service he had been called to do for Castor, his lord and master.

"I'm done," Harig said, surveying his work. The altar Harig had worked on had been thoroughly cleaned of wax. He threw the brush into the bucket, where it landed with a splash, spilling some of the holy water onto the stone. "Since you feel so moved to do this grunt work, finish the last one."

"You should feel honored to be allowed to cleanse the holy altars," Cetrite said. "Though menial in nature, any small service we can perform is worthy in the great god's eyes."

"It is as I thought, then. You won't mind finishing," Harig said, tone reeking of satisfaction. "I am going to eat before the kitchen closes."

Cetrite watched sullenly as the other made his way up the steps and out of the great worship hall.

"You feed your belly," Cetrite hissed. "I will feed my soul."

He turned back to the task of cleaning and scrubbing free the wax, which seemed uncommonly stubborn. Later, he would use the broom to sweep up the drippings. The scraps of wax would be returned to the temple candle maker.

Cetrite dipped his scrubbing brush once more into the holy water of the bucket and then returned to his vigorous scrubbing. As he worked, he absently muttered scripture, something he had long since done. Cetrite found it not only calming to the mind, but also relaxing to the soul.

An hour later, Cetrite was done. He surveyed his work, feeling a sense of pride. All three altars had been thoroughly scrubbed clean. He had even gone and ritually scrubbed the altar that Harig had already worked on. The black marble of all three altars fairly gleamed. Cetrite felt renewed, as if the task had cleansed his soul as well. Around the altars lay the wax drippings. He dropped his brush into the near empty bucket and reached for the handle of the broom when he heard something from behind.

It was a soft scratching sound, as if some small animal was behind the great god's statue. Frowning, he scanned for the creature. In the dim light, he could see nothing. The fires illuminating the great worship hall had burned low, but truly his eyes were not what they had been. Cetrite let another breath hiss out. With age, he had lost much more than his youthful vigor.

He straightened up, prepared to investigate. It was not unknown for pests to get into the temple, but it was rare for them to penetrate this far. So deep under the mountain, there was no food to be had anywhere nearby.

The sound grew louder and the old priest realized that it was no animal. Someone was behind the statue. He scratched at his jaw, wondering if Karf had come to finally kill him. He fingered his athame. Did he have the strength to fend off the strong bull? Cetrite was no stranger to fights. He had won more than his fair share over the years. In fact, his broken tusk was a testament to a contest over a stronger male in which he had prevailed. There was more to winning than brute strength.

"Come out," Cetrite called. "Though my eyes are not nearly what they once were, I can hear you well enough."

"Can you now?" a voice hissed back in reply.

Cetrite's brows drew together. Though the words were easy to understand, the sound of the voice was alien to his ears. Cetrite abruptly shivered and realized with a start that the temperature in the worship hall had dropped considerably. A frigid draft of air blew around his feet. A slight mist rolled over the ancient stone.

What was going on here?

"You can hear me," the voice hissed from behind the statue, "now look upon me."

A dark form separated itself from the shadows and stepped into view, illuminated by the dying fires.

Cetrite's eyes widened. He dropped to his knees, barely even feeling the pain this time. He abased himself before the minion from his god. Like a tidal wave, emotion washed over him and he wept at the singular honor bestowed upon him by Castor.

"Thank you, my lord, my great, great god," Cetrite called with his forehead pressed against the cold stone that was growing more frigid by the heartbeat. "Long have I waited for your return. Long have I remained faithful. My life's work, my faith, my trust have been fulfilled. For that I thank you with all of my heart."

Cetrite could hear the minion move forward, one uneven step at a time. The cold intensified with its proximity.

Cetrite kept his forehead pressed firmly to the stone and began to pray.

"Are you faithful?" The minion moved even closer.

"Yes," Cetrite said fervently. "Though only a rudimentary, and not without sin, I have kept the faith as best I can, my lord."

"We shall see about that."

Cetrite felt a light touch upon the back of his head and immediately a great force pushed its way into his mind. His consciousness fled in terror as the minion sifted through his memories. The minion's power infused his being, and with the intrusion came indescribable pain. Cetrite had never felt such agony, but at the same time was elated, for he was being touched by a measure of his god's power. The minion was a direct connection to Castor. It was a holy disciple, and for that Cetrite felt singularly honored.

The old priest cried out in agony as the minion probed deeper. The pain, he told himself, was transitory, and so he endured it. At last the light touch upon the back of his head withdrew and the agony ceased. Silence followed. Cetrite cried unabashedly. These were not tears of pain, but of joy.

"The flock has wandered," the minion hissed with a terrible anger that Cetrite could almost feel. "Though I did not believe it, I have seen it through your eyes. My lord is disappointed. However, you spoke truth. You alone, lowly priest, remained faithful. For such devotion, and strength, Castor rewards you."

Cetrite felt another touch on the back of his head. Instead of pain, he felt a sense of warmth flow into him, diving deep into his soul. His aches and many pains vanished in a heartbeat. His mind became clear like it had never been before as the power of the god he loved with all his heart continued to flow into him. It was an exhilarating experience. Cetrite felt rejuvenated, reinvigorated.

The touch withdrew and the minion stepped back. Cetrite almost protested as the flow of power ceased. With the touch had come an intense joy, a direct conduit to his god. It had been severed and yet Cetrite found there was something else there in its place. He could sense it, deep down, something that had not been there moments before. It was the direct connection to Castor that he had wished for, a ball of warm energy that burned brightly amongst the darkness. He could touch it with his mind, and when he did, the power flared. He'd been infused with a measure of Castor's power. He had been judged worthy.

"Look upon me," the minion commanded.

Cetrite sat back on his knees and gazed upon the minion. Twisted as it was, it had clearly once been human. Castor's touch had turned it into something else, transforming it into something new, something beautiful to Cetrite's eyes.

"I have come from a different time to right a terrible wrong," the minion said. Cetrite's heart soared to new heights at this admission. "The High Father has sent an agent of evil, a human male, to keep me from accomplishing my task. He must be stopped. For this, I require your assistance."

"You have it, my lord," Cetrite said without hesitation. "My life is Castor's to command."

"Good," the minion said. "It is time for the Horde to return."

Cetrite felt intense joy at hearing those words. The scripture spoke of the Horde and the promise that came with its return. Nothing—no race, no kingdom, no other god—could stop the power and unity of the Horde. Like a great tide, the Horde swamped everything.

The minion dragged its gaze around the Great Hall, before it settled upon the statue of Castor. Cetrite felt that its eyes lingered on the sword with the dried animal blood. After several heartbeats, the gaze turned back upon Cetrite.

"It is time we restore the faithful to their proper place," the minion hissed, and Cetrite could almost taste the anger and rage infused with those words. "Tonight, we will purge the unfaithful from this temple before moving on to greater things. This night, your athame will finally taste the blood you so crave and it so deserves. With its use, you will be suffused with more of Castor's *will*."

How he had longed to hear these words. They touched his soul. Cetrite glanced down at the hilt of his sacrificial knife. His hand had strayed to the handle. Cetrite gave start, for the hand was not his own. The gnarled knuckles had straightened. The wrinkled and slack skin had tightened and smoothed out. The age marks were gone. He blinked in astonishment as he moved his arm. The muscles bulged, as they had in his prime. He felt his face and was astonished to find the skin smooth, taut and firm. The bruising and split lip that Karf had given him were gone, healed. His hand inadvertently brushed against his broken tusk and found it once again whole.

Cetrite's gaze returned to the minion. Castor had given him back his youth and strength. The great god had returned and Cetrite would do his utmost to fulfill his will.

The minion turned, moving over to the statue. It rested a hand upon the statue's leg. The hall was filled with the sound of a great crack that echoed loudly against the walls. This was followed by a bell tolling throughout the temple. Dust shook loose from the ceiling and filtered downward in a stream as the bell tolled again.

Cetrite tore his gaze from the minion to Castor's lantern. Incredibly, the black, lifeless marble began to emit a soft, pale blue glow. Within a handful of heartbeats the light intensified to a strong radiance. The entirety of the worship hall was bathed in holy brilliance. It was everything and more that Cetrite had dreamed.

The minion looked back upon the priest. "Together, we shall bring back Castor's *will* into this world. But first, as you have cleansed these altars, so too will we cleanse the unfaithful from these hallowed halls."

"Yes, my lord," Cetrite said and pulled forth his sacrificial dagger. He glanced in the direction that Harig had gone, licked his lips, and wondered whose blood his athame would taste first, Harig or Karf?

Chapter One

The night air was cool, and a serious improvement over the dank chill of the dwarven underground. Stiger rode in the back of the empty supply wagon as it bounced uncomfortably along the moonlit dirt road.

Stiger had drawn his legs up and held onto the side of the wagon, which seemed to hit each and every rut and pothole as it trundled slowly, almost painfully along. It was an uncomfortable and jarring ride as the two mountain ponies pulled him inexorably onward toward what would, he was certain, become his new prison. He would've gladly walked, but the commander of his dwarven guard had not permitted it. Instead he rode, while they marched the miles away.

Stiger rested his back against the teamster's box, his gaze on his guard. There were eleven dwarves marching behind the wagon, armed with swords and wearing the heavy armor that he had come to associate with dwarven infantry. A twelfth, wearing a simple tunic that appeared stained with drink and a tattered purple cloak, drove the wagon. Stiger suspected he was a civilian.

The pace was slow, but Stiger had nowhere to be. He had stepped back in time through the World Gate just a week before, and with that fateful step, his life, his purpose had ground to a halt.

The man he had come to save was dead. The minion had killed him before Stiger and Father Thomas had even arrived. Castor had won. It was that simple. With Delvaris's demise, the future would never be the same. He could not set things right in the past, nor could he return to his time. For the first time in a great long while, Stiger was without orders, without duty, and without a plan. No one required saving and no one needed killing.

Stiger smelled smoke. He looked to the left and in an overgrown field fifty yards away he saw a military encampment. His eyes took in the neatly ordered tents, the dwarves sitting around campfires, the sentries on duty. He counted thirty tents in all, which told him the military formation inhabiting the camp was at least company strength. The wagon continued past, slowly working its way one bump and jolt at a time farther down the road.

"Ho," the teamster called out unexpectedly. "Ho'up."

The wagon slowed to an unexpected stop. The ponies took an extra step, and the wagon lurched forward another two feet before stopping. This was followed by a light clunking sound as the teamster engaged the wagon's brake.

Stiger's guard detail were called to a halt. The commander of the guard stepped up to the back of the bed and motioned for him to get down. Stiger glanced around and saw to the front of the wagon what appeared to be a small farm. He estimated it was around two hundred yards from the dwarven camp they had passed. There were only two buildings, a medium-sized barn and what looked like a two-room farmhouse. Stiger also saw a chicken coop, springhouse, a pen for pigs and another for sheep. Yellowed light leeched out from the shuttered windows.

The teamster and commander exchanged a few words in dwarven that Stiger could not understand. Then the teamster gave a shrug of his shoulders and climbed down off the driver's box. He took a moment to stretch out his back and then stumped off toward the dwarven camp.

Stiger had assumed he was being moved to a new cell, but the dwarves had taken him out of the mountain and into the valley. He had asked where exactly they were going, but his guard did not speak enough common to make the answer intelligible, or more likely hadn't bothered enough to tell him.

Stiger noted several guards positioned around the farmhouse. They were looking in his direction.

"So," Stiger said to himself with dawning realization, "this is my new prison."

"You," the commander said in the common tongue, drawing Stiger's attention. The dwarf's accent was quite thick and harsh. Stiger did not know his name, but he was an older dwarf, with his neatly braided beard reaching down over his chest armor. He had an unforgiving and intolerant air about him. Under the moonlight, the gray of the dwarf's beard almost seemed to glow with a pale ethereal light. The commander placed his hands on his hips, before pointing at the ground with one hand. "You, come. Now!"

Not liking the dwarf's attitude, Stiger glanced around again, stalling. The bastard could wait until he was good and ready. The dwarf gestured impatiently for him to get out of the wagon.

The dwarf raised his voice. "You, come, now!"

Stiger doubted very much if the dwarf could speak more common than that. Stiger climbed slowly out of the wagon's bed and dropped onto the ground. He reached back in and grabbed the scabbard of his sword, slipped the strap over a shoulder, and settled the weapon in place. Stiger's hand came to rest upon the hilt, and he felt the comforting tingle run up his arm and into his body. The dwarf took a nervous step backwards. Several of the dwarves' hands slid to the hilts of their swords. By their grim expressions, they looked like they meant business.

Stiger removed his hand and held it up for them to see he meant no harm. He could not understand why they had let him keep the sword. The dwarves had taken everything else, his armor and all of his possessions, including his purse. They had left him only with his tunic, his boots, which were thoroughly worn out, and the sword. Thoggle had insisted he keep the sword with him at all times, saying it was dangerous to anyone else but him.

"You go," the dwarf said and pointed toward the farm. "You go, now."

"And if I refuse?" Stiger asked. He'd grown weary of being treated as a prisoner with no semblance of respect. For a week the dwarves had kept him locked in a cell under their mountain. His only visitor had been Thoggle, who had told him just how screwed up the future had become, and that had been on the first day of his confinement. How Thoggle knew this, Stiger wasn't certain, but he was sure it had something to do with Delvaris's untimely death. No one else had spoken to him or visited, other than to deliver bland, tasteless food and to remove his waste. Stiger took a step toward the older dwarf. "What will you do if I refuse, friend?"

"That would be an unfortunate turn of events," a gravelly voice said with a hint of amusement.

Stiger turned. Thoggle stood just to the front of the wagon. The wizard leaned heavily upon his staff and appeared thoroughly amused. Unlike the other dwarves, Thoggle was clean-shaven. Stiger spared a glance at his guard. They had shifted their gazes to the wizard, regarding him almost as warily as they did Stiger.

Stiger made his way over to the wizard. Thoggle was the last person he had expected to find here. The wizard's amusement slipped from his face and he said something to the commander, who shot Thoggle a scowl by way of reply. Thoggle waved him away and then turned his back on the guard, facing Stiger directly.

"I apologize for your treatment. Your keepers were given instructions not to talk or interact with you," Thoggle said. "In fact, the thane made sure to assign dvergr who did not speak your tongue, or at the very least whose ability to do so was limited."

"Why?"

"We can't have them knowing who you are or where you came from." Thoggle gestured at the farm behind them with his free hand. His other hand clutched at the staff. "We are moving you here amongst your own kind. You should find this place more comfortable and—er—pleasant."

Stiger's eyes briefly ran over the humble farm.

"I don't expect you will let me go?" Stiger asked, looking over at Thoggle.

"No," Thoggle said. "The thane has placed an entire company here for your protection."

"My protection?" Stiger asked.

"Your protection. You will be watched day and night."

"Why?"

"Because it is too dangerous to allow you to roam around with Rarokan at your side." Thoggle pointed toward Stiger's sword. "It is safer in your possession and you in ours."

"I see."

"Do you?" Thoggle asked sarcastically. "Had you not quarreled with the thane and questioned his legend, things would be less difficult for you. Your argument with Brogan nearly became physical. To satisfy his wounded legend, the thane could have challenged you. We are very lucky I was able to successfully intervene before things spun completely out of control, for Brogan has a terrible temper and an unforgiving nature."

Stiger felt himself scowl, recalling the heated argument with the thane, dwarven warriors pouring into the Gate room with swords drawn, Thoggle stepping between him and the thane. Father Thomas had grabbed his arm and pulled Stiger aside as the dwarven warriors surrounded the two of them. The thane had been spitting mad and so had Stiger.

"You have made it quite problematic, not only for yourself, but for me as well. The thane has become heavy-handed in his treatment of you. Should you ever be granted an audience, it might be best to remember you are in his domain and not your own. You do not dictate to the thane. His word is law."

"He should have let us chase after the minion," Stiger said. He still felt angry and bitter.

"There were two noctalum after the creature," Thoggle said. "I seriously doubt you and a paladin could have done better at chasing it down."

"You don't know that," Stiger said. "Now it's gone and on the loose. There will be trouble."

"That may be so," Thoggle said. "For now, you need no longer concern yourself about it. Castor's servant has left the valley."

Stiger wondered how the wizard could be so certain about that.

"Where is Father Thomas?" Stiger asked. He had not heard from or seen the paladin since the Gate room.

"He is where he needs to be," Thoggle said, "and you are where you need to be."

Stiger felt the rage bubble up. It took him a moment to get a handle on it. He glanced around the farm once again. If they meant to keep him here, he was sure there were much less pleasant places to be. Being out from under the mountain was a relief. Besides, if he wanted to, he could always sneak off. Eli had taught him how to move stealthily about. Studying the guards' positions around the farm, Stiger had no doubts he would be able to slip away some dark night.

"Before you consider absconding and making for the hills," Thoggle said, almost as if he had read Stiger's thoughts, "I placed a tracking spell upon your person. The thane insisted. Stray more than five miles from this spot and I shall know of it. More importantly, I will know exactly where you are. Trust me, you don't want me to come looking for you. Since I have personally intervened upon your behalf with the thane, I expect you to behave yourself. Do not make me regret having done so."

Stiger supposed he had been too transparent. He gave a reluctant nod of understanding.

"Now that we understand each other, I think it time to introduce you to your host." Thoggle turned and began moving painfully toward the farmhouse. He had a terrible limp and leaned heavily upon his staff with every step.

As Stiger walked with the wizard, he noticed the eyes of the guards positioned around the house upon him. They appeared just as unfriendly as those of the detail who had brought him here.

"The homeowner is a widow," Thoggle said, "and from what I understand a good and honest person."

Stiger said nothing as they neared the farmhouse. A deep and terrible sadness took hold. His life and everything he had known was done and over. He stopped. Thoggle stopped also and turned to look back at him, raising an eyebrow in question.

"Are you certain?" Stiger asked. "There is no going back? The future has been irrevocably changed?"

"One can never be certain about anything," Thoggle said, drumming his fingers on the worn wood of his staff. "You are a man out of his time and, as I've already told you, a paradox. I cannot open the World Gate to send you home. I am sorry for that. Truly."

The wizard turned toward the farmhouse and then hesitated.

"I would ask you not to speak of the future to anyone," Thoggle said. "Though I suspect much has been altered already, there may yet be the possibility to repair some, if not all, of the damage."

Stiger's gaze snapped back to Thoggle at that.

"I need more research to be certain," Thoggle cautioned. "I promise you I will make every effort to set things right. In fact, your paladin and I will be working on it together."

The news that Father Thomas would be helping was somewhat encouraging. Though Stiger thought Thoggle did not sound too hopeful.

"Ogg said I was only to speak of such things to you," Stiger said. "It is why I told you what had occurred prior to our stepping through the Gate."

"My future apprentice was wise to give you such guidance," Thoggle said. "By revealing details to anyone else, including the thane, you risk adding to the damage the minion has already wrought." Thoggle paused and then gave a half scowl. "You may do so only if you feel it is absolutely necessary. And in necessary, I mean life threatening necessary. Then you will tell me after. I will judge whether I must cloud and befuddle their memories. This is very important, especially if I am to even begin to attempt to set things right. Tell me you recognize the importance of such discretion."

"I understand," Stiger said, though in truth he could not see how things could get much worse, or what the wizard could do to repair things. Delvaris was dead and there was a minion of Castor out there. Stiger almost shuddered at the thought of such a dread creature on the loose, even if it had left the valley.

Creaking on hinges that were badly in need of an oiling, the door to the farmhouse swung open. Yellowed lamp light spilled out into the yard. A woman in her twenties, in a blue summer dress that had seen better days, stood framed in the doorway. She was a little shorter than Stiger, and somewhat on the skinny side. Her brown hair had been pulled back into a ponytail, opening up her face. She was no beauty, but far from ugly. Plain or just ordinary could be the best way to describe her. Her mouth was turned down in a shallow sort of frown that seemed somehow a permanent feature. Stiger read a deep sadness in her expression, but there was something else there, too. She held herself erect and in a manner that spoke of an inner strength and natural confidence.

"Ah, Sarai," Thoggle said. "I bid you good evening."

"Thoggle," she said in a voice that was firm. Her gaze shifted from the wizard to Stiger. "Is this the man you told me about?"

Stiger found her brown eyes were quite penetrating as she studied him.

"He is indeed. May I introduce Bennulius Stiger."

"It is a pleasure to meet you," Stiger said, offering her a slight bow. "Please call me Ben."

Her expression cracked a little and the frown lines around her mouth loosened a tad. Her eyes lingered upon his face. For some reason he could not fathom, Stiger suddenly felt self-conscious and almost reached up to the scar on his cheek. He had no doubt he was intruding upon her home, and him a rough and tumble soldier. It could not be a comfortable prospect for her to have him under her roof.

"I welcome you to my home," Sarai said.

"Since I will be imposing upon you," Stiger said, making a sudden decision, "I will work to earn my keep while I stay with you."

"That will be most welcome," Sarai said. "There is always work that's in need of doing on a farm."

"I am no stranger to hard work." Stiger thought she sounded far from convinced. He knew actions spoke louder than words and he would just have to show her.

"Well," Thoggle said, "I think you two should get on just fine. With that, I believe I will take my leave."

"I've put on a stew. It should be done shortly. Thoggle, would you care to join us for dinner?"

Stiger had not noticed before, but now that she had mentioned it, he could smell the delicious aroma of the stew on the air. The dwarven fare had been bland and overcooked. He felt the rumblings and stirrings of hunger at the prospect of a decent meal.

"As tempting as your kind offer is, unfortunately, my time is most limited," Thoggle said. "I have responsibilities elsewhere tonight."

"Another time, then," she said, sounding disappointed.

Thoggle gave her a half nod.

"Oh, one more thing," Thoggle said to Stiger. "Captain Aleric, in command of the company protecting you, will be by tomorrow to introduce himself. He was called away to consult with the thane. You can trust him. He is a good and fair officer."

Stiger gave a nod.

Sarai stepped aside and gestured for Stiger to enter. "Would you care to come in?"

He started forward but was arrested as the wizard reached out a hand.

"Remember what we spoke of." Thoggle looked at him meaningfully. "Discretion is best."

"I will remember," Stiger said and stepped into the house.

Stiger sat up and shook off his sleep. He cracked his neck and looked around, stretching as he did so. He had slept on the kitchen floor by the fire with a couple of blankets and an old pillow. It wasn't the worst place he had ever slept, but it was better than being under an open sky with nothing other than your arms for a pillow, or being in the barn with the animals. He had done that on occasion and it was never a pleasant experience.

The room was dark with early morning gloom. It was also quite cold. The fire had long since gone out. The stones still radiated heat, but not enough to make any real difference. Stiger looked around. The door to Sarai's room was closed. Before he had fallen asleep, he had thought he'd her heard her weeping softly. But in truth, he wasn't quite sure.

He stood and made his way over to one of the shutters and opened it. The hinges squeaked loudly. Stiger almost cringed, for he did not wish to wake Sarai. The sky was lightening with the first rays of dawn. He shivered as the cold outdoor air flooded in. He closed the shutter part way.

With a little bit of light, he cast his gaze around the kitchen. The first order of business was to restart the fire.

He laid on several fresh pieces of wood and spent some time rekindling the fire. He was rewarded for his efforts a little while later with a good blaze that snapped and popped in a satisfying manner. The fire rapidly spread its warmth throughout the small kitchen, beating back against the cold.

Stiger picked up the blankets she had given him, folded them neatly, and placed both on the table. He pulled a stool out from under the table and sat down. Stiger stared into the flames, thinking on all he had lost and left behind in the future. There would be no going back. That was certain. More than that, he was bothered by his failure to save Delvaris. It ate at him something terrible. There had been absolutely nothing he could have done to stop the minion from killing the legate of the Thirteenth Legion and yet, even knowing that, it troubled him. Ogg sending him back to this time had been a pointless effort.

The door to the bedroom opened and Sarai peered out.

"Good morning," Stiger said, standing. "I hope I did not wake you."

"I am an early riser," she said. "I've always been. Did you sleep well?"

Sarai moved into the kitchen and up to the fire, where she warmed herself. She wore the same dress from the night before. The original blue dye had faded considerably and the fabric appeared a bit threadbare. Despite that, Stiger thought it looked good on her.

"Yes, thank you," Stiger said and then hesitated. "I regret the necessity for imposing upon you."

"Think nothing of it," Sarai said. She waved a hand at him. "Truth be told, my life's been a little quiet of late. So this is a nice change. It will be good to have another pair of hands around to help manage the farm." She paused. "Would you care for breakfast? I am going to make some oatmeal."

"Yes, please," Stiger said. "Can I help?"

"You've already started the fire," Sarai said and placed a bucket on the table. "Would you mind drawing some fresh water from the well?"

Stiger crossed over to the door and grabbed his boots. He sat back down on the stool as he slipped them on.

"Those are in a sad state," Sarai said as he laced them up. "I'm good at mending things, but not boots."

Stiger glanced down and had to agree that his boots appeared quite sad-looking. They were badly scraped and scuffed up. Part of the leather was missing along the side of his left boot, and his foot could be seen underneath. The soles had also worn through in a number of spots. The useful life of his boots was rapidly coming to an end. They had been with Stiger so long that saying goodbye to them would be like losing an old friend.

"I used them hard," Stiger said. "They saw a lot of marching."

"You're a soldier?" She pointed at the sword in the corner. "Thoggle told me not to go near that. He said it was a dangerous relic from another age and only you should be the one to touch it."

Stiger must have scowled, for she suddenly looked away.

"I should not have pried," Sarai said. "Thoggle said not to."

Stiger became irritated with the wizard and decided to throw caution to the wind. She seemed honest enough. He would return that favor with candor of his own.

"Yes," Stiger said. "I am an officer in the emperor's service. Or at least I was."

"Mal'Zeel?" She said. "Until your legion arrived, Mal'Zeel was just a distant place that people spoke of occasionally."

"The Thirteenth is here?" Stiger asked, suddenly interested. "In the Vrell Valley?"

She nodded. "Their encampment is just a few miles away. I've even seen your legionaries at the market in Venera."

Stiger sat back on the stool as he considered what she said. After a moment, he decided it did not much matter. It wasn't his legion, but Delvaris's. Stiger's time as a soldier was over. He stood and grabbed the bucket and stepped outside. A dwarf standing guard near the door looked over and their eyes met. Stiger saw no warmth there, just wary caution.

Ignoring the guard, he started across the farm yard to the well. This was the first time he had seen the farm by the light of day. The barn had boards that were rotting away and the clay-shingled roof needed some serious attention. Everywhere he looked, from the pigpen to the chicken coop, the farm had a rundown look to it. He could readily see the rough patchwork Sarai had done. He glanced back to the house. It needed work as well. Stiger had learned it took a lot of labor to maintain a farm. Managing it by herself, it appeared as if Sarai was just barely holding on.

Stiger turned his attention back to the task at hand. A bucket was attached to a rope and sat on the ground next to the well. Using the rope, Stiger gently lowered the bucket down to the bottom, where he jerked it to get some water inside and then hauled it up. He repeated the process several times until the bucket Sarai had given him was full. He gazed around the farm once again. The planted fields were neat and well kept. Beyond that, weeds were nearly everywhere, with ivy even growing up the side of the barn. Ivy could be destructive.

He might be a prisoner, but at least he could make himself useful here.

Stiger walked back to the house and stepped inside, closing the door behind him. Sarai took the bucket and poured the water into a copper pot and then carefully hung it over the fire from one of the chains. She turned and looked back at him for a long silent moment. Oddly, Stiger felt somewhat uncomfortable and shifted his feet. He was suddenly reminded of his mother looking down her nose at him when he was a child. Stiger's mother had been a strong, stern woman, almost as unforgiving as his father. But she had given him one thing, and that had been her unconditional love. For that, Stiger would be eternally grateful to her, for he had not gotten any from his father.

"Last night, you did not come with anything other than that sword," Sarai said. "Will your things be arriving today?"

"I'm afraid this is all I have," Stiger said. "The dwarves took all I had. Though, to be fair, I did not come into their hands with any spare clothing."

"Well," Sarai said, "you look a sorry sight. Your tunic's dirty and quite stained."

Stiger glanced downward at himself and suddenly felt embarrassed. His tunic was still stained with dried orc blood. He would need to wash it.

"I have a spare tunic for you, along with pants," she said, moving by him and into the bedroom. As she passed him, Stiger thought he could detect the faint fragrance of roses on the air. He had known other women to use rosewater on their hair and had always liked the scent.

Sarai emerged a few moments later with a tunic and pants. She had also brought a pair of sandals. She hesitated a heartbeat before handing them over to Stiger. The tunic and pants were of poor-quality wool, but were well sewn and made. It would do.

"Off you go." She nodded toward the bedroom. "Time to change out of that dirty thing."

Setting down the sandals, he stepped into the bedroom and closed the door. Stiger slipped off his old tunic and pulled on the one she had given him. It fit well, though he found the wool a little itchy. He pulled on the pants, which were also a close fit. Stiger tied the ties tight, then returned to the kitchen.

Sarai stiffened at the sight of him. Her hand went to her mouth as her eyes brimmed with tears. She half turned away to conceal her grief.

"This is your husband's, I take it?" Stiger asked.

Sarai nodded.

"He caught the fever last winter." She paused. It was clear to him her husband's loss was still an open wound. "He was gone before I knew it."

"I'm sorry," Stiger said.

"So am I." She cleared her throat and wiped her eyes before handing him back the empty bucket. "Would you mind gathering some eggs from the hen house?"

Stiger took the hint and stepped outside. The same dwarf was still there. Their eyes once again met. Stiger shot the dwarf a wink and started off toward the chicken coop. As he walked, he looked around the farm, making a mental list of what he wanted to accomplish this day.

Chapter Two

Stiger hammered away, driving the nail in while the dwarf held the board securely in place. He pulled the last nail from between his lips and hammered that one in too. Stiger and the dwarf stood back and regarded their work. The old rotten sideboard lay on the ground behind them, along with ten others just like it.

"It looks good," Stiger said to the dwarf, whose name he had learned was Geligg.

Geligg nodded his satisfaction with their work and said a few words in dwarven. Unable to speak common, Geligg understood hand gestures well enough. When Stiger had asked for his help, the dwarf had readily set his shield down and without hesitation lent a hand.

Stiger was pleased with his work. The barn looked much improved and had lost its dilapidated look. Well, some of it. With Captain Aleric's approval and an escort, he'd scavenged the wood for the repair from an abandoned farm a mile away. He had learned from Sarai that the family that had lived there had died from fever a few years back. The barn had been old and decaying. The locals had picked over the farm rather thoroughly for any usable material, but Stiger had managed to scavenge ten good boards from what was left of the barn and another twenty from the house for siding.

"When I was ordered to take my company here to watch over you, I had not envisioned my boys being pressed into manual labor."

Stiger turned to see Captain Aleric standing just behind them. The captain was also studying their work. Geligg immediately straightened to a position of attention, shooting his captain a guilty look. Stiger could readily sense the dwarf's unease.

Aleric was wearing a simple tunic and cloak. The cloak's pattern was green, yellow, and brown. He carried a sword that was a little longer than a legionary short sword. The captain's brown hair had been close cropped and, along with his temples, his beard was beginning to gray. There was a sternness and correctness to his manner that spoke of a professional soldier confident in his ability. His arms and hands were nicked with tiny scars, a sure sign of a lifetime of arms training.

"Do you mind me borrowing them occasionally?" Stiger asked, glancing over at Geligg. He hoped he'd not gotten the warrior in trouble. "There is a lot of work and your boys are just standing around all day watching me. It can't be very exciting work."

Aleric spoke in dwarven to Geligg. It sounded like an order, and sure enough, the warrior grabbed his shield and stepped away, resuming his assigned position a few feet from them.

"Exciting is something we experienced soldiers tend to avoid," Aleric said.

"Too true," Stiger said. "Boring is better, but at the same time a busy soldier is one who doesn't get into trouble."

Aleric gazed around the farm. "You've been here just two weeks and this place already looks much improved."

Stiger placed his hands on his hips and surveyed the farmyard. Yes, it had only been two weeks, but it somehow seemed longer. The farmyard looked vastly different. Stiger had first cleaned up the yard before starting work on the barn and house. He'd uprooted all of the weeds, which had gone right onto the compost pile. Then he had begun removing anything that had been lying around. That included stones and old farm equipment that had long since served its purpose and was now simply junk. Sarai had helped him with most of it, silently toiling at his side. He wasn't accustomed to working alongside a woman, but this was her place. Who was he to tell her no?

"Orderly is better, don't you think?" Stiger asked Aleric. He had also stacked the firewood, which had been left in a pile by the splitting stump. This morning he had made it his job to work on the exterior of the barn, replacing worn-out and rotted boards.

"I do," Aleric said.

Stiger glanced over at the barn, thinking on what needed to be done. He next planned on organizing and cleaning out the interior before starting work on the roof. According to Sarai, it leaked badly. He also wanted at some point to repair the pasture's fencing, which was a mess. That was a big job and Stiger wasn't looking forward to it.

"Sarai was kind enough to put me up," Stiger said to Aleric. "It is the least I can do for her."

"That is very noble," Aleric said, turning his gaze from the farmyard back to Stiger. "You gain much legend from helping the widow. My boys can assist you if they wish. However, I want to be clear. They will not do the work for you."

"I would not expect them to," Stiger said, fully understanding the captain's position. "I will only ask for their help when I need to. Otherwise I will do the work myself. Is that fair enough?"

"Most," Aleric said and then got to the business at hand for his visit. The captain only came by when he had business to discuss. "I will be sending over one of my boys tomorrow."

"Oh?" Stiger was curious as to why.

"I thought it might be good for you to learn our language," Aleric said. "It will help you to get to know and appreciate my people better. Perhaps it may also save on any potential misunderstandings, if you get my meaning."

Stiger gave it a moment's thought. He had nothing pressing, only the farm work to occupy his mind, which on most days was quite troubled. He decided it would be a good diversion, and also at the same time would bring a convenient extra pair of hands for jobs like the barn. "I think I'd like that. Captain, I accept your generous offer."

"Very good," Aleric said. "His name is Theogdin. He will be over sometime after dawn."

"Is he on punishment detail?" Stiger wondered if Aleric was sending him his problem child.

"He should be, but no," Aleric said. "Theogdin is one who needs to have a something to do or he gets himself in trouble. He also speaks common, which should help with your instruction."

"I will do my best to keep him busy for you," Stiger said.

Aleric gave him a satisfied and somewhat pleased nod.

"Good day," Aleric said and moved off toward the dwarven camp. Geligg relaxed a fraction after his captain passed. He puffed out his cheeks and shot Stiger a relieved grin.

Sarai exited the house a short while later. She walked over to him and examined his work on the barn. She smelled of freshly baked bread. The smell of it had been on the air all morning.

"It looks good," she said, glancing over at him and crossing her arms. "When my husband and I came to live here, the house and barn were already a wreck. It took a lot of effort getting the house livable. We never quite got the barn where we wanted it. My husband wasn't very good at making repairs, but he was a good farmer and taught me to tend the fields."

Stiger had to agree that Sarai knew what she was doing when it came to farming. There was not a weed in either of her two fields. She was growing potatoes, lettuce, carrots, and peas, which for her were all cash crops. When the harvest came, Sarai would sell them at the market over in Venera, the nearest town. Each field was neat and orderly, with the first shoots of the planted crops having spouted.

Even her personal garden was exceptionally tidy. Sarai had a wide variety of vegetables planted. From this she would provide herself food for the coming summer and fall. Some of her produce would be jarred or stored for winter in the springhouse behind the barn.

"One thing the legions teach you is how to construct buildings," Stiger said. "Once you learn that, you can easily do maintenance, and that's all the barn was needing. I will give the interior and roof some love over the next few days."

Sarai turned to him and her brows drew together.

"I wanted to..." Sarai stopped. She began again. "I'm grateful for the work you've done."

"You're feeding me and putting a roof over my head. The least I can do is help you out."

"It's more than I expected," Sarai said. "The bread should be done soon, but I've got some time. What are you planning to do next?"

"Well," Stiger said, pointing behind them. "I'm gonna carry these old boards over to the woodpile. In a few days,

I will get around to breaking them up. We can use them in the fire."

"Sounds good. Let me help you carry them over." Sarai bent down and picked up one of the heavy boards.

Stiger almost smiled. She was a hard worker and never seemed to stop. Even after sunset, she frequently kept working by candlelight, sewing, mending things, or preparing food for the next day. Sarai had a fierce, determined spirit. It was something he could well appreciate and respect.

For much of the work he'd done, Sarai had toiled alongside him, only retiring to the house to prepare food for the two of them. Stiger was a terrible cook, and knew that was being kind. Cooking was one thing the legions had failed to teach him. As an officer, it was a simply a skill he never needed to learn.

Sarai, on the other hand, was an exceptional cook. She'd even taught him how to make bread, and Stiger had thoroughly enjoyed the experience. She had promised to teach him how to make oxtail stew. He was looking forward to that.

Stiger watched her for a moment as she carried the board away. She had an inner beauty that shined forth in her attitude and approach to life. He bent down to pick up a couple of the old boards and started after her. Together they moved all ten boards over to the woodpile. As Sarai was tossing down the last one, she grabbed at her hand.

"Bleeding gods," Sarai said, examining her hand.

"What is it?"

"A splinter is all," Sarai said with a frustrated breath, "a large one, too."

"Let me see." Stiger stepped closer and took her hand in his. The skin on the top of her hand was soft, smooth, and warm. Her palm, when he turned it over, was hard and calloused from a lifetime of manual labor. His own palms looked the same, but that was mainly from sword and shield work.

"That's a big splinter," Stiger said, looking at her palm. Using his nails, he carefully drew out the sliver of wood. She did not flinch, nor look away. A small bubble of blood appeared as he took out the last of the splinter. When he was satisfied he'd gotten it all, he looked up to find her eyes searching his face. Their eyes met. She blinked, as if he'd caught her doing something she ought not, and pulled her hand back. She sucked at the wound, eyeing him for a moment more with an inscrutable look.

"I need to check on the bread," Sarai said and left him, walking quickly to the house. He followed her with his eyes as she made her way back inside. The scent of fresh bread mixed with rosewater remained behind.

Stiger set the shovel down and wiped sweat from his brow. The sun from the warm spring day beat down upon him. The last few weeks had seen the temperature increase almost daily. It was so hot he had brought a bucket of water with him. Sarai had loaned him a large wooden ladle, which he dipped in the water and brought to his lips, drinking it dry. He dropped it back into the bucket, where it landed with a soft splash.

Stiger had finished his work on both the house and barn before turning his full attention to the pasture's fencing. Much of it had deteriorated badly, which meant Sarai's horse and cow could not properly graze for fear of having them wander off. She had resorted to tying them to the fencing that was still sturdy enough to hold them. She used a long rope, which allowed them to graze somewhat. Unfortunately, this was not a satisfactory solution, for both animals regularly got themselves tangled.

A good number of the fence posts were rotted, and in places the fence had completely collapsed. Others had shifted with the ground, leaning at odd angles, and needed work to be righted. When he started the project, Stiger estimated that twenty-five posts would need to be dug up and replaced. That did not count another twelve that required resetting. At the time, that had not sounded too bad. It turned out to be a very difficult job. Before digging out a post, he had to dismantle the fencing around it. This took a lot of time. It required careful attention, so the good pieces could be reused when he rebuilt the fencing.

Stiger waved away a fly and glanced down into the hole he was digging around the post. He had spent the last two hours digging and he'd only managed to remove five posts. The day had turned very warm while he'd been at it. Combined with his exertions, he was sweating like a farmer's prize pig fleeing a predator. Stiger stripped off his tunic so that he wore only his pants and sandals. Shedding the wool tunic brought a modicum of relief. He returned to his digging.

A cloud interposed itself between the sun and the land. With it, Stiger's mood abruptly darkened. He'd been at the farm for four weeks now. He still felt terrible about Delvaris. Stiger had dedicated his life to service and the High Father, but everything he had worked toward was now gone, stripped away with a simple step through the World Gate. That was a difficult thing to accept. But the more time he spent at this farm, the more he had come slowly to accept his fate.

The dwarves seemed unable to decide what to do with him and so he remained their prisoner. He was a man out of his time.

He resumed digging, tossing aside one shovel full of dirt at a time as he worked his way around the post. purposely made sure to keep himself busy. He worked from near sunup to sunset. The work helped to ease the frustration with his current situation. But it gave him plenty of time to think, and that was a curse, too. In truth, it felt good to be doing something, anything. That he was helping someone else besides himself made the burden he bore just a tad easier.

Sarai was really the only reason he'd not gone mad with rage at his predicament. He'd been surprised to find he enjoyed her company. She seemed to enjoy his as well. Sarai was the only bright point for him.

They both in a way were shattered people with deep hurts that cut to the soul. Late at night, he heard her occasionally weeping for her husband. Stiger had been tempted to go to her to offer what comfort he could but did not want to intrude upon her grief. No matter how much he wanted to, he felt he did not know her well enough to take such liberties. It pained him to listen to her.

Grief could be intensely personal, and he'd tread carefully whenever the subject of her husband came up.

Stiger put the shovel aside as the post tilted a little and shifted to the left slightly. He reached down and first pushed, then pulled, jerking it back and forth to loosen the post up, at first straining to free it. The ground did not want to give up the post. He pulled harder. The post resisted a moment more, then came fully free. Breathing heavily, he dropped it on the ground, where it landed with a thud.

"How's it going?"

Stiger looked up and saw Sarai crossing the field to him. A gentle gust of wind stirred the waist-high grass in waves, rippling around her as she closed the distance. Stiger wiped sweat from his brow. The breeze was a nice relief to the heat.

"As well as can be expected," Stiger said as she neared. "These posts are proving more difficult a foe than I had anticipated."

She came to a stop to his front. "It will be nice to let the animals graze freely and not have to check on them throughout the day. Untangling Misty is tricky work. She gets impatient and likes to kick."

Misty was Sarai's horse. She used her to ride to market once a week. Sarai was quite fond of the animal, setting aside time each day to brush her down or go for a short ride. She loved the horse, and as far as Stiger could tell, the horse was quite fond of her, too.

"If we don't get them out here grazing," Stiger said, "this pasture will become thoroughly overgrown with brush. Then we'll have a heck of a time clearing it. I've already seen a few saplings I will need to pull up."

Sarai glanced around the pasture and gave a slow nod. "Once we get them both out here, they should make quick work of the grass."

"There were several good-looking posts at that farm where I got the boards for the barn," Stiger said. "In a day or two I will head over and bring a few back. Once we have them, it should be a day or two of effort, maybe a little more, before the pasture is fully enclosed."

Stiger leaned down to the bucket and grabbed the ladle for another drink. Out of the corner of his eye he saw her stiffen. Suddenly uncomfortable, Stiger straightened. She moved around, first to his side, craning her neck for a better view of his back, and then stepping fully behind him. He closed his eyes and shook his head slightly. He should have thought better than to remove his tunic.

"Dear gods," Sarai gasped.

"The gods had nothing to do with it," Stiger said, on guard and angry with himself for not thinking. The last thing he needed was to frighten her. Sarai likely thought him a criminal.

He felt the light touch of her fingertips upon his scarred back and flinched as if the contact were painful. It had surprised him, was all. She pulled her hand back and then returned it.

"Who would do such a thing?"

Stiger turned to look upon her and saw the horror in her eyes. Her gaze shifted from his face to his chest. A finger reached out to one of the larger scars on his breast. She traced its puckered surface. He had gotten that in battle while serving with Third Legion, just before he'd come south. Then her hand went to his face and her index finger tentatively touched the scar Sergeant Geta had given him.

"You've been through a lot." There was a tenderness in Sarai's expression and eyes that Stiger had not expected.

"Yes," Stiger said gruffly.

"You've suffered. I can see it in your eyes."

Not trusting himself to speak, Stiger gave a slow nod.

"Your back. Who did that to you?" Sarai asked when he did not answer, allowing her hand to fall to her side.

"A man with no honor scourged me," Stiger said. The thought of it kindled his anger. But at the same time, he found the look in her eyes surprising. What he saw there wasn't fear or loathing, but something else. The horror was not directed at him but what had been done to him.

"Why?" she asked, her gaze locking with his.

Stiger took a deep breath. He had not spoken on this for many years and suddenly found it was almost too painful to do so. And yet, he could not help but answer her. Something urged him on, almost as if deep down he wanted to get the burden of the injustice off his chest. Looking into her deep brown eyes, he felt he could tell Sarai anything.

"A man under my command committed a crime," Stiger said, his voice harsh with the emotion of memory. "After investigating, I thought him innocent. He wasn't, but I didn't know that at the time. The evidence against him was circumstantial at best. I set him free. That should have been the end of it."

"But it wasn't," she said.

"No. The general in command of my legion learned of it. Regardless of the evidence, he wanted the man punished. I protested and was overridden. The general desired to make an example of my man. For the scope of the crime, the punishment prescribed was cruel, and unjust. It was all designed to get to me because the general and I have a not-so-pleasant mutual history. He wanted to embarrass and cause me grief. To do that, he ordered three hundred lashes of the whip. Such punishment typically cripples those few who manage to survive such an ordeal."

Stiger fell silent a moment as he recalled that fateful time so long ago. He could still feel the first few searing blows that had landed on his back, almost wincing as if it had just happened. He looked into her eyes and saw Sarai was intensely focused on him.

"When the day came to administer punishment, I offered to take the man's place."

Her hand went to her mouth and her eyes widened. "And this general accepted?"

"He did," Stiger said. He had planned on one day having a reckoning with Lears, but the opportunity had never presented itself. Now, he knew it never would.

She moved around behind him again, to gaze upon his back. Stiger felt her palm touch his back tenderly. Once again, he could not help but flinch.

"Does it hurt?"

"It itches on occasion," Stiger said. "But no. It no longer causes me pain."

She put a hand on his shoulder and turned him around to face her. She was very close. Stiger could smell the rose-water over the aroma of the fresh soil and grass he had dug up. It was intoxicating.

"Where I come from," Sarai said, "only slaves are punished in such a manner. How did you survive this?"

"A friend of mine nursed me back to health," Stiger said, thinking on all Eli had done for him. "It took months, but he managed it, just barely. I caught a bad fever and almost died."

"He must be a very good friend."

"The best," Stiger said, his throat suddenly thick with emotion. "I expect I will never see him again."

Their gazes remained fixed and both fell silent. Stiger found her brown eyes deep and compelling. He abruptly took a half step forward, grabbed her about the waist, and pulled her against him. He kissed her, pressing his lips against hers. He shocked even himself by the move, which was wholly spontaneous. She stiffened and he feared she would pull away. Then Sarai relaxed, as if the air had left her body. Stiger felt her kiss him in return as she gave into it, her lips soft and warm against his. Her mouth opened and their tongues met and explored. Stiger lost himself in that kiss and sensed the same from her.

After a long moment, Sarai pulled away from him and placed both hands on his chest, while her eyes searched his face. She pushed slightly and Stiger reluctantly released his hold upon her hips.

Stiger realized his attraction to her had been growing slowly, day after day, but he'd been blind to it until this very moment. His heart was hammering away. She had an indefinable inner beauty and goodness that radiated forth. He was drawn to it, like a moth to a flame. He recognized that now. This attraction was something he'd not felt for a very long time, and yet with Sarai it was something more, something different. They were kindred souls. Both had suffered terribly. Perhaps it was that suffering that had brought them both together. He was rocked by the realization of how he felt. He had thought her simple and uneducated, but she knew more of the world than many of the nobles in Mal'Zeel. Her face, which had once seemed plain and ordinary to him, was lovely. Her eyes were bright and her cheeks were flushed. In that moment, Stiger desired no one else but her.

She took a breath that shuddered.

"Losing my husband almost broke me," Sarai said and touched her heart. "I lost my daughter soon before. She had just turned two. I can't tell you the pain."

Stiger blinked. He had not known she'd had a child. The silence between them stretched. He was afraid to speak, lest he break the spell between them.

"I was a whore," Sarai said and her voice took on a hard edge. "That is what I am, a whore. You need to understand that before you take this any further."

Stiger had not been prepared for such a revelation. He was at a loss for words.

"My mother sold me into prostitution when I turned fourteen. It was awful, terrible. When I was able to escape, I fled and then I met this wonderful man, a slave. He was a common field hand. We came to Vrell, two runaway slaves looking for safety, and the dwarves let us into the valley.

They gave us this farm. All they asked in return was a tenth of our harvest."

Sarai gave a sob, a tear running down her cheek. Stiger wanted to reach out and wipe it away, but he restrained himself. He did not want to interrupt her as she bared her soul to him.

"It was perfect, a dream compared to the life we'd known, and then the only two people in the world I loved died." She paused, glanced down toward the ground before looking back up at him. "I have no family, no one to care for me. My nearest friends live in town and they're only acquaintances to whom I occasional sell produce. After my husband and child passed I had no one. I still have no one."

She fell silent. Nothing Stiger could say seemed appropriate, so he waited for her to continue.

Sarai gestured around them as tears brimmed her eyes. Her hands shook slightly. "Then you come. The dwarves dump you on me. They offered gold to take you in. I have no money to speak of. Thoggle said you are a man of noble birth who had suffered, a great leader of men who had lost everything and everyone he cared about." Sarai's words came out as a torrent, as if the floodgates had opened. "He said you were someone who needed to be hidden and my place was perfect. How could I turn away someone who had suffered so? How could I take his money? I refused but took you in." Her look hardened. "I will never sell myself to anyone again. I thought you would just lie around all day, but no." She tapped his naked chest with a palm. It was almost a slap. "You went to work fixing this and that. You threw everything you had into it." She paused and choked back a sob. "You a noble and me just a common girl, a whore. You should not want me."

Sarai had said the last with such self-loathing that it tore at Stiger's heart.

"I am a killer," Stiger replied, almost shocked by the admission of his own words. "I've ordered countless men to their deaths. I've killed and murdered with my own hand, all in the name of service, the empire, and the High Father. You are a whore. I ask you, what does it matter in the end? I am a killer."

"Thoggle told me you were a good man. Such a man wouldn't want me." Sarai said the last in barely more than a whisper.

"I do want you," Stiger said, and with those words, he knew it to be completely true. She was the one he wanted.

"Despite being faithful, the gods have cursed me for my sins and have taken both my husband and child. I'm not worthy of your attention."

"You are, and I don't care what you were," Stiger said and took a step toward her. She stepped back, as if afraid of his touch.

"What happens when you go? Besides fixing up the farm, what mess will you leave me with? I will be alone again. Tell me. I can't bear to lose someone else I care for."

Stiger found he had to clear his throat before he could speak.

"I don't think I'm leaving," Stiger said. "I can't ever go home. My noble birth no longer matters. Who I was is done and over. I've lost everyone I care about. There is nothing to go back to. My life as a soldier, as a killer, is over. The dwarves just don't know what to do with me, which is why they put me here."

Her brows drew together and the frown lines around her mouth deepened. Her gaze was just as piercing as it had been the night they'd met. It was as if she were trying to divine whether or not he was lying to her.

"I'm—" he started to say, but she put a finger to his lips. Her touch was unexpected.

"Don't," Sarai said and it came out a half sob. "Don't say anything more. Don't ruin it."

Stiger reached up and took her head in his hands and drew her close. He kissed her again and she responded. It was long, passionate, heartfelt. She shuddered as he placed his arms around her and drew her to him. She pressed against his body as if she wanted to melt into him. Stiger held her, his face in her hair. They remained that way for some time, each holding the other.

Sarai pushed him away and abruptly laughed as she wiped tears from her eyes. She wrinkled her nose at him.

"You stink pretty badly."

Stiger glanced down at himself. He was very sweaty and dirty.

"There's a pond just two miles from here," Sarai said in a firm tone. It was almost as if she were talking to a young child. "I want you to go bathe. If you leave now, you should be back in time for supper."

Stiger frowned. He wasn't done with the day's work. He'd been bathing daily out of a bucket drawn from the well. He'd thought that had been enough.

"I have some soap back at the house." Sarai pointed a finger at him and wagged it. "You are to take a proper bath, understand me?"

"My work?" Stiger gestured toward the fencing.

"It can wait."

"But the dwarves?" Stiger said.

"Go speak with Aleric," Sarai said. "As long as you have an escort, they let you go where you will. They allowed you out to that old run-down farm. Bowman's Pond is not that far. I don't think they will mind." Sarai paused and looked at him down her nose. It was a very meaningful look. "I want you to take a bath."

"I believe I will go find Aleric," Stiger said with a sudden grin.

"You do that," Sarai said and shot him a wink. Her eyes were red and puffy. In that moment, he thought her the most beautiful thing he'd ever seen. She spared him another look and then turned back for the house.

Stiger watched her walk away. She held her hands out to caress the tall grass that rippled around her as another gentle gust blew by them. In her faded blue dress, she looked very fine to him. Something he'd thought long dead inside him had stirred awake. His pain and frustration at his current circumstance had faded. Watching her, it almost felt as if he had a future once again, something perhaps to look forward to.

Stiger turned toward the dwarven camp. As he did so, he saw his guards who were standing just thirty yards away begin moving with him. They had seen everything. One of them gave him a thumbs-up and grinned. Stiger put the dwarf from his mind.

It was time to find Aleric to arrange an escort, for he needed a bath.

Chapter Three

Stiger picked up a battered wooden bucket. The handle had long since broken off. He tucked it under an arm and stepped out into the yard. Before he had taken three steps from the barn, more than a dozen chickens came running at breakneck speed. They crowded around his feet, clucking eagerly, a few even bold enough to rub up against his legs as if they were cats.

He chuckled and tossed a fistful of feed, old corn, onto the grass at his feet. The clucking intensified and the chickens went mad. He threw out another fistful before emptying the remainder of the bucket into the long grass.

The chickens scratched and pecked frantically, in search of the dried kernels. Stiger watched the frenzy a moment before moving over to the henhouse. He stuck his head inside and his nose wrinkled at the powerful stench of chicken manure. It was nearing that time again when he would need to muck out the henhouse. It was not one of his favorite chores, but a necessary one.

The manure was an excellent source of fertilizer for the farm's garden, but that did not mean he had to enjoy the task. Careful where he put his feet, Stiger stepped inside. He had to bend over, as the ceiling was rather low. Four shelves lined the back wall. Each held five roughhewn nesting boxes. Large enough for one hen, each box was lined with straw. This he would also need to change out.

A brooding hen on the second shelf squawked at him in irritation. There were three other hens loitering about inside the henhouse.

"Easy, old mother," Stiger said to the bird. Despite his soothing tone, she stood up in her nest, flapping her wings and exposing a number of eggs, several of which were different hues. There would be eggs from multiple hens amongst her future brood, as multiple females would have laid their eggs in her nest. The hen squawked louder as he came nearer.

"I'm not here for your eggs," Stiger reassured her as he moved over to the empty nesting boxes.

He set about checking each nest. There were plenty of fresh eggs. Looking carefully amongst the hay, he rapidly cleared out the nests, filling the bucket halfway with eggs. Before he deposited an egg into the bucket, he tested each to make certain the shell was firm. Bad eggs with parchment-thin shells would go into the compost pile along with the shells from the good eggs.

Satisfied with his haul, he set the bucket on the ground and checked the pan of water on the floor. Chickens, very much like people, preferred to drink clean water. The pan was usually fouled. It was half full and surprisingly clean. Regardless, he resolved to draw some fresh water from the well and change it out later, when he was done with his other tasks around the farm.

As Stiger left the henhouse, the brooding hen scolded him the entire way out. Once outside, he took a moment, savoring the cool, fresh morning air free from chicken manure. The sky was clear and blue with only a handful of clouds. Movement drew his attention to the left.

Sitting on his haunches, the dog was back.

Tongue hanging out of its mouth, it was a great big mangy thing, with long gray hair that was matted, tangled, and dirty. It was the largest dog Stiger had ever seen. He could not place its breed. Despite its fearsome size, the dog had a sad look about it, almost as if he had lost his best friend.

"You again." Stiger grunted in an unhappy tone. "Time to move on, friend."

The dog just continued to stare at him.

Stiger gave a slight shrug and walked back to the barn. He felt the animal's eyes track him the entire way. He had appeared two weeks ago and showed no signs of desire to move on.

Once inside, he placed the bucket next to another on a battered work table. This second one was heavy with milk. Stiger had filled the bucket from their only cow a short while ago, before freeing the animal into the back pasture behind the barn. In the chill air, a slight hazy steam rose from the surface of the milk. He cast his eyes over the buckets, satisfied with the morning haul.

His stomach rumbled. Sarai would be out shortly to collect them. Breakfast would follow within the hour. Most days she served oatmeal and tea for the morning meal. Today would include eggs, milk, cheese, and bread that she had baked the night before. To break up the monotony of standard fare, Sarai usually set a nice breakfast twice a week. It was these meals that he looked forward to.

He moved over to a small cart that had been placed by the wall and wheeled it over to the cow's pen. As he went for the shovel, he stopped to look over a series of nets hanging from the ceiling, heavy with drying walnuts.

"Soon," Stiger said, patting one of the bags affectionately before moving on. He had harvested his first walnuts a little over two weeks ago. His hands were still stained a somewhat unpleasant light green. Removing the husks and worms from the nut had proven not only a time-consuming process, but also an educational one. It had been a first for him, and he was proud of his work. He would enjoy it more so when the time came to consume the nutmeat.

Stiger took the shovel in hand and mucked out the cow's stall before moving on and cleaning out the horse's too. Both animals were out in the farm's back pasture. It was small but now completely fenced in. There was little chance of them escaping, as he had repaired the fencing.

Stiger climbed a ladder up into the loft and dropped a fresh bundle of hay down to the floor, along with one of straw. It landed with a heavy thud and a small cloud of dust. He made his way back down, dragged the straw over, and untied the coarse burlap strips that held it in place. He threw some fresh straw down on the dirt floor of each stall before placing the shovel in the bed of the cart. He made sure to set the burlap strips aside for future use. Stiger surveyed his work before wheeling the cart outside and back into the morning light.

The dog had not moved.

"What?" Stiger asked it as he wheeled the cart over to the garden compost pile. The dog's gaze followed him. "What do you want from me?"

The dog tilted its head, long tongue hanging out of the side of its mouth as he continued to watch him with an unblinking, watery gaze.

"This isn't your home," Stiger said to it. "There are plenty of other places in this valley. It's time you went on your way."

The dog said nothing.

"That dog likes you."

Stiger turned to see Sarai striding from the house. Her long brown hair was tied back in a tight bun. She flashed him a smile. Stiger loved that she wore her feelings plainly. It was something that he, growing up amongst the aristocracy, had never known. Honesty and openness were things to be treasured.

Sarai wore a simple gray wool dress that had been patched over in numerous spots. It was her work dress, an old thing that she preferred to wear while gardening or doing work outside.

"I think the dog would like anyone who fed him," Stiger said, following her with his eyes as she went into the barn to retrieve the two buckets. He raised his voice a little. "Perhaps if you stop feeding him he will find a new home and leave us to ourselves. It's just a thought."

"He's a lot like you," she said, reemerging and holding the two buckets. "When I found you, all you needed was a little love."

"Is that so?"

"I'm fond of you both," she said as she made her way toward the house. "He stays as long as he likes. Best make friends with him then, eh?" She stopped in the doorway and looked back at Stiger with a firm look. "I take it you understand me?"

"I do," Stiger said, somewhat sullenly. "That I do."

"Good," she said. "Now give him a name."

Sarai offered him a wink, before disappearing inside.

Stiger looked over at the mangy dog, who returned his gaze with one of sad equanimity.

"The lady says we should be friends." The dog simply continued to look at him. "Before you accept, you should know my other friend is an elf."

Chuckling to himself, Stiger took hold of the shovel and began scooping the manure out of the cart and onto the compost pile. The compost not only stank, it steamed. Stiger made quick work of it, carefully using the shovel to scrape the last of the manure out. He returned the cart and shovel to the barn.

When he emerged again, the dog was still there. It had a small stick in its mouth. He thought the animal looked hopeful as he walked up. It dropped the stick on the ground and gave a soft whine.

"The lady says I should name you?" Stiger gazed down at the animal. Sitting on its haunches, its head came up above his waist. It was very large for a canine. "Well? Any suggestions? No? OK… you are now Dog. Got that?"

The dog lowered his head to the stick and whined.

Stiger bent down and picked it up. He threw it, expecting the dog to chase after it. Instead, the animal just sat there watching him.

Stiger let out a long breath. "Aren't you going to go get it?"

The dog just looked at him with those sad, watery eyes that seemed uncommonly deep with both emotion and intelligence.

"Have it your way then, Dog," Stiger said and walked over to the pigpen. Four large pigs were still clustered around the pile of slops, hungrily feasting. He had fed them earlier, along with the sheep. Stiger eyed them a moment before continuing on to the woodpile on the other side of the barn. Dog got up and padded after him.

The old axe, head sharp but rusted, was embedded in the tree stump where he had left it the day before. Next to the stump lay a serious pile of wood ripe for splitting.

The pile was almost as tall as he was. Stiger had chopped down several dead trees and then, using the horse, had dragged them over. He had sawed them into manageable sizes, steadily growing his woodpile. The saw work had been the hardest part, one that had left his back, legs, and arms aching for days. The axe work was the easiest part.

Removing the axe, Stiger picked up a piece of wood and placed it on the stump.

Crack!

The rusty axe neatly snapped the piece in two.

Wielding the axe was good, clean work.

Crack!

Fall was almost upon them. The leaves had just begun to change. All it would take was a serious cold snap and that would be it. Stiger was looking forward to that. Fall was his favorite season, generally not too hot and not too cold.

Over the last few weeks, he had split at least five cords of wood. He hoped to have at least two additional cords split before the weather really turned cold. Stiger paused and took a moment to glance up at the forbidding mountains that surrounded the valley. The tops were already coated in a thick carpet of white.

He had learned from Sarai that winter in Vrell could be tough. Stiger had spent more than a few cold winters in the field. Much of that had been with his old company, the Seventh. As the snow piled up, he well knew the value of having a good fire. He glanced back at the house. A fire and a good woman to keep a man warm was all he needed these days. A slight smile sneaked its way onto his face as he thought on her.

Stiger returned to his work, but not before his gaze flicked to Castle Vrell, or as the dwarves preferred to call it, Grata'Kor. His thoughts darkened for a moment and the smile slipped away as he took in the distant gray speck of the fortress. Letting out a heavy breath, he returned to his work.

Crack!

He split several more pieces, quickly working up a sweat. Stiger reached for another piece of wood. A growl stopped him halfway to it. He looked at Dog, who was staring off to his right. Stiger followed the animal's gaze.

"Theo." Stiger straightened as the dwarf, one of his many guards, approached. He liked this dwarf. The others not so much, as they were stiffly formal or refused to communicate with him. Theo had a sense of humor and a relaxed attitude. Out of habit, Stiger glanced around. No more than thirty paces away in any direction stood one of his minders. They wore their heavy armor and were armed with an assortment of battle axes and swords. Theo only wore his tunic.

"My name is Theogdin," the dwarf said in harshly accented common. "I've told you before, only my wife called me Theo. Why do you insist on calling me that?"

"It's easier than Theogdin," Stiger replied in the dwarven tongue.

"You speak better with each passing day," the dwarf said in his own language, though his tone was still a bit grumpy. "You sound better than most humans who simply manage to mangle our tongue. Perhaps with time you will increase your legend by speaking it even better?"

"These daily visits help," Stiger said and picked up the piece of wood he had been reaching for. "I find them and your instruction quite diverting."

Crack!

"That dog is still here," Theo said, stroking his long brown beard. Like most of his kind, it was tightly braided. "I thought you were going to get rid of him?"

The dog gave out a low, menacing growl aimed at Theo. The sad eyes were now intense and fixated on the dwarf. Theo turned to regard the dog.

"Sarai said he stays." Stiger looked over at the dog, who continued to growl. It was as if he were following their conversation. "Dog, stop that."

Almost instantly, the dog ceased its growling and lay down, placing its head between his paws. Stiger noted how the animal's eyes never left the dwarf.

"He listens to you," Theo said.

Stiger returned to his work.

Crack!

"Why?" Theo asked. "Why does she want to keep him?"

The dog growled again, but only briefly.

Stiger shot Theo a look before rolling his eyes and picking up another piece of wood.

"A woman gets what she wants, is that it?" the dwarf grunted as Stiger gave a nod of affirmation. "You don't like dogs?"

Crack!

Stiger straightened and looked over at the dwarf before glancing at the dog. "For hunting, yes. As a pet, no."

"Hunting?" Theo's gaze traveled over to the dog. "He does not look like a hunter, but a scrounger."

"No, he doesn't have the look of a scrounger," Stiger said. "He's more beggar than anything else."

"How do you use a dog to hunt?" Theo asked. "In the mountain, we keep small dogs only to find rat colonies to be dug out."

Stiger allowed the axe head to rest on the ground as he turned fully around to face Theo.

"Well," Stiger said. "It's not just one dog, mind you, but many. Unlike this one here, there are several breeds trained to chase and corner game."

"Why chase?" Theo seemed confused by the concept. "Why not bait and trap? Chasing seems much more difficult and a waste of one's time."

"Sport," Stiger said. "It is the chase that is fun. We use horses and beaters and follow the dogs until the animals are cornered."

"It does not seem very sporting," Theo said. "Now, noseball is a sport. That is worth watching."

"Yes," Stiger said, picking the axe back up. "I've seen your noseball. I don't know if I would call it a sport. It is more of a beating than anything else."

"You've seen noseball?" Theo appeared surprised by that. "When? Where?"

Suddenly mindful he had said too much, Stiger turned back to the task of splitting wood.

Crack!

Theo moved around the stump so that he faced Stiger.

Crack!

"Tell me," Theo said, stepping up to him and placing a thick six-fingered hand on Stiger's shoulder before he could reach for another piece of wood.

"I do not wish to speak of it," Stiger answered and then let out a heavy breath of frustration. "I mean it."

"There is a lot you do not speak about." With a disgusted look, Theo released Stiger's shoulder. He stomped over to a large uncut log and sat down on it.

"Thoggle asked me not to speak of it," Stiger said, though he knew Theo was already aware of this. "To be fully truthful, Thoggle insisted I say nothing."

"Thoggle is without legend," Theo said, a displeased look coming over his face. "He does not follow the Way and meddles too much with the thane. There are many who do not like it."

"As a wizard, he must be learned and wise," Stiger said. "Surely your thane sees value in his counsel."

Theo said nothing to that. After a few moments, Stiger resumed his splitting and allowed the silence to grow. He worked his way through several more pieces before the dwarf broke the silence.

"You are a warrior, no?"

Stiger lowered the axe again and glanced over sourly at the dwarf. Theo was short, even for a dwarf. That said, he was broad-shouldered. He had an expression that spoke of a mischievous nature and also, perhaps, an inner sadness. It was really the eyes that conveyed the latter.

"Don't bother denying it. I saw your armor," Theo said, "and that magic sword that burned Geligg."

"I am sorry about that," Stiger said, and he meant it. "I did not wish to see him injured."

Theo shrugged. "Thoggle told him not to touch it. He needs to listen better, even if it is to one without legend."

"How is he?" Stiger asked. He had not known the sword would injure another so by simply picking it up.

"He is good as new. The paladin healed his hand." Theo laughed. "My captain has him on latrine duty. I think he hopes that Geligg will listen better in the future."

"That is good to hear."

"That he has been healed or is on latrine duty?"

Stiger barked out a laugh.

"Ah, so you can laugh now." Theo pointed a finger at him. "When I met you, you were less fun than one of my people on blood feud."

Stiger gave a slight nod to that as he considered the dwarf's words. It was true. After everything that had happened, his mood had finally lightened somewhat. He glanced around the farm. He felt more relaxed than he had for a very long time.

"So," Theo said, breaking in on Stiger's thoughts, "you are a warrior, then?"

Stiger hesitated and glanced toward the house before returning his eyes to Theo. He was certain the dwarf knew this already. He wondered where Theo was going with this line of questioning. "I was but am no more. I gave that life up."

"Bah." Theo waved a hand. "Once a warrior, always a warrior. The paladin says you are a great fighter and leader of men. He claims you have accumulated much legend."

"Father Thomas speaks too much." Stiger returned to splitting his wood. "He should keep his mouth shut."

"Maktalon."

Stiger looked back over at Theo and sucked in a breath. "I don't know that word."

"It is…" Theo thought a moment and switched back to common. "Another word for what you call the World Gate. You came through it. You are a Maktalon traveler. There has not been one for a good long time."

"I came through it, as did Father Thomas," Stiger said. "So what?"

"My grandfather, a great warrior by the name of Shoega, fought with the humans to close and seal the Gate," Theo said. "Perhaps you have heard of him?"

Stiger shook his head. "I do not know the name."

"It matters little." Theo shrugged. "I never knew him myself. He died years before I was born. My father told me of my grandfather's tales of the world Tannis and of fighting the Horde. He gained much legend for himself, our family and clan. He was a great warrior."

Stiger knew that dwarves were long-lived, but here was a dwarf whose grandfather had walked another world. It was crazy just thinking about it. Perhaps Shoega had even seen Rome. Such a thought would have once seemed absurd, but no more.

"Did you come from Tannis?"

"No, I did not."

Theo gave another shrug of his wide shoulders. "My grandfather fought alongside a great leader of men. Perhaps you heard of him? His name was Karus. He helped to form the Compact. He too was a Maktalon traveler."

Stiger studied the dwarf for several moments. Theo had named someone Stiger knew of and was even reputedly distantly related.

"No one has come through the Maktalon for a long time. With the Gate sealed, I understand what you did to be impossible, and yet you and the paladin came through anyway. Where, I wonder, did you come from?"

Stiger did not answer but split another piece of wood.

"Your arrival has created a lot of excitement amongst my people." Theo paused a moment and pointed a stubby finger at Stiger. An intense look came to the dwarf's eyes. "I think you have come to restore the Compact."

"You think too much," Stiger said, growing cold at the Theo's perceptiveness.

"Perhaps," Theo said.

The dog growled again, drawing their attention. Theo let out a quiet groan and stood, stiffening his back as his captain approached.

Stiger offered a nod to Captain Aleric. The dwarf captain wore his heavy armor but had not donned a helmet. Like others of his race, the armor was painted in his clan's color pattern: green, yellow, and brown. Theo's colors, oddly enough, were purple, the thane's own.

"How are you today?" the dwarven officer asked in near perfect common.

"Well," Stiger answered in dwarven, to which the captain gave a pleased nod. "I am well. You can't ask for more than that, now, can you?"

"Theogdin has been a good instructor of our tongue," Aleric said with a glance at Theo. "He does his legend good."

"If I had wanted to be a teacher, I would have become one," Theo replied.

Aleric scowled at Theo.

"Thank you for loaning him out to me," Stiger said, before Aleric could reply. "It has been an honor to learn from him."

The captain sucked in a deep breath. "It keeps him out of trouble and complaining about missing his son." The dwarven officer turned to Theo. "What was your boy's name again?"

"Garrack," Theo said, drawing a sharp look of surprise from Stiger that neither dwarf appeared to notice. "My boy's name is Garrack, and I will raise him to be a warrior fit to fight alongside the thane."

"I have no doubt you will," Aleric said and then turned to face Stiger. "I come to inform you I have received word that in a month we will be relieved. You will have a fresh company to watch over you."

"I wish I could say I was sorry to see you go," Stiger said. "I do not like being a prisoner. My word of honor ... my legend should be sufficient for you and your thane. Should it not?"

The captain shifted his feet uncomfortably, before he cast his eyes around the farm. "This isn't a prison. There are no bars locking you up."

"Am I free, then?" Stiger pressed. "Can I leave the valley?"

"No," Aleric said. "I cannot allow you to go, at least until the thane says so."

"Then I am your prisoner," Stiger said, with some frustration. They had had similar talks before. "As much as if you had locked me in a cell."

"You are the guest of our thane," Aleric responded stiffly. "Instead of keeping you under the mountain, we have placed you with your own kind ... as a comfort."

"Captain Aleric," Sarai said in greeting as she emerged from the house. They all turned to look at her. "Will you be having breakfast with us this morning? Ben gathered fresh eggs."

"Sarai," Aleric switched to common. "I bid you good morning, but am afraid I must decline. I will be drilling my warriors shortly."

Sarai's eyes slid over to Theo. "I hope you can excuse Theogdin. He is a pleasure to have around."

"I can," Aleric said stiffly, though his manner seemed to say he wished otherwise. "Theogdin is free to join you."

Theo caught Stiger's eye and winked. He had been escaping from drill a lot lately, using Stiger as an excuse. In truth, Stiger enjoyed Theo's company, though he would have happily traded the dwarf for his friend Eli.

"And you, Theogdin, will you be kind enough to join us?"

"Gladly," Theo said with a broad smile and then looked over at Stiger and switched back to dwarven. "If she can say my given name easily enough, why can't you?"

"You will always be Theo to me," Stiger said back to the dwarf. "Always."

Chapter Four

Stiger's eyes snapped open. For as long as he could recall, he had been a light sleeper. He was lying on his back. The room was nearly pitch black. The small clay brazier in the corner had long since run out of fuel and no longer shed even a modicum of light. Next to him and under the covers of a thick wool blanket lay Sarai. An arm thrown around him, she was snuggled close, her head resting upon his naked chest. Under the blanket, the heat from her body was agreeable. Sarai's breathing was steady, relaxed.

Something had woken him. He was sure of it. Not moving a muscle, he simply listened. With the dwarven company guarding and watching the farm, he seriously doubted there was an actual threat about. The dwarves took their duty seriously. Still, Stiger had long since learned that it was better to be careful. He waited and continued to listen.

After several moments, he heard the jingle of armor, followed by a muffled voice speaking in the harsh tongue of the dwarves. Stiger could not make out what was said. This was almost immediately followed by heavy footsteps that became fainter with every step.

Stiger mentally relaxed. It was only the changing of the guard, something that regularly happened right before dawn. The dwarves were nothing if not predictable and reliable. He sucked in a breath and let it out slowly.

Sarai stirred slightly. He wrapped an arm around her and pulled her close. She gave off a soft half moan and snuggled in. Stiger closed his eyes. He could feel her chest rise and fall, the warmth of her skin radiating against his, the touch intoxicating. He had become content, happy even, and desirous of it not coming to an end. After all of these years, he had finally found happiness... as a prisoner.

Stiger closed his eyes and allowed himself to slip back into sleep. He woke sometime later to find the room had brightened a tad as dawn approached. Animal pelts had been hung over the closed shutters to help keep in the heat. Despite that, light had begun to leak in.

Stiger could now make out the bedroom he shared with Sarai. It was small, meager like the rest of the two-room house, nothing at all compared to the luxury with which he had been raised, back in Mal'Zeel. His boyhood home had been a near palace. Sarai's home was a hovel by comparison. Stiger found it simple, and charming. As his eyes roved around the dim bedroom, he wondered how much that feeling had to do with her.

There were two windows and four large trunks that had been pushed up against the walls. These contained Sarai's clothing, a few of her treasured possessions, and the belongings of her late husband. Besides the bed and a bucket as a chamber pot, a small, rickety three-legged stool was the only other piece of furniture in the room.

After a time, Stiger forced himself to pull away. He slipped from under the covers and out of bed. The cold air was a shock and it snapped him fully awake.

Sarai mumbled something incoherent, rolled over, and pulled the blanket closer. The door had been left open to the kitchen. The stones of the fireplace undoubtedly still radiated some heat, but it was no longer sufficient to reach into the bedroom and combat the cold.

Stiger grabbed a tunic from where he had tossed it on the stool the night before. He slipped it on, the wool doing little against the chill of the room. He gave an involuntary shiver. Sarai had laundered the tunic the day before and it still smelled clean, though mercifully it was no longer damp. Like the rest of the clothing he had been wearing, it had belonged to her late husband. Despite being cut from poor material, the garment had been well made. Stiger glanced over at the bed and the sleeping woman. When he had been brought here as a guest, some sixteen weeks before, he had felt like an intruder. Now, things were very different.

"I shall happily spend the rest of my life with you," Stiger whispered to himself as he regarded her, before turning away and stepping carefully across the floorboards, lest they creak overmuch.

The kitchen was slightly larger than the bedroom. Though it was humble, it had a charming manner that spoke of Sarai's complex personality. A large wooden table dominated the center of the room. It served not only for food preparation, but also dining. Shelving along one wall held battered pots, pans, and mismatched plates. One shelf had a row of carefully organized jars and cooking implements. Dried summer herbs and onions had been hung from the ceiling in numerous places. A cask filled with flour rested against a wall. The room was neat and tidy. Everything had a place.

Along the back wall was a large fireplace, with a number of hooks and iron chains for cooking. Next to it was a small oven for baking bread, a luxury for such a modest home. It meant that, more often than not, they had fresh bread.

The floorboards were spotlessly clean, as was the rest of the kitchen. Sarai preferred cleanliness and order, something the legionary in Stiger could well appreciate. Had Stiger performed a formal inspection, he would be hard-pressed to find dust.

He cracked one of the shutters a fraction to allow in a bar of dim light. He did not wish to welcome in the cold more than he had to. With sufficient light, he moved around the table to the fireplace. The pieces of wood he had laid on the previous evening had burned up and turned to ash. As expected, the stones still gave off some heat. Stiger held his hands out to warm them before rubbing them together.

From the small pile of wood next to the fireplace, he laid on several pieces, carefully stacking them to produce the best effect for a fire. He prided himself on his ability to set a good fire and almost regarded it as a form of art.

"If you are going to do something," Stiger said to himself, "might as well do it right."

From a bucket, he took a bundle of dried kindling and shoved it into the thick pile of ash under the pieces of wood he had stacked. He followed this up with another bundle. Using a poker, Stiger moved the ash around and exposed the hot embers, which glowed a sullen orange-red. From the same bucket, he pulled out a fistful of dried leaves and, using the poker, pushed them into the embers and underneath the kindling. A few moments later, the leaves caught, flaring brilliantly as they curled in upon themselves. Then the kindling started to burn.

A copper pot full of well-drawn water sat waiting on the table. Using an iron hook set into the stone of the fireplace, careful lest he spill any and spoil his efforts, Stiger hung the pot over the growing fire. By the time Sarai climbed out of bed, it would be close to boiling and ready to make tea and oatmeal, which she had also set out.

Stiger pulled a stool out from underneath the table and sat down on it. The stool creaked alarmingly as it accepted his weight. He faced the fire and settled in to watch, something that had become his routine since arriving here. It cracked and popped as the blaze took hold. He found the flames comforting, not only with the heat they soon began to shed, but also the light. The fire slowly brightened the kitchen as the blaze grew.

Stiger had spent many a lonely evening seated before a campfire, staring into the flames. This, in a way, was no different. Only then he had always had an urgent purpose waiting for him the next morning. Rarely had he ever truly been worry-free. These days, Stiger found it hard to care for anything other than Sarai and making her happy. Still, he found he was not without regrets and dark thoughts that continued to haunt him through the passage of time.

Stiger rubbed at his eyes, which were a little dry. Nearly sixteen weeks ago, his purpose in life had unexpectedly and inextricably changed. He was no longer the man responsible for leading other men into battle, hoping and praying that he had made the correct decision. He let out a long breath. He had finished with that life and, if he had anything to say about it, he was done with killing, too.

At first his attitude had been different. He had refused to accept his fate. He had resisted, even struggled against it. But in the end, he had come to accept it. He was separated from his time, cut off from the life he had known and felt called to live. He had failed in his duty and was trapped in the past.

Stiger had been sent back in time to put things right. He had been unable to do so. The minion that had proceeded him through the World Gate had managed to kill Delvaris first. With his passing, the future was undoubtedly altered beyond repair. Even if he could return through the Gate, which the dwarven wizard Thoggle insisted was now impossible, things in Stiger's time were not the same, and would be more favorable to Castor. Stiger let out a long, slow breath. The wizard had called it a paradox. In fact, he had directed that term at Stiger and had stated he could not understand why Stiger even still existed.

According to the wizard, Stiger was now an impossibility. Stiger wondered if the sword had something to do with it. Stiger had never heard of a paradox before Thoggle had mentioned it, and in truth he did not fully understand it. But he understood the damage done, especially after Thoggle had explained things. There was no going back to the life he had known.

He was a man out of his time.

"All things considered," Stiger said softly to himself as he glanced toward their bedroom, "it could be worse."

He drummed his fingers on the table as he turned back to the flames. His thoughts darkened, even as the room brightened. Over his long years of service to the empire, so many good men had died under his command that he had long since lost count, or perhaps the real truth was that he had long since ceased trying to count. Varus, Bren, Erbus … the list went on. Each death came with a hurt, some more than others. Though he had come to accept loss, the emotional wound it opened never fully managed to heal. It lingered just out of reach and with it came the terrible guilt at having survived when others had not.

Stiger found it odd, ironic even, that every step he had taken since he entered service had led him to this small farm in the Vrell Valley. He had come to terms somewhat with his failure, the first in a great long time for him. If he was honest with himself, there had been little he could have done to change things. He had stepped through the World Gate and emerged on the other side only to discover he had failed. There had been nothing to do other than rage at the injustice and the fickle nature of Fortuna.

Stiger heard Sarai stir in the bedroom, the bed creaking as she climbed out. He listened to her soft footsteps. There were several heartbeats of silence and then he heard her relieving herself in the waste bucket. It was a strong hiss that proved surprisingly long in duration. She let out a contented sigh as she finished. Amused, he laughed.

"You drink more water than anyone I've ever known," Stiger called into the other room. "And I mean anyone, including Eli, and he guzzled the stuff."

"Water is good for you," came the reply. She stepped into the kitchen completely naked, her small, firm breasts perky, the nipples erect in the cold air. Stiger felt a stirring as the orange firelight played over her supple body.

"Brooding again, I see." She checked on the water over the fire before looking back at him. "On what this time?"

"The usual," Stiger said.

Sarai rolled her eyes and used the poker to prod the fire a little, sending up a spray of sparks into the chimney and out of view. Stiger found himself admiring the view.

She looked back at him again, this time with sad eyes, and shook her head. "You should let it go. You've traveled here to me. Your life, your future, is with me. It is as simple as that. There are some things you can change, but this is something you can't."

"Though my time as a soldier is done," Stiger said, "I don't know if I will ever be able to let it all go, not completely." He paused, drawing in a deep breath. "Much has happened. On the battlefield, I have left behind too many comrades and friends." He paused and sucked in another deep breath. "Some I even knowingly sent not just into battle, but to their deaths. It is something that will always be with me."

"Was it all necessary?"

Stiger was silent several moments as he considered his answer. "At the time, I thought it was. Now, with what has happened… I am not so sure."

"Ben," she said, with a slight scolding tone, "you can't blame yourself for things you have no control over."

Stiger gave her a shrug in reply.

She stepped over to him and looked down into his eyes. A hand reached up to his close-cropped hair and stroked it, her eyes never leaving his. A smile slowly found its way onto her face. Stiger felt his heart quicken. She reached down and took his hand, large in hers, and cupped her breast with his palm. Stiger felt the hard nipple rub against his skin.

"Let me help you forgot your worries and find peace," she breathed, leaning down. She kissed him hard and long, her tongue boldly exploring.

"You already have," Stiger said, when they came up for air. "You already have… my love."

The smile returned to her face. Silently, she drew him to his feet and led him into the bedroom.

Stiger slid back out of bed and drew on his tunic. Sarai lay under the wool blanket. Her eyes followed him as he moved about the room, drawing an old leather belt around his tunic to help keep the warmth in. The clasps of the belt were wearing thin and nearing the end of their useful life. It was something else that had belonged to her late husband.

"I thought, perhaps..." Stiger paused to look at her. "I might go up to Bowman's Pond today."

"Fish would be more than welcome on the dinner table," Sarai said, stretching underneath the blanket and letting out a near purr of satisfaction. She sat up in bed, the blanket falling to reveal her nakedness as Stiger came over to her. He gave her a passionate kiss and held it for a prolonged moment before straightening.

"With luck, I will bring home more than one," Stiger said.

"That would be nice," Sarai said, amusement dancing in her eyes. "Let's hope your fishing skills have improved. The last time you went, you came back with a fish that could only be called a mere snack, or perhaps even bait."

"I was proud of that fish," Stiger said with an indignant grunt. "It is the pond that is lacking."

"Well then," she said, "if that is so, better make certain you catch more than one fish this time."

Stiger went into the kitchen, threw another couple of pieces of wood on the fire. The water had been boiling for a while now. Sarai came out. She had thrown on a gray dress that had seen better days. Using a thick towel to keep from being burned, she grabbed the handle and removed the pot from over the fire, setting it with practiced ease on the flagstones at her feet. Stiger sat on a stool and put his sandals on, lacing them up his calves and tying them tight.

"When you go, take that sword with you," Sarai said.

Stiger looked over at his sword. Rarokan rested in its scabbard in the corner. The lacquered runes and figures on the hilt were illuminated somewhat by the firelight. Since he had arrived in this time, the sword had not once spoken to him. It had remained sullenly mum, no matter what he said to it. Stiger wondered if it was brooding as well.

"I don't like it being here," she said. "It makes me uncomfortable."

"It is just a sword," Stiger said. Despite a warning from Thoggle to limit what he told others of the future, he had made the mistake of telling her about it and how Rarokan spoke to him on occasion. Early on, he had made the decision to conceal nothing from her.

"No," Sarai said. "It is anything but. It is a magic sword, perhaps evil even."

Stiger's eyes swept back to the sword sitting in its scabbard. It was very possible she was right, though he was sure Father Thomas would have warned him against it as an implement of evil were it so.

"I will take it with me," Stiger conceded.

"Good," she said. "When will you go?"

Stiger stood. "I think after I finish feeding the animals and breakfast with you."

"I will pack you a lunch of bread and cheese."

Stiger gave a satisfied nod. She was a fine woman and had a kind soul. His eyes followed her as she moved about the kitchen. This was not the first time he had been in love, but it was different with Sarai. He would be proud to have her as a wife. They would grow old together and share the remainder of their days. That is, if she would have him, which he knew she would.

"You should bring Theogdin as well," Sarai said, as he stood. "You need another friend besides that dog."

"I thought I already had one." Stiger winked at her.

"I am your lover," she said seriously. "Theo can be your friend. He is a good one, that dwarf."

Stiger considered her for a moment, grunted, and stepped out into the cold. The guard was standing just outside the door. The dwarf looked over at Stiger with no hint of emotion on his heavily bearded face. Yet, Stiger had gotten the feeling that most of his guard were deeply suspicious of him. Or perhaps they disliked him, as he had given affront to their thane? He gave the warrior a brief nod, which was curtly returned. No words were exchanged. Another guard stood a few feet away. Stiger ignored him and set off for the barn. He had work to do before he could set out for Bowman's Pond.

Chapter Five

Stiger put the small shovel down. He sorted through the pile of dirt, pulling out several of the larger worms that he judged suitable, and placed them in a small burlap bag. Theo stood a couple of feet away and watched him curiously.

"These little buggers will get the fish biting nicely." Satisfied with his haul, Stiger stood back up. Bag in hand, he shook it slightly for emphasis. "Nothing better than worms for bait."

"If you say so." Theo looked unconvinced. "You dragged me all the way up here. Tell me why you think this is fun again?"

"Dwarves don't fish?" Stiger looked at Theo with mild surprise. "I find that hard to believe."

"I don't fish," Theo said and gestured at the bag in Stiger's hand. "Some of my people do this sort of thing. However, I am a warrior, not a fisherman. I have dedicated my life to protecting my people. I gain much legend."

"That doesn't mean you can't enjoy the simpler things in life from time to time," Stiger said. "Does it?"

"I enjoy plenty of the *simpler* things in life," Theo said.

"Like what?"

"Drinking with my mates," Theo said, "for one."

"I might have guessed that one," Stiger said. "It seems soldiers in all armies love to drink when given the opportunity. It helps to pass the time and soften the edge of a hard life."

"That it does," Theo agreed. "What do you legionaries drink?"

"Wine," Stiger replied, "and cheap beer. When in camp, legionaries get issued a daily wine ration."

"No spirits?" Theo said.

"No, the hard stuff is rare and too expensive for the average legionary."

"I see," Theo said. "Do they fish, too?"

"Some do. When time permits and a fresh body of water is available. It helps to supplement rations and creates a little variety."

"I have never seen the need"—a sour look crossed Theo's face—"to, ah, fish. But as you say, a little variety may be worth something now and again." Theo paused. "Those of my people who do fish for food use nets. You get more fish that way with less work." Theo's sour look returned, and then he suddenly cocked his head to the side, a curious expression crossing his face. "Have you done this sort of thing often?"

"No." Stiger began walking over to where he left the fishing rod. "Sadly, I'm not very good at it, but I've learned to enjoy it."

"Who taught you to fish?" Theo followed after him. "Your father?"

Stiger paused and glanced back at Theo for a moment. He dropped the bag softly to the ground, and then reached for the rod. "No, my father did not teach me to fish. He never had the time for such things."

"Who, then?"

"A friend of mine," Stiger said, half turning back to Theo. "An elf, actually."

"An elf?" Theo laughed loudly, drawing the attention of several of the nearby guards. "You can't be serious? Elves have not been seen in centuries."

"Yes, I am," Stiger said, removing the string and hook from a pack he been carrying. He quickly fished the string through the small metal loops on the homemade rod and tied it off. He secured the hook to the other end of the line. Carefully looped, he held the extra line in his hand. "He is a good friend."

Theo regarded Stiger for silent moment. It was clear that the dwarf was wondering if he was being toyed with.

"I even lived amongst the elves," Stiger said, with a quick look at Theo.

"I see." Theo's tone still held a trace of doubt. "Elves are not highly thought of by my people."

"I know."

"When my people came to this world," Theo continued, "along with yours, the elves betrayed us."

"How so?"

"For a time," Theo explained, "they fought with us, but when it mattered most, they stood apart. They went their separate way, turned their backs upon both our peoples. In the eyes of mine, they lost much legend."

Stiger read real anger in Theo's expression. Though Theo had likely never met an elf, he clearly harbored hard feelings that had been passed down from his father and likely his grandfather before him. Stiger had never known Eli to be anything but honorable. However, the other elves that Stiger had become acquainted with were far from predictable in their behavior. Eli had explained that his people looked at things differently, a result of their longevity. Stiger reminded himself there were always two sides to a story. He wondered for a moment what the elven side was. Then decided it didn't really matter to him. His time of concerning himself with such events was over. Stiger gave a slight shrug of his shoulders and turned away, moving toward the water. He had tired of the conversation. It was time to begin fishing.

The pond was good sized and ringed almost completely around by young trees. Thick, low-lying brush grew almost right up to the edge of the water. A few yards into the brush, on the far bank, were the stone ruins of an old house and barn. Stiger had explored these the last time he was here. They had been abandoned long ago and there had been nothing of value left. Time and the elements had claimed nearly everything.

The roof of the barn had collapsed, along with part of the stone wall facing the pond. The stones from this wall had fallen in a large pile, over which grass had begun to grow. Of the one-room farmhouse, the entire roof was gone and all that remained was a mere shell. The chimney was intact, but it looked far from solid. A strong wind might take it down.

What had once likely been cultivated fields and pastures was now overgrown forest filled with young trees, choked by low-lying brush. The pond, Stiger suspected, was probably artificial and had been for watering animals.

Giving Stiger and the dwarves plenty of space, several ducks drifted across the placid surface. He considered the ducks, wondering how he could trap them. The opportunity to present a duck to Sarai was very tempting. It would be a welcome addition to their fare. Had he a bow, the ducks would have been easy targets. Unfortunately, Sarai didn't own one. At the very least, he would need to construct a trap of some kind. He resolved to think on how he wanted to do it over the next few days, for he enjoyed roast duck immensely.

The pond and surrounding forest was a peaceful enough setting. It was isolated and very quiet. Several weeks ago, when he had been restless, Sarai had suggested he take a hike and catch her a fish. After negotiating with Captain Aleric, Stiger had set out with a small guard for an afternoon of fishing.

It was a good hike and even better exercise, as it took some effort to get to Bowman's Pond. It wasn't the distance that made the hike challenging, as it was only around four miles from Sarai's farm, but the elevation. The grade was very steep, at some points even requiring a bit of scrambling, as parts of the path had washed away with the spring rains.

The pond was located on a small mountain ledge. The ledge was several miles in length and, as near as Stiger could tell, at least one mile in width. The last quarter mile of the hike, though over flat ground, was through young forest that was quite thick with brush, making even the flat portion of the hike a challenge.

Emerging from the trees, Stiger paused for a moment, surveying the peaceful setting. Bright afternoon sunlight reflected off of the surface in a dazzling show. A series of large stones spread out from the edge into the water. Stiger made his way over to the spot. He stepped from the bank to the first stone and then from one to another, until he was on the last one, around seven feet from shore.

He sat down on the rock, which had been warmed by the midday sun. The chill air had retreated, and it was almost uncomfortably warm. Stiger understood that feeling was partly the result of the exertions from the hike up.

The water looked refreshing and he contemplated jumping in for a swim. At the farm, he had been cleaning himself using a bucket of cold well-drawn water. Hiking up, he had worked up a sweat. A dip was not a terribly bad idea, he thought as he hooked a worm. It might even be enjoyable, but would have to wait until he was finished. He did not want to scare the fish. Satisfied the worm was secure, he cast the line out into the water and sat back to wait for the inevitable bite.

After some hesitation, Theo followed him out onto the rocks, sitting down on a large, smooth one to his right. Stiger glanced over at the dwarf, who looked uncomfortable being so close to the water. Theo returned the look with one of mild irritation.

"I don't much like water," Theo said, without a hint of embarrassment. "Not one bit."

"For bathing?" Stiger cracked a grin at the dwarf, who shot a scowl back at him.

"I like bathing well enough," Theo said, adjusting his tunic as he leaned back using a hand to prop himself up.

"You could have fooled me."

"Ha, ha," Theo said and then gestured out at the pond. "It's large bodies of water like this that I do not much care for."

"You can't swim," Stiger said, contemplating his friend, "can you?"

"No," Theo admitted. "I've spent most of my life under the mountain. Any underground lakes or ponds like this one here are bitingly cold and usually very deep. Sometimes the water is even poisonous and can give you painful burns." Theo paused to swat a fly away. "Don't get me wrong, there are places where the waters run warm from the blood of the mountain. Those pools are usually very shallow and worth taking a dip in. It helps one to relax. Now that I heartedly approve of."

Stiger had never heard of such pools and wondered what they would be like. Perhaps akin to a bathhouse, where the waters were heated? It had been a good long while since he had seen the sight of an imperial bathhouse. He looked back at the pond and then over to Theo.

"This pond isn't that deep," Stiger said, gesturing out at the placid water. "I could teach you easily enough to swim, if you wish. Who knows, you might even one day teach your son."

"My son?" Theo whispered, his expression turning inscrutable as he studied the water for prolonged moment, before turning his gaze around to his fellow dwarves. Ten of Stiger's guard were spread out along the bank and in the trees, several of which were watching them closely. Wearing their heavy armor, they looked hot and uncomfortable. Stiger almost felt sorry for them—almost. He was, after all, their prisoner.

"Perhaps another time," Theo said.

"In the legions," Stiger said, "it is a requirement that every recruit learn to swim. I myself have had need of that skill more than once, and when it mattered, too."

"By nature, my people are not the best swimmers," Theo said. "We are too heavy, you see, big boned, and tend to sink. It takes a lot of effort to swim a short distance."

It was Stiger's turn to bark out a laugh.

"I don't find that very funny," Theo said, which only caused Stiger to laugh even harder.

"It is not funny." Theo went red in the face.

"No, I suppose it is not," Stiger said, reining in his amusement and holding up a hand. "My apologies. Still, I would be willing to teach you. Swimming is a valuable skill to learn. You never know when you might need it."

"I have no doubt about that and ... I may take you up on that offer," Theo said, lowering his voice. He looked meaningfully at the nearest of his comrades. "But not today. I don't wish to make a fool out of myself."

Stiger understood and the two fell silent for a time as he waited for the fish to bite.

Basking in the warmth of the sun and tugging occasionally at the pole to attract the fish, Stiger did his best to enjoy the peaceful setting. He felt a lessening of the heat as a light breeze worked its way by. He gave the pole another soft tug.

There was a scuffing sound behind them that caused Stiger to turn.

"Your dog has followed us," Theo said.

"Yes, he has," Stiger said, "hasn't he?"

At the edge of the pond, the dog sat down on his haunches next to a dwarf and stared straight at Stiger. The dwarf patted the dog's head, eliciting vigorous tail wagging. This was followed by a scratching of the animal's neck. The dog craned his neck, clearly enjoying the attention.

"Have you given him a name yet?"

"Dog," Stiger said, giving the pole a slight tug. No bites yet.

"Yes, it is a dog," Theo replied and then it hit him. "Wait ... you named your dog Dog?"

"It seemed fitting."

"You could have been a little more original, don't you think?"

"Fishing requires a semblance of quiet." Stiger spared the dwarf an unhappy look before returning to his fishing.

He grew silent and over the next hour refused to be baited into further conversation by Theo.

Dog eventually made his way out onto the rocks. He laid down on the nearest one, just behind him, and promptly went to sleep. Stiger eyed the dog for a bit, which was lying on its side, soaking up the sun and snoring softly.

Stiger closed his eyes and listened to the sounds of the forest around him, something that Eli had taught him to do. He breathed slowly in and then out, calming his mind, centering his being. He took another series of breaths.

There were a number of birds calling out, some of which he could identify, others not. He could hear the insects. Somewhere nearby, a deer rubbed its antlers against a tree, close enough that he could hear it clearly. A breeze worked its way through the trees, causing limbs to sway and creak. The leaves rustled with its passing.

Stiger opened his eyes. For a moment he recalled his time living amongst Eli's people. The peace and tranquility of the land that they had shaped to their will was not only beautiful, but as near perfect as one could imagine.

In a way, that was why Stiger had repeatedly returned to Bowman's Pond. It reminded him of another happy time in his past… well, really his future. He gazed around at the guards spread out along this side of the lake. Eventually, the dwarves would come to the conclusion that he did not need guarding, and with a little fortune they would leave him to live with Sarai. At least he hoped so. He couldn't imagine being watched for the remainder of his days.

Stiger returned to his fishing, giving the line another gentle tug. Nothing was biting. He dreaded returning to Sarai empty-handed. He cocked his head to the side.

Something wasn't quite right.

It was more a feeling than anything else. At first, he could not put his finger on exactly what was bothering him, but then it hit him. Had it not been for Eli's training in the ways of the forest, he might have missed it. The sound of nature on the other side of the pond had gone unnaturally silent.

The birds on his side of the pond, having become accustomed to the intrusion upon their domain, still called to one another. The breeze was still there, periodically coming and going with soft gusts. However, the birds no longer called to each other from the far side of the pond. Even more telling, the insects had fallen silent as well.

Stiger chewed his lip as he thought it over. After several moments, he decided they were being watched. Of that, he was sure.

A low guttural growl from behind set his hair on end. There was danger afoot. Stiger gave the fishing pole another gentle tug, as if nothing were amiss, and glanced casually over at Theo, who had turned slightly to look back at the dog. Their eyes met when the dwarf looked back.

"Theo, don't make a show of it, but we are being observed," Stiger said in a near whisper. He gave the pole another tug. "Someone's on the other side of the pond."

Theo said nothing, but his eyes flicked in the direction indicated.

As casually as he could, Stiger studied the far bank, but could see nothing amongst the overgrown brush along its edge. There was enough of it that anyone with a little skill could easily conceal themselves. The sunlight reflecting off of the surface of the pond from this angle made seeing anyone along the opposite bank only that much more difficult. He wondered who was watching them, and why.

Dog's growl became deeper, louder, meaner. Stiger sensed the dog standing up.

"Dog," Stiger snapped quietly, looking back at it. "Down."

The dog immediately ceased his growling and lay back down.

Our enemy comes…

The voice he had not heard in some time hissed in his mind. Stiger froze, feeling the uncomfortable sensation of ice running slowly down his back. His hair stood on end.

The fire of their black souls calls out to me. Do not deny me… Wield me…

Stiger swallowed. He had left the sword back amongst the trees. Without it, he suddenly felt terribly naked. He scanned the far bank, wondering again who it was. The sword had named them the enemy. Stiger silently cursed. He had become complacent. He had thought himself done with killing. His anger began to swell at himself and those who wished him ill. All he now wanted from life was to be left alone. And yet, here he was… once again facing a grave danger.

"When I say"—Stiger gave the pole another gentle tug—"we make a break for the shelter of the trees. Got me?"

"Are you serious?" Theo's tone was low and Stiger heard the skepticism. "All because your dog growled?"

"There is danger out there," Stiger said. "I am certain of it."

The dwarf gave a low, disbelieving grunt and glanced back at his fellow dwarves, most of whom appeared bored, though a few were diligently looking their way. "Bah."

Before Stiger could make a suitable reply, he heard the not-so-distant twang of a bow. Instinctually, he rolled to his left and plunged half into the water of the pond. A sharp crack sounded from where he had just been, followed by the immediate clatter of an arrow as it skittered across the rocks behind him.

The water was ice cold, but the suddenness of the attack was even more shocking and sobering.

Incredibly angry at himself for letting his guard down, for becoming complacent, Stiger dragged himself back up onto the rock and set off at a run, half crouched across the rocks toward the safety of the trees. An arrow hissed by his head. There was another crack just behind him, and ahead an arrow buried itself into a tree with a hard thud, quivering with spent energy.

Theo called out an oath, scrambled, slipped, and splashed into the shallow water behind him. Dog began barking madly. Shouts rang out from his guards as they reacted to the unexpected attack.

Diving the last few feet, Stiger threw himself behind the thickest tree he could find as yet another arrow thunked into its wooden bark on the opposite side. Breathing heavily, he glanced around and saw his sword in its scabbard where he'd left it just three feet away and leaning against a tree. Stiger risked a glance out. He saw movement in the brush on the other side of the pond, but nothing more. He could not see who the attackers were, but it was clear there was more than one, if not many.

Theo crashed down behind a tree a few feet away, completely soaked and wide-eyed.

"Who in the great fiery caverns are they?" Theo glanced out from behind the tree. "By my beard, that was a close thing."

Stiger glanced over at the dwarf. Theo was uninjured. He looked back toward the far bank of the pond. Dog, standing on the rocks, continued to bark madly. Amongst the trees behind him, the dwarves were calling to each other, readying themselves. There were no more arrows, which meant the attackers had either fled or were coming to attack. Stiger leaned toward the latter.

A strange, inarticulate battle cry sounded off to his right. Stiger's head snapped around. Whatever was happening was concealed by the brush and trees. He heard the ringing clash of arms.

It drove him to action. Stiger made a sprint for his sword, running out into the open, hoping no more arrows came his way. His hand closed on the pommel. It was the first time he had drawn the sword since he had stepped through the World Gate weeks before. The familiar electric tingle ran from his fingers and palm right up his arm and into his being.

The power of the sword surged and for a moment time seemed to slow. Stiger sucked in a breath and let it out. The action seemed to take an eternity. A falling leaf caught his eye. It floated with an incredible sluggishness toward the forest floor.

Then, with a near audible snap, the world began moving again at its normal speed. The sound of the fighting had spread out and Stiger remembered he was standing in the open. With a flick of his arm he threw the scabbard off. The exposed blade exploded into brilliant blue fire that roared silently, with tongues of blue flame licking at the air.

Stiger turned to his left. The fighting there sounded closer. Amongst the greenery, the backs of two of his guards were barely visible, flashes of sunlight reflected from their armor. He moved in their direction and emerged to find the two dwarves locked in combat with five opponents fighting amongst waist-high brush.

Orcs.

What were they doing here?

Stiger at first was shocked to see them. He hesitated a moment, faltering. And then with a sudden clarity he recalled the vision the sword had shown him of the battle fought against an army of orcs, of Delvaris defeating the minion at the cost of his own life. Realization slammed home. The killing of Delvaris had changed nothing in this time, not the events already in motion. The orcs were still coming to take the valley. These must be advance scouts.

Stiger studied the fight before him. The orcs wore black leather armor with brown pants, and were essentially light infantry. They wielded long, wicked-looking swords that had a slight curve for slashing rather than jabbing. They carried no shields. Bows were slung across their backs, as were light packs. This reinforced his feeling they were in all probability scouts.

The dwarves, on the other hand, had come armed to the teeth and heavily armored by comparison. Though outnumbered, this difference in kit was not inconsiderable, and they were managing to hold their own—just barely. The body of an orc lay twitching on the ground as the five attackers moved around the two dwarves with the intent of surrounding and overwhelming them. An injured orc was attempting to crawl away from the fight, dragging a long tangle of intestines after him, some of which had caught amongst the brush.

Stiger's anger at himself for not realizing that the orcs were still coming for the valley and the surprise of their attack exploded into a thundering rage. The frustration of his failure and everything that had occurred since he had arrived through the World Gate came to the surface. The sword flared brilliantly and throbbed in his hand, its power screaming for release.

Roaring his rage for all to hear, he charged forward at the nearest orc, which had turned to face him. The creature's eyes narrowed. The orc took a step back to gain room, and then another, bringing its sword down to strike at him as it did so. Stiger brought his up. When the two blades met there was a terrific flash, followed by an audible crack. The orc's sword shattered to bits, the pieces hitting Stiger's chest, stomach, and leg.

The orc stared stupidly at the stump of the sword. Before it could react and recover from the shock, Stiger jabbed forward and into his opponent's chest. There was an awful sizzling sound as the sword slipped in with ease, as if Stiger were cutting butter with a hot knife. The hilt of his sword warmed in his hand as the orc's eyes immediately glazed over and a final breath escaped from its lips.

Stiger shoved his opponent roughly back and off his sword as another orc turned to face him. The sword came away bloody, but that changed as the greenish blood bubbled and boiled away into a black smoke. Stiger faced the new threat and dropped into a combat stance.

His opponent's eyes went from Stiger's face to the sword and back. Stiger saw a grim determination steal over in the other's look. Without understanding how, he knew instinctually that this was no mere scouting party. They had come specifically for him. The orc advanced. It bared its tusks at him and tossed its sword from hand to hand as it closed the distance. It was an attempt to confuse Stiger as to which side the first strike would come from.

I hunger for its soul, the sword hissed. *Take it and we become stronger, more powerful, unstoppable.*

Encouraged, Stiger took a step forward to meet his enemy, an unaccustomed eagerness driving him to the killing. He felt his scar along his cheek pull tight as a grin formed on his face. He took another step, hungry for the orc's death, its promised soul.

There was a sudden flash of gray as something large shot by Stiger's face, literally flying through the air. The surprise of it stopped him in his tracks and he blinked. Dog, jaws open, slammed into the orc, knocking him backwards and into a big bush. Down in a tumble they went, Dog growling like a wild animal, powerful jaws snapping, teeth ripping. The tumble ended with the orc on his back and Dog on top. The orc screamed in fear.

Shocked, Stiger's anger fled in a flash. He watched in horrified fascination as Dog, with one snap of his jaws, tore the orc's throat clean open, exposing spinal bone and abruptly cutting off the scream. Blood sprayed across Dog's fur and into the air in a sickening arc before rapidly ceasing. The orc went limp.

To Stiger's immediate right, one of the dwarves wielding a battle axe buried it deeply in the chest of an orc he was facing. The orc roared in pain and it snapped Stiger back into the fight and away from Dog. He turned as the other dwarf went down, bodily knocked over by a large orc. The orc, standing over the struggling dwarf, raised his sword for a finishing strike.

Stiger stepped forward and used his sword to block the killing blow. Their swords met with a powerful clang. The enemy's sword did not shatter. Stiger's sword still glowed, but it had lost the blazing blue fire it had at the beginning of the fight.

He felt the blow communicated to his hand, which tingled a bit. He gripped the hilt tighter and jabbed forward. The orc jumped back to avoid the strike and swung his long sword in a slashing attack aimed for Stiger's neck. Stiger danced to the side and brought his sword back up and neatly blocked the strike. The orc kicked out with a booted foot. It connected painfully with Stiger's side, sending him reeling several steps back.

With a savage roar, the orc pushed forward to continue his attack. Stiger managed to block another strike, his hand aching painfully from the repeated blows. Dog leapt onto the orc's back, taking it to the ground, jaws snapping closed on the left shoulder, teeth sinking deeply. The orc screamed in maddened pain and attempted to shake the animal off. Dog held on and shook his head, tearing skin and shredding muscle.

Stiger took the opportunity and drove his sword into the creature's back. The sword sizzled once again and Stiger felt the hilt grow warm in his hand. The warmth seemed to flow up his arm. The creature collapsed to the ground, twitched once, and died.

The immediate action around them ended as the dwarf still on his feet dispatched the last opponent. Stiger could still hear fighting off to the right. It was concealed by the trees and brush. Stiger looked down at Dog. The animal appeared very different than the sad-looking thing that had been hanging about the farm, following him around like a lost soul in search of a friend.

The dog, though the same size, seemed somehow larger, fiercer. There was a ferocious look in its eyes as it gazed up at him. Orcish blood stained the fur around its mouth and chest. Perhaps, he was just seeing Dog with new eyes. Maybe it had always been a killer.

"Good boy," Stiger said, breathing heavily from the exertion of the fight. He hesitated, then reached down a careful hand, patting the animal's head. "Good boy."

The intense gaze softened and the tail gave an enthusiastic wag.

There was an agonized cry through the trees where the fighting was still going on. The dog's head snapped around and it bounded off, quickly lost from sight. Stiger glanced over at the dwarf who was still standing. The warrior gave him a nod and bent down to help up his comrade, who had been having trouble getting to his feet due to the weight of his armor. Stiger returned the nod and headed toward the fighting.

He pushed his way through the brush. The fight ahead sounded quite spirited. The forest was filled with dwarven oaths and cries of alarm and rage. Stiger heard the orc tongue mixed in with the sound of weapon on weapon. Then Dog was amongst them, barking and growling viciously.

A few heartbeats later, Stiger pushed through a thick bush and emerged into a scene of chaos. There were orcs all around, too many to count. Five dwarves struggled mightily to fend them off. There were several bodies already down on the ground, all enemy. As Stiger cleared the brush, he saw Dog take another to the ground, jaws snapping and working as the animal tore flesh and muscle from an arm.

Theo was a few feet to his left, tightly engaged by two orcs. Unlike the others, Theo had come in only his tunic. He had not been on duty, but had still carried a sword. The dwarf fought with no less intensity than the others. Stiger rushed to his aid, attacking one of the orcs pressing Theo. He stabbed deeply into the back of the creature's thigh. The sword punched clean through the muscle, the tip emerging from the other side. He must've hit an artery, for a gush of greenish blood poured out, down the leg, and onto the ground as he drew his blade back. The sword came away coated in blood and bits of skin. As it fell to the ground, mortally wounded, the orc dropped its weapon and gripped its leg. To be sure, Stiger followed up with a strike to the unguarded belly. The orc grunted as the blade went in and roared in pain before choking as blood poured from its mouth.

There was no time to wonder why the sword had not sizzled or killed the orc outright. The intensity of its glow had faded, now barely perceptible.

An orc came crashing through the brush, rushing him. Stiger brought his sword up to block the slashing blow swinging down toward his head and at the last moment dodged to the right and into the orc's path, at the same time bringing his sword around, point up. The orc's sword whistled through empty space a half heartbeat before the two of them crashed violently together. Stiger's sword plunged deeply into the other's belly, easily penetrating the hardened leather armor. The orc grunted. Hot blood poured over Stiger's hand and arm.

The force of the impact drove Stiger to the ground, the weight of his enemy hammering his shoulder painfully into the forest floor. The creature's momentum carried the orc forward, over and beyond him. Its head smacked against the trunk of a tree with a deep, hollow-sounding *thunk.*

A little dazed, Stiger rolled painfully onto all fours. He looked for his opponent.

The orc was unmoving.

Stiger had lost his sword. He stood, a little wobbly at first, then looked around for his weapon. He did not see it and figured it was likely under the orc he had just taken down. The desperate fight was still raging unabated. There was no time to roll the creature over or hunt for the sword. To do so might expose him to attack. He bent down and picked up a thick stick, really a branch, at least three inches around and four feet long. Theo was closely engaged just a few feet away. The orc had its back to him. Stiger moved forward, stepping around a thick prickly bush and taking aim, slammed the stick into the back of the creature's head. The blow was so powerful that the stick broke upon impact. The orc went down without a sound.

"Thank you," Theo said between breaths and glanced down at the unmoving orc, "for that."

The two dwarves that Stiger and Dog had helped emerged from the brush and joined the fight. Shouting battle cries in their own tongue, they came on. One lowered his head and charged, striking the back of an orc with his helmet. The creature gave an *umff* and fell forward to the ground, the breath having gone from its lungs. The dwarf calmly raised his battle axe and swung downward at the neck, almost taking the head off with the strike.

Stiger glanced around, looking for an opponent. Where moments before there had been lots of the enemy, now there were only a handful. There was a shout from one of the orcs. The call was repeated and with that, they turned as one and fled into the trees.

An injured orc tried to flee with the others but could only manage a slow hobble, painfully dragging its wounded left leg. A dwarf with a battle hammer stepped up behind him and swung, smashing the creature to the ground with a powerful blow. The orc lay still, its back half caved in where the blow had landed. The dwarf spit on his dead enemy for good measure.

"Cowards!" Theo yelled at them. "Come back and let's finish this!"

A severed forearm in his mouth, Dog looked up at the fleeing orcs, who were disappearing into the trees and brush. He dropped the arm and bounded after them, barking madly, and was quickly lost from view as he plunged through the brush. A moment later there was an agonized cry, and a deep thud as a body crashed to the ground somewhere off in the trees, followed by growling and the terrified screams of Dog's latest quarry.

"I must admit it, I like that dog," Theo said to Stiger, gulping air and struggling to catch his breath. "No matter what you say, he is a hunter, that one. I think Sarai is right. You should keep him."

Stiger gave an absent nod. The dog's sudden ferocity had certainly been surprising. A moment later, he thought of the combatants and glanced around at the dwarves. A dwarf to his left finished off a wounded orc with a quick stab to the throat. The orc choked for several moments as green blood fountained up into the air. Then the creature went limp and the flow of blood ceased.

"Is anyone hurt?" Stiger asked them in dwarven.

The dwarves checked themselves over. A number shook their heads or replied no.

"I am," Theo remarked, with some surprise. He was glancing down at his leg where there was a shallow cut around four inches long.

"That will need to be cleaned out." Stiger bent down to examine the wound. "And, I am afraid, stitched up."

"You should have worn your armor," one of the dwarves said to Theo.

"That's just like Theogdin," another dwarf said, with a deep chuckle, "always doing things the hard way."

"It was more fun without it," Theo said, and pounded his chest with a fist. "I gain much legend from this!"

Stiger looked in the direction of the pond, wondering if the archers were still there. He and the dwarves were concealed by the brush and trees, but that did not mean they were safe. There was absolutely no doubt in his mind. The orcs had come for him. With that thought, the anger returned.

Yes, the sword hissed in his mind, *feel the anger mount... grow... feel it, embrace it.*

Stiger almost jumped. He looked around for the weapon with more than a little concern. A scream rang out from amongst the trees, followed by shouts. Stiger's head came up. Dog had clearly taken down another.

The realization that the orcs had come to assassinate him rekindled his fury. All he wanted was to be left alone, but they had come for him. How dare they? Worse, he knew they were coming for the valley, and that not only threatened Sarai but his planned future with her.

Stiger found his weapon under the body of the orc he had killed. It took some effort to roll the creature off it. Taking it in hand, the sword began to glow softly again.

"Once a killer," Stiger said to himself unhappily, his eyes on the glowing blade, "always a killer."

"What was that?" Theo asked, looking over at him.

"Nothing," Stiger said, taking a step toward where Dog had disappeared. "We need to clear the area around the pond to make sure they are truly fleeing and not regrouping."

"No," one of the dwarves said. Stiger could not recall his name but knew he was the equivalent of a corporal and currently in charge of the guard detail. "My orders are to keep you safe. We return to the farm."

Stiger looked at the dwarf for a moment and considered refusing. Would they actually try to stop him? Could they? Once in the trees, he could easily disappear. Eli had trained him to conceal himself when needed and move through the forest like a ghost. Once free of them, he could hunt the enemy as Dog was doing now.

"I too would like to track them down," Theo said, before Stiger could reply, "but our duty is clear. The attack has been stopped and legend satisfied. We must get you back to the farm where we can better protect you and Sarai." Theo gazed at him meaningfully.

Stiger looked beyond Theo and into the trees where the orcs had fled. A long, hungry howl from Dog sent shivers up his spine. From the looks of the others, Stiger understood they felt the same. Though he longed to join the chase, and the anger coursing through him almost demanded it, reason won out... as did his concern for Sarai. He swallowed, forcing the rage back down.

Stiger stepped over to the nearest body. The orc was an impressive creature. Standing up, it must have been at least seven feet tall. Intricate tattoos covered the animal-like face, head, and arms. The tattoos appeared to continue under the leather chest armor. The orc was bald, and had likely shaved its head, giving it a sinister look.

"You're right," Stiger said, looking up as Theo joined him. "There may be more out there that we don't know about, and we know they can use bows."

Theo gave a satisfied nod that smacked of intense relief.

Stiger shot a sudden grin at Theo. "You know, until they started shooting at us back at the pond, I never knew you could move that fast."

Theo seemed about ready to reply and then looked back toward the pond. "They could still be out there, as you say... How badly do you want your fishing pole?"

Stiger glanced back toward the pond and chuckled. He suddenly looked around at the dwarves.

"I thought there were ten of you?" Stiger said. "I only count eight, excluding Theo."

The dwarves became immediately concerned. A quick search found the missing two no more than twenty feet away. Both had been brutally cut down, with one having had his throat slit. It looked to Stiger as if the orcs had gotten the jump on them and taken them by surprise.

"They were good boys," Theo said sadly as he closed the eyes of one.

"The best," the corporal said, before turning to his dwarves. "Make litters. We shall not be leaving them here."

A long distant howl rang through the woods. Dog was still on the hunt.

Chapter Six

Stiger stepped out of the barn. The air was comfortable, not too hot or cold. The sky was gray and overcast, and it looked as if they might get some rain later in the day. His dwarven guard stood just a few feet away, looking more diligent and determined than ever. The nearest glanced in his direction, and when their eyes met, the dwarf's expression hardened. Stiger eyed him for a prolonged moment, feeling the stirrings of anger.

It had been two days since the ambush at the pond. Upon Stiger's return, he had discovered oversized boot prints around the farmhouse, larger than a man's and slimmer than a dwarf's. Farther away from the house, some of tracks appeared to be several days old. This had led to a heated argument between him and Captain Aleric. It had almost come to blows, with both Stiger and the dwarven captain becoming apoplectic. The dwarves had clearly not been performing their duty, at least up to Stiger's standards. The captain had been hard-pressed to defend himself, especially with some of the tracks coming right up to the house and barn, where his dwarves had been posted.

The orcs had been watching the farm. That much was certain, and there had been no denying it. Worse, they had likely followed Stiger's party to the pond. Since the argument and the attack, the guard around the farm had been doubled. A second dwarven infantry company had also arrived to provide additional security. There were dwarves everywhere. Stiger was watched even closer than before, though it was now clear they were more invested in protecting him than worried about Stiger escaping. Captain Aleric had even wanted to station his dwarves inside the farmhouse at night. Stiger liked none of it. His anger at both the attack and the lapse had left him simmering. This had all frightened Sarai terribly.

Stiger's hand strayed to the hilt of his sword, which he had taken to wearing at all times. He felt the welcome tingle that came with direct contact and was comforted.

He removed his hand from the hilt as he shifted the bucket from one hand to the next and continued on into the henhouse, where he collected nine good eggs and returned to the barn. He diligently mucked out the stalls. As he was finishing, Theo arrived, limping from the wound he had received.

"How's the leg?"

"Hurts," Theo admitted with a shrug. "I've had worse."

Stiger eyed the dwarf as he limped into the barn. His limp seemed more pronounced than it should have been for such a shallow cut.

"You are playing it up," Stiger accused. "That cut on your leg wasn't all that bad."

The edges of Theo's beard curled slightly. He lowered his voice and switched to common tongue after a careful glance at the nearest of his comrades. "I'm on light duties until it heals." Theo shot Stiger a wink.

"I see," Stiger said. "Then what are you doing here?"

"Official business, I'm afraid," Theo said. "Unfortunately, my captain considers walking here from camp light duty."

"That's, what, a two-hundred-yard walk?" Stiger looked at Theo, faintly amused.

"About that."

Stiger grunted, took hold of the cart and wheeled it outside. Theo limped along behind him, putting on a show for his comrades.

"I think he might be on to me," Theo said with a shrug.

"Why did he send you over?" Stiger suspected that Aleric was still smarting after their argument. Hence the dispatching of Theo. He likely carried bad news.

Theo switched back to dwarven. "I am to inform you that you will be getting visitors today."

Stiger stopped and turned to look back at Theo. "Who?"

"The senior tribune from the legion. The captain told me his name, but honestly, I forgot it," Theo said without any hint of embarrassment. "Father Thomas and..." A frown washed over the dwarf's face. "Apparently Thoggle too, maybe even that Centurion Sabinus. I don't like him. He's too serious and is always checking up on you."

Stiger stopped the cart midway to the compost pile. "Checking up, how?"

"He comes by regular-like to get reports on you from the captain," Theo said. "You're going to have a lot of company today. It should be pretty exciting for you."

"The attack at the pond likely got their attention," Stiger said, thinking that his definition of exciting differed greatly from Theo's.

Theo glanced around at the extra guards. "It may have escaped your notice, but it got everyone's attention. If rumors can be believed, the thane has even ordered the clans to assemble their warriors. They are marching to the valley. That's not happened since we first came to this world."

Stiger resumed wheeling the cart over to the compost pile. Theo followed, his limping causing him to move slower. He looked at Stiger for a long moment.

"Well, my duty here has been done. I'll be off, then." Theo huffed out a breath and started back toward the dwarven camp, hobbling along. "Back to relaxing before a fire with a mug of good spirits, or whatever I can mooch at camp that doesn't involve me laying out silver."

"Any idea on when they might arrive?" Stiger asked Theo.

"Soon, I was told. Sometime this morning." Theo stopped and half turned back. "My advice as your friend ... is to be civil to Thoggle."

"To one without legend?" Stiger almost laughed. For some reason Stiger could not fathom, the dwarves despised their wizards, but here he was being told be polite and respectful to one.

"I mean it," Theo said, tone sobering. "True, he is without legend, but he does have the ear of the thane." Theo glanced around the farm in a meaningful manner. "I do believe this arrangement is much better than having you secured in Old City. The population of the city has been slowly declining over the years, and ... well, let's just say it's not as nice as it used to be. There are only a few hundred dvergr remaining, and those are an unfriendly lot, especially to humans. They'd happily lock you in a room, for your own safety, and then forget where the key was."

"Is there much chance of that?"

"After your little spat and the attack at the pond, Captain Aleric wrote the thane about it," Theo admitted. "He feels it may be best to move you to a more secure location. So perhaps it is best for you to be polite and not disagreeable to one of the few that the thane listens to. I don't know about you, but I think that may be a wise course of action."

With that, Theo turned and left. Stiger watched him go. He let out a long breath and grabbed the shovel to begin emptying the cart. Stiger paused after dumping a shovel full of manure onto the pile. He spared a quick glance around the farm. He felt an odd attachment to the farm, almost as strong as what he had with Sarai. Stiger's eyes lingered on the small house. He had fixed the roof. His gaze slid over to the barn, which he had helped fix up, patching its age-worn boards and then rebuilding or repairing much of the interior. Stiger's eyes returned to his growing pile of split and stacked wood. The farm was now home. Theo was right. This was indeed better than being locked up in Old City, even with all of the guards constantly underfoot.

Stiger returned his mind to the task at hand. He worked quickly and efficiently, shoveling out the manure. As he was finishing up and scraping the cart clean, something made him turn to look back at the barn. Like a ghost, Dog had appeared. Stiger stopped what he was doing and eyed the animal carefully. Dog spotted him and padded his way leisurely over. The dog sat down and gazed up with unblinking eyes, long tongue lolling out from the right side of its mouth. Dog wagged his tail in the dirt and grass, as if to say, Hello there friend. Stiger wasn't sure, but he thought he detected a satisfied air about the animal.

"Where've you been?" Stiger asked, tossing the shovel into the cart. He had not seen Dog since the day of the attack and had wondered if the animal would ever return. After seeing the other side of Dog, Stiger had even half hoped he would never see him again. No luck there, he decided.

"So, are you going to answer me?"

Dog gave a small, clipped bark followed by a whine and looked guiltily away, breaking eye contact.

"I hope you got the rest of them buggers," Stiger said, and he meant it.

Dog turned his gaze back to Stiger and gave a single bark, tail wagging enthusiastically. Stiger felt himself frown as he looked on the animal. He talked to a sword and now it seemed to an animal as well.

Was he going insane?

Stiger shook his head, glanced toward the heavens, and then wheeled the cart back into the barn. Dog followed along like an obedient pet, looking nothing like the animal who'd ripped out the throat of an orc at the pond. The dog's sad appearance had returned, and the fearsome, vicious killer was absent, as if it had never been.

Returning the cart to its place, Stiger emerged from the barn, Dog still walking along at his side. He noticed the nearest guard, one of the dwarves who had accompanied him to Bowman's Pond, take a careful step away. The dwarf's eyes fell uneasily on the animal. Stiger almost laughed but restrained himself, for he had seen firsthand the true killer nature the animal had displayed. Stiger did not understand how, but he sensed the animal was no threat to him—only his enemies.

Stiger made his way over to the woodpile, intent upon working out some of his frustration. The dwarves followed at a discreet distance and set up positions within ten to fifteen feet of him. There was another larger cordon just out of sight and roving patrols even farther out. The orcs would have a difficult job of sneaking back up to the farm.

As Stiger reached to pick up the axe from where its head was embedded in the chopping stump, Dog gave a low growl. He glanced at the animal, who had lain down in the grass. Dog's head was up and he was looking intently in the direction they had just come.

Stiger turned and froze.

Menos, otherwise known as Sian Tane, was standing no less than thirty paces away and looking squarely at him.

Stiger straightened and let out a long breath. This was not how he had expected his day to go.

Menos was a tall, thin, and pale man. Though describing him as a man was far off the mark. Menos was noctalum, the first race the gods had created. He was fair with near perfect features, much like those of an elf. His ears were even pointed as well. His pupils were silver, as was his beard and long straight hair that ran down his back. Menos wore a long gray robe that was well cut with rich, smooth fabric. A delicate black and gray crown rested upon his head. Despite the silvery hair, he had the appearance of being in his prime.

Stiger felt suddenly uneasy, for he knew the true nature of this creature. Their eyes met, and Stiger felt his mood abruptly sour. Here was trouble, and Stiger hated trouble. They regarded each other silently for several moments, then Menos moved forward. He seemed to glide across the ground as he approached. Stiger's dwarven guards took one look at the newcomer and almost as one fell to a knee, bowing their heads. The nearest trembled in the presence of the noctalum as he brushed by. Menos paid them no mind. He strode up until he stood within four paces of Stiger and stopped.

Dog's growling ceased as Menos's eyes fell upon the animal. A slight hint of a smile twitched the noctalum's beard, and even managed to touch his eyes. He held out a hand, palm upward. Dog stood, approached, and sniffed cautiously at the proffered hand, then emitted a soft whine. Using the same hand, Menos brought it slowly around and up to the top of Dog's head, where he scratched affectionately.

The dog's tail began wagging happily. Stiger had the uncomfortable feeling that the two recognized each other.

After a few heartbeats, Menos withdrew his hand. Dog seemed disappointed for a moment, then shook himself and padded back to Stiger, where he sat at his side and stared at the noctalum. Menos turned his gaze back upon Stiger.

"You are lucky to have been blessed with such a companion," Menos said, eyes returning to the animal only briefly. "Lucky indeed, for a human."

"I know what you are," Stiger said. He was no mood for small talk. Though the dwarves bent knee before the noctalum, Stiger refused to do so. He realized he should show some sign of respect, but Menos's condescending manner irritated him deeply.

Menos raised an eyebrow at that but said nothing.

"Should I call you Menos, caretaker of the World Gate, or is it Sian Tane, the noctalum, the dragon?" Stiger cocked his head to one side as he regarded the other and waited for a response.

Menos let slip a raspy chuckle that betrayed no hint of surprise or actual amusement.

"You are as bold as the paladin let on you would be," Menos said. "Impudent too, especially as you know me and I not you. One would think you would show more respect and deference to one of my kind." Menos fell silent for a number of heartbeats. "It has been a great long time since someone challenged me as openly as you do."

Stiger said nothing to that and just waited. The dwarves remained kneeling, almost seeming to hold their collective breaths.

Menos gave a slight shrug. "However, I prefer you address me as Menos when in this form."

"Then that is what I shall call you," Stiger said, and inclined his head slightly. "Welcome, Menos."

"I cannot read you," Menos said plainly.

"You mean you tried invade my mind?"

"I made an attempt," Menos admitted without any hint of guilt or surprise. The noctalum gestured toward Stiger's sword. "But that insult to life you carry has prevented me from learning more about you."

Stiger felt himself scowl.

"You and the paladin told the wizard everything, but he tells me little," Menos said. "I do not like that."

"I was warned against revealing too much," Stiger said, "by Thoggle and another wizard."

"It seems you keep interesting company."

"I have been known to," Stiger said, "and it has included a pair of noctalum."

Menos fell silent, though his gaze did not waver. Stiger returned it.

"I wonder who this other wizard is?" Menos wagged a delicate finger when Stiger declined to answer. "It matters little. The advice you were given is wise. Though I must admit I am sorely tempted to learn more of my future. Curiosity is a fire that is hard to extinguish amongst my kind." Menos paused and shot a glance toward the house, almost as if a thought had occurred to him. "Perhaps you shared more than just a home with the woman who lives here? Is it possible you told her more than you should?"

Stiger felt his eyes narrow. He became alarmed at the prospect of the noctalum invading Sarai's mind. She deserved no such thing.

Menos gave a cold laugh. "I see my intuition is quite correct. Your kind has its predictable weaknesses."

"You will not search her mind," Stiger said firmly, his anger building at the thought of such an invasion. "Do we understand each other?"

The noctalum regarded Stiger for several heartbeats and then gave a nod, perhaps more to himself than to Stiger's demand.

"You have nothing to fear," Menos said. "Though my desire to do so is strong, I will not probe her mind, nor will my mate. You have my word on that."

"Thank you," Stiger said.

"I do it not for you," Menos said.

"What do you want?" Stiger had seriously tired of the noctalum's game. "Tell me or be gone."

"Know that I tolerate your disrespect because it serves my interests." Menos's tone became hard. "One day that may no longer hold true."

Stiger clearly understood his meaning. Still, his anger was up and he had difficulty caring, especially after the creature had threatened Sarai. How dare he? It was odd, for deep down Stiger knew he should fear the noctalum with every fiber of his being.

"Thoggle very much desires me to stay away from you," Menos said. "My mate, Currose, feels as he does. So naturally I thought I would come anyway… to offer you a warning,"

"A warning," Stiger said. "About what?"

"I am sure you know this already. The blade that protects you is a very dangerous weapon. But you probably do not know that it is just as dangerous to you as it is to those you face in battle, if not more so," Menos said with a slight gesture toward the sword. "You are the one destined to wield Rarokan, but if you're not careful, the sword will wield you."

Stiger did not enjoy the thought of that. Ogg had warned him of the same thing. Though surprisingly, now that Stiger thought of it, Thoggle had said nothing on the subject.

"I have had another give me similar advice," Stiger said.

"Good," Menos said. "You are somewhat aware of the dangers, then."

"Who chose me?" The thought popped out before Stiger could think of a better way to phrase the question.

"Why, your god, of course." Menos stepped over to Stiger's growing pile of split wood. He picked up the axe, examined it for a moment and then returned it to its place on the stump and then looked back up at Stiger. "The one you call the High Father, the one your ancestors from Earth named Jupiter. It was he who bound the soul of the betrayer, a dwarven wizard named Rarokan, to the sword. It was Rarokan who set everything in motion and forced the gods down their destructive path."

Stiger could not resist a look down at the sword, suddenly feeling incredibly uncomfortable with it being so close to his person. He wanted nothing more than to shed himself of it.

Menos noticed Stiger's discomfort. "Yes, he is in there and has been trapped for more than an age."

"A wizard is in my sword?"

"He isn't just any wizard," Menos continued. "Rarokan was a High Master, one of a handful of the most powerful of wizards. The High Masters not only have the ability to move through space, but time as well. Not even the noctalum were granted that ability, which is why we created the World Gates." Menos paused, sucking in a breath. "A High Master wields incredible power, the extent of which wizards like Thoggle can only dream of and guess at."

"Why are you telling me this?"

"Why?" Menos arched an eyebrow. "Knowledge is power. For you to have a chance against a mind such as Rarokan, you must first understand what you face. It is this understanding that I have come to share. I fear a great many lives may depend upon it."

"Speak on." Stiger rubbed his jaw, not wanting to hear more, but at the same time he knew he must. He gave a nod for Menos to continue. "I am listening."

"Rarokan, as I have said, was once one of the most powerful wizards in existence. To attain such power, one first needs terrible ambition. Once attained, there is a terrible temptation to use the power in ways it was not meant to be used." Menos took a step closer to Stiger, silver eyes intense. "Rarokan thought he knew better than the gods and meddled where he ought not. As punishment, his soul was torn from his body and imprisoned within an instrument that brings death—something he can still inflict upon others but will never know himself. It is a horrendous price to pay for one's ambitions, but I'm led to understand that he knew in advance the cost of his folly and went ahead regardless."

"What did he do?"

"Like you, I have revealed perhaps too much," Menos admitted. "Only know that his actions were base enough for both the High Father and another to hand him a punishment far worse than death and eternal damnation."

Stiger once again glanced down at his sword, almost as if seeing it for the first time. It was strange to think there was a soul bound up within the hard metal. And yet deep down, for some reason it seemed he had always known. The sword in a way was alive.

"Rarokan's mind and soul are trapped within that blade," Menos continued. "Be warned, he is no less dangerous than he was prior to his imprisonment. The wizard, though confined and limited, is still powerful, almost beyond imagining. Just as before, he feeds off of the souls of others and in turn spends their energy. Though he can no longer cast spells, he has the ability and power to reach beyond the sword itself, including into your mind."

Stiger remained silent as he considered the other's words. He liked none of what he was hearing.

"As he stole the souls of countless beings to amass his power," Menos said, "so too will he try to claim yours. Thoggle desired I not reveal this next part to you, as he feels it is far too early for such things." Menos closed his eyes. "I cannot penetrate your mind. However, judging by the anger I sense radiating from your aura, Rarokan has already begun his conquest." The noctalum opened his eyes and looked deeply into Stiger's. "So… in the end it seems I was quite correct to come to you and offer fair warning."

Stiger was horrified. He closed his eyes and thought of the sword. In his mind he asked, *Is this true?*

Yes, came the reply, *you are mine and I am yours. Together we are one weapon. Together we can change things. Together we can become stronger than the gods.*

Stiger opened his eyes and stumbled back a step, in shock.

"He tells you truth, I see," Menos said, eyes narrowing. "Doesn't he?"

Stiger gave a reluctant nod.

"It is no less than I would expect, for all deception begins with a little truth," Menos said. "You must not let him dictate your destiny. Take control before it becomes too late."

"How do I stop him? He is a wizard and I am just a man."

"If I am not mistaken, you are a fighter," Menos said. "Isn't that correct?"

Stiger gave another nod.

"Then fight him you must, with all the strength you can muster. You have been chosen by your god." Menos paused and then added, "As was he. Yet you are the one meant to use him, not the other way around. Bend Rarokan to your will, for destiny has been laid upon you and is yours to dictate. The gods have given you freedom in this, and with it comes a power all its own. You can master it, and make your *will* matter."

The answer was not what Stiger had been looking for. It didn't tell him how to do what Menos suggested. He had a sense—or, more accurately, a fear—that the sword was listening to every word the noctalum was saying.

I listen through your ears, the sword confirmed, sounding almost amused. *I see through your eyes. We are one. We are the same.*

"I won't use it," Stiger said, unslinging the sword and setting it down on the wood pile. "I won't ever touch it again."

Stiger thought he heard the distant echoes of a mad laugh, cackling with amusement, but was unsure.

"Carry the blade with you or not, it matters little." Menos gave him a sad look. "You were inextricably linked the moment you shared power. The bond is secure and permanent. He is as much a part of you now as you are of him."

Stiger glanced down at the sword in mounting horror. He understood the truth in the noctalum's words. The bond with the sword was permanent. There was no way to sever it.

"No," Menos said, "there is nothing you can do to cut the link, except perhaps die. In such an event, his purpose would end as well, but he would continue throughout all eternity, adrift with his failure or success, depending upon how you look on it." The noctalum paused, eyes sliding to the sword. "Still, in balance, Rarokan's heinous acts and self-sacrifice, if you can call it that, now give our cause hope when before there was none."

"Hope?" Stiger asked. All he felt was despair. The gods were once again turning his world upside down.

"There is a summit coming between the dwarves and orcs," Menos said, abruptly switching subjects, as if the previous one was now of little concern to him. "I will not be attending, for I loathe orcs with all of my being. I have sworn to kill each and every one with a black heart I set my sight upon."

Stiger blinked as the noctalum's train of thought shifted. He gave a slight shake of his head and looked at Menos, comprehending what had just been said. He could not think of a more ridiculous idea.

"They are coming to take the valley," Stiger stated with certainty. "I've told Thoggle this."

"I know," Menos said, "though Thoggle has not told me. I can sense Castor's minion at work, its power growing as well as the *will* of its followers. With each passing day, Castor's strength is increasing upon this world. Where before it was but a footprint, now it is the entire foot."

"So why even bother with a summit? What can be accomplished?"

"There has long been a peace between dwarves, humans, and the orcs in this area," Menos said. "I understand there is some optimism on both sides that they can avoid the war that is coming. It was not the dwarves, but the orc king who requested the summit."

"King?"

"Yes," Menos said. "I am told his name is Therik and he rules over all of the tribes, a first for one of his kind. He apparently has some honor, though I personally find that difficult to believe."

"I see," Stiger said. "And he thinks he can stop what's to come?"

"Brogan, thane of the dwarves, certainly hopes so," Menos said. "We fast approach the time when the Last War shall return. Thoggle knows this, but I think he desires to believe otherwise, or at least to delay things a little longer."

"Why tell me all this?" Stiger said.

"Beyond my giving you fair warning?"

"Yes."

"I had hoped by coming here you would reveal something of my future," Menos said. "Though you have told me little, you confirmed much that I had speculated on. I thank you for that and consider our meeting having borne some fruit."

Menos paused again and sucked in another deep breath.

"Before I take my leave, I have something else to share with you," Menos said, almost as afterthought. "Thoggle has cast a web upon you."

"A web? What is that?"

"It is a spell specifically tailored to your being," Menos explained. "He spun it after you arrived here. To your kind and others, you shall appear as if you were Delvaris himself and not as you really are. You will look and sound the same to yourself, but for others who knew you not before the spell was weaved... you shall be Delvaris, almost as if the man had been reborn."

Stiger sucked in a breath. "Why would he do that?"

"Why indeed?"

"Sarai?" Stiger glanced toward the house. "She sees me as I am, then?"

"It would seem so."

"With my coming here and the death of Delvaris, Thoggle told me emphatically the future has changed," Stiger said. "So did... the other wizard, now that I think on it."

"Did he?" Menos seemed interested. "Did they indeed?"

"Thoggle called me a paradox," Stiger said. "Or maybe it was that I had caused one. I am not sure."

Menos was silent for several moments, clearly thinking on what Stiger had said. "You may be, and you might not be."

"That's a bit cryptic," Stiger said. "I was hoping for something a little more helpful."

"Thoggle is a Master of his order," Menos said. "He is not a High Master and does not see time in such a manner as his betters do. Like Thoggle, noctalum have a limited vision of both the past, present, future, and the flow of the in-between. Perhaps the future you came from is still there, remaining linear and untouched, not bent, twisted, or altered beyond recognition. It is possible that all that happens in this time was meant to be, and for you is both your past and rightful future. Or it could be something altogether different."

Stiger felt a sudden surge of hope for the first time since he had arrived in this time. Maybe he hadn't failed after all? Then something occurred to him and his thoughts darkened once again.

"The sword showed me a vision." Intrigued by Menos's line of thought, Stiger fully threw caution to the wind. "It showed me Delvaris fighting and dying on a battlefield. That didn't happen. As you well know, he died before the World Gate."

"Interesting." Menos was silent for several heartbeats. "Since it was Thoggle who convinced Brogan to attend this summit, and especially considering the casting of the web, it seems the wizard has a plan. I will have to ponder on your words and will speak with the wizard. I might be able to provide additional counsel before Thoggle decides to tamper with my memory."

"He can do that?" Stiger said, surprised.

"Not without my willing participation," Menos admitted. "But I will allow him to do so, if I believe it will permit the future to play out as it was meant to. That is ... if he can convince me it will. If not, then I shall intervene in a way only the noctalum can."

Stiger rubbed his jaw. He thought intensely on what Menos had just said. It was clear that, as suggested, Thoggle had plans for him. Why else make him appear as Delvaris? The hope continued to grow. A great heavy weight began to lift off his back.

Perhaps there was still a chance to set things right, to restore the future to what it had been. Or maybe it had never been altered, and the past, as Menos had said, was playing out as it was supposed to. Stiger didn't know for sure. This was all incredibly confusing to consider. There was just so much he didn't understand or couldn't be certain of. He gazed at the farmhouse and suddenly felt a wash of sadness mixed with extreme reluctance roll over him. Menos followed his eyes.

"I was told that Thoggle is on his way to see me, along with Father Thomas and the senior tribune of the legion," Stiger said. "I suspect they will desire me at this summit."

"That is possible," Menos said. "As wielder of Rarokan, and with the mark of destiny, you are an expected central figure in events to come."

"I want nothing to do with this summit, or what is going to happen when the orcs come out of the mountains," Stiger said. "I have had enough suffering. For the first time in my life, I am truly content. I wish to set my burden aside."

"Happiness, contentment, suffering," Menos said, drawing Stiger's gaze back. "Destiny has its stamp upon you, as it has been placed upon your line ever since Rarokan meddled. No, you cannot put the burden aside, for the gods are not yet finished with you. Even I can sense that." Menos fell silent for a prolonged moment. "You can choose to do nothing, resist their will—it is your right. But by doing so, you may not find the continued happiness or the contentment that you so desire. Instead you may find yourself suffering worse than you could have ever imagined. You must choose, one way or the other. Nothing is guaranteed, as nothing is certain. Though your kind is short-lived, life should have taught you that by now."

"I may very well choose to do nothing then," Stiger said.

"As I have said, that is your right."

The two fell silent for several moments.

"I have had enough dealing with evil gods, minions, and orcs." Stiger glared at Menos.

"Whether you take up the challenge or not is up to you, but I am afraid the other side will still see you as a threat to be countered."

"That was why I was attacked two days ago?" Stiger said, rubbing his chin and looking in the direction of Bowman's Pond. "They wanted to eliminate me … to remove the threat to their plans. Isn't that right?"

When Menos did not answer, Stiger looked over to find the noctalum gone. He glanced around and saw no one. It was as if Menos had vanished into thin air. The dwarves were still kneeling and had not risen. Dog had placed his head between his paws and gone to sleep. Stiger felt himself frown in irritation. Why couldn't things ever be simple?

Now, the sword hissed in his mind, *you just begin to understand…*

Chapter Seven

Crack! The piece of wood split neatly and satisfyingly in two. Stiger reached for the next piece, while shooting an annoyed glance at the nearest of his guards. Once he had begun splitting the logs, the dwarves had resumed their positions.

Crack! Another piece split.

He had been at it for at least an hour and had worked up a good sweat. Stiger wiped his brow with the back of his arm to keep the sweat out of his eyes. Stiger's old sergeant from Seventh Company, Tiro, had introduced him to wood splitting as a way to work out some frustration. Stiger wished he had Tiro around to talk to, or even Eli. His friend would have some comforting, wise advice. Tiro would provide the gruff kind.

So, he said silently to the sword, *I am stuck with you.*

Nothing.

I know you're in there. Speak to me. Are you as vile as the noctalum made you out to be?

Irritated that the sword did not immediately answer, Stiger started to reach for another piece.

I am Rarokan, High Master of the Blue, the sword responded with a suddenness and intensity that caused Stiger to almost drop the piece of wood he had picked up. He took a calming breath and placed it on the chopping stump. Stiger hefted the axe as the sword continued, *I fight the ilk of the dark gods.*

"So, you aren't evil, then?" Stiger almost laughed. The nearest dwarf looked over at him with a question in his eyes. Stiger realized he had said the last aloud.

Some would consider me so. Without all of the facts, they ignorantly judge me.

So, Stiger said, *tell me, then.*

I fight the gathering darkness that is even now sweeping over all things. Long have I planned. Long have I waited. It is nearly time for action. It is nearly time for the tide to be rolled back.

That did not answer my question.

The sword remained stubbornly silent. Stiger split another piece of wood.

Why me? he asked the sword.

Why not?

Stiger felt himself frown at the cheeky response. He resumed his splitting, working his way through a dozen more pieces.

Why me? Stiger asked again. *Why would the gods choose me? Why not someone else?*

Stiger wondered if it would answer his question or avoid it. More of the puzzle had been filled in, but there was just so much he did not know.

I traveled the pathways of time, searching world after world. I looked and looked, until at last I was ready to give up. Then I discovered a clue that led me to an unexpected place. It was one that should have been obvious from the start. So, following the clue, I willingly broke the Covenant, one of the key rules for my kind, and searched humanity's cradle world, Earth. It was there I found what I was looking for, what I needed.

And what was that? Stiger thought back.

There is strength in your line, latent power in your blood that makes you and those who came before you and those who will come after suitable. No matter what the noctalum says, the gods did not select you. I chose you.

Stiger split several more pieces. He knew that he should feel proud that he had been chosen, but he felt more conflicted about it than anything else. The truth was he did not fully understand what it all meant, but what he got was that he was somehow special and the gods had taken notice.

Correct, the sword hissed. *There is a measure of Jupiter within you, a tiny divine spark, if you will, making you very special indeed.*

The High Father?

Yes... where nearly all other humans have lost it, a small portion of the light of creation yet remains, lingering inside of you. I arranged for the line of another with the spark to merge with your line, making that diminutive portion greater, stronger, more profound. Stiger could sense the satisfaction emanating from the sword. *Then, I added destiny's touch and you became more important.*

You are saying I have some of Jupiter's power inside me?

Even as I was punished for these actions, it is what made you acceptable to Jupiter, it is why he selected you as his champion.

Stiger missed the piece of wood he was aiming for. The axe head stuck firmly into the chopping stump, splitting part of it aside. He worked it free and stood there a moment. With every little piece of information, Stiger felt more trapped. He closed his eyes and took a deep breath.

What is it that you expect me to do?

Stiger waited for reply. The sword remained silent.

I grow tired of this. Answer me.

Nothing from the sword.

It enraged Stiger.

Good, the sword said, *feed your anger, embrace it... for you will need it. Your rage fuels our connection and helps to cement our bond. Your anger frequently wakes me from my long-tormented slumber. Yet, this conversation has expended too much of my will... As the bond between us continues to strengthen, the effort to communicate will become easier... as will unlocking your potential. But my time now is growing short. Soon I must return to my restless slumber amidst the nothingness.*

I am done, Stiger said to it.

Are you? the sword hissed, with a mocking laugh. *I think not.*

You desire to control me, Stiger said. *You never will.*

I already do and I always have. You are mine and I am yours. We are now one will.

Stiger felt chilled by the statement. He felt the presence that inhabited the sword leave. It was the first time he had truly ever felt Rarokan's distinct consciousness and knew that the conversation with the wizard was over. Strangely, it left him feeling less than whole, as if he were missing a part of himself.

He resumed his chopping at a more vigorous and strenuous pace. His hands began to ache from the repeated strikes. The friction from the handle was starting to rub his palms red. Still, he continued.

Stiger only stopped when he heard horses and turned to see who it was. There were three riders approaching, moving steadily down the dirt track that led to the farm. The track ran parallel with their small pasture and, filled with potholes, was a poor excuse for a road. The riders rode along the fencing that stretched around the small pasture behind the barn. Their single cow and horse happily grazed on the grass, uncaring and unconcerned as the visitors passed.

Stiger recognized Father Thomas. The paladin wore a simple brown priestly robe. His two companions were legionaries, their armor and helmets reflecting bright flashes of sunlight. One was Centurion Sabinus and the other a tribune whom Stiger had yet to meet. Much like Sabinus's, the tribune's armor was of an older type, though it was that of a senior officer and not a centurion. Stiger had seen such ancient armor displayed in his family's ancestor room, along with the wax death masks of his important forebears. Around the tribune's chest, a pale blue ribbon denoted his rank as the senior tribune for the legion. It would be him to whom command would have fallen after Delvaris's death.

Stiger saw no sign of Thoggle.

Dog woke as the sound of the hooves became louder. The animal stood, shook itself, and growled, low and guttural, at the newcomers.

"Fat lot of good you are, as a watch dog, that is," Stiger said to it. The animal glanced up at him before returning to watch the riders.

As they turned their horses into the farmyard, Father Thomas spotted him standing next to the woodpile. The paladin offered him a friendly wave. Sarai stepped out of the house as the riders came up. They exchanged greetings as the three dismounted and secured their horses to the hitching mount.

As he rounded the side of his horse, the tribune came to a complete stop at the sight of Stiger. He stared for a long moment. Then he said something to Sabinus that Stiger could not hear, pointed, and immediately made his way over, trailed by Father Thomas and the centurion.

Clearly in his late twenties, the tribune was tall, thin, and in excellent shape. His arms were muscular and his face fair, yet weathered. The tribune's helmet hid the color of his hair, but his eyes were brown and sharp. He had a confident manner of someone accustomed to command. The tribune's armor and red cape were of excellent quality, which established that he was from a wealthy house. He wore the ring of a senatorial family, and Stiger figured he was likely a year or two away from receiving an appointment to legate.

"What is this?" the tribune demanded of Stiger in the common tongue, all color drained from his face. He untied the straps of his helmet and lifted it off his head to reveal short-cropped brown hair that was matted. He was starting to go prematurely bald. "Great gods, it can't be, can it? No, this is impossible."

Stiger's irritation only increased. It had begun with Menos. The sword had only contributed to his mounting frustration, and now this indignity, thanks to Thoggle.

"I'm not sure what you mean?" Father Thomas said, before Stiger could say anything. Stiger noticed that Father Thomas's eyes skipped from the tribune to Dog, seeming to widen before snapping back to the tribune.

"You told me we were coming to see this Stiger you keep speaking about," the tribune said and turned back to address Stiger. "You died. I saw your body. There was no chance of survival. How can you possibly be alive?"

Stiger dropped the axe and pinched the bridge of his nose, feeling a headache coming on. If Thoggle had been present, he could have gladly strangled the wizard.

Sabinus looked between Stiger and the tribune, his eyes narrowing. In the old tongue, Lingua Romano, he said, "Sir, you mean to tell me you know this man?"

"Of course, I know him," the tribune said, still speaking in common, turning to Sabinus in an irritated manner. "By the gods, man, you know him as well." A deeper look of irritation stole over the tribune's face. "Centurion, standing orders are to speak common. When around the dwarves we need to appear open with them. Get into the habit of using common, which most all of them speak."

"Yes, sir," Sabinus said, switching to common. "Sir, the first I saw him was when he came through the World Gate, no more than four months ago."

"Are you having a jest with me?" The tribune became heated. "How could you not know our legate?"

Father Thomas cleared his throat. "Ah… I believe I can explain."

All eyes turned to the paladin.

"Tribune Arvus," Father Thomas said, "the wizard Thoggle cast a spell on Stiger here so that he appears as Legate Delvaris."

"I can confirm this is so," Stiger said unhappily. "I'm none too happy about it."

"It is like that illusion spell over the entrance to Old City," Father Thomas continued in a pleasant tone. "Once you see it, the spell no longer works. It is why Sabinus and I see him as Stiger and you see him as Delvaris."

"Magic, you say?" Arvus said, appearing highly skeptical. "Such trickery makes me terribly uncomfortable."

"It's most unnatural," Stiger said.

"Exactly," the tribune said, in agreement. He peered closer at Stiger's face, as if doing so would pierce the magic of the spell. "You are this Stiger, then?"

"Yes, that is correct," Stiger said. "I am Bennulius Stiger, at your service, sir."

"This is so unusual," Arvus said, with a glance thrown to Sabinus. "If I am to understand correctly, you are a legate"—he paused and looked to Father Thomas for confirmation—"from the future, as impossible as that sounds. Do I have that right?"

Stiger gave an unhappy nod. "You do."

"It is not my intent to offend in any way, but I've never heard of your family, sir," Arvus said. "I assume since you are a legate, you come from good blood, a senatorial family perhaps?"

Stiger almost grinned at the tribune, thoroughly amused, and turned to Father Thomas. "Traveling back in time seems to have its advantages. I must say, this is truly a welcome pleasure."

"I would imagine so," Father Thomas said with a wry grin.

"What do you mean?" Arvus asked, brow furrowing. "Could you kindly explain?"

"In his time," Father Thomas said, "the legate's family has achieved some, shall we say, *renown* across the empire. Everyone of consequence knows of the Stigers."

"As soldiers?" Sabinus asked. "Or as politicians?"

Stiger understood what the centurion was after. Sabinus wanted to determine whether the Stigers were known for their political acumen or military accomplishments. There were plenty of political hacks like General Kromen, power-brokers in the senate with little to no military experience looking to increase their prestige with an appointment to a legion.

"Centurion," Father Thomas said, "they are known for their battlefield victories and conquests in the name of the empire. Legate Delvaris is actually one of Stiger's ancestors."

"Are you, sir?" Arvus asked Stiger with some interest. "Do you have much experience in the field?"

"I myself was at a battle Legate Stiger commanded," Father Thomas continued, drawing back Arvus's attention. "The battle was hard fought and against overwhelming odds. I am pleased to say it was a complete victory."

Stiger wondered why the paladin was working so hard to establish his credibility with the tribune. He was afraid he knew the answer to his own question.

"I see," Arvus said, straightening and turning back to Stiger. "Then it is a pleasure to meet you, sir... no matter who you look like."

Arvus took a step forward and extended his hand, which Stiger took. The grip was firm, and though the tribune still looked uncomfortable, it was clear he was a gentleman through and through.

Dog stood and shook himself before padding up to Sabinus, tail wagging. The centurion smiled and patted the animal's head before giving him a scratch on the neck.

"How did you find Delvaris's dog?" Sabinus asked.

Stiger looked sharply at the centurion, before his gaze shifted the Dog.

"He found me," Stiger said. "Just showed up at the farm."

"What are the odds of that happening?" Sabinus said, shaking his head.

Stiger shared a questioning look with Father Thomas. He was starting to believe there were no such things as coincidences. The paladin shifted his gaze to Dog and his eyes narrowed.

"According to the letter confiscated with your kit," Sabinus said, "you have been given command of the Thirteenth. Legate Delvaris had a matching letter in his possession. As incredible as it sounds, we are told both are one and the same. I assume that letter referred to you, sir?"

"Yes, that is correct," Stiger replied and let out a long breath, returning his attention to Sabinus and Arvus. He saw a warning glance from Father Thomas. "But I am afraid my Thirteenth is not your legion."

"I don't understand," Arvus said. "There is only one Thirteenth and we are encamped just a few miles from here."

"You are quite correct on that point, tribune," said a raspy voice. Stiger saw Thoggle approaching. All eyes turned to the wizard, who, like Ogg was beardless, as if he had freshly shaved. Thoggle gave off the impression of a dwarf entering the later stages of his life. His face was lined and wrinkled. The gray hair on his head was patched and had thinned almost to nothingness.

The wizard walked with a bad limp, which caused him to move slowly, almost painfully. His black robe concealed whatever injury or malady affected him. He leaned heavily upon his staff for support as he moved. Like Ogg's, the staff was wooden and had a misshapen crystal mounted upon it. The bottom of the staff was capped in metal, which gave off a soft thudding sound as he moved forward one painful step at a time. "I sincerely apologize for my tardiness. I am afraid I was unavoidably detained."

Arvus's eyes narrowed. Stiger got the sense that the tribune was deeply uncomfortable in the wizard's presence.

"Technically," Thoggle continued, addressing Arvus, "it is the same legion, in his time, that is. Roughly three hundred years ahead of ours, to be exact."

Thoggle waved his hand in Stiger's direction as the tribune looked from the wizard to Stiger.

"Magic." Arvus gasped and took a step back, his fist going to his mouth. After a moment, he pointed a finger in Stiger's direction. "I would never have really believed it had I not seen the transformation with my own eyes. You are most definitely not Delvaris."

"I never pretended to be." Stiger gestured toward Thoggle. "That was the wizard's work."

"Correct, and fully I confess my guilt," Thoggle said. "I feel compelled to admit I cast the spell upon him without his approval, or even his knowledge."

Sabinus turned on Thoggle. "Why would you do such a thing? It demeans and disgraces the memory of a great man."

"I had to act before more set their eyes upon him, including the soldiers of your legion. Legate Delvaris's death was unexpected," Thoggle said, "and should never have happened the way it did at the hands of a servant of Castor. The minion traveled into our time to change things... and make events in the future more favorable to its dark god. That is the problem we face. To put things right and to save everything, he," Thoggle said and pointed a hand at Stiger, "must become Delvaris."

"I don't like the sound of that," Stiger said, though it only confirmed his suspicions, as did the conversation with Menos. He glanced over at Father Thomas. "It smacks of Delvaris reborn, doesn't it?"

"Yes," Father Thomas said, and gestured at the wizard, "but we feel it is necessary."

"You must assume Delvaris's identity," Thoggle insisted. "In essence become the man, keeping to much of what you know he did and in short finish his work here in this time. You must not stray far from the path Delvaris set."

"Impersonate him?" Stiger said, feeling deeply unhappy. His headache was becoming worse. "There is no honor in that."

"Honor, legend," Thoggle said, "such words matter little under the circumstances."

"Your own people feel you have no legend," Stiger said. "Perhaps it should come as no surprise you would care so little for such things. But it does just the same."

Thoggle turned his gaze upon Stiger and a look of extreme weariness passed over the wizard's face. When he spoke, he sounded much older than he had moments before. "Don't make the mistake of thinking that because my people feel I have none, that I am without legend. Legend, honor ... they are words. Actions speak louder."

"They do," Stiger conceded, feeling somewhat rebuked. "I've met more than a few who mouth such words for matters of convenience."

"Of course actions matter," Father Thomas said and then turned to Stiger, steering the conversation away from rocky ground. "Thoggle's spell would not affect those who knew you before the casting, like Sabinus or Sarai. For those who don't know you as Ben Stiger ... well, they would see Legate Delvaris, not only in name but look and sound as well."

"I am uncomfortable with this notion," Arvus said, a look of distaste crossing his face. "Very uncomfortable."

"You are uncomfortable?" Stiger shot a look at the tribune. "You don't know the half of it."

"Kindly take no offense with this, but I don't know you," Arvus said. "I don't care what your orders from Atticus say or your appointment to the legion, whether in my time or yours. No matter the machinations of the wizard and paladin, you will not command the Thirteenth. With the death of the legate, that is rightly my responsibility and trust."

"It must happen this way," Thoggle said to Arvus. "Should he not assume Delvaris's mantle, all will be lost. It is why we asked you to conceal the legate's death from your men. I have to ask. Do they still believe he is traveling with the thane?"

"They do," Arvus said. "The men still believe Delvaris is traveling with Thane Brogan to the dwarven capital deep in the mountains. As discussed, we have told them he is expected to return any day. Though I must say I feel this deceit impugns my honor."

"It is necessary," Father Thomas said. "We have a plan to set things right."

"I have my doubts," Arvus said. "The High Father's scripture teaches the gods gave us freedom of choice. As such, it stands to reason the future is wholly unwritten."

"That is where you are mostly wrong," Thoggle said. "With the paladin and Stiger here, we potentially know what will happen if we do nothing, and what could happen if we try to fix things. We must work to repair the damage done by Castor's minion. That is all that matters."

"I need to hear more," Arvus said. "I cannot do as you say without compelling proof."

Thoggle gave the tribune a long look and was silent for several heartbeats. "I dare not tell you much, but be assured that the future of your empire and my people is at stake. If you doubt me in this, ask the paladin."

Arvus looked to Father Thomas and raised his eyebrows in question. "Is it as dire as he says?"

"I am afraid the wizard speaks truth," Father Thomas confirmed. "The empire is at risk, and should we not act, evil will almost certainly triumph."

Arvus looked as if he wanted to argue the point with Father Thomas. Stiger could see the struggle in the other man's eyes. A paladin was the direct holy representative and conduit of the High Father. His word was above reproach.

"And this man can save us?" Arvus gestured toward Stiger. "Are you so certain?"

"Certain, no, but let us all hope he can fix things," Father Thomas said.

"Our enemy has already taken an interest in eliminating him," Thoggle said, "which suggests they recognize his value too."

"The ambush at the pond," Stiger said.

"Yes," Father Thomas said, "they came to kill you and I think it's fair to say that they will try again."

"You ask too much," Stiger said. He desired no part of any of this and simply wanted to be left alone. But, he knew deep down that Castor would never leave him be.

Father Thomas sucked in a breath and let it out slowly before meeting Stiger's gaze, as if he could read thoughts. "My son, for those called to serve, we are asked to sacrifice. Some may even be asked to make the ultimate sacrifice to do what is right."

"Like Father Griggs?" Stiger asked, feeling suddenly helpless. "If so, I think I would prefer to pass on that fate. Now that I consider it, if I am to end up like him, I'm inclined to not go along with this charade."

"You must," Thoggle said, and tapped his staff on the ground with a soft thud. "For without you, all is lost. I thought I made that abundantly clear."

"You can cast a spell to make anyone look and sound like Delvaris. Find someone else," Stiger said with a quick glance toward the farmhouse. Sarai was standing in the doorway watching them. She was too far to hear what was being discussed, which Stiger felt was a small blessing. He turned his gaze back to Thoggle, thinking it ironic that they were discussing the fate of their world in a farmyard, just feet from a compost pile that stank terribly. Stiger pointed at the tribune. "Pick Arvus here to save you. He's keen on leading his legion against impossible odds. This is his chance. Let him take on this burden."

"There is no one else," Thoggle said. "You are it. Destiny's mark is upon you."

It was as he had feared. Stiger rubbed his jaw in frustration. It always seemed to come down to him. Just when he had found happiness, it seemed that he might lose that too. Stiger stole another glance toward the house and his eyes met those of Sarai. The problem was, he did not wish to give up what he had found.

"Menos essentially said the same thing," Stiger admitted.

"He was here?" Thoggle asked, taking a shuffling half step forward. "Menos was here?"

"A short while before you lot arrived," Stiger said.

"I wish he had respected my wishes," Thoggle said with a deep scowl. The wizard tapped his staff on the ground.

"At least he gave me warning about Rarokan," Stiger countered. "That's more than you did."

"Did he mention the summit as well?" Thoggle held Stiger's gaze for a moment, then rubbed at his eyes with his free hand, the frustration clear. "Of course he did. Why wouldn't he?"

"Yes, with the orcs," Stiger confirmed.

Thoggle smacked the butt of his staff hard on the ground. "Though well-intentioned, the noctalum should have known better than to interfere."

"You both should know better," Stiger said with heat, looking from Father Thomas to Thoggle. "Negotiating with the orcs is a mistake. There is no point treating with them."

"The thane feels otherwise," Arvus said to Stiger, crossing his arms. "The dwarves apparently have a long history with the tribes that, admittedly, is not without trouble, but overall has been fairly peaceful."

"It is a mistake," Stiger repeated. "The attack on my person only proves that there will be further trouble. If you think otherwise, you delude yourself. The people of this valley will suffer for it."

"We take this threat seriously," Arvus said. "The entirety of the legion, along with our auxiliary cohorts, has been moved into the valley and a dwarven army is being called up. Should negotiations fail, the orcs will find they have bitten off more than they can chew. That said, the king of the orcs has requested a meeting on neutral ground. Though it is detestable to meet with such loathsome creatures, the thane has accepted the invitation and I feel honor-bound to participate and represent the empire's interests. I will be sending Sabinus here, along with a century as escort. Father Thomas will be going as well, and he has requested quite forcefully that you also attend. Which is why I am here. I wished to meet you first before giving my blessing."

"Now why would you want that?" Stiger looked pointedly, first at Thoggle and then Father Thomas.

"I feel called to bring you," Father Thomas said simply, and then gave a shrug. "It seems the High Father desires you to go."

Stiger rubbed the back of his neck, feeling that he was losing control. No, he had already lost control from the moment he picked up Delvaris's sword. "And the thane approved this? He will let me out of the prison he put me in?"

"He did," Thoggle said. "And you were never a prisoner."

"You could have fooled me," Stiger said.

"This was for your protection," Thoggle said. "With a minion on the loose, it was my idea. I knew there was a strong chance our enemy would come for you." Thoggle paused and sucked in a breath. "It is why I made sure you had the sword close to hand."

"You could have told me," Stiger said.

"I did," Thoggle said.

"No," Stiger said with a quick glance at the nearest guard ten yards away. "You told me a half-truth that my guard were to protect me, not why."

"Blame me," Father Thomas said, "if you are to blame anyone. It was I who convinced Thoggle to conceal the nature of the threat from you, until it materialized or we could get a handle on it. We thought we would have more time, but the attack has shown otherwise. Events with the enemy are proceeding faster than anticipated."

"We had hoped," Thoggle said and gestured back at Sarai, "that you would find some peace here, helping you become more centered with your being."

"What does that mean?" Stiger was feeling manipulated and he did not like it.

"Burdened with the world on your shoulders, you were hanging on to too much anger," Father Thomas said. "We felt you needed to find yourself again, in a way remove the burden you were carrying."

"Rarokan's influence was growing too rapidly," Thoggle added. "We both sensed it, felt it. I am sure the noctalum could detect it too, hence his visit. Had we told you in advance, saddled you with additional concerns, the chance of you finding any semblance of peace would have been minimal. Even I can tell you have found it, and been grounded by it." Thoggle's gaze flicked to the sword. "When it matters most, I hope that peace and grounding will save us all."

Stiger knew honesty when he heard it. He did not have to like it, but he understood it.

"You will not mislead or lie to me again," Stiger said. He hated when others tried to shield or spare him from unpleasantness. Stiger looked at the paladin. "Tell me we have an understanding."

"Upon my lord, the High Father," Father Thomas said, "you have my word."

Stiger turned his gaze to Thoggle.

"I cannot give you what you wish," Thoggle said. The wizard took a shallow breath and let it out. "There are things I know, or may become privy to, that you can never learn, nor do I dare share. Such is the way with my service to my god."

Stiger did not like Thoggle's answer.

"I am not going," Stiger said.

"You are," Thoggle insisted, and there was a hard edge to the wizard's tone.

"No, I am not." Stiger was becoming enraged again.

You must go, the sword hissed and its presence returned with a vengeance, *for it has already happened.*

Stiger grew cold at the words, and the feeling of being trapped only intensified. There was more to it than simply not wanting to go and turning his back on what was about to occur here in the valley. The sword had shown him what had happened to Delvaris. Stiger now understood that vision he had been shown might very well not have been his ancestor. The feeling of being roped in by destiny and the gods was growing by the moment.

I won't let you fall to the shadow, the sword hissed, *I cannot allow that to happen.*

The words did little to assure him. In fact, they did the opposite. Stiger also understood that if he went with them to this summit, he would potentially lose everything he had gained over the last few weeks—contentment he had found with Sarai—especially if he died at the minion's hands.

"No," Stiger said firmly, and every eye was upon him. "I have given enough. My time as a soldier is over." Stiger began stalking toward the house and Sarai, who looked on with concern.

"Are you sure this man is the brave soldier you told me of?" Arvus asked of Father Thomas.

Stiger stopped and looked back.

Dog stood and gave a low, menacing growl, eyes locked upon Arvus. The tribune took a step away from the large animal as it stood.

"Dog, down," Stiger snapped absently. Dog ceased his growling and sat, but his eyes never left Arvus.

Stiger eyed the tribune for a long moment, his anger simmering. The man seemed competent enough, and may have seen action; however, his words still pricked at Stiger's sense of honor and self-worth. In fact, they struck too close to home, to his sworn duty and his promise to the High Father.

There was a long moment of silence before Stiger spoke. He forced his pride down. "I have led men in battle. I have led many thousands of men, in fact. I have watched more good boys than I can count die or become horribly maimed upon my orders. I fought alongside dwarves, elves, and gnomes. I've directly faced servants of the dark gods and done battle with them. I've fought orcs and with my own hands personally sent them into the shadow." Stiger fell silent for a few heartbeats, all eyes upon him. He cleared his throat. "You can question my bravery all you wish, but I know who I am and your opinion of me changes nothing. The orcs are coming to take this valley."

Stiger pointed at the forbidding Thane's Mountain, which towered above the other peaks. Its top was coated in white.

"Make no mistake. They come for the World Gate and with them will be their evil priests, wielding Castor's dark magic. Worse, they will be accompanied by a minion, an evil being of terrible power devoted to Castor's service. I have already seen such horrors and, with the paladin, have even fought one. You, sir, have not." Stiger took a deep breath. "I grow weary of such things."

There was a general silence after Stiger had spoken. No one seemed to desire to break it. Thoggle glanced at the ground and tapped his staff with his thumb absently. Arvus even looked uncomfortably away.

"Then"—Sabinus cleared his throat, boldly speaking up—"don't you think what you have found with Sarai is worth fighting for?"

Stiger turned a hard look upon the centurion. Sabinus met his gaze with one of matching steel. Stiger felt something in him wanting to go with them to the summit, nudging at him, tugging him forward, but at the same time something else was screaming for him to remain with Sarai. In short, he was torn by duty, service to the empire, his god, and love.

"You have more experience against orcs than any of us," Sabinus continued. "I think you should most definitely go and lend us your expertise. It is the honorable and right thing to do. I suspect you know this."

Stiger said nothing.

Father Thomas stepped up to him and placed a hand upon his shoulder. He leaned forward and whispered so that only the two of them could hear. "I know you feel called to go as well. The High Father speaks to you. You cannot deny it. The presence of the dog is proof enough."

Stiger's eyes went to Dog, who had laid back down and gone to sleep. He looked back over at the paladin. Their eyes locked and Father Thomas held his gaze a moment before stepping back.

"The thane's party will depart in the morning," Arvus said. "Sabinus will come to collect you. Go, don't go. It is your choice. After what you've told me, I have wasted enough time here. I need to get my legion ready for a fight."

With that, the tribune turned away and walked toward his horse. Sabinus looked at Stiger and gave a nod before turning away too, leaving Father Thomas behind with Thoggle.

"You have told Sarai everything," Thoggle said once the others were out of earshot. It wasn't a question.

"Yes," Stiger admitted. "You will not harm her."

"No, I will not damage her in any way," Thoggle said, looking extremely weary once again. "I had warned you against such disclosures. If it becomes needed, I will cloud her memory. That may affect her feelings toward you."

"Let's hope it does not come to that," Stiger said.

"Let us hope," Thoggle said.

"About going . . ." Father Thomas said and let the rest of what he was going to say hang on the air as he clearly reconsidered what he wanted to say. "Those orcs that attacked you are of the Theltra, a religious order of warriors in direct service to Castor. They answer only to the priestly caste and not the king. That is why the thane feels there may still be some hope. Thoggle and I think so as well."

"I will speak with Sarai about it," Stiger said to them.

"I would expect nothing less," Father Thomas said. "Sabinus and I will be here in the morning to collect you, sometime after dawn. I pray that you join us."

Stiger gave a tired nod, turned away, and walked to Sarai. There was a sorrowful look in her eyes.

"We have a lot to discuss," Stiger said when he came up to her.

She nodded and together they entered the house.

Chapter Eight

Stiger laced up his sandals and tied them tight. Leaning back on the stool in the kitchen, he looked up at Sarai. A tallow candle on the table provided the only other light source in the kitchen besides the fireplace. It was early morning, and the sun was just coming up. Though the air outside was chill, they had been awake for a while and had restarted the fire two hours before.

Sarai was busy placing carefully wrapped bundles of food into his saddlebags on the table, next to which lay his armor. Stiger watched her, feeling pained at their coming parting. She was fair but rather plain looking, someone who would not stand out in a crowd. And yet, to his eyes and heart, she was a beauty. His hand absently reached up to his cheek and touched the damaged skin. With the scar, he knew he was no looker himself.

Stiger admired her inner strength, determination, and intelligence. It was something he could appreciate. After her husband's death, she had survived and managed the farm herself.

"I've packed plenty of that cheese you like," she said. "The dwarves make an interesting cheese that's full of holes. They are quite fond of it. I am not sure you will find it to your liking."

"Good," Stiger said. "I will only be gone a few days. Yours should be fine." He didn't really enjoy the cheese she made, but he led her to believe he did. It was a small untruth that purchased her some measure of happiness.

"I've also put in a loaf of fresh bread and some of that salted pork that I bought at the market last week," Sarai told him as she tied the last saddlebag closed.

She made good bread and it was a welcome addition. The salt pork was not.

"It's not much, but it is enough."

"I have to go to this summit," Stiger said. "You know that I don't want to, but I feel that I must."

"I know, Ben," Sarai said. "I don't want you to go either, but with everything you've told me…" She fell silent and looked down at the floor. "It frightens me terribly. You should be there, where you can make a difference."

"Father Thomas and Thoggle seem to think I can do some good," Stiger said.

"I know you can as well," Sarai said. "I feel much better knowing you are going. This valley is my home. If we need to fight to keep it, then so be it."

Stiger eyed her silently. His hand gripped the table. Though he should only be gone a few days, he would miss her terribly.

Stiger stood and placed the stool under the table where it belonged. He eyed his armor. The dwarves had brought it the previous evening. He had not seen his armor since he had arrived. Next to it was a small bag of his possessions that the dwarves had confiscated as well, including the purse he had carried on his person after stepping through the Gate.

He placed a hand upon his armor. He had an uncomfortable feeling that once he put it on, he would be crossing a line. Once he stepped over, there could be no going back. The happiness he had known would soon be at an end.

Stiger hesitated, grinding his teeth and hating himself for what he must do. He had made his decision. Now it was time to see it through. Stiger picked up his armor and slipped it on. He had forgotten the heavy deadweight that came with wearing it, but the armor felt like an old friend. Shrugging his shoulders to get comfortable, he began fastening it up tightly and making sure to tie off the straps using a double knot. Sarai came over and helped. Stiger allowed her to finish up. He said nothing as she worked. He just admired her. As she finished the last knot, she looked up at him and their eyes met. There were tears in her eyes.

"After my husband died…" Sarai said in a near whisper. She swallowed before continuing. "I never thought I would find love again, never ever."

Stiger grabbed her and pulled her close against his chest and held her, kissing the top of her head as she tucked under his chin. She gave a slight shudder, then after a moment stepped back and wiped her face. The chest plate on his armor was wet.

"I know," he said, his voice gruff as he eyed her.

"I have given you my heart," Sarai said.

"And I have given you mine," Stiger said.

Stiger slipped on his greaves as Sarai picked up his folded blue cloak, shook it out, and then stepped behind him, clipping it on. The dwarves had cleaned and mended the cloak's numerous holes and the frayed ends. The cloak looked new, as it had on the day he had taken it from Delvaris's tomb.

The sound of horses approaching told him that it was almost time to go. He stepped over to the corner, where Rarokan was leaning against the wall. After a slight hesitation, he picked up the sword by the lacquered scabbard and slipped it on. He turned and saw her studying him.

"My soldier," she said with a note of pride. "You look the part, the dashing leader you told me of and I always believed you to be."

There was some talking outside and then almost immediately a knocking on the door.

"I will be there shortly," Stiger called out in the language of the dwarves, not wishing to part so soon.

Stiger stepped over to the small bag containing his possessions. There wasn't much, just a leather-bound dispatch pad, charcoal pencil, the gold torc he had taken in personal combat with an orc, and his purse. His pipe and the remainder of his personal items waited in the time from whence he had come and would likely never return. Stiger placed the dispatch pad and pencil into his cloak pocket. Using a thick leather tie, he affixed the gold torc to his chest armor, where he had worn it before.

Stiger hefted the purse, feeling its weight. The coins within chinked. It was only a small sum. He glanced up at Sarai. To her, it would be a fortune. He tossed her the bag, which she caught.

She opened it and her eyes went wide at the sight of the gold coins within.

"If you see the need," Stiger said, "spend what you will. I mean that."

"Promise that you will come back to me," she demanded, throwing the purse onto the table as if it might burn her. "Ben, swear to me upon your honor and love for me that you will come back. You must come back to me. I cannot lose another I hold dear."

"I will, you have my word on that," Stiger said. "If it is the last thing I do, I shall return to you."

He grabbed the saddlebags and threw them over his right shoulder. Tucking his helmet under an arm, he unlatched the door and swung it open and found himself face to face with one of his guards. The dwarf stepped back and to the side as the cold air flooded in.

Centurion Sabinus and Father Thomas were mounted and waiting in the yard. Stiger stepped through the doorway and stopped. Captain Aleric and his entire company were drawn up in ranks, all two hundred. Sarai followed him out. An order was shouted. The company, with their captain standing to their front, snapped to attention. Stiger studied them for a prolonged moment. He had not expected this show of respect, especially after his heated argument with Aleric.

Stiger made his way over, passing slowly before the ranks, studying the dwarves. Their armor was polished and maintained perfectly. The captain offered Stiger a smart salute. Stiger drew himself up and dutifully returned it, fist to chest, legionary style. Stiger made a point of running his eyes once again over the company.

"I already know they can fight, but your warriors look good, Captain," Stiger said in dwarven. "Very good, indeed. You have a fine company."

"Thank you," Aleric said and puffed up at the compliment.

"As we discussed last evening, you will keep Sarai safe." It was not a question, but an understanding.

"I will," Aleric affirmed. "Upon my legend and our lives, we will watch Sarai until you return."

"Thank you." Stiger turned away back toward the farmhouse and hitching post, where he had left Sarai's horse saddled and ready to go.

Misty was a young brown mare that Sarai had acquired the previous spring. Stiger had risen well before the sun to brush the animal down and saddle her. The horse was a good mount, but she wasn't Nomad. He had no doubt she would meet his needs over the next few days. He secured his helmet to the back of the saddle and then worked on the saddlebags behind his blanket. Stiger made a point to check that everything was secure, especially the saddle.

Most horses Stiger had known had the unfortunate tendency to breathe in when being saddled. When the horse finally exhales its saddle ends up loose, which is certain to dump the rider. Sure enough, Misty was no exception. The saddle was slightly loose. He undid the strap and cinched it tighter. Satisfied that all was secure, he untied Misty from the hitching post and with practiced ease swung himself up and onto her back.

The horse took a few nervous steps. Stiger tightened his hold on the reins and Misty stilled. He was in control here, not the horse. Stiger shifted himself back a little, finding a better seat. The saddle was old and the leather badly cracked in places. It showed its wear, but it was well broken in and comfortable.

The horse knew that they were going for a ride and pawed at the ground in eager anticipation.

"Easy, girl," Stiger soothed, patting the horse on the neck. "We will be on our way soon enough, but then, before you know it, you will be missing your warm barn stall and quiet pasture."

Sarai walked up to him. He leaned down and gave her a kiss, not caring about those watching. She stepped back, a tear spilling from one eye and running down her cheek. Stiger cleared his throat, jerked slightly on the reins, and pulled Misty around toward Father Thomas and Centurion Sabinus.

The centurion offered him a salute, which Stiger dutifully returned.

"I'm pleased you decided to join us, sir," Sabinus said.

"I suspected you would come around," Father Thomas said. "Truthfully, I knew you would. You have an incredible sense of duty."

Stiger was about to respond when the sound of another horse drew their attention. Theo came riding up on one of the stout mountain ponies that Stiger had seen the dwarves use. Theo's mount appeared well-provisioned and, more telling, his friend was wearing his armor. Theo's helmet had been tied to a saddlebag and bounced slightly, as did the dwarf.

"And where exactly do you think you're going?" Stiger asked Theo.

Theo gave a scowl. "I thought that might have been a little obvious."

"It was my idea," Aleric said, stepping over to them and switching from dwarven to accented common for the benefit of the centurion. "Theogdin will act as a go-between for you and the thane's party." He paused. "It is my sincerest hope that he will provide an invaluable service to you in negotiating the prickly temperament of my people."

"As in," Stiger said, "he may keep me from irritating your thane again?"

"I can only hope," Aleric said. "It would please me greatly for there to be peace between you both. Trouble is in the air, and as old allies, our peoples must work together, even if your legion is not here to restore the Compact and resurrect the alliance."

"I wholeheartedly agree with you, Captain," Stiger said. "Truth be told, I am not terribly unhappy that Theo is coming along. It will be good to have a friend along for the journey."

Theo, on the other hand, did not appear to think his captain's idea was all that grand.

"However, he is injured." Stiger gestured at Theo in a halfhearted manner. "Are you certain about him going with us?"

"He is terrible at faking," Aleric said with a half shrug. "It's a shallow cut and given time will heal just fine, whether lounging about in camp causing trouble or on the back of a pony keeping you company and also doing his best to steer you out of trouble."

Theo shook his head in a disgusted manner as Stiger offered him a knowing grin.

"I appreciate you sending him along," Stiger said to Aleric. "I am sure he will prove an invaluable addition to our party."

"Knowing Theo, as I do," Aleric said with a dramatic breath, "he may very well get you into trouble, but at least he won't be causing me any grief for a few days."

"Right." Stiger looked to the paladin and Sabinus. "Shall we get a move on? I believe we have some distance to cover today."

"We do," Sabinus agreed, shooting Theo an amused expression before returning his gaze to Stiger. "We will be meeting up with our men at Bridgetown. We shouldn't keep them waiting longer than required."

"Why, centurion, don't you know?" Stiger said. "Waiting is a requirement of service to the empire."

"Oh, I've learned it well enough," Sabinus said. "'Hurry up and wait' should be the Thirteenth's motto. We were ordered down to Vrell in a rush, but only to sit tight for months on end doing nothing once we made it down here.

Oh, and I almost forgot, if we hurry we may catch the thane's party in Bridgetown. If we miss them, we will meet up with them in Old City."

"Well then," Stiger said and set Misty into a slow walk with a gentle nudge, "let's get a move on."

Sabinus started his horse forward, as did Father Thomas. Theo spared Stiger an unhappy look as he passed by. Theo nudged his pony sullenly into a walk, bringing up the rear.

"Good fortune," Captain Aleric called after Stiger.

"Thank you," Stiger said. "I will take all that I am offered."

Sarai was standing in the doorway as he rode out of the farmyard. He raised a hand and waved. She waved back.

He suddenly had the uncomfortable sense he would never again see her in this life. Stiger puffed out his cheeks and offered up a brief but silent prayer to the High Father, begging that the great god look after and make her a definite part of his future. He desired nothing more than to grow old with her.

An excited bark drew his attention back toward the farm. Dog came loping over, slowed, and began padding along next him. Stiger glanced down at the animal for a moment as he turned his horse onto the road. The others were riding just a few feet ahead. Stiger steered his horse around an overly large pothole with a fieldstone sitting in the center and then looked back down at the dog.

"Coming along, I take it?"

Dog gave a vigorous wag of his tail and then sprinted energetically ahead, quickly passing the others. It seemed that wherever Stiger went, Dog intended to go as well.

Stiger nudged Misty into a faster walk and caught up to Sabinus and Father Thomas.

"Taking the dog?" Sabinus asked, a slight frown crossing his face. "I heard about what he did at Bowman's Pond. Hard to believe that shaggy thing Delvaris kept around has a violent side. Well, I guess he's yours now."

"He's not my dog," Stiger said.

Dog was several hundred yards ahead of them now. Tail wagging vigorously, he disappeared into a small stand of trees.

"I think he more adopted me than anything else. In a way," Stiger said, "I think he is his own person. He goes where he wills."

"I agree with you on that point," Father Thomas said, eyes on the spot where Dog had disappeared.

"Why the rush to get here?" Stiger was curious to know why the Thirteenth had been sent south. He had assumed it had something to do with the orcs coming to take the valley, but now he was not so sure. Why hurry down here months before any threat was known and then have them wait?

"I honestly don't know," Sabinus admitted. "Emperor Atticus gave the legate his orders personally. But beyond that, there is not much to tell. The legate did not share what exactly our orders were. The most believable rumor is that a delegation of dwarves arrived in the capital asking for assistance, though I didn't hear that one until we arrived at Vrell. Heck, I had no idea dwarves were real until we got to the fortress at Grata'Kor. Also, the dwarves did not seem very keen on letting us into the valley... so I would rule that rumor out."

"Knowing legionaries," Stiger said with a sudden chuckle, "I imagine there are hundreds of rumors running about camp."

"More like thousands." Sabinus seemed amused and then sobered. "With the death of the legate, the only one who knows for sure why we are here is Tribune Arvus, and he's not told me or the camp prefect of his orders. When I asked, I was told to mind my own business. All he has let slip is that we have come to represent the empire's concerns with the dwarves."

"If I had to make a serious guess," Stiger said, "the Thirteenth is here to honor a treaty, called the Compact."

"A treaty?" Sabinus seemed shocked by this news. "A treaty with the dwarves?"

Stiger gave a nod.

"It dates back to the founding of the empire," Father Thomas said, "and the time of Karus."

"That's incredible," Sabinus said. "The empire has a longstanding treaty with the dwarves?"

"Yes," Stiger said, "we do."

"Why have I never heard of it before?"

"Knowledge of the treaty was intentionally suppressed. After many centuries, it was forgotten by all but a select few," Father Thomas said.

"What is the purpose of the treaty?" Sabinus asked.

"The Compact was created to protect something of incredible importance to both the dwarves and our empire," Father Thomas said.

"The World Gate," Sabinus guessed, snapping his fingers.

"Very good," Father Thomas said. "You have seen the Gate room and what came through it. You understand the danger it represents."

"Yes," Sabinus said. "Brogan explained, but I still think it incredible that you could actually travel to another world like our own."

"It is," Stiger agreed. "I was surprised to learn Rome was a real place, just on a different world."

"Not just mythology, it seems," Sabinus said

Stiger looked over at Sabinus, a thought occurring to him. The empire's borders in this time were hundreds of miles from Vrell, perhaps even more than a thousand. "Did you have any problems marching to Vrell? It is a long way from friendly territory, is it not?"

"Oh, it is," Sabinus confirmed. "The only real trouble was the Tervay. Once we got past them, no one wanted to mess with a small army of over thirteen thousand moving through their lands. And we moved quickly in the event they changed their minds on that point."

"If I recall," Stiger said, "the Tervay were a collection of barbarian tribes, is that right?"

"Were?" Sabinus gave a chuckle. "I keep forgetting. This must be ancient history for you."

"Somewhat," Stiger admitted and then shrugged. "I guess you can say it's now current history for me."

"True," Sabinus agreed. "We marched into Tervay lands with four other legions, the Seventh, Ninth, Tenth, and Fourteenth."

"That must have been an incredible display of imperial might," Stiger said, marveling and thinking back to his time fighting the Rivan in the North. Though there were four legions fighting in the North, the most he had ever seen together were two in any one place.

"It was impressive," Sabinus said. "The marching column, from the vanguard of the first legion to the rearguard of the last legion, stretched for over one hundred miles. At least that is what our cavalry scouts told me. Not counting the camp followers, all five legions and auxiliary cohorts numbered somewhere around sixty thousand men. I've served eighteen years, sir, and I've never seen the like."

"How did it go when you entered Tervay lands?"

"Predictably," Sabinus said, "they came out to fight. It was rugged terrain, steep hills, lowland swamps, and mostly forested with no real roads to speak of. They are savages, really." Sabinus fell silent a moment, thinking. "Despite being thorough barbarians, tough bastards they are, sir. During the first few days of the campaign, due to the terrain it was very hard to maintain organization and set lines."

"I can imagine," Stiger said. "I've fought over ground like you are describing. It naturally lends itself to the defense."

Sabinus grinned. "That's what we did, sir. We dug in and they foolishly came at us. They'd never seen legionaries before and, as hairy-assed barbarians, were totally lacking discipline, and they came at us in a shrieking mob. Some of the new recruits shat themselves, but the veterans knew what was what. We slaughtered them, like felling hay, and broke them in just a few hours. When the order came to break away and strike out on our own, it was a surprise. As the other legions pursued the Tervay deeper into their lands and back to their villages, the Thirteenth slipped away, marching south straight through their lands and out." Sabinus scowled slightly. "We were getting regular messengers updating us on the progress of the campaign. That continued up until a month ago, but then stopped. We've had no word from them since. It has me a little concerned, sir."

"What did the latest dispatches report?"

"The last dispatch mentioned the Tervay had abandoned their villages and took to the forests. They were conducting small-scale raids, or had holed up in hill forts," Sabinus said. "The campaign seemed to have bogged down, with supply becoming a problem, sir."

Stiger recalled reading about how it had taken four years of bloody fighting to subdue the Tervay. What he had not known was that the Thirteenth had been part of the initial thrust into Tervay territory. He suspected that, much like the scrubbing of the Compact from history, there had been an organized effort to remove the Thirteenth's mission as well.

"You wouldn't know what happens, sir?" Sabinus asked.

"I do," Stiger said.

"Can you tell me? I have friends fighting there."

Stiger spared a glance over at Father Thomas as they clopped along. The paladin gave a shrug.

"We will eventually subdue the Tervay," Stiger said, "but it will take time and prove costly."

Sabinus grimly nodded. Stiger regarded the centurion. What Stiger had just told him was likely nothing Sabinus had not already suspected. Besides, if things played out as they had in Stiger's time, Sabinus would not be returning to the empire in his own time, but in Stiger's.

"In the end," Stiger added, "they will supply some of our best auxiliary cohorts."

"That's something, at least."

"What he tells you of coming events," Father Thomas said, drawing the centurion's attention, "you must share with no one. Much depends upon the future playing out as we need it to."

"I understand, Father."

They rode in silence for a while, Theo still dragging and bringing up the rear. Stiger spared a glance back at the dwarf. Head down, he was muttering to himself and clearly sulking. Stiger knew he would soon get over it. The irrepressible Theo would return.

Putting Theo's unhappiness from his mind, Stiger scanned for Dog along the roadside, which was bordered by a small thicket of trees and brush. He saw the animal far ahead, smelling a bush. A moment later the dog plunged headlong into the brush and was lost from view.

Despite leaving Sarai, it felt good to be back on the move again, traveling. His mood lightened with each passing mile and he began enjoying the ride. Stiger found that the valley had not changed much in look or tone from when he'd seen it in the future. The buildings were different, of course, but basically the same in style. The valley was agrarian, with impressive vineyards majestically climbing the steeper slopes. Of the farms that they passed, most were small and humble. People came out to see them as they rode by. Most were human, but Stiger was surprised to see the occasional dwarven family tossed into the mix. Though the people were exceedingly pleasant and friendly, only the most cursory of greetings were exchanged as they rode by.

The outskirts of Bridgetown came into view around noon. Smoke rose from the tight cluster of buildings just down the road. Father Thomas and Sabinus stopped their horses nearly on the edge of town. Stiger could see legionary sentries posted, just a few yards ahead.

"Remember," Father Thomas said, "the men will see you as Legate Delvaris. You need to act as if you are him. Should you fail, they may lose confidence in you as a leader."

Stiger gave an unhappy but curt nod of acceptance. "Easier said than done, since I've never met him."

"You look like him," Sabinus said, "despite that scar on your cheek. You both might have been brothers. You sound like him as well."

"That still doesn't help me much, now, does it?" Stiger said.

"I will coach you," Sabinus said, "and point out people you should know. It is why Father Thomas wanted me along. I will also provide advice now and then, should you wish it."

"Good," Stiger said, "then you stick close. Since I don't have any junior tribunes handy, you are now my aide. Until further notice you are detached from your regular duties. Understand?"

"Perfectly," Sabinus said. "I guess it is as good an excuse as any."

"Tell me about the century waiting for us."

"Fifth Century, Second Cohort," Sabinus said, glancing at the sentries who were undoubtedly wondering why they had stopped. "Centurion Pixus commands. He is a good man, and reliable. Pixus has served in this legion for nearly twenty years and, like most other centurions in the Thirteenth, came up through the ranks. You can count on him, but more importantly, he will know you."

"Is he married?"

"No," Sabinus said.

"How does Delvaris handle his men?"

Sabinus thought a moment before answering.

"The legate is stiffly formal, proper," Sabinus said, "a gentleman with a deep-seated sense of honor. He is fair and makes a point to listen to his officers. Once he has solicited advice, he considers it, then decides on a course of action. When the decision is made, he sticks with it and doesn't brook further questioning or debate."

"What about under combat conditions?"

"Cool as the most solid winter ice, sir," Sabinus said. "Nothing ruffles him."

"Sounds like my kind of man," Stiger said. "I would've liked to have met him."

"He was the best of officers, sir," Sabinus said. "I respected him very much."

"All right." Stiger nudged his horse forward. "Oh, one other thing. What did Delvaris call Dog?"

"I don't think he ever had a name for him," Sabinus said with a frown. "He just called him Dog or the dog, like you do. It's why I thought you called him that."

Dog had returned a short while before and was walking along next to Stiger's horse. Stiger glanced down at the animal and wondered on the odds he and Delvaris had given the animal the same name. The coincidence was unnerving. Dog abruptly took off, running madly for another stand of trees twenty yards off. Then he was lost from view again as he plunged into them.

"He must have seen a rabbit," Sabinus said as they neared the sentries.

"A squirrel or something," Stiger said. "With all the preparations this morning, I don't think Sarai got around to feeding him."

The sentries snapped to attention and saluted. Sabinus, riding next to Stiger, leaned close. "Rather than saluting, Delvaris waves casually. Rarely, if ever, does he return salutes, sir."

Stiger nodded and held his hand up as they rode past. The legionaries' eyes were on him. Once past, Stiger released a breath he had not realized he was holding. He focused his mind on what was to come. As if heading into battle, he made a point to study his surroundings.

Bridgetown was larger than it was in Stiger's time. There were at least thirty buildings, most of which had grass thatched roofs. Besides the small houses, there were also a number of barns and storehouses.

Unlike the village Stiger knew it to be in the future, Bridgetown looked to be more of a small, prosperous town surrounded by cultivated fields that had already been harvested or were about to be. It was certainly a growing community. A goodly number of children came out to watch them as they made their way into town.

Stiger even spotted a smithy and next door a farrier, where in the future there had been none. There were also a couple of taverns. The first one they passed. The second one was in the exact same spot as Malik's. This tavern was, however, a completely different building, and much larger, too. Sabinus led them to it.

A sign hung out front proclaimed, *Standing Bear Tavern.* Next to the sign, painted on the wall was an image of a large black bear standing on its hind legs. It wasn't a very good painting.

Fifth Century had been waiting before the tavern. Sighting Delvaris, they jumped to their feet and rushed forward. The men gave a cheer as Stiger and his party rode up to the tavern. Stiger offered what he considered a suitable wave.

He noticed that there were dwarven infantry waiting, too. They were lounging about and did nothing more than glance in his direction, then resume their conversations and dice games. Stiger noticed that a few of the legionaries gave the dwarves black looks for their lack of concern.

Sabinus called out an order that cut above all the noise. The men gave them space, and they continued on to the hitching posts.

"With all of these dwarves around, I would assume the thane is inside," Father Thomas said, coming up to Stiger. "Shall we go see him?"

"Let's get this over with," Stiger said, dismounting. He felt very uncomfortable pretending to be a man he wasn't. Though the legionaries had given them room, their eyes were still upon him. He quickly tied Misty to the hitching post, where several dwarven ponies were secured.

"Centurion Sabinus." Father Thomas turned to the officer. "I think it best if you wait outside. There may be matters discussed that you should not hear."

"Got it."

Father Thomas led the way. Behind them, Theo had dismounted and was securing his pony.

A centurion carrying a vine cane exited the tavern as they were nearing the door. Stiger took the centurion to be Pixus, who stiffened to attention and saluted.

"Centurion," Stiger greeted.

"Nice to have you back with us, sir," Centurion Pixus said in a firm tone. The centurion was a tall man in his mid-thirties. He had a rugged look about him. His short-cropped hair was brown, as were his eyes, and his neck was thickened from years of service. Pixus also had a small zigzag scar above his right temple that was slightly purplish in color. The man was clearly a veteran and exuded a natural confidence that Stiger warmed to immediately. Stiger's eyes strayed to the six phalerae, awards he had received for valor.

Pixus also carried a well-worn traditional vine cane. Such symbols of status and rank had mostly fallen out of practice in Stiger's time.

"Thank you, Centurion Pixus," Stiger replied. "It is good to be back."

"Yes, sir," Pixus said. "I am sure it is."

"Would you check in with Centurion Sabinus? He is over there by our horses. I'd like no trouble between our men and the dwarves, especially since we will be traveling with them over the next few days."

"I will, sir," Pixus said, "and there will be no trouble."

"Very good," Stiger said, dismissing the centurion. Pixus moved toward Sabinus.

Father Thomas opened the door and held it. Stiger made his way into the tavern's large common room, which was dimly lit and slightly hazy from wood smoke. The shutters had been opened to allow in fresh air and light. Even so, several oil lamps hung from the ceiling to augment the natural light.

Stiger estimated there were twenty communal tables, with an assortment of battered benches and stools. A large fireplace along the left wall had a good-sized fire going. The chimney apparently needed cleaning, as it leaked an inordinate amount of smoke into the room.

Surprisingly, the common room was nearly empty. This likely was by design. Stiger spotted Thane Brogan seated at a table by the fire, with a dwarf to his right and left. Thoggle sat opposite the thane. There was no sign of the proprietor about or, for that matter, any servants.

The thane stood as Stiger and Father Thomas walked over to the table. The dwarf on the thane's right came to his feet as well. Thoggle remained seated. A moment later, the door behind them banged open and in walked Theo, moving a little too stiffly, and not because of his armor. Stiger suspected his friend was saddle sore. Theo spotted the thane and started over toward them.

"Our last meeting wasn't as pleasant as I would have preferred," the thane said in near perfect common, shooting a quick glance over at Thoggle, who nodded in a pleased manner. The thane looked back to Stiger. "Perhaps, since we are going to be traveling companions for the next few days, you would care to join me in a drink?"

"I would be honored," Stiger said, understanding that this was as near an apology as he was likely to get from the thane. "It's been a long ride. A drink is more than welcome."

There were several large pitchers on the table, as well as six clay jars for drinking. The thane picked up one of the pitchers and poured out two drinks of red liquid.

"I prefer spirits," the thane said, "but as this tavern only caters to humans, all they have here is heated wine and some piss poor excuse for beer that's more swill than anything else. I would recommend against it."

He picked up a jar and handed one to Stiger. Since the thane had not poured anyone else a drink, including the paladin, Stiger understood the underlying significance. He was being singularly honored by the thane of the dwarves.

"Thank you," Stiger said, accepting the clay jar. "Wine is preferable, then."

"Damn right it is. Let us salute." The thane raised his jar. "To a pleasant journey and a productive summit with those bloody heathenistic savages."

Stiger raised his as well and drank respectfully after the thane started in on his jar. Stiger found the wine to be of superb quality and very smooth. There was a fruity hint to its taste. He had not enjoyed a fine wine like it in months—Sarai hadn't been able to afford the good stuff. He took another sip and savored the drink.

"You already know Thoggle," the thane said, placing his empty jar down on the table with such force it cracked the clay vessel. "This is my advisor and lifelong friend, Jorthan. I value his counsel as much as I do Thoggle's."

"It is a pleasure to meet you," Jorthan said, though his eyes seemed to say otherwise. The thane's advisor wore a belted tunic, pants, and thick black boots. He was clearly not a warrior. Jorthan's long blond hair was tied back in a pony tail. His beard reached down his belly and over his belt. Unlike most other dwarves Stiger had met, Jorthan's beard had no braids or ties and was free-flowing.

"It is an honor, Jorthan."

"Captain Taithun," Brogan said, gesturing to an older dwarf who had been sitting to his left. The captain wore his armor, minus the horse-hair plumed helmet, which rested on an adjacent table. An ugly scar ran across his forehead. The captain had the look and confident manner of a battle-hardened veteran. "Taithun commands my escort and personal guard."

"It is a pleasure to meet you."

"And I you," Taithun said in a gravelly voice.

The thane took Stiger's empty jar and poured two more drinks. He handed the full jar back to Stiger.

"Your turn," the thane said. "I want to hear a human toast to our success."

Stiger eyed the thane a moment as he rapidly thought on what he wanted to say.

"Let this summit be a success," Stiger said, switching to dwarven, "for if it is not, then we shall happily kill bucket loads of orcs and send them on to their dark master for a fitting welcome."

The room fell silent for several heartbeats, the thane's eyes narrowing at Stiger.

"That is as fine a salute as I've heard. I will drink to that!" the thane finally said and threw back his wine, downing it in one go. Stiger took a sip, savoring the taste.

"You speak our language," the thane said, sounding somewhat pleased. "To use a human word, you honor us."

"Theo here has been a good teacher." Stiger gestured toward his friend, who was standing quietly a couple of steps behind. "It is he who honored me with his teaching."

The thane looked past Stiger, and an unhappy look passed across his face. Theo shifted his feet nervously at the sudden praise and attention.

"Still causing trouble, Theogdin?" the thane asked.

"No more than usual, my thane," Theo replied.

"He is my first cousin." The thane gestured with his empty jar at Theo. "The kind that starts the drama at close family gatherings, making them doubly insufferable affairs."

Stiger looked over at Theo with a raised eyebrow.

"I'm not that bad," Theo protested.

"I am truly sorry for that," Stiger said to the thane. "I have relatives just like him. We try to keep them as far away as possible. Is that why he's posted to Captain Aleric's company?"

Jorthan stiffened, and the thane leaned back slightly, rocking on his heels.

"I told you this one was smart," Thoggle chuckled. "He may be onto something there, Brogan."

The thane let loose a guffaw that turned into a deep belly laugh.

"I can tell we're going to be good friends," the thane said. "All good friendships should start with a fight." The thane glanced over at Jorthan and placed a heavy hand upon Stiger's shoulder. "When in our teens, Jorthan and I were both sweet on the same girl. At the time, I couldn't stand the sight of him. With such things, as they naturally do, it all came to blows."

"You hit like a gnome," Jorthan said.

"Is that so?" the thane asked with a broad grin that seemed more challenge than anything else. Removing his hand from Stiger's shoulder, he flexed his left arm and cracked his knuckles before making a fist.

"What happened to the girl?" Stiger asked. "Who got her?"

"That's the ironic part," Jorthan said. "She wasn't interested in either of us. We beat each other silly and the next day she was taking walks with old Daggins—well, I suppose he was young back then."

"So were we," the thane said. "That beating we gave him for stealing our girl was worth it."

"I don't seem to recall it being much of a beating. He got in a few good licks that left us both with black eyes. It was more a draw than anything else, made worse that it was two on one."

Brogan and Jorthan chuckled at their shared memory, before the thane turned his gaze back to Theo.

"Legate," the thane said, eyes still on Theo, "I accept your apology for Theogdin."

"Now that's just not fair," Theo said, which caused the thane to grin.

"Sit," the thane said to Stiger. He gestured at the table. "And drink with us, for the road awaits and we have a long way to go."

Stiger took a seat across from the thane. Theo shot Stiger a sour look as he sat down on a stool to his right. Stiger gave him a wink in reply.

"It is good to know that you have a sense of humor," the thane said to Stiger. "It seems that our journey together may not be as tedious as I had thought."

"If you pour me another drink of that fine wine," Stiger said, "I will toast to that."

Chapter Nine

Stiger stepped out of the tavern, blinking under the bright early afternoon sun. His belly was full from a hearty beef stew that had been thick with carrots, leeks, and potatoes. The stew had been good, but not overly great. For an out-of-the-way tavern it was acceptable and, after the plain diet of living with Sarai, more than welcome. Stiger had also shared several jars of wine with the thane and Theo. When he had stopped his drinking for fear of becoming drunk, the thane had continued with Theo, downing jar after jar.

After the filling meal and drinks, Stiger was feeling quite good and, truth be told, a little sleepy. The temperature had warmed as the sun climbed higher into the sky. It was almost too warm and caused him to yawn. The sky was clear, bluer than the ocean and with only a handful of puffy white clouds slowly making their way across the sky. All in all, it was a perfect day for travel.

The legionaries from Fifth Century had formed up into a double column for march. Marching yokes, javelins, packs, entrenching tools, and shields lay on the ground by their feet. Centurion Pixus stood slightly apart and was speaking with Sabinus, who held the reins of his horse.

The dwarves had also formed up on the edge of town, along the road that led off toward Thane's Mountain. Brogan's escort numbered at least two hundred. Jorthan had told Stiger they were an elite company from the thane's personal guard. All were handpicked warriors from the best of the best—veterans.

Stiger's gaze traveled up to Thane's Mountain. It was tall and imposing, and it dominated this end of the valley. His thoughts drifted to all that happened in this area before he had traveled back in time. The desperate fight against the orcs just across the river weighed heavily upon his mind. It sobered him somewhat, and he wondered what was in store for him in the coming days and weeks. Stiger was seriously worried, for it felt like he was walking not only in his own steps, but now Delvaris's too. Stiger moved his gaze to the ridgeline across the river. The Sabinus in Stiger's time had told him a battle had been fought on that very spot; Stiger had waged his own here. Was he destined to now fight Delvaris's battle, too? It certainly felt like it would be so.

Mood now subdued, Stiger moved to his horse. Father Thomas exited the tavern behind him and went for his own, which the paladin had secured to a hitching post several feet away. Stiger untied Misty and mounted up. Theo and the thane came out a few moments later, singing a bawdry tune together in dwarven. So bad was their singing, Stiger only managed to catch a third of the words they were cheerfully belting out. Both dwarves had consumed a great amount of wine and it showed not only with their walk, which was unsteady, but also in their tune.

Stiger pulled Misty back and away from the hitching post. He shifted about as he did so, finding a comfortable seat, then shrugged his shoulders slightly. The straps from his armor were rubbing somewhat uncomfortably on his skin. Stiger had forgotten about the chafing. This evening he would be quite sore.

"Take care of my thane, will you?"

About to ride over to Sabinus and Pixus, Stiger checked himself and brought Misty to a halt. The horse sidestepped in apparent disappointment as Stiger looked down to find Thoggle. He had not seen the wizard leave the tavern, or even approach for that matter.

"You're not coming with us?" Stiger found he was somewhat surprised by this, but not overly much. The only other wizard he had known, Ogg, came and went at will. Why should it be any different for Thoggle?

"Alas, no," Thoggle said. "Should I attend, our enemy would surely notice my presence so far from my regular haunts. You see, Castor's minion can sense my *will*...you might call it power, or my aura. It is rather imprecise, meaning the creature cannot tell exactly where I am, but it will have a general idea."

"You can sense it, too?" Stiger asked.

"I can."

"And where is Castor's minion now?"

Thoggle turned to the west and gestured with his staff. "That way, deep in the mountains, perhaps two hundred miles, give or take ten or so."

Stiger found it uncanny that the wizard knew where the minion was, could sense it. It made him somewhat uncomfortable. A thought occurred to Stiger as he looked down on the wizard.

"Why don't you go deal with it, then?" Stiger said. "Kill it and end the threat, send it back to Castor. We would not have to go through with this summit."

"It is a little more complicated than that," Thoggle said, looking up at him with tired eyes. Stiger got the sudden impression that a mountain weighed upon the wizard's shoulders. "I cannot do as you suggest. It would be unwise."

Stiger grew irritated, but at the same time, Thoggle had just given him a nugget of information. Perhaps the wizard would be willing to share more?

"I grow weary of getting half answers and having to piece things together," Stiger said. "If it is so complicated, kindly explain it to me, then."

Thoggle shifted his staff and stared up at Stiger, eyes narrowing.

"Very well," Thoggle said. "You know the gods' war, right?"

Stiger nodded. "We are caught up in their struggle."

"That is correct," Thoggle said. "The minion and I are given by our respective gods the potential to use *will.*" Thoggle held out his hand, palm upward. A tiny spark of blue light appeared, hovering an inch or so above the skin. It grew rapidly into a small ball, hissing softly and spitting soundless sparks. "Think of it as power, and with it comes certain additional abilities. Our *will* is somewhat different in that our gods are disparate entities." Thoggle closed his hand and the ball of light extinguished itself. "Are you following me so far?"

Stiger gave another nod.

"Good," Thoggle said, seeming pleased. "It is important that you understand. Should I directly confront Castor's minion, it is possible I may defeat the creature. However, the outcome of such an encounter would be seriously in doubt. The minion knows this as well. And as such, it will not yet willingly choose to confront me directly, nor shall I it."

"It is too dangerous for either of you to contest the other?" Stiger asked.

"Yes. In place of a direct conflict, we shall use proxies, hoping for an advantage to develop. Besides, I am most likely not the best person to challenge it. From what you and Father Thomas have told me, we know Delvaris faced it."

"In that vision I was shown, he died," Stiger said, unhappily.

"And defeated the creature," Thoggle said.

"So, I must face it." Stiger was not eager to share Delvaris's fate.

Thoggle nodded gravely.

"You work, in a way, like the gods themselves," Stiger said, "meaning you use others to fight your battles."

Stiger thought he detected surprise in the wizard's eyes as they blinked. Or was it anger? Whatever it had been passed in a flash.

"I meant no offense," Stiger said. He had just drawn things to their logical conclusion. "It was just an observation."

"A good one," Thoggle conceded and shifted his grip on his staff. "And you are more correct than you realize. The minion and I have tasks that need to be completed, things that must be done. We dare not risk a direct confrontation."

"I see," Stiger said, wondering what those tasks were and who had set them. He suspected that he knew the answer to that. His hand strayed to his hilt, and his eyes shifted to the distant speck of the fortress that guarded the valley. "Father Thomas and I defeated a minion in Grata'Kor. I used the sword to do that."

"I know," Thoggle said, his eyes resting uneasily upon Stiger's sword. "Father Thomas told me. Rarokan is a powerful and dangerous relic, a tool forged directly by the gods." Thoggle shifted his staff. "And yes, it has the power to end a minion of Castor. The blade also has the *will* to do much more. Yet, even with it... we should move carefully and confront the creature on our terms, when we have the best chance for success. Until then, we must prepare and work to stack the board to our advantage." Thoggle tapped his staff on the ground. "That means we must work to counter and frustrate Castor's plans."

"Which is why you put Brogan up to the summit, even though you dare not go yourself?"

"Correct," Thoggle said. "If we can keep the orcs from organizing, we buy ourselves time to prepare. And more importantly, it is our understanding the summit is being held without the knowledge of the orc priests. As a result, with a little fortune, the minion will be ignorant of our attempt to drive a wedge into the unity it is struggling to create amongst the tribes. Which is why, should I go, our enemy will become curious as to why I have strayed and send agents to investigate. I am certain we both can agree we don't want that happening."

"You really believe that something can be gained from going, then?" Stiger was surprised that the wizard, knowing all that he had told him of the future, the orcs, and what was to come, would still hold out hope. It was a mad plan, but if it worked…

"What I believe is immaterial," Thoggle admitted with a slight shrug. He shifted his staff from one hand to the other. "Without the attempt, we will never know what can be gained, now, will we?"

"There is that," Stiger said. "However, you risk not only my life but the lives of all those going, including your thane. Have you considered what can be lost in this venture?"

"I have," Thoggle said, "and as you suggest, there is risk. However, the summit is being held on neutral and ancient holy ground. It was chosen with great care and is a site that even the minion and most orcs would choose to avoid." Thoggle paused and sucked in a breath. "It is far from orc lands, but not so distant from our own. Should something happen, I can easily be called upon to help by Jorthan." Thoggle's gaze moved to the thane.

The thane and Theo finished up their tune, striking a particularly terrible high note that was almost painful enough to shatter glass. Song finished, they slapped each other fondly on their backs.

Thoggle continued. "The thane has also dispatched pioneers to scout the surrounding area about the summit. At the very least, there should be some warning if the orcs mean to betray us."

Stiger considered the wizard for a long moment. "I hope you are right."

"I do too," Thoggle said, gaze traveling back to the thane. "As I said, make sure the thane comes back."

"Thank you," Stiger said and hesitated a moment. "I appreciate you taking the time to explain."

"To be victorious, a general must see the land he is fighting over," Thoggle said. "I did nothing more than show you the lay of the land." Thoggle turned away and then paused, looking back. "I also disabled the tracking spell. I wasn't completely truthful with you. It would also have prevented you from leaving the valley, in a painful way, had you tried to do so." Thoggle's eyes flashed with amusement. "You are your own man now and may go where you wish."

Not waiting for a reply, Thoggle turned his back on Stiger and began painfully stumping back toward the tavern. Jorthan stood in the doorway watching Stiger with an unfathomable expression.

"Now this," Theo said, coming up and slurring his words slightly, "is how all journeys should begin."

The thane walked over to where his dwarven escort was holding his pony. Jorthan started after him. The thane's escort drew themselves up, making ready as shouts were called out by their officers.

"Will you be able to ride?" Stiger asked Theo, who had attempted to pull himself up into the saddle and utterly failed, slipping right back down to the ground.

"Stupid animal," Theo groused, barely managing to stay on his feet. He fixed a bleary-eyed gaze on Stiger and wagged a thick index finger. "None of your negativity, now. Nope, don't need none of that. Happy thoughts only. Got me?" Theo made another attempt. This one failed also. He pointed an accusatory finger at Stiger and shook it. "You say nothing. Don't distract me. I will get it eventually."

Stiger leaned forward in the saddle and grinned at the struggling dwarf.

"Would you like a boost?"

Theo glared at Stiger before making a third go at it. He succeeded and mounted his pony. He wavered precariously, and Stiger wondered for an alarmed heartbeat if the dwarf would slip out of the saddle. After a few moments, Theo seemed to get his bearings. He made a tremendous effort to hold himself steady, though he had to lean forward with both hands and hold the pony's neck for stability. Once he was sure of himself, he reached for the reins to pull his horse around, only to discover that his horse was still tethered to the hitch.

"Wouldn't you know it?" Theo said with disgust.

Stiger slapped his thigh, thoroughly amused.

"I fear it will be a long ride for you, my friend," Stiger said. "I'm thinking you will come to regret that drinking session soon enough."

Sliding off his horse, Theo spared him a dark look. The dwarf untied his horse and took the reins in his hand.

"It's like when you go for a walk," Stiger said. "First you put on your sandals, then you walk. It is a simple enough concept."

"I'll remember that," Theo said, pulling himself successfully back up into the saddle. "Very wise advice. You know, you may want to consider becoming an oracle or scholar or something like that. Your talents are clearly wasted as a warrior. I am going to ride with the thane today, instead of you. He's more fun."

Stiger wheeled his horse around. Sabinus waited a few feet ahead with Pixus. The centurion of the Fifth idly tapped his vine cane upon the ground. Stiger started over. Next to the two officers stood the standard-bearer, who had been engaged in conversation with them. Both centurions offered Stiger a salute. The standard-bearer simply straightened. Mindful of staying in character, Stiger waved back at them.

"Have the men eaten?"

"Yes, sir," Pixus said, "I saw to it that they did. Canteens have been filled as well. We are ready to march."

"Excellent," Stiger said.

"Is he going to make it?" Sabinus asked of Theo, clearly noticing how the dwarf swayed dangerously in the saddle with every step his pony took. Theo passed them by in a not-so-straight course as he followed in the direction of the thane. He shot Stiger another dark look with bleary eyes.

"I would hazard eventually," Stiger said, "and if not now, later, when he sobers up."

A shout rang out ahead, followed by a clatter, and then the dwarven column began to move forward, unit and clan standards fluttering in the breeze at the head of their column. A moment later, the dwarves broke into a rousing marching song as they stepped off and began moving down the road.

"Shall I give the order, sir?" Pixus asked. The centurion had not brought a horse, and it was clear he would march with his men.

"Let's allow the dwarves to get some ways ahead," Stiger said. "Their legs are shorter than ours, and judging by their pace, they are accustomed to moving slower than we are."

"Very good, sir," Pixus said. "I will give the order to move out when they are a sufficient distance ahead of us."

"Perfect."

Stiger's attention was drawn to Father Thomas, who had dismounted and was speaking to a man and woman just a few feet away. Curious, he moved his horse over to the paladin. The woman was holding a baby in her arms. Wrapped in a coarse brown blanket, the child, who could not have been more than a few days old, looked pale and sickly. The infant's lips were a bluish color.

The mother and father were clearly distressed. Stiger read a hopelessness mixed with terrible pain and suffering in their eyes. It was nothing he had not seen before, but it still pulled on the strings to his heart.

"May I hold your baby?" Father Thomas asked gently.

"Yes, Father," the woman said. Her eyes were red and puffy from crying. Sniffling miserably, she handed the baby over, hesitating at the last moment. It was as if she was afraid it would be the last time she held the child in this world. "He just won't feed, Father."

"We've not had a priest about these parts for a long time," the man, clearly her husband, said. "It was a miracle to find you passing through here."

Father Thomas cradled the baby and nodded absently. Opening the blanket, he was silent as he made his examination. The baby hardly moved as he poked and prodded it. The child seemed to struggle for every breath with a low rasping sound that was quite pitiful. It was as if the baby was about to give up on life, which Stiger supposed it was. The paladin wrapped the blanket around the baby and laid the back of his hand on the child's forehead before looking back up.

"What is the child's name?"

"Fin," the father said. "He is our third boy. Each died in infancy. We are hoping you can offer the child a blessing and the last rite. I..." The father's voice caught and he cleared his throat. "I fear he won't last much longer."

The child's mother broke down, covering her face, shoulders shaking. Her husband looked over at her, clearly hurting. He reached out an arm and drew her close. She turned into his chest, sobbing loudly. Stiger felt incredibly moved by the scene and at the same time helpless. Life could be hard. Fortuna was a fickle mistress. His own mother had lost a child due to sickness.

"I will offer a blessing," Father Thomas said, placing his hand to the child's forehead, "but I will not yet perform the last rite."

"Father," the man said, "please. I beg you. Give us this small comfort, before he passes over into the lord's keeping."

Instead of replying, Father Thomas closed his eyes, lips moving in silent prayer. Stiger watched and could almost feel the divine power welling within Father Thomas. It made the small hairs on his arms stand up as he realized he was looking upon a true wonder in the making. The paladin was channeling the High Father's divine power, he was sure of it. Stiger had only seen such a thing happen a handful of times before, and it never ceased to amaze him. But what was more shocking was that he could feel the paladin's power.

The baby's gray skin slowly gave way to a healthy, pale-reddish hue. As if ink on parchment in the rain, the blue seemed to run from Fin's lips. A couple of heartbeats later, the baby gave off a loud, hungry cry, and with that Father Thomas opened his eyes. Stiger was surprised to see tears there. The paladin smiled down at the healthy-looking child in his arms and rocked the boy a moment.

"A miracle." The child's father fell to his knees and clasped his hands together, praying loudly. The mother wept uncontrollably, this time with joy, as Father Thomas gingerly handed Fin back to her.

"The High Father has passed along a blessing of healing," Father Thomas said, a weary edge to his voice. The effort had clearly taken a toll. There was an ashen look to his cheeks and his fiery red hair seemed not as bright. "He rewards your faith, mother. I ask humbly that you continue your devotion and raise your child to love our god, for he is special in the High Father's eyes, as are we all."

"Thank you, Father," the mother said, almost crushing the baby to her chest and rocking him slightly. "Thank you, oh, thank you."

Father Thomas reached out a hand and touched her cheek, smiling softly. "Your gratitude should go to the High Father. I am but his humble servant."

"It will," she said, giving her baby a kiss. "I will thank the High Father for the rest of my days for his blessing and raise my boy to love our lord."

With that, Father Thomas turned away and mounted his horse. The smile slipped from his face and was replaced by an expression of near exhaustion. His shoulders slumped slightly as he sat there silently, simply breathing in and out. Then the paladin shook himself and looked around. He saw Stiger walking his horse over and gave a slight smile.

"The High Father's *will* has been done," the paladin said simply and glanced back on the family. "They will know a happiness today that I pray they will not soon forget."

"Yes," Stiger said, eyes still resting on the small family. The husband and wife were hugging. They were all crying, even the baby. "The great god rendered a kindness to them."

"A simple reward for faith, my son."

"Simple?" Stiger asked. "I don't think so. It looked like it took a lot out of you."

"The child was almost to the boundary from whence there is no return," the paladin said. "It took effort to pull him back and set things right."

"And the High Father desired that child healed?"

"Oh, yes," Father Thomas said. "Without the High Father's blessing, there would have been no healing. All I can do is ask for my god's assistance." He glanced over at the family. "Though I am called to confront great evil, this small service brought me great joy."

The paladin's gaze swung up to Thane's Mountain and a grim expression came over him. Stiger followed the gaze. They both remained silent, considering the mountain.

"Reminiscent of how things began once before, traveling to that mountain." The paladin looked over at Stiger. "Isn't it?"

"Yes," Stiger said. He had been thinking the same thing. He had first gone with Braddock. Now, Stiger was traveling to the mountain with Braddock's father. It was all too similar. "That last time, things did not go as expected. Perhaps this time it will end with us going back to where we belong."

"I wouldn't plan on it," the paladin said.

"You believe we are stuck here?" Stiger said. He already had come to that conclusion, but he wanted to hear it from the paladin. "In this time?"

"I do, my son," Father Thomas said. "I do not see how we can return. This is now our time."

Stiger scratched at his jaw and studied the mountain.

"That's not such a bad thing," Stiger said.

"I don't quite follow you."

"Do you think if I survive what is to come...?" Stiger stopped. He could not bring himself to continue.

"Ah, that," Father Thomas said. "You are wondering if you will be able to go back to Sarai?"

"Something like that," Stiger said and pulled his canteen from a saddlebag. He unstopped it and took a swig, more to wash the taste of wine out of his mouth than anything else. "Something very much like that."

"It is not simply surviving," Father Thomas said. "We must prevail over the evil that is even now growing amongst the orcs."

"If a life with Sarai is the reward for defeating the minion," Stiger said, shaking the reins in his hand slightly, "then I will make certain that we do."

The paladin did not immediately answer.

"I am afraid it is not likely to be as easy as that," Father Thomas said.

"It never is," Stiger said, thinking of his conversation with Thoggle.

"All right, you lovely bastards, yokes and shields up," Pixus called loudly to his men. "Time for a little hike."

The dwarves had marched out of the town and were half a mile down the road. Stiger watched silently as the men grabbed their shields, which were in their protective canvas covers, and slung them over their backs. Heavy yokes were hoisted up and settled into a comfortable position on the shoulder.

Carrying his own shield on his back and yoke on his shoulder, Pixus walked up and down the length of the column, checking his men to make sure all was ready and in order. He returned to the front of the marching column and nodded to the standard-bearer, who moved into position.

"Forward," Centurion Pixus called out loudly to his men. "March!"

Stiger watched the eighty-some legionaries of Fifth Century begin to move forward, sandals rhythmically crunching the dirt of the road. It was a familiar sound, something he had not heard for quite a while. It was also, in a way, comforting. And yet, he had the increasingly uncomfortable feeling he was heading down a path from which there was no return. Destiny, fate, and duty were dragging him onward, and he hated it.

"An old sergeant once told me, 'Nothing worth doing right is ever easy,' " Stiger said.

"It sounds like something a good sergeant would say," the paladin said.

"So far," Stiger said, "that's proven apt advice."

Stiger nudged his horse into a trot, leaving the paladin behind. He caught up with the men, passing by the century's mule train and bringing Misty to a halt midway along the column. Stiger looked them over. Most of them appeared to be long-service veterans with a handful of youths tossed in, likely recent recruits. Stiger made a decision. He dismounted and, leading his horse, marched alongside the men. At the head of the column, Sabinus saw what he was doing and stopped his mount. He waited for Stiger to catch up and then himself dismounted.

"What are you doing, sir?" Sabinus asked in a near whisper while leading his horse alongside Stiger's. The centurion had made sure to put himself between Stiger and the men.

"Sharing the miles with the men."

"Delvaris never did that."

"Well, I do," Stiger said. "It sets a good example. Besides, I need the exercise. It has been too long since I took part in a good march and felt the ache in my legs at day's end."

"Sir, please," Sabinus said. "It may unsettle the men."

"They will become accustomed to it," Stiger said, adding a firm undertone so that it was clear he had made up his mind.

Sabinus fell silent with a heavy breath, and together they marched, leading their horses by the reins. The column passed the last of the buildings, leaving Bridgetown behind. The road ahead took them through the farm fields that surrounded the town. To their side, the men were at first silent as well. This was most likely the result of their legate being so close. Then, as time passed, they began to talk, and the regular friendly banter of an extended march began to take hold.

As they approached the bridge, Stiger saw it was a work of stone, highly arched at the center. The bridge was nothing like the wooden one in the future. The hobnails of the men's sandals cracked loudly on the paving stones as they made their way over its span. It was an impressive structure, and it reminded Stiger of some of the grand bridges back in the empire's capital. A lot of engineering went into its construction. Thinking on the structures he had seen in Old City, and the apparent quality with which the bridge had been built, he decided it was dwarven work.

Stiger made a point to peer over the edge. The river looked much deeper than it had when he had last seen it. Mountain-fed and clear, he could see straight down to its rocky bottom. He glanced over at Sabinus, recalling what the centurion's future self had said about his recollection of the battle that happened here, in this time with Delvaris, and about how the legate had refused to destroy the bridge as the orc army advanced. Stiger felt abruptly chilled, realizing that Sabinus may very well have been speaking of Stiger himself and not Delvaris. There was no doubt in his mind that when the orcs came, he would meet them here on this spot, as he had done in the future.

"Halt," came the unexpected shout from ahead. "I said bloody halt!"

The column ground to a stop, snapping Stiger back to reality. Pixus and several men were clustered about a mountain pony just ahead. One of the men was holding the reins. As he and Sabinus made their way forward, Stiger saw a dwarf lying on the ground.

"I found him like this, sir," Pixus said, stepping aside. "He's alive. I checked. He's just drunk is all."

Theo was passed out on the ground, clearly having fallen off his pony. The dwarf was snoring loudly. Stiger shook his head in both amusement and disgust. He considered what to do. He obviously couldn't leave Theo here. His friend would never forgive him.

Captain Aleric had been right to send Theo along. After the talk with Thoggle, Stiger understood difficult days lay ahead. He would likely need all the help he could get from the dwarves, and Theo would assist with that. He rubbed his jaw and glanced at the pony. Strapping Theo to his mount with all of that armor he was wearing was not an option. Removing the armor wasn't, either. It would take too long.

Stiger glanced around and spotted a small grove of young trees twenty yards away. There were several saplings.

"Have a litter fashioned," Stiger said and pointed at the grove. "There are a couple of smaller trees over there. We will use his pony to drag him along until he wakes and is able to ride."

"Yes, sir," Pixus said and called out some orders. A section of men snapped to.

Less than thirty minutes later, the column was back on the march. They followed the road up the small ridge. The dwarven column was no longer in sight. Dog reappeared, coming up from behind at a run, barking as he came and then slowing to a walk next to Misty. Stiger glanced down at the animal and wondered what he had been up to. Tongue lolling, Dog seemed to be enjoying himself.

"Welcome back," Stiger said to him. Dog gave a clipped bark and sprinted ahead, rapidly climbing the slope of the ridge.

"He sure likes to run," Sabinus said.

"Seems that way," Stiger agreed. His legs had started to burn with the climb.

At the top of the ridge, Stiger stopped and glanced backward the way they had come. The ridgeline and bowl appeared much as it had in his time, with only a few minor differences. The grass was taller, and green. Winter was not yet upon them. Beyond the bridge, he could see the tops of the buildings from Bridgetown, smoke from the chimneys rising slowly up into the sky. With little wind, the fire smoke hung over the town like an ugly pall.

"What is it?" Sabinus asked, having also stopped. He was looking curiously at Stiger. "Is something wrong?"

"I fought a battle here. Our defensive positions ran atop this ridgeline," Stiger said, eyes roving where he had ordered his defenses set. In his mind, he could still hear the clash of arms and screams of that desperate fight. The memory of the battle was still fresh and hot.

Sabinus's eyes narrowed and he studied the terrain. "With the elevation, it is good ground, sir."

"Yes," Stiger said, starting to walk once again as the tail of the column caught up to them. Theo was being hauled along at the very end, just after the century's mule train. A legionary had been tasked with leading his pony. "It is exceptional ground."

Chapter Ten

"I am not sure what to say," Pixus said, clearly at a loss for words as they entered the mountain gates that ultimately led to Old City.

Passing the massive stone gates, he and his men were looking around, agape, staring in awe at their surroundings. Only discipline, or perhaps it was the simple momentum of the march, kept the men moving ever forward. They craned their necks around, looking at everything.

"This is absolutely astonishing," Pixus continued. "Ten years from now, should I live long enough to make it to a veterans' colony, no one would believe me. They'd think I was telling exaggerated tales over cups."

"They'd never believe us now," Sabinus said to Pixus. "Gods, this is my third time through here, and I hardly can trust my eyes that this is all real. I never in all my imaginings thought such things were possible."

"It is fairly impressive," Stiger said. He was leading his horse and walking alongside Pixus. Sabinus was to his right. Father Thomas was ahead somewhere. The paladin had ridden much of the way with Jorthan and had appeared to be deep in conversation with the thane's advisor when Stiger had last seen him.

"Fairly?" Pixus asked. Stiger glanced over at the hardbitten veteran and their eyes met. There was a questioning look there. "Just fairly, sir?"

Stiger gave a slight shrug.

The entrance tunnel into the mountain spread out before them. A double row of support columns to either side traveled the length of the great hole. The columns reached upward to the ceiling, sixty feet above. The floor was smooth from centuries of use and the wear of untold numbers of feet. Large fire pits, spaced out every few yards, provided sufficient light to see. Even before they had stepped through the gates, the cold of the mountain had flowed outward in an eager, if not unwelcome greeting. It was as if the cold emanated from a deep crypt, the chill of the dead reaching to pull them over to the other side.

So huge was the tunnel that the fire pits did absolutely nothing to combat the underground chill. They only served to illuminate the way, like a row of beacons, and light the carved reliefs on the walls that stretched from floor to ceiling. Though he had seen it all before, Stiger still found himself deeply impressed.

The tunnel was considered an extension to the defenses of the fortress, Grata'Jalor, which lay ahead and guarded not only the way into the mountain, but also the World Gate. Stiger's eyes once again searched out the murder holes, hidden amidst the carved reliefs, and the numerous trapdoors above, at least those he could see and identify in the shadows. There were also metal portcullises, suspended above by thick, rusted iron chains. The dwarves had done their best to create the perfect killing ground, and Stiger pitied any enemy who tried to force their way into the mountain through the tunnel, for it was a death trap in waiting.

"This," Stiger said to Pixus, "is nothing compared to what you're about to see."

The centurion looked over at him, clearly with some skepticism, and then, like his men, returned to studying the surroundings as they marched deeper into the mountain. A hush had fallen over the men, despite the noise of marching feet, clattering wagons, and dwarven voices.

The tunnel was busier and livelier than the last time Stiger had come through. That had been hundreds of years in the future, when Old City had been thoroughly abandoned for years. Now there were dwarves seemingly everywhere, either moving in or out of the mountain on business. The legionaries marched past slow-moving wagons and carts, dwarven teamsters wrapped heavily in fur or wool cloaks and jackets, clan colors proudly displayed for all to see. The wagons were pulled by teams of oxen, others by mules or work horses. The sound of their heavy hooves on stone echoed loudly throughout the chamber, as did the rattling and clattering of wagon wheels on stone. Stiger found it almost as noisy as a battle. The thousand sounds together created a cacophony that was nearly deafening.

The dwarven teamsters paid them little attention, though a number did stare with what Stiger took to be disgust or suspicion at the sight of humans entering their sacred mountain.

It had surprised Stiger to see the massive stone storehouses out in front of the mountain well-maintained and clearly in use. Prior to entering the mountain, they had passed by a caravan with over a hundred wagons preparing to depart for some unknown destination. The caravan wagons had nearly all been completely loaded, most having heavy tarps secured over their loads.

"The legate is right," Sabinus said to Pixus. "Wait until you see Grata'Jalor."

"The fortress that you told me of?" Pixus said, sparing his fellow centurion a look. "The one that guards this city of theirs?"

"Yes," Sabinus said and shot Stiger a warning glance to say no more. "That's right."

"I still find the concept of an entire underground city difficult to swallow," Pixus said. "Even after setting my eyes upon all this."

"As did I," Stiger said.

"What is that?" Pixus was pointing just ahead toward one of the large open fire pits. He was gesturing at a small diminutive creature busy taking split wood from the back of a cart and tossing it into one of the fire pits. The creature moved efficiently and with haste, seeming to want to finish its task rapidly.

"That," Stiger said with a heavy breath, "is a gnome."

"A gnome?" Pixus sounded as if he could hardly believe what he was seeing, not to mention hearing. "I thought they were just fancies of imagination, sir. Creatures that lived only in myth and tale?"

"Like dwarves?" Sabinus asked him. "Up until a few months ago, we all would have said they weren't real either. Remember our surprise when we saw our first dwarf?"

Pixus nodded absently and stepped nearer the fire to get a better look. Stiger and Sabinus went with him.

The gnome turned, its black eyes glittering in the firelight as the three humans approached. Stiger had always found it slightly disturbing that gnomes had no pupils. The small creature, half the size of a dwarf and painfully skinny, was dressed in a simple tunic of plain brown wool. The tunic, patched over in numerous places, was made of coarse material and draped down past its knees, almost to the creature's black boots. The gnome's skin was an ashen color that could almost have been described as gray.

Stiger idly wondered if the creature's pallor was a result of it spending much of its life underground. The gnome ran a hand through its short black hair as it said something in a harsh, clipped tongue that Stiger did not understand but supposed was gnomish. Whatever it had said didn't sound very pleasant.

"I wouldn't get too close," Theo said, coming up from behind. The dwarf was leading his pony. Red-eyed and hair askew, he looked terrible. "The vicious little shits can be dangerous when provoked."

Theo had woken about an hour before. Showing no signs of embarrassment, the dwarf had dragged himself off the litter, detached it, and mounted his pony. Stiger suspected that he was still somewhat drunk, as his cheeks were flushed and he swayed slightly as he walked.

"That little thing?" Pixus asked, clearly in disbelief. "It can't be much stronger than a young child. Why, there's no doubt I could overpower it with ease."

"They have a mean streak," Stiger said.

"A mean streak doesn't adequately describe their temperament," Theo said to Pixus. "Oh, and when dealing with gnomes, it's not the individual that you have to worry about, but all of them devious, evil little monsters."

Theo casually gestured at the next fire pit, where five more gnomes were working. They had allowed the fire to burn out and were shoveling ashes into a cart. Two of the gnomes were inside the fire pit working. Another wagon, stacked with wood, stood nearby.

"How many of them are there?" Pixus asked, eyes moving from the work detail to the gnome before them.

"Too many," Theo said unhappily. "Thankfully the little monsters mainly keep to themselves and live deeper into the mountains than my people. We dvergr try to have as little to do with their kind as possible. However..." Theo gave a shrug. "They are inextricably tied to my people, as we are to them."

"They really are dangerous?" Pixus sounded extremely skeptical. "I'm sorry, but I am having difficulty believing that."

"I've seen them fight," Stiger said, "and, centurion, you don't want to be on the receiving end of a pissed-off gnome."

"You fought alongside gnomes?" Theo turned, clearly surprised. "Wha—?"

The gnome, looking at the humans, spoke again. Theo's head snapped around and away from Stiger. The dwarf's expression turned murderous.

"You little piece of goblin dropping," Theo said to the gnome in dwarven, taking a half step forward, "keep your mouth shut before I rip out that filthy tongue."

"What did it say?" Sabinus asked.

In the face of Theo's rage, the gnome held its ground. It cocked its head to one side.

"You don't want to know," Theo said in a heated tone, switching back to common. "They are unpleasant creatures who once worshiped a dark god. You could say in a way we adopted them in the hopes they would become more pleasant. After a couple thousand years, they may never be fully redeemable, nor do I think they even care to be."

"Filthy half-man," the gnome spat back, switching to Theo's language. It pointed a small finger at the dwarf. "You tarnish your legend by—" The gnome spoke a series of words that Stiger didn't understand, but since it gestured at the legionaries he assumed it was referring to the humans. "I even question your—" The gnome spoke another word Stiger did not know. "You should shave now. Save your relatives the time and become a beardless wonder."

Going red in the face, Theo uttered an animal-like roar and lunged at the gnome. It nimbly danced out of reach, laughing wickedly at him, which seemed to enrage Theo to new levels. Head down, he began chasing the gnome around the fire pit, swearing in dwarven. At least Stiger assumed the words were curses, because he didn't know them.

Dog padded up to Stiger and sat down. The dog, like the rest of them, watched the show, as did the gnomes from the next fire pit. They hooted and hollered, seeming to encourage their mate along.

The gnome, for its part, intentionally slowed, just enough for Theo to make a grab, and then sped up out of reach. It was clearly playing with the enraged dwarf. The third time around the fire pit, Stiger doubled over in laughter at the comical scene, as did Sabinus and Pixus. The men had also stopped and were watching. After a bit, it occurred to Theo that he could not catch the gnome, as the creature was faster and nimbler than he was. Theo was also wearing his heavy armor, which restricted his movement and slowed him down significantly.

Theo came to a stop, chest heaving and out of breath. Sucking in great gulps of air, he rested an arm on the wooden cart carrying firewood. The gnome turned its back on Theo and hiked up its tunic, exposing a small buttocks, which he joyfully wiggled about. The gnomes at the other fire pit died with laughter, as did the humans.

"Oh," Theo said, with a black look at the human officers, "I see. You seem to think this very funny?"

"It was," Stiger said, recovering, "at least until you stopped chasing him."

Pixus and Sabinus exploded into another bout of laughter.

"Ha, ha, ha," Theo said with disgust.

"Theo," Stiger said and wiped a tear from his eye, "I don't think I've laughed that hard in years."

The gnome had stopped its mooning of the dwarf. It glanced over at its fellows before turning back to face Theo. An evil smile formed on its face. It too began to laugh and point at Theo in obvious mirth, clearly poking the bear further.

Theo's eyes swept unhappily over the gnome and then the others on the work detail. The dwarf's eyes narrowed. His hand casually slid over the firewood and gripped a largish piece. Before Stiger could react, Theo hurled it with near perfect accuracy. The gnome moved to dodge, but had reacted too late. The piece of wood connected solidly, knocking the small creature down hard.

Everyone stilled, staring at Theo in shock.

"Now that," Theo said with a great hearty laugh, "was funny, and how you deal with the ungrateful little bastards."

Laughing, the dwarf turned his back on the appalled humans and returned to where he had left his pony. Picking up the reins, he started down the tunnel, whistling loudly and seemingly greatly pleased with himself. Not once did he glance back.

None of the other gnomes moved to assist their injured mate, but quickly went back to what they had been doing, as if such violence was a regular and expected occurrence. Bruised and clearly battered, the gnome picked itself up. It dusted off its hands.

There was an ugly cut that ran along its cheek, bleeding freely. The gnome's blood looked almost black in the firelight. Its eyes followed as Theo continued on, then it turned a malevolent look upon the human officers and held it for a long moment. The gnome spat bloody spittle on the ground.

"I think... we may wish to keep moving," Sabinus said, glancing back at the men. "Brogan will have gotten ahead of us again."

"Who gave you permission to halt?" Pixus roared at his century, suddenly enraged and stomping toward them like an erupting volcano. "Who gave you that bloody order? I certainly didn't. There is nothing to see here. Get your sorry asses moving."

The men instantly began moving again.

Stiger started after them, leading Misty. Sabinus walked alongside. Stiger couldn't help but glance back at the injured gnome. Heedless of its injuries, the small creature had returned to its task of tossing the wood into the fire.

"I understand the gnomes are allies of the dwarves," Sabinus said. "Yet, from what I've seen, they don't seem to get along all that well."

"I don't pretend to understand it myself," Stiger said, "but it seems their relationship is rather a complicated one."

"I would agree with you there, sir," Sabinus said, gaze sliding over to a pair of gnomes pulling an empty cart along in the direction of the entrance. "Perhaps Theo can explain it better to me, after he calms down."

"Maybe," Stiger said, though he harbored his doubts. From what he had seen, the gnomes appeared to be slaves to the dwarves, but he understood that was not the case. They were unsteady allies that worked together for some common purpose.

"Sir." Sabinus lowered his voice a little. "I feel I must caution you about revealing too much to Pixus. He may become curious about when and where you fought alongside gnomes. It could lead to some uncomfortable questions."

"Noted," Stiger said, irritated with himself for slipping. "I will have to watch myself."

Passing the second set of massive stone doors that guarded the inner side of the mountain, they entered the unbelievably giant cavern that housed Grata'Jalor. Stiger and the legionaries came to a stop, thoroughly amazed at the sight that greeted them. Pixus said nothing about his men coming to an unordered halt, as even his jaw dropped.

Hundreds of rounded support columns, each the size of a house, climbed upward toward the ceiling and disappeared in the darkness above. The roof of the cavern was perhaps a thousand feet in height. Massive open skylights admitted shafts of daylight that beamed straight down into the cavern, almost like rays of blessed light from the heavens.

Stiger's eyes settled upon the fortress of Grata'Jalor, almost a quarter mile distant. It was ringed by a wide, dark chasm, much like an aboveground castle might have a moat. Yet Stiger knew that there was no water in this moat, just an impossible drop into darkness.

Torches glittered as pricks of light from the citadel's walls. Sentries could be seen walking their rounds along the perimeter, appearing small in the distance.

A drawbridge spanned the chasm to the castle. Three wagons were moving across, traveling in the direction of the citadel. From this distance, they looked like children's toys. On the other side of Grata'Jalor lay Old City, a place Stiger knew would be all but abandoned in a few years.

"Sir," Sabinus said, drawing his attention. "Heads up."

The thane, Jorthan, and Father Thomas were walking his way, along with Theo.

"Pixus," Sabinus said, half turning toward the other centurion. "See to your men."

Pixus took the hint and stepped away, ordering his men to fall in.

"From here..." Brogan said and gestured off to the left on their side of the chasm toward another gate about half a mile away. This gate, one big door, was closed and half the size of the main gates that led in and out of the mountain.

In the gloom, Stiger had not seen it. "…we will take the Haritan Road. This will see us to Stonehammer Hostel, where we will spend the night."

"We won't be staying in Old City?" Stiger was surprised by this and had assumed they would. At least before moving on to wherever the summit was being held.

"No," the thane said, "that would take us well out of our way." Brogan turned to Jorthan. "How far would you say it is to the Stonehammer?"

"I've not been there in nigh seventy years, but if I recall, the hostel should be a good three, maybe four hours' walk," Jorthan replied and then turned to Stiger. "From the Stonehammer, we will take the Kelvin Road, which will bring us most of the way to our destination."

"So," Stiger said, thinking it through, "we will climb up out of the mountain then and onto this Haritan Road?"

"The road," Jorthan said, "is not aboveground, but under. It makes negotiating your way through the mountains in these parts easier. The Kelvin Road takes us under several mountains and then down into the foothills and finally the forest. Where we are going, there are no aboveground roads or easy trails that travel from here to there. This is the quickest way."

Stiger recalled that he had been told the dwarves had completely tunneled out this area. He'd forgotten that they had such roads. He could see the advantage of going straight from point to point, without having to worry about mountains, hills, and forest or winding difficult trails. Still, it must have been difficult work to construct a road like that. His eyes moved around the cavern. The dwarves seemed very good at digging.

"I've been meaning to ask. What is the name of the place where the summit will be held?" Stiger asked.

"Garand Kos," Jorthan said. "It was one of the first settlements when our people and yours came to this world. It has long been abandoned, but its ruins stand as a monument to cooperation. I feel—"

"Yes, yes," Brogan said impatiently. "Thank you for the history lesson, Jorthan. Your ancient stories are doubtless of little interest to him."

"Yes, my thane," Jorthan said and bowed his head respectfully, though Stiger thought he detected a twinge of well-concealed irritation in the advisor's tone.

"We travel underground for at least three days," the thane explained. "The Stonehammer will be our last stay in civilization, at least until we return. After it, we will camp along the way, but I promise it won't be that bad, as I have arranged for supplies to be brought with us."

Stiger wasn't too terribly keen about spending the next three days underground. The mountain was cold, damp, and dark. Had there been an easier way, he would've gladly taken it. Unfortunately, the dwarves had selected the site for the summit, and they were the only ones who knew how to get there.

"Right," Stiger said, eager to be on his way. "Let's get a move on, then. The sooner we start, the quicker we will be there."

"If only it were that simple." The thane balled his thick fists. "Tell him, Jorthan, for the thought of their slight irritates me much."

"I am afraid we must wait a short while," Jorthan said in an unhappy tone. "It seems the gnomes bringing us our lanterns are slightly delayed. I'm told they will be here within the hour."

"Gnomes," Theo grunted, "always going out of their way to make simple things difficult."

"Bah!" Brogan spat on the stone at their feet. "I should have just sent some of our own people to the storehouses to avoid giving them such an opportunity."

Jorthan's tone was patient. "As I said, they are undoubtedly making a statement with this as an inducement to reconsider their latest offer."

"Statement." The thane fairly seethed with anger. "I tell you it is an insult. I will give them a statement. I should replace their entire council. See how they like that as an offer. Ha!"

"They would not dare offend you, my thane. This is nothing more than a negotiating tactic and was, I can assure you, not meant as an insult," Jorthan said somewhat apologetically. He turned back to Stiger, ignoring his thane. "We are negotiating a number of important contracts with the gnomish council. Usually they choose other means of delay to make their point, a slowing of metallurgic coal deliveries, for one. They do not typically play games that affect the thane directly." Jorthan shot a glance over at Brogan. "I fear they may have miscalculated this time."

"Miscalculated," Brogan said, turning on his advisor and speaking in dwarven. "After this, we lower our latest offer and stick with it. See how that settles with them."

"My thane," Jorthan said, "perhaps it is best to consider a subtler response." Brogan and the Thane started speaking about the specifics of an agreement, or lack of one, in their own language.

"Waiting again, it seems," Stiger said to Sabinus.

"Looks like we will be taking a break then, sir," Sabinus said. "Shall I pass that on?"

"Would you see that Pixus has the men fall out?" Stiger said. "Make sure they do not wander. This is not our mountain and I do not wish to cause offense by some unintended slight."

"Yes, sir. I will see to it." Sabinus drew himself up, saluted, and stepped away.

Stiger turned back to the thane and Jorthan to find Brogan studying him with a critical eye.

"You have them listening to you, already," Brogan said in dwarven. "Thoggle told me that might take a little longer, at least for the ones who know you are not Delvaris. It seems you do indeed have a commanding presence."

With that, the thane turned and walked abruptly off.

"An hour, maybe more, then we shall be on the road," Jorthan said and followed, leaving Stiger with Theo and Father Thomas.

"Brogan is warming to you," Theo said. "That is the closest I have ever heard him come to complimenting a human, and he doesn't like your people. Then again, I could be reading into it." He paused and sucked in a breath, looking Stiger hard in the eye. "My cousin appears a simple enough fellow, but he is as complicated as getting water out of a deep mine without using pumps. That bit with the gnomes and their contract negotiations was purely for show. I warn you now. He is a sly one, a user of people. He can be devious to get what he wants." Theo stopped and glanced around before returning his attention to Stiger. "It is why I try to avoid the family gatherings and, when I am compelled to go, cause trouble. I don't care to be used either. You may, as you humans say, desire to stay on your toes."

Theo patted Stiger on the back. What should have been a friendly pat, coming from a dwarf, was actually more of a pounding. Stiger was thankful for his armor as Theo walked off after his thane.

"I am inclined to agree with Theogdin," Father Thomas said as they watched Theo move in the direction of the other dwarves. "Brogan would not have served as long as he has without being very intelligent and crafty."

"And how long is that?"

"Jorthan tells me Brogan has been thane for nearly two hundred years," Father Thomas said.

"A long time." Stiger whistled. A few feet away, Fifth Century were setting their yokes down.

"That," Father Thomas continued, "is close to setting a record amongst their kind, and he's only middle aged for a dwarf. So, he has many more years to go."

"How old is he?"

The men began sitting down, grateful for the unexpected break. They started to rummage through their haversacks.

"Three hundred and twenty-two," Father Thomas answered and then rubbed his hands together for warmth. "He came to the throne at what the dwarves consider a young age and was able to hold it. I am told he is also a warrior of uncommon skill, matched with a keen intellect. You should heed Theo's advice and watch yourself with him."

"I will," Stiger said. It seemed everyone wanted to use him for something. Perhaps that was just how the things worked and he had not realized it 'til now.

Father Thomas rubbed his hands together again. "It certainly is chilly."

Stiger agreed, but said nothing. He had only been gone a few hours but was already missing Sarai, and the simplicity of the life they had shared together. He had come to find comfort in her presence.

"My son," Father Thomas turned, "I know you are unhappy with your role, but what you do is for the greater good."

Stiger breathed shallowly in and out, his eyes on the paladin.

"We will find a way to defeat the minion and Castor's efforts," Father Thomas said. "We do that and we can set things right."

"Has it occurred to you that Delvaris never killed the minion?" Stiger asked. It had been on his mind a lot lately. "What if it was me? What if I was the one who took the mortal wound in battle and not Delvaris? Have you thought of that?"

Father Thomas appeared troubled and hesitated before replying. The paladin glanced down at his feet before looking back up.

"I have," the paladin said in a voice that was almost whisper. "We have, yes."

"So," Stiger said, realizing that the paladin was speaking of Thoggle too. They had both come to the same conclusion. "I may very well die setting things right."

"That is a possibility," Father Thomas admitted. "But I will do my utmost to keep that from happening."

"If I die," Stiger said and paused, following the logic through to its natural conclusion, "I am the High Father's champion, and Restorer of the Compact. If I die, then who will make the decision when the time comes? Have you and Thoggle thought of that, too?"

"We have," Father Thomas admitted.

"And?"

"We're still working on solving that little problem," Father Thomas said. "Not only do you have to live, but you will need to return to the future, where you belong, for when that time comes."

"I would say it is a large problem then, wouldn't you?"

It was the paladin's turn to fall into an uneasy silence. He closed his eyes for a few heartbeats and then opened them. "Faith, my son."

"Faith?"

"Faith in the High Father," the paladin said. "You must have faith, for with it will come hope that, with his help, we will triumph over evil."

Stiger played with a loose stone using his foot to roll it around.

"In the past I put my trust in the High Father," Stiger said, looking back up at the paladin. "No matter how difficult things got, I never turned away from our god. I believed with all of my heart and soul. That doesn't mean I've never questioned. But lately I have been doing a lot of doubting."

"We've all doubted now and then," Father Thomas said in a kindly manner. "It is what makes us human. If you recall the teachings in the Book of Emlire, our god expects, in fact demands us to question ourselves, our actions, and our faith. Doing so brings you closer to him. My son, there is nothing wrong with that."

"Even if I struggled against bearing this burden?" Stiger shifted his feet slightly and kicked the small stone away. "Even if I did not heed when called?"

"Even then," the paladin said. "When first called, I resisted myself."

Stiger let out a long breath.

"Long ago, shortly after I entered the service," Stiger said, "I made a vow to the High Father. I am honoring my vow by putting my trust once again in the great god's keeping."

"You don't know how much it pleases me to hear that."

"I will do my duty," Stiger said firmly.

The paladin gave a nod.

"But know this," Stiger said. "At the same time, I wish to return to Sarai."

Father Thomas did not speak at first, and his gaze flicked away for a heartbeat. "I shall pray for that, my son."

They fell back into an uneasy silence, studying their grand surroundings.

When Stiger said nothing further, Father Thomas rubbed his hands together, once again working to gain warmth. "I think I will go get my gloves."

The paladin took a step away and then stopped.

"We will speak again on this later. If you wish."

Stiger nodded and watched as the paladin made his way over to his horse and began opening a saddlebag in search of his gloves.

A low whine drew Stiger's attention down toward his feet. Dog was sitting next to him, almost touching his left sandal. The dog was looking toward the citadel and appeared somewhat distressed, emitting another whine that was part whimper.

"I don't like being down here either," Stiger said and reached down a hand to rub the top of Dog's head. "But this is where we need to be."

Chapter Eleven

There was solid double rap on the door, followed by a deep growl close at hand. Stiger opened his eyes. The light from under the door was just enough to see the ceiling and the walls of the tiny room.

"Dog, quiet," Stiger snapped and the growling ceased.

There was another knock.

"Excuse me, sir?"

"Yes, what is it?"

"Centurion Pixus is waking the men, sir," a voice said from the other side of the door. "He told me you would want to know, sir."

"Thank you," Stiger said.

Out in the hall, he could hear the voices as Pixus and his optio went from door to door, rousting the men. The legionary moved off, his footsteps trailing away.

Stiger's legs ached abominably. Yesterday's march, the first in a good long while, had been hard, but he had persevered. He stretched and sat up, rubbing his eyes. Out in the hall someone walked hurriedly by, eliciting another low growl from Dog.

"I said stop it," Stiger snapped, looking over at the large shadow that was the animal. Dog grew quiet again. "Good boy."

Stiger shifted. The ache in his calves and thighs was quite painful. He groaned softly.

"You're getting old," Stiger said to himself, reaching for the lamp. He took up the flint and steel and lit an oil-soaked taper with practiced ease, then touched the flame to the wick of the small clay lamp. The wick caught almost instantly and the light grew.

Simple, plain, and austere, the room he had been given was small, much like one would find in a monastery. Despite that, it was rather warm, comfortable, and, more importantly, clean. There was no bed. Dwarves, from what Stiger had observed, did not seem to believe in them. An old, thick rug with a red and brown pattern stretched from wall to wall, making the floor a significant improvement over the cold stone below.

Two cushions stuffed with goose down and a blanket had been left for sleeping. The blanket was wool and moderately coarse, but a welcome addition that Stiger had elected to use over his own. The interior walls had been plastered over to keep the heat in, and a small hole little larger than his thumb emitted heated air without a hint of smoke. The hot air hissed softly as it blew. A rounded piece of corkwood hung by a chain next to the hole. Stiger had not needed to plug it. The heat was enough to combat the pervasive chill of the underground and kept his room comfortable. Stiger had seen dwarven heating before, so it had not been a shock to him, but it had been to Pixus and his men.

Overall, Stiger had spent a pleasant enough night and felt rested, though sore. Dog was curled up in the corner. Head resting over a paw, his eyes were fixed upon Stiger, watching his every move.

"Sleep well, boy?" Stiger asked.

Dog just watched him, his deep, watery eyes unblinking.

"That's what I thought."

Legs aching with strain, Stiger pulled himself to his feet. He stretched, trying to put the pain from his mind and work out the stiffness. Stretching, though painful, often helped to loosen up the muscles. Stiger's earliest weapons instructors had taught him the importance of stretching. Sergeant Tiro had reinforced and ingrained it further.

"I am definitely getting old," he said to himself. Stiger found it took him longer to bounce back from serious exertion than it had just a few years before. He felt the hand of age upon his shoulder, a most unwelcome friend. On cold mornings, the joints in his knees ached. "And... you're getting too soft. Time to toughen up."

He decided that only more marching would be the cure to his ailments. That and further exercise. Once his legs warmed up, the pain would lessen some.

Stiger relieved himself in the bucket that had been provided by the keepers of the hostel, a team of elderly dwarves who upon arrival had fallen all over themselves greeting their thane and his guests. Stiger had gotten the impression that such a visit was very rare.

He put his sandals on, lacing them up and tying them off so that the fit was both comfortable and firm. His armor was next. Predictably, it had rubbed him raw and would again today as the march continued. He knew in a few days' time he would barely notice, but until then, wearing the armor would be supremely uncomfortable.

Stiger patiently laced up his armor, cinching it tight, before tying off each strap. He checked to make sure the straps were tight and secure. He took a moment, shrugging his shoulders around until the armor fit just right.

Willfully putting the discomfort from his mind, he slipped on his sword and then clipped his cloak in place.

Satisfied that all was in order, he folded the blanket he had been given and placed it in the corner, then smoothed out the rug as best he could.

The previous evening, Stiger had performed a full toilet, which had included a shave. Not without a little satisfaction, he felt his jaw and found it still mostly smooth, with only the hints of budding stubble. He always felt like a new man after shaving.

Stiger collected his few possessions, returning them to the saddlebags. He was careful not to disturb the food Sarai had packed, nor the precooked rations Pixus had provided him with. He checked about to make sure he had missed nothing. Picking up his pack and saddlebags, Stiger opened the door and then blew out the lamp. Lastly, he grabbed his helmet.

"Atten-SHUN," a legionary called loudly out when Stiger stepped out of his room. The other legionaries in the hallway snapped to attention and put their backs to the wall.

"Carry on," Stiger said, looking first one way and then the next. Oil lamps set in mirrored recesses lit the spacious hallway in a muted, yellowed light. The stone walls had been plastered over. Theo had explained that the dwarves preferred plaster to not only help insulate their buildings, but also to muffle sound. The plaster was clearly showing its age, with exposed stone visible in numerous places.

"Dog," Stiger called. "Come."

Dog poked his head out into the hallway, almost tentatively at first, and then followed after. Stiger turned in the direction of the common room, the men making space for him and Dog, who trailed along behind. There were no dwarves about. They had been quartered in a different part of the hostel. As he made his way down the hallway toward the stairs, Dog received a friendly pat from more than one man as he padded by.

A goodly number of the men already had their armor on. Pixus had seen to it that his century had visited the washing rooms the night before, meaning all they had to do other than gather their kit was suit up.

The hostel had aqueduct-fed water, and as a result, the legion's fetish for cleanliness had been satisfied. Pixus's men were presentable, and from what Stiger could see their kits were well-maintained. Always one for setting the example, Stiger had personally cleaned and polished his armor before going to sleep.

The air in the underground was not only cold, but surprisingly humid. Stiger could only imagine how the rust would grow on metal if not looked after on a regular basis. Rust was the enemy of every legionary.

Stiger had been surprised at the sheer size of the Stonehammer Hostel. He had expected something small. In fact, it wasn't even a building at all, but a complex that had been carved into the bedrock of the mountain. From what he had been told by Theo, there were more than five hundred rooms on ten different floors. In its heyday, the hostel had been regularly packed with visiting travelers and traders.

Stiger worked his way down the stairs, descending three flights to the level that housed the common room. The stairs continued down farther, bending out of sight. Whether they traveled to another floor with additional guest rooms or a basement, Stiger did not know.

Following several legionaries, Stiger moved through a series of hallways, past innumerable doors, until he came at last to the common room. If the Stonehammer had been a military establishment, the common room would have been a mess hall. It was crammed with stout, long tables and benches that showed their age, well-worn and battered by years of use.

Large multi-wick lamps mounted to the walls with mirrored recesses provided much of the light. Thick candles on the tables augmented the effort. The strong smell of tallow mixed with fresh bread hung heavily on the air.

Stiger found the room packed with both legionaries and dwarves. Brogan's escort only wore their tunics and had not donned their armor. It was understandable. Legionary armor was far less bulky than the dwarven kind, which attempted to protect nearly everything and was quite cumbersome.

A good number of the dwarves were civilians, mostly men. There were a number of females in the mix, along with a handful of older children, clearly distinguishable by their lack of beards.

Colored tapestries hung down the walls, adding color and helping to muffle sound. Despite that, the common room was crowded, noisy, and surprisingly welcoming. With all the bodies, the room was warm. Stiger liked it.

Sabinus saw him and worked his way over.

"Did you sleep well, sir?"

"I did," Stiger said, his stomach rumbling at the smell of fresh bread. "You?"

"Not so well, sir," Sabinus said.

"That's a shame," Stiger said. "I've always been able to sleep at will, something I picked up long ago while on campaign. Sleep whenever you can get it."

"Agreed," Sabinus said and then frowned. "Usually that's not a problem… it's just being underground makes me a tad uncomfortable, if you know what I mean?" Sabinus turned and pointed. "They've set a table with food along the back wall, sir."

Stiger looked. Legionaries and dwarves had lined up, waiting their turn.

"They don't have coffee, do they?" Stiger didn't smell any. Sarai had only been able to afford a weak black tea. After years of service, he had missed coffee as a morning staple served by the legion's cooks. Stiger had forgotten how much he had looked forward to his morning coffee.

"I'm afraid not, sir," Sabinus said. "Sadly, they don't even have tea."

"Did Pixus bring any, perchance?"

"No, sir," Sabinus said. "As you know, we're traveling light, with the mules only carrying bare essentials. The men are carrying just seven days of precooked rations, nothing more."

"A small tragedy, then," Stiger said. "Where are you sitting?"

"Over there, sir," Sabinus said. "Pixus has already fed himself and is rousting the last of his men. He will be joining us soon enough." Sabinus shifted his feet. "Ah … I hope you don't mind, sir. I've invited the optio and standard-bearer to share breakfast with us."

"Good thinking," Stiger said. "I look forward to meeting them."

"I've already served myself," Sabinus said. "If you wish, I can take your things over to the table."

"Thank you." Stiger handed his pack, bags, and helmet to Sabinus. "I will be over shortly."

"Yes, sir."

Dog abruptly left Stiger as Sabinus moved away toward his table. Stiger watched as the animal rapidly worked his way toward the kitchen door, where an older dwarf wearing an apron stood silently watching the common room with a distinctly unhappy expression. The dwarf was idly playing with his beard. Stiger recognized him from the previous evening when they had arrived. He had made a point of feeding Dog.

The dwarf's expression cracked as Dog approached with its tail wagging enthusiastically. He had clearly made a friend in Dog, whose head came up to the dwarf's upper chest. Dog licked vigorously at his face, which elicited a hearty laugh.

The dwarf patted the top of the dog's head, and then scratched at his neck with both hands. Dog soaked up the attention, craning his neck this way and that for more scratching. His hind leg began to work, as if he were scratching himself. The dwarf turned and held open the kitchen door. He and Dog ducked inside, the door closing behind them.

"I hope he's got something good for you," Stiger whispered and made his way over to the table with the food. The dwarves and legionaries stepped respectfully aside for him.

The table contained several large wicker baskets filled bread rolls and cheese wheels. The cheese had been sliced neatly into smaller wedges. Sarai had been right; the dwarven cheese was riddled with holes. It was curious stuff, and Stiger was looking forward to trying it. He liked a good cheese. There were also pitchers of beer and water, along with a stack of wooden mugs.

Stiger grabbed a battered wooden plate and threw two rolls on it and a small wedge of cheese. He then poured himself some water and made his way over to the table where Sabinus was with Pixus's optio and standard-bearer. The three men stood respectfully. Stiger waved them back down as he set his plate and mug on the table.

"Sir, I would like to introduce you to Optio Mectillius and Signifier Lerga," Sabinus said.

As legate, Stiger should have known all of his officers by sight. He wished belatedly he had thought to ask Sabinus their names.

"I know their names," Stiger said. "I've seen them both on parade more than enough." Stiger gave a nod, hoping his bluff worked. It was almost an embarrassment that Sabinus had to feed him their names. Stiger consoled himself in the knowledge that he was only playing at being their legate. He took a seat opposite Sabinus.

"Yes, sir," Mectillius said, with no hint of disbelief. "Good to have you back with us, sir."

Stiger gave another nod and took a healthy bite of his bread roll. The optio was an older man, who absently reached up to scratch at one of the pock scars that tracked their way across his cheeks. Mectillius had a hard look about him. From what Stiger had learned about Pixus, the optio was likely very competent. Pixus seemed the sort not to tolerate incompetence or laziness in the men he commanded.

Chewing his bread, Stiger found it to be fresh and good, but not as fine as Sarai's. He washed it down with a drink of water and then took another healthy bite.

"What the dwarves have been able to accomplish is truly incredible, sir," Mectillius said. "Don't you think?"

"Yes," Stiger agreed, "it is. They seem to dream large."

"I thought Mal'Zeel couldn't be outdone," Mectillius said. "The public buildings, temples, and the palace of course, after all this..." He shook his head in dismay.

"Granted, what they've done is impressive, but I don't think I could ever live underground," Sabinus said, finishing up his roll with a swallow and chasing it down with some water. "It's just too cold and dark."

"I couldn't either, sir," Mectillius said to Sabinus. "I need the sky over my head, the sun and moon. I'd even take the open sky on a frigid winter night over this... though the heated air in the rooms was nice. Wish we had that back at our garrison."

"Optio, I will be sure to add that to the list of requested improvements," Stiger said, with some amusement. "Just as soon as we can figure out how they did it."

"Should I note that, sir?" Mectillius asked, and pulled out a pad and charcoal pencil.

"Good one," Stiger said.

Mectillius returned the pad and pencil to his cloak pocket. The optio took a deep breath, glancing around.

"I also wouldn't want to fight underground." Mectillius looked over at a table full of dwarves. "Without that bunch to show us the way, it would be easy to get turned around and lost."

"It is rather mazelike," Sabinus said in agreement.

"What you've seen so far is nothing," Stiger said. "The city under this mountain, Garand Thoss, is a site to behold. Talk about a rabbit warren. As their cities go, the dwarves tell me it is on the small side."

"I'd love to see that, sir," Lerga said, speaking up for the first time. Stiger eyed the man for a moment. To be promoted to his current position, he would have had to be a respected man who had distinguished himself. In essence, he was an optio in training and a junior officer.

"Well," Stiger said, "perhaps one day you shall."

Pixus entered the common room, following after several legionaries, much like a sheepdog herding its charges. Sabinus called out to the other centurion, waving a hand. Pixus spotted them and made his way over, weaving between tables and around people.

"Good morning, sir," Pixus said.

"Morning," Stiger said back to the centurion as he took a seat. Stiger glanced around. He had not yet seen the thane. "I understand you've been up for a while. You wouldn't know where the thane is? I haven't seen Brogan yet."

"I was told he is dining in his quarters," Pixus said.

"And the paladin?"

"Father Thomas is still in his room," Pixus said. "He is saying his prayers, sir. I did ask him if he wouldn't mind conducting a short service this morning. The men should find it comforting. I figure we can have it right before we march."

Stiger gave a nod. He saw no problem with a service. Being in the profession they were in, the average legionary tended to be somewhat religious, if not devoutly so. Many went out of their way to honor the gods whenever the opportunity presented. It did not do to ignore and offend the gods, especially when Fortuna could step in at a moment's notice and cock things up.

"Jorthan came to find me before I woke the century," Pixus reported. "He said we would be departing shortly after breakfast, sir."

"I can't wait to see the sky again," Sabinus said, slapping a hand on the table.

"Aye," Pixus said in earnest agreement. "It's not right for us to be here."

Stiger eyed them a moment as he took another drink. He stole a quick glance about at the legionaries scattered in small groups around the common room. Pixus's men had purposely sat away from the officers. There was nothing wrong with that, and it was quite normal. No one wanted to attract the attention of an officer. But those nearest looked ill at ease, if Stiger was any judge. He could well sympathize with them. He did not wish to be here either.

"I agree, sir," Mectillius said. "It's not natural, us being this far beneath the surface. Some of the men are feeling claustrophobic. All of the sounds down here too, the echoing and such, is not right and gets on the nerves."

Stiger returned his attention to the table and took a bite of his bread. He considered the officers before him as he slowly chewed. He did not like the tone, or the direction the conversation was taking. If there was to be any chance at setting future events right, Stiger was stuck on this path he was going down and needed their help. More importantly, he desired very much to succeed so that he could eventually return to Sarai.

His eyes flicked from Sabinus to Pixus and then back again. If the officers felt this way, then so did the men, and probably more so. The last thing Stiger needed was a failure of morale in a desperate moment. This sentiment, he decided, needed to be addressed. Not only did he feel an example had to be made, but a purpose and expectation laid out for them as well. They needed to accept being here as their duty and it had to start now, before the attitude worsened and became entrenched.

"Right or wrong," Stiger said. His voice was firm, but not so loud that it carried beyond their table. He pointed a finger down into the table and tapped it. "This is where we need to be. If duty requires us to spend more time here, in this tomb under a mountain ... well, then so we shall. Is that understood?"

"Yes, sir," Pixus said and everyone at the table sat up straighter, including Sabinus. "You're right, of course. It was not my intention, nor my optio's, to imply otherwise."

Stiger took a slow drink from his mug as he eyed Pixus and the others. He placed the mug down on the table. "This mission, this summit that the dwarves have cooked up with the orcs, is important. Should it fail, the orc tribes will flow out of the mountains with their blood up. They will wash against our lines like the tide during a storm, rising higher and higher with each surge." Stiger paused. The real

Delvaris had not told the legion of their purpose for coming down south to Vrell. Stiger decided he would share with them what he thought their purpose was, what he needed it to be. And he intended to make it painfully clear just what was at stake. "Has anyone here ever seen an orc?"

They all shook their heads in the negative.

"The average orc warrior stands over six feet tall, and is powerfully strong," Stiger said. "In a fight, they are a determined enemy."

"Have you ever faced an orc, sir?" Mectillius asked.

"Yes, he has," Sabinus said, speaking quickly before Stiger could respond. All eyes at the table turned on the senior centurion, including Stiger's. "The legate was with a party of dwarves just a few days ago. They were ambushed in the forest by a party of orcs."

"You were, sir?" Pixus asked, with some surprise. "I didn't hear about that."

"Yes, I was," Stiger confirmed, his gaze flicking to Sabinus. He was grateful for the centurion's timely intervention steering him out of dangerous waters. "But know this. No matter how fearsome they look, or how strong and determined they can be, orcs can be killed. I can attest to that, as I've personally done it. Like any other creature the gods made, they die just the same when you stick 'em with a few inches of steel."

Stiger fell silent and took another sip from his mug.

"Sir," Mectillius said. "It's that serious, isn't it?"

"Yes." Stiger made a point of meeting everyone's gaze at the table. "And now it is time to tell you why the Thirteenth is in Vrell."

Pixus, Mectillius, and Lerga eagerly leaned forward. Sabinus shot Stiger a cautioning look and gave a slight shake of his head. Stiger ignored him.

"The empire has a long-standing treaty with the dwarves," Stiger continued, "the Compact. There is something under this mountain that is of incredible importance to the empire and to the dwarves. I can't tell you what it is, not yet, at least. The orcs want it. We're not going to let them have it." Stiger poked his finger down into the table again. "That is why we are here."

Pixus leaned back and shared a glance with his optio and then one with Sabinus.

"It is why we marched all the way down here, brother," Sabinus said to Pixus, "and left the rest of the army to deal with the Tervay."

"Then I guess, sir..." Pixus said, turning his gaze back to Stiger. There was a flinty look to his eyes. "... this is where we belong then, underground with the dwarves, until you say otherwise."

"That's right." Stiger approved of the centurion's change in attitude. Hopefully it would become infectious and the men would buy in, too. Stiger swept his gaze around the table. "No matter how uncomfortable it is for us being here, for the good of the empire we must make do."

"I take it, sir," Pixus said and blew out a breath, "you don't think the summit will be a success?"

"I have my doubts," Stiger admitted and hesitated as he gathered his thoughts. "Though it is noble of the dwarves to think that they might be able to reach an accommodation, achieve something noteworthy, and avoid unnecessary bloodshed, I believe that there is a strong chance the talks will ultimately fail. One way or another, it will likely come to a fight. That said, I still see the need to try so I will assist in such efforts, especially if it means we can save lives by avoiding the fight I foresee as coming."

"While we are here," Sabinus said, "Tribune Arvus is preparing the legion for that fight."

"So," Stiger said, drawing everyone's attention back to him, "once we get to where the summit is being held, you all must keep your eyes open and stand ready for the unexpected. I don't want to be caught with only one sandal on."

"Do you expect the orcs to betray us, sir?" Mectillius asked.

"I understand that such a betrayal is unlikely," Stiger said, and considered telling them about the minion. He decided against it. Worrying about orcs was enough for them. "The orc king apparently has some form of honor. However, I don't want to trust my life or yours on that. Do you?"

No one said anything for several heartbeats.

"Sir," Pixus said. The centurion took a deep breath. "I would like to tell the men what you've told us. Do I have your permission?"

Stiger thought about it and then shook his head. "I shall tell them myself, after Father Thomas's service and before we march."

"I appreciate that, sir," Pixus said, looking somewhat relieved. "Coming from you, the men will take it all the more seriously. Have no fear, sir. Once we get to the talks, my men will keep their eyes open. Next to Sabinus's cohort, these are the best men in the legion." He shot a glance over at Sabinus, and a slight smirk traced its way onto his face. "Perhaps even better than his best century, now that I think on it."

Mectillius and Lerga broke out in broad grins, looking over at the senior centurion. Even Stiger almost grinned at Pixus's cheek in poking a senior officer. He suspected the two men had been friends for years.

"Only in your dreams, my friend," Sabinus said, pointing a finger at Pixus. "Your boys can't hold a candle to mine. That is for certain."

"Care to make a wager on that?" Mectillius said gamely. "Ever since our last pay, I've got a few coins that have been burning a hole through my purse, sir. What say we put some of your coin against mine?"

The mood at the table lightened, and Stiger found himself grinning at the exchange between the officers. It seemed that no matter the time period, there was always a healthy competition between units.

Sabinus chuckled, leaning back on the bench. "I don't need to wager my hard-earned money against yours, Optio. I know my boys are better. That's all that matters to me."

"Is that so?" Pixus said. "Seems like more of an excuse to not prove it than anything else."

"An excuse?" Sabinus said and his eyes narrowed. "All right, then. When we return to camp we can hold a contest to show who's the best."

"What do you have in mind?" Pixus asked, suddenly very interested, a sly look in his eyes. "What type of contest? It had best not be writing, as most of my boys don't know their letters."

Before Sabinus could reply, a shout rang out in dwarven. Almost as one, Brogan's warriors stood. They began carrying their plates and mugs over to a table near the kitchen door, where they stacked them. In a stream, the dwarves moved off toward their wing of the hostel, likely to don their armor and gather their kit. Stiger was pleased that Fifth Century would be ready before Brogan's escort. It would also allow time to address the men.

"Well," Stiger said, standing. So badly did his legs ache, it took effort to keep from groaning. "I believe it's time for us to go as well." Stiger paused and looked at both Sabinus and Pixus for a long moment. Here was the perfect excuse to give Fifth Century something to think about and look forward to. Perhaps it might even partly take their minds off being underground. "Gentlemen, I do believe we will revisit this conversation. Pixus, you may wish to consider sharing this upcoming contest with your men." Stiger paused and looked between the two officers, a grin tugging at the corners of his mouth. "I have no doubt that together we can come up with a suitable challenge and settle this important question once and for all. Don't you agree?"

"Aye, sir," Pixus said, grinning broadly at Sabinus. "Such an opportunity to show up First Cohort is just what my boys need to take their minds off of being under the mountain… that and your coming talk, sir. It should give them a little motivation."

"Good," Stiger said, pleased.

Sabinus looked none too happy, likely about the challenge, but he nodded as well. The honor of First Cohort was now at stake.

"Centurion Pixus," Stiger said. "Would you be kind enough to have your men fall in, out on the road? I will speak with them after Father Thomas's service."

"Yes sir," Pixus said. "And thank you, sir, for telling us what's what and why we came."

Stiger gave a nod as he stuffed his last roll and uneaten cheese wedge into one of his cloak pockets. He finished the water in one swallow and turned away, carrying his plate and mug to the table, where he stacked them with the others. Stiger visited the food table and grabbed a second bread roll, taking a bite.

"Plates and mugs go over there," Pixus hollered, pointing. "Stuff what you've got left in your mouth and fall in outside. Anyone keeping me waiting will be on a charge. I promise you, punishment detail will not be a joyful experience."

Chapter Twelve

"Yes, sir!" the men shouted as one.

Stiger was just wrapping up his talk to the men. He gave a satisfied nod, the massed shout echoing off the walls of the tunnel. Listening to the echoes as they retreated into the distance, Stiger wondered how far the sound would carry.

Fifth Century was assembled around him in a half oval. Pixus had gathered his men just to the side of the entrance to the Stonehammer. Its wooden double doors were painted a bright red. Above the door, an exquisite hammer had been carved into the stone. Wielding the hammer was a stone dwarf in the motion of striking at a wall, clearly at work digging a tunnel.

The hostel was located at what looked like a key junction of four tunnels, three of which were smaller than the one they had taken to get here. The space was large, with stables opposite the Stonehammer's entrance. Five heavy-duty wagons were parked, one next to the other, just off to the side of the red double doors. Large tarps covered the contents of their beds. Stable hands were leading a team of oxen out of the stables toward the wagons.

An open skylight in the direct center of the junction, some seventy feet above, provided the tunnel's only illumination. It told him how deep in the earth they were, but not where. Stiger found it more than a little odd to not know where exactly he was. It was a new experience for him.

Water cascaded down from the skylight in a waterfall, meaning it was raining. The dwarves had thought of this eventuality, and a large drain with a rusted iron grate was located directly under the skylight.

Stiger brought his attention back to the men. All eyes were upon him. They had seemingly accepted what he had just told them about their mission and what was at stake. Despite their apparent enthusiasm, he knew they would be concerned. Any sane person would. He just hoped their sense of duty and discipline would see them through whatever was to come.

"When we reach Garand Kos, I expect you to treat the orcs with respect. That said, I want you to keep your eyes open. I am not expecting trouble, but best be prepared should it find us. Understand me?"

"Yes, sir," they shouted again as one.

"Anyone wanting to bring us trouble will receive it back in kind," Stiger told them. "That happens, we show them our shield wall and give them some good steel."

The men gave another hearty cheer, the sounds of it echoing off the walls of the stone chamber.

Stiger waited for the cheer to die down. "Centurion Pixus, kindly form your century for march."

"Aye, sir." Pixus turned to his men and pointed using his vine cane. "Fifth Century, you heard the legate, fall in."

The men broke up, quickly moving to where they had left their shields and yokes. Stiger watched them, with Sabinus at his side. The centurion held the reins of both Stiger's horse and his own, which the stable hands had groomed, fed, and saddled.

"Well said, sir. They were hanging on your every word." Sabinus handed the reins over to Stiger.

"It has been my experience…" Stiger said, rubbing Misty's forehead in an affectionate manner. He had always liked horses. "…if you clearly lay out the mission and your expectations, the men perform better."

"Agreed."

Stiger looked over his horse. He had secured his saddlebags before his talk. He checked his saddle, making sure it was cinched tightly, giving it a good pull. The saddle did not budge.

"I tell you," Stiger said, turning to watch the men as they started forming a double column for march, "though I feel compelled to go and give the talks a chance, I don't feel good about this. My experiences with the orcs have been…shall we say, negative at best."

"Yes, sir," Sabinus said. "I've never had dealings with orcs, so I will take your word on it."

"They worship a dark god," Stiger said.

"Castor," Sabinus said. "Father Thomas told me, sir."

"What good can come from consorting with such filth?" Stiger looked over at Sabinus, the senior-most centurion of the Thirteenth. "I ask you, how do you treat with creatures that worship such evil? Surely their hearts are just as black as their god?"

"I don't know, sir." Sabinus appeared troubled. He glanced over at Brogan's escort, which had formed for march. "The dwarves have had dealings with the orcs. They've managed to keep the peace. That may be something to think on."

Stiger considered the centurion's words. "You're saying that perhaps the orcs are not so bad?"

"I did not say that, sir. They may be perfectly awful." Sabinus paused to suck in a breath. "It may be a possibility they can be negotiated with, as the dwarves seem to think."

"Maybe," Stiger said. "I guess we shall see if they are correct."

"Very rousing speech," Theo said, coming up to Stiger. "I am deeply impressed. Who knew you could speak more than a half dozen words at a time, eh?"

Stiger chuckled. "Started drinking already?"

"No." The dwarf frowned. "I've not had a drop since I got up, just some water. Why do you ask?"

"You fairly reek of drink," Stiger said. "And to be completely honest, you look terrible."

Theo glanced down at himself. "All because I did not clean my armor? I think it looks all right." He brushed at a spot of dirt on his chest plate. "Maybe it needs a bit of a wipe down, but not much."

"I am not talking about that," Stiger said, though now that Theo had mentioned it, the dwarf's armor was in a sad state. It looked nothing like the thane's personal guard, who were well turned out and appeared quite sharp.

"Then what?" Theo looked exasperated.

"Your eyes are bloodshot," Stiger said, "your hair isn't combed, and there are several ties missing from your beard. You stink a bit, too, and not just from drink. You look like you woke up in the stable with the animals."

"Oh, that." Theo reached up and touched the parts of his beard that were unbraided. "It is possible I consumed a little too much. Besides, Brogan and I made a late night of it, telling stories, swapping tales and such. My cousin can be engaging when he desires."

Stiger shared a glance with Sabinus, who rolled his eyes.

"Are you serious?" Theo protested, looking between the two of them, aghast. "The thane's buying. Granted, Brogan holds his drink better than I, but I'd be foolish to pass up such an opportunity when it's free."

"Clearly you've never heard of the concept of moderation," Sabinus said, stifling a laugh. "Tell us the truth now, have you?"

"Where is the fun in that?" Theo said. "It's a good way to drown your miseries when you want to. Surely you legionaries drink?"

"Oh, we do," Sabinus said, "and on occasion very heavily and even to excess."

"Well then, what is the problem?" Theo asked, appearing to be thoroughly mystified.

"We typically don't overdo it before a long march," Sabinus said, "like you have."

"Or drink overly much while on one," Stiger said, piling on. "Such behavior makes the day only that much longer and more difficult."

"I am on detached duty," Theo said. "Captain Aleric made me nothing more than a glorified hand-holder to keep you out of trouble with Brogan. Which, I think, I am managing quite well, thank you."

"You are?" Stiger scoffed. "How?"

"By keeping my cousin entertained," Theo said. "I thought that would be obvious."

"Right," Stiger said, far from convinced.

A shout from farther down the tunnel saw the dwarven contingent begin the day's march, the front of the column moving before the tail like an accordion. The walls began to echo with the crunching of many footsteps. They turned to watch Brogan's escort move out.

Brogan and Jorthan rode at the front of the column, just ahead of the standard-bearer. Riding by the skylight-turned-waterfall, the light from above fell on the thane. He looked impressive in his armor and purple cloak. The color seemed to drain away from his cloak the farther Brogan rode from the light until it looked black. The dim light in the tunnels seemed to leach all color.

"Don't they just look superb?" Theo said in a flat tone.

"They do," Sabinus said. "The thane has a fine guard. That much is clear."

"All shiny and perfect." Theo's tone was laced with a deep disgust. "I thought Aleric's company was bad, second rate even. My captain likes to have us polish, too." Theo pointed at Brogan's escorts. "Not to their standards, but at least the stuffy bastard's main focus was on fighting. You can say much about my captain and his many flaws." Theo wagged a finger at Stiger and Sabinus. "One thing you can't claim is that Aleric has neglected his duty by failing to drill his dvergr to fight. Next to maintaining kit, he's all about drill, training, and hard, backbreaking work. Aleric's kind of fanatical about it, now that I think on it. It is one of the reasons I don't like him much, either."

Stiger looked over at Theo with more than a little concern. He turned his gaze back to the marching dwarves, wondering if what his friend said was true. Surely not.

"They can't fight?" Sabinus asked the question on Stiger's mind.

"Oh, I am sure they can fight," Theo said. "You can't get into the thane's personal guard unless you are a veteran who has seen some action."

"So," Sabinus said, seeming confused, "I don't understand, then?"

Theo gave a great sigh.

"The last time any of them lovely bastards saw action was at least twenty years ago." Theo's hand came to rest on the hilt of his sword as he regarded his fellow dwarves. "The most they've had to do is guard against unruly dinner guests and look smart on parade or for show at the thane's palace. They're damn fine at it, too."

Stiger ran his eyes over the thane's escort again, this time with fresh eyes. It was not what he wanted to hear. He had expected deadly competence, but now he was not so certain.

"And the thane knows this?" Sabinus asked.

"He hasn't seen any action since that time either, a minor uprising of the lesser races, goblins and such filth," Theo said. "No, Brogan is quite ignorant of his guard's shortcomings. You see, he has complete confidence in Captain Taithun, a combat-hardened veteran of advanced age. The sad truth of it is both are living on memories of who they were, not who they currently are. I fear the same goes for Taithun's company as a whole. They think they are better than anyone else because they polish their armor better."

"This is not a joke?" Stiger asked, hoping Theo was playing with him. "Tell me honestly now."

"Sadly, no. Look at that fine bastard." Theo gestured to Captain Taithun marching to the side of the column. "Looks beautiful as a peacock, strutting his stuff before the girls... only there are none of the fairer sex about, just his warriors. I think he shines his armor to perfection for self-satisfaction alone."

Taithun was large for a dwarf and wore the thane's colors with obvious pride. He walked with a slight limp and his beard seemed grayer than the others, almost wholly white. In the gloom of the tunnel the beard seemed to glow. Stiger read confidence in his manner as he marched with his men.

"He's a doddering old fool," Theo said, an underlying note of disgust creeping back into his voice. "He, like his thane, lives in the past. Taithun carries his legend on his sleeve, very prim and proper." Theo spared Stiger an unhappy look. "He does not like heavy drinking either."

"At least that's something," Sabinus said.

"Last night, Brogan asked me if I wanted to join Taithun's company." Theo stomped a boot on the ground. "Can you believe it? Me?"

"What did you tell him?" Sabinus asked, raising an eyebrow. "I hope it was a yes."

"I told him no," Theo said plainly. "I'm staying with Aleric."

"You'd pass up all that free drink?" Sabinus asked. "I find that hard to believe."

"Bah." Theo waved a hand. "I'd have to spend hours shining and polishing my kit! Then they'd have me stand around all pretty-like for hours on end."

"I can see the trade off and it doesn't sound all that bad for you," Sabinus said. "Drink for looking somewhat presentable and not being required to work all that hard. A cushy assignment like that and you passed it up?"

Theo turned his gaze upon Sabinus, his eyes narrowing.

"You really hate me, don't you?" Theo asked Sabinus.

"What?" Sabinus asked, shooting Stiger a look of question, clearly confused.

Theo ignored the look and jerked a thumb at Stiger. "If this brooding fool is half correct, the talks with the orcs are a waste of time, and in the end it will all come down to a big fight. Do you really think I'd rather be in Taithun's company? Trust my life to a crusty old beard who's not had a serious drilling or thought in his head in who knows how long? No thank you."

"All this time," Stiger said, unhappy thoughts on Brogan's escort as he turned to Theo, "I've thought you a complete slacker."

"You got that part right," Theo said with conviction, "but when it matters, no one will see me shirk from a good fight. No one!"

"I never expected you would," Stiger said and meant it. Theo had already shown his bravery during the fight at the pond.

"Oh, yeah, I almost forgot," Theo said, suddenly. "While breakfasting with Brogan, he asked if you would ride with him this morning."

"You didn't think to pass that along sooner?" Stiger demanded, alarmed to think he might have inadvertently offended the thane. Most of the dwarven column was already lost to view, having moved out and into the tunnel that was the Kelvin Road. "Perhaps it would have been best to tell me before the march began?"

"It kind of slipped my mind," Theo said, without any hint of embarrassment. His hand ran through his beard again. He yawned. "Well, I think I might take your advice and clean up a bit before setting out. If the thane asks for me, tell him I should be along sometime around noon."

"I will try to remember," Stiger said. "That is, if he asks."

"Great," Theo said enthusiastically and started off for the entrance to the Stonehammer. "I knew I could count on you."

Stiger shook his head, thoroughly irritated at Theo.

"I had best catch up with the thane." He looked over at Sabinus. "If you have need of me, you know where I am."

"Yes, sir," Sabinus said. "Sir, do you think Taithun's dwarves can fight?"

"I don't know." Stiger paused, a hand on Misty's saddle. "I don't like it. If it goes sideways at the summit, and Taithun's dwarves crumble, we may be on our own."

"I wish we had brought more men," Sabinus said.

"Wishing is one thing," Stiger said. "Making do with what you have is another."

Stiger pulled himself up and into the saddle. He glanced around at his surroundings and spotted Dog, sitting by the double-doored entrance to the Stonehammer and watching all of the activity. The old dwarf who had fed him stood by his side, idly scratching Dog's head.

Father Thomas, wearing a priestly robe, stepped out of the hostel, making sure to close the door behind him to keep the heat in. He spoke a word to the dwarf and started off for the stables, passing another team of oxen that was being led out. The stable hands had to wait for the last of the thane's escort to pass them by, along with the three supply wagons that had arrived sometime in the night. These rattled and clattered their way after the last of the dwarves.

"Forward march," Pixus called, pointing with his vine cane. The century stepped off after the dwarves.

"Dog, come," Stiger called as he nudged Misty forward into a trot and quickly passed the men by. With a bark, Dog bounded after him.

Stiger was thoroughly irritated at Theo. The last thing he needed was to insult the thane further, especially considering they had got on cordially since the tavern in Bridgetown. The thane had even asked Stiger to sit on his right side during the feast last evening, which Father Thomas had explained was an honor in dwarven culture.

The feast had been a pleasant enough affair, though the food was bland and lacking in taste. Most of what had been served consisted of roast meat and potatoes. The meat had been slightly overcooked for Stiger's tastes. The drink, on the other hand—of which there had been beer, wine, and spirits—was exceptional. Stiger had partaken of the wine and enjoyed it very much.

Still, all things considered, Stiger was grateful to Theo for the warning he had passed along. He now knew the thane's escort was of questionable quality. If it came to trouble, Stiger could only be sure of Fifth Century. At least he hoped he could. He had not seen them drill or fight, either. However, he had confidence in Pixus as a leader, and the men appeared steady enough.

Stiger gave Pixus a nod as he rode by.

"Make sure you speak with Sabinus about the thane's escort," Stiger told him.

"I will, sir."

"We will speak on it later," Stiger said and then he was past.

He turned Misty into the side tunnel, now their main route to Garand Kos. Having caught up to the tail end of the dwarven column, Stiger saw that the road ahead was lit with lanterns hung from the ceiling every hundred yards. The lanterns provided just enough light to make the way visible. However, it was fairly dark between lanterns, giving the road an ominous look.

As he continued past the escort, which stretched at least two hundred yards from front to tail, Stiger idly wondered who was responsible for the lighting of the lanterns and the refilling of oil. It was surely a serious undertaking.

The dwarves and humans had been issued several dozen lanterns of their own, along with flasks of oil, to help supplement the light when needed. As Stiger came upon the first ceiling lantern, he was astounded to see it was magic, a ball of light unnaturally suspended within a glass case. He'd seen such devices before, but the tunnel seemed to go on and on, disappearing into the gloom of distance. The expense to light it must've been incredible, for true magical items were rare wonders and therefore, in Stiger's experience, priceless.

As Stiger rode along, steadily overtaking the dwarven column, he noticed the left wall of the tunnel was wet, glistening in the magical light. The wet patch lasted for twenty yards. Water ran onto the stones, which had sagged a little, allowing a puddle to form. Misty splashed through it, the dwarves on his right marching in and out of the puddle without a concern. The temperature was very cold, causing breath to steam slightly. The dwarves, like the legionaries of Fifth Century, wore sandals instead of boots. Stiger could only imagine how frigid the water was.

The Kelvin Road's tunnel was smaller than the one that they had taken to the Stonehammer, and yet it was at least twenty-five feet from wall to wall, more than enough for two wagons to pass one another. The walls curved outward from the ground. The ceiling of the tunnel was rounded, with stone support arches spaced every ten feet. There were numerous places where either the ceiling or wall had been patched in repair, ranging from small fixes to work that had clearly involved entire sections of wall or ceiling.

The road itself was smooth stone paving. The roadway was shaped in such a manner that it was sloped, with the center being slightly raised and higher than the edges, though there were places it had begun to sag. The stones had been placed with precision so that they appeared almost seamless under the dim light.

The engineering feat of constructing such a tunnel—or really, as the dwarves called it, a road—was remarkable. Stiger had no idea how long it would've taken to make this underground way, but figured it must have been centuries.

The dwarves looked at him curiously as he made his way past. Stiger's eyes stole over them, noting their neat, snappy appearance and their age. All were older. With Theo's warning fresh to mind, he could not help but feel deeply concerned. It was something he knew he could not bring up with Brogan. To do so would surely insult the thane.

He increased Misty's pace, quickly trotting up to the front of the column, where he found the thane riding with Jorthan. The thane turned in his saddle and raised an eyebrow at him curiously.

"Good morning, Thane," Stiger greeted, nodding his head respectfully.

"And to you as well, Legate," Brogan replied as Stiger slowed his horse to ride alongside him.

"Thank you for inviting me to ride with you," Stiger said.

"I thought it might be good for us to share the miles and," the thane said and looked over, the reins of his pony held lightly in his right hand, "get to know one another better."

"I very much appreciate that opportunity." Stiger turned his gaze to the thane's advisor. "Jorthan, a good morning to you as well."

"Thank you, Legate," Jorthan said. "Your salutations are most welcome. We have an open road before us and it is a fine day for a ride."

"How far does this tunnel go?" Stiger asked.

"The Kelvin Road," Brogan replied, "travels for thirty-five miles. There are several other smaller roads that branch off this one, before it terminates at a place called Garand Toll. We will be taking one of the branch roads to Garand Kos, say around twenty miles from this spot."

"Thirty-five miles?" Stiger asked. "And the road is this size the entire way?"

"Yes," the thane said, rather proudly. "Kelvin is a main artery. For many centuries prior to the gradual emptying of Garand Thoss, it was a key trade route to the south. One could almost say Garand Thoss became wealthy off this road."

"A remarkable achievement, for sure," Stiger said. "Are there many more like it? Main arteries, as you call them?"

"Yes," the thane said, "and even grander than this one. Sadly, what with my people leaving this region for better lands deeper into the mountains, these days the Kelvin is a road infrequently used. It does not see the regular maintenance it so deserves." The thane pointed at a rockfall to the side, where a number of the ceiling tiles had fallen. Someone had pushed the debris off and out of the way. "I see the day approaching when this fine road shall deteriorate to the point where it is either impassable or unsafe to use. Such is the way with change."

As if to underscore Brogan's point, Stiger's horse splashed through another puddle, this one smaller than the last. Several ice-cold drops of water splashed down upon him from above. He glanced up and thought he heard the sound of running water over the loud echoes of boots and the clopping of horses on stone.

"Is that water I hear?" Stiger asked, looking over at the thane. "It almost sounds as if we are riding under a river."

"You do hear water," Brogan answered. He pointed towards the ground as they continued to ride. "The water is not above us, but below. There is an extensive runoff system beneath this road. It is what keeps the Kelvin mostly dry and this tunnel from flooding with groundwater."

"Runoff system?" Stiger said, glancing around. "Like a sewer or an aqueduct?"

"Very much so," Jorthan said, joining the conversation. "If you look there, just ahead, you will see drains along the floor, next to each support."

Sure enough, he saw a metal grate, next to the support column that ran up along the wall. Under the dim lighting, he had missed it. He now understood why the road was raised in the center, as it was guiding any water that entered the tunnel down to the drains.

"When the road was first constructed," the thane said, as the grade of the road began to slope gradually downward, "the tunnel that was originally dug was far larger than what you now see, at least another twenty feet beneath us. The drainway was constructed first and then the road was placed above it. Our engineers are quite good at these sorts of things."

"You would be surprised," Jorthan said, "at how much water accumulates in the runoff system. In more populated areas, not only do we use the runoff as a source for our drinking water, but also to power mills, grind flour, and saw wood, amongst other industrial activities."

"There was once a sawmill at the end of the Kelvin Road," Brogan said, "where the runoff system dumps into a river. By the time it reaches the mill, the force of the water is very powerful. At its prime, it was quite the operation. Had we more time, I would gladly offer to show it to you after we finish with the summit."

Stiger turned slightly, shifting in his saddle and studying the thane for a prolonged moment before he replied.

"So, you also have doubts about the talks bearing fruit?"

"I do," the thane admitted after a slight hesitation. "By the gods, I do."

They fell into silence for a time, simply riding along and keeping their own thoughts. The grade became sharper for a short while as the road took them deeper. Then it flattened out again.

"I have met with King Therik," Brogan said, finally breaking the silence. "For an orc, I found him to be surprisingly intelligent and thoughtful."

"Truly?" Despite himself, Stiger was curious. "Have you met with many orcs?"

"A few," Brogan said. "They are not as long-lived as my people. Most were weak chieftains that had united a handful of the tribes nearest our lands. Orcs despise my people and yours. They think themselves a superior race. And yet, these chieftains desired to remain strong in the face of their own tribal neighbors. This was more important to them than their disdain and hatred of us. They were more interested in trading and keeping the peace than wasting their warriors against ours."

"Therik is different?"

"Very. He is a strong leader and the first to unite all of the tribes, at least the ones we know about," Brogan said. "According to our informers, amongst his people, all bend the knee to Therik. Even their priesthood fears him. For the most part he, too, desires to avoid hostilities and has kept his people out of the valley. The exception being trade missions, of course. Over the years, he and I have communicated regularly by messenger and met face to face a handful of times. I have had no cause to ever question his word, nor his intentions." Brogan looked over at Stiger. "The worst issue we've had in recent years is the ambush on your person. I intend to speak with him about that, even though he likely can do little, given what's happening to his people."

"The problem we have," Jorthan said, "are the religious zealots motivated by their priesthood. With the arrival of Castor's minion, they have gained much support from

Therik's people in recent weeks. The orcs are growing restless."

"That is a real problem for us," Stiger said.

"It is Therik's problem as well," Brogan said, "and why he has requested these talks. His control over his kingdom is rapidly being eroded and undermined. I fear he will not be able to contain the zealots much longer. The proof of the breakdown in his authority is the attack on you at the pond and a few other minor raids on our caravans passing close to orc lands."

"That is why you have called for your army to be assembled," Stiger said to Brogan.

"Yes, I have called on the clans," Brogan said, "for, as you correctly surmised, I do not expect the talks to bear much fruit. The best we might be able to hope for is keeping a number of the tribes from the fight."

"How many warriors do you have in the valley?" Stiger hoped the number was substantial.

"Around two thousand in the region and close at hand," Brogan answered. "That includes the garrisons of Grata'Kor and Grata'Jalor. We will be able to call up another thousand militia. All told, when the army comes up, the clans should provide us around fifty thousand warriors."

"I see," Stiger said. It was a ray of sunshine. "When will your army arrive?"

"The majority of it within the next three to four weeks," Jorthan answered, "the rest in twelve to twenty, mostly support at that point."

If the orcs struck before the dwarves arrived, it meant the legion would be the only real force capable of contesting them. Stiger suspected they would be badly outnumbered.

"What of the gnomes?" Stiger asked. "Do those numbers include them as well?"

Both Brogan and Jorthan looked over at him, something approaching shock in their eyes.

"Why ever would you want that?" Jorthan asked. "Gnomes are nothing but trouble. I would never recommend calling upon them for aid."

"We may need them," Stiger said simply. "Should the orcs move before your army arrives, we will need all the help we can get."

"The gnomes have not fought at our side since we came to this world from Tannis," Brogan said. "To ask them to do so may be unwise and give them ideas we don't want them having."

They passed through a road junction. The crossroad was unlit. Stiger had seen a dozen just like it. The dwarven underground was a virtual rabbit warren of tunnels. Only a handful of other roads had been lit. There were no signs or markers that Stiger could see, and yet the dwarves seemed to easily know what tunnel went where. Occasionally they passed parties of dwarven traders or gnome work parties, but for the most part the road was empty.

"Can you speed up the arrival of your army?" Stiger asked.

"I have already sent messengers to my chieftains. You must understand, the clans are spread out, deep in the mountain range," Brogan explained. "Many of my warriors have a long way to come, and before they set out, supplies have to be gathered to support them."

"What about the gnomes?" Stiger asked. "Do they have as far to come?"

"Your fascination with those despicable creatures concerns me," Brogan said.

"There is a gnomish city within a week's travel of Garand Thoss," Jorthan said, sharing a look with his thane. "Should the need arise and the situation becomes desperate, I am sure we can call upon their aid. Though the thane and I will need to speak on how best to do this, if and when the time comes."

"As Jorthan said, gnomes are most troublesome." Brogan frowned. "I hesitate to ask them to join us, for they are difficult to control. All it would take is an incident between my warriors and the gnomes… then you might see our combined army fighting itself, doing the work of our enemies."

"I see," Stiger said. "Let's hope the orcs give us the time we need then, for the bulk of your army to arrive."

"More importantly," Jorthan said, "no matter how pessimistic we are on the summit, let us all pray that something comes out of these talks. For, should they fail, it is clear many on all sides will die. And our numbers are far fewer than you humans. We cannot afford such losses as your armies regularly face."

The thane cleared his throat loudly and shot Jorthan a look that Stiger could not fully see. The thane's advisor sat up in his saddle.

"That is an interesting animal you have there," the thane said, clearly desiring to change the subject. He gestured at Dog, who was walking alongside Stiger's horse. "Quite the pet."

"He's not really a pet," Stiger said, unsure how to best characterize his relationship with Dog. The animal had adopted him, instead of the other way around.

"I heard what he did during the ambush," Brogan said. "Though he does not have the look, you are correct. He is not pet, but an attack dog, a warrior in his own right."

Stiger glanced down to his side, where dog walked between the thane's horse and his own, head held low, sniffing the ground as he went, tail occasionally giving a vigorous wag. "He certainly doesn't have the appearance of one."

Brogan stroked his braided beard a few times as he looked on Dog, and then his gaze shifted back to Stiger.

"There was a time," the thane said, "when my people, like yours, had paladins, servants of the gods we honor. I don't remember many of those tales, but I seem to recall one I heard my grandfather tell of a paladin on another world. He was dvergr and had a great big dog as a companion." The thane turned to his advisor. "Jorthan, you were there for those stories. Do you remember the one I am talking about?"

"The paladin's name was Survil," Jorthan said. "I used to love those old stories your granddaddy told us. When I grew older, I sat down with him and took the time write them down."

"You did?" The thane looked over at his advisor with ill-concealed surprise. "Truly?"

"I thought it was important to preserve such tales," Jorthan said with a slight shrug of his shoulders. "They are part of history, our people's heritage, and should not be forgotten."

"Jorthan is something of a historian." The thane turned back to Stiger. "He and our scholars spend a great deal of time sharing and recording all that has occurred. It is tedious, but I suppose necessary."

"Those unfortunates who fail to learn from past mistakes," Jorthan said, a hard look stealing over him, "are destined to repeat them."

Stiger glanced over at the thane's advisor. As a lover of history himself, he wholeheartedly agreed with the sentiment, though at the same time he felt chilled by it. Destiny was forcing him to walk in Delvaris's footsteps. With each movement forward, Stiger felt as if he were being dragged toward Delvaris's fate.

"Yes, yes," the thane said impatiently to Jorthan. "You are always telling me such wise things. I do on occasion listen. Now, speak about Survil's dog, will you?"

"That tale your grandfather told concerning Survil and his dog seems to be true." Jorthan looked over at his thane.

"He told true tales?"

"I have confirmed it through other sources, historical texts to be exact, that specifically mention this paladin and other characters in his tales as real people who lived and breathed as you and I."

"And here I thought he made many of them up," Brogan said, with an amused expression. "So the dog was real, too?"

"Survil indeed had a large, shaggy dog, like this one here." Jorthan fell silent as his gaze traveled down to Dog. "I find the descriptions of Survil's companion eerily similar to yours. It is believed that the animal was a gift from his god, but we cannot be certain of that. The dog was supposedly not only incredibly intelligent, but had a warrior's heart."

Stiger glanced down at Dog. He had never seen another like him. "And you think he is a gift from a god, then?"

"I wouldn't know how to tell for certain," Jorthan said. "However, since events around you are central to the gods' interests, I find I cannot easily dismiss the possibility."

"He is the largest dog I have ever seen," the thane added. "If half of what I've heard is true from the ambush, you are a lucky man indeed, for you have been gods blessed."

Stiger was tired of people telling him that. He felt himself scowl and glanced down at Dog again, who seemed oblivious to their conversation. Could it be?

Stiger looked back up and over at Jorthan, as he maneuvered Misty around a hole in the road. "What God did this paladin serve?"

"We call him the Wolf God," Jorthan said. "I believe, in your religion, he is second only to the High Father."

"You're speaking of Mars?" Stiger asked. "The god of war?"

"I am," Jorthan said. "Mars is but one name of many he carries, and he is god of much more than just war."

Stiger did not bother to reply, but his gaze fell back down on Dog, who was padding along with them. He showed no indication that he either understood or was anything other than just an animal. The thane caught his look, drawing Stiger's attention.

"Only time will tell of his true nature," Brogan said.

"Or," Stiger said, a thought occurring to him, "I could always ask Father Thomas for his thoughts."

"The paladin would know more of these things," Jorthan said. "That much is for certain."

Stiger's gaze returned once again to Dog. Without even having to ask Father Thomas, he felt he already knew the answer.

Chapter Thirteen

Stiger moved back into the stall, carrying several handfuls of hay from one of the supply wagons. He tossed these onto the ground before Misty. The dwarves had also provided him a bag of oats and an empty bucket. Every horse he had known loved oats, and Misty was no exception. She had her nose deep in the bucket and was happily munching away.

Stiger glanced around the stable that had been carved into the bedrock of the mountain. It consisted of one long central shaft with stalls for animals on each side, perhaps as many as thirty. The stone stall walls came up to chest height, at least for a man, oddly allowing the animals to see one another and interact.

Four oil lanterns provided the only light in the cavernous space, and it wasn't much. The stables hadn't been used in many years.

Prior to bringing the animals inside, a team of dwarves had worked hurriedly to clean out the space. A layer of undisturbed dust and debris had covered everything. Cobwebs had stretched from ceiling to floor and every which way. Some of the webs were disturbingly thick, almost the width of his finger. Stiger dreaded encountering the spider that had spun it. He did not much care for spiders.

The dwarves had found tools, including brooms and shovels, in a closet. They swept the dust and debris out and onto the road.

Those same dwarves were now busy caring for the ponies. Two legionaries were tending to the four mules from the century's train.

Sabinus was in the next stall over from Stiger, grooming his horse. Stiger was pleased to see the centurion doing his own work, instead of assigning it to the men of Pixus's century. He was alternating between humming and whistling a tune Stiger had never heard. Sabinus wasn't very good at either. Stiger had almost joked with him that it was a good thing he had entered the legions. Almost. He did not know Sabinus well enough yet to take such liberties. So, he remained silent and listened as he worked on caring for Misty. He had to admit, besides the centurion's poor skill at music, it was a catchy tune.

"I picked up Azerax in Iveria, about a year ago," Sabinus said, without looking up. "She cost me a pretty little fortune. She comes from working stock, but she was worth every talon. I couldn't ask for a more loyal and steadfast horse."

Sabinus patted Azerax's neck affectionately and then resumed his brushing.

Stiger glanced over, hearing the pride in the centurion's voice. It made him think on his own trusty mount, Nomad. Stiger felt a pang of sadness of his loss.

"You have a fine horse, centurion," Stiger said.

"Thank you, sir."

"A good horse is like that," Stiger said. "Care for her and she pays you back tenfold."

"True," Sabinus said. "I don't often get to ride. I usually march with the men, or when in camp I'm stuck attending to the legion's business. Sadly, on most days she's picketed with the rest of the mounts and rather neglected."

"So," Stiger said, "when you can, it is an absolute joy to ride."

"Exactly, sir." Sabinus looked up. "Dead on right."

"I know the feeling only too well myself," Stiger said as he looked over the job he had done at brushing Misty down. He was quite satisfied with his work. He had made sure to completely remove the dust and dirt from her coat.

Stiger had been amazed at how much dust there was under the mountain. Combined with the chill, more than a few of the men now had a sporadic cough. The dwarves seemed wholly unaffected. Perhaps, Stiger considered, they were just accustomed to it, as this was their natural environment.

He ran a hand along Misty's back. Her coat was smooth. Before they set off tomorrow, he would groom her once again. Between now and then, anything that found its way onto her coat and under the saddle could easily rub her raw, resulting in sores and infection.

Stiger checked the mane and tail. He had made sure to brush both. He set about carefully picking the hooves clean, making certain they were free of any rocks and debris that might have become stuck during the day's ride. Thankfully there had been no rocks, but he found some trapped grit. Cleaning the hooves kept a horse from bruising herself as she walked.

Stiger looked over the saddle, which he had hung on the stall wall. Using a small towel he had wetted earlier, he wiped it down, removing the dust. The saddle was a sad piece of work, past its prime. At the same time, it was well broken in and made for a comfortable ride. Once clean, he hung the saddle on a pair of hooks set into the wall just outside the stall. Sabinus's saddle, having also been cleaned, hung just below it.

Lastly, he turned to the water trough. There was running water in the stables. It flowed in and out through a basin on the back wall, at the far end. The water came from the runoff system Brogan had mentioned. After having cleaned the trough free of filth, he drew several buckets and filled it. Still focused on the oats, Misty ignored the water. Stiger knew that would not last. The ride this day had been a long one.

"Well, I'm done here," Stiger said to Sabinus, returning the brushes to his saddlebags, along with the small wool towel he had used for the cleaning of the saddle. He had squeezed out as much water as he could. The towel was still damp and would need to be set out tonight to fully dry.

"I will be along shortly, sir," Sabinus said, making long brushstrokes along his horse's back, all in the same direction. "I'm almost done here."

Throwing the saddlebags over a shoulder and tucking his blanket under an arm, Stiger made his way out of the stables and crossed the Kelvin road to where they would be camping. One of the magical lanterns hung overhead, bathing this stretch of tunnel in a pale-yellow light that never flickered.

There was a small pull-off just beyond the stables, where the supply wagons had been parked. The teams of ponies had been unhitched and moved to the stables to enjoy a night of well-earned rest. Theo's pony was the only animal not in the stables. Its reins were tied to a wheel of one of the wagons. Stiger shook his head and continued on.

A simple green door granted access to the campsite. The paint on the wooden frame was faded and in places peeling. The door, standing open, had seen better days. It was warped slightly at the bottom and did not completely close. A team of dwarves was busily unloading burlap bags and casks from the wagons. They were carrying them from the pull-off across the road into the campsite, which was essentially a smaller, untended version of the hostel. Stiger stepped aside to permit one of the dwarves, carrying a large and seemingly heavy sack, to pass him by.

Two legionaries stood to either side of the entrance. Against Taithun's protests that they weren't needed, Pixus had stationed his men there anyway. The legion had certain rules that had been proven out over a very long time, and by posting sentries, the centurion was adhering to them. Stiger approved of the centurion's diligence, even down here in the dwarven realm, where it was safe. As Stiger made his way past them and inside, both sentries snapped to attention and saluted.

Brogan called this camping. It wasn't. The small complex consisted of three floors. Each floor contained one large, open communal room, with four fireplaces spaced evenly about. There were a few smaller rooms on the main floor, including what looked like a kitchen with an oven. The dwarves had taken the first floor. Brogan had assigned the legionaries the second for the night.

Stiger found Theo, standing just inside the entrance, watching the tumult. The dwarf was absently playing with his beard as he watched his fellows preparing the large room on the main floor, making it habitable. Dust was heavy on the air, a result of some vigorous sweeping. It was clear the entire complex had not been used in many years.

The fireplaces, each along a wall, had been lit, spreading their light and heat. So far underground, Stiger could not at first understand where they had gotten the firewood. Then he saw dwarves and legionaries emerging from a side room, well-seasoned wood in their arms. Clearly someone long ago had set in a supply.

"A quaint setting," Theo said, glancing over at him. "Don't you think?"

Theo looked more presentable than when Stiger had seen him last, earlier that morning at the Stonehammer. His beard was neatly braided, but his armor was once again dusty, likely from the ride. He had clearly just arrived, several hours after when he had suggested he would catch up with them.

"Better than sleeping on the road, I suppose," Stiger said.

"You can say that again," Theo said and then nodded toward the thane, who was seated before a fire and enjoying a drink with Jorthan. "It appears I got here just in time. The work's almost done."

"It seems that way," Stiger said. "I'm surprised you're not already in there, drinking up the thane's supply of spirits."

Theo turned slightly to better see Stiger's face.

"You disapprove?" the dwarf asked after a moment.

"You may wish to moderate your consumption a tad," Stiger suggested.

"How can you say that? I am the soul of moderation," Theo said, with a glance back toward the thane.

"Of course, you are," Stiger said.

"You and Sabinus set me on that path," Theo said with a straight face and then gave a heavy sigh. "Look here. We're out in the middle of nowhere. It wouldn't be bad if we were traveling through settled lands. Unfortunately for us, Garand Kos lies in lands we long since moved away from, which means no resupply of drink until we return to Old City. The thane's supply of spirits won't last beyond the summit, as there is bound to be a feast of some kind."

"Better to get what you can now?" Stiger asked. "Is that it?"

Theo shot him an exaggerated look that reeked of hurt, as if Stiger had injured the dwarf's sense of pride.

"Right." Stiger started up the stairs. "I will see you tomorrow, Theo."

"That's Theogdin."

"It's Theo," Stiger called back over his shoulder.

Stiger climbed the stairs to the first landing, where the communal washroom was located. It had running water and, more importantly, a latrine. There were seats where one sat to defecate or urinate into a channel several feet below. Fast-moving water flowed through the bottom of the latrine, carrying waste away. It meant the sound of running water was a constant. The room also smelled of mold. Back home Stiger had seen similar facilities in imperial cities, so it was not a surprise the dwarves had something similar.

He stepped inside. An oil lantern had been set on a small ledge above the door. It provided the room with some weak light. Along one wall, water flowed out of two holes at chest level and cascaded down into a large basin with several drain holes at the bottom.

He put his hands into one of the streams. The water was ice cold. He washed his hands, then splashed some on his face and cleaned away whatever dust had accumulated from the ride. The bitingly cold water felt good, but at the same time, it made his hands ache.

Stiger stretched out his back. It had been a good long while since he had spent so much time in the saddle. His butt and legs ached. He was looking forward to lying down, pulling his blanket up, and catching some shuteye. But, there was still work to be done. His armor was very dusty and required a cleaning. He was also sorely in need of a thorough washing himself. He would attend to both later, before turning in for the night.

He left the washroom and made his way up the stairs to the second floor, arriving to a frenzy of activity similar to what he had witnessed below. He glanced around at the large room the dwarves had assigned them. It was essentially box-shaped, fifty yards wide and another fifty long. A series of plain, rounded stone columns as thick as a man supported the ceiling.

Three of the four fireplaces in the room had been started. There was nothing ornate about them. They were purely functional, as was the room. Two legionaries were working on the fourth fireplace.

A team of legionaries was busy carrying enough firewood up their stairs to keep the fires fed throughout the night. They were stacking the excess wood next to each fireplace. Pixus and Mectillius stood in the center of the chaos, orchestrating the men. They appeared to have things well in hand.

Already the large room was warming. The firelight gave it a cheery glow and fought back against the pervasive gloom of the underground. Pixus had found three old brooms and put a detail to work sweeping up the thick coating of dust that lay on everything. They were almost finished. Dust hung heavy in the air, a natural result of their efforts. It tickled at Stiger's nose and he found himself resisting a sneeze.

Stiger made his way over to the nearest fire, where several sturdy-looking stools sat. Dropping his saddlebags and rolled-up blanket on the floor, he cleaned off one of the ancient-looking wooden stools with a hand and eased himself down onto it. Clearly made for a dwarf's width, the stool creaked but took his weight. He leaned forward and held out his hands to catch some of the warmth from the growing fire. They still ached from the cold water and air. Relishing the feeling of the heat, he stifled a yawn.

"Might I join you?"

Stiger looked up to find Father Thomas. The paladin grabbed a stool, brushed off the dust, pulled it over to Stiger, and sat down.

"Suit yourself," Stiger said.

"I have, haven't I." Father Thomas gave a good-natured laugh. "One of the perks of my station. I answer only to the High Father."

"I can see the advantage to that." Stiger glanced over at Father Thomas and shot him a wry look. "However, I have found he is a demanding master."

"A loving one, too," Father Thomas said. "Never forget that. You have been blessed with an extraordinary life."

Stiger eyed Father Thomas. With Sarai, he had gotten a glimpse of what an ordinary life was like, and it did not seem that bad. It had been quite good with her. He turned back to the fire, wishing he had some tobacco, for a pipe sounded good right about now too.

"A long ride today," Father Thomas said, kicking his feet out onto another stool. "Ah ... now that feels good, very good."

"We've come a long way," Stiger said. "You could say all the way back to the past."

Running a hand through his red hair, Father Thomas laughed, drawing a curious look or two from the nearest legionaries.

"That we have," the paladin said, "and I'm afraid we've got farther to go."

Dog came over, seating himself between Stiger and the paladin. He laid his shaggy head on Stiger's thigh and looked up imploringly. Reaching over, Stiger absently started scratching the dog's neck. Almost immediately, Dog's back right leg began to work, as if he were scratching himself.

Stiger noted Father Thomas's gaze swing toward the animal. The paladin regarded Dog for several heartbeats, an inscrutable expression crossing his face. Father Thomas chewed on his lip as he turned back to the growing fire.

"He's special," Stiger said to the paladin, "isn't he?"

"Special does not begin to adequately describe what he is," Father Thomas said, without turning away from the fire. "My connection to the High Father allowed me to recognize his nature the moment I saw him."

Stiger paused in his scratching. "And you said nothing?"

"Sometimes it is better to learn for yourself that something is special," Father Thomas said, "rather than being told from the start. It allows one to better appreciate it."

Stiger was not pleased with the answer, but he understood the paladin's meaning.

"Tell me about him," Stiger said

"What do you want to know?" Father Thomas's tone grew weary.

"Why would Mars send me a dog?"

"How do you know it was Mars?" Father Thomas looked over, suddenly very interested.

"I don't know that for sure," Stiger admitted, with a glance down at the dog. "Jorthan told me of a dwarven paladin named Survil. Apparently, Mars sent Survil a dog for a companion."

"I've read of his life and, yes, he did have a dog that was very special, somewhat like yours." Father Thomas nodded and then closed his eyes. The paladin breathed in slowly and let it out. He continued to do so, almost as if he had fallen asleep. Stiger waited, understanding that Father Thomas was searching his feelings. It was something he had seen before with Father Thomas and another paladin, Father Griggs.

When the paladin finally opened his eyes, he took a deeper breath and then let it out. "It is possible Mars dispatched him… though, I cannot be certain which god lent you such a powerful servant." Father Thomas jabbed a thumb at Dog. "He is a naverum, one of the guardians of Olimbus. They serve all of the gods and at the same time none."

"Olimbus is where the gods reside," Stiger said, leaning back on his stool and glancing down at Dog. "He guards the heavens?"

"That is what we are taught in the holy texts." Father Thomas nodded, his gaze returning to the dog. "I am aware of only a few accounts concerning the naverum. Survil's is one. Naverum typically only appear during times of crisis and great need. It is thought that, in a way, naverum are their own agents, working independently for some common purpose. What that purpose is," Father Thomas held out his hands palms up, "I unfortunately can't tell you, as I don't know. Having a naverum as a companion is considered a great blessing. However, throughout all of the accounts, one thing always remains constant. Whenever naverum appear, they have always attached themselves to a paladin."

Stiger looked up and their eyes met. "I am no paladin."

"No," Father Thomas agreed. "You are not. You are something else."

"And what is that?"

"I shouldn't have to remind you of something you already know," Father's Thomas said, an amused smile playing across his face.

Stiger looked at the paladin and raised an eyebrow, encouraging him to continue.

"You are the High Father's champion, of course," Father Thomas said.

Stiger felt himself frown at the paladin, the scar on his cheek pulling the skin taught.

Dog gave a soft whine and nudged Stiger's hand. Stiger absently began scratching again. He studied the animal resting its head on his leg. He couldn't believe that such a sad-looking creature could be what Father Thomas said. He rubbed his jaw with his free hand, feeling the day's growth. No matter what he looked like, Dog was certainly special. Of that, he was sure. Somehow, he sensed it as such.

"I wonder..." Stiger said to himself, gaze shooting to Father Thomas. Very much like Father Griggs, Thomas consulted his feelings on a regular basis in the search for answers. Stiger recalled what Marcus had done in the Gate room, looking inward to sense outward. The dwarves had named him Rock Friend after that...

It was something Eli had attempted to teach, but Stiger had never fully succeeded at. Perhaps he, too, could seek answers? He had not tried since he had lived with the elves. He was becoming more attuned to things like Dog's nature and Rarokan's presence. Was it possible that he might now be able to succeed?

"If one listens close enough," Eli had once told him, "you may hear answers to hard questions."

Eli had been speaking about talking to the forest. Stiger's gaze traveled back to the paladin. He figured it was worth a try.

Closing his eyes, he focused on centering his being. He used the technique that Eli had taught him and quieted his mind. When he was in this calm state, he had been trained to listen to his surroundings—the forest, the wind, the animals—searching for anything out of the ordinary. It was a basic skill that all rangers learned and, according to Eli, led to the next level of understanding.

To his elven friend's chagrin, Stiger had never been able to achieve that next level of skill necessary in the elven mind to become a full-fledged ranger. It was supposedly how they became one with the forest and gained a better understanding of the nature of things. This time, however, he was going to attempt something slightly different from what his friend had tried in vain to teach him. Stiger wasn't even sure it would work.

Breathing steadily, he worked to calm his mind, to put all concerns from his thoughts. Stiger felt his aches and pains from the day's ride fade. Ignoring the noise around him, he reached deep within himself and continued.

Stiger lost track of time. The noise around him receded; the talking steadily faded. He cast his mind adrift in the void, like pushing off from shore in a boat.

He sensed something ... the familiar touch of Rarokan's mind. It was close at hand, the sword's presence and its attention partly focused on the conversation Stiger had been having with the paladin. The rest of Rarokan seemed shrouded in a deep fog, almost as if asleep. For a moment, it startled him that he could sense it so clearly. So much so, he almost lost the calm feeling keeping him centered. With some effort, he pushed past Rarokan and continued his search for the truth he sought, casting his mind farther outward. He had never before attempted something like this, but somehow it seemed like the right thing to do—to search one's feelings, something beyond a simple gut check.

At first, there was nothing ... then he felt more. It was almost akin to a burning light amongst the vast darkness of the void. Again, without fully understanding, the light in the darkness became Dog's presence, or perhaps it was the animal's soul he was truly feeling. He studied it.

The light seemed to become aware of him. A tentacle of incredible brightness reached out towards him. It connected with his own being. For a moment, he sensed a mind of staggering intellect, clearly beyond his comprehension. Stiger shuddered in fear.

The tentacle of brightness flashed like a lightning bolt striking a tree. There was a resounding crack. It was a clear warning.

STOP! he heard in his mind.

So powerful was it that Stiger jumped, almost falling off his stool. His eyes flew open in shock. His breathing came hard and fast, as if he had held his breath for an extended period of time. His forehead was wet. Stiger reached up and wiped at his brow. It was coated in sweat. In fact, his entire body was drenched. A terrible tiredness tugged at him.

Blinking, he looked down at Dog and found the animal gazing back up at him with those same brown, watery eyes. There was a powerful intelligence there, and Stiger knew without a doubt this creature was somehow divine in nature. There was simply no denying it. Dog was indeed special, and he was no servant of Stiger's.

"You sensed truth," Father Thomas said softly, with a sad undertone. "He is indeed naverum. I am certain you know that without a doubt now. I would in the future recommend against doing what you just did. It is dangerous, and your mind has not been trained to handle what you will encounter in the Void."

Speechless, Stiger just looked back at Father Thomas, unsure what to do or how to respond.

"One might say you are cursed with Rarokan," Father Thomas said, "but you have been equally blessed with a naverum. I almost wonder if each balances out the other?"

"Cursed and blessed." Stiger swallowed. "Is this my fate? Is this what a destiny is?"

"You have powerful weapons and allies at your side for whatever is coming. That much is certain."

Stiger reached down and touched the hilt of his sword. The familiar electric tingle ran through his hand and up his arm, into his being. It was comforting yet frightening, for the sword meant to dominate him. The room, lit only by firelight, appeared to brighten considerably, and the tiredness he felt moments before eased a bit. At the same time, he placed his other hand upon Dog's head.

An unhappy hiss sounded in his mind. It emanated from Rarokan. Dog gave a low, menacing growl. Stiger removed his hands from both. Dog ceased his growling and set his head back down on Stiger's thigh. The hissing died away as well, and a measure of the fatigue returned. The two clearly did not like each other.

Father Thomas looked over at Stiger and regarded him for several heartbeats. The paladin's gaze slid back to the dog.

"There's a very good chance he can understand everything you and I say," Father Thomas said. "Naverum are reputed to be incredibly intelligent beings."

Stiger looked down. Dog gazed back up at him, raising his eyebrows, almost as if in question.

"Can you understand me?" Stiger asked Dog.

Dog just stared back at him with that same unblinking gaze. It was clear there would be no answer. After a moment he nudged Stiger's hand, and when Stiger did not move, the animal nudged it yet again.

Stiger absently resumed the scratching.

I can hear you, Rarokan hissed in Stiger's mind, sounding somewhat amused. *And I can understand you as well.*

I know, Stiger said silently back at it, thoroughly unamused.

Good, the sword said. *Though I sleep deeply, know that I am always listening. You have but call to wake me, for I am ever with you. We are one.*

Stiger considered Rarokan's words for a moment. Perhaps Rarokan might provide some answers?

What god sent this naverum? Stiger asked. *Was it Mars?*

To that question, I have no answer, the sword said. Stiger sensed a hesitation, as if Rarokan was deciding to share additional information. There was, Stiger felt, the mental equivalent of a shrug and then the sword spoke. *I knew Survil, and Mars most definitely did not send his companion.*

Stiger continued to scratch Dog's neck. Father Thomas, completely unaware of this side conversation, returned his gaze to the fire.

I would recommend sending the naverum back. Rarokan sounded annoyed and somewhat disgruntled. *But alas, I have come to the conclusion he won't leave. He is here to stay, and we may as well accept it…*

We? Stiger asked.

Now I must rest, for this communication has taxed me greatly. Feed me soon, rebuild my strength, for it is flagging.

With that, Stiger felt the presence of the sword leave him once again, and with its departure came a vast relief. At the same time, he was troubled. Though he was supposedly the High Father's champion, Stiger was feeling thoroughly out of his depth, and with each passing day it was not getting any easier.

Stiger took a deep breath and turned his gaze to the fire. He did not want to be anyone's champion and certainly did not feel like one. He let the breath out, shoulders sagging a little with exhaustion.

"I will do what I've always done," Stiger said softly to himself as he continued scratching Dog. "I will soldier on."

Father Thomas looked over at him. "That, my son, is why you are the perfect champion for our god."

Chapter Fourteen

Brogan, hands on his hips, surveyed the hulking door before him. Rusted hinges, each the size of Stiger's fist, were attached to thick metal supports and bracings that ran down the seam of the backside of the stone door. A team of five dwarves waited expectantly just behind their thane.

"Open it," the thane ordered and stepped aside, moving over to stand by Jorthan.

Two worked to lift the heavy locking bar at the bottom of the door. They grunted with the effort. It wouldn't budge, as it had rusted together with the support. They stopped. One of the two gave it a good kick, and then again for good measure. The second kick seemed to work it free, as the bar rattled loose. They lifted it aside, setting the bar out of the way along the side of the passage.

All five dwarves pulled, struggling to open the door. Grunting with effort, they strained. At first, nothing happened. The massive door refused to be budged. It was made of solid stone, yet that was not what seemed to hold the door in place. The door seemed so ancient that any oil lubricating the hinges had long since dried out, the corrosion cementing the moving parts in place.

"Pull," one of the dwarves shouted to the others. "Come on, lads! All together now, pull!"

With a groan and a staggering screech, the ancient hinges gave a tad. Then the door began to open, first a sliver and then one painful half inch at a time. Dirt and dust cascaded down the seams as the opening became larger.

Light from the outside world flooded into the tunnel, as did a distinctly warm breeze. The bar of light was so bright that Stiger and the others were forced to shield their eyes.

The aroma of vegetation and moist, rich soil flowed inward, overcoming the musty smell of the underground. It reminded Stiger of what he had been missing these past few days—the outdoors. The smells triggered recollections of his time with Eli, traveling elven lands, moving through the forest, and learning the ways of the ranger. Stiger felt a pang for that long-ago phase of his life. He missed those simpler times, when everything had been neatly black and white.

"A sight for sore eyes, sir," Sabinus said to Stiger. "I can't tell you how much I've missed the sky."

"It is," Stiger agreed, glancing over at the centurion and then at the thane. Brogan was standing with Jorthan, speaking a few words. They were watching eagerly and with barely contained impatience. Father Thomas stood next to Sabinus. Dog, like a well-heeled animal, had sat down at Stiger's side.

The door seemed to screech madly, as if in horrible pain. The stone walls of the tunnel only served to magnify the sound to the point where it was almost excruciatingly loud.

The tunnel that had led to this exit to the surface was sort of like a switchback, snaking its way down to the road below. It was just large enough for one wagon. As the door continued to screech and scream its way open, Captain Taithun and the front of the column waited patiently just behind them.

Jorthan gave a nod to whatever the thane had said, and then Brogan stepped over to Stiger.

"We had to take this side tunnel," Brogan said, raising his voice to be heard over the screeching. "The main route into Garand Kos was intentionally collapsed long ago."

"On purpose?" Stiger glanced over at the thane.

"Yes," Brogan yelled. "When the decision was made to abandon the city, and the last of the population left, it was brought down. This door will let us out into the edge of the foothills, just on the outskirts of the city. It has been well-hidden and was built years after the evacuation." Brogan glanced around the tight confines of the tunnel, lit by lamplight and now growing sunlight from the outside. "These days, as you can see, we use it only rarely."

Stiger nodded, wondering why the dwarves felt the need for a hidden entrance. But more importantly, he desired to know why the main tunnel had been collapsed. Clearly, they feared someone gaining access to their system of underground roads and tunnels. The question was, who? He figured it was likely the orcs.

The screeching of hinges reached a crescendo, making further talk impossible. Covering his ears with the palms of his hands, he resolved to ask about it later when time permitted.

Stiger turned back to the door. It continued to open, one very painful inch at a time, the dwarves straining under the effort. When it was wide enough for a person to pass, Brogan half turned and gestured for Stiger to follow.

The thane stepped forth, with Stiger on his heels. It was the first time in three days Stiger had felt sunshine on his face. It was a wonderful feeling. The air was also much warmer.

Stiger looked upward. The sky was near a perfect blue, with puffy white clouds scudding slowly along several thousand feet above. He looked downward at his feet. The soil was damp, almost muddy, which meant it had recently rained. A few colored leaves graced the ground, a sure sign that fall was upon them and also that they were at a higher elevation than they had been in the Vrell Valley, for the leaves there had yet to begin to turn.

He squinted, allowing his eyes to fully adjust, and then carefully studied his surroundings. They had emerged onto the side of what looked to be a steep hill. Behind them was a sheer rock face. The door had been set into it. It was clear there had once been some sort of a road that had traveled by this spot, snaking its way farther up the hill and out of sight. A few feet from the tunnel entrance, the road had become completely overgrown with brush, except where the last of the uneven paving stones impeded growth. It almost appeared as if the ground were slowly swallowing the stones, one at a time.

"Garand Kos." Brogan gestured expansively with both arms outward and into the distance. "A truly sacred place. Here your people and mine made their original mark upon this world. First City to both our peoples."

"First City," Stiger breathed, head coming up. "Can it really be?"

The side of the hill upon which they stood was part of a ridgeline that rose around three hundred feet above a large, flat, tree-filled expanse that stretched out for as far as the eye could see. An unending sea of trees spread out below them. The canopy of leaves was spattered with fall colors.

About a mile distant, amongst the trees, lay the remains of what appeared to have once been a great city. Garand Kos was now thoroughly overrun by forest. A wide stone wall cut a line through the trees, encircling what Stiger took to be the city itself. In several places, sections of the wall had completely crumbled and collapsed. The battlements of the wall had been worn down and smoothed by weather and the ages. Inside the walls, the shells of hundreds of buildings could just be seen poking up above the trees. The tops of the walls or the columns that had supported roofing were all that was left. A few crumbling towers were still visible in the distance.

Stiger's eyes roved hungrily over the remains of the city. He figured from what he was seeing that it was large enough to have held nearly one hundred thousand people, perhaps even more. There was no telling how much the forest obscured of what had been outside the walls. For all he knew, there could have once been rolling farmland where now there were only trees.

"That," Sabinus said, coming up next to Stiger with Father Thomas at his side, "is something you really don't see every day."

"Indeed," Father Thomas said, excitement in his voice. "If this is First City, down there, somewhere, is the original temple on this world to the High Father. It was built on the orders of Amarra, High Priestess of the Faith."

"Amarra," Sabinus said, shocked. "The original Amarra? Truly?"

Father Thomas gave a nod.

"It's all down there, paladin," Brogan said. "And my people helped yours construct that temple. We did it together, honoring the god instrumental in helping us come to this world."

Stiger shook his head slightly, somewhat at a loss for words. He was looking upon a city almost as fabled as Rome, something he thought he would never see. It was all incredible.

"The City of Sout," Father Thomas said. "This great city has been lost for ages." Father Thomas's eyes shone with excitement. His hands shook slightly. "We are truly blessed this day. My order has been searching for this holy place for ages. We knew it was somewhere in the South, but not where." Father Thomas suddenly chuckled. "Truth be told, I still don't know where we are."

"Having been underground for three days," Sabinus said, "I'm all turned around too. Thane Brogan, you wouldn't care to enlighten us?"

"No," Brogan said simply, "I would not. This city is sacred. It should not be disturbed or visited without good cause."

"I guess if word got out, treasure hunters would eventually come," Stiger said.

"That could not be tolerated," Brogan said. "This city is now a tomb. Many of our people who came here from Tannis chose upon their deaths to return and be buried here. This door we just passed through is called the Grieving Gate."

"If the accounts of my order are correct," Father Thomas said with a look over at Brogan, "this, my children, after arriving on this world, was the city our two peoples claimed as their own. Down there, somewhere, Karus built a shrine. Within it, he set the standard of the Ninth, entombing it for all time."

"Karus," Sabinus said, "as in the first emperor? He was here?"

"Oh yes," Brogan said. "In a way, you could say the start of your empire began here, with the taking of this city."

"So, Karus did not build the city?" Stiger asked, looking over at Brogan. He wondered if the standard of the Ninth was still down there. It would be something to see, perhaps even to take back to the capital. He had a suspicion that to hunt for such a relic would be frowned upon by the dwarves and perhaps even the gods. The more he thought on it, the more he understood the Ninth's standard would remain here. It was a holy relic and deserved, like the bodies of the ancestors, to not be disturbed.

"No," Brogan said, "he did not. The humans that lived here were called the Kelsey. When my people and yours arrived, the Kelsey proved hostile. Together our peoples crushed them and took their cities and lands for our own." There was pride in Brogan's tone. "It was an exciting time. I wish I had been alive to witness it."

"What happened to this city?" Sabinus asked. "Why abandon such a place?"

"For a while," Jorthan said, moving nearer, "our peoples lived in harmony. However, yours became, shall we say, restless. There were tensions between our peoples. A few short years after the conquest of the Kelsey, Karus decided to leave for new lands. The elves had a hand in his decision to leave us. Sadly, this ultimately led to the sundering of the Compact, the shattering of the alliance between our two peoples."

"Karus went off to found the empire, then," Stiger surmised. Here was another reason for the dwarves to hold a grudge against the elves.

"He did," Jorthan said. "And in time my people, unaccustomed to living aboveground, also sought richer lands. Those few that were left behind could not long sustain the great works that made civilized life comfortable. With the passage of time, the roads, aqueducts, sewers, and baths all crumbled. Everything that civilization had delivered, within a few short years, fell into ruin."

"The few who still call these lands home," Brogan added, "are scattered and isolated, living in small primitive forest villages, thoroughly ignorant of their great past or even, for the most part, of each other."

"I had an elf tell me once that with time, all things change," Stiger said, feeling a keen sadness. "I would have very much liked to have seen this city in its prime, not as a mere shadow of its past glory, nothing more than an ancient and crumbling ruin."

Until recently, First City had been no more than myth. Stiger wondered if the same thing had happened to Rome. Was that city a ruin also? Was it a sad monument to a past age of grandeur and wonder?

"Does the temple still stand?" Father Thomas asked of Brogan and Jorthan.

"The remains of it should," Jorthan said. He studied the city for a long moment and then pointed. "I believe it is out that way, toward the center, near what is left of Karus's palace. See that crumbled spire there? That may be it. Our pioneers are expected to meet us here shortly. They should be able to give you more precise directions."

"That would be most welcome," Father Thomas said fervently. "I want to see it."

Stiger glanced upward again and breathed in deeply. It certainly felt good to be back out under an open sky. Judging from the sun, he figured it was perhaps an hour past noon. Turning his eyes back to the forest, his thoughts darkened. He could not help but wonder what threats were hidden out there amongst its vastness. He blew out a slow breath. Like a cloud blocking the sun, a bad feeling had suddenly overtaken him. An army could be concealed amongst not only the ruins of the city, but the forest itself. Should the orcs mean them ill, things could go very badly. Then again, Brogan could be right and the threat minimal, but Stiger had long since learned to trust his gut. And his gut told him to be on his guard.

Looking down upon the dead city, any eagerness he had felt passed over to a deep, lingering concern. Stiger now felt anything but the excitement of Father Thomas, or the pride of Brogan at past accomplishments. The feeling of unease became more acute. He shook his head slightly, attempting to dismiss the feeling. Perhaps he was just overthinking things. After all, he had only ever faced orcs in battle. Never had he dealt with them as civilized beings, which, from what he had seen, he seriously doubted that they were or could ever be. Maybe that was what he was worried about, seeing the orcs for more than just heathen barbarians.

Stiger turned and glanced back into the tunnel, as the screeching ceased. The door had been fully opened. Taithun, who had been speaking with one of his dwarves in the tunnel, stepped out, as did the first of the dwarves behind him. The captain's eyes narrowed with the bright light. He walked with a confident swagger up to his thane. Taithun looked over Garand Kos.

"It has been a long while since I set my eyes upon this place, My Thane," Taithun said in dwarven.

Brogan gave an absent nod, but said nothing. His eyes also ran over the city. Both seemed deeply moved.

"I am growing old," Taithun said, wiping at an eye. "It is good to have made this journey. It pleases me greatly to see this place one last time and does much to restore my spirit. I only wish I could live to see the restoration of the Compact as foretold by the Oracle."

Brogan looked over at his captain for a heartbeat. Stiger saw a tender fondness in the thane's eyes that had not been there a moment before.

"As do I. This place has special meaning for our people. I should require all of my chieftains to regularly visit," Brogan said. "They fight and squabble like children over insignificant toys. Perhaps it will remind them of how we came to this world and why we are here."

"My Thane." Jorthan cleared his throat and shot a warning glance over at Stiger. "Perhaps we should get settled in the city below."

The thane looked over at Jorthan and scowled. He looked behind them at the front of the column, his dwarves waiting patiently. "You are right. No sense in remaining here, even if our pioneers are late."

"We will need to clear this road for the wagons," Taithun said, glancing down the hill. "It is much overgrown. Either that, or we must carry our supplies down."

"We can leave a party to deal with the road," Brogan said. "Fifty of your dvergr should make quick work of it. I want to get down into the city well before Therik arrives."

"Yes, My Thane." Taithun bowed his head respectfully. "I assume you will be paying respects to your ancestors?"

"I mean to visit the tomb of my grandparents," Brogan said, "if that is what you mean."

"Very good, My Thane. I shall detail an honor guard for you," Taithun said. "Will you be going now or after your talks with the orc king?"

"Before, I think," Brogan said. "There may be little time after."

Stiger approved of the thane paying his respects to those who came before. Honoring one's ancestors was important. Stiger had been raised in such a manner and had regularly made devotional visits to the family's ancestor room. In this room important items were kept, including the wax death masks of his forebears, at least those who had served the empire with exceptional distinction. Growing up with it all, including the antique armor, swords, and shields... tokens of those long-dead souls had served as motivation to the young Stiger to serve as faithfully as those who had come before him. It had lit a fire in his own soul and distilled in him a need to serve the empire he loved.

Two dwarves emerged from the brush ahead, as if materializing from thin air. These were likely the pioneers Jorthan had mentioned. Unlike Taithun's warriors, the pioneers wore brown boots and soft leather armor over simple tunics. No clan colors were present in their dress. Stiger assumed this was to help them blend into the forest. Both were armed with swords. They fell to a knee before their thane and bowed their heads respectfully.

Brogan regarded them silently for a long moment.

"Rise and report."

"My Thane," one of the dwarves said in dwarven, "the city is empty, occupied only by wildlife. We could find no sign of orcs either inside the city or outside within a range of twenty miles. There is a human village, thirty miles to the east, but we think they do not visit here often."

"And Therik?"

"The orc king has not yet arrived."

"Have you located his party?"

"We have, My Thane," the dwarf said. "We are shadowing their approach. He should arrive sometime this afternoon. He travels with twenty warriors and retainers. We believe them to be ignorant of our presence."

"Excellent," Brogan said and clapped his hands together. He turned to Stiger and hesitated. "Legate Delvaris." Brogan said the name as if using it was somehow distasteful. "May I introduce Hogan, captain of my pioneers."

The pioneer turned, eyeing Stiger as if sizing him up. Hogan had a tough, hardened look about him, and unlike the other dwarves, his skin was tanned and weathered from exposure. He had the appearance of having been outdoors much of his life. His beard was tied and woven neatly into a single braid, and his brown hair had been bleached a sandy blondish color by the sun. Hogan stepped forward and offered a hand, which Stiger took. Hogan's grip was firm, but not crushing.

"It is an honor to meet you," Stiger said in dwarven.

Hogan's eyes widened slightly and then he smirked.

"The honor is mine," Hogan said, speaking in the old tongue, Lingua Romano. It was Stiger's turn to be surprised. Hogan gave a slight shrug. "I acquire languages, as some people accumulate friends."

"He has no friends. Make sure you don't take it personally, but he does not like anyone." The other pioneer, also speaking in the old tongue, stepped forward. He offered his hand. "I am Lieutenant Merog."

Stiger shook, finding the grip also firm, confident.

"He's right, I don't like anyone," Hogan admitted and shot a sour glance over at Taithun. "Not even my own kin."

Taithun scowled, but said nothing.

Merog shot a smirk at his captain. "He only tolerates me because I get him out of the hole he so often digs for himself."

"And because I forced him to take you on," Brogan said. "You caused too much trouble for your family to allow you to remain at home. Your father begged me to take you into my service and make a true dvergr out of you." Brogan gave an exaggerated sigh. "It must be a restless spirit that runs deep within your side of the family."

It was now the thane's turn to receive an unfriendly look from Hogan.

"It is, cousin," Merog conceded with a slight shrug of his shoulders. He nudged Hogan with his elbow. "I have the bug of wanderlust, don't I?"

Hogan said nothing, almost as if the last were not directed at him.

"I work each day on his social skills," Merog said with a grin directed at his captain. "It may not seem so, but he has shown remarkable improvement. I really think that's why the thane sent me to the pioneers."

Hogan went red in the face, but he still remained silent.

"If you say so." Brogan rolled his eyes.

"My senior centurion, Sabinus," Stiger said by way of introduction when Hogan and Merog's attention returned to him.

Hogan gave a nod, then offered his hand.

"And Father Thomas, paladin to the High Father."

Hogan and Merog turned their gazes on Father Thomas. They bowed in an exceedingly respectful manner.

"How excellent. We are now all acquainted," Brogan said, sounding suddenly impatient. "Captain Taithun, as Jorthan so rightly suggested a short while ago, it is time to move down and into the city."

"Yes, My Thane," Captain Taithun said and snapped out an order to those waiting just behind him. The dwarves immediately began marching out of the tunnel. Once they hit the overgrown road, they slowly began working their way down as best they could. The captain spun on his heel and walked back into the tunnel.

Stiger watched the dwarves, thinking. His gaze slid over to the pioneers and then the forest below. He gestured for Sabinus to step aside with him.

"I can't quite believe we are here, sir," Sabinus said. "I honestly never thought First City was real."

Stiger's gaze slipped back to Brogan and his pioneers. The thane, Jorthan, and Father Thomas were speaking with them. Hogan turned and motioned back into the city, using both of his hands to point something out. Stiger's gaze moved back to the city overrun by forest.

"It apparently is," Stiger said, returning his focus to Sabinus.

"Do you think we might be able to search for the Ninth's standard while here?" Sabinus said. "I'd love to see it."

"I don't think that would be such a good idea," Stiger said. "If Karus left it here, he meant for it to remain here, otherwise he would have taken it with him." Stiger paused. "We have to move beyond our reverence for this place."

"Sir?" Sabinus's brow furrowed. "I am afraid I do not understand."

"Do you see any open ground down there within the city walls?" Stiger asked him. "Or, for that matter, anywhere?"

Sabinus turned, scanning the city and then looking beyond it. "No, I do not. All I see are trees and ruins, sir."

The orcs had already proven that they could sneak by Captain Aleric's dwarves. Though Stiger suspected that Brogan's pioneers were skilled, he wasn't about to take a chance they had done a shoddy job of scouting out the area. The pioneers certainly weren't elven rangers, who could speak to the trees themselves. More importantly, Stiger wanted to impress this upon Sabinus. "There are trees everywhere. No matter what Captain Hogan says, anyone with a bit of skill could sneak in."

The centurion turned his gaze back onto the city. He held it there for several long heartbeats, eyes raking the ruins and trees before looking back. Stiger could now read the concern in the other's eyes. It was what he had wanted to elicit.

"When Fifth Century comes up, the men will be just as amazed and awed as we are," Stiger said. "We need to keep them focused, professional, and on the task at hand. They must remain diligent, for should the orcs mean us ill, any slacking could prove fatal."

"Yes, sir," Sabinus said, sobering. "I will do what I can and, knowing Pixus, he will stay on his boys to keep their eyes sharp."

"The men have brought entrenching tools, correct?" Stiger knew that they had. He'd seen several men with picks, axes, and shovels attached to their marching yokes. He wanted to get Sabinus thinking defensively.

"Yes, sir," Sabinus said. "It's part of their standard kit and something all centuries usually travel with."

"Well, then," Stiger said, "when we get down into the city, you and Pixus find a good defensible spot."

"A fortified marching encampment, then?" Sabinus asked.

"Exactly," Stiger said. "I don't know about you, but I do know I will feel better sleeping at night with a trench and wall between me and whatever else is out in that forest."

Sabinus fell silent, his eyes once again roving over the city.

"I quite agree with you, sir," Sabinus said. "It will be done."

"Excellent," Stiger said. "I am counting on you."

Hogan and Merog broke off from Brogan and started down the hill, making their way alongside the column of Brogan's escort. Father Thomas moved over to Stiger and Sabinus. There was a bounce in the paladin's step that had not been there in the tunnel.

"My son," Father Thomas said to Stiger, "would you care to go with me to the High Father's temple? After speaking with Hogan, I believe we've identified it below."

The paladin pointed with a hand at a large stone building around a mile and a half off. The roof had long ago collapsed; however, a number of thick white marble columns yet stood, poking up from amidst the trees. It was clear that the building had been very large but, like everything else in the city below, was now only a ruin, just a shadow of the past.

"As Brogan goes to honor his ancestors, I believe it will be good to pay our respects to our god," Father Thomas said. "Don't you agree?"

Stiger thought about it a moment. The temple to the High Father in Mal'Zeel was a true wonder. In his youth, it was a place Stiger had often visited with his mother. He had fond memories of those times, before things had turned sour, all the result of a poor choice by his father.

"I should like to see the High Father's temple," Stiger said and meant it. He glanced around and saw Dog sitting a few feet away, gaze focused intently down into the trees. Dog's tail started to wag. Stiger wondered if he had seen something worth chasing, perhaps a squirrel or something else. Or it could have been just the forest and all the smells that begged for exploration.

"Dog," Stiger called. "Come."

Dog immediately got up and walked over.

"Shall we go, then?" Father Thomas was clearly eager to be off.

"Excuse me, sir," Sabinus said. "After what we spoke on, I would feel more comfortable if you two had an escort. Once Pixus comes up, he can organize a detail."

"You are quite correct," Stiger said and then turned back to the paladin. "It won't kill us to wait a little longer."

"No," Father Thomas said, his gaze swinging longingly out toward the city. The dwarves continued to march by them. Fifth Century was still down below in the tunnels. "I suppose it won't."

Chapter Fifteen

"This, my son, pleases me greatly," Father Thomas said, wiping away tears with the hem of his robe. "Standing here is a dream come true."

Stiger and Father Thomas were standing in the middle of what clearly had once been a temple. Most of the walls had come down, thoroughly collapsed into mounds of rubble and ruin. A layer of dirt, thick with vegetation, topped most everything. Aside from small patches of exposed stone, the temple was almost completely covered by a carpet of greenish forest moss.

Stiger stepped up to what looked to have been a marble basin. He had seen such basins before. Instead of holy water, it was filled with dirt. Ivy had taken root, spilling out and down the sides of the basin and spreading outward in many directions. It had worked its way across the floor and started to climb several of the broken columns.

It wasn't just ivy that grew here. Plants, brush, and even whole trees had grown up inside the temple. Stiger glanced upward at the sky. There was nothing left of the roof, other than smashed clay tiles that poked up and out of the dirt on the floor. Stiger was careful where he placed his feet, lest he trip and turn an ankle.

The great pillars that ringed the building had collapsed as well. Most had fallen outward, with only two having come down inside the temple. All that remained were the stumps and the foundation of the temple itself.

As they had moved through the city, Stiger noticed in some places there was a complete lack of any stone blocks, walls, or piles of debris. It appeared as if, long ago, some enterprising individual had intentionally removed the marble blocks for repurposing elsewhere. Stiger had seen this happen before, so it did not overly surprise him. At some point in the past, nearby peoples had likely scavenged the city for fresh building materials. Why work to make new materials when you could just take what you needed?

The forest was doing its best to reclaim what people had once worked so hard to build. The temple, like the surrounding area, was so choked with growth that it had taken them some effort to make their way here. Climbing over walls and mounds of debris and forcing their way through thickets of brush, they had traversed a veritable obstacle course. By the time they had arrived, Stiger had found himself sweating profusely.

He glanced behind him at the file of men Pixus had assigned as an escort. They had had just as difficult a time, maybe more so, as their shields repeatedly caught in the low-lying brush. Stiger had allowed the men the opportunity to rest. They had gratefully set their shields down.

Dog sniffed, weaving his way in and out of the brush and bushes. Stiger turned. He had just lost sight of the paladin. He saw a rustle of brush and figured Father Thomas had pushed through the large bush.

"Oh my," Stiger heard Father Thomas exclaim. Curious, Stiger followed and found himself standing in an open space. There was a coating of dirt on the floor, and very little grew here besides isolated strands of grass.

He moved aside some of the dirt with a foot and found an aged and cracked marble flooring less than an inch down. The flooring was surprisingly intact. He reasoned the thick foundation of the temple had helped to keep it so.

"This must've been the exact center of the temple, the beating heart, if you will," Father Thomas said, gesturing around with both hands held outward. He stopped and pointed. "The priests would have conducted religious services here for the masses. If I had to make a guess, just ahead there would've been the High Father's altar, and behind that, *his* statue."

All that was left was a large brush-covered mound where the back wall of the temple looked to have collapsed, falling inward. Stiger found the ruins of the city somehow sad and the temple even more so. A student of history, he understood that cities rose and fell. And as Eli had so often reminded him, the world was constantly changing.

"What seems permanent," Stiger said to himself, channeling Eli, "is in reality not."

The empire, as it expanded, had conquered entire peoples, sometimes absorbed existing cities. Other times, depending upon the circumstances, destroying cities and enslaving entire populations. Stiger was sure that the people who had once lived here could never have imagined what it had become, a massive ruin, a decaying reminder of a past his own people had long since forgotten. He shook his head sadly.

On the other hand, Stiger found it fascinating that Karus the Great had once lived here. He had often wondered what Karus had been like. He was reputed to have been a great warrior and leader of men, a true soldier of Rome. Was Stiger, even now, walking in the great man's footsteps? In this very temple, perhaps? It was a captivating thought and one that sent a slight thrill through him. Stiger suspected that if what Father Thomas had told him about this being the very first temple was true, there was a good chance that he was indeed walking in Karus's footsteps, and even Amarra's.

"Were there something left over other than just ruin …" Father Thomas said, sounding a little disappointed. The paladin turned to Stiger. "… I would very much like to have seen the High Father's statue."

"I would've enjoyed seeing it as well," Stiger said, and in truth he would have.

"It was reputed to be a masterpiece beyond comparison," Father Thomas said, "made by Adava's own hand. The holy texts speak of it, you know, as do some of the histories of my order."

"My father once owned a small Adava," Stiger said, recalling the bust of Legate Dio.

"What happened to it?" Father Thomas asked.

"With our fall from grace, it was confiscated by the emperor," Stiger said with a shrug. "I imagine it is decorating some corner of the emperor's palace."

Father Thomas gave a nod, as if the answer had not been unexpected, and resumed his explorations of the temple.

"Your order makes a record of history?" Stiger said, a thought occurring to him. "You have your own historians, histories, then?"

"We do," Father Thomas admitted, sounding a tad grudging. When Stiger failed to respond and simply waited for more, the paladin gave a slight sigh. "We try to record as much as possible. However, what we do record is never shared or disseminated outside of the church."

"Why not?"

"Knowledge is power," Father Thomas said. "As a son of a great house, you above all people should recognize that. It is no different in my profession; sometimes a little information can make all the difference."

Stiger thought on what Father Thomas had just told him, kicking at a small tuft of grass. The paladin, having picked up a stick, used it to part some of the brush that grew over the mound that had once been the back wall.

"The statue may still be under this." Father Thomas sounded hopeful as he probed with his stick. "Though I imagine it is in a thousand pieces by now."

"You order has recorded events from when this city was populated?" Stiger said.

"We have a few accounts from that time, mostly fragmentary at best." Father Thomas looked over and then returned to surveying the mound, covered in a mass of entangled greenery. An oak tree grew out of the very top of the pile. "My order did not arise until after the founding of the empire."

Stiger had suspected as much. He glanced around and then turned his attention back to the paladin.

"I do not agree with the church's practice of withholding information," Stiger said. "Most histories of the empire's founding were written hundreds of years after the events had occurred. Essentially, the historians were recording spoken tales that had been passed down through families or referencing older works that no longer exist. My tutors pointed this out. They taught me to question everything as a way to determine fact from fiction and to better make an informed opinion. As such, it makes the veracity of those histories hard to verify. We don't know what actually is true. Think of everything your order's accounts could teach from this time and those of the early empire."

"My son," Father Thomas said, straightening up and turning to face Stiger. "Though I find your argument is cogent and I fully sympathize, some things were deemed best forgotten, lest they lead to trouble."

And there it was. Someone had made the decision. Stiger wondered who it had been. The church? One of the emperors? A wizard?

"I recall what Ogg had said," Stiger said. "Specifically, steps were taken so that our people intentionally forgot the past or really our coming to this world. Is that part of it?"

"Yes."

"That, too," Stiger said, "in my opinion, was a mistake. Had we known, think how better prepared we could have been."

"The same goes for our enemies, as well," Father Thomas said, and then heaved a great sigh. "Would you have better armed them with information?" Father Thomas paused, giving Stiger a long look. "Well, there is nothing to be done about it now. Those decisions were made centuries before you and I were born. We have to work with what we have been given."

"I suppose," Stiger said, still unhappy. There was so much that he did not know.

The paladin returned to his explorations of the temple. Stiger, hot from their hike to the temple, simply watched. He could hear his escort farther back, obscured by the brush, talking amongst themselves. It sounded as if they were playing a game of dice.

Like a young boy, Father Thomas in his excitement scrambled up the mound where the altar would have been. He worked his way through the plants and brush until he reached the tree at the top, a young oak. The mound was only six or seven feet high. Holding onto the trunk, he looked in all directions. Stiger down below had his view obscured by the brush and ruins and could not see anything beyond a few feet.

"Do you realize," Father Thomas said, "that this city was once a place where our people lived with the dwarves, in unity and harmony?"

"Not until we came here," Stiger said. "Heck, until we came to Vrell I had no idea that dwarves were real or, for that matter, that Rome was anything but myth and legend, a fabled city lost to the ravages of time. Again, that knowledge should never have been suppressed."

Father Thomas seemed to deflate a little at that. "Only a select few were permitted to know the truth. It was for the best, or perhaps really it was meant with the finest of intentions."

Father Thomas climbed down and stepped up to Stiger. He cast a glance toward the legionaries, who were half hidden by brush, and lowered his voice.

"Our kind, humans," Father Thomas said, "as you are aware, have been known to serve more than one god, including the dark ones. I know you know this for a fact, because of your experiences with Father Griggs in the North." Father Thomas took a breath, clearly considering what he wanted to say next. "It was thought at the time by those in power that it might be best to forget certain things," Father Thomas said and held his arms out to indicate the temple and, by extension, the city, "so that when it mattered, and the time came for such things to be remembered, those who held the knowledge would have the advantage."

"It certainly doesn't feel like we have the upper hand," Stiger said. "It seems to me when it mattered most, Castor's minions have always been one step ahead of us. I would point to the death of Delvaris as an example of this."

"It certainly appears that way, but you must have faith, my son. Castor has expended great power attempting to take the advantage away from us, to hinder our ability to fulfill what must come." Father Thomas laid a hand upon Stiger's shoulder. "With each defeat, he becomes weaker on this world and our side grows in strength. Look at the allies we have gained."

Stiger gave a reluctant nod.

"You must also consider," Father Thomas said, almost as an afterthought, "that there are other alignments that are working against both us and Castor, such as Valoor."

"The Cyphan," Stiger said, as he thought on what Father Thomas had just said. He snapped his fingers. "And the Rivan?"

"They and their gods have an interest in what we pursue as well," Father Thomas said. "You should also know we are not the only ones working to make sure that things succeed in favor of the High Father and our alignment."

"What?" Stiger's head came up. "Who?"

Father Thomas withdrew his hand and studied Stiger a long moment. "My son, I don't know everything, but prior to us stepping through the World Gate, there was another paladin, Father Orsin, who was dispatched to assist them. Please don't ask me more on this, for, in truth, that is all I was permitted to know."

Stiger was intrigued to hear this, but as the future had already been altered, he was unsure what effect, if any, this would have on their current circumstance and plight.

"Now," Father Thomas said, "shall we pray, for we came not just to sightsee, but also to pay our respects."

The paladin bowed his head in silent prayer.

Stiger eyed him a moment and took his cue. He also bowed his head.

High Father, Stiger prayed silently, *thank you for allowing me to see your temple, and this city where Karus and Amarra lived. I thank you for your favor and ask that it continues. If at all possible, please help these talks show some fruit. In my absence, please look after Sarai and help me make a speedy return to her.*

He was about to add to his prayer when a shout drew his attention back the way they had come. Father Thomas looked over as well, a scowl upon his face.

"Where is the legate?" a voice hollered insistently.

"Over there," one of his escort answered.

Stiger spared a glance with Father Thomas and then made his way in the direction of the person looking for him. He pushed through brush and came face to face with a legionary coming the other way. The man was out of breath and sweaty, his cheeks heavily flushed. He had clearly run here.

The legionary snapped to attention and offered a salute. Stiger waved it away.

"Speak," Stiger ordered, wondering with no little amount of trepidation what bad news the man carried.

"Centurion Pixus ordered me to report the orcs are arriving, sir," the man said. "He asked me to bring you right away, sir. The thane would like you present before they arrive. He told me to emphasize that point."

Stiger, feeling some relief at there being no bad news, looked back at Father Thomas, who had followed him. "It seems our explorations and respects are to be cut short."

"I have fulfilled one of my lifelong desires," Father Thomas said, no hint of disappointment in his tone. "I should very much like to return to this hallowed place. Perhaps there shall be time later?"

"Maybe," Stiger said. "If you do manage it, kindly say a prayer for me and Sarai."

"That I will gladly do, my son," Father Thomas said and flashed Stiger a cheerful smile.

"Dog," Stiger called, not seeing the animal. "Come."

There was a loud rustling of brush and Dog emerged, a good-sized hare in his jaws. He padded happily up to Stiger and dropped the dead animal at his feet, almost as if it were an offering. Dog wagged his tail with seeming satisfaction.

"Good catch," Stiger said and bent down to pick up the hare. He tossed it to one of the men of the file, who caught it. He knew the men would appreciate the break in their rations. "When you cook it tonight, see that Dog here gets some."

"Yes, sir," the man said. "Thank you, sir."

"That suit you?" Stiger asked Dog, for he had just given away the animal's kill.

Dog gave a clipped bark, tail still wagging.

"Lead on," Stiger said to the legionary. His escort, having picked up their shields, closed up around them.

"Yes, sir," the legionary said. "I will show you the way, sir."

They worked their way out of the ruins of the temple and onto the remains of an overgrown street. It had once been paved, but tall grass and brush now choked it. The remaining paving stones were few, and only a handful even remained visible. The collapsed buildings lining the road were now mostly covered mounds, with a few walls poking up out of the ground. The mounds looked uncomfortably like overly large graves. They were everywhere one looked.

The legionary led Stiger, Father Thomas, and the escort through the city on an unerring course. After about a half mile, they came to what Stiger thought could have been the remains of a central, open forum that was mostly free of the choking brush. But in truth, it could have simply been a crossroads. Time had been hard on the city.

It was here they found the dwarves.

Captain Taithun had formed his warriors up into a line four deep. Standards for both the thane and clan fluttered under a slight breeze. These had been set into the ground just to the front of the formation. The sight of the dwarven escort was striking, especially after the sun poked out from behind a cloud. Sunlight reflected off the dwarves' armor like little blinding flashes of lightning. Fifth Century was notably absent. Only Pixus and Sabinus were present.

Brogan, Jorthan, and Taithun were standing with the two centurions, casually talking. As he walked up, Stiger wondered where the remainder of the men were.

"Legate and Father Thomas, so good of you both to join us," Brogan said, turning. "I trust you were able to find the High Father's temple?"

"We did," Father Thomas said. "It was a true blessing to spend a few minutes there."

"Very good," the thane said and then turned to the business at hand. "My pioneers have informed me Therik's party has entered the outer city and should be joining us shortly. It seems that the orc king has remained true to his word. We have been unable to detect anyone attempting either to enter the city or, for that matter, skulking about. They assure me we will have sufficient warning to return to the safety of the tunnels should Therik attempt to cross us."

"That certainly is good news," Stiger said. He again wondered how competent Hogan and his pioneers were. Had they missed something? He certainly hoped not. Stiger excused himself and stepped aside to speak with the two centurions as Father Thomas engaged Jorthan and the thane in conversation on what they knew concerning the abandonment of the city.

"Where are the men?" Stiger asked.

"Setting up a fortified encampment," Sabinus said, "as you ordered, sir."

"We found the remains of a large building. It was possibly a warehouse, but you can't tell for sure," Pixus said and pointed behind them. Through the brush and trees, Stiger could see nothing. "It is about two hundred yards that way. I hope you don't mind, sir. I selected it as our campsite. The walls only come up to your lower chest." Pixus used his hand to demonstrate the height. "But they run almost all the way around. More importantly, they are in relatively good shape and solid. As we speak, my boys are cleaning out the interior and digging a trench around the outside. Tents will be last, after we have our defenses in place."

"Excellent work," Stiger said. He was pleased to learn Pixus was using what was available to them to make the encampment that much better fortified. He glanced up at the sky. Dusk was only a couple of hours off. He wondered how secure the camp would be by nightfall. "I am certain the site you picked is more than acceptable."

"It should take us three to four hours, sir," Pixus said, as if he had read Stiger's thoughts. "Our camp should be in good shape by then."

"Taithun seemed a little put out," Sabinus said, with a glance over at the captain.

"About what?" Stiger asked.

"I think the dwarves are not too pleased with us digging in, sir," Pixus said. "He gave me a little grief about it. Seems to think it might give Therik's bunch the wrong idea."

"Taithun also seemed to take it as an insult to their pioneers' skill, sir," Sabinus said. "At least until I explained to him that what Fifth Century was doing was only standard procedure. He still did not like it."

"I see," Stiger said, and glanced over at the dwarves. "Well, I would not worry too much about what Taithun thinks. Should the thane complain, I will handle it. Better to be safe than sorry. Understand me?"

"Yes, sir," Pixus said.

They come.

Like an out-of-control wagon on a steep hill, Rarokan's presence returned. The rage, hunger, and yearning for blood flowed as a torrent of emotion into Stiger's being. So strong was the tide of emotion that his knees went weak and he almost fell. Stiger felt his hand, of its own accord, reach for the hilt. He struggled to stop it. With not a little effort, he managed to pull his hand away.

Give them what they deserve—death.

Stop that, Stiger shouted silently at the sword and pushed back, trying to plug the flood of emotion with his willpower alone. Instantly, the rage and eagerness for bloodshed withdrew, or perhaps he had somehow forced it back. Stiger was not sure. However, the presence of Rarokan remained, hovering on the edge of his awareness.

As you wish.

"Are you all right, sir?" Sabinus asked.

"Yes, yes I am." Glancing at the hand that had gone for the sword, Stiger knew he was not fine. Rarokan had sought to gain control. It had almost succeeded.

"You've gone very pale, sir," Sabinus said, his concern plain. "And for a moment there, I thought you might collapse. Are you certain you are fine? Have you drunk enough water today?"

"I have a headache," Stiger said, hoping it was a sufficient enough excuse. "It's being out in the sun, after days spent underground in dim lighting. That's all."

In the hopes they would let the matter drop, he took several steps away from the two officers. He felt their worried eyes upon him and did his best to act as if nothing had happened. Father Thomas broke off his conversation and stepped over to him, a similar look of concern written on his face.

"I felt that," Father Thomas said without preamble. The paladin shot a wary glance down at the sword. "I felt the upwelling of power. What happened?"

"Rarokan," Stiger said quietly to the paladin. "He senses the orcs approach. He wants blood, and very badly, too."

"I see." The look of concern in Father Thomas's expression only deepened. "I fear he desires much more than that."

"The sword's hatred caught me by surprise, is all," Stiger said. Honesty was the best policy, particularly if he wanted to keep his mind. "I tell you, it was difficult to withstand. He sought to control me."

"You must resist him," Father Thomas said, "fight against him with all of your being and deny Rarokan the control he seeks."

"Easier said than done," Stiger said.

"Use your heart." Father Thomas laid a hand upon Stiger's chest armor, next to the torc he had taken in battle.

"My heart?"

"Your love for the High Father, for Sarai, for your empire, whatever works," the paladin said. "Think of that first. There is power in love. Use it as a weapon. When it becomes difficult to withstand, as it just was, you can always seek out help, and ask for it. Our god will listen and lend you strength."

Stiger felt himself frown at the paladin. Father Thomas wanted him to pray when the sword assaulted his mind? It sounded absurd. Stiger regarded the paladin for several heartbeats, understanding the paladin was deadly serious in his advice.

"I shall keep it in mind."

"Do so," the paladin said. "Much counts on you wielding the sword, not the other way around."

A shout rang out. Their heads turned. Therik's party had come into view, moving around a ruin barely thirty yards distant and entering the forum.

"Thoggle warned me this may happen," Father Thomas said. "I am here for you and will do what I can to help. Do not hesitate to call upon me. There are certain things I can do to render you assistance. Do you understand me?"

Stiger gave a grateful nod and then turned to study the approaching orcs. There were around twenty of them. They didn't march in formation, but walked in an unorganized group. They looked nothing like the warriors that Stiger had fought. These did not have the wild, outlandish dress or appearance he had come to expect. Instead they were dressed as civilized beings, wearing an assortment of tunics, pants, and shirts. Only a handful wore armor. The orcs were still alien-looking, but it was a shock not to see them dressed in a crazed manner or maddened by battle rage, with hair limed back and eager to throw themselves upon the shield wall.

What was even more surprising to Stiger was that mixed in amongst the orcs were a handful of well-dressed humans. They wore similar attire to the orcs. Eyeing them, Stiger wondered what kind of a person would willingly consort with such vile creatures. At their sight, he recalled Father Thomas's words about humans serving other gods. It was chilling to think a man would willingly serve the likes of Castor or another dark god. But as the paladin had reminded him,

Stiger understood the truth of human nature. Some preferred to serve their own self-interest over doing what was right.

Therik's party came to a halt around twenty paces from Brogan. Stiger moved over and joined the thane. Brogan's eyes were upon one orc in particular, who stepped forward from the group. Stiger took this one to be Therik.

Another large orc, this one wearing armor, positioned himself directly behind the king. He carried a large standard emblazoned with an image of a black stag. The warrior proudly planted the standard in the ground. Stiger took it to be Therik's personal banner.

Brogan took two steps forward and spoke in dwarven. "I have come at your request, King Therik. We come in peace, to talk with the king of the tribes."

"I thank for honor you show by coming to our call," Therik said in a rough but passable dwarven. The orc king's voice was a deep baritone and filled with confidence. "And I thank you for coming to meet me. We also come in peace to speak with thane of clans."

It surprised Stiger that the orc spoke the language of the dwarves, but then again, he had been told that Therik was different from others of his kind. Stiger reminded himself to stay on his toes.

"I have brought with me a representative of the Mal'Zeelan Empire, a proven leader of men," Brogan said and gestured back toward Stiger, who took a half step forward. A look of distaste appeared briefly on Brogan's face, before rapidly being covered up. "This is Legate Delvaris."

Therik's eyes swung over to Stiger, as did those of his party. At first there was mild interest, then Stiger read a flash of surprise, followed by anger. One of the orcs behind the king said something loudly. Another gave an animal-like roar of anger. The others began shouting, gesturing, and pointing at Stiger, speaking amongst themselves.

Dog, sitting at Stiger's side, growled menacingly and stood, ears back and teeth bared.

Brogan looked over at him, a clear frown forming on his bearded face.

"Dog," Stiger ordered firmly, looking down at the animal. "Down."

Dog ceased his growling and sat.

"How you get that?" Therik demanded in the common tongue. The king took two steps closer to Stiger. He pointed directly at Stiger's chest. "How you get that? I must know."

For a moment, Stiger was unsure what the king meant. Then it dawned upon him, and his hand went to the gold torc that he had hung on his chest armor. He fingered it a moment, considering his response.

Brogan flashed him a warning glance.

"I took it in battle," Stiger said, deciding that honesty was the best action he could take. "I killed the orc to whom this belonged."

The king's eyes seemed to bore into him, almost as if Therik was trying to determine if Stiger was lying. Several in his party looked ready to draw their weapons. Then the king's gaze swept over Taithun's dwarves. Stiger read calculation in the orc's eyes. Therik turned and said something that sounded quite harsh in his own tongue to those behind him. They stilled, all eyes shifting from Stiger to their king.

"To get that..." Therik's hand went up to his own neck, where he pulled down the front of his tunic to reveal a golden torc nearly identical to the one that Stiger wore. "You must kill chieftain. To lose a *hoharithan,* without losing one's life, is to lose what you call honor. No chieftain would stand such loss without giving life."

"He died well," Stiger said.

Brogan's eyes fell upon Stiger in clear dismay and rage. Gnashing his teeth, the thane looked ready to explode. Before he could say anything, Therik continued.

"My people want kill you for such a brazen display and attempt to provoke my anger. There can be but one *hoharithan*. I tell you now, I not seek your life. You show honor by coming, and great courage by displaying that." Therik pounded his chest with a large fist. "I show you same, chieftain killer. You keep battle prize, for now. I give you warning. One day I may challenge you and take it from your lifeless corpse."

"And I give you fair warning," Stiger said, "many have tried to take my life."

"We have much in common, I think." Therik gave a bark of laughter that was part snort. "But you have not faced me, yet."

"Let me know when you want to try," Stiger said.

Therik grinned and then gave a respectful nod, which Stiger returned. The orc king sucked in a great breath through his nostrils, shot a hard look at his followers, who shifted uncomfortably, and then returned his attention to Brogan.

The tension seemed to drain away and Stiger relaxed a little.

"The journey here was long. We make camp now," Therik said, switching back to dwarven. "After the sun goes down, and moon up, we talk, then we feast, yes?"

"We are camping over there." Brogan pointed to a spot a hundred yards away, where the wagons had been parked. A team of dwarves was busy erecting tents. "Where will you make camp?"

Therik glanced around, clearly looking for a suitable spot.

"There," Therik said, pointing at a nearby building that only had three remaining walls standing at shoulder height. "Good?"

"Acceptable," Brogan said. "We will meet back here after sundown and talk. As the moon climbs high in the sky, we shall then feast."

"I find that good," Therik said. "We bring the wood, fire, and food. You bring more food and spirits? We share. I have a taste for dwarf spirits, make sure you no forget."

"I will do so," Brogan said, "and I've made sure to bring a supply of the kind you prefer."

"Done," Therik said with a satisfied nod. The orc king shot Stiger a look, then turned away, walking boldly toward the ruin where he had said he would camp. The orc with the standard picked it up, eyed Stiger a moment, and then turned to follow his king. Stiger noticed a number of hostile looks thrown his way from Therik's followers, before they too followed their king.

"You could have ruined everything by wearing that thing," Brogan said furiously. The thane clenched a fist. "Had I realized what it was, I would have demanded you leave it or at the very least conceal it."

"But I didn't ruin things, did I?" Stiger said, rather than admit he had not known that the torc was, in orc culture, the sign of a chieftain's rank. Stiger sucked in a breath. The orc king was not what he thought he would be.

"Watch your insolence with me, human," Brogan spat, "or I may kill you myself."

Brogan spared Stiger a last furious glance and stomped off toward the dwarven camp.

"That could have gone better," Father Thomas said. "You do have a certain way with people that seems to bring out intense dislike."

Stiger rolled his eyes at the paladin.

"He will get over his anger," Jorthan said.

"Brogan or Therik?" Stiger asked.

"Both. Though if I am any judge, I believe you earned Therik's respect. I understand that not to be an easy thing. Make sure you don't lose it."

Jorthan turned away and followed after his thane.

"Did you really take that in battle, sir?" Pixus asked, stepping closer with Sabinus.

Sabinus threw Stiger a warning glance.

"I did," Stiger said. He decided to change the subject. "How about you show me the camp you are building?"

"Yes, sir," Pixus said and led the way.

Let's provoke the orc king further, the sword hissed.

Stiger had almost forgotten the sword's presence.

No, Stiger said to the sword. *We are here to talk only.*

It will come to killing soon enough, the sword said. *The followers of Castor cannot be trusted.*

Chapter Sixteen

Stiger scrambled up onto the mound. Grass and small bushes grew thick over the mound, a few corners of fallen stone blocks poking up and out of the soil and vegetation.

A soft breeze stirred the leaves of the nearest trees. In his armor, Stiger was uncomfortably hot from the afternoon sun and his exertions. The breeze was more than welcome. Atop the mound, he took a moment to survey his surroundings. He thought the mound had once been a decorative wall.

The mound ran in a curving line to his left for another twenty yards, before becoming obscured by the encroaching forest and brush. To his right, the ruins of the wall disappeared into a grove of trees, which had grown up closely along both sides.

He looked to his front at the remains of the structure that the wall had once apparently enclosed. Despite the growth of brush, trees, and tall grass doing its best to conceal its nature, Stiger thought it might be an amphitheater. The backside of one at least.

It consisted of a small hill that seemed unnaturally rounded, with a series of stone columns jutting up from its top. Most of the columns had broken, while others had fallen over or were tilted at odd angles by ground settling. They had the appearance of being decorative, not load-bearing, which meant they had never held a roof. He had seen imperial amphitheaters of a similar style.

Curious, Stiger carefully worked his way down the other side of the mound, watching where he put his feet. The rubble and ruin of this ancient city was dangerous enough. Add to that the low-lying brush and ivy that seemed to run over nearly everything, the prospect of turning an ankle became very real.

Stiger paused. He untied his canteen and took a hearty swig of water. Stopping it back up, he returned the canteen to its place on his armor harness.

Stiger took a breath of fresh air, savoring it. The air was free of the decay and mustiness that had pervaded the underground. He glanced once more around, enjoying the solitude of the setting.

It had occurred to him a short while after Therik's arrival that he was no longer under guard or immediate supervision. Theo had even decided to camp with the dwarves. After Stiger had toured the budding legionary encampment, he found there was nothing for him to do. Had he actively contributed to the construction of the encampment, as legate, it would have seemed odd and potentially raised uncomfortable questions.

So, while Pixus and Sabinus worked Fifth Century and oversaw the building of the camp, Stiger had quietly snuck off to do a little exploration. This was the first time he had been on his own since stepping through the World Gate. It felt wonderful to once again be his own master, even if it would only be for a short time.

Deer tracks, perhaps half a dozen in total, tracked the ground before him. He bent down to examine them. They were fresh, made within the last few hours. Amongst the undergrowth, he had already seen numerous game trails and a wide variety of tracks. Stiger understood, with all of the brush and grass, this was the ideal environment for deer and other animals like boar, for there was plenty to feed on.

He worked his way up to the hill, pushing through the grass and stepping around thorny scrub oak that had grown up nearly to the height of his shoulders. Instead of climbing the hill, he followed it around until, as expected, he came to a large gap. This would have been one of the entrances.

Time had worn away the walls of the entrance, nearly filling the gap in, but there was still a path of sorts. He made his way through the rubble-strewn entranceway, making sure his footing was secure, the debris unshifting before taking each step.

Sure enough, it was an amphitheater, and a good-sized one at that. He estimated it could have held more than two thousand spectators. Stopping just inside, Stiger discovered age had not been a kind friend. The amphitheater was in terrible shape. Grass, bushes, and young trees grew all together, looking more like a wild thicket than a stage for theater. It was all thoroughly overgrown.

The spectator benches were still in good shape, if a little uneven in places. One section had thoroughly collapsed, as the foundation at that point had given way. Looking over the collapsed portion, Stiger wondered if the amphitheater had underground spaces. He decided that if it did, it would be too dangerous to explore.

He climbed up the stone benches, stepping from one to another, until he came to the last row at the highest point, just beneath the columns. Grass and small bushes grew between the benches. Brushing away the layer of dirt that lay atop the stone, he sat down and relished the feeling of being off his feet.

"How long has it been?" Stiger asked the empty amphitheater. "How long has it been since someone sat here and enjoyed a show?"

There was no answer, of course, just the sound of the breeze rustling leaves and the call of song birds. Stiger contemplated the setting before him. He found it exceedingly peaceful. He could hear no voices, just the wind and birds, many of the same sounds one found deep in the forest, well away from people.

He wondered what plays had been performed here. Would he know any of them? At one time in his life, Stiger had enjoyed theater. That had been before he had become a soldier. It had been years since he had attended a show.

"Aegisthus," Stiger said to himself. It was a play that was reputed to be ancient, even predating the empire. The Aegisthus was considered a traditional play, and regularly performed around the time of the High Holy Days. It was said to have been consistently enjoyed since the time of Karus. Had that play been put on in this ruin of an amphitheater?

Stiger had brought his haversack. He opened it and removed some of the precooked rations that Pixus had supplied, salted pork and hard cheese. He took a bite of the pork, chewed, and swallowed. He was about to take another bite when movement in the bushes below near the center of the amphitheater caught his attention.

A large animal was working its way through the brush, rustling loudly and disturbing branches. Was it a deer? Stiger went still. Of large game, besides deer, he had seen bear and boar tracks, too.

Nose pressed to the ground and sniffing along, Dog emerged into view. The animal looked as if he were hunting something. Stiger knew what he was looking for. After several moments of intense sniffing, Dog looked up and spotted Stiger. He gave an excited bark and bounded up the stone benches.

"Easy, boy," Stiger said with a laugh as Dog jumped up on his chest, almost pushing him back to the next bench, licking madly at his face. "Easy there. Come on now."

Dog's enthusiasm subsided as Stiger began scratching at his neck. It also helped that he fed Dog a piece of the salt pork, which was almost instantly wolfed down. As Stiger chewed on his cheese, Dog settled himself down next to him on the bench. They sat together for a long while, with Stiger alternating between scratching and rubbing the dog's neck. Stiger was enjoying the peacefulness and quiet of their setting. Dog's presence was also comforting.

As they so often did, Stiger's thoughts turned to Sarai. He wondered what she was doing at this moment. The afternoon was wearing on. He figured she would soon likely begin preparing her supper. He wished he were there to enjoy it with her and not here in this long-dead city. Dog, perhaps sensing his mood shift, placed his head down upon Stiger's leg and gave a soft whine.

Stiger glanced down at the animal.

He felt absolutely no threat from Dog, only a sense of reassurance, perhaps even empathy. And yet, he got the exact opposite from the sword. Both had been sent to him by a god. The High Father, whom Stiger worshiped and honored, had arranged for the sword to come into his keeping. Stiger found that more than a little ironic. He had sworn to the High Father, and in return the god had given him a sword that had a mind of its own and wanted nothing more than to dominate him.

Glancing down at Dog, he had questions that needed answering.

"Who sent you?"

Dog did not answer.

"Are you here to protect me? Help me?"

Dog again did not answer, just lay there with his head on Stiger's thigh.

"Not one for a lot of words, are you?"

Eyes closed, Dog started to snore slightly.

Stiger let out a slow breath and turned his gaze back to the amphitheater. Small birds flitted in and around the brush. He watched as they played and chased after one another. One with bright blue feathers landed on a bush with small red berries just a few paces away. The bird eyed Stiger and Dog for a few moments, head twitching this way and that as it looked at him with first one eye and then the other. Apparently deciding they were no threat, it deftly pecked at the red berries, neatly picking one. It swallowed the berry, then took wing and flew off toward the center of the amphitheater, quickly disappearing amidst the brush.

The city, once teeming with people, had become a refuge for animals. In a way, Stiger found that fitting. Nature was reclaiming what human and dwarf had in effect borrowed. He knew with certainty that Eli would have enjoyed the thought of it too.

A soft growl disturbed his thoughts. Dog had raised his head and was looking down toward where Stiger had entered the amphitheater. Stiger sucked in a breath and was immediately on guard. An orc stood below. Not just any orc, but Therik.

Hands on his hips, Therik quietly surveyed the amphitheater. He seemed completely unaware of Stiger, until his gaze tracked around. The king froze and then looked about once again, this time appearing to scrutinize his surroundings thoroughly, as if searching for hidden threats or the possibility of ambush. He eventually returned his gaze to Stiger and gave a slight shrug.

"You here alone?" Therik said, taking a few steps nearer before climbing over several of the stone benches.

Dog's growl intensified. The orc ceased his forward movement, gaze falling warily upon the animal.

"Call your dog off," Therik said.

"Quiet," Stiger said absently, wondering why the orc had come. Dog continued to growl. "That's enough."

Dog fell silent, but his gaze never wavered from the orc king.

"You alone here?"

"Yes," Stiger answered in dwarven.

"You speak the language of the little ones," Therik said, switching to dwarven. "That is good. Makes it easy to speak. Common is a difficult tongue." Therik glanced around. "Like you, I alone."

"You snuck off, too?" Stiger said, supposing that the orc had taken the opportunity also to wander off without an escort. At least he hoped that was the case. If Therik was looking for trouble, he had certainly found it.

Stiger sensed Rarokan intently paying attention.

"Yes," Therik said. "It is a rare thing to be alone."

"And yet in the middle of this ancient city," Stiger said, "we just happen to chance across one another? And by ourselves, too?"

Therik's eyes narrowed. For several heartbeats he said nothing, then he gave a bark of laughter.

"Yes, human," Therik said. "I made off while my people were busy making camp. And no, this is not chance meeting. I was looking around. I saw you and decided follow so we might speak."

"Honesty, then?"

"Honesty," Therik said, with a firm nod of the head. "Nothing more than you have shown me."

"I appreciate honesty," Stiger said. "And those who are direct."

"Very well. If that is what you wish," Therik said matter-of-factly. "The priests have spread word about you. They want you dead. They want it badly."

"Is that so?" Stiger tensed up and felt a prickle of anger. Dog sensed it, for he stood.

"No need to worry," Therik said.

"And why is that?"

"I will not take your life this day," Therik said, and then grinned, displaying his large sharpened tusks. "Perhaps tomorrow or the day after, but not today."

Stiger relaxed slightly, realizing the orc was playing with him. Dog sat back down as well.

"Should the priests learn I speak with you and did not seek your life," Therik said, sobering, "then they happily take mine."

"You would let them?"

Therik gave a growl, not unlike Dog's. "They could try."

"They've already attempted as much with me," Stiger said.

"I know." Therik pointed toward the space next to Stiger on the opposite side from Dog. "May I sit?"

Stiger was surprised by the question, but after a moment's reflection gave a nod.

Therik made his way up the last few benches, giving Dog some healthy room as he crossed in front of them. He cleaned off the stone, brushing aside the dirt, before sitting some three feet from Stiger. They were silent for a time. Stiger wondered why the orc king had come. Taking a bite of the cheese, he reached over and offered the rest to Therik.

"Thank you," the orc king said, accepting the offering. Therik finished the cheese with one chew and swallow. "You humans must have no taste. That terrible cheese."

"It is army food," Stiger said. "It is meant to feed you, keep you going, not taste good. If a person finds it tasty, there is either something wrong with them or something not quite right with the food."

Therik laughed, snorting through his nostrils. "Much truth in that, I think."

"Agreed," Stiger said, amused.

"This looks like pit for fighting," Therik said, gesturing outward with his hand.

"It is for…" Stiger paused. He did not know the word in dwarven for theater. "Play."

"Play?" Therik's forehead ruffled. "I do not understand."

"Acting," Stiger said, in the common tongue. "People pretending to be others. They put on a show for the masses."

"Ah," Therik said in dwarven. "I know of this. Not for fighting, then?"

"No," Stiger said, "this is not a gladiatorial arena."

"Gladateria?" Therik said, stumbling over the word.

"Gladiatorial," Stiger corrected. "Men fighting for show, or condemned criminals hoping for their freedom by being the last man standing."

"My people have this, too," Therik said. "We go to watch. It is very entertaining. Sometimes, sadly, fighting is not real. It is like this play you speak of."

"We have fake fighting, too," Stiger said, thinking it odd that their peoples had something in common. "It can be expensive to lose good gladiators."

"Owners no like lose money," Therik said. "When they lose, they become unhappy. They complain." Therik let out an explosive breath. "Everyone brings problems to me. Sometimes, I wonder what they do before I came along."

Stiger gave a nod, pulled out his canteen, and took a swig of water.

Therik held out his hand expectantly. The orc king did not carry a canteen. Stiger hesitated, thinking it somewhat odd he was sharing not only conversation but his food and water with an orc. He handed the canteen over. The orc took a modest gulp. Therik returned the canteen.

"Why have you come here?" Stiger asked, looking over, as he stopped the canteen closed. He set it down at his side.

"Why here," Therik said and pointed down into the stone bench, "or why speak to Brogan?"

"Brogan," Stiger said. "Why have you asked for talks? By doing so, if I understand correctly, you put yourself at risk. Am I right in that?"

"Why anger priests?" Therik asked. "That is what you want to know?"

"Yes, exactly," Stiger said and looked over. "Brogan tells me why he thinks you are here. I want to hear it from you, in your own words."

Therik placed both hands on his thighs and leaned forward slightly, partly turning toward Stiger.

"I come to stop war," Therik said plainly.

"It has already begun," Stiger said, just as plainly.

"That is where you are wrong. It never ended. Gods war and be fighting a very long time."

"Why go against your god, then? You defy Castor, by just speaking with me."

"Castor is not my god," Therik said, with deep feeling. The orc king flexed his jaw before spitting on the stone bench to their front. "I tell you, he is not my god."

Stiger wasn't sure what to think, so he settled for challenge.

"You expect me to believe that?"

"Believe, don't believe," Therik said, looking away. He waved a hand in dismissal. "It is up to you."

"How can you say Castor is not your god?" Stiger asked. "Unless I have it wrong, you orcs serve him."

"Castor is Castor's god. The gods' war brings nothing to my people, only destruction, death." Therik's tone reeked of a deep-seated anger. "It was I. No one else united the mountain tribes. I did this. We now build cities, and work together." Therik pounded a fist into the palm of his hand. "For first time, my people live in peace. Yes, there are petty squabbles, but we no longer war amongst ourselves. And then you come, along with—" Therik said a word Stiger did not understand, becoming more passionate. "Now, with each day, more and more tribes go over to the priests." Therik's face twisted with disgust. "Even my son listens to their poisonous words. All that I have built is but inches from the cliff face. It balances on knife's edge."

Breathing heavily and worked up, Therik abruptly fell silent, eyes sweeping the amphitheater once again.

"I come to stop war," Therik said, in a near whisper. "I come to stop war."

"I am afraid we waste our time here," Stiger said. "There is no stopping the fighting to come. I know that."

"I don't know that." Therik's tone was forceful. He looked over and Stiger read pure anguish in his face. "My kingdom fall, and the war go on and on unless we can stop Cetrite and the mishkathol."

"Cetrite? Mishkathol? I do not know those words."

"Cetrite is High Priest," Therik said with a tone that reeked of disgust. "*Mishkathol* is gods blessed. Both are bad."

Stiger froze for a heartbeat. His hand began moving toward the sword until he realized that Therik was not speaking about him, but someone else. So caught up in the emotion of the moment, the orc did not notice the move.

"Gods blessed?" Stiger snapped his fingers in sudden realization. "You mean the minion, the direct servant of Castor? It is gods blessed?"

"Yes," Therik said, slapping a palm on the stone bench. "It has much medicine. The mishkathol must be stopped. If we do not, with it come Horde, massed strength of my people. Then there be lots of death and suffering, for all."

"I've seen that," Stiger said softly, averting his gaze. "I've fought against your Horde and I have no desire to see it again, ever."

"What?" Therik said, eyes narrowing with skepticism. "How can be? How can you be here? Nothing survives Horde."

"I did.'

"Impossible," Therik said. "The stories tell of Horde as being unstoppable as a rockslide."

"Believe, don't believe," Stiger said, turning Therik's words back upon him. Stiger fingered the torc affixed to his chest armor. "Fighting the Horde is where I got this little prize."

Eyes upon Stiger, Therik fell silent. He was clearly in deep thought.

"What did you call it? The creature, Castor's servant?" Stiger asked.

"A *mishkathol*," Therik said in a subdued tone. "It is *will* of Castor in flesh and blood."

Stiger sucked in a breath and regarded Therik. He made a decision.

"You should know, I have faced one of Castor's minions," Stiger said.

"A mishkathol?" Therik's expression now turned to one of utter surprise. His tone was filled with awe. "You fought one?"

"Alongside a paladin of the High Father," Stiger said. "Together, we defeated it and sent it on to its master."

Therik just stared at him for what seemed like a long time.

"I should disbelieve you," Therik said, "but I do not. I see now why Brogan brought you and why priests want you dead. You are dangerous."

"I have come to kill your mishkathol," Stiger said. "It is why I am here."

"You bring hope," Therik said, brightening considerably. "It is why I called these talks. I wished to find hope."

"You have that wrong," Stiger said, with a heavy breath. "Where I go, death follows. I bring death."

"Until I unified tribes, my people thought same of me." Therik fell silent again, seemingly lost in thought.

Dog leaned his head back down on Stiger's leg and closed his eyes, going to sleep. Stiger glanced down at Dog, surprised, and felt himself frown. He looked back up at the orc king. Like Dog, he felt no threat from Therik, and it was more than a gut feeling. The orc king had been completely honest with him. He was certain. As incredible as it was to believe, Therik was here hoping for a way to defeat his own god. Stiger ran a hand through his matted hair. He was rocked by this sudden revelation.

"What tribes have you fought?" Therik asked after a time. "Were they of western plains? We've heard tale of brothers and sisters but have had no direct contact."

Stiger glanced over at the orc and felt sadness for him. Therik appeared almost civilized. He had never expected to relate to an orc. Still, like everyone else not of the Mal'Zeelan Empire, Therik was, in essence, a barbarian. As an orc, he was considered even lower than that, a mindless savage. Stiger was beginning to find that was not necessarily the case.

"Why do your people desire the return of Castor?" Stiger asked, instead of answering the king's question.

"Desire?" Therik snorted out a laugh. "There is no desire to it. Castor has returned and his priests have regained their medicine. It is fear that motivates my people, fear of Castor. That and priests' sacrificial knives. It has always been way. Most do not understand we are no better than slaves to a hard and unforgiving master."

"But there are those who believe?" Stiger asked. "Those of your people who have faith. Are there not?"

"Of course," Therik said. "Until mishkathol returned, most only said words. They did not feel with heart. With coming of Castor, there are many who are blinded by faith to a god who cares not for his people. Castor does nothing for us, and for that, he never be my god. If I could kill all of his priests with my own two hands, I would."

"So," Stiger said, "what will you do, then?"

"Tonight, you, me, and Brogan speak important words," Therik said. "We must kill mishkathol. We do that, and war ends. My people be free to build better future." The king heaved a great sigh. "If you are to kill mishkathol, then I have a plan. Together we end the war."

Stiger thought of all he knew from the future. He did not have the heart to tell Therik that he suspected it was already far too late.

Therik stood and pointed at Stiger's golden torc. "As I told you, those I brought with me want to kill you for that. They see you wearing that as insult to people. By killing you, it will return honor to chieftain you took it from. They are loyal to me and not act without my order. Continue to wear it proudly, for though it is an outrage, it also gives you standing."

"And in your eyes?" Stiger asked.

"In mine..." Therik opened his mouth in a sudden broad grin, a long red tongue snaking around his lower left tusk and briefly caressing it. "You killed a mishkathol and look to kill another. For that, I consider you a brother, even if you are only a lowly human."

Therik began climbing down the stone benches.

At the last one, the orc king stopped, turning back. "You are not like humans I have known. Human tribes in my kingdom are weak, fearful." The king pointed a finger at Stiger. "You not fear me. For that, I like you. Even so, I kill you one day. I promise."

With that, Therik turned and continued on. Stiger watched the king of the orcs as he made his way out of the ruined amphitheater and was soon lost to sight.

Do not let him fool you, for you cannot trust him, Rarokan hissed in his mind. *Orcs are of the Horde and pawns of the dark gods. They are the enemy. Better to be safe. He is alone, unprotected. We should follow and kill him now. Take his soul before he can act against us.*

Stiger felt the sword's hunger well upward from within. The power flowing in to him rapidly becoming a flood, a torrent of rage.

"Stop that," Stiger said through gritted teeth as he struggled to resist the urge to pursue Therik. The power battered violently at him, seeking to overcome his resistance. Stiger pushed back hard, but it wasn't enough to hold off the deluge of hate and rage. He realized with a sinking feeling that the sword was rapidly overcoming his mind, his control. Desperate and recalling Father Thomas's words, he thought of the High Father and the urge almost immediately receded, as if the threat alone of calling upon and receiving aid from the great god was enough to cow Rarokan.

Stiger's breath came in great gasps. Dog was looking up at him and whining softly.

"It's all right," Stiger said, patting his head.

Dog seemed to understand and once again laid his head upon Stiger's thigh.

Danger past, Stiger sat there for a time, breathing steadily and attempting to slow the hammering of his heart. He forcibly calmed himself, contemplated his words with Therik, and the struggle with the sword.

"Nothing is ever easy," Stiger said to himself, "and it's not likely to get any easier."

Chapter Seventeen

As Stiger stepped up to the fire, Brogan cast him an unhappy and impatient glare. Stiger had inadvertently kept Brogan and Therik waiting. It had taken him longer than expected to return from his explorations. Ignoring the thane, Stiger took a seat, sitting cross-legged on the rug between Father Thomas and Sabinus. He could feel the hard stones amidst the grass beneath the rug. He shifted about for a more comfortable position and then stilled.

"Cutting it kind of close," Father Thomas said, "aren't you?"

"I've made it," Stiger said, shrugging his shoulders. After his talk with Therik, he had remained in the amphitheater thinking about all that weighed heavily upon him—himself as the High Father's champion, Sarai, the sword, and everything fate had thrown his way.

The sun had just passed behind the trees. Highlighted by the clouds, the sunset sky was a brilliant orange mixed with deep hues of purple. The temperature was still somewhat warm, but the onset of the coming night was beginning to leach the warmth from the air.

Though it wasn't a large blaze, the fire crackled and popped loudly. Brogan and Jorthan had a rug of their own just to the left. Facing them from across the fire was Therik, seated next to an elderly orc. Brogan, with a heavy breath, settled himself next to Jorthan. The thane carried a large mug, which he made a show of gazing into before taking a slow sip.

"That is Karan," Father Thomas said in a low tone and nodded toward the elderly orc. "He is advisor to Therik. Jorthan explained that Karan raised Therik after his mother and father were killed in a raid by a rival tribe. He is one of the king's most trusted advisors."

Stiger gave Father Thomas a grateful but curt nod. He turned his attention to study Karan. The orc's face was lined with age. The skin had gone from a healthy greenish color like Therik's to a pale, faded green that seemed almost translucent. It hung on his arms like a burlap sack that had been used well beyond its prime. The orc's hair had also lost any color and was now a dull, rain-cloud gray. Despite all that, Stiger read cunning and intelligence in the creature's eyes as Karan carefully studied those across the fire.

Stiger sensed Rarokan waking, its presence hovering in the background. The sword was clearly interested in what was to be said. Stiger also felt its hunger for blood, but that was sullenly muted and subdued, which was something of a relief.

Brogan took another long sip and then placed the mug down at his side. He smacked his lips and wiped his beard around his mouth with the back of his forearm before looking up at Therik. There was a calculating expression on his face as he considered the king for a few moments.

"We know why we are here," Brogan said finally in a tone that was almost hostile. "The priests are stirring up your people something fierce. By all indications you are in a desperate position. If this is not a correct assessment, I would like to hear what is."

Therik opened his jaw slightly, as if taken aback. Therik returned Brogan's gaze with a flinty one of his own. He reached up a hand, running a thumb along one of his sharpened tusks. The firelight gave the white tusks a yellowed hue. It was clear by how he had stiffened he was unhappy with Brogan's approach.

"Your spies have always kept you better informed," Therik said, after a slight hesitation. "I wish my spies and informers were as good."

"No doubt," Brogan said. "We've kept the peace between our peoples, and I desire very much to continue to do so. You asked for us to come, and we have. Let us speak plainly on matters and not beat around the brush."

Therik looked over at Karan, who gave a slight nod. With that, Therik returned his attention to the thane.

"It is as you say. I need your help," Therik said simply, though it was clear the admission was a grudging one.

Stiger suspected the king loathed being in the inferior position. Such a statement smacked of weakness.

"I don't speak dwarven," Sabinus whispered, leaning close to Stiger. "What are they saying?"

"It is probably not a bad idea to begin learning," Stiger whispered back. "Don't you think?"

"I will get right on that, sir," Sabinus said in the same hushed tone. "Do you think Theo would teach me?"

"Father Thomas and I will explain everything later," Stiger said. "As to Theo, I don't see why he would say no. Ask him tonight at the feast."

"That I will, sir," Sabinus said.

"What do you want from us?" Brogan said.

Therik hesitated and looked back over at Karan. They exchanged a few words.

"Speak up," Brogan continued in the same brusque tone. "I am hungry. I do not wish to sit here all evening waiting for you to get around to whatever it is you want."

Therik worked his jaw a moment, clearly irritated at the thane's manner. Stiger sensed Therik had expected more courtesy than he was receiving. He noticed the orc king flex his left hand, as if he desired very badly to hit something. Stiger could guess what that something was. Karan leaned near and whispered into the king's ear. Therik said something back that sounded harsh and jabbed a finger toward Brogan. The advisor gave a nod.

"We wish you to help us kill the mishkathol," Karan said, turning to Brogan. He spoke dwarven exceptionally well, in a voice made raspy by his advanced age.

"And Castor's High Priest," Therik added. "That help keep peace."

Brogan scowled at that and looked over at Jorthan with a questioning glance.

Playing idly with his braided beard as he studied Therik and Karan, the thane's advisor whispered something to Brogan. The thane said something in reply. Jorthan gave a shrug and then shook his head.

After a few moments of this back-and-forth with the thane, Jorthan responded. "I'm afraid, Karan, we do not know that word. What is a mishkathol?"

"He means the minion," Stiger said, having tired of the whispering games. He looked over to Brogan. "He wishes our help in killing Castor's servant, the creature that came through the Gate before me and Father Thomas."

Brogan sucked in a startled breath and turned his gaze back to Therik. Clearly the thane had not expected this request from the orc king.

"That is my desire," Therik said, leaning forward. "Should it live, Horde return."

"The Horde," Brogan said in an unhappy tone, sharing a look with Jorthan. "It has been a long time since my people faced the Horde, and never on this world."

"When that happens, there no holding people back." Therik's tone dropped slightly. "We have war."

"A war of a kind not seen since your peoples and ours came to this world," Karan spoke up, with a glance that traveled from Stiger to Brogan.

"You would kill the representative of your own god?" Father Thomas asked. "I find that most difficult to believe."

"He is no god of mine." Therik pointed at Stiger. "I told him same, he who has powerful medicine."

Brogan turned his head to Stiger, as did Father Thomas and Jorthan. The thane's expression turned thunderous and his jaw worked for a moment before he spoke.

"You had talks without me present?" Brogan's tone was low and menacing. He appeared ready to stand.

"I was exploring the city," Stiger explained, before hard words could be said and further accusations made. "It seems King Therik was doing the same." Stiger slid his gaze over to Therik. "We met by chance and spoke but briefly."

The thane's face became mottled with rage. Stiger could almost read his thoughts. The thane would have expected him to say something. Unfortunately, there had been no time. He had only just returned from his explorations, which was why he had been late. Brogan would not have known that. The thane likely thought Stiger was playing a game of his own.

"What do you mean, Castor is not your god?" Father Thomas returned his attention to the orc king. The paladin cocked his head to the side. "If you would, kindly explain that to me."

"Castor brings suffering," Therik said, becoming passionate. "My people know peace because of me. We build cities. We do great things. Castor wants Horde and sends his mishkathol with powerful medicine. All I have done, all my people have done ... be blown away like leaves on the wind."

Brogan placed both hands in his lap. He considered the orc king. Jorthan leaned in close and whispered again to Brogan, who showed no reaction to his advisor.

"When you say medicine," Jorthan said, "you mean magic?"

"Magic, power, medicine," Karan rasped. "It is all the same."

Brogan was silent a moment. "Should we be the ones to kill the minion, war will still come. Your people will see us as the ones responsible. Surely they will want blood."

"My thane is correct. It will be the same result," Jorthan said, "and may even prove uglier, since this is all tied to your religion."

"We orcs respect strength above all else." Therik flexed a powerful arm, showing his bicep muscle. "This brute strength." He touched a finger to the side of his head. "This thinking strength." Therik brought his palm to his chest. "Strength of heart."

"How does that change things?" Jorthan asked.

"Without minion, and high priest, people return to me," Therik said, touching his chest again, but this time with a fist. "By killing it, you show strength and medicine of your two peoples. Chieftains have no choice but to come crawling back. I only one with strength left. They beg my mercy. Understand me?"

"I do," Father Thomas said. "However, I am inclined to agree with the thane. Killing the minion will leave hard feelings, especially if it is seen as an assassination."

"Some remain angry and want blood," Therik said with a slight shrug of his impressive shoulders. "So?"

"Most will accept it as your strength." Karan sucked in a tired breath, as if the effort to breathe had suddenly become difficult. "They will not admit it, but privately they will be relieved. No one but the most devout wants the Horde."

Therik swung his gaze to around. "If we don't try, war come anyway. We work together, yes? This is a threat to all our peoples."

"Caused by your people." Brogan, a hostile look in his eyes, pointed a stubby finger at Therik. "Not ours."

"By Castor," Therik said.

Brogan picked up his mug and took a sip before returning it to his side.

"How do you propose we do this?" Brogan asked in a tone that was almost insolent. "Already your tribes have begun assembling for war. The priests have called, and your people, for the most part, have willingly answered. I am told your army is thirty thousand strong and gathering around Castor's main temple at Berke'Tah just forty miles west of Vrell. The minion is there, as is Castor's high priest. Both are well-protected. So, tell me, Therik, how do you propose we do this?"

Therik leaned back, eyeing the thane. "You knew of gathering and still you come?"

"I came," Brogan said, placing both hands upon his hips. "Yes, I came knowing ten tribes is all you have left. The rest have gone over to the priests. Your power has been severely eroded. How long will those tribes remain loyal? I fear it is only a matter of time until you lose all of your support."

"Therik," Jorthan said, "you will shortly have a choice to make if you are to hold onto your kingdom. The priests have seen to that."

"I have made my choice," Therik insisted, his tone outraged, and pounded the ground before him with a fist. "I come here. I come to work with you."

"You have a plan?" Stiger asked Therik. He did not like Brogan's approach, or his tone. It almost seemed as if the Brogan and Jorthan were intentionally goading the orc king into a rage. He wondered what they were up to. "If so, I wish to hear of it."

Therik looked over at Stiger, almost with an expression of relief. A tongue snaked out around one of his tusks and remained there a moment. "Of course I have a plan. But I still need help and your medicine."

"Go on," Brogan said with a quick glance over at Stiger. The thane's eyes narrowed. After a moment, the thane returned his gaze to Therik. "We are listening. Tell us of this plan."

"First, I tell you your numbers are wrong," Therik said. "Forty thousand have joined gathering at Berke'Tah. With each day, more warriors come in from mountains. Soon there be sixty thousand gathered."

"I don't like the sound of that," Stiger said in a hushed voice to Father Thomas.

"Nor do I, my son."

"In a week's time," Therik continued, "there be strong raid on your valley."

Stiger sat up straighter, eyes narrowing, as his thoughts immediately went to Sarai.

"Is meant to provoke you into war," Therik continued. "Cetrite, high priest, means to unite tribes in a holy battle upon both of your peoples. Raid draws your"—Therik pointed to Brogan—"army out onto the surface, where it be exposed. There it be destroyed. After, everything is for taking. Cetrite has promised clans your rich valley, but also your city, and both castles."

"How do you know my army is even assembling?" Brogan asked.

"Please," Therik said, waving a hand of dismissal. "You are not only one who hears things. You know we gather our army. So, you gather your army. We have informers and spies, too, Brogan. Your army is on march. I know this as true and so does Cetrite. Do not bring shame and deny it."

Stiger shot a glance over to the thane. Brogan appeared none too happy with Therik's revelation.

"You are forgetting the legion," Stiger said.

"No, I am not." Therik turned his gaze upon Stiger. "During raid, legion be attacked with many warriors. No hope for you humans. This way, Cetrite keeps your army from coming together with Brogan's army."

Stiger didn't like the sound of that either. He leaned back, thinking. They had to get warning back to the valley before it was too late. He glanced over at Brogan and caught Jorthan's eye. Clearly the advisor was thinking the same thing. Messengers would have to be sent as soon as possible.

"I still do not hear of this plan," Brogan said. The thane's tone was heavily laced with irritation. "Tell me of it or stop wasting my time."

Stiger felt himself frown slightly, the scar on his cheek pulling tight. Why was Brogan being so belligerent?

Therik's fist clenched again, clearly angered. "Forkham Valley."

"What of it?" Stiger asked, a chill coming over him as he recalled the desperate rescue he had led, battling Castor's priests, their magic, and the dark temple dedicated to Castor. He had seen good people sacrificed to Castor. It had left him sickened, a sight he knew he would carry to his grave.

"Cetrite be visiting temple there," Therik said. "It is to be same time as raid on valley. Where Cetrite goes, minion follows. They never part. They go to place honor on temple to Castor and offer blood sacrifices for war."

"Go on," Brogan said.

"During big raid on valley, there is opportunity to strike." Therik paused to suck in a breath and turned his gaze fully on the thane. "Brogan, my allies are few. I"—Therik tapped his chest—"can guide a small group into valley through secret tunnels to minion at temple. I have warriors I trust to do this, but not many. With your warriors and mine, we stand a chance of success." Therik pointed at Stiger. "He must go, too."

"Why him?" Brogan asked, eyes narrowing as he shot Stiger a look of suspicion.

"Him strong with medicine," Therik said simply.

Brogan frowned as he glanced over at Stiger.

"To have survived a mishkathol," Karan said, "he would have great medicine at hand. There is no other way."

"Castor fears him," Therik continued. "There be bounty upon his ears and head. It worth much, very much."

"He," Karan added, "fought a mishkathol, and survived. That is why he is feared. That is why he is wanted dead."

Brogan and Jorthan looked over at Stiger in apparent shock. Stiger's eyes went from Karan to Therik. The last bit had not surprised him. He knew Castor wanted him dead. However, he was alarmed by what Therik was asking of him.

He felt the sword's interest in the conversation grow. Pangs of its terrible hunger began to stir at the prospect of facing the minion and Castor's priests.

"How do I know this is not a trap?" Stiger said.

He was fairly certain it wasn't but wanted to hear the answer anyway. Stiger felt Therik was being open and honest, but he still had some lingering doubt. After all, the king was an orc, and therefore the enemy. It was possible Therik had been intentionally sent here to lure him out and into Castor's lair. Perhaps by doing so, the orc king was proving his loyalty to Castor. Stiger studied Therik for a long moment. If he was being set up, then the orc king was a fine actor.

"You don't," Therik answered Stiger, then directed his gaze at Brogan. "You know me. We have treated fairly with each other for many years." Therik clasped both hands together. "We have built trust. Refuse me and I be forced to go over to Castor. I no more than puppet king. Trust in me."

"Our kingdom will be lost," Karan said, voice so raspy with age it cracked slightly, "and yours will be in peril and next to the chopping block."

Brogan leaned back, stroking his beard as he contemplated Therik across the fire, which cracked and popped. A slight breeze stirred the flames and swirled the smoke. The arrogance that he had displayed was gone. He shared another look with Jorthan, whispering something to his advisor. Jorthan said something back, to which Brogan gave a shallow nod.

"We will discuss your proposal," Brogan said. "In the morning we will give you our answer."

"I expect nothing less," Therik said and stood. He offered a hand to Karan and helped the old orc to his feet. Everyone else got up as well.

"When you say yes," Therik said, "we discuss plan serious-like."

"If we say yes," Brogan said.

"You will. We meet back here in two hours to feast under moon," Therik continued. "Make sure you bring the spirits and discuss this not with those I brought. I trust them less with each day. One of them may try to sell me to priests."

"We will keep this amongst ourselves," Jorthan said.

With that, the king of the orcs turned his back and left, stalking off the way he had come. Karan gave a slight bow of his head to Jorthan before following after his king. The elderly orc walked stiffly and slowly off.

"What do you think?" Brogan asked Jorthan as Stiger, Father Thomas, and Sabinus stepped over to the thane. "Do you think he speaks truth? Is it possible he is willing to turn on his god?"

"It has to be a trap," Jorthan said with a disappointed look at Karan's back. "Their plan is reckless, and risky, My Thane. I am almost certain Therik has been put up to this by the priesthood. I would advise against any consideration of accepting his proposal. We should continue as we had planned."

Stoking his beard, Brogan looked over to the paladin, clearly seeking his input.

Father Thomas hesitated. "Therik strikes me as desperate."

"That he is," Jorthan said.

"His plan may be reckless," Father Thomas said, "but I suspect his motives are honest. He stands to lose all and will do anything to keep what he has. I believe he speaks truth."

"My thoughts as well," Brogan said, then turned to Stiger. "And you? What are your thoughts?"

"I don't like the thought of going into a dark temple on this raid of his," Stiger said, "but for it to be successful, both Father Thomas and I will need to go ..."

"You can't tell me you are considering his mad plan?" Jorthan said angrily, looking between Stiger and Brogan. "Even if they are being truthful, one way or another it is a suicide mission. Whoever we send will stand little chance of returning, even if you do manage to kill the minion and Castor's high priest."

"What are you talking about?" Sabinus asked Stiger, having not been able to follow the conversation.

Stiger explained, quickly bringing Sabinus up to date.

Brogan switched to common so Sabinus could understand. "We send a small force with Therik. Risk a few. Should it prove successful, we will save many." Brogan paused and addressed himself to Jorthan. "It may be worth it to see what happens."

"You are not the one risking your skin, though, are you?" Sabinus jerked a thumb at Stiger and Father Thomas. "They will be."

"You dare question my legend?" Brogan's tone increased in volume and he took a half step toward the centurion, who held his ground. "I will stick your head on a pike for your insolence, human dog. How dare you speak to me like that? I am thane!"

Stiger was about to intercede when Jorthan spoke.

"He does have a point, My Thane," Jorthan said, with an overly loud chuckle. "Those going will be at significant peril."

Brogan shot Jorthan a hostile look, as if his advisor was interfering where he ought not.

Jorthan ignored it and continued. "They must journey into hostile lands and sneak into a dark temple. Once they accomplish that feat, they will confront not only a high priest who wields magic—or, as Therik says, medicine—but also a powerful servant of Castor, the minion."

"It will indeed be a dangerous enterprise," Father Thomas said.

"You want a fight," Stiger said suddenly, looking from Jorthan to Brogan. It all made sense now. "The antagonistic approach with Therik. You came here not to seek peace, but to pick a fight."

Brogan and Jorthan shared a look.

"Not quite a fight," Brogan said. "But I won't deny we had other plans."

"Why?" Sabinus asked, perplexed. "Why the deception, then?"

Stiger's mouth fell open as it dawned on him what the thane intended.

"You are not planning on letting Therik leave," Stiger said to Brogan. "Are you? That is why Hogan is here and your pioneers have come in force. You aren't looking to secure this site. It is deep in your lands, far from orc territory and fairly safe. You brought Therik out here to kill him."

"Is this true?" Father Thomas's voice bordered on angry. Stiger had never seen the paladin livid before and felt the power within the paladin bubble up. He wondered for a moment if the others could feel it as well.

Brogan and Jorthan exchanged another look.

"You speak of legend," Stiger said, irritated that Brogan had not been open with him on his intentions. "How does assassination pass your sense of legend? You brought them here under the guise of a parley. All along, you intended to betray that trust."

"Therik is an orc," Brogan said with a slight shrug, as if it were of no real concern to him. "He is of the lesser races, our enemy. Your enemy, too. Legend does not apply to them."

"I don't see it that way," Father Thomas said.

"Does your legend apply to us?" Stiger asked. "Or does legend only matter amongst dwarves?"

Jorthan cleared his throat loudly, drawing their attention.

"Perhaps I can explain," Jorthan said. "For years we have worked to keep the tribes fragmented. We encouraged disputes between them. We financially supported tribe against tribe, sometimes funding both sides in a blood feud. Anything we could do to keep the tribes from uniting, we did. As long as the orcs were preoccupied with each other, they left Vrell alone. That has always been our objective. Whenever a king or leader would arise and start unifying the tribes, we shifted and focused our attention on undermining his base. In this way we have been able to keep the orcs weak, with no chance of developing into a serious threat."

"Then Therik came along," Stiger said. "That all changed, didn't it?"

"He is different," Brogan said. "Therik managed, despite our best efforts, to unite all of the tribes under his banner. And it is as he himself said: They now work to build things. In short, they prosper like never before and have become strong."

"When we realized we could not weaken his position," Jorthan said, "we changed our strategy. We worked with him to keep the peace, while at the same time preparing for war. For the last five years we have been building up our army. It was our understanding that once Therik's kingdom became powerful enough, he would turn his gaze our way."

"We had intended to provoke a war long before they were ready," Brogan said. "To protect Vrell and the World Gate, we would strike first. We would hurt them in such a way that they would not soon seek to challenge us for years to come, perhaps even decades."

"You decided not to try for peace?" Father Thomas asked.

"Since we have come to this world," Brogan said, "my people have fought several wars with the orcs. There is no living peacefully with them. Believe me, we have tried."

"You heard Therik," Jorthan said. "Orcs respect strength. We were going to show it to them."

"Only, the war came early," Stiger said. "The minion arrived and you're not quite prepared, are you?"

"We had expected to have another couple years," Jorthan said.

"Why kill Therik, then?" Father Thomas asked. "I don't understand that. With the minion present, ready or not, you now have your war. And if I understand correctly, you may be better prepared than the orcs."

"The minion was unexpected," Jorthan admitted. "We had not planned on it."

"So," Stiger said, thinking it out. He glanced in the direction Therik had gone. "You decided to eliminate Therik because you have what you want, your war. Keeping him alive is more dangerous. Is that it?"

"By all accounts and reports from our spies," Brogan said, "he is a genius on the battlefield, a natural leader. If I don't have to face him in battle, especially if the orcs are coming anyway, all the better. Do you understand now?"

"We had not planned on allowing him to return to his people," Jorthan said. "Our provoking him was designed to get him to reveal more information about his current position than he normally would. For instance, we learned their army is larger than we knew. With the minion and this high priest running things, allowing Therik to go back is too great a risk. Even as a puppet king, he would be their field general. Why allow our enemy to retain such an asset?"

"I have two hundred pioneers sealing a ring of steel around us," Brogan said. "After the feast tonight, Therik and his entire party were to be killed. Taithun was to see the deed done, Hogan to ensure none escaped."

"But," Stiger said, looking at Brogan, "you are now having second thoughts?"

"I am," Brogan admitted. "I had not expected Therik to turn on his own god. It might make more sense to go through with Therik's plan, especially if the minion can be killed. Should such a venture prove successful, some of the tribes would clearly want revenge. We'd punish them severely, of course."

Jorthan's expression became unhappy and he shot a scowl at his thane.

"But that would still leave Therik as king," Sabinus said, "with a good part of his army in place. They would still be a threat to you."

"An accident could always be arranged for Therik and his son," Brogan said with an unconcerned shrug. "In the end, the tribes would fragment, which is what we want. Without Therik or his son, there is no clear heir. The next decade would see the tribes consumed in fighting each other for dominance. Our goal of keeping Vrell safe and secure would be achieved."

Stiger rubbed his jaw as he regarded the thane. He was, as Theo had said, extremely devious. The thane was playing a hard game, which Stiger understood all too well. The empire had done the same in manipulating its neighbors. Stiger had even participated in such efforts of playing tribes and small kingdoms against one another. That said, he did not much care for the idea of crossing Therik. Contrary to his expectations, Stiger had begun to like the king, and thoughts of assassination bothered him greatly.

"Does Thoggle know what you planned?" Stiger asked.

"No," Brogan said. "The wizard thinks we came only to talk."

"I will have no part in the assassination of Therik," Father Thomas said firmly, anger plain in his voice. "And I will not allow you to proceed."

"Will not?" Brogan asked, turning on the paladin with a shocked expression. "You would prevent me from killing the enemy?"

"I would," the paladin said in a quiet tone that raised the hair on the back of Stiger's neck. "I supported these talks because Thoggle and I thought they might bear fruit. They have. Therik has brought us an opportunity. It should be seriously considered. And if discarded, the orc king will be allowed to leave. I will not stain the High Father's honor with an assassination on holy ground. This city, as you well know, was consecrated in the High Father's name. It is why Therik agreed to this place. Outside of a temple, it is the one area that Castor's priests and minions may not go. You will not betray that sanctity."

Brogan stared hard at the paladin. His gaze flicked over to Stiger.

"Oh, very well," Brogan said, giving in. "But if we let him go, it may prove bad for us in the long run."

"We will just have to take that risk," Father Thomas said.

Jorthan looked as though a thought had occurred to him. "From what Therik says, I take it you both have already confronted and defeated a minion. Is that true? Would you willingly face another?"

Stiger shared a glance with the paladin.

"It all comes down to that," Stiger said, coming back to the task at hand. Despite Brogan's machinations, he still had a job to do. "I fear I must face the minion. Whether that is in a dark temple or on the field of battle, the creature must be taken down."

"You will not face it alone, my son." Father Thomas rested a hand on Stiger's shoulder. "Like the last time, I will be there at your side."

"What if it kills you?" Sabinus asked Stiger. "I saw that monstrosity when it murdered my legate. What then if the same happens to you?"

"It may." Stiger had seen that future, too. He turned his gaze back to Father Thomas. "Do we go to it or allow it come to us?"

"How do you know it will come?" Brogan asked. "If we don't go through with Therik's plan, it may just send him and his army at us and remain behind. And why do you have to face it?"

Stiger was about to respond when Father Thomas laid a hand upon Stiger's forearm and shot him a meaningful look.

"This centers around the restoration of the Compact," Father Thomas said to the thane. "We've both come here because of it."

Brogan blinked, then pointed a finger at Stiger. "Are you here to restore that which has been sundered? Is that why you have come through the Gate?"

"I've already restored the Compact," Stiger said, "not here in this time, but the future."

"The future?" Excitement danced in Brogan's eyes. All hints of irritation and anger had left him. He looked over at Jorthan. "The oracle's prophecy is true."

"It seems so, My Thane," Jorthan said, just as excited.

"As you know," Father Thomas said, "the minion coming to this time has changed events in the future. However, much was kept from you. You must tell no one of what we speak. If you do, and we are successful in repairing the damage, any loose words may fundamentally change what must come."

"We will say nothing," Jorthan promised fervently, clearly eager to hear more. "Both my thane and I shall swear it to the High Father and all the other gods we honor."

Brogan looked over at Jorthan, his lips drawing together in a thin line.

"And you, Thane Brogan?" Father Thomas pressed. "Will you swear, as your advisor suggested? For if you refuse, Thoggle will almost assuredly alter your memory, including of what you already know. By the High Father, he may do so anyway, even if you do promise."

"He wouldn't dare," Brogan said, though the conviction was somewhat lacking in his tone.

"Thoggle made it plain to me that he would alter your memory if you refused me," Father Thomas said.

"He would," Jorthan confirmed. "Thoggle may be without legend, but he always follows through on his promises."

Brogan gave a firm yet sullen nod. "I swear upon my legend and the gods I honor I will reveal nothing of what you tell me." Brogan jerked a thumb at Sabinus. "What about the centurion here?"

"He has already given me his word," Father Thomas said and rubbed his hands together. He turned to the fire and held them out a moment, warming them. Then turned back. "At Castle Vrell, we defeated a minion of Castor, approximately three hundred years in the future. Another escaped us. With the help of a wizard, it opened the World Gate to travel here to your time. It came to kill Legate Delvaris with the intention of changing what is to come. We traveled back after the creature to stop it. Tragically, we did not arrive in time. That last bit you know only too well." Father

Thomas paused and sucked in a breath. "Now, what you do not know is that we must fix the damage done, for should we fail, the Compact will never be restored and someone else, quite possibly an agent unfriendly to our two peoples, will have the power to manipulate the World Gate. That is what is at stake. The High Father has chosen Stiger as his champion. It will be his honor to read the High Father's intentions and choose to unlock the Gate"—Father Thomas paused and glanced over at Stiger—"or leave it sealed. That is why Castor wants him dead, for the god desires the Gate for himself."

A silence fell upon them. Even Sabinus, who knew much of what had been revealed, seemed stunned by this additional information. Stiger felt uncomfortable as their eyes fell upon him in wonder.

"That certainly puts things in perspective," Jorthan said. "And if I am correct, this is why you are taking Therik's proposal seriously? You are looking for an opportunity to get to Castor's minion."

"Exactly," Father Thomas said. "We must kill the minion. With its death, Castor's strength on this world will diminish greatly. If we are successful, we will have the time and ability to set things right, or so Thoggle believes."

"Champion?" Sabinus said, eyes upon Stiger. "You are a holy warrior, like the paladin?"

Stiger turned an unhappy gaze upon Sabinus.

"He is the High Father's champion," Father Thomas said in a hard tone, before Stiger could reply. The paladin turned to look upon the two dwarves. "He is the one named by your oracle, the Restorer of the Compact."

The dwarves' excitement had shifted over to what seemed like awe. Brogan's eyes had gone wide, then narrowed as he tilted his head. It was as if he were seeing Stiger for the first time. Jorthan brought a hand up to his mouth and played with the beard in a speculative manner. It made Stiger feel even more uncomfortable. Yet, at the same time, his mind raced. The sword had shown him what had happened to Delvaris. Having assumed Delvaris's mantle, Stiger understood that fate was now his. There was really only one option open to him.

"It does put things nicely in perspective, doesn't it?" Stiger looked at Brogan. "And it is why we have to take Therik up on his offer to guide us into that dark temple. We must go kill the minion and this high priest, Cetrite."

Chapter Eighteen

"An impressive camp," Taithun said to Pixus as he gazed around. The captain had removed his armor and was wearing only a gray tunic. A purple belt denoting his clan colors had been cinched around the middle. He was walking around with his arms behind his back.

Upon his return from meeting with Brogan and Therik, Stiger had found Pixus providing a tour to the captain, conducting him about the camp. The centurion had patiently answered Taithun's questions about the camp, equipment, training, food, the legion's supply system, and the men. Taithun seemed genuinely interested in what Pixus had to say.

Stiger was sitting a few feet away, resting on a fallen stone block. The site Pixus had selected for their camp was an old building, the interior of which had long ago collapsed. Judging from the size, it appeared to have once been a warehouse, but it was hard to be certain. The truth was it could have been anything. The walls, what remained of them, were quite solid, though they were showing their age through weathering and cracks. The top-most blocks had been worn smooth by years of exposure to the elements.

The walls came up to around four feet. The roof, had there ever been one, had long since caved in and was nowhere to be seen. Stiger rather suspected it was now buried beneath their feet. The interior of the ruin had been choked with small trees and brush. Fifth Century had spent considerable effort ripping up the vegetation. They had done a good job of it, too. Ivy, which had grown up thick on and over the walls, had been pulled off and uprooted.

A trench had been dug around the outside of the walls to a depth of seven feet. The men were now busy erecting the last of the tents behind him. A team was digging a series of latrines on the backside of the camp, while a wood party had built up quite a supply and several campfires had already been set.

Stiger opened his haversack and pulled out the last of Sarai's cheese. All that was left were several wrapped bundles of salted pork. He eyed Taithun and Pixus a few feet away as he broke the cheese up into manageable portions. He took a sip from his canteen.

"Very impressive work," Taithun said, "and in so short a time, too."

"Thank you," Pixus said. "Setting up a marching encampment is something our men are trained to do."

It was clear the tour was coming to an end as they had finished near the entrance gate. Taithun gazed once again around the camp.

"What happens when you don't have walls like these?" Taithun asked.

"We build dirt walls," Pixus said, "using what we excavated from the trenches. Then we set a wooden barricade over the top of it. We got fortunate today and it saved a lot of time."

"I still don't understand why you feel the need to fortify your camp, especially here," Taithun said. "Our pioneers have cleared the city and the surrounding lands. Were there any threats out there, we would know."

"I have no doubt about that," Pixus said in a carefully neutral tone. The centurion was being quite diplomatic. "This is simply our standard practice—procedure, if you will. Since we've been underground the last few days, you've just not seen us do it."

Stiger took a bite of his cheese as Taithun glanced his way. The cheese was not terribly good, but Stiger was hungry and had felt like a snack. He chewed without much enjoyment, but it did remind him of Sarai and home.

What with the march here, his explorations and the meeting with Therik, it had been a long day. Stiger's legs ached and he was looking forward to turning in after the feast. Chewing slowly, he peered into his haversack in the hopes of avoiding conversation with Taithun and took another bite of the cheese. It really was quite terrible. The alternative was some of the salted pork. Over his years of service, he had developed an intense dislike for the stuff, so much so that Sarai's terrible cheese was preferable.

"Legate Delvaris, are you regularly in the habit of making your men work, just so they have something to do?" Taithun asked Stiger.

Stiger considered the elderly captain for a long moment as he slowly chewed. He got the sense that Taithun was not attempting to be offensive and had meant nothing by the comment. The old dwarf had asked the question without malice or sarcasm. He seemed interested in hearing what Stiger had to say. Stiger had been hoping to avoid joining the conversation.

"Busy boys don't cause trouble," Stiger said simply, quoting his old sergeant Tiro and wishing Taithun would go on his way so that he could have some peace before the feast.

"Normally I would agree with such sentiments. But in our current place, what trouble could they get into out here?" Taithun gestured around them with his arms out wide.

"Captain," Stiger said, having tired of the conversation, "you may have confidence in your pioneers. However, it has been my experience that when in strange lands you can never be too careful. These are my men and I feel it is better to be prepared."

Taithun shook his head slightly. "You have that wrong. These aren't strange lands. They belong to my people and are known to us. We are at least three hundred miles from orc lands. I might add that it would be difficult, if not impossible, to march through the impenetrable forest that surrounds this ancient city."

Stiger took a breath. He had learned there was no such thing as an impenetrable forest. Eli had taught him the truth of that.

"They are unfamiliar to us," Stiger said, after a moment's reflection. He decided to end the conversation and added a hard edge to his tone. "Captain, you are more than welcome to set up your camp however you wish, without any fortifications and defenses. I prefer to have some basic security. Not only that, it is good exercise and practice for the men."

"I've seen enough," Taithun said stiffly before turning to face Pixus. "Centurion, thank you for the tour. It was most educational."

"It has been my pleasure," Pixus said.

"Legate." The dwarf captain gave Stiger a curt nod and stepped away toward the gate.

Stiger watched Taithun as he stomped over the bridge that led out of the encampment, disappearing out into the darkness. He decided he did not much like Taithun. The dwarf had an arrogant air about him that reeked of certainty and correctness, while being blind to other alternatives.

Over his long years of service, Stiger had met many an officer like him. Stiger reflected that Theo's opinion of Taithun might have colored his.

He had not seen Theo all day. His friend had not been at the meeting either, meaning Brogan had not invited him. Stiger wondered what the dwarf had been up to. He broke off another bite of cheese and chewed. Sensing Stiger was in no mind to talk, Pixus excused himself and stepped away, leaving Stiger alone with his thoughts.

As he was taking the last bite of Sarai's cheese, Dog appeared and made his way over the bridge. One of the sentries bent over and patted the animal's head. Dog stopped briefly and licked at the hand before padding his way into the encampment.

Dog padded right up to Stiger and sat down. Facing him with unblinking eyes, tongue lolling out of the side of his mouth, Dog looked him square in the face. Stiger had never known a dog who had been able to meet his gaze and willingly hold it for a prolonged time. Usually, they looked away after a few heartbeats, as if uncomfortable. Dog was clearly different.

He was still having some difficulty believing that Dog was divine in nature. Every time he looked at the animal, he saw only a large, hairy dog. And so, he treated it as one.

"And where have you been?"

Dog gave a clipped bark, tail wagging in the dirt. He snapped his jaws.

"Hungry?"

Dog gave another bark and snapped his jaws again. Stiger chuckled and opened his haversack. He pulled out one of the wrapped chunks of salted pork. He unwrapped it and tossed it up. Dog jumped and snatched it right out of the air. He gobbled it down in a heartbeat. After the meat was gone, the animal looked back up at him expectantly.

"At least one of us enjoys salted pork," Stiger said, securing his haversack and tying it closed with a double knot.

Dog snapped his jaws again.

"That's all you're getting," Stiger said. "You'll just have to go catch something yourself."

Dog gave a soft whine.

"You could always try begging from the men," Stiger suggested. "And there was that rabbit you caught earlier. I ordered the men to share it with you."

Dog, seeming to understand, walked off toward the tents and the men.

"Excuse me, sir."

Stiger turned to find Mectillius.

"We have a tent for you, sir," the optio said, "right over there. It's not much, I am afraid. Not like your regular tent, sir."

Stiger looked where indicated. A small one-man tent stood amongst the communal tents. The side flap was open and had been tied back. There was just enough room that he would be able to stand up inside. He knew there would not be a cot. He would be sleeping on the ground, using his arms for a pillow.

"It is better than spending the night out in the open," Stiger said. "I am sure it will be fine. Thank you, Optio."

"Yes, sir." Mectillius turned to go.

Stiger glanced up at the dark sky.

"Optio?"

"Sir?"

"Have all of the sentries been posted yet?"

"Not all of them, sir," Mectillius said. "The men are still working at setting up the camp. Would you like me to put them out?"

"I would," Stiger said and then thought of something else. "For the feast, I will require an escort."

"Centurion Sabinus thought of that, sir. He has already spoken with Pixus," Mectillius said. "He has ten picked men. They are readying themselves as we speak."

"Good," Stiger said. "They will not be partaking in the feast, if you understand my meaning."

"Do you expect trouble, sir?" Mectillius asked.

"No," Stiger said. "But I don't want to take that chance."

"Yes, sir," Mectillius said. "The men will keep a clear eye. I will make sure of it."

Stiger gave a nod of thanks and Mectillius left.

He glanced down at his armor. It was dusty from the day's travels and dirty from his explorations. To say it needed some attention would be an understatement. He had no intention of going to the feast without wearing it. No matter what he thought of Therik, there was no way he planned on fully trusting an orc or, for that, matter Brogan. It bothered him that the thane had been preparing to kill Therik.

Stiger picked up his saddlebags and removed the brush and towel he used for cleaning his armor. He also had a small bag of sand, but now was not the time clean down to that level. He glanced down at his armor. It was presentable enough. He would just have to make do with a good wipe down and a little bit of scrubbing. He put the brush and towel down next to him on the stone block and then began untying the laces, loosening his armor up.

Stiger finished brushing. He blew on the metal to remove the last bit of grit that had become tucked in a groove, then leaned back and looked over his armor. It hadn't been a deep cleaning, but it was enough. Despite having only spent an hour at it, he was pleased with his work. The sky was completely dark now. The moon had begun its nightly climb into the sky. It provided just enough light to see.

All work on the camp had ceased sometime within the last half hour. Several fires had been set, both inside and outside the camp. Those fires on the outside were for the watch, to help make sure that no one approached unseen. The men sat around campfires or before their tents in small groups, eating and cleaning their kits. There was much jawing, interspersed with the occasional laugh.

Stiger looked up and glanced around. He found the sounds of the camp somehow comforting. The army had been his home for a long time, at least until he had met Sarai.

Stiger saw Sabinus make his way across the makeshift bridge and into the encampment. The centurion spotted him and made his way over. Sabinus appeared to be in a good mood.

"Good evening, sir," Sabinus said. "Lovely night."

"Been out exploring?"

"No, sir," Sabinus said and glanced off into the darkness beyond the walls. "I was inspecting the trench. Though I'd love to have a look around some tomorrow, if there is time. To think, Karus walked the streets of this city."

"I know what you mean," Stiger said. "It is kind of surreal when you think on it."

"You poked around a bit, sir," Sabinus said. "Do you think there is anything worth finding?"

"No." Stiger returned his brush and towel to the saddlebag. "Not without doing some serious digging, that is for certain. This city's been abandoned too long. It's all overgrown and ruin."

"I think you are right on that. Other than fallen stones and broken pottery shards, there is not much left." Sabinus shook his head. "One of the men digging the trench found a small silver coin about four feet down."

"A coin?"

"It was old and corroded. I had a look at it," Sabinus said. "You can't make out what it was, but I let him keep it as a memento."

"That's nice," Stiger said. "I bet he was the envy of all the men."

"I wonder how long it will take him before he melts it down or trades it for drink money." Sabinus let out a sigh. "Still, I think I would enjoy a walk before we return, just to say I've done it and had a look around."

"This city would have been something to see at its prime," Stiger said, then glanced up at Sabinus. The centurion's armor was dusty and dirty, just like his had been. "You'd better get to cleaning that. I expect the feast to begin in about an hour. At least that's what Taithun said when he stopped by. Apparently, the food isn't ready yet."

"Armor tonight, then," Sabinus said, "instead of tunics?"

"Armor," Stiger said.

"I will get right on it," Sabinus said and headed off. Stiger watched him walk away.

Father Thomas emerged from a tent wearing his armor, the beautiful sabre at his side. He walked over to Stiger.

"Ready for the feast?" the paladin asked him.

"Don't you look just all pretty," Stiger said, with a sudden grin.

"It is important to look one's best," Father Thomas said, "when attempting to spread favorable impressions of the High Father to the heathens."

"Do you think the orcs will be impressed?"

"With my armor and sword?" Father Thomas said. "Maybe."

"Last week," Stiger said, hefting his armor and setting it upon the ground, "if you'd told me I'd be dining with an orc delegation, I would have thought you crazy."

"I believe I would have said the same," Father Thomas said.

"Sir!"

The shout rang out from the front of camp. Stiger's head snapped up, as did everyone else's. He saw one of the sentries calling for Pixus, who was halfway across the camp. "Sir, something is happening!"

Armor chinking, Pixus hurried over. Stiger shared a glance with Father Thomas and then picked up his armor. Standing, he hastily shrugged back into it. Father Thomas left him and jogged after Pixus.

Stiger looked up. He could not hear what the sentry was saying to Pixus. But it did not matter. He knew without a doubt there was trouble. He began hurriedly lacing up the armor, cinching it tight as he went.

Shouts outside the encampment rang out. They sounded panicked. He reached down and grabbed the sword by the scabbard and slipped the harness on. He had left his helmet back where Misty was picketed but gave it no thought. He moved towards the gate.

Two legionaries ran into camp. Breathing heavily, they came to a stop before their centurion and gave a salute. Both men pointed in the direction of Brogan and Therik's camp, speaking rapidly.

Stiger walked over, working to finish tying off the straps to his armor. He didn't run or jog. He had long since learned to project a sense of calm, as if nothing were amiss. He did this for the benefit of the men. A panicked leader did not inspire confidence.

"Report," Stiger ordered, tone rock hard as he came up to them. Pixus, Father Thomas, and the legionaries turned to face him.

"Sir," Pixus said, "it seems a group of pioneers came running through. As they passed our boys, they shouted the word 'orc.' It's not much to go on, but these"—the centurion gestured at the legionaries who had just run into camp—"thought they saw an armed party moving in the direction of the other camps after the pioneers came through."

Stiger turned to the two men.

"That's what we saw, sir," one said. "There was a lot of them and they were moving all sneaky-like."

"Could you tell who they were?" Stiger asked.

"No, sir," the other legionary said. "They were sneaking through the trees and brush. It was hard to make them out and we wasn't going any closer, sir."

Stiger rubbed his jaw and glanced out at the forest beyond the camp. He could not see much other than trees and ruins. Stiger found he couldn't blame the two for not getting a closer look. Had they done so, they might have been killed. Instead, they had done the correct thing and reported.

"What were you two doing out there?" Stiger asked of them. Pixus had dismissed most of the men of the century to look after their kit.

"Punishment detail, sir," Pixus answered for them. "I had them gathering wood. They were the last two of my boys out, besides Mectillius's detail. I sent the optio to fetch water about half an hour ago."

"How many men did he go with?"

"Ten boys and two mules."

"This cannot be good," Father Thomas said. More muffled shouts could be heard in the distance. Stiger could not tell if they were dwarves or orcs. Whoever it was seemed alarmed.

"No, not good at all," Stiger agreed and then turned his gaze back to the two legionaries. "If you had to guess, who do you think they were?"

"I thought they were orcs, sir," said one of the men.

"And you?" Stiger asked the other.

"In the darkness, I couldn't see very clearly. I took his word for it, sir."

Stiger shared a glance with Father Thomas.

"You are thinking Brogan went back on his word to me?" Father Thomas asked. "Aren't you?"

"You have to admit it is possible," Stiger said. "Though I would not have expected such after what you said."

"I wouldn't either," Father Thomas said in an unhappy tone.

"Call the men to arms," Stiger ordered Pixus.

The shouts in the distance grew in intensity.

"To arms!" Pixus roared, turning away and moving back toward the center of the camp. "Form up! Full kit, including javelins. On me! Now!"

A moment later, a massed shout rose up from the darkness, somewhat muffled by the trees. This was followed by a sound Stiger was only too familiar with. Battle. He stepped across the bridge and out before the camp, scanning the trees. He saw nothing, but that did not mean anything.

There was another massed shout, followed by a loud clash. This one was also muffled by the trees, but it sounded farther away. Stiger heard animal-like roars mixed in with the shouting and clatter of arms. He had heard those roars before. Orcs in battle.

Stiger felt the sword's presence and interest return.

The nearest fighting seemed like it was in the direction of Brogan's camp. For all of Therik's talk, and the thane's machinations, had it been a double-cross, then? From the sound of it, Brogan, instead of Therik, was the likely target. Taithun had just left the camp and he'd not been in his armor. Had it been Brogan going back on his word to the paladin, Taithun would never have visited. He would have been with his warriors preparing to attack Therik's camp.

Stiger scanned the darkened trees, mind racing. Therik had not brought enough orcs to overwhelm Taithun's company, even if there were no defenses on the dwarven camp. Who was attacking whom? Fifth Century's camp had not been assaulted. Why? What was going on?

Glancing back on the walls of the camp, the legionaries of Fifth Century were falling in, hastily pulling on their armor and equipment. Men who already had theirs on were assisting others. Pixus and Sabinus crossed over the bridge and stepped up to Stiger. Father Thomas trailed after them, but stopped a few feet short of Stiger. The paladin's attention was fixed in the direction of the fighting.

"Your orders, sir?" Pixus asked, a hard look to his face as he tried to peer through the darkness and trees to see what was going on.

"We have seventy men on hand?" Stiger asked, as he considered sending scouts out. "Is that right?"

"Sixty-nine, sir," Pixus said. "Not counting the officers and Father Thomas."

The sounds of the fighting behind the trees grew louder. It appeared as if the dwarven camp was under serious assault, but he just wasn't sure. He had no idea what was going on, and that frustrated him.

Stiger was leaning towards it being Therik that had crossed Brogan. If so, the legionary camp could fall under attack at any moment. He felt torn. Should he take the men and go to the aid of Brogan or at the very least venture out from behind the walls? If he did go to determine what was going on, and the camp came under assault, he may not have enough men left behind to hold it. Stiger bit his lip. He could send scouts out to reconnoiter. He had no idea of the enemy's numbers or, for that matter, even who they were. But sending scouts out would take time, and if the dwarven camp was indeed under attack, such a delay might ruin any chance he had of making a difference.

Stiger met Sabinus's eyes. He saw a similar indecision in them. Sabinus clearly understood the situation. It was this shared understanding that drove Stiger to act. He glanced around their camp, knowing he had to do something. But what? And then, it hit him.

Nothing was holding them here. There was absolutely nothing worth defending other than the camp itself and their supplies. The encampment's only value was in the strength of its defense.

"We will take the entire century out," Stiger told the two officers. "I believe Brogan's camp to be under attack. We will venture out to his aid."

"And leave the camp undefended?" Sabinus asked, clearly shocked by the idea. "Are you certain, sir?"

"The only thing of value, other than the supplies we brought with us, is ourselves," Stiger told them. "We built this camp to protect ourselves and we don't have any camp followers to watch over. So there is no good reason to leave a guard. Besides, I don't think whoever is out there is here for our salted pork. Do either of you disagree with me on this?"

Sabinus shook his head.

Stiger looked between the two centurions. Pixus shook his head as well.

"All right, this is what I am thinking," Stiger said. "We don't know how many of the enemy are out there or even who the enemy is. This camp is our fallback position. It is defensible and, if need be, we can hold it through the night. We take the entire century and march in good order to the dwarven camp. If they are under attack, we render what aid we can to the dwarves, then assess the situation. I would appreciate your thoughts, gentlemen."

"It's got to be orcs, sir," Pixus said.

"I think so, too," Stiger said.

"What if there are too many of the enemy?" Pixus asked.

"We turn around and come back here posthaste," Stiger said. "I do not think that'll be the case. If there were an overwhelming body of the enemy nearby, Brogan's pioneers would have spotted it. No, this assault force must be relatively small, perhaps a few hundred at best. Questions?"

"Your plan is good enough for me, sir," Sabinus said.

"No questions from me, sir," Pixus said.

"Very good, then," Stiger said. He looked back at Pixus's century formed up inside the fort. Each man held a javelin and his shield. Helmets were on. In the firelight they looked grim, and ready for action.

The enemy is near, Rarokan said softly, and Stiger chilled. *Feed me. Together we grow stronger.*

It was orcs. He was now sure of it.

Stiger felt his anger at Therik's betrayal grow. He sensed that the sword was feeding his anger and he allowed it to build, intensify. If the opportunity came to kill Therik, he would. His hand reached down to the hilt and he felt not the normal tingle. A surge of energy flowed into his being. The darkness lightened just a bit.

Use my strength, Rarokan hissed. *Use it to make you powerful.*

"We take everyone," Stiger said. "We leave no one behind. Have your century fall in outside the fort and send a runner, if you would. I'd like Mectillius and the water party found and given a heads-up."

"Yes, sir," Pixus said and moved off, shouting orders to his men.

"This may be a very bad idea," Sabinus said, so that only the two of them heard.

"Yes, I know," Stiger said. "Leaving the safety of our fort is not ideal, especially in the darkness. However, we have no idea where we actually are." Stiger paused a moment, scanning the darkened trees around them. "The dwarves are the only way to get back to Vrell. We must go and help them. If you have a better idea, I'd love to hear it."

"No, sir, I don't." Sabinus shifted his feet uncomfortably, glanced down at the ground and then back up at Stiger. "Yours is as sound a plan as any."

"I assume," Father Thomas said, joining them, "you intend to go to the assistance of the dwarves?"

"I do," Stiger said, and paused. He stepped nearer the paladin and lowered his voice. "You sense orcs too, don't you?"

Father Thomas cast Stiger a wary look and gave a nod.

Fifth Century was already in motion, the men double-timing it through the gate and over the bridge, spilling out before the camp. They rapidly fell into a line of battle, facing the sounds of fighting.

The paladin drew his saber. "Shall we go see what good can be done?"

"Agreed," Stiger said and drew his own sword.

Chapter Nineteen

Formed up into a double line around twenty yards long, Fifth Century pushed forward through the brush, trees, and ruins of the city. The organization of the line was sorely tested. Forced to repeatedly break ranks, the men stepped over rubble and around bushes and trees. They even climbed walls and debris piles when they had to. In the darkness, lit only by a moon that kept disappearing behind the clouds, more than a few lost their footing and had to be hauled back to their feet by comrades or, worse, by their officers. There were curses and muttered oaths all around.

Pixus and Sabinus called out orders, continually shouting at the men to maintain ranks as best as possible. They coaxed, cajoled, and threatened—whatever it took to keep the line together.

"Barus," Pixus hollered, "you had best get that sorry thing you call an ass back in line, before I kick it there."

"You men," Sabinus shouted a moment later. "Come on, dress yourselves smartly or I will see you on a charge."

"Julius," Pixus shouted at a man who had fallen to his hands and knees, having become tripped up in the brush. He had even dropped his shield, an unforgiveable sin. The centurion's tone reeked of a weary exasperation. "I swear, it's not that hard. Use the tools the gods gave you, man. They would be your feet. How about staying on them for a change?"

"Sorry about that, sir," came the reply as Julius scrambled back to his feet.

"You'll be sorry when we get back to camp," Pixus called back. "Latrine duty for you."

"Yes, sir," Julius said, sounding not only embarrassed but dejected.

Marching just ahead of the century, Stiger understood there was no helping it. When he had given the order to advance, the disorder was nothing more than he had expected. His sense of uniformity and perfection were offended nonetheless. He gritted his teeth and allowed the two centurions to handle the integrity of the line while working hard not to interfere more than he had to.

Dog paced along at his side and weaved his way unerringly through the brush. Sometimes Dog came so close that he brushed Stiger's side.

"You stay with me throughout this," Stiger said to the dog, glancing downward, concerned with what was ahead. A battle was no place for a dog, even if he had been sent by a god. "You got that? Don't you go wandering off or get distracted. You hear me?"

Dog ignored him.

The fighting ahead grew louder and more chaotic with each and every step. The legionary encampment had been barely two hundred yards from where the dwarves had set up their camp. Yet in the darkness and through the brush and trees, it seemed to take forever to close the distance. The prospect of the coming fight made time seem to stretch longer.

Stiger felt the need to hurry, but understood from experience that hastening the formation's pace, especially at night, would be a mistake. On the battlefield there was strength through organization. The more organized and disciplined a force, the better the chance to accomplish objectives, whatever they were. So he restrained the urge to move the century into a faster pace, instead settling for a steady, solid advance.

The sword, however, seemed overly eager for battle, its hunger building with every passing heartbeat. Stiger could feel the mounting pressure in his chest, almost as if it were a palpable pain. The sword's urge was rapidly becoming a compulsion for him. It had also begun speaking to him again.

Wield me!

No, Stiger thought back at it.

Take me into battle. Sate me!

The mental pressure by the sword increased dramatically. Stiger felt his resolve weakening.

No, Stiger growled back to it in his mind, forcing every ounce of willpower into mentally pushing back. *Stop it. I need to command so we can get through whatever is waiting for us. Stop it!*

The hunger immediately slackened, but it was still there, hovering in the background, as was a sullen, hateful rage directed at the enemy.

I can wait.

Taking a deep breath of relief, Stiger offered up a quick prayer to the High Father, asking for help to withstand the sword's will. He commended his soul into the High Father's keeping.

"Spare as many of these fine men as possible," Stiger added in a whisper. "High Father, help me guide Fifth Century through what is to come."

Prayer complete, Stiger focused on what was ahead just through the brush. The harsh clatter of weapons, oaths, animal-like roars, and cries of agony, rage, and fear were all too plain. Then, Stiger pushed through a large bush and saw the dwarven camp. He almost missed the step.

Without any defenses, the camp was thoroughly overrun. Amidst dozens of campfires and tents, the scene before Stiger was one of chaos. Orcs were everywhere, both before and among the rows of neatly ordered white tents. Several of the tents had collapsed, and a couple were even on fire. The fighting had spread beyond the confines of the camp, disappearing into the darkness. As the moon slipped back behind a cloud, Stiger found it hard to tell, but he estimated there to be as many as four hundred orcs, maybe even five hundred.

The firelight from dozens of campfires gave the fight a strange and eerie look, even ominous. Just past the first of the campfires, shadowed lumps littered the ground. Stiger knew them to be bodies.

The orcs had apparently charged into the camp, then the fighting had moved its way deeper inside and amongst the many tents. It pained Stiger to see so many fallen dwarves. It was clear, Taithun's boys had been caught thoroughly by surprise. And yet, even so, there were a surprising number of orc bodies scattered haphazardly amongst those of the dwarves.

The dwarves fought in small groups and clusters, cut off from each other. There was no unified cohesion to the defense. It was desperate and ugly, and there appeared precious few of Brogan's escort left. Despite that, they were still giving the orcs a hard time of it.

Most of those dwarves still alive and on their feet fought in their tunics, holding only swords and shields. Very few wore their armor. Here or there, a handful had managed to don helmets. One dwarf was even completely naked, but for the long red beard that stretched down to his navel.

Stiger tore his gaze away from the fight and studied the space between the camp and Fifth Century. It was fairly open ground, with long grass and a few isolated trees. He recognized it as perfect for small formation fighting and was grateful for that. It would do nicely. Stiger came to a stop to allow the line to catch up with him.

"Not good," Father Thomas said to his side.

"You can say that again, Father," Pixus said, coming up.

Father Thomas's eyes roved the fighting to their front. "I am afraid we are in serious trouble here."

Stiger glanced over at the two and found he could not disagree with the paladin's statement. He looked for Sabinus and saw him over with the men on the right side of the formation. The terrain on that side had been rougher, more broken up. In the darkness, the senior centurion had taken it upon himself to make certain the men stayed in line and none became separated.

"Halt," Stiger called loudly. The fighting was only twenty yards to their front. He cupped his hands to his mouth. "Sabinus, on me!"

Sabinus hustled over.

Stiger knew he did not have much time. Shortly his formation would be spotted by the enemy. If he was to have any success, he had to strike before the orcs became aware of his presence and could react to it. He turned to the two officers, pointing ahead of them at the fight.

"We are going to push into the dwarven camp to try to determine if Brogan still lives. If he does, once we have the thane, we will pull back to our encampment."

"And if he's already dead, sir?" Sabinus asked. "What then?"

"In that case, we will save as many as we can," Stiger said, with a heavy breath. "So, make sure the men allow the dwarves through the line. Understand me?"

"Yes, sir," both officers said, in near unison.

"Pixus," Stiger said, "take the left flank. Sabinus, I want you on the right. As we push forward, we are bound to push the enemy out to either end of the line. Make sure none of the bastards get in around and behind us. I don't want to have to worry much about our flanks."

Both centurions nodded.

"Very good," Stiger said. "Take your positions."

"Yes, sir." Pixus moved off.

Sabinus gave another nod and stepped off, too.

"Any orders for me?" Father Thomas asked, a grim smile spreading across his face. It was plain to Stiger that the paladin had made a poor attempt to lighten the mood.

"If I were bold enough to give you orders," Stiger said wryly, "I am not certain you'd listen to me."

"There is a lot of truth in that." Father Thomas chuckled.

"In that case, do your own thing, Father," Stiger said with a sidelong glance over at the paladin.

"Oh." Father Thomas flexed the grip on his saber. "I plan to."

Stiger turned, first one way and then the other, looking, studying his line. Drawn up under the moonlight and lit by the yellowed light of the nearest fires, the men of Fifth Century looked good, solid. Stiger waited until both officers were in position on either end of the line.

It was time.

"Draw swords," Stiger called. Rarokan was already in hand. The sword didn't glow, but he felt its keen interest in what was about to occur. The hunger throbbed in the background, eager for battle. But at the same time, the feeling was muted. Stiger thought he detected a sullenness mixed with a bit of resignation. There was an understanding present, the keen mind of the wizard recognizing Stiger's need to lead, not fight directly. For the moment, it seemed willing to allow him to command.

"Ready shields," Stiger called as loud as he could. His voice cracked a little. It had been a long time since he had shouted this much. The shields came up.

Once again, he looked first left and then right. Night actions were always the most difficult. It was easy to become confused and turned around. Accidents under such circumstances were common. Stiger once had even seen friendly units fight each other. It was why most commanders avoided night actions whenever possible, and why Stiger checked and then double-checked everything again before giving the order to proceed.

Stiger took a deep breath. There was no turning back now. He was committed.

"Advance!" Stiger shouted.

The line moved forward, stepping off, and Stiger allowed it to flow around and past him. His job was to lead, not fight in the line with the men. He was taking Fifth Century into a dangerous position where they could become completely surrounded. He had to remain focused. In the darkness, even with the sword brightening his vision, the fighting was confused. It was messy, disorganized, and ugly. Dog started growling.

Stiger shifted his gaze and ran his eyes along his line of men, their backs to him now. He got the sense that they were nervous about the impending action, unsure even. It was just a feeling, but having repeatedly led men in battle, it something he had learned to notice and pay attention to.

"They can be killed like any other living thing," Stiger hollered as loud as he could to the men in an attempt to reassure them. He rapidly began pacing behind the line as it continued to steadily advance toward contact. "When you come upon an orc," Stiger shouted, "stick it good, really good. They may look big and nasty, but they die just the same." Stiger paused, took a deep breath, and shouted the next as loud as he could. "We're gonna give these animals an introduction to the legion. We're gonna show them why our enemies fear us. They're going to learn why the legionary is the biggest and meanest bastard walking the land. We're gonna show them our shield wall and the tips of our swords! Can you hear me, you bastards?"

The men gave a tremendous shout, and for a moment, just a moment, it drowned out the sound of the fighting across the dwarven camp. The combatants, both friend and foe, looked around in surprise. The dwarves gave up an impassioned shout of elation at the sight of the advancing legion line.

The orcs, stunned at the appearance of Stiger's formation, at first appeared to hesitate. It cost them dearly, as the dwarves tore into them with a renewed and desperate fury. The hesitation lasted only for a moment. The orcs, greatly outnumbering their enemy, turned back to the task at hand, slaughtering the disorganized and unarmored dwarves. It was as if they had collectively decided to ignore the threat of Fifth Century bearing down on them.

Stiger watched it all dispassionately. Any anxiety he had felt moments before was gone, vanished. In its place was a cool resolve. He was focused on the task at hand—and that was killing. The distance closed from ten yards to five, and then the shield wall slammed into the first of the orcs. Shields bashed violently forward at the enemy. Swords jabbed or punched outward. Stiger saw the first orc fall, and then another. The advance continued over their bodies.

An orc came running out of the darkness, leaping over a campfire. He hurled himself bodily into the line. The legionary receiving him saw the charge coming, braced himself for it, and smashed back with his shield at the very moment the orc reached the line. There was a deep, hollow thump and Stiger saw the legionary's shield flex slightly with the impact, then spring back. It was as if the orc had run headlong into a stone wall. The orc went down hard. He did not rise, and a moment later the line advanced over him.

To his left, the shield wall parted and admitted a dwarf who was bleeding from half a dozen cuts. Exhausted, chest heaving mightily, the dwarf fell to the ground and dropped his blood-coated sword. Stiger met the eyes of the injured warrior. The dwarf held out a hand imploringly, silently asking for help. Stiger shook his head slightly and turned his attention back to the fight as he stepped past. He had to stay focused on the fight.

The line parted again, and more dwarves were passed through. These were uninjured, but just as spent.

"Help your wounded," Stiger called to one of them and pointed at the injured dwarf lying helplessly on the ground some five yards behind. One of the dwarves gave a nod of understanding and moved over to render what assistance he could.

Stiger scanned the battlefield as the century continued to drive deeper into the fight. The racket to his front increased in volume as they met more resistance. The orcs began throwing themselves not only against dwarves, but also at the legionary shield wall.

The enemy carried a mixture of swords, spears, and war hammers. They were large and intimidating. However, the orcs wore only a simple studded black leather chest armor with pants. It could only be described as light armor, the sort of lightweight protection that scouts would wear. They carried no shields. For the moment, against the better-equipped, trained, and disciplined heavy infantry of the legion, it was an unfair contest, even considering their superior numbers.

Stiger swung his gaze from left to right, taking in all of the action as the Fifth drove deeper into the dwarven encampment. His line, twenty yards in length, did not extend the width of the fight, which had spread out beyond the confines of the dwarven camp. The farther Stiger pushed forward, the more orcs they passed by who would be able to get around on either side of his line. This included dwarves as well, who were struggling for survival. It ultimately meant that the deeper he pushed forward, the more dangerous it would become for the Fifth. It was not an acceptable situation.

Stiger glanced around, understanding he had a problem that would compound itself with every step forward. To the right, an orc attacked the man at the very end of the line in the second rank. The legionary saw it coming and turned, raising his shield. He blocked the attack and then countered, jabbing outward with his short sword. The strike took the orc hard in the belly. The legionary pulled his sword back, opening up the creature's stomach. The orc fell on its back, screaming in agony as it held its destroyed stomach with both hands. Without hesitation, the legionary stabbed a powerful blow downward, killing it. The orc twitched a couple times and went still.

Sabinus clearly saw what had occurred. Stiger was pleased to see the centurion take the initiative and immediately order men in the second rank on his end of the line to form a flank guard of sorts. Sabinus formed a new line of ten men, almost at a ninety-degree angle to the main line, which faced forward and continued the advance, making the formation look more L-shaped.

Father Thomas apparently had also seen what had occurred on Sabinus's side of the line. Without a word, the paladin left Stiger and joined the right flank's action. Stiger followed Father Thomas's progress along the line. As the paladin arrived, an orc approached, attempting to get behind Sabinus's new flanking line.

Father Thomas placed himself in the orc's path along the extreme flank. The creature pointed a large metal hammer at the paladin, said something, and then charged. Saber in hand, Father Thomas calmly stood his ground. The orc raised its hammer above its head to strike. The paladin just stood there, as if scared into immobility. He did not even crouch or cringe. Stiger could hear the creature's triumphant shout of victory over its opponent.

The orc brought the hammer down in a crushing blow that would surely kill Father Thomas. At the last minute, the paladin nimbly dodged aside and around the creature. The saber flashed from the light of a nearby fire as it slashed outward toward the creature's exposed belly. The orc stumbled onward a few steps, then crashed to the ground, where it lay still and unmoving.

Satisfied the right flank was in good hands, Stiger glanced to the left side. Pixus had not yet set a flank guard, as the enemy had not tested his flank. Stiger, unwilling to give them the opportunity, stepped forward and tapped a man on the shoulder in the second rank. As he did so, the line to his left broke open to move around a campfire. Once past the campfire, the line closed up again. Stiger, ten feet away, could feel the fire's heat.

"Sir?" the legionary asked.

"Tell Centurion Pixus," Stiger hollered to be heard over the battering of shields and clash of arms, "to detail men to protect his side of the flank. I don't want any of the enemy getting in around and behind us. Understand me?"

The legionary gave a nod. He was young and his eyes were a little wild. They darted nervously around. Stiger chalked that up to facing orcs for the first time. It was even possible this was the boy's first fight.

"Repeat it to me," Stiger ordered, adding steel to his voice. He knew the effect it would have. The eyes of the young legionary widened. It was better the boy fear his own officers more than the enemy. "Speak up! I want to hear what you will tell your centurion."

"Yes sir." The legionary stiffened almost to a position of attention. "Centurion Pixus is to form a flank guard so the enemy does not get around behind us on his side of the line. Is that right, sir?"

"You got it, son," Stiger said, "and pass along my compliments to your centurion as well, will you?"

"Yes, sir." The legionary gave a hasty salute and dashed off.

Stiger looked up over the ranks at the fighting. He saw a tight knot of dwarves being heavily pressed, just twenty yards ahead. One of them held the thane's standard. It waved about wildly in the air as the dwarf who was holding it used the sharpened end as a long spear. Over the shoulders of his comrades, he was stabbing the vicious weapon at the enemy.

Stiger studied the knot of defenders. The dwarves were clustered tightly around the standard-bearer. They were fanatically defending, giving up ground grudgingly. They were not quite surrounded, but Stiger could see it was only a matter of time 'til they were. He hoped they were protecting more than just the standard, but their thane as well.

Pierced through the chest by a heavy blade, one of the defenders fell. Another dwarf took a hammer to the face, eliciting a sickening spray of blood that spattered across his fellows. So tight was the press around the knot that the deceased dwarf was held upward.

The orc that had killed the dwarf gave a roar of irritation, reached forth, gripped the dead dwarf's tunic, and threw him bodily aside, knocking several of his own over in the process. Free to strike at the next dwarf, he raised his hammer to attack, but one of the defenders holding a shield stepped forward and slashed outward with an axe, cutting the orc deeply in the thigh.

The orc screamed in pain and fell backward, disappearing beneath the crowd of orcs behind him. Eager to get at the dwarves, the mass of orcs gave no thought to their wounded. Stiger had seen this before. He understood that any unfortunate enough to become wounded were likely being trampled to death by their own side.

As Fifth Century drew closer, Stiger finally saw Brogan in the midst of the knot of dwarves, fighting alongside his warriors. Stiger gave a thankful breath of relief at the sight of the thane. There was no sign of Jorthan. Wearing only a blood-spattered tunic, carrying a shield and sword, the thane was calling out battle cries and oaths as he fought.

Brogan's long beard swung about as he worked his sword and shield, blocking blows aimed to kill him while looking for an opportunity to strike. In the blink of an eye, the thane laid open an orc's belly. He screamed out his exultation before jamming his sword into another. He then brought his shield up and stepped back as the knot of defenders fell backward several steps with him.

A dwarf to Brogan's left fell, and a heartbeat later another to his right went down. Stiger had seen enough.

He understood there was no time to waste. Brogan and his defenders would not last much longer.

As the mass of the enemy before the shield wall compressed, Stiger's front rank had slowed its advance. The legionaries were now struggling for each step forward. The time had come to bring some order to the killing. He would make it more efficient—more of a killing machine.

"Lock shields," Stiger hollered. "Close order, now! Tighten up that line. Lock those shields."

The shields thunked together in a ragged clatter.

"Prepare to push," Stiger called to the left and then repeated himself to the right. He waited a five count to give the men time to ready themselves.

"Push!"

Together, the legionaries shoved forward, throwing their shoulders into their shields, and took the prescribed half step. The sudden advance forcibly pushed the orcs before them. Shields scraped aside and swords jabbed outward. There were cries of pain and agony. The shields closed up again.

"Push!"

Another half step and the shield wall scraped aside. Again, there were screams. The shields closed up.

A loud clatter to the left mixed in with cries and screams snapped Stiger's head around. He saw that Pixus had ordered a javelin toss from the second rank along his side of the line. It had been aimed at a group of orcs attempting to flank the formation. The men in the second rank had been holding the first rank's javelins. Pixus called for a second toss. They pulled their arms back, aimed, and released. The javelins arced up into the air and slammed down amongst the group of orcs. From the screams and scattered sounds of impact, he knew it had been a successful toss. The second toss broke the group, and they disappeared into the darkness, undoubtedly looking for easier game to tackle.

Stiger was gratified to see Pixus had gotten his message and, like Sabinus, had set a second line to cover the formation's left flank. Satisfied that all was well in hand there, he turned back to the line and the fight to his front. The killing machine needed to continue its advance.

"Push!" Stiger yelled.

The line advanced, and once again, after the half step, shields parted. Swords punched out. There were more screams as the legionaries stepped over dead and wounded orcs.

"Push!"

Relentless, the advance continued, as Stiger knew it would.

To the left side of the line Stiger saw a wounded orc who had fallen and been passed over by the first rank reach out and grab at the back of a legionary's leg, causing the line in that spot to the buckle. A legionary in the second rank stabbed downward with his javelin. The orc released the leg and grabbed at the javelin, which had pierced its belly. Another javelin darted downward into its throat, killing it. From that point onward, any orc the front rank passed over, whether dead or alive, received a poke from a short sword or javelin in the second rank.

The first of the men went down. An orc wielding a spear had reached over the shield wall and thrust downward, taking the man through the neck. Like a felled tree, the legionary stiffened and then toppled backwards, taking the spear with him.

The man directly behind in the second rank dropped his javelin and, drawing his sword, took the vacant place in the first rank, bringing his shield up as he came on. He blocked a blow with his shield and stepped into place. The legionary did not miss a beat, as he jabbed outward with his short sword, taking an orc in the arm.

Another man on Sabinus's end of the line went down. Still the relentless advance continued, the machine chewing up the enemy before it. Stiger called out one push after another and then the shield wall parted. The legionaries of the first rank admitted Brogan and ten of his weary defenders, including the standard-bearer, who was badly injured. Stiger was relieved to see that Theo was one of those who had been fighting with the thane. His friend appeared unhurt. He was covered in orc blood, his sword fairly dripping with it.

"I thought you'd never get here." Theo flashed a relieved grin. He gave Stiger a wink as he made his way over to Brogan. The thane had planted the tip of his sword in the ground and was leaning on the hilt. He looked exhausted.

"I will work on my timing," Stiger called back to Theo.

"Do that, because yours is terrible." Theo paused. "On second thought, it's not so bad."

That brought out a chuckle from Stiger.

The shield wall parted in other places and dwarves were admitted through. Without Stiger having to ask, Brogan ordered those uninjured of his dwarves to the flanks. There they helped to provide security.

Stiger called several more pushes, hoping to shove the orcs back to the point where he might encourage them to temporarily disengage. That would allow him room to maneuver.

Abruptly, the sounds of fighting to the immediate front of the line died down.

Apparently understanding that they were, for the moment, outmatched by the armored killing machine of

Fifth Century, the orcs before his line had begun backing away. Stiger was certain that they had never seen anything like the legionary century. The thought of such killing efficiency made him proud. Pixus had trained his men well.

"Halt," Stiger hollered, bringing the advance to a stop. The legionaries in the front rank, breathing heavily, brought their shields up defensively. They watched the enemy but went no farther.

"What are you doing?" Brogan had come up to Stiger. Theo was with him. The thane had a small cut on his brow. It bled profusely, running down his face and onto his beard. He was also splattered with orc blood and greenish bits of gore. Thin strips of skin hung from the thane's sword. "Why are you stopping? We must kill them all."

Stiger studied the fighting around the century. They were still badly outnumbered, even with the surviving dwarves, many of whom had made it through to the safety of the century. Of those, Stiger estimated there were at least forty.

Out of the near two hundred Taithun had marched in with, forty was a paltry number. Stiger was reminded of his time as a lieutenant, when his captain had led a mad dash out into a field after a broken company of spearmen. Exposed and in open ground with no cover, much of the Seventh Company had been run down by enemy cavalry, who, until the moment of the charge, had approached unseen. The thought of such slaughter born of thoughtlessness made him angry.

Instead of responding to Brogan, Stiger's eyes swept the battlefield. He came to the conclusion he had underestimated the number of orcs. There were more than five hundred, and that was likely a conservative estimate. Many of the enemy had stopped fighting and were busy looting bodies, tents, and the supply wagons. Fights had even broken out amongst them over loot.

Outside of the bubble of order he had created, there were still a handful of dwarves who remained cut off. They were fighting desperately for their lives. He understood that when the fighting around the century slowly died out, as it most certainly would, the orcs would turn on his legionaries. Then, the Fifth would be in serious trouble. Seventy legionaries against several hundred of the enemy, no matter how well-armored, were not good odds.

The orcs were now giving the century a wide berth. Stiger understood their hesitation was only temporary. All it would take was someone on the other side with authority to take control, establishing some semblance of order, and the enemy would be on him. However, the unwillingness of the orcs to press him created the opportunity he had desired.

"It's done here," Stiger said, turning back to the thane.

"How can you say that?" Brogan demanded of Stiger.

It was clear the thane's heat was up. Brogan wiped blood from the cut on his forehead out of his eyes. If it had been his men out there, Stiger wouldn't want to leave either. Still, Stiger knew his duty and had to impress that upon Brogan.

"Look around," Stiger said, pointing with his sword. He felt his anger mounting. "They outnumber us, and there may be more out there in the darkness we don't know about. We must pull back to my encampment. It is the only thing to do. There, with its defenses, we stand a chance to hold until morning."

"No," Brogan yelled back at him. "We have to punish them for this betrayal! We have to make Therik pay!"

"Brogan," Theo said and placed a hand on the thane's arm. "He's right. It is over. Listen to the legate. We've lost here."

"Never." Brogan shook Theo off and advanced on Stiger. "Now is the time to hit them back!"

"No," Stiger said.

Brogan raised his sword, as if he were working himself up to strike.

Ears back, with teeth bared, Dog growled and placed himself directly between Stiger and the thane. Brogan was clearly beyond caring.

Brogan's sheer pig-headedness enraged Stiger. He had lost good men coming to Brogan's rescue and with every moment they delayed in withdrawing, even more were put at risk. The anger shifted over to a full-blown rage, and he took a step nearer the thane. Rarokan fed him power and Stiger enjoyed the feeling of it. He even welcomed it. Stiger reached out and grabbed Brogan's tunic with a fist, twisting it, as he pulled him closer. The move appeared to surprise Brogan, and the thane's sword lowered.

"We must pull back if we are to have a chance for survival," Stiger yelled at the thane and shook him slightly. "I lost good men rescuing you. Don't let their sacrifice go to waste. It is time to withdraw."

The thane blinked, and Stiger saw his eyes shift away from him to Rarokan. The sword had begun glowing a bright, fiery blue, small tongues of flame licking at the air. Stiger released the thane and took a step back, abruptly realizing he had gone too far. He forcibly calmed himself, controlling his breathing, pushing back on the flow of power from Rarokan. The sword's fire slackened, but the blade still glowed ever so slightly. The power of Rarokan receded from whence it had come.

"It's over, Brogan," Theo said, tugging on Brogan's shoulder. "We must pull back."

Brogan tore his gaze from Stiger's blade to Theo and then looked around. His shoulders slumped, seeming to deflate. He glanced back over at Stiger, giving a miserable nod.

"You are right," the thane said in a low tone. "It is time to give up the field."

Satisfied the thane had seen reason, Stiger glanced around as Brogan moved off toward the rear of the formation. It was indeed time to withdraw, and it needed to happen quickly.

"Second rank," Stiger hollered, "about face."

The second rank neatly spun around.

"Thoggle told Aleric's company your sword was magic," Theo said. "He warned us never to try to take it or touch it, said it was dangerous. Until now, I never fully believed it."

"Even after it burned Geligg?" Stiger asked, sparing his friend an unhappy look.

"Even then," Theo said with a shrug. "I didn't see it actually burn him, so I guess it made it harder for me to believe ... if you know what I mean."

The noise of the fight had diminished some, especially with the orcs no longer challenging the century. He looked over toward the left flank and then the right. Sabinus and Pixus both saw what he was doing and rearranged the flank guard to help cover the formation as it withdrew.

"Second rank, advance five paces," Stiger ordered. "First rank, prepare to fall back in good order."

Stiger saw Sabinus had detailed several men to help the wounded dwarves and legionaries move back toward the encampment. Brogan had called on those dwarves who were either walking wounded or had not yet joined the flank guard to assist the injured as well. They already had a good head start on the century, something Stiger was grateful for.

"Thoggle should have warned us that it wasn't just the sword that was dangerous," Theo said, and then glanced over at the thane. "I have a feeling Brogan knows that now, too. I would—"

"Mind if we save this for later?" Stiger could not believe his friend wanted to have this conversation now. "I need to get us out of here and back to my camp before those buggers out there turn on us."

Theo gave an understanding nod. "Of course."

Relieved, Stiger turned back to studying the battlefield. Watching the disorganized enemy and the fight beyond the bubble of the Fifth, Stiger gave the order for the formation to move. They began a slow, steady withdrawal from the battlefield, one rank marching forward and the other stepping backward, shields facing the enemy. Several dwarves caught outside the formation realized what was happening. They made a desperate dash for the century. Two made it to safety. Five others were cut down well short.

The rage he had felt toward Brogan glowed white hot again. This had been a senseless slaughter. Had Taithun bothered to fortify his camp, the dwarves might have stood a chance. Now, such thoughtlessness had placed Stiger and Fifth Century in serious jeopardy, for Stiger expected the enemy to come for him next.

Watching the orcs closely, Stiger stepped with the formation as it moved steadily backward. In the darkness behind him, those cut off fought on. It killed him inside to leave those dwarves to die, but there was simply no choice. The enemy had superior numbers. He could not remain here or make a futile attempt to rescue them, losing even more than he would likely save.

The formation moved back through the trees and brush. The dwarven camp disappeared from view. Even as it did, the fighting died down and, a moment later, ceased in its entirety.

"First rank," Stiger called, "about face."

He waited for his order to be executed. All of the legionaries of the Fifth were now facing in the same direction. It was time to move with haste.

"On the double," Stiger called. "March."

The formation began moving rapidly back through the trees and brush, armor chinking as it crashed forward toward the safety of the legionary encampment. There was no pursuit. That didn't surprise Stiger. The orcs were disorganized and were now likely more interested in looting the dead and the camp behind them, searching for spoils.

Mectillius and the water detail had returned and were waiting for them when they arrived back at the camp. Stiger was pleased to see the optio and his men alive and well. It appeared Mectillius was just as relieved to see them.

Stiger handed command back to Pixus and instructed the centurion to bring his century back within the safety of the camp. Within a short time, Pixus's men were streaming over the bridged trench and through the entrance. Stiger waited until the last of the men and dwarves made their way through before stepping up to the bridge. He was left with Brogan, Theo, and Father Thomas. Sabinus had just followed after the men.

Dog sat down by Stiger's side. He glanced down at the animal. Dog's ears were up and his intense eyes scanned the darkness in the direction they had just come.

Now that he reflected on it, Stiger was surprised that Dog had stayed by his side throughout the entire fight. Dog abruptly glanced upward at him, almost as if he were reading Stiger's mind. He got the sense that the animal was disappointed not to have been set free to go after the enemy.

Stiger sucked in a breath. There was a hunger in those eyes that Stiger found akin to Rarokan's.

"You too?" Stiger asked him, letting the breath out.

Dog did not answer. After a moment, the dog looked away, returning to scanning the darkness.

"I suppose a thank you is an order," Brogan said, dragging Stiger's attention away from Dog. The thane's tone was grudging and somewhat subdued. "Thank you."

Stiger felt the anger that had burned in his breast slowly begin die down. It left him feeling weary and slightly ill at the thought of what had just occurred. So many dwarves had needlessly died. He wondered how many men he had lost.

"You would've done the same for us," Stiger said. "What of Jorthan? I've not seen him."

Brogan shook his head, and a look of grief overcame him.

"And Taithun?"

Again, Brogan shook his head. "He was one of the first to fall." The thane cleared his throat. "Both had been with me for many years. I shall miss them dearly."

"I'm sorry for your loss," Father Thomas said with sadness, laying a comforting hand upon the thane's shoulder. "Over the past few weeks, I am proud to say I got to know Jorthan well. He had a good soul. I will pray for their spirits as they cross over to the other side."

"Though he was no warrior," Brogan said, "in the end, Jorthan picked up a sword and stood with the rest of us. He earned himself great legend." He gave a heavy sigh. "It came at the cost of his life."

The thane fell silent.

"Before we left," Stiger said, "Thoggle told me Jorthan had a way to summon him. If things went balls up, which I believe we can all safely agree they have, Jorthan was to call on the wizard for aid. Now that he is gone, can you summon the wizard? I would think we could use his help about now."

Brogan was silent for a long moment, and Stiger's heart plummeted. He knew the answer even before Brogan spoke.

"I have no way of calling upon Thoggle." Brogan heaved a great sigh. "Sadly, any such means would have died with Jorthan."

It was as Stiger had thought. Rubbing his jaw, he turned to the paladin.

"And you, can you reach Thoggle?"

"No," Father Thomas said. "I cannot."

"That is downright disappointing," Theo said, which Stiger thought was an incredible understatement.

A victory cheer went up in the direction of the dwarven camp. It was accompanied by individual roars. It almost sounded to Stiger as if someone was giving a speech and the orcs were responding to it. Was it their king? Was Therik basking in his victory over the dwarves? Was he even now working them up into a frenzy for a final assault on the legionary encampment? It was a sobering thought and one that pricked at Stiger's anger. Despite the sword telling him otherwise, he had felt he could trust the king. It had been a mistake. Hopefully, it would not be his last.

"I guess," Stiger said, feeling terribly unhappy, "we are on our own."

No one said anything to that.

Taking a deep breath, he glanced once more in the direction of the enemy, concealed by the darkness and brush. He turned and walked over the planks that bridged the trench into the camp. He sensed the others following, as well as Dog.

Pixus had men standing by, waiting for them. Once everyone was inside the camp, they quickly took in the planks. A rough wooden gate made of thick logs was manhandled into place. Landing with a heavy thud, it neatly blocked and sealed off the entrance. The thud had the sound of finality to it.

He turned around, studying the walls of the encampment. They looked sturdy enough. The camp was well-fortified. The enemy would have a hard time of it. Stiger was pleased to see the men had already been dispersed to each wall. They waited in anticipation of the assault that Stiger was certain would shortly come. It was only a matter of time until the orcs got organized.

He was about to say something to Brogan, then paused. In the distance, there was the sudden clash of arms. The sound of the fighting continued and grew, which meant it was not stragglers. From out in the darkness there were shouts.

Sabinus came over to Stiger. "That sounds as if it is coming from the orc camp."

"It must be some of Hogan's boys," Brogan said bitterly and turned to face Stiger, shooting a glance toward Father Thomas. "After you both talked me out of my plans for Therik, I dispersed his pioneers. They were to scout outward, beyond the city." Brogan looked back out into the darkness. "As his pioneers were dispersing, Hogan must have stumbled upon the enemy, for he sent us warning, though it only arrived just moments before the orcs did." Brogan fell silent as they listened to the distant fighting.

"It seems Hogan was able to call some of his boys back together," Theo said. "It is the only explanation. They must be hitting Therik now."

Stiger agreed with that assessment.

"I hope he hurts them something good," Brogan said.

Stiger looked at Brogan and discarded what he had intended to say. He turned and saw Pixus waiting.

"Your orders, sir?"

"Check over your men," Stiger said. "Make sure any wounds are tended to. You and I both know there are those who get injured but don't become aware of it until later. Have everyone look themselves over." He paused. "Also, while the enemy gives us the time, see that your men get watered and fed."

"Yes, sir." Pixus saluted and left.

The fighting in the distance had died off. No longer could they hear the clash of arms.

"What now?" Brogan asked in a whisper as he stared out into the darkness beyond the walls. Stiger got the sense that the thane had meant that for himself alone, but Stiger decided to answer him anyway.

"Now we wait for their attack," Stiger said. "We bleed them good and hurt the enemy as much as possible. When dawn comes, we will see if we can break out and make it to the safety of the tunnels. Then your people can guide us back."

Brogan turned to him, and his expression for a moment hardened, but then the thane of the dwarves gave a reluctant nod of acceptance.

Stiger turned away. His mouth was terribly dry from shouting. He also had a foul taste. He stepped over to the stump where he had left his canteen and saddlebags. Unstopping the canteen, he sat down on the stump and took a long drink.

Chapter Twenty

"It's too quiet, sir," Sabinus said in a hushed tone so that only Stiger could hear. The nearest of the men was only feet away. The centurion was peering out into the night, his hand resting absently on the hilt of his sword. "Just too bloody quiet."

Stiger scanned the darkness beyond the wall he was leaning upon. He saw nothing other than the watch fires, which had been set just past the lip of the outer trench. The fires had died down for the most part and now barely provided any useful light. They were a dismal and somewhat disheartening sight.

Stiger took a deep breath and sucked in some of the crisp air. A slight breeze rustled the leaves of the nearest trees. An owl hooted in the distance, while insects buzzed or chirped loudly away. He glanced upward. Stars set against a blackened sky poked out from around the scattered clouds that slid slowly by high overhead. The moon had disappeared behind one large cloud. Its outline could be seen straight through the cloud. Another breeze blew by, this one a little stronger. It seemed very much a peaceful night. But it wasn't.

Eying one of the dying fires, Stiger let out an unhappy breath. Sabinus had been on him to send parties out to build up the watch fires. He had demurred. Sending men over the wall was not only risky, it was a bad idea. They had few enough defenders as it was. He could not afford to lose the very men he would need to hold the wall, for Stiger believed the enemy was surely out there, concealed in the darkness. The question was, where? And more importantly, what were they up to?

To his left and right, legionaries from Fifth Century manned the walls, as did a handful of dwarves. They had returned from rescuing Brogan at least two hours before. Once it had become clear that the enemy would not immediately test him, Stiger had stood down half of the century from the walls. Those men were now busy working, while the rest kept a keen eye staring out into the night.

Stiger had already walked the walls himself. To keep from unsettling the men, he had intentionally positioned himself by the gate. Here he stood with Sabinus by his side, as if he had not a concern in the world.

He looked over the nearest sentry and was pleased with what he saw. The man's gaze was fixed outward, scanning the darkness for any hint of the enemy. The legionary was holding his javelin's neck, the butt of the fearsome weapon resting in the dirt at his feet. The man's shield had been leaned against the wall, ready when needed.

Though he was a man out of his time, Stiger could easily relate to Pixus's men, especially after the fight. Soldiers were soldiers, no matter the time period. Even better, these men were legionaries. Their armor was of a different design, one that was more archaic, in that the cuirass was made out of chain mail, instead of steel segmented plates. It was still more than familiar to him, especially since many of the allied auxiliary cohorts Stiger had worked with over the years favored the old-style chain mail. The helmet, though incredibly similar, was more functional and less ornate than those used in Stiger's time.

The men of Fifth Century were professional soldiers and Stiger felt comfortable amongst them. For the most part they used many of the same weapons and tactics that his own men had used three hundred years in the future. The shields and short swords were nearly identical, which meant their tactics were similar to those Stiger was familiar with.

One of the nearby men shifted his javelin from one hand to the other. Yet another difference was that the legions in this time still used the traditional heavier weapon, which Stiger preferred over the short spear. In the old tongue, this weapon was called the pilum.

Stiger glanced around again. Yes, he felt as comfortable leading these men into battle as he had his own. The legions, whether in the past or future, were formidable fighting machines. They were filled with disciplined, skilled, and professional soldiers. Out of time or not, just by being amongst them, Stiger almost felt as if he were home again.

That thought caused him some concern. Sarai's home had become his and he had given up this life, putting his time as a soldier behind him. Instead, Stiger had been unexpectedly drawn in even deeper. He now found himself more accepting of Delvaris's fate as his own. Stiger rubbed the back of his neck. If a return to the legion meant he could help keep Sarai safe, he would willingly pick up Delvaris's mantle and wear it proudly. And yet, at the same time he felt as if the more he came to terms with this fate, the further from Sarai he would be driven. Stiger wasn't sure he was prepared to sacrifice Sarai for destiny. Was it really worth it?

Though he wanted to fight and rail against the injustice, Stiger suspected it was.

A loud sneeze to his right shook him from his thoughts. In the near silence, it seemed like a shout. He glanced over and saw a dwarf wiping at his bulbous nose with a handkerchief. The dwarf stood next to a legionary, who was shaking his head with dismay. The dwarf gave an apologetic shrug.

Forty-eight of Brogan's dwarves had survived the assault on their camp by the orcs. Of these, four had come in after the century had returned to the safety of the encampment. The rest of Brogan's escort was gone. Stiger had found it more than a little disheartening to see these once proud dwarves humbled in defeat. Despite his dislike for Taithun and irritation with Brogan, they were his allies. He needed them, no matter how unreliable the dwarves in this time were proving to be. Should they survive the next few hours, Stiger wondered if Brogan would learn anything from what had occurred here in this dead city.

"Bloody dwarves," Sabinus muttered, before turning his gaze back out into the darkness. "Well, it *was* quiet."

"They're out there," Stiger said in a low, steady tone, without glancing over at Sabinus. "Don't you doubt that. They are out there."

The chinking of armor caused Stiger and Sabinus to turn. Pixus was moving steadily along the wall. He stopped just feet from them to speak quietly to several men. The centurion's voice was a barely whisper. Stiger could not make out what was said. Pixus pointed at a javelin that had been set against the wall, then at one of the legionaries, tapping the man on the chest. He jerked a thumb at Stiger. The legionary hastily snatched it up and stood to attention. Pixus said something further and then, wearing a hard, irritated expression, moved on. Stiger almost chuckled, for he knew the hard-as-nails centurion act was all for the benefit of the men. Pixus was certainly as anxious and unsettled as the rest of them. He, like the other officers, wouldn't permit the men to see his true feelings.

"A lovely evening," Stiger said to Pixus, loud enough for the nearest man to hear.

"That it is, sir," Pixus said. The centurion sucked in a deep breath and let it out slowly. "By the seven levels, I wish every night was as fine as this one."

In the distance, thunder rumbled.

"Sounds as if the weather's gonna improve on this night as well," Sabinus added with a chuckle.

"I hope it does, for it will make any assault on our walls just that much more difficult. We had a nice little fight, sir," Pixus said in a confident manner. "We gave those savages a solid thrashing. It was the beating they didn't want but deserved." He gave a dramatic sigh. "I expect that when they get off their asses for a go of it, we will give them another good whipping." Pixus bounced lightly on his toes. "Yes, sir, a very fine evening indeed."

That brought a slight smile to Stiger's face. He had to struggle to conceal it as the closest of the men glanced over. Pixus was a man he could like.

The centurion spared a quick glance around him and then drew nearer. He lowered his voice a bit. The show was clearly over. It was time for business.

"I've got the wounded tended to, sir," Pixus said. "Father Thomas helped with the sewing and the bandaging of those more grievously injured."

"He did not heal any of the men?" Stiger was surprised by that.

"No, sir." Pixus gave a slight scowl as he placed his hands upon his hips. "I asked about that. He said now was not the time. I then asked when would be the right time, and he said he did not know."

"I see," Stiger said, thinking on the effort it took for the paladin to heal serious wounds. There always seemed to be a cost for such miracles. "I am certain he knows his business better than we do."

"Yes, sir," Pixus said, the scowl slipping from his face with some apparent effort. Stiger got the sense the centurion was hopping mad about the paladin refusing to heal his men. Stiger could understand that.

"All right, let me have the bad news," Stiger said. If Father Thomas felt this wasn't the time for healing, he saw no need to grouse about it further. He turned the focus on the subject he had been dreading. "How many casualties did we take?"

"Ten of the dwarves are injured," Pixus said. "Their wounds range from minor to serious. Of those, two aren't ambulatory, nor will they be anytime soon."

"And of our boys?" Stiger asked, knowing that when it came time for the century to move, the wounded were sure to slow them down.

"Six walking wounded, four non-ambulatory, sir," Pixus answered. "All four have serious leg wounds." Pixus ran a hand through his short-cropped hair and shook his head slightly. "One I expect will not survive the night. Merax is a good man, a veteran of twenty-two years, sir."

"Not Merax," Sabinus said and turned to Stiger. "He has a woman and daughter amongst the followers. Cutest little thing you ever saw." Sabinus shook his head sadly. "Merax isn't too bright, but he's a good soul, and as steady as they come, sir."

"Fortuna can be a cruel mistress," Stiger said, now fully understanding the centurion's irritation with Father Thomas.

"She can be a right bitch, sir," Pixus agreed. "He was due to muster out next year."

"That's unfortunate," Stiger said. "How many did we lose?"

"I saw four go down," Pixus said. "Before we withdrew, I or Mectillius made sure they were finished. There was no time to recover their remains." Pixus fell silent for a heartbeat. "After a count, which I did myself, I have two additional missing."

"Six then," Stiger said.

Pixus gave a grim nod.

Stiger swung his gaze out into the darkness and tapped the top of the wall lightly with his fist. It was slowly crumbling with age. Gods, Stiger thought, losing even one man was costly. And yet, six was not too terrible a number. In truth, when he had seen the dwarven camp overrun, he had expected the butcher's price to be even higher. They had gotten lucky.

Yet men had given their lives, and it pained him no less. That it was necessary never made it any easier. Stiger rubbed his jaw and glanced around the interior of the camp. He could not afford to dwell upon those unfortunate souls. He had the heavy responsibility of looking out for the living. They were relying upon him to lead them out of this mess that the dwarves had gotten them all into. Worse, Stiger wasn't even sure he would be able to do it. He was fairly certain there would be a steep cost for whatever was to come.

Stiger was silent for a few moments. "We shall have a memorial service for the fallen later. When we've returned to the legion, we will see to honoring the dead."

"Yes, sir," Pixus said. "I had expected as much."

Stiger considered his next words. Sabinus and Pixus waited patiently.

"I want you to rig litters for the mules," Stiger said. "Those unable to walk will be coming with us. I do not intend upon leaving anyone behind."

"I've already given the order for that, sir," Pixus said and gestured vaguely behind himself at the other end of the camp, where the horses and mules were picketed. "The litters are ready, sir, and hitched."

"Very good," Stiger said, well pleased with the centurion's initiative. Pixus was, as Sabinus had vouched, a first-rate officer. Should Pixus survive his term of service with Fifth Century, he was the kind of man who would likely see himself ultimately promoted to command of First Cohort or even at some point achieve camp prefect, a rank all centurions strove for and coveted. First, however, he needed to survive, and being an officer of the legion was by no means a safe position. Casualties amongst the officer corps always ran high. Officers were expected to set the example and lead from the front.

"And the loading of the mules?" Stiger asked.

"As you ordered, sir, they are being loaded with food and what water we have on hand. Mectillius returned with enough water for two days. Everything else not considered essential is being abandoned, including the tents. We should be ready to leave within a short while, if not immediately."

Stiger wondered for a moment on the centurion's choice of words by mentioning the tents, then it hit him.

"Leaving your personal tent, I take it?"

"Yes, sir," Pixus said, with an unhappy look. "It's been with me for a long while. Good-quality material, sir, well cut and sewed. I had just had it weatherproofed. Even on the worst of nights she kept me dry. I've never had a tent treat me so well, sir."

Stiger had lost a fine one himself, during the campaign against the Rivan. Losing his tent had felt like he had lost an old friend. He could well understand the centurion's attachment to it. Still, with the loss of the dwarven supply wagons, all available space was needed for their food supply, which the dwarves had helpfully added to after arriving and setting up camp. More importantly, Stiger knew that they would shortly need the additional space the tents had been taking up. When he tried to break out, this space would go to any that became seriously wounded and unable to move under their own power. He could not imagine a scenario where the enemy just let them walk out uncontested.

"Do we have any spare tents back at the main encampment?" Stiger asked Sabinus, sure that that the legion quartermaster would have replacements. "Good-quality ones, not the musty standard issue stuff from the quartermaster."

"I can think of a nice one, really good quality, sir," Sabinus said, scratching his jawline with his index finger. "We took it from the Tervay, after overrunning one of their camps. It's a bit large. Must have belonged to one of their chieftains or princes, or whatever those hairy barbarians call their leaders. I believe it was slated for sale, along with the other booty we seized. It's probably worth some good money, say four or five gold talons at least."

"I see." Stiger turned his gaze back upon Pixus. "When we make it back, that tent is yours, centurion. Consider it as compensation for your loss."

Pixus's eyes bulged. Fifth Century's centurion opened his mouth and then closed it. Stiger had genuinely surprised the man and was enjoying the moment. It was but a little pleasure in the middle of a dire situation. More importantly, Stiger was communicating to Pixus that he expected to get them back.

"Sir," Pixus said, "are you sure about that? My tent only cost half a talon."

Stiger thought for a moment before replying. Half a talon for Pixus, a commoner who had clearly come up through the ranks, was a fortune. Stiger well knew the Thirteenth would never return to the empire. He was certain there was no chance any of the spoils the legion had seized from the Tervay would ever be sold for prize money. It would mysteriously disappear, just as the Thirteenth had.

"As long as you don't sell it," Stiger said, "the tent is yours. If at some point you don't want it... well, then you can sell it and repay yourself the half talon. The rest goes to the legion's strong box."

Stiger looked over at Sabinus, who gave a subtle nod that Pixus did not catch. Stiger was gratified that the senior centurion of the Thirteenth approved.

"I feel this is an equitable arrangement," Stiger said. "Of course, if you don't want it... I will understand."

"Oh no, sir," Pixus said, bouncing on the balls of his feet. "I don't believe I can pass on this. I heartily accept your generous offer."

"Excellent," Stiger said, pleased with himself. He turned his gaze back out beyond the walls of the camp and his thoughts abruptly blackened with the night.

"Are you thinking of leaving tonight?" Sabinus asked the question that was clearly on both centurions' minds.

"I would have expected an assault by now," Stiger said simply, his eyes raking the darkness.

"Yes, sir," Sabinus said with a glance to Pixus. "We both think it odd they've not tried our defenses yet."

"Or showed themselves," Pixus said.

Stiger turned to face both men.

"I don't see that we have a choice," Stiger said. "We have to get out of here. If the enemy has not yet become organized, my thinking is it would be best to go before the sun comes up."

"But, sir," Sabinus protested, "you said so yourself. They're out there. What if they are waiting?"

"Before we make any movement," Stiger said, "I would send scouts over the wall to find the enemy."

"And they'd likely die in the process," Pixus added, sounding none too happy about the idea. "The bastards are probably watching us now."

"Centurion," Stiger said, "if you have a better suggestion, I'd love to hear it."

"No, sir," Pixus said. "I just wanted to make sure the legate understood the risk to our scouts."

"Now that the watch fires have burned low," Stiger said, "they stand a better chance of leaving the camp unseen."

"So that is why you wouldn't let me send a detail out to add wood to the fires?" Sabinus asked.

"Partly," Stiger said.

"Wouldn't it be better to wait until after the enemy assaults our encampment?" Sabinus asked. "We all agree they're out there. We just don't know where at the moment. Why waste our scouts? We have food and water. Let's just wait them out until they strike."

"You're forgetting about the coming raid on the valley and their intention of directly attacking the legion," Stiger said, voice hardening. "My initial thinking was that they'd have come for us by now. We'd be able to bleed them a bit, and thin their numbers before making a break for it." Stiger swept an arm out toward the darkness. "It's been over two hours and they haven't tested our walls yet, nor shown themselves."

"Perhaps," Sabinus said, "having taken a look at our defenses, they've had second thoughts?"

"The orcs might be smarter than we give them credit for," Pixus said. "I'd not want to assault this camp, at least not without making serious preparations."

"Scaling ladders, bundles of sticks and such." Sabinus nodded. "They could be doing that now and most likely are."

"That's very possible," Stiger said.

"The problem as I see it, sirs," Pixus said, "if we make a break for it sooner rather than later, we just don't know how many of them bastards are out there, waiting."

"From what we saw over at the dwarven encampment, we do know we are outnumbered," Sabinus said. "We have strong defenses here, including a trench and stone walls. Even if they make preparations for assault, the enemy has to overcome them first, which will not be easy."

"All right," Stiger said. "You both clearly understand our current position. Not only is the valley at risk, but also the legion. Our priority must be to get a warning back, and before it becomes too late. So, the question I am putting to you: Do we stay and allow the enemy to assault us, or do we make a break for it as soon as possible? Do we dare take a chance and wait 'til morning?"

Stiger looked to Pixus first. The centurion rubbed the back of his neck as he clearly considered his answer. Though he had given his thoughts and spoken freely, he suddenly looked uncomfortable having been asked his direct opinion on the matter by none other than his legate.

"My advice ... well, we go, sir, and as soon as possible," Pixus said. "It's dark out, and as you know, any action at night is a difficult thing at best. Ours tonight was the first night action I ever saw that was not even a partial cock up. With luck, we may be able to slip away and get a head start on any pursuit. That is, if they are not out there, waiting for us to make a break for it. Which means, no matter how much I dislike the thought of doing so, we have to send out scouts first to locate the enemy."

"Thank you, centurion." Stiger turned his gaze over to Sabinus, looking for his position, though Stiger suspected he already knew it.

"What of Brogan?" Sabinus said.

"What about him?" Stiger asked.

"Shouldn't we be getting his thoughts as well?"

"We did this his way," Stiger said. "That did not work out so well. Now it is my turn. I will of course consult him, but this decision is mine to make. Now, your opinion, sir?"

"We stay," Sabinus said firmly, "and remain until morning. Then, send out scouts. With the light, they will have a better chance of survival. If it's clear, we leave. As Pixus rightly said, night operations are asking for everything to go to pot. It's better we leave during daylight hours. Being able to see what we are marching into will, in my mind, be the key to successfully escaping. If they attack our camp this night, we know we have the advantage in defense. They do not have the same in assault and it will prove costly for them."

Sabinus fell silent. Pixus appeared to have nothing further to say. Both men were professionals and they apparently saw no reason to argue their points further, which surprised Stiger. Then Stiger realized that this was a result of Delvaris's leadership style. He recalled what Sabinus had told him. Delvaris solicited opinions from his officers and then made a decision. They were simply waiting for that decision.

Both arguments were sound. Both had merit. Regardless, Stiger understood the ultimate decision, as usual, lay with him. If he chose poorly, it would translate into blood and death. Heck, if he chose correctly it would likely see the same. He eyed Sabinus a moment, wondering what the centurion would do if Stiger chose against him.

The senior centurion of the legion knew Stiger was not actually Delvaris. Pixus did not.

"Thank you, gentlemen," Stiger started, but stopped when a sentry just feet away hissed out a warning. The sentry was intently gazing outward. Stiger moved over to the man.

"Look, sir." The sentry pointed out into the darkness. "Someone's out there, sir."

Gut tightening, Stiger followed the sentry's finger. The man had good eyes, and it took Stiger a moment of searching. The moon had slid behind a cloud, making it difficult to see much more than darkness. Then, he saw it… movement. But was it an orc or dwarf?

The moon had moved behind a particularly dense cloud. No matter how much he squinted, he could not make out the person moving around approximately thirty yards away. It did appear as if the individual was doing his best to move without being seen. Stiger reached his hand down to Rarokan, touching the hilt. The darkness brightened a little and Stiger could better see. The solitary figure emerged from the shadows. It was a dwarf, and he was moving stealthily toward the gate in a slow, steady manner, moving from tree to tree. Whenever possible, he sought out the darker shadows.

"Pass the word," Stiger said quietly to the sentry. "A friendly is coming in. No noise is to be made. Is that understood?"

"Yes, sir," the man said and moved off, speaking to the next sentry several feet away.

Stiger turned his gaze back to the dwarf, who was slowly approaching the trench. As he came nearer, Stiger saw that it was Hogan and his jaw tightened.

The sentry returned. "Go fetch the thane," Stiger said to him, and the legionary immediately jogged off.

"May I come over?" Hogan asked quietly, with a nervous glance behind. It told Stiger volumes about what was out in the darkness, just out of view.

"Yes," Stiger said.

Hogan quickly climbed down into the trench and then clambered up the other side. He held his hands out. Stiger and Sabinus had to reach over the other side, armor scraping on the stone. They hauled him up and over the wall. For his size, Hogan was surprisingly heavy.

"A little hazardous out there," Hogan said, dusting his hands off and brushing the dirt from his pants.

Brogan jogged up with Father Thomas. The thane's head was bandaged in a white cloth. "Hogan," Brogan said, anger heavy in his tone. "What the blazes happened? Taithun's dead, Jorthan's dead. So many died because of your failure. Explain yourself, before I have you executed."

Hogan seemed unruffled by his thane's rage, not to mention the threat of his imminent death, which surprised Stiger a little. Brogan wasn't the forgiving type. The scout captain regarded his thane for a heartbeat, his expression concealed behind his beard.

"We did not miss them," Hogan said, "even after you changed the plan, I had scouts covering the city and just beyond it. Any large body coming in from beyond my ring of eyes would have been spotted with plenty of warning to spare."

"Well then"—Brogan placed his hands on his hips—"explain it to me then. How could this happen?"

"They didn't sneak into the city while we were here, sire," Hogan said and then pointed downward. "They arrived from under our feet."

"What? Through our tunnels?" Brogan said. "All roads leading to the city were collapsed. The only road left is the one we came in on, and I know they did not come that way."

"We scouted the underground spaces, and, as you say, all other roads were pulled down. They are still collapsed. We even checked what remains of the sewers and aqueducts. All were either impassable or showed no signs of activity," Hogan said, then heaved a sigh. "In the last hour, we've found where they came out and think it was one of the old mines. It's on the edge of the south side of the city. Those mines lead nowhere, just down to the deep. It seems the orcs either burrowed into an existing mine, or located it, digging the entrance out weeks, if not months, ago and then concealing the entrance, with themselves inside. I think that the most likely explanation. They must have been waiting, with no sign for us to find that they were already here."

"In an abandoned mine?" Father Thomas asked.

"It would seem so," Hogan said. "We saw no need to check the mines, as they don't connect with any of the roads. They're all dead ends and, to be honest, there are simply too many to check."

Stiger sucked in a breath, his anger at the pioneer fading. He would not have thought to check a mine. With no outlet, and no evidence anyone had been in the city, why bother? Stiger saw that the thane's rage and anger subsided a little, too. Hogan, however, did not seem to be in the mood to waste any further time with explanations.

"How soon can you be ready to leave?" Hogan asked them. "I think the only reason the orcs did not immediately attack this camp was because it is fortified. That will not last much longer." Hogan turned and pointed beyond the walls. "They are conducting some sort of religious ceremony over at their king's camp. We think they have a priest with them, too."

"A priest, you say?" Father Thomas said. Stiger thought the paladin seemed surprised by that revelation. "Are you certain?"

"No," Hogan said. "We're not certain of much at this point. My boys have tried to get close for a better look but have been unable to do so." Hogan gave a shrug. "There are just too many orcs in the city. When they finish with their little service, whenever that happens, I expect them to turn their attention this way."

"Do you have any idea how many there are?" Stiger asked.

"At least six hundred, maybe more," Hogan answered. I've recalled all of my pioneers, but they won't get here for some time. I've only got fifty of my boys at hand."

"We can leave now," Pixus said, speaking up. "My century is ready to move."

"Good," Hogan said.

"I assume they are watching, waiting for us to make a break for it?" Stiger said.

"There are five lookouts watching your camp," Hogan said. "There were six, but to get in here I was forced to silence one." Hogan rested his hand upon the hilt of his dagger. The scabbard had blood running down the side. "That is another reason to get moving sooner rather than later. We don't want them to discover my handiwork too soon and raise the alarm. My guess is once the scouts see you leaving, they will run to tell Therik and then the chase will be on." Hogan paused and suddenly grinned, something that seemed out of place on the scout's face. "My pioneers are in position to silence the rest of their scouts. All they are waiting for is word from me. If everything works out, you can get back to the road before they know you are gone."

"Okay." Stiger turned to Pixus. "Let's get the men quietly formed up and ready to move. Impress upon them they are to make as little noise as possible. We don't want to tip our hand. Our lives depend upon it."

"Yes, sir," Pixus said. "I will make sure they understand."

"Good," Stiger said. "Sabinus, kindly assist Pixus, will you?"

Sabinus gave a nod and hurried off with Pixus.

Stiger turned back to Hogan.

"Silence those lookouts," Stiger said curtly. "Once they're down, we move."

Hogan nodded, gave his thane a hard look, and then stepped back up to the wall. He nimbly slipped over the side and slid down into the trench, then slowly climbed out the other side. Without sparing a glance back at the camp, he set out and quickly disappeared into the darkness and brush.

"I ordered Taithun to clear the trail to the road," Brogan said, "so that the wagons could get down to our camp. Once the orcs discover their fellows are dead, they're likely to have no trouble following us."

"Yes, I know," Stiger said. "I expect Therik to come after us. It will be an ugly affair. I will make sure of that."

"I am pleased we understand each other," Brogan said. "I will get my boys ready to move as well."

"Brogan," Stiger said as the thane made to step away. "Once we make it to the road, we need to send a rider back to Old City. They must have word an attack on the valley is imminent. The legion needs to know as well. It has to be one of yours, someone who knows the way."

Brogan gave a nod of agreement. "I will have someone ready. That is, if you have a horse?"

"We do," Stiger said.

"Good," Brogan said and started off without another word.

As he glanced back out into the darkness, Stiger could hear the muffled sounds of the men beginning to assemble behind him. After a moment, he shot a look over at Father Thomas, who had remained behind.

"I thought, for a short time," Stiger said, "that I might actually be able to trust Therik. It was more than just a gut feeling, if you know what I mean."

"I do," Father Thomas said, with a sad shake of his head. "I also believed him trustworthy, or at least that he meant what he was saying." Father Thomas placed a hand upon the wall. "This attack was planned out in advance."

"It would have to have been, if Hogan is to be believed."

Father Thomas turned to face Stiger. "We both come from the future. We are aware of some of the events that occurred here in the past, such as the final battle where Delvaris fell, defeating the minion along with the orc army."

"What you are getting at?"

"The minion is of our time," Father Thomas said. "It too would know of events that had occurred here in the past. Perhaps it even has knowledge of things of which we are ignorant."

Stiger felt himself go cold.

"You're saying," Stiger said after a moment, "that the minion had knowledge of the summit in advance? It set this ambush for us? With Therik's help?"

"That is a distinct possibility," Father Thomas said. "We cannot discount it, nor dare we try."

Stiger found he could not disagree with the paladin, and if true, this certainly complicated matters. If the minion knew of past events, then they couldn't count on meeting the enemy where Delvaris had fought his battle.

"Why did you not speak of this 'til now?" Stiger asked.

"I had not considered it," Father Thomas admitted, "until I heard what Hogan had to say. I should have thought of it sooner."

Stiger thought of a line Sergeant Tiro had been fond of using. "In war, there are always a lot of shoulds."

"Yes," Father Thomas said, "there are, aren't there?"

Stiger turned and looked over the camp. Most of the men had been assembled. The horses and mules were being brought up with their litters for the wounded. It was almost time to go. Stiger gazed out into the darkness with more than a little concern.

Once before he'd been pursued by an enemy, hounded and hunted for many miles. Though it had worked out in the end, it had been an exhausting and harrowing experience. He had an uncomfortable feeling that he would shortly be running for his life, with the enemy nipping at their heels. And they had a long way to go.

Chapter Twenty-One

Chest heaving from the exertion of the climb, Stiger came to a halt. Despite the chill night air, he was hot, sweaty, and somewhat out of breath. Glancing back down the slope, he decided he needed more exercise. In a column of two, the men of Pixus's century continued to flow by him and into the entrance that led to the underground.

The opening of the tunnel looked blacker than black, almost ominous. From its depth spewed a colder flow of air. It felt refreshing, but at the same time Stiger found it wasn't. The cold of the underground would be with him as an ever-present companion for the next few days, chilling him to the bone. The only warmth would come from marching and the occasional fire—that was, if they had time to stop.

"Seems like we slipped away without detection," Sabinus said, having made his way up the hill to him. The centurion was breathing heavily. "Hogan's boys did their job, that's for sure."

Not wishing to waste breath as he recovered, Stiger remained silent. He had to agree that Hogan had come through. The enemy's scouts had been efficiently eliminated. A short time after Hogan had given the all clear, the century had marched out of the encampment.

"The climb wasn't so bad." Sabinus cracked his neck before taking out his canteen. After a quick swallow, he offered it to Stiger, who took a grateful swig before returning the canteen.

"It was the pace you set," Sabinus continued. "If I may say so, a real punisher, sir. Almost as bad as a route march, but shorter."

Stiger glanced over at the centurion, wondering if Sabinus had said that for his benefit. After a moment, he decided the centurion was serious. Sabinus was sweating just as profusely as Stiger and appeared almost as winded.

"Route marches are always the worst and that's what's essentially ahead of us," Stiger said. "A forced route march." Stiger almost groaned at the thought of how far they had to go. "Don't worry, I'll slow things up. We have a lot of ground to cover and something more manageable will be called for. That said, we will march in longer intervals with shorter breaks."

"I had figured as much, sir," Sabinus said and then brightened. "The good news is the dwarven road is straight and level. That should make it a tad easier for the men."

Stiger looked behind them into the trees, where the dwarves had ripped up the brush along the old road. They had also felled trees and removed the stumps so the wagons could pass. Even in the dark, it was a path a blind man could follow. He glanced upward. The cloud cover had thickened up considerably, completely hiding the moon. As a result, he wasn't able to see much farther than a few feet.

Thunder rumbled, sounding much closer than before. The air, though chill, was humid. It wouldn't be long before the rain started. A flash of lightening somewhere off to the left illuminated the clouds for a fraction of a heartbeat. Stiger counted slowly. The thunderous crack came at the number five.

"There is a bright spot," Sabinus said.

"Oh?" Stiger glanced over at the centurion. "What is that?"

"At least we won't have to worry about being rained on, sir." Sabinus glanced in the direction of the tunnel entrance.

"There is that little mercy," Stiger agreed. "While marching, I've been rained on more times than I can count."

"It's never much fun," Sabinus said, "marching with your feet wet, cold, and muddy. Worse, the rain eventually seeps through your armor so that every part of your body is soaked and cold. You only have your helmet for protection to keep your head dry." He tapped his helmet with a finger. "This damn thing's a real pain in the neck." He paused, sucking in a breath. "If I had only known before enlisting, I honestly don't think I'd ever have gone through with it." Sabinus paused again. "Upon reflection, I was a stupid kid who thought he had all the answers. Sir, I probably would have joined anyway."

Stiger chuckled. He had heard such sentiments before. The allure of being a legionary was a strong pull for a headstrong youth. Only after they had enlisted and been sworn in did they realize the gravity of what they had done.

"We were all young and stupid once," Stiger said, thinking of his own youth. He had joined, following in his father's footsteps—a man who had ruined their family name. Even after all this time, Stiger's anger for his father was still hot.

"You know," Sabinus said, "at first I thought I'd made a huge mistake. Basic training does that to everyone. It gets you questioning yourself on why you joined. But honestly, the legion made me into the man I am today, sir. I owe the empire a debt I can never fully repay. It is why, before the legion marched south, I signed on to a new term of service."

"A debt?"

"Had I not joined," Sabinus said, "I would likely have ended up knifed in the slums of Mal'Zeel, another forgotten thug who had joined a gang. That or disease would have gotten me. Yep, I owe the legion a lot."

Stiger gave a nod.

"I love what I do," Sabinus continued. "It's not everyone that loves their job so much they look forward to it each morning."

"And the killing?" Stiger asked. "The losing of men under your command?"

"Not that. You never get used to that, sir. I hate that part, though it's necessary. Still, in general I love not only what I do, but the legion as well."

"I understand," Stiger said, and in truth he did, only too well. The legion became a good home to so many who had not known one.

Tongue lolling out the side of his mouth, Dog emerged from the darkness and padded up to him. Dog sat down and leaned his head against Stiger's thigh. Reaching down, he absently tousled the long hair on the dog's head before scratching at an itch on his chin. Stiger returned his gaze to scanning the darkness. It was frustrating that he couldn't see much. He touched the sword's hilt and the darkness brightened just a little. It didn't help. He couldn't see much farther than he had a moment ago. Hopefully, the orcs would have the same problem.

"You are certain they will follow?" Sabinus asked, thoughts turning to what lay down below them in the forest.

"Yes," Stiger said and pointed at Brogan. The thane stood a few feet away. He wore a thunderous expression that matched the rumbling of the coming storm. Hogan and Merog were with him, as was Theo. Theo and Merog were speaking with another pioneer Stiger did not know. "The enemy wants the thane dead, and badly, too."

"I see," Sabinus said, turning his gaze to Stiger. "And what about you, sir?"

"That too." Stiger wiped sweat off his forehead with the back of his forearm. His helmet had become loose, and the heavy thing had been shifting about slightly with every step. It was not only annoying but uncomfortable. He quickly undid the straps and then tied them tight once again. He gave the helmet a slight tug to make sure the fit was snug.

The thane spotted them and made his way over. Hogan was at his side. Theo and Merog followed a moment later, after finishing up whatever they had been discussing with the pioneer, who immediately went back the way they had just come, and in a hurry, too.

"Legate," Brogan said in common, tone hard and cold. There was an unforgiving look to the thane's eyes. Stiger understood his rage was directed at their current situation and Therik. Stiger did not take it personally.

"A pioneer just arrived," Brogan continued, "with word the religious ceremony the orcs were conducting has ended. They seem to be feasting to their success at the moment."

"A feast?" Stiger asked Hogan, surprised. The captain of the pioneers didn't even seem winded in the slightest by the climb and pace, though Brogan most certainly did. There was a heavy sheen of sweat on the thane's face. The bandage on his head was soaked with sweat. A dark-red stain had seeped through the center, where Brogan had been cut.

"As crazy as it sounds," Hogan said. "They don't seem in too much of a hurry, do they?"

"They will be," Stiger said, "once they figure out we've gone."

The last of the men in the small column marched by and into the blackness of the tunnel entrance. The mule train came next, each being walked single file up the hill.

"I seem to recall that door can be locked from inside, right?" Stiger nodded toward the huge stone door that stood open a few feet away.

"It will lock," Theo said. "Once everyone's through, it will be sealed behind us."

"That won't hold them for very long," Hogan said. "A few hammers and some effort is all it will take to break through."

"Aren't you just a ray of sunshine," Stiger said, though he had suspected as much.

"I'm always telling him that, too," Merog said, jumping in, which drew an unhappy look from Hogan. It didn't stop the lieutenant, who rounded on his superior. "Hogan, you need to be more positive. Think happy thoughts or perhaps less pessimistic ones or I don't know—something."

"Happy thoughts?" Hogan turned on Merog, eyebrows rising just a tad. Hogan pointed at the tunnel. "I will be happy when that door is closed and they are on their way to Old City."

"Is that all it takes?" Merog asked.

"All what takes?" Hogan asked, clearly confused.

"To make you happy?"

"Really?" Hogan shook his head in dismay. "You think this is a good time to play with me?"

"I only hope that door will buy us a head start," Stiger said, amused with the two. It reminded him of his time with Eli.

"With luck, it will take a while before they notice we've gone," Sabinus said. "Especially with them feasting, gaining us even more time."

Hogan turned a scowl upon Sabinus but said nothing. The captain's expression told Stiger much.

"I will make Therik pay for this." Brogan clenched his fists. He was breathing heavily, and not just from the climb. He shook a finger into the darkness, as if he were talking to Therik directly. "I will extract a terrible vengeance upon your people for this base betrayal. By my legend, on that I promise."

Stiger glanced over at Brogan. He found the thane's attitude more than a little ironic. Only a few hours before, Brogan had been the one planning to betray Therik. Still, Stiger understood that there were more important matters than revenge. He decided to hit the matter plainly, knowing there was a strong chance that, with Brogan's current ill temperament, the thane might take offense.

Stiger had already made the decision to become an active participant in events and help shape them, rather than be reactive. It was time he reinforced that, for only in that manner would Brogan see him as an equal partner in what was to come.

"First," Stiger said in a firm tone that exuded self-assured authority. He put as much steel into it as he could, without being rude. Just plain steel and resolve. "We need to make it back to safety. What Therik did here is only a prelude for what is to come. They will strike at the valley, and I would say it will happen sooner rather than later."

Brogan gave Stiger a funny look, his bushy brows coming almost together. He was clearly wondering what Stiger was getting at. Just the same, the thane turned to Theo.

"Did the messenger get off?" Brogan asked.

"Yes, My Thane," Theo said, with a quick glance over at Brogan. "I saw to it as soon as the horse was ready. I sent

Talik. He left before we marched out of the camp. Talik knows what's at stake and should make excellent time."

"Talik's a good dvergr. He's reliable and levelheaded. It was a good choice." Brogan gave Theo a pleased nod before turning back to Stiger.

"You are correct," Brogan said, giving a little. "We must not get ahead of ourselves. With the messenger out, our sole objective is to return to safety. Then, I shall have my revenge."

"Protecting the valley is the most important thing," Stiger said, with just as much firmness as he had used a moment before. He was simply pointing out the obvious, but at the same time knew it would upset the thane regardless. "Only then can we think on a reckoning. Are we agreed on that?"

Stiger saw Theo roll his eyes, as Brogan's popped with anger. Both Hogan and Merog stiffened. Stiger could imagine the thane's irritation at having been corrected in front of others, and by a human to boot. The thane worked his jaw for a moment and then his eyes narrowed.

"We protect the valley," Brogan said finally, as if giving in to the inevitable. "We will do this together. Once the threat is over, then jointly we shall seek our revenge. Are we agreed on *that*?"

The thane extended his arm, hand open, and held out in expectation.

Stiger glanced at the proffered hand a moment, understanding the thane was giving his word. This had to do with dwarven legend. Brogan would expect Stiger to give his word as well, essentially committing him to a course of revenge, should they survive. If Stiger refused the thane, he would be giving offense. There was too much at stake.

He felt he did not have much of a choice. Stiger clasped the thane's forearm tightly.

"Agreed," Stiger said. "We protect the valley, see it safe. Then we will make Therik pay for his sins. That sound good?"

"It does," Brogan said and released Stiger's arm. Clearly pleased, he patted Stiger on the shoulder armor. It was more of a blow than a pat, and Stiger found himself grateful for his armor. "We do this together, like Karus and Garath."

Stiger did not know who Garath was, but he gave a nod. Theo let out a soft breath in what seemed like relief. Stiger noticed that Hogan and Merog had done the same. He wondered for a moment what Brogan would have done had he declined. Stiger was now committed on a path of revenge, just as Braddock had vowed against the Cyphan.

The last of the mules passed them, each led by a legionary, entering the tunnel one at a time. Behind them, they dragged along makeshift litters. The injured were having an uncomfortable ride, several calling out or groaning loudly with each bump. There was no helping that. Stiger saw Misty was amongst them, pulling a gravely injured dwarf who was mercifully unconscious. Father Thomas came next, walking just behind the last mule.

"Father," Stiger greeted, "how are the wounded?"

"I'd rather not have moved some of them." The paladin stepped aside to join them.

"It was our chance to escape the trap Therik laid for us," Stiger said.

"At some point, I will need extended time with the wounded," the paladin said. "I've bandaged and patched them up as best I could. Some of them need more, the High Father's blessing."

"I see," Stiger said.

"I have refrained from healing anyone so far," the paladin said. "Such blessings always take a toll. I don't want to be napping when you need me most, especially if the orcs have a priest with them."

And there was the reason Father Thomas had refused Pixus. Stiger completely understood and agreed with the paladin's decision. Though he had faced priests before with Rarokan, Stiger felt more comfortable with Father Thomas there by his side.

"Can it wait a few hours?" Stiger's thoughts drifted to the man with the family. He had checked in on the injured legionary, and for Merax it was a serious as Pixus had made it out to be. "I want to put several miles in before taking a break, gain as much ground as possible while we have the opportunity."

Brogan cleared his throat, drawing their attention. "Though it pains me greatly to see suffering, I agree with the legate. When we can, Father, we will stop. Then you can tend to the wounded and give the High Father's blessing as you see fit."

"What must be, will be," Father Thomas said, quoting a line of scripture that Stiger recognized. "He who patiently waits will be rewarded."

The paladin gave an understanding nod that was filled with more than a little sadness. Without another word, Father Thomas started after the mules and the wounded. He disappeared into the black hole that was the entrance to the underground.

"My boys and I will do what we can to delay the enemy," Hogan said. "Hopefully, it will buy you another hour before they start working on the door. Maybe a little more if we get creative. I don't have that many on hand to give it a more serious effort."

"Any time you can gain us is appreciated," Brogan said.

Stiger looked between the two dwarves, worried that Hogan was thinking of intentionally sacrificing himself for them. An hour gained was not much. Stiger didn't see such a sacrifice for so short a time as worth it.

"Don't worry about us," Merog said, perhaps reading Stiger's concern. "Really, they're more interested in you. With that said, I have no intention of allowing the orcs the satisfaction of looting my corpse. Or his." Merog jerked a thumb over at Hogan. "Though if he fell in battle, it might improve his sunny disposition a little." A grin played its way across the lieutenant's face, the corners of his beard along the cheeks turning up as he looked over at his captain. "I've had my eyes on that dragon-bone dagger of yours for some time. I believe your grandfather brought it all the way from Tannis. When you die, can I have it?"

Hogan rolled his eyes at his lieutenant, though Stiger did notice his hand drift protectively down to the hilt of the dagger. The gesture caused both Merog and Theo to chuckle. Brogan's stern, angered expression cracked slightly.

Clearly embarrassed, Hogan pulled his hand back and then turned to Stiger and Brogan.

"We will make life difficult for them," Hogan said. "When it becomes too much, my boys and I will melt back into the forest."

"It is what we do," Merog said and gave a half shrug. "We're good at it, too."

Stiger liked the thought of that much better. Scouts, such as Brogan's pioneers, were not meant to fight in the line. They were more valuable being used as they were meant to be, the eyes and ears of the army, striking only in isolated spots when the odds favored them. Though he had thought poorly of Hogan and his pioneers, he silently wished them luck, for they would be left behind and there were a lot of orcs out in the forest.

"Two hours would be better," Brogan said.

Merog glanced sharply at the thane. Hogan, however, did not bat an eye.

"We will do what we can, My Thane," Hogan said and then hesitated. "You should know, I have sent a messenger to Maas. It is only a day from here at best. Perhaps, they will be able send significant aid and meet you somewhere along the way."

Stiger noticed as Brogan stiffened. The thane, however, said nothing, which troubled Stiger.

"Is that a dwarven city?" Stiger asked, wondering what the problem was. "Perhaps it makes more sense to go there first?"

"It's a town, and it is in the opposite direction from where you need to go," Merog said. "From here, the only way to get to Maas is through thick forest. There are no trails. It would be very difficult on your men and easy for someone who is not familiar with this forest to become separated, turned around, and lost. Worse, the orcs would be nipping at your heels before the sun comes up, which is something we are trying to avoid by sending you into the tunnels."

"A single rider they will ignore," Hogan added, "but certainly not the entire group. You stand a better chance underground than you do above."

"Perhaps I am missing something," Sabinus said. "If Maas is in the opposite direction, how will any aid from them reach us in time?"

"There is a road, the As'ur'Ay," Hogan said. "It is a smaller tributary that intersects the Kelvin about halfway to Old City. It is possible that my messenger will make it in time for the town to muster their militia. If they hurry, the militia just might be able to meet you along the way. That is, if they feel so inclined to help."

"What do you mean, *if* they feel inclined?" Stiger did not like the sound of that.

"Gnomes." Brogan spat on the ground. "Maas is a gnome town. Much of the land around Garand Kos belongs to the gnomes. It was one of the reasons we thought there would be little trouble from the orcs."

"Bloody gnomes," Theo said with disgust.

"Any help from them will cost me dearly in the future," Brogan said, heaving a great sigh.

"Will they come?" Sabinus asked. "They wouldn't just ignore our need, would they?"

"Who knows?" Theo said. "With gnomes you just never know what the little bastards are thinking. And trust me, you don't want to know what goes on inside their heads. No one does and no one can figure them out."

"We're giving them a chance to kill orcs," Merog said. "Personally, I think they will jump at the opportunity. They will come. I will bet good coin on it."

"Possibly," Hogan said. "As Theo said, it's quite difficult to tell gnome thinking sometimes, but I thought it worth a try."

"Oh, they will come," Merog insisted. "The little bastards hate orcs. The only question is whether they will arrive in time to help."

The rearguard marched up the road, Mectillius leading them. They looked tense, as if they were expecting orcs to explode from the darkness. Shields and swords were held at the ready. The optio started ordering the men to spread out, clearly intending to protect Stiger and the thane, until Stiger held up a hand stopping him.

"Optio," Stiger said, "get the men into the tunnel and down to the road. We will be along shortly."

"Yes, sir." Mectillius saluted and snapped out an order. The rearguard began to rapidly file their way into the tunnel. At the entrance, Mectillius stopped to look back a moment and then followed his men into the darkness, disappearing as if crossing over the veil of the living world and into that of the dead.

Stiger knew it was time to go into the tunnels. He glanced up at the sky, seeing no stars, for the cloud layer was very low, thick, and dark. Thunder rumbled loudly for a long moment. It reminded Stiger briefly of the sound of a cavalry charge. He sucked in a deep breath, savoring the smell of the trees and fresh air. In moments, he would willingly plunge back into the cold, damp, and musty underground.

A harsh horn ripped across the air. Stiger's head came around, as did everyone else's still outside the tunnel. The horn sounded a second time. It blared a long, mournful note, coming from the direction of the legionary encampment.

Dog stood and growled, taking several steps forward.

"Dog, stay," Stiger snapped.

Dog glanced back at him, then sat back down. Ears up, the animal continued his low growl.

The horn sounded again. This time, the tune blown changed. It sounded more like a call to hunt.

Stiger ground his teeth.

"It seems, My Thane," Theo said and extended an arm toward the tunnel entrance, "it is time to go."

"Very well," Brogan said. He gave Hogan a look, nodded, and then stomped off toward the entrance to the underground. Theo turned as well, arching an eyebrow at Stiger.

"You should go, too," Theo said.

"I will," Stiger said. "In just a moment."

Theo shook his head slightly and made for the tunnel.

"I will see you inside shortly," Stiger said to Sabinus, dismissing the man.

"Yes, sir." Sabinus walked over and entered the tunnel, following after Brogan and Theo.

A team of dwarves stood just inside. They looked anxious and were ready to close and seal the door. One motioned to Stiger to hurry. Stiger ignored him and turned back to the two pioneers.

Hogan and Merog looked curiously at Stiger, clearly wondering why he had remained behind.

"Hunt well." Stiger held out his hand to Hogan.

"Always," Hogan said, taking the hand and shaking it vigorously. "Don't you doubt that none."

"It is what we do," Merog said with an infectious grin and shook as well. "We will buy you that hour, perhaps a little more, before they start working at breaking that door down. Just make sure our thane gets back to safety. Will you? He is not of my clan, but I respect and love him as if he were."

"I will," Stiger said.

"With any luck," Hogan said, turning to look over the stone door, "you will have four—" Thunder rumbled loudly again. When it subsided, the captain continued. "You will have four…maybe six hours, if it rains, before they can break through and come after you."

"That should give us the start we need," Stiger said. "Take care."

"Always," Merog said with a twinkle in his eye.

Stiger gazed once more out into the darkness. Garand Kos, First City, lay shrouded in darkness and hidden from view. Once again, the great city was lost to his people. No one would ever truly believe he had been here. Stiger let his hands fall to his sides. He stepped away, walking rapidly through the entrance and once again back into the underground.

"Dog, come."

Dog trotted after him, rapidly catching up.

Once inside and clear of the door, he turned back to look. Hogan and Merog had not wasted any time. Both pioneers were gone. Like wraiths, they had melted away into the darkness. It reminded Stiger of Eli and his friend's skill at concealment. He felt a pang of loss for his good friend. Stiger wished Eli were here with him now, for he could use the elf's help.

One of the dwarves threw back the hood of a lantern. In the darkness of the tunnel, the abrupt light seemed awfully bright. Stiger wondered for a moment if the enemy could see it up on the ridge, but then realized that with all of the vegetation outside in the forest, such a thing would be very unlikely.

"Push," one of the dwarves shouted to the others. As one, grunting and straining, the team of four dwarves pushed. Each had a hand on a thick metal bar meant for gripping, set on the inside of the door. The hinges screeched painfully as the door slowly began to inch and grind its way closed. Stiger glanced around. Nearly everyone else had already made their way down through the tunnel to the road below, including Brogan.

Stiger stood there with Dog and watched. He wanted see the door closed. He needed to be sure that the entrance was sealed and locked. It was irrational, he knew. Still, knowing it had been done would make him feel better. It would be one less worry weighing him down. So he waited and looked on as the door screeched and ground its way closed, one painful inch at a time.

Curiously, Theo had remained behind as well. Their eyes met briefly and then returned to the door.

After what seemed like an eternity, the screeching ceased with a heavy thud as the door finally closed. Sweating and grunting with effort, the dwarves picked up the heavy locking bar and dropped it in place. It landed with a deep, solid clang that echoed and reverberated through the underground like a funeral bell tolling for the recently deceased.

Listening to the echoes as they raced off into the tunnels, Stiger thought the tolling might be instead for the soon-to-be deceased. Had they just sealed themselves in their tomb? He certainly hoped not.

The team of dwarves took a slight breather, then began gathering up their weapons and shields, clearly preparing to join their fellows down upon the road. One picked up the lantern and held it forth for light.

Stiger absently rested his hand upon his sword hilt, feeling the comforting electric tingle move lightning fast from his palm up into his arm. The darkness receded as lantern light brightened, almost painfully so. With it, he felt his anger flare.

Let them come, Rarokan thundered in his mind, *for I am hungry, angry, and more than ready to spill blood.*

"Let them come," Stiger said softly to himself. He turned and started down the tunnel, the team of dwarves and Theo following after him.

Chapter Twenty-Two

One of the many magical lanterns lighting the road hung just overhead. It shed pale, ethereal light downward upon the resting men and dwarves. Sitting with his back against the tunnel wall, Stiger chewed on a piece of salted pork. It was tough, overly dry, and too salty for his tastes. The worst part about salted meat was that after you ate it, it tended to make you incredibly thirsty. On a hard march, thirst was something you generally wanted to do without.

Back armor scraping against the tunnel wall, Stiger shifted slightly, attempting to make himself just a little more comfortable. He had called a break a short while before, their first since returning to the underground. They would remain here for five hours and then push onward.

No one was up and about. Most had their backs against the walls of the road. A few had literally dropped their kits and fallen to the ground, immediately going to sleep, using their packs or arms for a pillow.

Stiger did not blame them in the slightest. They had had no sleep for well over a day. They were dog-tired.

As he chewed, he looked around. Most were asleep. A few, like him, were taking the opportunity to eat before surrendering and settling in to sleep. He would have pushed on farther, but the men were nearly blown. Heck, he was just as blown, and they had a long way to go. Everyone needed rest.

Worse, one of the wounded had expired a couple of hours past. Merax had succumbed to his wounds. Stiger felt terrible about that, but there had been no helping it. He resolved to check in on the man's daughter and wife once they made it back to the legion. Life was hard enough as a camp follower and even worse without a husband or patron. He would do what he could to ensure they did not unduly suffer over his loss.

Father Thomas had warned that if they did not stop, more of the gravely wounded would die if not tended to. So Stiger had reluctantly called their first extended break.

He shifted one of his legs and almost groaned with the effort. Gods, his legs ached. He took a moment to massage his left calf, which had started to cramp. After a moment, he relaxed, placing his back once again against the carved stone wall. He let out a soft sigh of relief.

The sound of running water from the runoff system could be heard amongst the subdued talking. It came from a nearby grate and had a relaxing and soothing quality to it. To his immediate right, a ten-yard stretch of the tunnel wall was slick with water slowly bleeding out of the walls and ceiling. From this, a small stream ran along the edge of the tunnel toward the drainage grate. It was one of the reasons he had chosen this spot. The sound of the water falling into the spillway and the running water below reminded him of the outdoors.

Stiger saw Pixus pull himself slowly to his feet. The centurion stretched, then looked about. Their eyes met. Stiger gave him a nod, which was returned. Pixus began moving about, checking in on each man still awake, speaking quietly so as not to disturb anyone already out.

Despite leaving his tent behind, Pixus had managed to bring along his vine cane. The cane was something Stiger knew to be incredibly important to the centurion. In Stiger's time, few bothered to carry the canes. Sergeant Blake had been one of the few and had taken exceptional pride in it.

In this time period, the vine cane's use was widespread amongst the legions. Virtually every centurion carried one. The canes represented the sacred trust placed in the centurionate by the emperor himself. In essence, a small measure of imperial power had been invested in each officer. The symbol of that power was the vine cane.

Watching the centurion make his rounds reminded Stiger of himself. That time seemed like an age past. So much had happened and changed since then. Stiger's simple world as a soldier had grown complex beyond recognition.

Pixus crouched down next to a legionary who had a bandaged head, speaking quietly with him. He was a damn fine officer and it showed in how deeply he cared for his men. That was something Stiger could well respect.

"Everything good?" Stiger asked when Pixus came past.

"Yes, sir," Pixus said. "Just making sure my boys are all right."

"Make sure you get some rest, too," Stiger said.

"I will, sir," Pixus said and stepped away.

Stiger took another bite of his pork, listlessly chewing. As fuel it was more than sufficient to keep him going. Salt was an excellent way to preserve meat. Pork was less expensive than beef, which was why it was the legion's preferred meat. He reminded himself it could be worse. Had they not had the pork, he would likely be gnashing his teeth on hardtack instead. That still didn't mean he had to enjoy it.

Curled up next to him, Dog lay asleep. His hind legs twitched repeatedly and he gave a soft whine. Stiger imagined Dog was dreaming about chasing something, perhaps a rabbit or squirrel. He reached out and absently scratched at Dog's neck. There was something calming about the animal's constant presence. Stiger had to admit he'd grown fond of the hairy beggar that seemed more beast than dog. In truth, he had difficulty remembering on occasion that Dog was something more.

As if sensing his attention, Dog abruptly opened his watery eyes and looked curiously up at him, cocking his head to one side, a floppy ear raised in question. Despite his weariness, Stiger chuckled, gently patting the animal's head a couple times. Dog licked once at Stiger's hand and then rested his head upon Stiger's thigh. A moment later, he closed his eyes again, going back to sleep.

Stiger resumed scratching Dog's neck and finished the last of the pork, swallowing it. He washed it down with a drink of water from his canteen. He regarded Dog for a time and decided the animal had the right idea. It had been one bitch of a day and he, too, needed sleep. Leaning his head back against the tunnel wall, Stiger closed his eyes and gave in to oblivion.

"Excuse me, sir."

Stiger's eyes snapped open. He blinked several times. Mectillius was standing over him. The optio looked tired. His armor was dusty and spattered with green and red blood. There had not been time for a cleaning of kit.

"Sorry for waking you, sir," Mectillius said. "You asked to be notified after five hours?"

"Is it already?" Stiger asked. "Seems like I just closed my eyes."

"I think we've all found time's hard to track underground, sir," Mectillius said. "No sun or moon to check the progress of the day. Seven levels, I am relying upon one of the dwarves, sir. I've no idea how he can tell the time down here, but he told me it's time. So, it's time."

"I see," Stiger said and held out a hand.

Mectillius hauled him to his feet. Stiger was stiff. His leg muscles were sore. Everything seemed to ache. He cracked his neck and felt a little better.

"Where is Pixus?"

"Over there, sir," the optio said, "sleeping next to Sabinus. I was about to wake him next."

Stiger looked in the direction indicated. Both centurions were asleep, with their backs pressed against the stone wall. Farther down the road, Father Thomas was with the wounded. They had been laid out on blankets in neat, orderly rows. The paladin was kneeling next to a dwarf, bent over as if he were praying.

Stiger glanced around the tunnel. Snoring was heavy on the air. As was the occasional cough from one of his men. No one—other than Mectillius, Father Thomas, a dwarf and Stiger—was awake. The dwarves had congregated just up the road a bit, with a slight separation from the humans. Brogan and Theo were asleep next to one another. Stiger stifled a yawn, wishing he could go back to sleep.

"Wake the officers and Brogan first," Stiger said. "Then you can roust the men."

"Yes, sir," Mectillius said and then hesitated as he was about to turn away.

"Speak your mind, Optio," Stiger said. "Let's have it."

"We've come about ten miles, sir," Mectillius said, with a glance in the direction they'd come. The magical lanterns set every hundred yards disappeared off into the distance. "That's an awfully long way. Do you really expect the orcs will follow us?"

"Yes, Optio, I do," Stiger said in a firm tone, wanting to put the matter squarely to bed. "Now, if you would kindly wake the officers, we have a long road ahead of us."

"Yes, sir." Mectillius saluted and moved off.

Stifling a groan, Stiger reached down. He picked up his canteen and took a healthy swig before stopping it. He swished the water around in his mouth, swallowed it, and set the canteen back down next to his helmet. He was incredibly stiff and sore, even more so than he had realized when Mectillius had hauled him to his feet. Straightening, he stretched out his back and then his legs. The pain wasn't too bad. It felt good to stretch.

Dog looked up at him quizzically for a moment, clearly wondering what he was up to. Then the curiosity faded and he laid his head back down upon the floor, returning to sleep.

Stiger walked stiffly over to the wounded. Father Thomas was on his knees, still bent over the same dwarf. Both hands were pressed against the dwarf's left thigh and the paladin was incredibly still. He didn't even appear to be breathing.

Not wishing to disturb the paladin, Stiger was about to walk away when Father Thomas exhaled an explosive breath, then breathed in deeply. To Stiger, he seemed like a downing man who had just fought his way to the surface, almost gasping at fresh air in relief.

After several heartbeats of simply breathing in and out, the paladin leaned back and his eyes fluttered open. For a moment his gaze remained unfocused. Then, blinking, he spotted Stiger.

Father Thomas had changed dramatically in appearance. He had aged since Stiger had last seen him, and that had only been a handful of hours ago. The paladin's hair was almost completely white, with a sprinkling of pepper. His face was gray and lined. So shocking was it that Stiger almost took a step back. The paladin's hands shook as he rubbed the back of his neck.

Stiger's eyes shifted to the wounded dwarf. He looked to be peacefully asleep, snoring softly. The bandages that had bound the wound lay in a heap at the dwarf's side. They were heavily soiled and stained an ugly reddish color. The leg itself was caked in dried blood. There was so much of it, Stiger wondered how much the warrior had left on the inside, or for that matter how he had managed to survive his wound.

No matter how hard Stiger looked, he could not see the injury or any hint of it. All that remained was an area clear of the dried blood, with smooth, unmarked skin that was perhaps a little too pink. It was as if the skin were newly made, which Stiger suspected it was.

"He is going to pull through, I take it?" Stiger asked, already knowing the answer. He had felt compelled to ask anyway.

"I was able to heal them all." Father Thomas's voice shook with weariness as he waved with an arm out toward the others. "At least those that were seriously injured and survived the journey here." He paused and cleared his throat. "The walking wounded will have to heal the old-fashioned way. I just don't have the strength for more, at least at the moment, anyway."

The paladin looked over at the dwarf he had just healed. He reached out and ran a finger along the fresh skin on the leg, almost as if marveling at his own handiwork.

"He will sleep for a few hours," the paladin said, voice trembling with exhaustion. "When he wakes he will be weakened, as healing such a fearsome wound takes some of his *will* as it does mine."

"I am sure he will be most grateful," Stiger said.

"His thanks should go to the High Father, for it was by his grace and this dwarf's faith in our god such miracles are made possible."

"Are you saying that if he did not believe in the High Father you would be unable to heal him?" Stiger asked.

"That, my son," Father Thomas said, "is a good question."

"Meaning you don't know," Stiger said. "Have you ever tried such a healing?"

"I believe it would be up to the High Father. I would not be able to be the conduit for his grace unless he willed it. That, my son, is what matters."

Stiger thought on that a moment. It sounded reasonable enough.

"What about you?" Stiger asked, understanding such healing took a tremendous toll. "I seriously doubt you will be able to march or ride."

Father Thomas moved himself stiffly from a kneeling position to one of sitting. It seemed to take a great effort, for he swayed slightly, as if dizzy. His eyes closed for several heartbeats, then opened and looked straight up at Stiger. It took him a moment to focus, but when he did, the paladin appeared confused. His eyes began to roll back. Stiger realized Father Thomas was on the verge of passing out.

He knelt next to the paladin.

"Lie back." Stiger eased Father Thomas to the ground. "Rest."

"But, my son," Father Thomas protested in a weak voice, the lids of his eyes clearly becoming heavy. He mumbled something incoherent.

"Rest easy, Father," Stiger said. "I'll have a litter rigged for you. We will take good care of you. On that, I promise."

"Thank you, my son," Father Thomas said in a shaky whisper, and with that his eyes closed. His breathing became deep and steady.

Stiger studied the paladin. He looked like an old man. The skin around his eyes had become heavily lined with age, looking very much like crow's feet. The skin on his hands had also become wrinkled and spotted with age marks. He had lost his youthful vigor.

With each healing, Father Thomas was giving part of his life force. How much more could Father Thomas take? It worried him, for Stiger was apprehensive about facing the minion alone. Could he defeat such a creature by himself?

When the time comes, I will be with you, Rarokan said, as if it were not a concern. Stiger realized the sword's presence had been with him since he had woken. *Fear not, for you are never alone.*

Stiger felt a comfort in that, but at the same time serious concern. He was becoming accustomed to Rarokan always being there.

He heard the scuff of approaching footsteps from behind and turned. It was Brogan, along with Pixus and Theo. Stiger stood, legs protesting as he straightened up.

Brogan gasped; the breath seemed to have caught in his throat. "What's wrong with him? How did this happen?"

"He's exhausted, is all," Stiger said and then gestured toward the dwarf lying next to the paladin. "He healed him and the others that were gravely injured." Stiger pointed at the nearest man, who slept as soundly as the dwarf at his feet. "I've seen this type of healing before, and it takes a terrible toll upon the paladin. Given time, he will recover."

"I certainly hope so," Brogan said, and then what Stiger had told him hit home. He gazed down at the dwarf and over at another one a few feet away. His eyes moved on to a legionary. All were asleep, but it was abundantly clear they had been healed of their gruesome injuries. The thane's mouth fell open just a little. The thane blinked rapidly.

"He healed Tommen. A miracle." Brogan stuttered a little as he spoke, awe plain in his tone as he gazed down at the healed dwarf.

"That is incredible," Theo said, stepping nearer and examining Tommen's leg. "Just incredible."

Brogan turned his gaze upon Stiger. "Stories tell of a paladin's ability to perform such wonders." He looked back down on Father Thomas and shook his head slightly. "My people have not had such a warrior priest amongst us since my grandfather's time. To be told one is such a thing, and to witness such a miracle is something else entirely." The thane glanced over at Theo. "We have been blessed this day."

"Truly," Theo said. Stiger noticed that despite his wonder on the healing, Theo appeared to be in a sour mood. The look he gave Brogan back was without warmth. The thane did not catch it.

Stiger glanced over at Pixus. The centurion was standing there silently. He did not look at all surprised.

"Centurion," Stiger said, "we're going to need a litter for Father Thomas."

"I will see to it, sir," Pixus said. His gaze flicked back to the paladin. "How long will he sleep, do you think?"

"I don't know," Stiger said, and in truth he didn't. "Perhaps a few hours or even a day or more. He needs to recover his strength."

Pixus gave a nod and moved off toward his optio.

Brogan shifted about, as if he had something he wanted say. The thane swallowed and then straightened his back.

"This miracle has moved me greatly." The thane gestured down at the sleeping Tommen. He then looked back at Stiger. "I will say it again. I owe you my thanks. Without you, my remains would now be moldering out in the open, forever lost to my family." Brogan gave a slight cough. "I shall not forget what you did for me or my people."

"Your thanks are not required," Stiger said. "I am certain you would have done the same for me had our roles been reversed. In fact, I would expect it."

The thane stared at him for a prolonged moment. "Of course, and yet I still feel compelled to tender my thanks just the same."

"As would I," Stiger said. "You are not in any way in my debt. We are allies. Let's not speak of this again."

"As you wish," Brogan said, a look of relief passing over him.

"On your feet, ladies," Pixus hollered, the shout echoing off the walls of the tunnel. There was a chorus of groans as the legionaries and dwarves stirred. "Time to once again use those wonderful things the gods saw fit to give each of us. Now, come on, ladies. On your feet."

"You heard the centurion," Mectillius called out, giving a legionary who hadn't yet stirred a not-so-gentle nudge with his foot. "Drop your cocks and grab your yokes."

Pixus prodded a legionary who had not moved with his vine cane. When the legionary failed to wake, the centurion smacked him hard on the side with the cane. That woke the man up. A moment later, he was scrambling to his feet.

"Varenus," Pixus said to the legionary as he shook his head. "I don't believe I've ever seen you move so fast. I may just wake you up more often with my vine cane."

Varenus looked in horror on his centurion, who gave him an amused wink and moved on to the next man.

Stiger turned back to the thane, who was gazing once more over those who had been gravely injured. Despite the commotion in the tunnel, they continued to sleep deeply. Stiger understood that had to do with the healing process.

The thane glanced up the tunnel in the direction they would be going and then back on Stiger.

"I think we should push hard," Brogan said. "Say another five miles before a short break and then another five after that. How does that sound?"

"Good to me," Stiger said. "When do you think your messenger will reach Old City?"

"If he makes decent time, and I have no reason to think otherwise, Talik should arrive sometime tomorrow," Brogan said. "With any luck, we will have a contingent of warriors from the garrison at Grata'Jalor marching our way soon enough."

"I will pray to Fortuna and the High Father to speed him on his way," Stiger said, glancing around. The legionaries and dwarves were beginning to fall in. Stiger saw a team had started to work on a litter to be pulled behind Sabinus's horse. He assumed this was for Father Thomas.

Brogan excused himself and stepped away towards his dwarves, who were readying themselves. Stiger rubbed at his tired eyes. They had such a long way to go, and he was certain the enemy was following. It had gone from a suspicion to conviction. They were coming. He felt it to be true. Soon enough there would be fighting.

They are coming, Rarokan said.

Stiger closed his eyes, feeling his stomach sink. This entire expedition had gone thoroughly to shit and there was nothing Stiger could have done. And it was about to get much worse.

"A bloody mess this is," Stiger said to himself.

"You've got that right," Theo said. Stiger had not noticed his friend remain behind.

"We will get out of it," Stiger said in an attempt to assure Theo.

"I won't," Theo insisted sourly. "Do you know what he did to me?"

"Brogan?" Stiger asked, confused and wondering what Theo was on about.

"Yeah, my bloody cousin," Theo said, spitting mad and clenching his fists. "I can't believe it myself. As if things could get any worse. It's just plain awful." Theo wagged a thick finger at Stiger. "I warned you he's a sneaky bastard."

"What did he do?" Stiger was becoming alarmed. He glanced in the direction Brogan had gone.

"He made me his advisor," Theo said with exasperation and threw his hands up. "Me!"

"What?" Stiger barked out a laugh, not quite sure he had heard his friend correctly.

"I am to take Jorthan's place. Can you believe that? Me? The thane's advisor? I can't possibly think of someone more unsuited. Can you? What am I supposed to advise him on?"

Stiger stared at his friend. There was real panic in Theo's eyes. Stiger burst out with another laugh. "You're pulling one over on me."

"Don't you laugh at me," Theo said, his disgust and anger growing more evident the harder

Stiger laughed.

"I think congratulations are in order," Stiger said, barely able to get the words out. "You went from babysitter—which, I might add, you stink at—to the thane's advisor. Good show, old boy. Way to move up in the world."

Stiger clapped Theo on the shoulder.

"I could use a good stiff drink," Theo grumbled.

"There are worse jobs," Stiger said, working to catch his breath. Then an amusing thought

occurred to him. "As the thane's advisor, think of all the free booze. Brogan's gonna be paying."

Theo froze as he considered Stiger's words.

"There is that," Theo admitted a little grudgingly. "I can see a slight upside to being his

advisor. But still… can you see me taking up Jorthan's position?"

Stiger actually could. Theo was sharp and shrewd. He had an interesting way of looking at the world. Brogan would have noticed it as well, which was why the thane had likely chosen him.

"You know," Stiger said, "now that I think on it, I believe you were right."

"About what?" Theo peered at him suspiciously.

"You were concerned the thane's supply of drink wouldn't last beyond the summit." Stiger chuckled. A few of the nearest men and dwarves looked over. "The orcs got the rest of Brogan's spirits."

"They did, didn't they?" Theo barked out a laugh of his own, finally becoming amused. "Let's hope they choke on it, eh?"

"If only," Stiger said.

Out of the corner of his eye, Stiger saw Dog abruptly get up. Looking back the way they had come, Dog bared his teeth and growled.

An icy sensation ran down Stiger's spine as he turned and looked. He could see nothing other than the magical lanterns disappearing off into the distance. Then, he thought he heard something.

Theo began to speak.

"Quiet," Stiger said.

He frowned. The men and dwarves around him were making too much noise.

"Quiet down," Stiger called out, then louder, "By the gods, quiet down!"

The voices and commotion died away, as everyone turned to look at him.

He thought he heard something again. Stiger cupped a hand to his ear.

A distant howl carried itself along on the walls of the tunnel, echoing up from somewhere far behind them. It was followed almost immediately by a louder yowl. Any last activity stilled with the howl. It sounded just like one of his family's hunting hounds.

Silence reigned.

Then a chorus of distant howls and barks echoed toward them. Whether it was from one or many, due to the echoes Stiger did not know.

"The hunt is on," Stiger said quietly to himself.

"You always seem to focus on the bright side of things, don't you?" Theo said with a deep scowl. "Has anyone ever told you? You're one gloomy bastard."

Ignoring Theo, Stiger spun around. The legionaries and dwarves were still hushed, seemingly frozen into inaction by the distant howls and barks.

"Centurion Pixus," Stiger called out loudly, "time to get the men moving."

Chapter Twenty-Three

"Get up!" Stiger reached down, grabbing the arm of the fallen legionary to help him back to his feet. The man just sat there, dazed and appearing thoroughly confused. He gave Stiger a quizzical look.

Baring his teeth at the enemy, Dog moved over to stand beside Stiger. Though the animal was growling, Stiger could not hear him over the noise of the fight.

"You stay here," Stiger said to Dog. He did not want him getting underfoot of the legionaries.

Stiger shot a glance toward the battle line, just feet away. Under the direction of Centurion Pixus, it was falling back toward them. He returned his attention to the fallen legionary. If he did not get the man moved and out of the way, he'd be trampled. Stiger released the arm and grabbed instead the armor harness. The legionary was nearly complete dead weight. Using both hands, Stiger hauled him to his feet.

"Stand up, damn you," Stiger shouted. The man stood, though Stiger still held him steady.

The line was almost on top of them. A legionary in the second rank stepped in front of them and, using his shield as a barrier, moved into the gap in the line, providing cover. Almost immediately, a sword hammered down onto his shield, sending a spray of splinters up into the air.

"Get to the rear," Stiger shouted at the dazed man, looking him square in the face. When he failed to respond, Stiger shook him roughly, hoping for some semblance of sense to return. Blood ran down the side of the legionary's face. It was coming from under the helmet, which had a large dent in it. The left cheek guard had been ripped away and was missing. The heavy helmet had saved him from a killing blow.

"Do you understand me?" Stiger demanded. "You need to get to the rear."

The legionary's eyes swung to Stiger's face. He blinked and his head lolled slightly.

"Sorry, sir," the legionary mumbled, while making a feeble attempt to wipe blood out of his left eye. Over the sound of the fight, Stiger could not hear what he said, but instead read it off the man's lips. The legionary's gaze became unfocused, but he managed to repeat what Stiger had told him. "Go to the rear, yes, sir."

Stiger released his hold. The legionary staggered as if he had drunk too much and swayed alarmingly. Stiger was bumped and nudged from behind by a legionary. He gripped the man's arm again, steadying him. Stiger dragged the dazed man back several feet, passing the third rank, and out of the way of the line.

Holding the man's arm, Stiger glanced around. The sound of the fighting inside the tunnel was intense and overwhelming. It was made unnaturally louder than it should've been by the close confines of the walls and all of the stone that surrounded them. The clash of weapons was magnified to a level Stiger had never heard. Screams and shouts were virtually drowned out by the echoing cacophony of the fight, which beat intensely down on the senses.

Stiger looked to the rear, past the third rank. The mules and horses had continued much farther up the road, pulling well ahead of the defending century. The litters they dragged behind them held the freshly injured and those who had been healed but had not yet woken. Father Thomas was among them, still unconscious.

Stiger had told the dwarves leading the mules and horses to continue on as rapidly as possible and to stop for nothing. It was safer for them this way, particularly if the Fifth Century broke. They were so far ahead, Stiger could barely make them out now, as they were passing between lanterns where the gloom of the underground lurked.

An injured legionary was limping along after them, trailing blood along the ground. He staggered in vain to catch up. Just ahead of him, a dwarf carried another legionary like a baby, following after the train. Such sights of injured men were nothing new to him, and yet it never failed to bother him.

Closer to hand, Stiger saw Mectillius bend down to help a legionary who'd slumped down to the ground and was cradling his arm. The optio pulled him to his feet and handed him off to a dwarf who had come over to assist.

Stiger's gaze swung over to Brogan and his surviving dwarves. Without their armor, Stiger was unwilling to put the dwarves into the line. Each had a sword and shield. A few even carried legionary shields.

Stiger and Brogan had organized a reserve that numbered a total of twenty-five effectives. Stiger planned on using them when his legionaries became spent. These dwarves had formed a single loose rank around ten yards behind the formation. The rest of Brogan's boys, most injured in some manner themselves, were doing what they could to care for the wounded legionaries.

Stiger's eyes stole over two dwarves working on a man who had been dragged clear of the line. Bent over the legionary, one was in the process of tying a thick bandage around the lower leg, while the other secured a tourniquet on the thigh. The legionary looked pale and trembled, not only from the pain, but also the shock. Both dwarves were spattered with blood.

"You," Stiger shouted at the wobbly legionary he still held firmly by an arm. He swung the man around to face the direction of the mule train. "Go that way, understand?"

"Yes, sir." The legionary's voice was a little louder. What Stiger could hear of it sounded badly slurred. He staggered off like a drunk toward the rear. After a few steps, a dwarf hustled over and took his arm, helping to guide him away from the action. Satisfied that the man was out of immediate danger and would be looked after, Stiger turned back toward the fight.

Fifth Century was organized into the three tightly compacted ranks. The first rank was locked in heated battle with the enemy, shields to their front. The shield wall ran the width of the tunnel and formed a nearly impenetrable barrier, which the enemy was trying with great effort and energy to overcome. Behind them, the second and third ranks, shields held to their sides, stood ready to assist or to move forward to battle, when a rotation of ranks would be called.

To the front of the shield wall, the tunnel was a seething mass of orcs. Mixed amongst them were a few humans. These came at the legionaries just as fiercely as the orcs. Without the ability to maneuver or flank, it was an ugly and brutal fight of pure endurance.

The first of the enemy had caught up to them a little more than two hours before. This had forced Stiger to halt the column and form the century for battle. The fight had been going on ever since. The enemy showed no sign of letting up.

Though the enemy held the advantage in numbers, as heavy infantry the legionaries had it in equipment. The enemy was the equivalent of light infantry, meaning they had no real armor and very few carried any sort of shield.

This qualitative advantage combined with the tight confines of the underground road had allowed Fifth Century to hold like a rock, falling steadily back, one measured step at a time. The legionaries were wreaking a terrible toll upon the enemy. The tunnel was really the perfect place for a fight. Had he more men, perhaps another century, there would have been no real risk of the enemy ever breaking his line.

Therein lay the problem. Stiger did not have the men he needed.

Every few feet, Pixus would call an abrupt halt and the shields would come together. A heartbeat later they would momentarily part and out would snap the deadly short swords. Whenever this happened, the enemy suffered and would inevitably fall back a few paces, or they would try to. Occasionally the press from behind was so tight there was absolutely nowhere to go for those at the front. When that happened, trapped, they fell in droves to the vicious short swords. Then the shields would lock together again in an impenetrable wall and the slow, steady retreat would once again continue, creating a brief gap between the enemy and the legionary shield wall.

To keep his front rank from becoming too worn down, Pixus rotated his line on a regular basis. It gave those fighting a short breather before being sent back into the action with the rotation.

The century had left a trail of bodies as it backed up the tunnel. Stiger estimated they had killed or injured several hundred. And yet the enemy came on with a fanatical and frightening intensity that Stiger found more than troubling. It was chilling.

He had hoped to get closer to Old City before the enemy caught up. He had lost the race, but there was no helping that now. They were committed to this fight, even if it meant help would likely not arrive in time.

Stiger's gaze swept over the enemy. He felt a stab of anger at the sight of Therik's standard waving above the mass of enemy just a handful of yards away. Though he looked, he could not see the orc king. He felt the sword's anger swell along with his own. If the opportunity came for personal combat with the king, he knew he would gladly seek it. He would make Therik pay for this.

Stiger rubbed his jaw and glanced backwards. He was wondering what was taking Sabinus so long to return. He had sent him up the road to scout a junction of tunnels. There was no sign of the centurion. Frustrated, Stiger turned back to the action, eyes settling upon Pixus. When the enemy had neared, Sabinus had politely suggested Stiger allow Pixus to fight his own century.

"As legate," Sabinus said, "your place is overall command."

"Is that how Delvaris would have done it?" Stiger asked quietly.

Sabinus gave a nod. "Trust your officers to do their job, sir."

Stiger had listened to the advice and held back. Though he had to admit to himself it had taken a lot of self-restraint. So, Stiger watched the action, occasionally giving an order or helping an injured man. Sabinus had been correct, of course. Stiger was the legate, the general. No matter how much he felt the pull to join the action, his role was now to keep an eye on the big picture. And truth be told, Stiger was very satisfied with how Pixus was handling his men.

Why hold back? Rarokan hissed, abruptly intruding upon his thoughts. *Draw me, feed me, awaken my will… complete the bond.*

Shut up, Stiger thought back at the sword. It had been talking to him sporadically since the fighting had begun. Not only could he feel it fueling his anger, the sword was exerting immense pressure on him to personally take the fight to the enemy. The pressure almost made his head hurt, as the sword sought with increasing strength to control his actions. It was only with extreme effort he had been able to resist.

Coming here, Rarokan continued, *to this time, has weakened me. My power is divided, maddeningly split. So too is my mind. Until we return to our own time, you must feed me. Only by doing so can I help you. Together we are one, together we are power, together we have a combined will. Use it. Use me.*

The flow of power from the sword increased. Stiger staggered a step at the intensity. With each passing moment, he was having increasing difficulty holding the sword's anger and desire in check.

He saw a man fall, pierced through the neck by a spear that had been thrown over the shield wall. It was frustrating to watch and do nothing. He should be fighting with the men.

Fight. The sword prodded him onward, and with it another flow of power actively fueling his anger. It was almost impossible to resist the urge to join the fight.

In a frightening turn, Stiger understood he was losing the battle of wills with Rarokan. It was becoming more difficult to withstand the assault on his mind. The flow of rage surged, and with it Stiger felt his sword hand, of its own accord, go for the hilt.

"No." Stiger ground his teeth in frustration, straining with all his might to resist. Only with a ferocious effort did he manage to stop and hold the hand in place.

Cease this now, Stiger ordered. *End it. This is not the time for me to fight. I need to keep my head and direct the action.*

At first there was no response. It was as if Stiger's willpower were a dam. Upriver the floodwater had built to dangerous levels. The water was threatening to spill over. Once it did, the dam would be compromised and there would be no turning back.

Wield me, strike at the enemy, become more than you are, the sword replied.

Do you understand me? By the gods, listen to me! Someone needs to direct the action or we are lost. Stiger gave voice to his rage. "Stop it!"

There was a hesitation, and then a slight lessening of the pressure. It was almost as if Rarokan was thinking things over.

I understand, came the sullen response, and almost instantly the urge and pressure abated, though the sword's presence in his mind remained. Rarokan was intently watching what was going on, looking for its chance. *I can wait a little longer.*

Stiger puffed out his cheeks and wiped sweat from his brow. He felt drained but at the same time thankful. Rarokan was no longer interfering with him. Stiger glanced around, studying the action. In his struggle with the sword, he had momentarily lost track of what was going on. Not much had changed, other than the line had drawn nearer. Stiger backed up several paces to give room to the third rank.

Pixus blew on a small wooden whistle, three short, rapid blasts. The front rank abruptly stepped back, moving to the rear, past the second and third ranks. The second rank, now the first, brought their shields up with a solid-sounding *thunk* and locked them tightly together. A moment later, the enemy pushed forward and hammered into the new front line in attempt to break its integrity. Pixus's men held and pushed back, throwing their shoulders into their shields.

Pixus blew on his whistle again, two short blasts. The shields scraped apart, just a matter of inches. Swords darted out, jabbing and poking. There were screams and cries of pain. Pixus blew again, this time a longer blast. When it ceased, the century resumed falling back, one steady half -step at a time.

Stepping over their dead, dying, and injured, the enemy was not as eager to close as they had been. A number of the enemy at the very front were clustered around a fallen orc. Stiger figured it had been a respected tribal leader. He felt some satisfaction they had taken him down. The legionaries were handling the enemy roughly, and anything further that they could do to affect the enemy's morale could only help.

A large orc stepped forward into the gap between the legionary line and the enemy. He looked upon the fallen orc for several heartbeats. Stiger noticed all eyes were upon this newcomer, who began to give a short address that seemed quite impassioned. There were roars and shouts of approval. The large orc turned, screamed a battle cry, and charged forward. The entire mass followed and the fight was back on.

Brogan and Theo stood just off to Stiger's left, watching the action. Both looked on with grim expressions. Stiger could well understand their concern, for in his mind he could see what was bound to happen, almost as if it already had occurred.

The intense pressure on his front line would eventually tell. The men would tire, and when that happened, the rate of casualties would increase. The formation's depth would thin next, going from three ranks to two. Then it would become perilous as the legionaries became exhausted and eventually blown. To give his men a badly needed break, he would be forced to throw Brogan's unarmored dwarves into line. Having only a shield for protection, they wouldn't last very long. Then the legionaries would be back, holding the line. At that point, it would only be a matter of time before the formation cracked.

There was a solid tap on his shoulder. He glanced over. It was Sabinus.

"I checked as you asked," Sabinus said, shouting into Stiger's ear just to be heard. He gestured behind them with a hand and pointed. "Back that way sixty yards is a cross tunnel, just as Brogan said."

Stiger had sent the centurion back to check. He wanted someone he could rely upon to give him an accurate idea of what the intersection of tunnels looked like.

"A cross tunnel?"

"Two roads coming together, at right angles," Sabinus said, making a cross with both hands. "Just like the others we passed getting to Garand Kos, only this junction is one of the larger ones."

"How wide exactly?" Stiger did not like the sound of that.

"A little over three times the width of this road here," Sabinus shouted back to him. "Negotiating our way through the junction is going to be tricky."

That was not what Stiger wanted to hear. With just the narrow confines of the road to deal with, the front rank was able to create and maintain a continuous line from one side of the tunnel to the other. When they hit this junction, they would not be able to easily do that without decreasing the depth of the formation to a dangerous level. Worse, Stiger would have to commit his dwarven reserves to extend the line, and that might not help either. Their flanks would still likely hang open. The enemy, with their superior numbers, might be able to get around them or—what Stiger considered a more likely possibility—crack a portion of the line that had become weak.

Stiger ran over the problem, looking for a solution. The current pace was measured and steady. Fighting withdrawals were tricky. Pulling back at a faster pace was not an option either, for that was a recipe for disaster, inviting the breakup of the organizational structure of the line. Whatever he did, passing through the junction would be dangerous. If not handled correctly, it could very well mean the breaking of the century.

Two legionaries in the front rank went down, and a third soon followed. The enemy, sensing both weakness and an opportunity, shoved forward hard, pressing against the shield wall and trying to widen the gap they had just created in the line. At the same time, the legionaries in the second rank stepped over their fallen comrades and attempted to put their shields forward into the hole. One of these men was brutally cut down in the attempt. He fell back and knocked another legionary behind him down.

Then Pixus was there, throwing himself forward and into the enemy. Shield held to the front, he shoved his way into the center of the gap. An orc barred his path. The centurion hammered his shield into the creature's face, knocking it off balance, before punching his sword into the orc's side. The creature screamed as Pixus gave the sword a savage twist before jerking his arm back. The injured creature was swallowed up in the press.

He continued his forward progress into the breach, bashing with his shield and slamming it into the face of a human who had taken the orc's place. The blow knocked him bodily back. The centurion stabbed outward again, this time at another orc, catching him in the stomach. The orc staggered backwards but had nowhere to go. His fellows, eager to keep the legionaries from plugging the hole, pushed him forward into the sword of another legionary to Pixus's right.

Pixus's efforts allowed the legionaries from the second rank to join their centurion, taking up positions on either shoulder. They brought their shields up to lock with his and for the moment the wall of protection had been restored. Orcs lashed out at the shields, battering away with swords and hammers. Stiger saw splinters fly from Pixus's shield as a battle axe tore into it. Heedless, Pixus fought on, scraping his shield aside, striking outward, and sticking an enemy.

The centurion glanced backwards, clearly intending to tell the man behind him to take his place. At that moment, two orcs reached forward and together gripped the top of the centurion's shield, pulling it downward. Another, seeing an opportunity, stabbed at Pixus with a spear. Pixus was caught off balance by the sudden assault. The tip of the spear slipped in around Pixus's collarbone and disappeared under centurion's shoulder armor.

Stiger watched in horror as Pixus dropped his shield and reeled backwards. The orc violently yanked the spear back and out, flinging blood up through the air. Pixus tottered in shock. The orc jabbed once again, this time striking the stricken centurion in the thigh, the weapon passing clean through, the spear point emerging just above the back of the knee.

The blow seemed to snap the centurion out of his shock.

Screaming in rage and pain, Pixus leaned forward and punched his sword into the orc's exposed neck. The sword slid in deep. The creature let go of the spear, which was still stuck through Pixus's leg, and fell forward to the ground.

Badly wounded and clearly in agony, the centurion stumbled backwards before falling to his good knee. Men from the second and third ranks rushed forward, one taking Pixus's place on the restored line while others helped to pull their officer to safety.

With the spear still embedded in his leg, Pixus was dragged well clear of the line. He was laid down on the dusty and grimy stone road. Sabinus reached Pixus before Stiger.

"Quickly, a bandage," Sabinus shouted to one of the men who had dragged Pixus clear. He knelt next to the injured officer. Blood flowed not only from the leg but out from under the centurion's tunic. The gray tunic was stained an ugly dark red. Sabinus pulled the tunic down, located the wound, and put his hand on the hole, attempting to staunch the flow of blood.

"Get it out," Pixus said weakly, blood frothing around his mouth. He attempted to reach for his leg. "Gods, it hurts."

"Lie still," Sabinus said. "We've got it."

One of the men pulled a bandage from a pack secured to his side and knelt down by the injured leg. Another prepared to pull the spear out. Blood pooled around the centurion's leg.

"What are you waiting for?" Shaking slightly, Pixus looked back up at his man. "Get it over with."

Sabinus gave a nod to the man, who slowly began to draw the spear out. Pixus gritted his teeth as it came free. Once the spear was removed, blood flowed thick and heavy out of the wound. The man with the bandage went to work, wrapping it around the leg tightly. As the man was finishing tying it off, Pixus arched his back. He cried out once and then went still. His eyes fluttered for a moment before rolling back.

Sabinus checked for a pulse. After several heartbeats, his shoulders slumped. He looked up at Stiger and the men, shaking his head.

Though he had known Pixus but a short time, Stiger felt terrible at the centurion's loss. He glanced around at the legionaries who had dragged their centurion to safety. All four were older men, clearly long-service veterans. They had long since been hardened to the horrors of war, and yet there were tears in their eyes. This surprised Stiger not at all, for Pixus had been a leader of men, the embodiment of the example of the glue that made the Mal'Zeelan legions so tough and formidable. It pained Stiger to see such a good officer brought down, but he knew now was not the time to grieve.

The fight behind them continued unabated. Stiger noticed that men from the second and third ranks had craned their necks around to see what happened. There were concerned looks on more than a few, and that worried him terribly. Morale was a tenuous thing. Losing a loved leader could easily sap the will to fight.

"Sabinus," Stiger hollered over the noise of the fighting. The senior centurion seemed not to have heard him. Sabinus leaned forward and closed the other centurion's sightless eyes. Stiger reached down and hauled Sabinus to his feet. The centurion shook him off. Their eyes met and Stiger read the naked anger directed at him for interfering with his personal grief. Stiger did not care.

"The men need a leader," Stiger hollered into Sabinus's ear and pointed back toward the line. "These men know you. Take a command of Fifth Century. Now, before it's too late."

Sabinus glanced around and took in the worried looks. Comprehension dawned. Already the third rank had lost much of its cohesion as men had begun backing away or breaking ranks for a closer look at Pixus. Sabinus apparently grasped the peril, for he gave Stiger a nod and then waded forward toward the line, hollering and gesturing at the men to face front. One man hadn't turned quick enough for the centurion's taste. Sabinus grabbed him roughly, shouted something in his ear, and then forced him around so that he faced front to help support the battle line.

Sabinus cuffed another legionary, who glanced back at Pixus. Sabinus shouted something at him before kicking at the leg of a third man to get his attention as well. Very rapidly, the men became thoroughly aware of the enraged centurion in their midst. They quickly returned their focus to their duty, and with that the dangerous moment passed.

Stiger turned back to Pixus. The four men who had dragged their centurion back had remained, standing there gazing down in shock at a man who had been an integral part of their daily lives. The line was still moving backward one half-step at a time. In a matter of moments, it would overtake them.

"Move the centurion to the side and out of the way," Stiger hollered to them. He pointed at Pixus and then the wall in case they could not make out his words. "Then get back to the line."

"Yes, sir," one of the men said.

Grabbing Pixus by the shoulders, they dragged him gently over to the side of the tunnel and left him there, propped up against the wall. It wasn't a proper place to leave him, but it was better than just lying sprawled in the road. Pixus had been a soldier and had died a warrior's death. There wasn't even time to say a proper prayer over his corpse, and for that Stiger was profoundly sorry. This certainly wasn't what the man deserved.

"In war," Stiger said to himself, shaking his head, "*deserves* have nothing to do with nothing."

Stiger returned his attention to the line, studying the action. Sabinus had things well in hand. He led the century calmly and coolly. There was a confidence in his actions that bespoke of years of experience. He was a rock, just as Pixus had been. In short, he was a legionary officer through and through.

Yet the men were clearly tiring. It was only a matter of time before the century started taking casualties at a higher rate. With no relief in sight, Stiger understood this was possibly the beginning of the end. He wasn't quite sure what to do, especially with the junction coming up. Though the enemy was numerous, they had to be tiring as well. At least he hoped so. Stiger spared one last glance at Pixus before the line passed him by and his corpse was lost from sight. Then he turned back to the action.

"One challenge at a time," he said to himself. "Deal with one problem at a time. First, the junction."

"Sir? Was that Pixus?" a voice shouted in his ear.

Stiger turned to find Mectillius.

"It was," Stiger said, and read the instant grief in the other's eyes. He leaned forward and shouted. "Now is not the time. We must be strong for the men. Do you understand me?"

"I do, sir." Mectillius straightened, a hard look in his eye.

"Good," Stiger said, and was pleased with what he saw in the other man. "I am promoting you to centurion."

"Me, sir?" Mectillius seemed taken aback.

"The Fifth is now yours," Stiger said.

"I don't want it this way, sir," Mectillius said, and Stiger read the sincerity in the optio's expression.

"I am sure Pixus didn't want to go the way he did either," Stiger said. "Nevertheless, you are now in command of Fifth Century. Do your former boss proud, by taking up his burden and looking after your men as he would."

"I will and thank you, sir."

"Go and help Sabinus," Stiger said.

"What about the wounded?" Mectillius gestured back at a group of five recently injured men right behind the formation. Some had major wounds. There were dwarves with them, helping to dress injuries.

"Get those who can still hold a sword and shield back into the line," Stiger said.

"And the others?" There was a look of concern in Mectillius's eyes.

If it became bad enough, Stiger knew he wouldn't hesitate to order the wounded finished off. Better that than leave them for the enemy. The time for such measures had not come—yet.

"I will speak to Brogan and have more of his boys pulled from the reserve to move them up the tunnel and beyond the coming junction. Make sure those who can fight get back to the line."

"Yes, sir, and thank you." Mectillius nodded his understanding and stepped toward the wounded as Stiger made his way over to Brogan and Theo.

"It is not looking good for us," Brogan said, his eyes fixed upon the action.

"No," Stiger said, "but it's not over yet."

"Your legion's fighting prowess has not been exaggerated," Brogan said. "I can see why my people formed the

Compact with yours so long ago and why your legions are so feared."

"Can you pull more of your boys out of the reserve to help with the wounded?" Stiger indicated the men he meant. Now was not the time for a discussion on the Compact or the legions. "The line will shortly overtake them. Can your boys help move them up the road a bit, beyond the junction?"

The crossroads was only twenty yards away now.

"We can," Brogan said and stepped over to the nearest dwarf. He pulled him close and spoke into his ear. The dwarf rounded up a number of his fellows from the reserve, and within moments the seriously injured were either being helped or carried up the road.

"Thank you," Stiger said when Brogan returned.

"How are you going to handle the crossroads?" Brogan asked.

"Very carefully," Stiger said, but the truth was he didn't yet know himself.

Now that he was near enough to see it fully, he looked the junction over. It was too wide to even attempt to extend his line to cover as much space as possible. Worse, if they moved back rapidly, the organization of the line would most definitely be tested. So intense was the pressure on the shield wall that if the formation broke, he understood only too clearly he might not be able to reconstitute it. With every moment that passed them by, the line edged closer to the junction and crossroads. Stiger was becoming frustrated. Then an idea came to him. He knew what he wanted to do.

He hurried over to Sabinus and Mectillius. So close to the fighting, the two had their heads together as Sabinus spoke to Mectillius.

"All right," Stiger said, getting their attention, "this is what we are going to do. I want you—"

"What?" Sabinus held a hand up to his ear. The noise was nearly overpowering.

With a gesture, Stiger drew Sabinus and Mectillius back several paces. He pointed behind, at the junction. "When we come to the crossroads, rotate ranks. Those coming off the line will break off and reform a line on the other side of the junction. Mectillius, you go with them and make it happen." Stiger pointed to where he meant so there could be no doubt. "Now, the fresh rank, along with the second, will push forward and advance, shoving the enemy back as hard as we are able."

"Advance?" Sabinus looked at him like he was mad. "You mean to attack? Are you sure, sir?"

"Yes," Stiger said. "We're going over to the attack. I am hoping it will shock the enemy enough to force them backwards a bit. You must hit them hard—very hard—for this to work. I intend to create a gap between their line and ours. Once we have some space, we withdraw and reform on the other side of the junction, where we will already have a line in place and anchored by Mectillius."

"What if we don't create the space we need to disengage the line?" Mectillius asked.

"We will deal with that if and when it happens," Stiger said. "Do either of you have a better idea?"

Sabinus shook his head.

"I don't, sir," Mectillius said.

"It's settled then," Stiger said. "Execute it."

The senior centurion gave a nod and returned to his line, shouting at the men of the second and third ranks, who passed along his orders from one man to the next. Stiger studied the formation as Sabinus allowed it to continue to back slowly up, nearing the edge of the tunnel junction.

The men were holding, but Fifth Century was under tremendous pressure.

With a little fortune, he was hoping he could temporarily shift the initiative to his side. Stiger tempered his anticipation. Fortuna could be fickle.

If his plan worked, he understood it would only be a brief respite. Once safely across the junction, the enemy would soon be back on them and the fight would resume. After that, the men would steadily wear down. It would only be a matter of time before the formation as a whole cracked. Then the real slaughter would begin, at the hands of the enemy.

Stiger looked down the tunnel, beyond the shield wall. It was hard to clearly see, but there had to be more than a thousand of the enemy, all packed tightly together. Those who had not yet seen action were waiting their turn or pushing their way forward to join the fight.

Stiger continued to back up with the line. Then he stepped into the junction. A large magical lantern hung above, brightly illuminating the center of the crossroads. He glanced down the side roads. Both were completely dark, without any light whatsoever. He could not quite remember coming through here but wasn't sure. Much of the underground looked the same, with many of the minor road junctions they passed appearing just like this one.

Stiger glanced behind to make sure the dwarves had gotten the wounded to the other side of the crossroads. They had and were continuing to help them farther up the tunnel. Brogan had formed twenty of his dwarves in a line just beyond the junction. Theo stood with them.

Brogan joined Stiger, both silently watching the fighting.

Dog was glued to Stiger's hip. Ever since the fighting had begun, he had stuck close at hand. Stiger spared a quick glance downward. Dog's attention was on the fighting, reminding him that was where Stiger's attention should be.

Stiger returned his gaze to the action and watched silently. Sabinus unexpectedly swapped ranks, breaking the routine Pixus had developed. Instead of calling a halt, he did the rotation on the move. The maneuver was pulled off flawlessly and seemed to catch the enemy by surprise. A moment later the third rank, which had just been the first, turned and jogged up the road, through the junction and past Stiger. Mectillius ran with them. The men looked haggard and tired. Even in the chill underground air, they were drenched with sweat. A number bled from minor cuts and wounds.

The enemy, realizing something was up, gave a massed shout and pushed at the legionary line, which was now only two ranks deep. At this moment, Sabinus gave the order to attack and the legionaries shoved forward, the second rank helping to push the first. They gave it all that they could. Shields hammered violently at the orcs. The deadly short swords punched out. Those in the second rank who still had javelins stabbed over the first rank at the enemy. Orcs screamed and attempted to strike back. It was an unequal contest. The legionaries had the better equipment, and the legionary shield was superior to anything the orcs carried. The legionary shield wasn't just a defensive tool, but a deadly weapon that could do fearsome damage in the right hands.

"Push!" roared Sabinus. "Push them!"

The noise in the tunnel increased in volume. Shouting, the men of Fifth Century pushed and then pushed again, attempting to give the enemy a shove backwards. It was incredible to watch, an inferior force attempting to bully a larger one. The enemy at first did not give. Then there was a little movement. That tiny bit of movement grew into a full step forward by the shield wall and then another.

As Stiger had hoped, the pressure along the line eased with every step. Sabinus kept the pressure up, screaming to the men to push. The legionaries advanced perhaps five yards, leaving a swath of enemy bodies behind them. Then the enemy gave fully and began backing up faster than the line could steadily advance. The noise in the tunnel quieted dramatically as the enemy disengaged.

Stiger found their backpedaling an encouraging sign, for it meant the enemy were also nearing their breaking point.

"Halt!" Sabinus brought his formation to a stop. He looked first left and then right, clearly making sure the line had stopped. "First and second ranks... about face." He paused, waiting for the movement to be completed. "On the double, march!"

Stiger turned to look back on the third rank, only ten yards away. They had reformed the line under Mectillius's direction and were waiting just ahead of the dwarven reserve.

Armor jingling and chinking, Sabinus and the men rapidly passed Brogan, Stiger, and Dog by. Sabinus jogged by as well. The orcs gave a howl of outrage but did not advance.

"Time to go, I think," Stiger said.

"Agreed," Brogan said, eyeing the enemy, who were just watching them.

They jogged to the safety of the new line. The men stepped aside to admit them, and Stiger made his way through the press to the rear. He turned back to watch.

A large orc, Stiger suspected the same he had seen earlier, stepped to the front of the enemy. He began shouting in what Stiger took to be the orc tongue and pointed a large sword at the new line. The orcs and humans amongst them roared like animals and charged.

"Shields up," Mectillius shouted.

Stiger glanced up at the ceiling, judging its height, and then he looked over the formation. There were around twenty who still had missile weapons.

"Javelins," Stiger shouted as loud as he could. "Watch the ceiling! Make your toss count. Release at will!"

Moments later, the javelins began to fly. The first landed short, skittering harmlessly across the road. The next took a human full on in the chest. He fell and was immediately trampled by the charging mass. Most of the rest hit home, causing another dozen or more casualties. It wasn't much, but it was something.

The orcs slammed into the shield wall. The men of the new first rank threw their shoulders into it as the orcs pushed and battered at the shields. Those in the second rank helped to hold the first in place. A few were forced back a step, but they redoubled their efforts and bashed back at the enemy. Swords jabbed out, seeking flesh and finding it. A hammer reached over a legionary's shield and connected with his helmet. The man went down. Without missing a beat, the legionary behind him took his place on the line.

The momentum of the charge forced those of the enemy at the front to be crushed against the shield wall. So tight was the press of bodies that most were unable to use their weapons and were helpless as the vicious legionary short swords repeatedly darted out, stabbing away remorselessly.

"That was a neat bit of work," Brogan shouted at Stiger.

Stiger glanced over at the thane to reply and was startled to find someone unexpected between him and Brogan. Stiger's hand went for his sword, as did Brogan's. Then Stiger relaxed a moment as he realized it was a gnome. He wore only a simple black tunic, but was armed with a small sword, a little shorter than a gladius. Stiger noticed Brogan relax as well.

But what was he doing here?

The little creature looked between the thane and Stiger, black, emotionless eyes inscrutable. Then, slowly, a cruel smile formed on its face. The gnome showed its tiny needle-sharp teeth. It said something that Stiger could not hear.

"What did you say?" Stiger asked in dwarven.

"Watch," the gnome shouted, in a squeaky voice that was hard to hear over the noise of the fight. Its smile grew wider. "Nasty orcs in trouble. Tunnel go boom."

Stiger's eyes snapped forward. He made a move for Sabinus to warn him, but a fraction of a moment later there was a tremendous earth-shaking roar that nearly tossed him from his feet. The shockwave of air followed a heartbeat later, then a wall of dust propelled by a hot gust of wind blew over them.

Stiger clapped his hands to his ears as they rang painfully. He was dazed and couldn't see. The dust cloud completely obscured the light of the tunnel. It was as if the blackest of nights had suddenly descended down upon them. He staggered backwards, wondering what the gnomes had done. Then it hit him and he recalled the exploding clay jars they had fired from their catapult. It was clear using their blasting powder that they had collapsed the tunnel somewhere ahead of his formation. There was a secondary crash that rumbled the road violently under his feet. More of the tunnel must have come down. The rumbling died off.

After several moments, the ringing in his ears began to subside as well. Stiger's ears popped. He was able to hear cries of alarm and shouts of pain. He coughed on the choking dust, as did many others. Then, mercifully, the dust cloud began to thin just a little. The light from the magical lanterns returned. Stiger was able to see the light from the junction ahead. It was as if he were in a thick early morning fog of dust. It caused the lungs to burn and eyes to tear. Half of the legionaries had fallen. Dazed, some were in the process of picking themselves up. Just ahead, several hundred of the enemy were doing the same thing.

"Gods no." Stiger's stomach did a backflip.

The gnomes had collapsed the tunnel behind the orcs, not on them, not over the junction itself. Though they had gotten some of the enemy, they'd not gotten them all.

"Shields!" Stiger shouted as loud as he could. Coughing, he rushed forward. "On your feet. Shields up!"

Only a handful of legionaries responded. Stiger knew time was not on his side. They were still terribly outnumbered.

"Reform, reform, hurry," Stiger shouted in between hacking from the dust. He shook several legionaries to get their attention. "Shields up, bring the line back together. Quickly now!"

"Get in a line," Sabinus shouted, joining him.

From head to toe, everyone was covered in a layer of white dust. The legionaries looked like ghosts as the line slowly began to reform. Not only were the legionaries of Fifth Century exhausted, but many were also thoroughly dazed and confused by what had just happened.

The dust cloud was rapidly settling down. Stiger's eyes swept over the enemy. They seemed in a similar state. Stiger heard an orc roaring what seemed like orders in his own tongue. He quickly spotted the creature. Stiger went cold. He wasn't certain, but covered in white dust the orc looked like Therik. He was busy dragging dazed and cowering orcs to their feet.

"Reform!" Stiger shouted, voice cracking from the shouting and dust. He hacked for a moment. "Hurry—"

A massed screeching shout stopped him in his tracks. Out of the darkness from both sides of the connecting road at the junction came thousands of gnomes charging madly forward. Like a tidal wave, they swept over the dazed and confused orcs. Stiger and the legionaries simply watched in numb exhaustion and shock. Bearing swords slightly shorter than a gladius, the gnomes took apart the orcs with a ferocity and intensity that was absolutely stunning. Stiger had never seen anything quite like it and had difficulty tearing his eyes away from the spectacle, which was over in a shockingly short time.

"It was big boom." Unnoticed, the gnome had come to stand next to him. Stiger glanced down. The gnome was looking on his brethren with what Stiger took to be more than a little satisfaction. "Surprise orcs, surprise humans"—it shot a glance at Brogan—"and surprise dvergr." The gnome snickered wickedly.

"It was a good," Stiger said in dwarven, suddenly finding himself grinning at the bloodthirsty little creature. "I think an unwelcome surprise to the orcs."

"Yes, yes," the gnome said, laughing in a high-pitched, squeaky kind of way. "Orcs very surprised. It was good joke on them. Ha, ha."

"I'm not sure they saw the joke," Stiger said.

"No," the gnome said and heaved a sigh, seeming to deflate a little. "They no have humor."

Brogan joined them. Hands on his hips, he looked over the carnage. The gnomes had killed every one of the enemy and were now busy either looting the bodies or dismembering and mutilating them.

Brogan turned his gaze onto the gnome, scowling. Though they had been delivered, and saved, Stiger thought the thane did not seem very pleased by the unexpected turn of events.

Dog padded up and started licking at the gnome's face, removing the white dust with each swipe from his tongue. The little creature gave a surprised laugh and patted the animal affectionately on the head.

"Good dog," the gnome said and glanced up at Stiger. "We like dogs."

"Dog, down," Stiger said. Dog ceased his licking of the gnome and sat down on his haunches.

The gnome reached out a small hand and patted the animal's side. Sitting or standing, Dog was taller than the gnome.

"I wish to thank you for your timely arrival," Stiger said. "I would know your name?"

The gnome looked up at him in what Stiger took to be surprise. A moment later, the gnome grinned and glanced over to Brogan.

"That," Brogan said, before the gnome could respond, "is Cragg. He is an outcast, even amongst his own kind. He styles himself a leader, but on most days, he is nothing more than a bandit."

"Bandit?" Cragg squeaked and pointed at his fellows. "I am leader."

Stiger's eyes went wide at the name. Could it be this was the same gnome he had known in the future? Were they that long-lived?

"A bandit," Brogan repeated.

"I good bandit," Cragg said indignantly, pointing a finger at himself. He then shook it at Brogan. "Bandit, no more. I save thane's life. You reward, no?"

Brogan looked thoroughly dissatisfied and unhappy. Gnome and thane stared at each other for several long moments.

"If I pardon you and your followers," Brogan said in a tired tone, "your people will object. There will be trouble for years to come."

"My people are sheep," Cragg said, seeming to push for his opportunity while the event was still fresh in the thane's mind. "They do nothing. I am rightful kluge. You reward me, now. I keep the people in order. You no worry. No worry."

Brogan worked his jaw a moment, glanced over at Stiger and then back to the gnome.

"I'd say he certainly earned a reward," Stiger said. "We were in serious trouble until his lot arrived."

"Oh, very well," Brogan said. "As you say, you are kluge."

The gnome gave a little jump for joy and then skittered away, dodging around legionaries and out amongst his own kind. The gnomes were still happily looting the dead. The legionaries looked on in numb shock, not quite believing they had been delivered.

The dust wasn't as thick, but it was still settling. Stiger could now see the road that had just come down. Around ten yards from the junction, it had been completely collapsed. Stiger wondered how many orcs had been crushed as the tunnel fell on them.

Cragg climbed onto the body of an orc that had fallen atop another, standing proudly upon its chest. It was a good perch for all of the gnomes to see him. He shouted something in what Stiger thought might be gnomish. The gnomes stopped what they were doing. All turned to look upon him. Once he had their attention, Cragg let out a long string of speech that lasted for a bit. He concluded by pumping a fist up into the air.

Silence followed but lasted only for a heartbeat. The gnomes began shouting wildly, jumping about in celebration. They punched their little swords and fists up into the air excitedly. The shouting solidified into a name.

"Cragg! Cragg! Cragg!" they shouted in unison, over and over again.

"I fear," Brogan said, "I may live to regret this."

Chapter Twenty-Four

Fifteen hours had passed since the gnome ambush. Stiger tied off the saddlebag, using a double knot to fasten it securely to his saddle. Misty stomped a hoof repeatedly. With all of the activity in the tunnel and the familiar weight of the saddle, she knew they were close to setting out and was more than eager to be off.

"Easy, girl," he soothed as he looked over the horse, making certain everything was where it needed to be.

Misty pawed at the ground and then looked around at him, clearly wondering what the holdup was.

"We will be on the move soon enough," Stiger said, patting her neck affectionately. "Your old, comfortable barn is waiting. There will be plenty of hay and oats. On that I promise."

He gave the saddle a hard tug and sure enough found it loose. Misty had been holding her breath once again.

"Trying to pull one over on me, are you?" Stiger asked the horse. The old leather of the saddle creaked slightly as he tightened the saddle straps. The horse whinnied, as if laughing at the joke at his expense.

Stiger next checked the animal's hooves for rocks or debris. Thankfully, they were clean and no picking was required. Satisfied all was in order, Stiger glanced around.

Sabinus was finishing up with his horse as well. Just behind the centurion, the survivors of Fifth Century prepared themselves for march. A series of gnome carts and wagons pulled by ponies had arrived an hour before. These were for the wounded. Blankets had been laid down in the beds to help make the ride a little more comfortable. Under the supervision of Father Thomas, the wounded were being carefully loaded.

The dwarves themselves were also preparing to depart. Now that the danger was past, both groups would be going their separate ways. Stiger had mixed feelings about that but understood why it was necessary. There was much to do and little time.

He cracked his neck, attempting to work out a crick. Sleeping on the hard stone of the road had taken its toll. Despite having rested at least twelve hours, he was still tired. Stiger glanced down the road, toward the junction where the gnomes had slaughtered the orcs, perhaps two hundred yards away.

The bodies of the dead lay where they had fallen. A handful of gnomes were combing through the bodies, poking about. At this point, the bodies had been thoroughly looted—what the gnomes were looking for, Stiger had no idea. He himself had searched through the dead, looking intently for Therik. He hadn't found the king's body. Stiger had reluctantly come to the conclusion the orc he had seen had not been the king. Was Therik buried under tons of rock? Or, more likely, was he still out there and on the loose?

Stiger turned his gaze back to the legionaries. Of Fifth Century, only twenty-two men were fit for service. Another twenty-one had been injured, with wounds ranging from light to serious. A good number of those who had held the line had been wounded in one way or another. Twelve of those could no longer move under their own power. After consulting with Brogan, Stiger had made the decision that all of the wounded would be brought back to Old City by the gnomes. This included any walking wounded. Thirty-seven men had not made it. The underground would forevermore be their tomb.

Stiger rubbed at his stubbled jaw. He badly needed not only a shave, but a proper toilet. He had given his armor a light cleaning, but, like him, it needed more attention. It would be good to properly clean up.

Stiger's gaze slid back over to the dwarves. The gnomes had brought enough ponies for the thane and five of his warriors. Brogan would be riding ahead to Old City, and the rest of the dwarves would hump their way back. Stiger spotted Brogan and Theo. Both were making their way over, weaving around wagons and carts. Cragg was with them. The gnome, due to his short stature, was nearly running just to keep up.

Stiger took Misty's reins and handed them to a passing legionary.

"Hold my mount," Stiger told the man. "Would you take her over to where the century will be forming up?"

"Yes, sir," the legionary said, taking hold of the reins and leading the horse off.

Stiger turned to face the thane.

"We're ready to depart," Brogan said, without any preamble.

The thane looked tired and haggard. Stiger was sure that he appeared just the same himself.

"Almost there ourselves," Stiger said, glancing over at the wagons where the wounded were being made comfortable for their journey back to the legion. He was able to see into the bed of one of the wagons, where two men had been laid out. A legionary climbed into the bed and began covering each in a thick wool blanket. Stiger was reminded of a father tucking children into bed.

"As discussed," Brogan said, "Theo will guide you back to the valley."

"And you go to hurry along your army," Stiger said. "I wish we were not splitting up, but I understand the necessity."

"You get back to your legion quicker and I to Old City. Time is no longer on our side," Brogan said. "I will send word of my progress."

"How will I reach you?" Stiger asked. "At some point, we will need to coordinate our actions."

"Send a messenger to Old City," Brogan said. "Your message will find me and I will respond as soon as I am able."

"That will work," Stiger said.

"Good," Brogan said. "I will meet you in the valley. You can expect me sometime within the next fortnight."

"Just make sure you don't take too long," Stiger said, with a sudden grin. "Depending on how fast Therik moves, we may need help sooner rather than later."

"I will come just as soon as I am able."

"I can ask no more," Stiger said and then glanced over at Theo. "Are you certain you wish to part with your advisor? Cragg offered to guide us back to the valley."

"Yes, yes," Cragg said, sounding eager. "I guide. No worries."

Brogan gave a highly amused laugh, though Stiger thought he read irritation in Brogan's eyes. "You'd never get there with this bandit. He has a warped sense of humor. You'd be lucky if he doesn't march you in circles."

"I am no bandit," Cragg said in his squeaky voice, sounding like an indignant child. He tapped himself on the chest. "I am kluge. I guide him to valley. My word is good. You know."

With a laugh, Brogan held up his hands.

"I only jest, Cragg," Brogan said to the gnome. "You people aren't the only ones with a sense of humor. Your word has always been good for me. But that is not the point. Theogdin is a liaison between my people and his." Brogan gestured at Stiger. "Since I'm sending him anyway, he can easily enough guide the humans to where they need to go. So, you can see there is no need for you or your people to go out of their way. You have done enough already."

Cragg did not look too terribly pleased but seemed somewhat mollified by the explanation. He gave an unhappy hiss and shook his head, but then nodded his understanding and acceptance.

"Theogdin goes with you," Brogan said firmly, turning back to Stiger. "When this is all over, you can return him. That is, if you so desire. I have no doubt that just as soon as he takes up his post, he will drink me poor."

"Brogan, you wound me," Theo said. "You know very well you will gladly do it with me."

Brogan gave a low chuckle. "I should have made you my advisor years ago."

The thane looked about, clearly ready to depart. He hesitated a moment and then offered his hand, which Stiger took and shook firmly.

"Good travels," Brogan said.

"You as well," Stiger said.

Brogan turned away, then stopped. "Theo, do try to stay out of trouble."

"Where is the fun with that?" Theo asked and when Brogan scowled, he gave a great sigh. "In light of the importance of my new position, I will endeavor to do as you ask."

Brogan gave a satisfied nod and moved off toward the ponies and his waiting escort.

Theo shifted his feet. Stiger glanced over at his friend.

"He aims to make something of me," Theo said. "I fear he has made it his project."

"I see," Stiger said.

"You should've asked him for something more than you got," Theo said as they watched the thane. "Brogan is rich beyond your imaginings. His mines are the deepest and have the strongest veins of gold and silver. It is why his family has held onto the reins of power for so long. They can buy most anyone they need, and those they can't... well, they can hurt economically."

"I already got what I needed," Stiger said. "There was no need to ask for more."

"You got what you needed?" Theo narrowed an eye at him, while cocking his head. "And what was that exactly?"

"His army," Stiger said, "and his help at defending the valley."

To kill the minion, Stiger understood he needed all the help he could get. Castor's servant would come at him with Therik's army.

"He would've given you his army regardless," Theo said with exasperation. "Well, he wouldn't really have given it to you, of course. He would just have sent it and used it alongside yours to evict the orcs from the valley."

"Really?" Stiger asked, turning his gaze upon Theo.

"Though we allow you humans to live there, you forget the valley is our land. Brogan is obligated to defend it. Since it falls under his own clan holdings, the valley's defense is tied to his personal legend. Then there is Grata'Jalor and the World Gate that need defending too. So, what exactly did you get?"

"An ally."

"Having Brogan as an ally is no small thing," Theo conceded. "I will give you that."

"In the end, it's the same thing," Stiger said, "isn't it?"

"For pulling his bacon out of the fire, you could have asked for gold, jewels, and still gotten his assistance," Theo said, seeming disgusted by the lack of opportunism. "You should have wrung him for everything he was willing to give, just like Cragg here. You could learn something from this former bandit."

Stiger glanced down at the gnome, who had been standing there silently, watching them. Cragg's black eyes shone under the magical light from above. Stiger got the impression the little gnome was exceedingly pleased with himself. He nodded his agreement to what Theo said.

"And Brogan needs you to help get his revenge," Theo said. "Additional leverage there, and you cast it aside."

"I have no need of riches," Stiger said, turning his gaze back to Theo. "Not at the moment, anyway."

"Of course you do," Theo said. "Everyone has need of money."

"Perhaps," Stiger said, and his gaze swung back toward the gnome. He regarded the little creature for a moment, thinking on what lay ahead.

"What?" Cragg asked.

"More orcs are coming," Stiger said. Here before him was another potential ally. Despite Brogan's disregard and disdain for them, the gnomes had already proven their worth to Stiger, both here in this time and in the future. "They come to take the valley."

"So?" Cragg said. "What means to me?"

"You enjoyed killing the orcs we brought," Stiger said. "Do I have that right?"

Cragg gave a tiny shrug, as if killing orcs mattered little to him.

"Don't let the murderous little bastard tell you otherwise," Theo said, gazing down at Cragg. "He and his kind hate the orcs more than us dvergr. They love killing their former allies."

"Never," Cragg spat back, becoming heated. He shook an angry fist at Theo. "We never allies. We slaves. Now we free. We kill, we murder, we hunt orcs for sport. Good sport too when dwarves allow." Cragg turned a nasty smile upon Theo. "And sometimes when they don't."

"Then come and help me," Stiger said. "Join me. Together we will kill thousands of orcs."

Cragg turned his black-eyed, pupil-less gaze on Stiger. He brought a tiny hand up and scratched the back of his head.

"We no fight for little people," Cragg said and pointed at Theo. "We no fight for thane." Cragg swung his tiny finger to Stiger. "We no fight for you. We no fight for anyone. Not anymore. I am kluge. I have what I want. Like he said, you should have asked thane for more. Stupid human."

The gnome spat on the ground between Stiger's feet.

Stiger restrained his anger.

"I'm not asking you to fight for me or the dwarves or anyone else," Stiger said. "I am asking you to fight with us, and for yourselves. I am giving you that opportunity."

Cragg did not immediately reply. He appeared to be mulling over Stiger's words.

"I think about," Cragg said. He gave a little shrug of his shoulders. "We come, we don't, I don't know."

"Fair enough," Stiger said, "but don't think about it too long or we will kill all the orcs without you. There will be none left for you and your people."

Cragg laughed at him. It was a dark sort of cackle, devoid of mirth. "Don't think me stupid, human. I think on your words. I promise nothing."

With that, Cragg turned and walked off toward the wagons and another gnome.

"Your effort was wasted on him," Theo said after the gnome was out of earshot. "He will come."

"You think so?" Stiger said.

"I do," Theo said.

"Why?"

"Brogan just gave the little bandit everything he's ever wanted but had not been able to get for the past century. When Cragg became kluge, he refused to bend knee to the thane. For that he was exiled. It created what you might call a bit of tension between my people and his. Now he doesn't have to bend the knee and swear fealty. Even better for his people, by recognizing him as kluge, Brogan has given the gnomes a place once again on the thane's council. For that alone, his people will think him a hero." Theo paused and glanced at Cragg's back as the gnome talked with another of his kind a few yards away by a wagon. "As Cragg himself said, he's not stupid. He's quite intelligent and as conniving as Brogan. Best you keep that in mind."

"So," Stiger said, "how do you know he will come?"

Theo gave Stiger a strange look. There was some calculation there, but also something else he could not identify.

"I tell you this, so you understand who you are dealing with," Theo said. "Despite what Brogan says publicly, he will want the gnomes to send their fighters with his army. Cragg, on the other hand, cannot allow us to fight without his people taking part. Sitting on his ass will reflect badly, not only amongst his own people, but on the council as well. If that happens, Brogan will hold a serious grudge against the mean-spirited bastard. No one—and I mean no one—holds a grudge like Brogan. Negotiations for the gnomes will be much more difficult than before. Brogan will hold their little noses to the grindstone on all sorts of contracts. Cragg's people will blame him for that and also the lost opportunity at killing orcs. So, he either joins the fight when Brogan calls, or he won't last long as kluge."

"Huh," Stiger said, suddenly feeling a little foolish. He had misread the situation. Never again would he make the mistake of underestimating a gnome or, for that matter, Brogan.

Theo suddenly grinned. "Besides, it's not often that orcs stray out of their territory and into ours. By treaty, the gnomes have long since been prohibited from hunting orcs on orc lands. Despite their disagreeable nature, they've abided by that little restriction we set upon them." Theo paused. "Brogan would not want you to know this, but our leverage with the gnomes is one of the things that has allowed us to keep the peace with the orc tribes. They fear the little bastards, and with good reason. I feel certain Cragg will come. When the call goes out, gnomes will eagerly pour up from the depths in numbers not seen since the Gate War."

"I hope you're right," Stiger said, "for I fear we will need all the help we can get."

"I am," Theo said with conviction.

The thane's party had mounted up. Riding at the head of his escort, Brogan wheeled his pony around and came by Stiger and Theo. The thane raised a hand in parting as he rode past. Nothing more was said, and nothing need be said, for each knew what the other had to do.

Theo watched his cousin ride off into the tunnel, a strange expression on his face.

After several moments of silence, Theo spoke. "Since we have all the supplies we need and are not burdened by wagons or the wounded, we should be able to make good time. We have a two-day trek from here that will lead us up and out of the tunnels to a small mountain trail. I chose this way for a very specific reason. Two hours on this trail will see us come out near Bowman's Pond. You'll be in Sarai's arms before you know it, and we may even have time to pick up that fishing rod you left the last time we visited."

Stiger was elated to hear that and laughed as they watched Brogan ride off down the road.

"If I recall," Theo said, "it was her fishing rod to begin with."

"Yes, it was," Stiger said, thinking how good it would be to see Sarai. He turned back to Theo. He saw a look of unhappiness there. It was quickly covered over.

"What's wrong?" Stiger asked Theo.

"In all honesty," Theo said, "I am somewhat disappointed I will not be returning to my company. Life is about to get very complex. Becoming entangled with my cousin is something I've been trying to avoid for a very long time."

Stiger was silent for a long moment. He had the sudden feeling Theo was acting. It was no different than an officer putting on a show for his men during a tense moment. The dwarf seemed to be overdoing it. Why was that? Stiger decided to probe a little.

"In exchange for giving up your old life... did you get what you wanted? From the thane, that is."

Now that Stiger thought on it, Theo was certainly not a typical grunt. Stiger wondered if Theo had ever really been a member of Captain Aleric's company. Throughout the entire journey to Garand Kos, he came and went at will. He was accountable to no one other than Brogan. Taithun hadn't even tried to order him about. Theo was far too smart, intuitive, and perceptive for a common soldier. He also seemed much better educated. There were so many signs he had not seen until this moment. It was something he would think further on. Stiger suddenly felt saddened. He would have to be on his guard with Theo.

Theo had not answered the question. He was studying Stiger with an amused expression. Stiger wondered if he had inadvertently given his suspicions away.

"Did you get what you wanted?" Stiger asked again.

"Oh, I got that and more," Theo said. "Don't worry about me."

"And what was that?"

"Do you really expect an answer?" Theo gave him a look of disapproval. He suddenly brightened, changing the subject. "I'm afraid you're stuck with me, at least for a few more days."

"Right," Stiger said, getting the hint. He turned his gaze to Sabinus and Mectillius, who were making sure the wounded were comfortable. Father Thomas was working alongside them.

The paladin had woken from his slumber when the gnomes had brought down the roof of the tunnel. Stiger supposed the blast would have been impossible to sleep through. Shortly after waking, Father Thomas had explained he was not recovered enough to attempt a healing on the injured. Still looking like an old man, the paladin seemed almost spent. Though he had regained much of his color, he moved about with a lethargy that Stiger felt was worrying.

Stiger started walking over toward them. Theo fell in beside him, as did Dog. The paladin gave Stiger a tired nod as he climbed down from a wagon bed and moved on to the next one.

"Sir," Sabinus said, clambering out of the same wagon.

Mectillius, standing by the wagon's side, straightened.

"How is it coming with the wounded?" Stiger asked.

"We've loaded all of them. They're as comfortable as we can make them, sir," Mectillius said. "The dwarves have assured us the gnomes will care for them on their journey to Old City."

"Once they reach the city," Theo said, "Brogan will arrange for surgeons to see to their needs. When they are well enough, they will complete the journey back to your camp. Your wounded will have the very best care we have to offer."

"I'm personally grateful for that," Mectillius said. "These men are my family. Thank you."

"Will the gnomes cause any problems for the wounded?" Stiger asked. He had some concerns about how the gnomes might treat the legionaries.

"Gnomes may not be the most pleasant of races, but your injured should be well cared for," Theo said. "Cragg gave his word, and to a gnome, one's word is all that matters."

"All right," Stiger said, feeling a little better about leaving the wounded in gnome hands.

"I've detailed the walking wounded to accompany them and help care for our boys, sir," Mectillius said. "Just to be sure, sir."

"Very good," Stiger said, glancing over the carts and wagons. Gnomish teamsters were sitting on the drivers' benches, waiting for the humans to finish their preparations. They looked neither impatient nor bored. In fact, he couldn't tell what they were thinking.

"Well then," Stiger said, looking at Sabinus, "if all is in order, I would like to get a move on. The sooner we return to the legion, the better."

"Yes, sir," Sabinus said. "I believe we are ready."

"Centurion Mectillius," Stiger said, "would you be kind enough to have your men fall in and prepare for march?"

"I will, sir." Mectillius drew himself up and saluted before turning on his heel and shouting, "Fall in."

The legionaries began to assemble a small column for march. Stiger looked them over. They had been through a terrible ordeal. Still, they were of the legion and held themselves proudly. Looking upon them in their antique armor, Stiger felt pride and a sense of belonging. He, too, was of the legion, and these men before him were some of the best soldiers that ever marched.

"I understand that you legionaries are issued a wine ration?" Theo was suddenly looking hopeful. "Do I have that right?"

"Forget it." Sabinus shot Theo a disgusted look. "We're not carrying any wine with us. At this point, all the men have in their canteens is water. I am afraid you are out of luck, old boy."

"I'm not talking about now," Theo said. "I'm looking forward to when we get to your camp. Do you think you will be able to spare me some wine?" He glanced back toward the piles of orc dead in the tunnel junction. "After what we've just gone through, I could use a drink, or two. Perhaps we can share a jar and toast our good fortune?"

"You're coming back with us?" Sabinus asked, clearly surprised. "You're not going back to your company?"

"No, he is not," Stiger said. He would speak with Sabinus on his suspicions later. "It seems the thane assigned him to us as a guide home and liaison. He will be with us for some time, I think."

"A liaison for drink?" Sabinus asked and suddenly chuckled. "Or did Brogan lend him out as a wine taster?"

"Very funny," Theo said. "Ha ha."

"I wasn't trying to be funny," Sabinus said, though he was having serious difficulty containing his mirth.

"All right, then," Stiger said. "It is time we got moving."

Chapter Twenty-Five

Stiger held Misty's reins loosely in one hand, almost letting them fall. He stared down at the valley, utterly at a loss. He couldn't believe what he was seeing.

They had emerged from the mountain trail onto the top of a cliff near Bowman's Pond, which was perhaps a quarter of a mile away somewhere to his left. It seemed as if everything was burning—all of the towns and villages, farmsteads, plantations, fields ready for harvest. In the early morning light, huge columns of smoke rose high up into the blue sky, turning it an ugly gray color. The smell of smoke, even this far away from the fire, was strong.

He shook his head in dismay. He was too late. The orcs had struck the valley hard. Gazing down at the smoke and destruction, Stiger wondered on how many had died.

His eyes scanned downward, searching for Sarai's farm. After a moment, he found it. His stomach clenched. It, too, had been burned. A plume of smoke climbed upward from where the house was. He could not see anything meaningful, for the smoke from the fire obscured his view and they were too far away to make out any real details.

A terrible, gnawing fear gripped him. At his side, as if sensing his thoughts, Dog gave a low whine. Stiger swung around and took a firmer hold on Misty's reins. He pulled himself up into the saddle.

"Wait," Sabinus called out, clearly aware of what Stiger intended. "Sir, you can't go alone. It may be dangerous!"

Ignoring him, Stiger turned the horse away from the cliff face and drove his heels in. Misty exploded forward, running for the trees. Barking, Dog chased after him. Stiger plunged back into the trees, seeking the downward slope into the valley. He found it. The wooded slope to the side of the cliff was steep but manageable. The cold fall air whipped about him as he worked his way as quickly as he could around the cliff.

From what he had seen from the top of the cliff, there was a large vineyard just below. From the vineyard he knew there would be a path that would take him to the base of the valley. Stiger weaved his way through the trees, working his way toward the vineyard. He was moving so quickly, branches occasionally slapped him in the face when he wasn't fast enough at batting them away.

He came to the edge of the wood, at the highest point of the vineyard. Stiger pulled Misty to a stop and, leaning forward in the saddle, looked down again into the valley. He judged he was only three or four miles from the farm. Dog caught up with him, barking madly and circling around Misty's legs. Though he was close to home, he had never come through the vineyard. Quickly, Stiger studied the way down, searching for a path.

He found it—at least he thought so. The vineyard had been constructed on a series of shelved terraces. He came to the conclusion he would have to ride around the edge of the first shelf, paralleling the vines, until he came to what appeared to be a path that lead from terrace to terrace right down to the valley floor. Stiger started Misty forward again. Dog ran ahead.

He followed the vines for two hundred yards before turning onto the path that led downward between the terraced fields of well cared for vines. The path was wide enough for a horse and cart. It was steep at points, but manageable. It was certainly not made for haste. He started down, carefully negotiating his way from terrace to terrace, going faster than he should until the path let out onto the grassy pasture slopes that preceded the valley floor.

It was a relief to be down. There was now only open land, broken by a handful of pastures and fields of wheat or barley between him and the farm, perhaps a little over a mile distant. He rode hard, passing a series of fields where the crops had been burned. In the distance, he could see the remains of farmsteads and plantations. Smoke climbed steadily upward from every structure in sight. A huge plume to the north told him the town of Venera had been hit and burned.

Stiger cut through a wheat field that had been burned, the edges of which still smoldered. He passed close to a scorched-out farmhouse and caught a glimpse of several bodies, including children, lying before the entrance. They were spaced out one after another over ten yards. It appeared as if they'd been killed while running for their lives. Black-fletched arrows poked out of their backs. The sight of the dead civilians spurred him onward. Like a vice, fear gripped his heart.

"Come on, come on," Stiger shouted, kicking Misty again, wanting the horse to go faster.

Hooves pounding, he turned her onto the hard-packed dirt road that led to their farm, steering around potholes and ruts in the road. Maddeningly, it seemed to take forever, but then the farm was in sight. He urged her onward.

The thick smell of smoke on the air seemed to get stronger with every yard. At the edge of the farmyard, Stiger yanked back on the reins. The horse skidded to a stop.

Misty's breath came hard, heavy, and ragged, steaming on the cold air. Sweat ran down her flanks as her breath gusted in and out. Foam had accumulated around her mouth. It dripped onto the ground, but Stiger paid her no mind. His eyes were on the farm. That was all that mattered.

As if in a dream, he slipped to the ground and released the horse's reins. Where before there'd been a quaint little farmhouse, only a burned-out, smoking shell remained, much of which had collapsed in upon itself. Surprisingly, the barn he had repaired and they'd worked on together still stood. One wall was charred black. For some reason, after being torched, the fire had gone out and the barn hadn't burned.

His eyes scanned the farmyard. There were bodies everywhere, orcs and dwarves. Aleric's boys had clearly not gone down without a fight. Many of the dwarves lay in lines, almost as if they'd gone to sleep next to each other. Wherever a line of dead was, a heap of orcs lay before it. At a glance, Stiger understood Aleric had managed to form his company for battle. The lines of dead meant they'd fought in formation. This also told Stiger the orcs had come to the farm in force. Only half of the dwarves seemed to be wearing any armor. That meant the attack had come as a surprise. The enemy's focus had been the farm and not Aleric's camp, some two hundred yards away. Stiger glanced over that way and saw the camp stood oddly untouched and undamaged. The tents were still arranged in orderly rows.

Dog padded up to Stiger's side and gave out a long whimper.

There was no sign of anyone alive. The orcs had come and gone. They'd left no survivors. Only a handful of carrion birds showed any life, and these were worrying away at the bodies.

As if drunk, Stiger took a staggered step forward and then another. Through sheer force of will alone, he continued forward, placing one wooden step after another. It was almost mechanical, as he stepped around and over the bodies. He found it a gruesome scene, some of the dead having suffered terrible wounds. Dried blood had dyed large patches of grass red or coated the dirt green. Whatever had happened here had occurred hours before, likely in the dead of night.

Nearer the barn, he came across their cow. She had been butchered for her meat. The pigs had also seen the same treatment. They'd been led out of their pen and also butchered. There was no sign of the sheep. Even the chickens were gone.

Stepping up to the barn, Stiger peered inside. It had been ransacked and looted. Most of the tools and tack for the horse were gone. The hay, set aside for the coming winter, had been taken as well. That, Stiger thought, was likely the reason the barn stood. Stiger's eyes swept the interior. The spare saddle, an ancient thing that was falling apart, had been taken too. He noted they'd even grabbed the cart. A pair of shovels and an old hammer were all that remained of the tools. His harvested walnuts lay upon the ground, scattered and discarded like a child's play stones.

Stiger turned away from the barn door and gazed upon the ruins of their once happy house. He knew what he would find there and hesitated to continue on. Like the house, his hopes and dreams had gone up in smoke. Knowing he had little choice, he made his way over.

As he came up to the ruins, he could still feel the heat of the fire that had claimed the house. It radiated from the stone foundation, pushing back on the chill air. Thin wavering and curling trails of smoke drifted upward from a few beams that yet smoldered, occasionally giving off a low crackle or pop.

The stench of the burned wood filled his nostrils. There was another smell there as well, something he had encountered before. He felt like vomiting. It was the sickly stench of charred and burned flesh. He entered what had been the kitchen. The fireplace still stood, as did the oven, appearing almost as if nothing had happened. Everything else was gone or nearly unrecognizable. It was shocking to see what had seemed permanent changed in such a way.

Then, he saw the body.

It was half buried under a pile of ash and debris. A blackened hand, fingers outstretched, poked up out of the ash, as if reaching out to him for help. What he could see of the body had been burnt beyond recognition, all except for some long brown hair. It had somehow escaped the inferno which had destroyed the house. He was certain it was Sarai.

"Oh, gods," Stiger whispered.

He had come back too late.

"I'm sorry," Stiger whispered, his throat catching with the words. "I am so sorry."

Tears blurred his vision. He fell to his knees amidst the ash and debris. When it had mattered most, he had not been here to protect the woman he loved. He lowered his head into his hands and wept uncontrollably.

"I should never have left," he cried out with the agony. Stiger pounded his fist upon a burnt floorboard, dislodging a cloud of ash and shaking the debris. "I should never have left you."

Dog came up behind Stiger. The animal sniffed at him and then placed its big shaggy head on Stiger's right shoulder. The touch surprised him and he stiffened. He sensed the animal was sharing its own sorrow at Sarai's passing.

Stiger couldn't take it. He shrugged the animal off. He wanted only to be left alone with his grief. The ache and heartbreak were so terrible, it was almost indescribable. His chest burned from the pain.

He was utterly gutted, devastated. It was as if a great big hole had been ripped from his soul. He cried out in anguish, sounding very much as if wounded in battle. He had known peace and joy. He had tasted contentment, something that had been absent from his life. It had all been ripped violently away.

Stiger felt betrayed. He had been let down by the god he had served, worshiped, and honored.

A feeling of absolute loathing stole over him.

He hated.

"I hate them all," he said. The senseless devastation the gods had wrought upon him gave way to an unmitigated rage. Stiger surrendered to it, relished it even. The tears went from those of grief and loss to rage. With effort, he tore his gaze away from Sarai's charred and unrecognizable body.

He pulled himself to his feet and looked around the destruction of the farm, studying his surroundings. By the woodpile, next to his split firewood, his eyes fell upon an orc standard that had been planted boldly in the ground. He recognized it immediately. It belonged to Therik. It was clear the banner had been intentionally left for him to find.

The sight of it made him ill. Stiger bent over and wretched, emptying his guts upon the ash. He straightened, wiping his mouth clean. He stared hard at Therik's standard, stoking his rage and hate.

"I will kill them all," Stiger whispered to himself. It was a promise. "I will make them pay for this. I will make them suffer."

Dog gave a growl that seemed filled with a matching anger.

And I will help you, the sword hissed. *We shall give them suffering beyond what they could have ever imagined possible.*

Stiger had resisted Rarokan's efforts for so long. Now he wondered why. The sword had been correct. Orcs could not be trusted. The summit had been a mistake. The orcs were the enemy. There was only one thing to do with them, and that was to kill them all.

"Agreed," Stiger said to Rarokan, his eyes moving back to Sarai's body. "First, there is yet something I must do."

I understand.

He stood and pulled his gaze from the body. Dog looked up at him with watery eyes. Stiger glanced down at those sad, sympathetic eyes and then walked woodenly toward the barn. He did not want sympathy. His hands shook from the rage. He had never known such utter loathing. Revenge was all that mattered now.

Stepping into the barn, he found an old shovel and laid his hand upon it. He closed his eyes a moment, not quite prepared for what he was about to do. Taking a deep breath, he stepped back outside with the shovel in hand.

Dog was waiting.

Stiger stumbled to a stop, abruptly and unexpectedly reminded of happier times, when he had looked upon the animal as just another hungry beggar in search of a meal. The sadness returned in a rush. He gave out a half sob, struggled, and then got a handle on his emotions. He continued on. Just beyond the woodpile, there was a lovely old apple tree.

Stiger hesitated a step, recalling a near perfect day not too long ago. It had been beautifully sunny with not a cloud in the sky. He and Sarai had been picking apples. Stiger could almost see her standing there, next to the tree, bag in hand. He shook his head and continued on.

Wormy fruit littered the ground. The tree produced so many apples, they had only collected what they could possibly use and a few bushels to sell or barter away at the local market. Stiger had intended to gather up the excess apples when time permitted. They would have gone into the pigs' slop. Now, like Sarai, they were destined to rot. The thought of it brought out the rage, which helped to overshadow the pain.

Sucking in a haggard breath, Stiger glanced around the tree. He selected a spot in the shade, four yards from the trunk. He hoped there weren't too many roots. Stiger bent his back and began digging, steadily tossing aside one shovel full of dirt at a time. The tears came again and he wept as he dug. Shovel after shovel, Stiger continued, working himself into a furious and unrelenting pace.

His breath came fast and hard. It felt good to do something, even if it was digging a grave. In a short time, he became thoroughly drenched in sweat, and still he continued on. As he worked, the rage gave way once again, shifting back over to sadness. He wept until his eyes hurt and no more tears would come. He had not cried like this since his mother had died during the civil war back when he was a youth. He continued digging.

The sound of approaching horses caused him to stop his work and turn. Theo and Father Thomas were riding up to the farm. Their horses appeared lathered and their breath steamed in the cold air.

Entering the farmyard, they spotted Stiger and came to a stop. Theo slowly slid off his pony. The dwarf eyed Stiger for a long moment, glanced around at the dead, and then made his way over to the farmhouse. A short while later, he returned with a grim expression and stomped over.

Their gazes met.

Theo laid a hand upon Stiger's shoulder, an unbelievably sad look in his eyes. It made it all feel worse somehow, knowing that another sympathized with his loss. Stiger resumed shoveling.

"She was a good and kind woman," Theo said. "She cared for you very much."

"There are no words," Stiger said, voice hoarse with raw emotion. "No words."

Theo patted him on the shoulder, turned, and walked off towards the barn, leaving Stiger and Father Thomas alone. The paladin sat upon his horse, his face drawn and pale. He seemed about to say something. Stiger held up a hand and shook his head violently in the negative, then turned his back on the paladin and resumed digging. After a few moments, Father Thomas climbed down off his horse and led it over to the barn.

Theo returned with a shovel.

"No," Stiger said. "This is something I must do myself."

"That, my friend, is where you are wrong." Theo stepped into the grave and, before Stiger could object further, began digging.

Stiger looked over at the dwarf for several heartbeats. He did not have the energy or the will to force Theo out, so he resumed his work. They dug in silence, working rapidly, and before Stiger knew it, the grave was ready to receive a body. Stiger glanced toward the house. He wasn't ready to let go. He knew in his heart he never would be.

Unspeaking, the two stood for a time, gazing into the grave.

"I lost my wife ten years ago," Theo said, breaking the silence. Stiger could hear the emotion hang heavy in his friend's voice.

Stiger looked up. Theo's face was a mask of grief.

"I did not know," Stiger said. He was unsure what to say other than, "I am sorry."

It sounded rather weak.

"So, my Traya," Theo started and stopped. He cleared his throat. "Traya was wonderful. We were fortunate enough that we grew up together. Our homes were within a stone's throw. As children we played all the time." Theo paused. "She was my oldest friend going all the way back to as far as I can remember. Even as we aged and grew to maturity, when so many others drift apart, we stayed close. I recall the day it dawned upon me she meant more than I'd ever realized. It is hard to describe how I felt, only that she was my best friend, and more than anything I wanted to grow old with her. From that day onward, there was no one else I was interested in. She was it."

Theo fell silent for a long moment, staring off into the distance. Stiger said nothing. He waited for his friend to continue.

"When I finally worked up the courage and asked for her hand, I feared she would say no." Theo smiled sadly. "You see, we were very good friends. I wasn't sure she desired anything more from me than friendship. When I proposed, Traya actually laughed at me. Can you believe that? I can tell you it came as something of a shock. I figured worst case she would say no, but laugh at me? Never." Theo chuckled, as if reliving the memory. "She was just nervous is all, and when she gets that way Traya tends to laugh. She accepted. I was elated beyond words."

Theo fell silent again, his eyes watering. The dwarf reached up and wiped a tear from his cheek as another ran down into his beard on the other cheek.

"She died giving birth to our son," Theo said. "After she passed, I could not bear to remain home. There were too many reminders of her. My loss was beyond words." Theo cleared his throat again. "I could not stay even for the sake of my son." Theo fell silent, this time for longer. "And so, I left him in the care of family and went to serve my thane." Theo drew in a shuddering breath and let it out. He looked over at Stiger, the sadness a mask of pain on his bearded face. "After all of this, and all I've seen over the last few days …" Theo cleared his throat again and gestured toward the grave and then around at the valley. "This strikes too close to home. I am thinking I made a mistake. My son deserves a father who is there for him, not one who blames him for the loss of his beloved. I should be there. I will be there for him." Theo looked up at the sky and his shoulders trembled slightly. "I will see this through, but after it is done, I shall return home. I will raise my boy and love him as he deserves, for life is too short for anything else. He shall grow into a proud dvergr, with much legend. I shall make him a companion fit for a thane." He lowered his tone. "And still, to the last of my days, I shall grieve for the woman I love with all of my heart. It is the only way I can honor her memory. That, and I shall live on as she would wish me to."

Theo once again fell silent, resting his hands upon the top of the shovel. He was looking down into the grave again. After a moment, he glanced up and their eyes met.

"So," Theo said. "I too have suffered unimaginable loss. There is nothing I can do or say to make it better, other than remain with you for this difficult goodbye. No one should have to go through something like this alone"—his voice dropped to a whisper—"as I did."

Stiger wasn't sure what to say. He swallowed, the emotion welling up again. It took him a moment before he could speak.

"Thank you," he managed.

"It is the least I can do for a friend," Theo said. "Shall we go get her?"

Though he was dreading this moment, Stiger nodded and turned toward the farmhouse. Before he could take more than two steps, he discovered Father Thomas carrying her across the farmyard toward them. Sarai was wrapped in the paladin's cloak. Stiger became angered that the man had dared to do something he felt compelled to do for himself, but then realized that Father Thomas meant nothing by it. The paladin only desired to help, and for some reason he could not explain, that made Stiger even angrier.

Father Thomas seemed to understand Stiger's feelings. He handed Sarai over to him. The cloak had been sewn shut, and yet the smell of burnt flesh was nearly overpowering, causing him to gag slightly. She felt incredibly light. A wetness had seeped through the bottom of the cloak. Stiger realized it was blood. He was suddenly grateful the paladin had sewn the cloak closed. He did not wish his last memory of her to be of charred and ruined skin.

Theo climbed down into the grave, and together they gently lowered her body down into it. Once she was at the bottom, the dwarf accepted Stiger's hand and clambered back out.

Stiger stared numbly down at the bundle resting at the bottom of the grave. This was all that remained of the woman he loved. She would rest beneath this tree for eternity. A gentle gust of cold air blew by, stirring the smoke and rustling the leaves of the tree above. The horror that had been wrought here would eventually be erased by the passing of time. It was a pleasant enough spot. He hoped her spirit approved and found a semblance of peace by it.

"Goodbye," he said in barely more than a whisper. He took up the shovel from where he had left it sticking out of the pile of excavated dirt. He began shoveling the dirt back into the grave. After a slight delay, while he silently watched Stiger, Theo also began to shovel.

It took a surprisingly short time to fill in the grave, much less than it had taken to dig out. As they were finishing up, Sabinus and Mectillius with the rest of Fifth Century arrived. Seeing what they were doing, the two centurions held back with the men, remaining at a respectful distance. For that, Stiger was grateful.

"I would like to offer a prayer for Sarai's soul," Father Thomas said quietly. "Would you mind terribly if I did?"

Stiger almost said no. Then, he remembered Sarai's deep love for the High Father. She would appreciate a prayer by the paladin. It was the last mercy he could grant her. He gave a nod and only half listened as Father Thomas began to say words for the honored and loved dead and those left behind.

His thoughts wandered back to the day he had left for the summit. He recalled their parting around the table in the kitchen, her closeness, the smell of her hair, the light touch of her skin on his, a parting kiss. He could picture her standing in the doorway, watching him leave. If only he had known he was abandoning Sarai to her fate. How he wished he had refused the call and remained. He should never have gone. Deep down he had known it was a mistake and still he had left. Stiger's fists clenched. He should have been here, at the farm. He might have been able to do something, anything.

Hindsight was always an unforgiving bitch.

As Father Thomas continued his prayers, Stiger felt as if he now had a hole in his heart. He could never forgive the paladin, Thoggle, Brogan, the High Father, or any of the gods for what had been done this day. They were all at fault. He had been left with a hole, not just in his heart but in his soul. There was nothing to fill it other than duty and revenge. After this, Stiger wasn't sure that he cared much for duty. That only left revenge.

The wind gusted, blowing by them and once again rustling the leaves overhead. Stiger did not feel the chill air. His thoughts were on Sarai and what she would have wanted. She had loved this valley. Through her, Stiger had come to love it as well. But now, Vrell had become a painful reminder of loss. Despite that, Stiger resolved to protect it. He would do it not for the gods, the dwarves, the oracle's prophecy, or destiny, but for Sarai. When it was safe… he would punish the orcs in a way that they would never forget, and the sword would help him do it.

I will, Rarokan affirmed. *We will make them suffer.*

Father Thomas had fallen silent. The short service was over. Stiger hadn't noticed. He glanced in Sabinus's direction. It was time to go. The peace of this place had been forever shattered. It would never be the same.

Stiger had a sudden recollection of the farm he had come across with Seventh Company, as young officer, near the Cora'Tol Valley. The Rivan had tortured and executed a father and his two young sons. Stiger had arrived in time to rescue their mother. As if it had only happened yesterday, he vividly recalled the bodies of the young boys. The image on that rainy night had been burned forever into his memory. It was the kind of thing you did not forget.

Stiger had left the mother at Fort Covenant, the place where Varus and so many other good men had died, leaving this world forever. Now, he suspected he understood what she had felt—utter devastation and a terrible loneliness.

Stiger wondered if the mother had also felt guilt at having survived her loved ones. Survivor's guilt was nothing new to Stiger. Over the years he had left comrades and friends behind. But this was somehow different. Stiger's guilt at living had abruptly become deeply personal.

Stiger wiped at his eyes, which no longer teared but were itchy and sore. He straightened his back and brushed past Father Thomas and Theo over to the woodpile and up to Therik's standard. He looked it over for several heartbeats before uprooting it from the ground. In a rapid movement, he broke the thick wooden shaft of the standard over his thigh. Then, in disgust, he threw it down onto the ground.

Stiger made his way over to Sabinus. He sensed the paladin and Theo following. Dog joined him too. One of the men held Misty's reins. She looked somewhat recovered, but still nearly blown from the brutal ride down into the valley. There would be no more hard riding today. She would not be pushed any further than a short, easy ride. Without saying anything, Stiger took the reins and mounted up. Sabinus did the same.

"It is time to return home to the legion," Stiger said simply to the centurion.

"Yes, sir," Sabinus said.

Stiger glanced once more around at the ruined farm, the bodies lying all around. He hated the idea of leaving the deceased dwarves just lying about for the carrion eaters. They'd died doing their duty and fulfilling Aleric's promise to Stiger to protect Sarai with their lives. Unfortunately, there were things that needed doing. Disposing of their remains would have to wait. He looked over at Sabinus and felt a terrible anger well up on the inside. "It is time to make the enemy pay for this."

Part Two

CHAPTER TWENTY-SIX

From the top of the hill, Stiger hauled back on the reins and surveyed the scene below. Sabinus brought his horse to a stop as well. Behind them, Mectillius called the century to a halt. Misty shifted her hooves, dancing sideways, as if uncomfortable. Stiger could understand the discomfort. She was not a horse trained for the sights, sounds, and smells of war. He took a firmer hold on the reins and she stilled. His hand shook, and he took a breath to steady himself.

The turf and timber walls of the legionary encampment stood just five hundred yards to their front. The walls were about twelve feet high. A staked barricade made the wall just that much more formidable, adding another three feet to its height. Square, roofed timber towers had been set along the walls every ten yards. From these towers protruded the snouts of deadly bolt throwers, pointing outward.

Before the walls, three trenches had been dug, each separated by ten yards of space. As legionary encampments went, it was quite impressive. The trenches made the position even more difficult to crack. A simple rule went that the greater the risk, the stronger the defenses. And in practice, the longer the legion stayed in place—and the Thirteenth had remained for a long time—the more powerful the defenses became. Arvus had clearly kept his men hard at work. The tribune had taken their conversation seriously about the coming threat to the valley.

The defenses weren't what had caught his attention. As if mute testament to the pure strength of the position, thousands of orc and human bodies littered the ground before, within, and in the gaps between trenches. Amidst numerous scaling ladders, bodies were clustered in piles around the base of the walls.

These enemy had come fully armored. Stiger found it troubling that they appeared similarly equipped, as if they had been organized professionally with an eye toward uniformity. This was something he had not expected to see from Therik's army. It was potentially a sign that the coming fight would be more difficult than he had imagined.

Behind them, Mectillius muttered a harsh oath. There were a number of exclamations from the men as well.

Stiger's eyes swept across the dead. The sickly stench of blood was heavy on the air. The apple tree flashed in his mind, along with Sarai's grave, and he felt his rage swell. Thousands of javelins stuck upward from bodies and the ground. Countless arrows stitched across the landscape, becoming thicker around the second trench, which clearly marked the encampment's effective killing zone.

Stiger's eyes roved the battlefield, picking out tiny details, such as small impact craters where ballista ball from the artillery had landed or bolts from the powerful throwers that had impaled individuals or groups. One orc had been hit so hard by one of the larger bolts, not only did it pierce his heavy chest armor, but the bolt had also pinned him helplessly in the air, suspended about six inches above the ground.

Stiger slid his gaze over the walls. Behind the staked barricade stood the sentries with their watchful eyes. A small cluster on the wall was looking their way. One man pointed, and then another disappeared from the wall. Stiger's eyes soaked it all in. From the looks of things, the fight had been very one-sided. Judging by the encampment's size, it had been constructed to hold not just the Thirteenth, but her auxiliary cohorts as well.

"Looks like the enemy made a good try at overcoming the walls, sir." Sabinus leaned forward on his saddle, also scanning the battlefield. "I daresay with this little bloody nose, they won't be trying another such assault anytime soon."

Stiger glanced over, gave a nod, and then returned his gaze to the battlefield. He had been worried about the encampment, but looking at the aftermath of the assault, he knew he need not have concerned himself. Stiger was very pleased to see that, at least here, the orcs had suffered badly. The multitude of dead before him only served to whet and stoke his appetite for more. He could readily sense Rarokan's pleasure as well, and the eagerness at what was to come.

Sabinus leaned closer and lowered his voice.

"When we get in there, sir," the centurion said, "you will likely be greeted by Tribune Arvus, whom you've already met, but also by Camp Prefect Salt."

"Salt?" Stiger looked back over at Sabinus. He had difficulty believing that to be the man's true name.

"His name is Publius Planus Oney," Sabinus said, "but he's been in the legion for ages and everyone, including Legate Delvaris, calls him Salt. If I had to guess, I'd say he's over fifty, but no one knows for sure. Nobody wants to ask him, either."

"Because he is a tough old salt, right?"

"Yes, sir," Sabinus said. "In the legion, there's no one that's tougher. Half of the centurionate are scared of him."

Sabinus nudged his horse forward. "They'll be wondering why we are sitting here, sir."

Stiger touched his heels to Misty's sides, setting her in motion. Behind them, Mectillius gave the order for the century to march. Theo and Father Thomas had been riding behind the century. When the men had stopped at the top of the hill, both had ridden off to the side of the century to get a better view of the battlefield. Stiger glanced back. Both were again moving and working their way forward to catch up to Stiger and Sabinus.

"Anything else I should know?" Stiger asked.

"Plenty," Sabinus said unhappily and glanced around, "but there's no time for all of that now. Keep me near you as much as possible and I will do what I can to help."

"I will," Stiger said.

As they continued to ride nearer to the camp, a horn sounded a particular call, four long blasts followed by an even longer one. It was customary to announce the legate's return. Since Delvaris had been absent for months, Stiger could well understand the hundreds of legionaries that began to appear on the wall a few moments later. They eagerly crowded the wall, peering out at him and his party.

A hearty cheer went up as the wooden gates started to swing open. The men gave another cheer.

"Delvaris was popular with the men," Sabinus said by way of explanation.

Stiger said nothing to that. He was not comfortable impersonating such a great man. But those feelings were secondary. The legion needed a legate, a combat leader, and he would give them that. Stiger had a job to do and he meant to follow through with it.

Before the gates had even finished opening, several teams of men raced out with long wooden planks and began bridging the trenches. A centurion followed after, shouting at them to pick up the pace.

"That's Centurion Titus Acillius Atta," Sabinus said, swaying in the saddle slightly as he steered his horse around a body. The orc had dragged himself around a hundred yards from the nearest trench before expiring. Sabinus glanced down sourly at the creature, whose end had been far from pleasant. "Atta commands a century in my cohort. You, or really Delvaris, decorated him twice since assuming command of the Thirteenth. He is very solid and reliable and possibly the bravest soldier I've ever had the pleasure to know. Eventually, should he survive long enough, I expect him to make senior centurion."

Stiger gave a nod of understanding.

They continued to ride closer, passing through the field of dead. It was a gruesome setting. Most had been killed by missile fire. A good number, however, showed signs of having been injured and then trampled. It was an ugly way to go, but Stiger did not care. A good orc was a dead orc.

Though he could not see the other side, the field of bodies seemed to run around the entire encampment, which meant the enemy had attempted all of the walls simultaneously. They had clearly brought a good-sized number to attack the legion. The questions in his mind was, where had the survivors gone?

Stiger guided Misty around several bodies as they neared the outer trench. The men from the encampment finished laying their planks. They began rolling the bodies that lay in the gaps between the bridges out of the way. Centurion Atta, using his vine cane as a walking stick, stomped out beyond the outer trench toward Stiger's approaching party. He turned and snapped an order to his men. They finished moving the bodies aside so there was an unobstructed path to the gate, then stood aside and snapped to a position of attention.

"Welcome back, sir," Centurion Atta said and offered a proper salute as Stiger reached him. The centurion was a boxy, compact man with a grim, plain face. He gave off the impression of being hard as iron. Stiger held his hand up in a half wave, as Sabinus had instructed was Delvaris's custom. Then Misty was clunking over the first wooden bridge. Tail wagging, Dog trotted along to the right of Stiger's horse.

"Atta," Sabinus greeted as he guided his horse onto the bridge after Stiger. "Nice to see that ugly mug of yours survived."

"It will take more than these savages to lay me low, sir," Atta replied.

"I'm certain of that," Sabinus said, turning in the saddle as he passed. "Knowing your kind and happy disposition, you'll likely meet your end at the hands of a drunk in a bar fight."

"Naw," Atta replied. "That'd never happen. Drunk or sober, I am the meanest bastard around, sir. You should know that by now."

Sabinus, along with Atta's men, gave an amused chuckle. Then they were past, with Theo and Father Thomas having caught up and riding just behind Stiger and Sabinus.

Stiger leaned over and looked down into the trench. It was filled with orcs. Some of the enemy were still alive, injured but living. They writhed in pain. He saw a good number had been impaled upon spikes set in the bottom. Likely they'd been shoved on them by their fellows as the orcs pushed forward toward the walls. He noted there had been no attempt at filling the trenches with sticks or bundles of brush to safely pass through. This told Stiger the enemy had not expected to encounter such obstacles, which meant they'd not done a proper reconnaissance on the encampment. It spoke of a lack of planning and preparation by Therik's army.

Stiger's anger burned at the live but injured orcs in the trench. It was creatures like these that were responsible for Sarai's death. He almost stopped to deal with them himself. He felt Rarokan pushing for it but clamped down hard on the urge before it could grow. He had things to do. Stiger had been ruminating on what he wanted to do during the ride and had a fairly good plan hatched out.

"We're gonna have to do something about that," Stiger said and pointed down into the trench at the orcs that still lived. One with a vicious stomach wound glared angrily at him. Greenish blood frothed at the creature's mouth as it bared its tusks in hatred. Stiger glanced over at Sabinus. "There could be some shirkers down there."

Sabinus glanced over the side of the bridge, a sour look on his face. "There could be."

Stiger swung his gaze around. He marveled at the number of javelins and arrows that dotted the landscape between trenches. It was quite incredible. He'd never seen so many missiles used to such deadly effect.

After such a fight, Stiger had expected to see groups of the followers sent out to help gather up the arrows and javelins for repurposing and possible reuse. They should also be happily looting the dead. He was surprised not to see them. Starting over the second bridge, he brought Misty to an abrupt halt.

"What is it?" Sabinus asked, stopping also.

"The followers," Stiger said and pointed at the encampment. "Where are they? Surely they're not inside. The encampment isn't big enough."

"Ah." Sabinus nodded in understanding. "After the tribune and I paid you a visit, he sent them out of the valley.

It was for their own protection and to limit the size of the encampment. They have their own camp just on the other side of Castle Vrell in the forest. One of the auxiliary cohorts is providing security. I've been there. It is a good camp, with a trench and solid walls."

It made sense to Stiger. Especially the part about limiting the size of the encampment. That meant less wall to defend if it came to a fight. At the same time, he also understood that it would not have gone over too well with the men. They were now separated from their unofficial families. The tribune was surely not a popular man. Satisfied with the explanation, Stiger started Misty forward again.

Rough-hewn scaling ladders lay by the hundreds haphazardly scattered about amongst the dead. Stiger felt the scar on his cheek pull tight as he smiled grimly. It was abundantly clear to him the orcs had not known who and what they were facing. He bet they understood now, and if they didn't, he would shortly do his best to educate them.

They clunked over the last bridge and then were through the gateway. The gate detail stood to attention. An older man, wearing the armor of a senior officer along with the chest ribbon of a camp prefect, met them just inside the entrance.

The prefect had short-cropped gray hair that had long since begun to thin. He appeared tired, but at the same time there was a confident air about him that bespoke a lifetime of hard and unforgiving service. He was, as Sabinus said, in his fifties, but his advanced age had clearly not slowed the man down. He was incredibly fit and looked ready to march those younger into the ground. Stiger warmed to him immediately. He was the kind of no-nonsense officer that Stiger had come to recognize and respect. Salt had reached his position due to competence and not politics.

"Welcome back, sir," the camp prefect said in a voice that sounded hoarse, as if he had recently done a lot of yelling.

"Salt," Stiger said with a nod and dismounted from his horse. A legionary ran over and took the reins. Stiger stretched out his back as Misty was led away. Behind him, Sabinus, Father Thomas, and Theo also dismounted. Legionaries jogged over to take their horses as well.

Tail wagging furiously, Dog jumped up on Salt, placing his big paws on either shoulder. The animal licked happily at the prefect's face. Dog's long tail was moving so fast it was a blur and shook not only him, but Salt as well.

"All right, all right," Salt said with affection, forcing the animal with some effort off him and back down. "Mangy old hound. I missed you, too."

Stiger recalled how Sabinus had recognized Dog as having belonged to Delvaris. It appeared that the prefect and animal were fast friends. What had Dog been up to prior to his coming to the farm?

Salt looked over and had the grace to color slightly as he dropped the tough, no-nonsense appearance for a handful of heartbeats as he patted the dog's head. Then the steel was back, as Father Thomas and Theo stepped up, joining Stiger.

"May I present Father Thomas," Stiger said, "paladin to the High Father. Father Thomas, I would like to introduce Camp Prefect Oney."

"It is an honor to meet you, Father," Salt said without missing a beat and shook Father Thomas's hand. He greeted the paladin as if the meeting were a common occurrence. Almost like true magic, paladins were extremely rare.

"Camp Prefect Oney," Father Thomas said.

"Call me Salt."

"Salt, then," Father Thomas said with a smile.

"Theo," Stiger gestured at the dwarf, "liaison from Thane Brogan."

Salt gave a nod to the dwarf.

"It is a pleasure," Theo said in common.

The camp prefect eyed Fifth Century as it marched in, passing them by. His eyes clearly noted the absent centurion and lack of numbers. Mectillius marched the century deeper into the camp, leading them toward their assigned tents. The newly minted centurion offered Stiger a salute as he passed by.

"Run into a bit of trouble yourself, sir?" Salt asked, raising an eyebrow.

"We did," Stiger said with a glance back at Fifth Century. "Pixus fell in battle. I have promoted Mectillius."

"Yes, sir," Salt said. There was a hint of disapproval in the prefect's tone. From it, Stiger understood there were clearly more senior men that had been waiting on the ladder rung to move up. Stiger's emotions were raw from losing Sarai. He did not care in the slightest, though a small voice in his head said he should. Stiger ignored it. He was the legate. His word was law. It was as simple as that.

Stiger looked around the interior of the camp. The tents and supply depots, which seemed unusually large to Stiger, were set well back from the walls. This was done so that, should the encampment become besieged, enemy artillery fire would have a more difficult time of reaching the vulnerable parts of the camp. Everything appeared neatly ordered and organized, just as it should be.

The men that had rushed to the wall still stood along the walkway on the rampart, the interior side being a gentle dirt slope that had been packed down. They were watching the discussion between their legate and camp prefect. This included the officers on the wall as well. Stiger understood the rumor mill would soon be hard at work.

Another cheer went up at the sight of Stiger looking their way. Stiger raised his hand to wave back. They cheered even louder. He then turned back to Salt.

"There are a number of wounded from Fifth Century," Stiger said. "The dwarves are transporting them to Old City. Once they're fit to travel farther, I have been told they will be sent on to us."

"I see," Salt said and nodded to Theo. "That is very kind of you dwarves."

"Think nothing of it," Theo replied.

Sabinus had been speaking with the legionary he had handed his horse to. Having finally sent the man on his way, he joined them. Salt gave the centurion a slight unhappy scowl and then returned his attention to Stiger.

"What happened here?" Stiger asked. "Tell me about the attack."

"They assaulted us early this morning, sir," Salt said. "Thought they could catch us napping. We received warning from the dwarves little more than an hour before they hit. The messenger said there might be a surprise attack sometime over the next few days. I didn't rightly expect it to come so soon, sir."

Stiger felt himself frown and glanced around. "Where is Tribune Arvus?"

"Dead, sir," Salt said matter-of-factly. He could have been discussing the weather. "Along with most of the junior tribunes."

"What?" Stiger asked, surprised. For the legion to lose the junior tribunes was unheard of. Junior tribunes were youths, coming usually from senatorial families. They came to the legion for experience and to see if army life was to their liking. They always served as the legate's personal aides or, as the regulars tended to call them, the messenger service.

"Arvus, dead?" Sabinus seemed rocked by the news.

"Dead as can be," Salt confirmed with an unhappy look.

"What happened?" Stiger asked. He had not wished the man dead, but at the same time, he realized that Arvus's death made his job of taking complete control of the legion a much easier task.

"As you already know, sir, the valley was raided last night," Salt said. "A village to the north of here was attacked. At the time, we didn't know what was happening and that we might even come under assault. The warning from the dwarves came later. All we could see were the fires from the town. It lit up the night sky something good. Tribune Arvus thought it was simply a fire that had spread. You know how civilians are with their cook fires, sir."

Stiger gave a nod. Fires were common occurrences in settlements. Sometimes, if not addressed immediately, they got out of hand. In his youth, a good portion of Mal'Zeel had burned down. It had ultimately taken an army of civilians working alongside the praetorian guard to stop the fire. The fire been so serious, a wide swath of buildings had been torn down in an effort to create a fire break.

"Well," Salt continued, "the tribune took two cohorts and a good number of the junior tribunes to help extinguish the fires. He figured it would be good experience for them. As they neared the town, they were ambushed. Near as I can figure, we were attacked around the same time they were. Only a handful of the men made it back, sir. They came in about three hours ago and brought the tribune's body with them."

Salt fell silent.

"Which cohorts?" Sabinus asked.

"The Ninth and the Fourteenth Altress Auxiliary Cohort," Sabinus said. "There were maybe a hundred survivors all told, mostly heavy infantry from the Ninth. I am afraid the light infantry suffered badly. The Fourteenth exists only in name now, sir."

"Tell me about the assault on the encampment," Stiger ordered.

"They hit us in the dead of night, sir, about two hours after the tribune departed," Salt said. "I may be old, but once the warning came from the dwarves and what with the fire lighting up the sky for all to see…I figured there was a strong chance something more was afoot and the legion might be in danger. I had the alarm quietly sounded and ordered everyone to the walls and the artillery manned. If I was wrong, the boys would miss out on a few hours of sleep. Well, I wasn't. Those animals out there snuck up in the darkness, maybe seven thousand all told. Our sentries spotted them as they moved into a step-off position around the encampment."

"Go on," Stiger said.

"Well," Salt said, "I had the boys play the helpless lamb, with everyone hidden behind the barricade and the sentries being the only ones to show themselves. When they attacked, charging and screaming like banshees, we sounded the alarm as if the camp was being roused to the danger." He chuckled. "I waited 'til they crossed the second trench and were well within missile range. We opened up with everything we had, including artillery. I put our slingers and archers from the auxiliaries to good use. We inflicted heavy casualties on them as they pushed up to and against our walls. When they tried to force their way over the top, we threw them back good. I am pleased to report they never even made it over the top. We easily repulsed them, sir. As they disengaged and withdrew back through our trenches, we kept the fire up, hot and heavy."

"And then?"

"Well, I figure they realized how strong our defense was and they'd not caught us napping like they expected, so they called it all off. It is also possible they misjudged how many men we had here in the encampment, for they were badly outnumbered. The bastards melted back into the darkness and we've not seen them since." Salt gave a shrug. "Afterwards, more fires sprung up around the valley. I understood it was a major attack."

"When did they withdraw?" Sabinus asked.

"About two hours before dawn," Salt said.

"What have you been doing since the attack?" Sabinus asked. It was not meant as an accusation, just a simple question.

"Rather than venture out without any intelligence," Salt said with an unconcerned glance in Sabinus's direction. He returned his gaze a heartbeat later to Stiger. "I thought it best to hunker down for the night and assess the situation in the morning. As soon as it was light enough to see, I put out the cat for the day, sir."

"You sent out the cavalry to reconnoiter?" Stiger asked.

"Yes, sir."

"We saw one of the squadrons in the distance," Stiger said. "Your decision was the correct one, Prefect. Well done."

"My thoughts exactly and thank you, sir," the prefect said without any hint that he'd ever had doubts. "I had no idea on the enemy's strength, only that from what we saw of the assault there were a lot of them creatures out there. I was taking no chances until I knew otherwise."

"And of the scouts you sent out?" Stiger asked. "What have they reported so far?"

"It seems that the civilians were hit fairly hard," Salt said. "Many buildings and fields were burned, though from the nearest village there are a surprising number of survivors. I understand the local militias put up a good fight of it. I am guessing—and, mind you, this is only a guess—that with the exception of our encampment, the enemy used light and scattered forces to cause as much mayhem and destruction as they could while sending their hammer to try and crack this nut." Salt held out his arms to indicate the encampment. "Though it looks right bad out there in the valley, the loss of life may be limited to some degree."

Stiger bit off an angry retort before he could voice it. He wanted to rage at the prefect, tell him there was nothing limited about Sarai's death. It took some effort but he managed to clamp down on his emotions. Deep down, he understood what Salt had said was a reasonable assessment and likely true. The man had meant nothing by the statement of what he saw as possible fact. Besides, he knew nothing of Sarai.

Stiger cleared his throat. "And the raiders? The orcs? Are they still in the valley?"

"From what we can tell so far, most seem to have gone south, sir," Salt said. "They appear to be leaving the valley, with all the spoils they can carry. They are moving in small groups up into the mountains. One of our squadrons caught up with one and ran them down. They reported the orcs had several wagons full of wine and meat they'd plundered." Salt paused and glanced back toward the parade ground. "I was preparing to dispatch four cohorts to see what can be done to help the civilians." He turned back to Stiger. "Now that you have returned, sir, how would you like us to proceed?"

Stiger looked over at the parade ground. A few yards off, he saw the cohorts assembling. Javelins and shields at their feet, the men were checking equipment, filling their haversacks with rations, and generally preparing themselves for march. He figured that if the orc raiding parties were heading south, there was a good chance they were making for Forkham Valley.

Go after them, Rarokan hissed with eager anticipation.

We will, Stiger said silently back to the sword.

Stiger's anger surged at the thought of a pursuit. He wanted revenge for what was done to Sarai. His hand sought out the sword hilt, the tingle running up his arm. The rage coursed through his veins. He would make them pay. But at the same time, if he followed them to Forkham—and he intended to—he would be treading in Delvaris's footsteps. With the loss of Sarai, he didn't much care anymore about that. All he wanted was to pay the orcs back in kind. Razing the temple and anything else in Forkham was but one step toward doing just that.

"Salt, I want you to prepare the entire legion for march," Stiger said, glancing up at the noon sky. "I would like to move in an hour or two, if we could."

"And where, sir, are we going?" There was no surprise in the prefect's expression. "Do you wish to leave a garrison to cover our supply? Or are we taking everything with us? If we are, I am afraid we won't be leaving in an hour or, for that matter, even two."

"We will be leaving a garrison," Stiger said. Moving the entire legion long distances took days of planning and preparation. Salt, however, was quite correct, and Stiger understood he had to start thinking larger. He would have to take care to be clear with his directions. "Fifth Century will remain, along with the Ninth and another of your choice.

The rest, including our auxiliaries, will march. And where most of us are going is a place called Forkham Valley, just to the south of here. That is where the orcs that did this are. We will be paying them a visit."

"Yes, sir," Salt said. If he wondered how Stiger had known, he didn't voice it. He clearly read the hard edge to Stiger's tone and stiffened his back ever so slightly. "The legion will be ready to march in an hour, maybe a bit longer, sir."

"Very good. I will be in headquarters. I need to change my tunic and grab something to eat. We will speak on operational details shortly. I will send for you when I am ready."

"Yes, sir." The prefect gave him a salute.

Stiger turned to Sabinus. "Centurion, you are with me. You two also." Stiger motioned for Father Thomas and Theo to follow.

He glanced around quickly, taking stock of where they were. This camp was almost identical to the ones he had known in the future, at least those in the North. Before traveling south, Stiger had never seen anything like the southern legions' disease-ridden camp. He was thankful this camp was clean.

"Dog, come."

Since they'd entered through one of the side gates and not the Porta Praetoria, the main gate, Stiger led the way through the streets, toward headquarters. Had they come through the main gate, it would have been a straight shot to headquarters along the Via Praetoria, the main thoroughfare of any encampment. The legionaries they passed stepped aside and came hastily to attention. Stiger paid them no mind. He continued on his way with Sabinus, Father Thomas, and Theo following.

This was only a marching encampment. There were no permanent structures. Headquarters was a series of large tents. As they approached the entrance, the four sentries on duty standing guard over headquarters snapped to attention, saluting.

The side of the administrative tent was completely drawn up and tied back with burlap straps to admit the light and air of the outside world. The administrative tent was the main point of entrance for headquarters. Here Delvaris and Arvus would have their office, along with the quartermaster, legion paymaster, and camp prefect. Six clerks were working diligently at camp tables when they arrived. The tables were stacked with wax tablets and rolls of vellum. The men ceased what they were doing, dropped their styluses, and stood to attention as Stiger made his way by them. Dog followed.

"Welcome back, sir," one of the clerks said, a tall, thin man who had gone completely bald. His nose had been broken and never quite healed right. Just off center to the left, it marred his features. He also was missing one of his front teeth. Stiger figured he was the lead clerk, as his table was closest to the legate's office. Stiger did not know the man's name.

Dog ran up to the clerk and began licking his left palm, which Stiger saw was closed into an ink-stained fist. The man opened it and fed Dog a small bit of bacon. There was a hint of a smile on the clerk's face.

"I need a fresh tunic," Stiger said. "Kindly send for one and have some food and drink brought to me. The legion will be marching shortly and I'd at least like to feel somewhat civilized before climbing back onto a horse."

Stiger paused and then glanced at Dog, who had wolfed down the bacon. The animal had sat down before the clerk and was looking expectantly at him. Dog snapped his jaws as if to say, "Feed me!"

"Also, send for some meat for my dog," Stiger said.

"Yes, sir," the clerk said. "I will call for your slave at once."

It did not surprise Stiger in the slightest Delvaris had kept a slave as a manservant. There was a very good chance that back in the capital, Delvaris, a man from an extremely wealthy and powerful house, owned hundreds of slaves, if not thousands. Slavery was widespread throughout the empire. Stiger had even grown up with them as a fixture in his household.

"Come," Stiger said to the animal and pushed aside the flap and stepped into his office, or really Delvaris's office, another tent. Dog walked in before Father Thomas, Theo, and Sabinus followed him inside. Sabinus dropped the tent flap back in place behind them.

Stiger felt as if he were trespassing. The feeling lasted only a moment before it passed. Delvaris was dead. As the man's direct descendent, it could be argued all of this now belonged to him. He glanced around. It was a large tent, of similar dimensions to the adjoining administrative tent. The fabric was of the finest quality. The rug that went from tent wall to tent wall was magnificent. The pattern depicted a likeness of Emperor Karus sitting upon the marble curule chair, a symbol of imperium. Stiger figured the rug had cost a fortune.

A large camp table occupied the center of the tent. A lit lamp sat atop it, as did an unrolled map. Along the left wall was a trunk that Stiger assumed was for important documents. There were several stools, and one that was slightly better in quality sat underneath the table. The others had been placed neatly against the left wall, waiting for use. Another smaller table sat along the right wall. On it rested a pitcher and two mugs.

Theo immediately stepped over, clearly hoping it held wine. He picked up the pitcher, peered inside, and then, with a look of disgust, set it back down with a hollow *thunk.*

"Really?" Sabinus asked and shook his head at the dwarf.

"It was a long ride," Theo grumbled.

Stiger went over to the center table with the lamp and map. It was a rough sketch of the valley from a camp scribe. Stiger glanced down at the map and studied it. The map wasn't as detailed as the one he had in the future, but it was good enough. He noticed the map ended at the southern end of the valley. It did not include Forkham. Dog went to a corner and lay down on the rug, curling up.

"Come over here," Stiger said, looking up at Sabinus, who had remained by the door.

Sabinus stepped over to the table. Stiger gave him a hard look and then lowered his voice so the clerks would not overhear. "Do you intend to cause me difficulty in what I must do? Will you stop me from taking command of the legion?"

Sabinus said nothing for several heartbeats, clearly weighing his thoughts. He responded in a hushed tone that was nearly a whisper. "After all that I have seen and learned, I do believe there are larger things at play."

"That's quite an understatement," Theo said.

Sabinus spared the dwarf an unpleasant look and then continued.

"Though I would prefer the real Delvaris, as legate, you clearly are the one meant to command. Father Thomas has vouched for you." The centurion glanced over at the paladin, who gave a curt nod of agreement. "He explained it is meant to be this way. The emperor's letter also makes it plain you are to be placed firmly in command. Though I dislike misleading the men and my fellow officers as to your identity, I will say nothing. I will do my best to follow your orders, sir."

Stiger suspected there was a catch to that assertion. "As long as?"

Sabinus pursed his lips. "As long as it does not unduly jeopardize the legion or put the empire at risk, sir. How is that?"

"Fair enough," Stiger said with no little amount of relief, accepting the centurion's conditions. He motioned the other two over and then tapped the map, pointing to the legion's encampment. "Now, look at this. We are here. When the enemy next ventures out, other than to simply raid, they will come in much greater strength, most likely in overwhelming numbers. Does anyone disagree with that assessment?"

"I concur, sir," Sabinus said.

"It sounds logical," Father Thomas said. "And we both know that is what will happen."

Sabinus looked sharply at the paladin before turning his gaze back to Stiger. Theo said nothing, but there was a shrewdness to his gaze.

"I think it is safe to say their entire army is not yet assembled," Stiger said.

"Why do you say that, sir?" Sabinus asked. "They clearly came at the encampment in good numbers."

"If Therik had his army assembled," Stiger said, "don't you think he would have used it and swamped these defenses? Or at the very least remained in the valley and bottled the legion up?"

"You have a point there," Theo said. "If Therik's army was ready to go, he would have sent everyone and not just raided the valley. No, he is waiting for greater strength and the priests to bless any major move against us."

"That is why we must strike first," Stiger said. "I believe we have a chance to hit them while they don't expect it and provoke a reaction. I want them to come at us with the forces they have on hand, not when they are good and ready."

"Provoke them how?" Sabinus asked, his eyes narrowing. "What do you intend?"

"It doesn't show it on this map," Stiger said, "but just off of the edge here, by Riverton, is a small valley by the name of Forkham. There is an orc temple to Castor there."

"You know of that?" Theo asked, with raised eyebrows.

"I do."

"Besides the temple," Theo said, "there is a town in that valley, too. Perhaps two hundred orcs live there."

"If I understand it correctly," Stiger said, "this temple is considered one of their holiest sites. I intend to attack their valley and raze the temple to the ground."

"Razing the temple will, I think, just piss them off," Sabinus said.

"That is what I am counting on," Stiger said. "I want to make it hard for Therik and the priests to resist the rage of their warriors over the destruction of the temple to their god. With any luck, he should feel compelled to make a move against us."

"How can you be sure about Therik's army and where it is?" Sabinus's brow furrowed into lines. "What if they are waiting for us to leave the security of the encampment?"

"He does have a point," Father Thomas said, looking meaningfully at Stiger. "They might be waiting for us to make such a move."

Stiger gave a slow nod and then looked over at Theo. "Brogan said Therik's army was assembling somewhere else. His spies had reported it as such. Where was that?"

"Berke'Tah," Theo said. "It is a large valley further to the north, four days away, nowhere near Forkham. It is where Castor's main temple resides and is deep in orc lands."

"Could they have marched the army here quicker than we did from Garand Kos?"

"Doubtful," Theo said. "The orcs don't believe in roads. They'd be stuck on mountain goat trails and paths. They'd also have to haul along their supplies. Any movement would be a major undertaking."

"I've been to Forkham and recall it being a very small valley," Stiger said. "I don't think Therik could put an entire army there. Do you?"

"You've been there?" Theo seemed shocked by this.

"Do you think they could fit Therik's army in Forkham?" Stiger asked of Theo, ignoring the other's comment. He did not feel inclined to explain further. "I am concerned about them hiding one and ambushing us."

"No," Theo said. "The valley is just too small and the path in is, as you likely know, confined. If there were any surprises there, you should be able to disengage and pull back to the valley. And if Therik starts his army from Berke'Tah, he is committed. Once he gets here, he must attack. Brogan's spies and informers have confirmed he does not have the supplies on hand for a sustained action. It is also likely why the valley was raided. Therik will need all of the food he can lay his hands on."

"Then at worst there may only be a portion of Therik's army in Forkham," Stiger said.

"I would agree with that statement," Theo said. "They may also be spread out through the handful of villages in the mountains around Forkham. You should have no problem getting in and out."

Stiger gave a nod and looked from face to face.

"It is settled. I intend to hit Forkham hard," Stiger said. "After the temple is razed, we will return to the valley and"—Stiger traced his finger back along the map heading north—"to here, where this river crossing is."

"Isn't that the river we crossed by Bridgetown?"

"Yes, it is," Stiger said.

"Where you fought your battle in the future?" Sabinus looked at him, eyes searching Stiger's face.

"And will fight another," Stiger said. He wouldn't be taking the entire legion to Forkham, but a good portion of it. "We will send our engineers and several cohorts to begin digging in and fortifying the ridgeline on the north side of the river. In addition, our artillery will be sent there as well. We will strike at Forkham, then fall back, moving our encampment as well. We will continue to fortify the river position until the orcs come for us. With any luck, the destruction of the temple and town should provoke the response I desire."

"If your plan works, it may mean we fight Therik without Brogan's help," Sabinus said. "What if Brogan doesn't arrive in time and we find ourselves outnumbered and in a bad position? What then?"

"We retreat to the mountain and the dwarves will seal us in," Stiger said. "You've seen those defenses. They are solid."

"Why don't we just go there first?" Sabinus asked. "Let the orcs hammer away at those big gates."

Stiger and Father Thomas shared a look. Stiger considered explaining further, but the paladin shook his head slightly.

"Because," Father Thomas said, "we must draw the minion out. The mountain is honeycombed with tunnels and mines. If we choose to fight inside the mountain, the orcs will go underground, and digging the minion out of a dark hole is, in my mind, not preferable. We may never find it and the vile thing will remain on the loose causing trouble for years to come. No, fighting on ground of our choosing will make it that much easier for us to draw it out and deal with it. That is the true purpose to bringing Therik and his army to battle. The minion must be killed."

Stiger was pleased that the paladin had grasped his plan and saved him from having to explain about the vision Rarokan had shared.

"This creature of Castor." Theo lowered his voice. "This is the one that killed the legate?"

"Yes," Stiger said. "Father Thomas and I must face it."

"And you think it will come?" Sabinus asked.

"I know it will," Stiger said, understanding it would very well mean his death if the vision Rarokan had shown him was true.

I shall not let you die, Rarokan said.

"And what of the people in the valley?" Sabinus asked. "What about them during all this? We will be effectively inviting an orc army into the valley."

After Stiger had conceived of his plan, he had given the people of the valley much thought as he rode to the encampment, but had not been able to decide what to do. They'd passed by burned villages and towns, along with numerous people who were now homeless. He rubbed his jaw as he considered the problem. The last time he had evacuated people to Old City, one of the dwarven chieftains had betrayed his thane. That had not worked out so well. Stiger wasn't about to make that mistake again. Then it hit him. There was a simple solution to this problem.

"I will dispatch our cavalry to advise and recommend that the people evacuate the valley," Stiger said. "We can arm them with any excess weapons we have on hand and send them out of the valley through Castle Vrell and to the encampment for the legion's followers. I am thinking we set the civilians up on the other side of the fortress, the forest side with the followers. The camp will need to be expanded, but it gets them away and out of the valley."

"The orcs won't get past the garrison at Grata'Kor," Theo said. "A thousand of my people hold the great fortress."

"I agree," Stiger said, thinking on the great walls of the castle that guarded the pass into the Vrell Valley.

"What about food?" Sabinus asked. "Without food, they will go hungry."

Sabinus was right, Stiger realized. He couldn't give them the legion's food, for the men needed it. Though the orcs had burned and carried much off, Stiger understood there would still be food and consumables in the valley.

"We encourage them to take as much food as they can carry. Once we relocate our own supplies to our new encampment, we can utilize our mules, carts, and wagons to help them move food and supply from the valley to the camp." Stiger paused and turned to look over at his friend. "Theo, do you think after all of this has blown over, Brogan will help with the food situation? Winter's coming and without a harvest, there will be starvation."

"He will," Theo said. "I am sure of it."

"Sir," Sabinus said, "this is all gonna take some time. Therik's army may come before we can accomplish all of this. Are you sure you want to strike today and provoke them sooner rather than later?"

"Yes," Stiger said. "I don't want to give Therik any more time to get his army together. Besides, by the time we reach Forkham Valley, it will be dusk, perhaps even early evening. If we wait until tomorrow, the orcs will likely come again tonight to raid. That will put the civilians at further risk and make moving them out of the valley even more difficult." Stiger paused a moment to suck in a breath. "The orcs had a busy time of it last night and will likely be exhausted and resting, if not celebrating. With a little bit of fortune, we will catch them by surprise."

"Might I make a recommendation, sir?" Sabinus said.

"Of course," Stiger said.

"Place Salt in command of fortifying the ridgeline. He's a taskmaster to be sure, but he knows his fortifications, sir. He has a lifetime of experience and is good at getting things done. Salt will make sure the engineers do things right."

"Very well, I will put him in charge then." Stiger lowered his voice and leaned nearer to the centurion. "What is the name of my lead clerk?"

"Nepturus," Sabinus said quietly. "He's a good man, was injured and disabled years ago. The previous legate before Delvaris kept him on because he can read, write, and do numbers exceptionally well. Most of your clerks were injured at one time or another and should have been mustered out."

"Nepturus," Stiger called out loudly.

"Sir?" The clerk, limping slightly, stepped through the flap and into the tent. Dog looked up and his tail gave a wag.

"Kindly send for the camp prefect and the chief of my engineers."

"Yes, sir," Nepturus said and left.

Dog, looking disappointed, lowered his head back to the rug.

A moment later the tent flap opened again and a tall older man wearing a slave's tunic came in. Dog looked up again, tail wagging. The slave was carrying a fresh tunic, belt, and a pair of boots. Stiger looked longingly at the boots. He had been wearing sandals for months now.

"Welcome back, master," the man said with a voice made raspy by age.

"Venthus," Sabinus said, "I believe the legate requested food as well?"

Stiger was grateful Sabinus had just given him the slave's name.

"I am sorry, master," Venthus said to Stiger, bowing his head. "The cooks are preparing a hot meal now. It should be here shortly."

"Excellent," Sabinus said and turned back to Stiger. "Sir, now that we have returned, I expect you will want me to take up my post as senior centurion of First Cohort?"

Stiger gave a nod.

"If you will excuse me then, sir," Sabinus said, "I need to prepare them for the march."

Stiger nodded again. Sabinus gave a smart salute, turned on his heel, and left.

"Do you have wine?" Theo asked hopefully, once the flap had fallen back into place.

"Of course," Venthus said. "I will bring some shortly."

"That would be most welcome," Theo replied with a broad grin. "If you keep the wine flowing, you and I will become good friends."

Venthus's lips pressed into a thin line at that.

"Leave those on the table," Stiger said.

"You do not wish me to dress you, master?" Venthus seemed mildly surprised by that.

"No," Stiger said, glancing meaningfully at Father Thomas and Theo. He had never been comfortable with others dressing him, and his two companions provided a ready excuse. "I will manage on my own today."

"Very well, master," Venthus said with a bow of his head. Then he looked Stiger up and down. "That rag of a tunic you are wearing, do you wish me to dispose of it?"

Stiger glanced down at the tunic under his dusty and ash-stained armor. It had belonged to Sarai's late husband. It was clearly out of place, and something a man such as Delvaris would never be caught wearing on his worst day. He felt a stab of pain at the thought of Sarai.

"Yes," Stiger said, deciding to make no excuse for his attire and how he had come by it. "And dispose of the sandals too. It will be good to get back into quality clothing."

"Yes, master," Venthus said. "Do you require anything else?"

"No, not at this time," Stiger said. "You may go."

"Very well, master," Venthus said and turned away.

"Oh, Venthus," Stiger called. "The legion will be relocating tomorrow at some point. I thought you would care to know."

"Thank you for the warning, master," the slave said. "I will begin packing your possessions immediately."

Venthus bowed and stepped out of tent, leaving Stiger with Theo and Father Thomas.

Stiger took a ragged breath, feeling thoroughly drained, and glanced down at the map on the table. The clothing the slave had brought partially blocked some of the map. Stiger placed both hands on the table. He hoped that his plan worked, for if it did and Therik responded as he wished, he would stand to slaughter many orcs. A trace of a grin slipped onto his face at that pleasant thought.

Chapter Twenty-Seven

Stiger strolled slowly through the town, Dog at his side. He was taking his time as he poked about. Occasionally, he peered into a building through an open door or window. The town was unnervingly similar to ones that he had known throughout the empire, with buildings that were wood-framed, plastered-over walls with arched tile or grass-thatched roofs.

Stiger found he was easily able to recognize some of the shops he passed. There was a blacksmith, tailor, brick maker, mason, and a woodworker, just to name a few. The town even had a tavern.

Don't let the town fool you, Rarokan said.

Stiger came to a stop at a cross street. His escort, trailing a few yards behind, also came to a halt. He peered down one street and then another. Groups of legionaries were busy searching buildings down the street to his left. *This could easily have been a human settlement,* Stiger thought. *It's just too similar.*

This is an orc town, Rarokan said.

The community that resided here had all of the appearances of being a peaceful one. There had been no defenses, no wall or berm. From Sabinus's latest dispatch, Stiger had learned the lead elements of the Thirteenth had climbed up to the pass and then swept through it, completely unopposed. They had descended upon the town, catching the inhabitants in their beds. There had been very little resistance.

There were legionaries everywhere he looked as he moved through the town. Somewhere ahead by the temple, Sabinus waited for him. Stiger continued on his way, slowly moving toward the center of town. He knew he was going in the correct direction, for the temple towered over all other buildings and it grew in size with every step closer. Stiger turned a final corner and came to a large paved public square. The temple occupied the far side of the square.

The temple was similar to the ones he had known in Mal'Zeel. Like most of the grand temples in the capital that honored specific gods, this one was very imposing. It was nearly five stories high and made of polished white-and-black marble. Massive columns ran completely around all four sides of the building. They had been engineered to hold up the stone-tiled roof. Each of these marble columns was brilliantly white. In the darkness, under the moonlight, they seemed to shine with an otherworldly light.

Surrounded by the small town, the temple seemed out of place in this valley. It was the kind of structure that belonged in a major city. As his eyes roved over the structure, Stiger decided Castor's temple had an ancient feel to it. It reminded him a little of Delvaris's tomb.

Why build it here?

It doesn't matter, Rarokan said. *All that does is that we will bring it down.*

Stiger's eyes ran up the several hundred marble steps that led to a great wooden door, the entrance to the temple. The door had been thrown wide open. A centurion stood before the entrance, Father Thomas at his side. Below them on the steps in a long double line was a century of men waiting to enter the lair of evil. Robes in a tangle, an orc priest lay sprawled on the steps just to the left of the centurion. A small stream of blood ran down the steps. The sight of the priest brought out a brief moment of pleasure in Stiger.

The paladin looked to be speaking with the centurion. Stiger figured Father Thomas was giving instructions about touching nothing for fear of being contaminated by evil. That was good, for Stiger remembered what had happened to Captain Aveeno, who had become corrupted and turned into a minion.

The temple was awe-inspiring, and for a moment, standing at its base, he could not help but feel impressed by the grandeur. Then his mood darkened. This was a temple to evil, a place Castor's spirit resided. Here the dark god was honored by his own.

The thought of it disgusted Stiger. He well remembered the sacrificial rites he had witnessed in this very valley three hundred years in the future. He could not for the life of him understand why anyone would want to worship a god that not only expected but demanded such things.

Stiger saw Sabinus waiting for him. He was speaking with another officer. The centurion spotted Stiger and walked over to join him.

"Impressive, isn't it, sir?" Sabinus asked, half turning to look back on the grand edifice.

"Not for much longer," Stiger said.

"Yes, sir."

Stiger tore his gaze from the temple and put his focus on the centurion. Sabinus looked troubled.

"What is it?"

"I find it strange, sir," Sabinus said. "The people of this town had no idea we were coming. Very few put up any resistance, whatsoever. The priest there was pretty much the only one who had any fight in him and he was an elderly fellow, barely able to hobble along. Father Thomas dealt with him. Of the populace, most simply surrendered. I did receive reports of a good number escaping up the slopes. That was expected, but after what happened to Vrell, I would have expected more fight out of them. Honestly, the prisoners seem stunned we are here at all. It's almost like they are living an isolated life, with no idea what happened in Vrell."

Stiger agreed. It was a bit of a puzzle to be sure, but at the same time the legion had achieved complete surprise. Being shocked was only a natural response. He was not about to look a gift horse in the mouth.

"What have you done with the prisoners?"

"We have them under guard on the other side of the town." Sabinus gestured vaguely toward the east. "Males, females, and children. A lot more of the latter, sir."

"How many would you say we bagged?" Stiger asked, perking up at the thought of prisoners.

"They've not been counted yet, but at least two hundred," Sabinus said and rubbed at his chin. "This is uncharted territory. I can't ever recall seeing an orc slave. Gods, I don't even know if they make good slaves."

"When I was younger, I once saw an orc fight in the gladiatorial games," Stiger said.

Kill them, kill them all, Rarokan whispered to him. *Allow me to take their souls and together we become stronger. We can complete the bond.*

Stiger felt a thrill of expectation. Like Rarokan, he wanted them to suffer.

"Really?"

"Yes," Stiger said, thinking back to his youth. "If I recall, the creature fought a bunch of criminals. It was the talk of the city for weeks afterwards."

"I'm afraid those we captured won't do for the fighting pits or games," Sabinus said. "I looked them over and they're certainly not warriors. I'm not even sure they would be good for the plantations or mines."

Once the Thirteenth had marched south, it had been lost to the mists of history. There would be no going home for the men. Sabinus did not know this, of course, and Stiger saw no reason to tell him. Thinking it through, he came to the conclusion there was no point in taking prisoners. They could not be sold as slaves back in the empire since the Thirteenth would be remaining in Vrell. He could do with the prisoners as he pleased.

"I think," Stiger said, glancing back up at the temple. It was a monument to pure evil. The sight of it made him ill. "We shall put the prisoners to death. Yes, that is what we will do."

"Even the women and children?" Sabinus asked, a look of distaste washing over his face.

"Squeamish?" Stiger asked, feeling his hatred for the orcs burn white hot again.

"Such measures are never enjoyable, sir."

"Centurion," Stiger said. "The latest dispatch I received from our cavalry back in Vrell reported the loss of life is steeper than Salt initially supposed. The bastards slaughtered entire families, including defenseless women and children. They wiped out the entire town of Venera. Three hundred dwarves and humans lived there. Don't you think they deserve what we are going to visit upon them? Don't you feel they've earned it?"

Sabinus was silent for several long moments.

"This may sound strange, sir. But I don't believe these people had anything to do with what happened in the valley."

"How can you say that?" Stiger demanded. "They are orcs, are they not? There before you stands a monument to a dark, vile, and twisted god. These barbarians, these heathens come here to worship and honor him. Do you know what kinds of rituals are performed just up those steps, at Castor's altar?"

Sabinus shook his head.

"I've seen their religious rites," Stiger said. "Trust me, you don't ever want to witness such despicable acts."

Sabinus swallowed. "I will take your word on that, sir."

"We shall put them all to death," Stiger said, swinging his gaze back onto the temple. "They deserve what is coming to them. It is that simple."

"Yes, sir," Sabinus said. "But that doesn't mean I have to be comfortable with it."

"No, it does not," Stiger said and then returned his full attention from the temple to Sabinus. "Unless, of course, you mean to challenge my authority."

"No, sir," Sabinus said, stiffly. "I still think you are our best bet. Nothing we do here jeopardizes the legion or the empire. I will continue to honor my word."

Stiger could tell the centurion was angry, though he hid it extremely well. *Good,* Stiger thought. *He should be angry.*

Stiger glanced around at his small escort. They had formed a protective cordon around him and stood at a respectful distance, looking outward for threats. Dog was wandering around sniffing the ground that led up to the temple. He seemed very curious about whatever he was smelling. Stiger looked back at Sabinus. In truth, he really didn't care whether Sabinus was angry or not. He just wanted the man to carry out his orders. Stiger had brought the legion here to destroy, and that was what he intended to do. Sabinus would lead that effort for him.

"I am thinking we put some of them to death by sword," Stiger said. "The rest will help us set an example."

"An example, sir?' Sabinus asked. "What kind of an example?"

"They will be crucified," Stiger said.

"Crucifixion?" Sabinus sounded shocked. He recovered quickly. "That, sir, will take a lot of time. We will have to cut down trees and shape them first. Nails will need to be scavenged from the town."

Stiger clenched his fists, his gaze boring into Sabinus.

"I am sorry, sir," Sabinus continued, unfazed. "I thought you wanted to come here, do our business as rapidly as possible, and then depart. The longer we remain in this valley, the riskier it gets." Sabinus glanced up toward the slopes that led to the mountains, which towered above. "The cohorts scouring the slopes have found it replete with tunnels and caves. They've spotted orcs hiding within them. My recommendation would be to conclude our business here just as quick as we can and return to Vrell. The objective, as I understand it, is to destroy, pull back, and draw the enemy out after us."

Calming himself, Stiger glanced up at the forested slopes of the small valley. In the darkness and under the moonlight, he could see fairly clearly. At the same time, he understood the sword was helping with that. It had been feeding him with a small, steady stream of power.

My power stores are low, Rarokan warned him. *You must use me soon.*

"So, there are eyes up there watching us?"

"Most assuredly."

"Perfect." Stiger felt the scar on his cheek pull tight as he smiled.

"Sir?"

"I want them to see what we do," Stiger said and then let out a frustrated breath. "However, you may be correct on crucifixion taking too long."

Stiger fell silent and swung his gaze away from the slopes to the temple again. After several heartbeats, he turned around in a complete circle, looking on the buildings that bordered the large square. Just as the orcs had destroyed the peacefulness of the valley, and the way of life that had existed for untold years, so too would he.

"We brought ropes and hooks," Stiger said, turning back to the temple. Anger and rage shook his voice. "I want that temple pulled down. I want it razed to the foundation. Not a brick or block is to remain standing. The town is to be demolished as well. The fields we passed coming in are to be burned." Stiger turned his gaze back up to the slopes. "Start with the town first. Leave the temple for last."

Stiger intended to enjoy every moment of the destruction of the town and temple.

"And the prisoners?" Sabinus asked. "When do you want the executions to begin?"

Stiger thought on that for several heartbeats.

"They are to be saved until after the temple has been razed." He swung an arm up toward the slopes. "Pull the men back down to the base of the valley."

"We're giving up the high ground?"

"There is little they can do to interfere with us," Stiger said. "By the time they get organized, we will be gone. So, pull our men back. I want the orcs in the hills to see what we are doing. Is that understood?"

"Perfectly, sir," Sabinus said.

"Excellent," Stiger said, "then kindly get on it, centurion."

Back ramrod straight, Sabinus snapped off a salute and stepped away.

Looking once again on Castor's temple, Stiger smiled. This was considered one of the orcs' holiest sites. Stiger had been told Castor's main temple, deep in the mountains, was at Berke'Tah. He would pay that valley a visit, too.

"One step at a time," Stiger said to himself.

Agreed, Rarokan said.

"Excuse me, sir?"

Stiger turned to find a legionary standing just behind him.

"Yes?" Stiger asked, irritated by the interruption. "What is it?"

"Centurion Nantus sends his compliments, sir," the legionary said. "He reports Second Cohort is in position covering the pass into the valley. There has been no sign of the enemy."

"Thank you for your report," Stiger said. "Dismissed."

The legionary saluted and left, returning back the way he had come. Stiger watched him for a moment, then looked around. Freshly arrived and still in their marching columns, two cohorts were twenty yards away. From their standards, Stiger saw they were the Eighth and Sixth, totaling nearly a thousand men. The centurions of both cohorts were gathering around Sabinus.

Theo walked up, coming from the direction of the pass.

"That was some climb," the dwarf said, wiping his brow with a small white towel. "I can see why my people don't often visit here... well, that and there being a temple to a dark god in this valley. Makes this place not too terribly inviting, if you know what I mean."

Stiger said nothing.

Theo frowned and stroked his beard as he regarded Stiger.

"You may not know the word yet, but Forkham in dwarven means *forsaken*," Theo said, using the common tongue for forsaken.

Stiger shot Theo an unhappy look.

"You've captured the valley," Theo said, his gaze falling on the temple. "Do you really plan on razing all of this?"

"We're going to pull it all down," Stiger confirmed and felt a thrill of expectation.

"How long will that take? That temple is much larger than I imagined. It also looks exceptionally well-constructed, and there are a goodly number of buildings. This all seems like an awful lot of work."

"We will remain here until the job is finished."

Send this fool away, Rarokan said. *Or kill him. I can tolerate his incessant ramblings no more.*

"Excuse me," Stiger said in a cold tone, for he too had grown weary of Theo's company. "I have things that need tending to."

He walked off, leaving Theo staring after him.

Over the following hours, Stiger walked through the town as it was systematically looted and destroyed. His escort followed at a respectful distance. Head hung low, Dog trailed along behind him. The sound of demolition was heavy on the air, as thousands of legionaries worked diligently at it. Utilizing ropes, hooks, and horse and mule power, buildings were pulled down. Others, too large to be easily demolished, were set on fire.

The light from the burning buildings lit up the small valley, driving back the darkness of the night. The firelight was so bright, Stiger could see orcs high up on the slopes, gathered in small groups. They were watching the legionaries work. The heat from numerous fires warmed the air, almost uncomfortably so, but at the same time it kept the cold at bay.

Stiger inhaled too much smoke and coughed as a light gust of wind swirled smoke around him. He glanced up at the orcs. There were dozens he could see. How many more were out there? What were they feeling? Was it anger and rage? Despair and suffering? Were their loved ones Stiger's prisoners? The thought gave him the briefest spark of warmth and happiness.

They suffer, Rarokan hissed, *not as you… but they suffer just the same.*

"I hope they do, for this is only the beginning," Stiger said to himself. "I want them to feel the pain, the loss, and the anguish at losing all they care about."

We will make them suffer.

Returning to the square, Stiger looked over at the temple, which was being saved for last. The thought of that house of evil coming down made Stiger feel good. Not only was he striking a blow at Castor, but he was also doing the world a service. He almost couldn't wait for the destruction to begin. At the same time, he did not wish to rush it. Stiger was thoroughly enjoying himself. He did not want it to end.

The prisoners were being held in a large field. He decided he wanted to see them and made his way over. An entire cohort was standing guard over the prisoners, huddled together in a frightened mass. There was a surprising amount of crying and wailing. It sounded all too familiar for comfort—almost human.

Stepping through the ring of legionaries guarding them, Stiger scratched at the scar on his cheek as he looked upon the prisoners. These wretches were not what he had expected. It was as Sabinus had said. The males were nothing like the warriors he had fought against. These looked small and puny, weak even. They were pathetic. Stiger found the sight of the prisoners very displeasing, nothing at all like he had imagined.

Don't let them fool you, Rarokan said. *They are the enemy. They are orcs. Creatures like these burned Sarai.*

Stiger's rage grew fiery hot. His hand reached down to the sword hilt and gripped it tightly. Rarokan was correct. These creatures deserved no pity, no comfort, and certainly no mercy. By worshiping an evil god, they had earned death. They had made their choice and so had Stiger.

"Sir, can I help you?"

Stiger blinked, snapping out of what seemed like a trance. He shook himself and looked over to find a centurion at his side. He did not know the man's name. Likely, this man was the senior officer of the cohort set to guard the prisoners. The centurion's gaze darted down to Stiger's hand. Stiger glanced downward and found he had half drawn his sword. He slid it back until the guard clicked solidly against the scabbard.

"No, I don't need any help," Stiger said. "I thought I would look upon our enemy."

The centurion turned his head to gaze at the prisoners.

"They don't seem that fierce, do they, sir?" the centurion said, with a look of disgust and revulsion. "Not like the bastards that tested the walls last night. It's almost as if these are a different race."

"Don't let your guard down," Stiger said. "They are the enemy. Make no mistake about that."

"We won't, sir," the centurion said.

"Good," Stiger said. "Carry on, then."

"Yes, sir." The centurion saluted.

Stiger took a last look at the crying and wailing wretches and then turned his back. He walked toward the temple, his escort following along behind. Tail hanging low, Dog padded silently by his side.

"What's wrong with you?" Stiger asked the animal. "We've taken an orc town and Castor's temple. We're doing good work today. So, I ask you, why so blue?"

Dog looked up at Stiger as they walked, gave a whine, and then resumed his sniffing at the ground. If the animal were human, Stiger would have described Dog's mood as despondent, depressed even.

Stiger put the animal from his mind as they arrived back in the town square. He was pleased to see work had finally begun on the temple. Much of the town had already been destroyed; the fires were even beginning to die down. Only a handful of buildings remained standing. He looked up at the temple. Men were on the roof, throwing ropes down to those below. Several ropes had already been secured to one of the corner columns, and a team of horses had been run up.

Looking upon the work in progress, Stiger saw no need to go inside. It was a temple to a dark god, one that desired nothing more than to end his life. As Stiger watched, more ropes were tied in place around the columns and in some spots hammered in with nails. Stiger watched the men work. Not only were legionaries skilled at building, but they were just as competent at destruction. It took no more than an hour's work to prepare the temple for demolition.

Father Thomas found him as the temple was cleared of men. A pair of centurions entered, checking to make sure no one was still inside. Stiger could hear their muffled shouts for everyone to get out. There were no replies.

As Father Thomas came up, Dog gave a soft whine but did not leave Stiger's side to greet the paladin.

"It took me a while to find you," Father Thomas said.

Stiger remained silent. He did not feel like talking, especially with the paladin.

"I made sure the men going into the temple took nothing and, more importantly, *touched* nothing," the paladin said and then chuckled. "I think I scared them something awful with my talk on what evil might befall them."

"Good," Stiger said. "Better safe than sorry."

They stood in silence for a bit.

"I am uncomfortable with this," the paladin said.

"Oh?" That surprised Stiger, and he looked over at the paladin.

"You aren't concerned?" Father Thomas gave him a funny look. "I find that surprising."

"Castor means me ill. I am only returning the favor."

"I was speaking of walking in Delvaris's footsteps," Father Thomas said and held out his arms toward the temple. "You are doing what we know your ancestor did, which is really what needs to happen to set things right. But I am uncomfortable with it just the same."

Stiger thought for a moment and then shook his head. "I am done worrying about that."

Father Thomas's expression became grave. "Explain what you mean."

"Castor has done his worst. He can do no more to hurt me."

Father Thomas regarded Stiger for several heartbeats before responding. "I do not believe I like the implications of that."

Send him away, Rarokan hissed. *Send the meddling paladin packing. We don't need him. You only need me.*

There was a tiny voice in Stiger's head that cried out a warning in protest. Stiger ignored the voice.

"I don't care what you think," Stiger snapped and then, with effort, calmed himself. "If you will excuse me, I would like to supervise the destruction of this vile temple."

Stiger began to walk away.

"I don't think I will excuse you, my son," Father Thomas said in a quiet tone.

Stiger turned back to the paladin, angered by the interference. Was he going to try to stop the temple's demolishment?

"My son, you should not throw your life away."

"Is that what you think I intend?" Stiger paused, the rage bubbling over. He laughed in the paladin's face. "Let me tell you what I am going to do." Stiger pointed a shaking finger at the temple. "I am going to make them pay for what they have done. I am going to send Castor a message. My dispatch will include the souls of all the orcs I can find. And when I run out, I am going to find more to forward on to the dark god. I am going to kill every last one of his followers. It will become the mission of my life. No"—Stiger shook an index finger up in the air—"let me correct that. It has become my mission."

Father Thomas took an unsteady step backwards.

"This valley is but a starting point," Stiger continued. His blood was up. "What we do here, now, will send more orcs into Vrell. Hopefully, Therik will bring his army and the minion will come along. When I break Therik and defeat the minion, only then I shall begin my hunt, my purpose. There will be no cave, no tunnel, no mountain, no hole deep enough, nor any barrier that stops me. I will do our world a service by removing every last orc. I shall have my revenge and then some."

"My son," Father Thomas said, "there is more at stake than just revenge."

"Is there?" Stiger asked. "For me, there is nothing more important. Everything that was dear to me has been snatched away."

Stiger's anger burned incredibly hot. He understood the sword was helping to stoke it. He did not care. In fact, he welcomed it. The rage gave him purpose and made him feel something other than loss and sorrow.

Open yourself up to me, Rarokan said. *Allow me to complete the bond. Do it now, before the paladin can stop us.*

He knew what he needed to do, for Rarokan showed him. It was so simple. Why had he not done it before now? All the wizard was asking him to do was a relaxing of his *will.* Stiger closed his eyes and did as instructed. He opened himself up fully, inviting Rarokan into his being.

The wizard's *will* flooded inward. The power was intoxicating, exhilarating. It filled him with strength and so much more. Stiger felt powerful. He felt a tingling in his fingers and opened his eyes. Tiny, almost invisible blue sparks jumped from finger to finger. He knew he could control the raw energy with a thought and simple flick of his wrist. Until this moment, he had not known what he felt each time he touched the hilt of his sword. It was *will,* the wizard's power source.

Is this what a wizard feels?

Yes.

The fires from the burning buildings had mostly died down. The dimming firelight cast long shadows about the base of the valley. With Rarokan's power thundering through his veins, the darkness retreated nearly in its entirety. It almost seemed like a dawning day, as the power continued to flow from the sword, filling the great gaping hole in his soul.

Stiger felt more energetic than he had in days. The aches and pains from the riding and marching were gone, as if they'd never been. The soreness that had come with wearing his armor had vanished. The tiredness from lack of sleep had disappeared. Stiger felt as if he were a man ten years younger.

"This isn't about revenge," Father Thomas said, snapping Stiger back to reality. The paladin was looking at him, as if seeing Stiger for the first time. "This should be about service, faith, and duty."

"I am done with that," Stiger said harshly. "I've given my life to service. What has it gotten me?"

Nothing, Rarokan answered. *Don't let him distract you. Continue to embrace the flow, let it shape you, mold you. The bond, the merging, is almost complete. Together we become stronger, more powerful. Together we shall get revenge.*

"Your service has gotten you much," Father Thomas said, anger clouding his voice. "You have been blessed by the High Father. You are almost first amongst men. I beg you, do not throw away what favor you have earned."

"Favor?" Stiger fairly roared at the paladin. His escort looked over with concern. Stiger ignored them. "People have been telling me I have been gods blessed. It's more like I've been gods cursed. Do you know how many friends and companions I've lost along the way? Do you know how many have died on my orders? And I did this all in the name of service!"

"How many more have you saved?" the paladin countered.

Stiger felt himself frown at that.

Father Thomas did have a point. He had saved a great number over the years, but at the same time he had lost those he cared for. That was painful. Worse, the woman he had come to love was gone. Where before he felt devotion, love, and kindness toward the High Father, now he felt nothing but a dull void.

Thoggle and Father Thomas had arranged for him to fall in love. This was their fault. The paladin was directed by the High Father. So, in a way, not only had Castor taken Sarai from him, but so too had the god Stiger honored. The High Father bore a portion of the blame.

Good. Now you begin to understand, Rarokan said. *Only now do you see how they manipulate and use others for their own selfish purposes. Together we can end this. With your spark and my ability, we can become as powerful as the gods and set things right.*

"This is about losing Sarai," Father Thomas said. "You are hurting. I know that."

"What do you know?" Stiger spat at him. "What do you know about loss?"

"More than you can possibly understand," Father Thomas said, anger roiling his voice.

He knows nothing, Rarokan hissed and Stiger felt a renewed wave of anger and hate bubble up. *Send him on his way. Stop wasting time with this fool.*

"Bah," Stiger waved a hand at the paladin.

"You are grieving," Father Thomas said. "I forgive you for what you have said."

"There is nothing to forgive," Stiger said. "We will seek our revenge. That is all that matters now."

"We?"

There was a loud creaking, followed by a tremendous crash behind them. One of the columns of the temple had been pulled outward. It slammed to the ground with earth-shaking force. Stiger felt the hard impact through his boots. A cloud of dust and dirt was kicked up into the air. The building groaned. He had not been paying attention and missed the start of the destruction. That pissed him off.

He shot an unhappy glare at the paladin and then turned to look fully on the temple. Teams of horses strained at their harnesses. Men shouted to one another as they worked. Whips cracked at the horses. What had likely taken years to construct and had stood for an age came down in less time than it took to eat a chicken dinner.

The roof and most of the other columns fell after three of the corner columns were pulled outward to the ground. With a crash and deep rumble, the numerous columns began to crack and then fall, knocking one after another over until the entire building fell down, kicking up a larger and far greater cloud of dust. The noise of it was nearly deafening.

At first Stiger could not see the result, then the dust began to settle. The satisfaction within his breast grew. The temple now looked much like it had when he'd last seen it in the future, a complete ruin.

Centurions began shouting orders. Further work at pulling down what remained of the structure ceased. Only six columns still stood, as did a small portion of the roof attached to them. Part of the back wall had also stayed upright. A handful of officers, Sabinus amongst them, reentered the ruin of the temple, climbing over debris and fallen columns, clearly intent on inspecting the damage. Men with fresh ropes and hooks followed after them. The next effort would see the destruction completed. Everything was proceeding as planned.

Stiger had enjoyed every moment of the temple's demolition. Rarokan was getting just as much enjoyment. Stiger began to laugh. The tiny voice in the recesses of his mind told him something was wrong. At first, he wasn't sure what it was. Then he knew. The laugh wasn't his. It was Rarokan's.

What was going on? Stiger attempted to speak but could not.

"You are mine," Rarokan answered him in a triumphant tone. The wizard was speaking using Stiger's voice. "As I prepared so very long ago, I have returned. You have given me everything. For that, I thank you!"

No. Stiger suddenly understood what had happened. The thought of it horrified him. It was too late.

Stiger was stunned. He was a prisoner in his own mind. His body was no longer his own. Rarokan had won.

Rarokan took a hesitant step forward, as if he were relearning how to walk. He took another and laughed deeply, thoroughly enjoying the experience. Stiger attempted to stop him but could do nothing. Rarokan had complete control over his body. Stiger felt panic and fear.

Then, Father Thomas gripped his upper arm.

"No," Rarokan roared and attempted to jerk Stiger's arm free, but the paladin's grip was incredibly firm. "You shall not take this from me!"

Time seemed to stop as a feeling of ice cold exploded through him. The cold surged forth from where the paladin's vice-like grip held his arm. It was met with fire and fury. Stiger cried out in agony, his vision going white as the paladin's power hammered into him. Father Thomas met Rarokan in a shocking confrontation of will and power. The battlefield was his mind. There was a titanic struggle going on within him, for possession of his soul.

The High Father struck at the wizard, who pushed back with all that he had. The wizard's attention was wholly focused on the paladin and fighting off the High Father's power. For the first time, all barriers between Stiger and Rarokan were down.

Stiger had not even realized there had been barriers. He could freely read the wizard's mind. It was like an open scroll. There were no partitions, no hindrances. Nothing stood in his way. All of Rarokan's secrets and knowledge were laid out as plain as could be.

Stiger saw his hand of its own accord reach for the paladin's throat. It seemed to move in an excruciatingly slow manner.

The wizard had lied to him. He saw that immediately. There had been no bond that needed to be completed. They had already been bonded from the moment Stiger had drawn the sword. Rarokan had also not needed more power. That had just been an excuse to accumulate more. He had been saving it, storing most of it away for more than two thousand years. The sword was not only a prison but also a storehouse, and Rarokan's store of power was vast. But why? Stiger searched deeper, looking for the reason.

Moving just as slowly, the paladin raised his own hand and managed grip Stiger's forearm. Fingers outstretched, Stiger's hand was stopped just inches from the paladin's throat. The open hand quivered with the effort as Rarokan attempted to break free of the paladin's grip.

Then Stiger saw and understood. Rarokan had hoarded his power for just this moment, this very encounter with the paladin. He had planned and anticipated this confrontation from the very beginning, long before the gods had confined him to his prison. His objective had always been to steal Stiger's body and subjugate his mind.

It was all a bid to escape from his prison. Rarokan planned for Stiger to take his place, imprisoned for an undying eternity within the sword the gods had forged. He saw that and more, so much more… He wanted to know it all, but he sensed there wasn't time.

Looking through Rarokan's mind, Stiger understood the source of the wizard's immense power. It derived not only from the life force of the fallen. The wizard had also been gathering souls for their divine spark. He saw from

Rarokan's memories that, upon death, this spark was supposed to return to the gods.

Rarokan had been instead keeping that for his own use, in turn spending the spark to generate power, something the wizard well knew was strictly prohibited by the gods. Every time the sword took a life, Rarokan not only became stronger and more powerful, but also more divine.

The horror of it shocked Stiger to his core. Those souls Rarokan took could never cross over the great river. They would never know rest, only pain and unending agony until the last remnant of their soul power was spent, their spark extinguished.

Then nothing.

Rarokan had twisted and resisted the purpose the gods had bound him with. By confining the wizard in the sword, the gods had inadvertently threatened their own existence, for Rarokan had gone mad and become terribly evil. Worse, the wizard had an unbridled ambition.

The pain of the struggle between paladin and wizard continued to lash at Stiger as he delved deeper into Rarokan's mind.

Stiger saw all of this in an instant. He understood why the wizard had selected Stiger's line, going back more than two thousand years. He saw it and was stunned by the knowledge. Stiger's own life force held a measure of the divine spark which most souls lacked. When combined with that tiny spark in his soul, it made Stiger almost unique. It gave him the ability to use *will*, a rarity amongst all peoples and races. It also made Stiger of interest to the gods, for through him and others like him, the gods could directly intervene in the affairs of mortals.

Stiger was astounded by what he had just learned. Rarokan, Father Thomas, Ogg, the minion—they all had the spark in their life force, each with their own unique abilities and skill to channel and manipulate *will.*

The pain of the battle raging in his mind lashed at Stiger in ever increasing waves, from his toenails right up to his hair. Everything seemed to be on fire. The pain was so intense, he could not draw breath to even scream anymore. It felt as if his soul were being ripped apart, as each power sought dominion over the other. Wizard *will* against a god's.

The pain intensified. He was frozen in place, screaming silently.

The wizard had planned for the fight against the paladin, but had he factored in Stiger? From Rarokan's mind, Stiger understood he now had the ability to channel *will.* But how? Could he, too, fight back, resist?

Pain lashed him again. Stiger desperately wanted them both out of his mind and pushed back at Rarokan. He shoved as hard as he could. Against such a titanic *will,* it was a puny effort, but the attempt seemed to surprise the wizard. Stiger pushed harder, more forcefully. The wizard divided his attention, splitting it between Father Thomas and Stiger. Rarokan shoved violently back.

Despite the pain, agony, and the effort it took, Sarai suddenly seemed to be with him. Her love rekindled the fire in his heart that had gone out. It was like a warm blanket on a cold night, soothing his shredded soul.

Had she reached forth from the grave to touch his mind, to once again be with him? It scarcely seemed possible. He could feel her love for the High Father, and instantly recalled Father Thomas's words. Stiger needed to pray, to ask for divine help if he was to have any chance. Would the High Father lend him *will*?

The pain lashed at him again as Rarokan shoved him harder, pushing him back down into the oblivion of the prison. Stiger felt himself losing the struggle. Father Thomas was also flagging. Stiger could feel it as the paladin's power began to wane. Rarokan could not win, for the world did not need another god of evil purpose, a god more powerful than Castor or perhaps even the High Father.

Help me, High Father, Stiger begged and pushed again at Rarokan. This time, the effort was stronger, almost as if the god were answering and lending him strength. Stiger felt the wizard give a little. The paladin gained ground, too.

No! Rarokan shouted in Stiger's mind. *You will not dislodge me. You cannot!*

Stiger pushed again, screaming silently as he did so. Father Thomas pushed as well. Rarokan gave even more. The struggle seemed to go on and on. Stiger steeled himself and pushed for all he was worth, throwing everything he had into it. This, he knew, would be his final effort, for he would not have the strength for another push.

There was what sounded like an audible crack.

Rarokan's resistance abruptly crumbled away. Stiger reeled on his feet and collapsed painfully to his knees, sucking in great gulps of fresh air now that he was free to once again breathe.

He was free!

The wizard was where he belonged, confined to the sword and in his prison. Stiger sensed that it was so. Rarokan was, once again, locked away and likely licking his wounds.

As quickly as the agony had begun, it was replaced with a cooling and calming sensation that flowed throughout his body. The paladin held his arm in a vice grip, so tight it hurt. A sense of serenity and peacefulness with the world settled in his soul. Stiger's rage melted away. He felt the crushing weight of his grief start to lift off his chest. He did not want to let go.

He blinked, tears rolling down his cheeks. Stiger found Father Thomas kneeling before him and looking into his eyes.

"I've never loved like this before," Stiger said, in a bare whisper.

"I know," Father Thomas said. "It was a cruel thing, Sarai's death. It should never have happened, but our enemy will come at you in any manner that it can."

Stiger gave a weary nod.

"We suffer," the paladin said, "so others will not have to. That is the service we are called to do."

"I felt her call out to me from beyond the river." Stiger wiped at his eyes. "She was with me."

"That has been known to occasionally happen. She is in the High Father's keeping and care," the paladin finally said. He closed his eyes for a long moment. "I sense … she waits for you."

"Will I see her again?"

"The holy books teach that in death we are reunited with our loved ones and ancestors," Father Thomas said. "I pray the same will happen to you, but only when it is the proper time."

Stiger took a breath that shuddered. The anger and rage were gone, completely. His grief was still there, but it had lessened somewhat and was more bearable.

"Rarokan?" Stiger said.

"The wizard sought to dominate your soul with the power of others, which I sense you now understand," Father Thomas said and stood. He helped Stiger to his feet. "Rarokan wields terrible power. You must take care." The paladin paused and gave Stiger a slight smile. "You know, this is the second time I stopped an assault on your soul. In truth, the High Father beat him back. I was his conduit. The next time will be up to you."

"How do I do that?" Stiger asked. "How do I keep him from taking over my mind? He is a wizard with powers and abilities I know little about."

"It is true, the war with him is far from over. After this battle, Rarokan's energy store is much depleted, though I daresay he has reserves left."

"That's not very helpful," Stiger said. "In fact, it is downright discouraging."

"I felt you struggle and fight," Father Thomas said and touched Stiger's chest armor with the palm of his hand. "You called upon our god and he granted you *will.* It was enough to force Rarokan back and into his prison. You only need to strengthen and focus your abilities, for the High Father has blessed you greatly. Do so, and you will be the master and he your servant, as it was always intended to be."

"But how?" Stiger asked.

"If you wish," Father Thomas said, "it would be my honor to teach you, to school you in the use of your mind."

Stiger thought about that. In a way, he felt like he had fallen overboard in a rough sea. On the verge of drowning, someone had tossed him a line and he was vainly reaching for it. Stiger gave a nod. There was no other option. He needed to learn, for he would not permit Rarokan to dominate him again. He could not allow that to happen.

A tongue licked his hand. Startled, Stiger looked down and saw Dog, tail wagging hard. He patted the animal's head affectionately. The tail wagged even more vigorously and he earned another lick. Stiger read happiness and relief in the animal's eyes.

"I can be a difficult student," Stiger said, glancing back up at Father Thomas. "But if you are willing to teach, I will learn."

"That is good, my son, for I've learned you never do anything the easy way, do you?"

Stiger shook his head, amused. He glanced around, remembering his escort. What were they thinking? What had they seen? His eyes widened.

Everything around them was frozen in mid-motion, as if locked in invisible ice. No one moved. The fire on the nearest building was unmoving, hot glowing sparks suspended in midair. Time had truly stopped.

"Oh, that." Father Thomas noticed his gaze and casually snapped his fingers. Time began moving again, as if it had never been arrested. "I merely took us out of phase. It is simple enough trick. It allowed me to do what needed doing without creating undue alarm."

"What?" Stiger asked. "You did what?"

"It is nothing," the paladin said. "Trouble yourself not on it. Just be thankful you are free and better armed for what will come again."

Stiger gave a nod and expelled a long breath. He rubbed the back of his neck, which had begun to ache. His joints abruptly felt incredibly stiff, as if he'd spent a cold night on the ground. Stiger cracked his neck in an attempt to work out the ache. He opened and closed both palms, then cracked his knuckles. It helped a little.

"Is it always like this?" Stiger asked, glancing over at the paladin.

"Sometimes the toll is much worse," Father Thomas said with a sympathetic look in his eye. "It all depends on what type of *will* that was required and used."

"There are different types of *will*?"

Father Thomas gave a slow nod.

Stiger was about to ask another question when a legionary exited the ruined temple with a purpose. The legionary spotted them and made his way carefully down the steps before jogging over. He hastily saluted.

"Sir," he said. "Centurion Sabinus requires your presence in the temple. When the roof came down, it opened a hidden room. He begs you come straight away."

"What did he find?" Stiger asked.

"I don't know, sir," the legionary said. "Only he and Centurion Prestus entered the room. I was ordered to fetch you, quick-like."

"I'm not sure I like the idea of entering a dark temple," Stiger said to Father Thomas. "We already know Castor means me ill."

"I will be with you, my son," Father Thomas said, placing a hand on Stiger's shoulder armor. "I will keep the evil away. Besides, this is your fault."

"How so?" Stiger asked, starting forward towards the temple and following the legionary.

"It was your decision to bring the temple down in the first place," Father Thomas said, with a smile. "Without that, Centurion Sabinus would never have found this hidden room, now, would he?"

"Rarokan had a hand in that," Stiger said.

"And here I thought you were one for taking responsibility for your own actions," Father Thomas said with a straight face as they started up the marble steps, carefully moving over the debris. Stiger could hear the amusement in the paladin's voice and also the tiredness.

Stiger actually laughed, and it felt good to once again discover amusement. He glanced over at the paladin, wondering what toll the intervention had taken upon the holy warrior. He looked no different than he had. There had been no visible aging.

Stiger stopped one step from the top and turned to the paladin, debris shifting under his feet. He caught Father Thomas's arm.

"Thank you," Stiger said. "Thank you for fighting for my soul and bringing me back."

"You are welcome, my son," Father Thomas said.

Stiger turned back to the ruined temple. Smashed to splinters with the collapse of the roof and walls, the heavy wooden door that had stood for untold years had been shorn off its ancient hinges. Ahead, several legionaries were standing on top of a larger pile of rubble that, if Stiger recalled correctly, was roughly where the sacrificial altar had been in the future. They were looking down into a dark hole in the rubble.

"Shall we go see what they found?"

Father Thomas gave a nod, and together they started forward.

Chapter Twenty-Eight

Stiger followed the stairs down, step after step, into the underground space beneath the temple. Dirt and debris from the temple's collapse littered the stairs. With the dirt and flakes of loose stone covering the steps, Stiger made sure to watch where he placed his feet.

Several steps ahead, Father Thomas led the way. Oily smoke from the paladin's torch trailed into Stiger's face. Holding his own torch up to see, he slowed his pace a little to avoid the smoke, allowing it to mostly rise over his head.

Every ten steps, the stairs came to a small landing before descending farther. There were no doors or exits, so they continued on. A glow from below them on the fifth landing indicated they were nearing their destination. Stiger's foot slipped as the debris gave way. He almost fell but managed to catch himself. Father Thomas stopped, half turning to look back.

"I've had enough of being underground to last a lifetime," Stiger said unhappily.

"I don't want to be here either," Father Thomas said. "However, I willingly serve the High Father. I feel the pull to find out what has been found."

"Let's get to it, then," Stiger said and they continued on their way. He figured they were at least fifty feet down, when they stepped onto the next—and what turned out to be final—landing. Sabinus and another centurion with a hard, heavily scarred face were waiting for them, along with a legionary. The legionary shifted uncomfortably. He drew himself up to attention.

"Sabinus," Stiger said as he looked down the darkened hallway ahead, lit only by flickering torchlight. "What have you found?"

"At first," Sabinus said and glanced meaningfully at the other centurion, "Prestus and I thought there was an entire complex down here, like the dwarves built under their mountain." Sabinus turned and pointed. "This hallway leads to only two rooms, sir. Both appear to be small chapels. If there are any other hidden passages or chambers, they are exceptionally well-hidden, for we couldn't find them. There seems to be no other way in or out."

Stiger gave an absent nod. The hallway was rectangular, running around twenty feet before terminating at a wall. It was at least six feet wide. There were two doors halfway down the hallway, one to the left and another to the right. A statue of what Stiger took to be Castor stood at the far end of the hallway. It was small, perhaps four feet high, and seemed to be made out of obsidian. The statue was so black, it gave the appearance of absorbing light. A well-used broom leaned against the wall next to the statue, as did a wooden bucket.

"Interesting," Father Thomas said with a glance over at Stiger. "Very interesting, isn't it?"

"That is not how I'd describe it," Stiger said. "Interesting always seems to lead to trouble with you paladins."

"It does, doesn't it?" the paladin said. His brows drew together. "Why do you suppose they dug down so deep?"

"We thought it strange also, Father," Sabinus said. "But then again, the creatures who constructed this follow the cult of Castor. They don't think like us."

"True," Father Thomas said. "It is a bit presumptuous to suppose we can understand the mind of an orc. Though if I had to make a guess..."

Stiger looked over at the paladin when he trailed off. His gaze became fixed upon the statue.

"You were about to make a guess?" Stiger prompted.

Father Thomas shook himself and then looked back over at Stiger. "I... ah, um, I was just thinking that perhaps whatever rites are performed down here, they are so heinous the priests dared not allow others to witness?"

"I don't like the sound of that." Stiger felt himself frown, the scar on his cheek pulling tight. "I don't like the sound of that, not one bit."

"It's just a guess." An element of excitement crept into Father Thomas's voice. "It is very rare to come across inner sanctums, such as this one. They can tell us a great deal about our enemy. I wish we had more time."

"Right." Stiger turned to Sabinus and Prestus. The last thing he wanted was to spend more time down here. "What did you wish to show us?"

"This way, sir," Prestus said. The centurion led them down the hallway, stopping at the door on the left, which was open. The door on the right was closed.

Father Thomas stepped past them and continued up the hallway toward the statue. He stopped before it and crouched down. Stiger took a step to follow, then stopped. He had not noticed until now, but the temperature in the hallway appeared to drop the closer he got to the statue. Stiger took another step. His hair stood on end and the chill intensified. He took a step backward, deciding to wait for Father Thomas.

The paladin stood, turned, and walked back to them. He cleared his throat. "I would advise against going too near the statue. It is best to proceed no farther than these doorways."

"That bad?" Stiger asked.

"That statue is something I dare not trifle with." The paladin sounded grave. "When we leave, we will want to bury the entrance. It may not be a bad idea to fill in the stairway with debris. The locals may not know about this subterranean chamber, and I sincerely hope they don't, for no good will come of anyone venturing down here."

"We will see to it, Father," Sabinus said, and gestured toward the doorway. "Now, let me show you what we found."

He led them into the chapel. It was small, with a row of a dozen stone benches. The benches ran up the middle of the chapel, with three feet of space to either side. The ceiling had been rounded into a curved arch. The floor, walls, and ceiling had been smoothed out, for Stiger could see no tool marks. He went to place a hand on the wall but thought better of it when Father Thomas shot him an unhappy glare.

Stiger settled for a visual inspection.

An overly large stone altar was at the far end of the chapel. Something lay atop it. A line of unlit candelabras stood along the left wall. Thick white candles sat in their holders, just waiting for a light.

"I can light a few of the candles," Sabinus said, almost as if he had been reading Stiger's thoughts.

"Touch nothing," Father Thomas said. "Disturb nothing. We are in a den of evil. There is no telling what is dangerous."

Stiger sniffed. There was a slight musty smell in the air and something else … blood. His eyes traveled in the direction the benches faced. He held his torch up for more light, shining it upon the altar. A body lay stretched across the stone top. Father Thomas and Stiger shared a glance before starting forward. The two centurions brought up the rear.

As they neared the altar, and the torchlight played more fully over it, Stiger saw the body was that of a large orc, most likely a warrior. The creature was naked and clearly dead. It had been tortured before it was allowed to expire. Blood was everywhere. It coated the altar and had run down onto the floor. The implements of torture lay against the base of the altar, as did what appeared to be small pieces and chunks of the orc's flesh and body.

Father Thomas lowered his torch, shining light on the floor. There were splashes of blood, along with tracks from the torturers who had walked through it. Stiger had not noticed before, but the blood trail led out toward the door. He glanced down and found he was standing in a dried puddle of blood.

Stiger stepped closer to the altar, his boots sticking to the floor. Stiger felt tremendous disgust at the sight of the body and almost turned away. He steeled himself and looked over the corpse. The orc's arms and legs had been broken. White bone poked out of the left leg. The knees looked like a hammer had been taken to them. The hands had been smashed and were horribly mangled. A few fingers were even missing, including a thumb on the right hand. The stomach had been cut open with dozens of small incisions, and the entrails had been pulled partly out. These too had been cut and sliced up. The orc's manhood had also been mutilated. Despite the creature being the enemy, it was one of the worst things Stiger had seen done to another being. It left him feeling revolted and somewhat sorry for the creature.

"Did you touch anything?" Father Thomas asked the two centurions, looking over at them. "Prior to us coming down here, did you handle anything?"

"No, sir, I didn't," Sabinus said and glanced over at Prestus, eyebrows raised in question.

"I didn't touch nothing," Prestus said. "I swear it."

"What about the closed door across the way?" Father Thomas asked. "How did you know that chapel is empty?"

"I did open the doors," Sabinus said, with realization and a dawning fear. He glanced down at his right hand.

"I will check you both over later to be certain you've not been tainted," Father Thomas said. "How about anyone else?"

"We are the only ones who have been in here," Prestus said.

"I posted the sentry at the landing to make sure no one else comes down other than us," Sabinus said.

"Good thinking. At least there are a few in this legion who can listen," Father Thomas said, with a sharp glance thrown over to Stiger. "Make sure you touch nothing as well. Your life may depend upon it."

"I always listen to your words of wisdom," Stiger said.

"I think that is still to be determined," the paladin said with a heavy breath and a slight frown. "We both know you like to do things the hard way."

Stiger rolled his eyes as the paladin turned back to the orc. He began a visual examination of the creature, holding the hissing torch close to the body.

Stiger glanced around the room, not quite understanding why Sabinus had requested his presence. Though what had been done to this orc was hideous and heinous, the priests had simply killed one of their own. As he saw it, this was likely tied to some arcane religious rite honoring Castor. Stiger was more than ready to leave. He fairly itched to be on his way.

Leaning over the body, Father Thomas, however, seemed a little more interested. He moved slowly and completely around the altar, taking his time, and was exceedingly careful to touch nothing. Stiger wondered what the paladin found so interesting. Perhaps, it was just an opportunity to study another religion's practices. After a time, Stiger grew impatient.

"You called us here." He turned to Sabinus. "I hope it wasn't just to see this body."

"Look closer, sir," Sabinus said. "Recognize anything on him?"

Despite his distaste, Stiger did as requested and joined Father Thomas in a closer examination. He began with the face. It had been beaten to a bloodied pulp. The mouth was open in a silent scream. The tusks had been pulled out. He saw them at the altar's base, by his feet.

The creature was apparently fresh, for Stiger noted greenish blood trickling from a cut along the jaw. It ran down onto the stone of the altar, joining the dried blood that thoroughly coated the floor. It told him the torture had been done recently, perhaps continuing up until the moment the legion had moved into the town.

Stiger recalled the elderly priest sprawled upon the steps of the temple. Had he been responsible for this sickening display? He found it hard to believe that one elderly orc had done all this by himself. He had to have had help. Where were the others? Where had they gone?

Stiger brought his gaze lower, moving to the neck and chest. He froze as the torchlight reflected on something metal around the neck. His hand holding the torch gave an involuntary shake. He had not seen it at first. The skin around the neck had swollen almost completely over the metal. But from what he could see, Stiger recognized it immediately. It was a gold torc and a near twin to the one that Stiger wore on his armor harness, the prize he had taken in battle. Stiger studied the orc's face as his hand touched his own torc.

"I think this might be Therik." Stiger glanced over at Father Thomas.

"I believe it is," Father Thomas said softly, straightening up.

"I recognized the torc," Sabinus said, "which is why I called you both."

"Good job," Stiger said.

"Thank you, sir."

"Why would they kill their king?" Stiger asked. "Especially after he did his very best to kill me and Brogan? Why go to all the trouble to do this? To torture him so?"

"That, my son," Father Thomas said, "is an interesting question, and one I am afraid we do not have the answer to."

"Perhaps because he failed," Sabinus said, drawing their attention. "Pardon my observation, but Castor does not seem to be a very forgiving master."

"That is one distinct possibility," Father Thomas conceded, "one amongst many I can think of."

"We've seen Castor's priests conduct a sacrificial ritual," Stiger said. "It looked nothing like what has been done to Therik."

Father Thomas continued his examination. "This, I am afraid, is altogether something different."

The paladin stretched out a tentative hand to touch the body. Stiger reached out and grabbed the paladin's wrist.

"Are you certain, Father?" Stiger asked, for he needed the paladin and could not afford to lose him. Stiger feared what would happen should he have to face Rarokan without the training Father Thomas had promised.

"I am quite certain," the paladin said and firmly removed Stiger's hand. Then, quite deliberately, he placed his palm gently upon Therik's naked chest.

Therik took a sudden gasping breath and arched his back. Everyone in the room jumped, taking a step back. Stiger shook his head slightly as his heart hammered in his chest. He could not believe that Therik still lived.

Bloodshot eyes fluttered open. Therik turned his head slowly, his unfocused gaze settling upon Father Thomas. Therik said something in his own language.

The paladin looked over at Stiger, who shrugged. "I don't speak orc, Father."

Therik cleared his throat. It was a pitiful sound, and he seemed to struggle just to do it.

"Kill me," Therik spoke in dwarven. It came out as barely more than a raspy whisper. "End my suffering."

The paladin shot Stiger a questioning look.

"Why did you betray us?" Stiger asked, stepping closer. Though the anger and rage had left him, Stiger wanted to hear why Therik had done what he had. What had been his thinking?

There was still the matter of revenge he had promised to Brogan. Gazing upon the shattered body of the king, Stiger realized that Castor's servants had punished Therik far more than he or Brogan ever could.

"We came to you openly to treat," Stiger said when Therik had not answered. "I want to know why you did it."

Therik's gaze flicked to Stiger and his eyes widened slightly. He blinked several times, as if working to clear his vision. The king looked between Stiger and Father Thomas, as if seeing them for the first time. "You are dream. You cannot be here."

"We are real," Father Thomas assured the king.

"No," Therik said, becoming excited. He body began to shiver. "Must be trick."

"It is no trick," Father Thomas said.

"Why did you betray us?" Stiger asked again, feeling somewhat surprised that he pitied the king's fate. Therik had to be in terrible agony. Stiger slowly drew his dagger, so the king could see. He would offer release for information. "Answer me and I will do you a kindness, something I feel you do not deserve."

Therik's gaze fell on the dagger, before traveling back to Stiger's face.

"I did not cross you." Therik coughed up bloody spittle. He groaned and choked a little, before coughing once again. "It was my son. I don't know how he knew… but he did." Cough. "My son betrayed. It was he who led Theltra against my camp and Brogan's. They killed Karan. I no betray. I came for hope."

Stiger stared down at Therik, wanting to disbelieve but couldn't. There was no point in the king lying. Therik was clearly dying, likely just moments away from taking his last breath.

The king's eyes sharpened. He looked intensely at Stiger and picked his head up off the stone altar with some effort. He groaned as he did it. "You should not be here."

"We came to destroy the temple," Stiger said. "Your people attacked Vrell and killed many."

Therik gave a moan that was half wail, then coughed violently, again arching his back in pain. He cleared his throat with some effort and spat out greenish bile onto his chest. Stiger thought it likely the king was slowly choking on his own blood.

"People of town had no part in that," Therik said with some force, struggling to speak the words. It came out slow and slurred. "They be peaceful, what you call"—cough—"civilized. They craft, they build, they not make war." Therik coughed again and then worked to clear his throat. It seemed to take a tremendous effort. "They nothing like mountain tribes. You came here to destroy and punish. Instead you start holy war."

"A holy war?" Stiger asked, going cold as the realization of what he had done sank home.

"You do Castor's work. Now, all tribes be united. You begin the Horde." Therik gave forth sob that seemed filled with not only suffering but a terrible, wrenching sadness. "Even in death, I fail people. Priests have won, Castor has won." He looked at Stiger and allowed his tortured body to relax back onto the stone. "Now… finish me. Please."

Stiger took a step back. He saw it now. The truth was plain. Therik had been honest in his dealings and intent. He was everything Brogan had initially said he was. Stiger had been manipulated into believing the broken creature before him had intentionally deceived.

In his thirst for blood and power, Rarokan had unwittingly helped complete the deception by fueling Stiger's rage and driving him onward to punish the orcs of Forkham. By coming to Forkham, Stiger had made a truly terrible mistake.

"What have I done?"

"You couldn't have known," Father Thomas said, turning to him. "There was no way to know."

"I should have," Stiger said, feeling utterly awful.

Castor's minion and priests knew that an attack upon Vrell would've provoked retribution on the nearest orc community. They had never intended to destroy the legion. The assault on the encampment had all been a show, to distract away from their real objective. They wanted to use the legion. The minion knew of the future. It wanted the temple razed by humans to galvanize the tribes and bring unity, without Therik.

Stiger had been encouraged and led along by the nose, following his ancestor's footsteps right into Forkham. They had murdered Sarai to ensure he followed through. They had even gone so far as to plant the king's standard on the farm.

His gaze fell upon Therik, whose dulling eyes were still on him. The king's breathing was becoming shallow and irregular. He understood with certainty the priests had left the king here for him to find. It was a message, and one that Stiger did not like, not one bit. They had also made an example of Therik for his efforts at peace.

Stiger had failed to save Delvaris, and now he had failed again. At least, it felt like he had. Stiger had wanted Therik's army to make a lunge into Vrell, and now they'd certainly come. By destroying the town and one of their most important temples, Stiger had given the orcs common cause to want revenge.

How many tribes would come? Would it be what they had on hand, as he hoped? Or would it be all of the tribes? Would they arrive before Brogan's army? Either way, he knew he would shortly have a fight on his hands, and he'd inadvertently given the orcs extra motivation to win it.

Stiger gazed back at Therik.

"I wonder," Stiger said to himself, as an intriguing thought hit him.

"What, my son?"

Stiger turned to the paladin, about to answer, then hesitated. He looked back on Therik. Was it possible? Stiger drew the paladin away from Therik.

"Save him," Stiger said simply to Father Thomas.

"What?" the paladin asked.

"Heal him," Stiger said, sheathing his dagger.

Thoggle had sent him along to the summit with the hope that something might come out of it. Perhaps he could still do something meaningful?

"Heal him, as you healed those injured in the underground. Just as you restored Sergeant Arnold's knee, heal him."

Father Thomas straightened, glanced at Therik and then up at Stiger.

"I can't do that," Father Thomas said, as if the very concept was absurd. "And this is more than fixing a simple knee."

"Why not?" Stiger asked.

"He is of Castor's ilk, a follower of a different god. The High Father would never bless such an attempt."

"Kill me," Therik pleaded, eyes sliding to Stiger's sheathed dagger in longing. A tear ran from one of Therik's bloodshot eyes down onto his battered and bruised face.

"He isn't a follower of Castor," Stiger said, pointing to the king. "He told us himself. What if it is true? It may be everything he told us was the truth."

Father Thomas scowled, considering Stiger.

"They left him here for us to find," Stiger said. "Let's turn this back on Castor."

"I don't believe I can heal him," Father Thomas said, uncertainty in his eyes. "Besides, even if I could, his injuries are likely beyond my ability to keep him on this side of the river."

"If you don't try, how can you know for certain?" Stiger felt that he was onto something. It was as if his gut was telling him this was the right thing to do. He sensed what he thought might be an encouraging nudge urging him on. He wondered for a moment if the gentle push came from the High Father.

"You must try," Stiger said. "What is the worst that can happen? The High Father will simply withhold his healing. Am I correct in that?"

Father Thomas glanced over at Therik. His lips formed a thin line.

"Very well, I will do as you ask." The paladin turned his gaze back to Stiger. "However, I warn you in advance..." Father Thomas paused to spare Therik a quick look. "He is an orc and, should this succeed, there may be unforeseen consequences."

"Such as?"

"I don't know," the paladin admitted. "To my knowledge, nothing like this has ever been attempted. No orc I am aware of has ever received a blessing from the High Father."

The paladin handed his torch over to Stiger and stepped back to Therik. He placed a hand upon the king's chest. Therik flinched.

"What you do?" Therik asked in a mere whisper.

"I may be able to heal you," Father Thomas said, gazing down on the mutilated orc. "However, for the attempt to succeed, you must pledge yourself to the High Father."

"I know nothing of your god." Therik coughed again.

"It is true you know little of the High Father. However, you can learn," Father Thomas said. "The High Father is a loving and forgiving god, not a vengeful one."

"I have failed my people," Therik said. "Can he offer forgiveness for that?"

"There is but one way to find out," Father Thomas said. "Will you accept his healing? If granted, will you pledge to learn more about my god?"

"I will," Therik said. "He may not like what he see in me. Castor did not."

Father Thomas smiled and then closed his eyes, bowing his head.

Therik's eyes rolled up and closed as well.

Stiger, Sabinus, and Prestus stood silently and watched, waiting. It was as if they collectively held their breath. The silence stretched. Sabinus let out a sneeze. In the silence of the chapel, it sounded explosive, causing Stiger and Prestus to start. Sabinus gave the other two an apologetic look.

The paladin began to mutter something. Stiger assumed he was praying. Time passed. Eying the paladin, Stiger did not sense a welling of power. Nothing seemed to improve. In fact, Therik's breathing became shallower and more erratic.

Stiger chewed his lip as he watched. A thought occurred to him and he sucked in a startled breath, tossing both torches he had been holding to the floor. They landed in a shower of sparks. He stepped up to the altar and hesitated a moment. Then he placed his hand on the paladin's. Father Thomas opened his eyes and looked over at him in question.

"Shall we do this together?" Stiger said. "As the High Father's champion and his paladin?"

Father Thomas's eyes widened a fraction.

"Let's try it," the paladin said. "As High Father's champion and me, his paladin."

Father Thomas bent his head over Therik. Stiger did the same, closing his eyes. He had never attempted anything like this before, so he decided to calm and center his being.

He reached within himself, going deep, using Eli's teaching to help focus his mind. When he felt at peace, Stiger offered up a prayer.

"High Father," Stiger said aloud in a clear tone. He poured all of his conviction and faith into it. "I humbly ask you grant your paladin the power to heal this orc, Therik, for he has turned away from Castor. Take him into your keeping and flock if you deem him worthy."

There was no reply, and no surge of power. Nothing whatsoever happened. Stiger was trying to make this a joint effort, for in some way he could not explain, he sensed it was the right thing to do. And yet, something clearly wasn't working. Stiger racked his mind. Then it hit him. How could he have been so blind? Rarokan had given him the solution. It was the divine spark that was part of his life force, the ability to call upon and use *will*.

"High Father, grant me your strength," Stiger said, adding to his prayer. He steeled himself for the next part. He had already made his decision. It was now time to reinforce it. He just hoped it worked. "I have strayed. For that, I humbly ask your forgiveness." Stiger paused briefly. "I will proudly take up your standard as your champion, whether you heal Therik or not. I am yours, forever in service, duty, and life."

Stiger felt a small spark flare in the darkness of his mind. It was like being on one of the dwarven underground roads, with a light far off in the distance. The light grew with intensity. Stiger recognized it as the High Father's power answering both of their calls. The light welled upward with frightening force, channeling its way through the paladin, though Stiger also felt a small measure of it coming through him as well.

Stiger could feel the paladin guiding the power, shaping it to his will and feeding it to where it was needed in

Therik's body, repairing the damage that Castor's priests had wrought. He did not understand how Father Thomas was doing what he did, but that did not really matter. Therik was being blessed by the High Father. He had been accepted and deemed worthy.

Stiger keenly felt the touch of the High Father. He was closer than he had ever been to his god. It was exhilarating, awe-inspiring, and at the same time frightening. He felt infinite depth and majesty of the High Father's mind brushing against his own. For a moment, it seemed the great god looked directly his way, and Stiger was filled with a sense of loving warmth, the kind a parent bestows upon a child. It lasted for both an eternity and a heartbeat, then the High Father's attention passed.

The closeness to his god and the flow of power was pure euphoria. He did not ever want it to end. Then, after a time, the power began to slack into a trickle before stopping altogether. The High Father's touch left him, the direct contact severed, and he was alone once again.

You will never be alone, Rarokan said to him. There was a sullen taste to the wizard's words in his mind. *For I am with you, always.*

Stiger's mood soured.

You lied, Stiger said, probing for the wizard's mind. The barriers were back up.

Yes, champion, Rarokan replied with disdain. *And that is the last time you shall read my thoughts.*

Perhaps, Stiger thought back.

There was no reply.

Stiger's eyes fluttered open. It took a moment for him to focus. He looked down upon Therik and saw the orc completely mended, whole and uninjured. The king slept, breathing deeply. A dark greenish color was returning to his unblemished skin. Therik was completely naked, with the exception of the torc around his neck. Stiger blinked. The torc had gone from a gold color to silver.

Stiger tore his gaze from the torc and shifted his position, feeling stiff and very tired. He looked over at Father Thomas and saw an utterly changed man. The paladin had aged at least ten years. His gray hair had thinned considerably. It had fallen out onto his shoulders and down around his feet, almost as if someone had just cut his hair.

Gazing upon Therik, the paladin gave a pleased smile and then his legs gave out. Stiger caught him before he could fall and gently lowered him to the ground. The paladin seemed to weigh almost nothing. "I think you know what comes next," Father Thomas said.

"A long rest, I take it?" Stiger said.

"The more difficult the healing, the more life force it takes," Father Thomas said. "Don't worry, I gave up more of mine so it would not take yours."

"What?" Stiger asked, alarmed. "Why?"

Father Thomas grinned broadly. "We were truly blessed today, for you and I have accomplished something that's never been done. We have brought an orc into the fold."

Father Thomas's eyes started to roll back.

"Rest easy," Stiger said, "for we shall carry you back with us."

"I expected nothing less from the High Father's champion," Father Thomas said, reaching a wrinkled and aged hand up to Stiger's cheek before lowering it back to his side. He closed his eyes and fell into a deep sleep.

Stiger eased the paladin's head to the floor and then stood, his joints and muscles protesting. It felt as if he had been holding the same position for hours. He saw that

Sabinus and Prestus were still there. Stiger wondered how much time had passed.

Prestus abruptly fell to his knees, both hands clasped together. Sabinus joined him a heartbeat later.

"Oh, get up," Stiger snapped.

"Praise be to the High Father," Prestus said in an awed voice that shook with emotion. "We witnessed a miracle."

Stiger gazed upon the veteran, a little surprised at the man's response.

"I don't know how else to describe it, sir," Sabinus stammered at first, "but you both were encased in white fire as you healed Therik. It was so bright, we had to look away."

Stiger did not like the look in their eyes, which shone with devout faith and belief as they gazed upon him.

"You named yourself the High Father's champion," Prestus said. "The paladin called you that as well. Is it true, sir? Are you gods blessed? Are we led by the High Father's champion?"

Stiger almost said no, then thought otherwise. He had pledged himself once again to the High Father and meant to follow through. There was no point in shying away or denying it.

"It seems, for better or worse, I am," Stiger said, with a wry expression.

There was a flash of light behind them. It lit up the chapel.

"The altar," Sabinus gasped.

Stiger looked around. The altar had turned from a rough granite to snow-white marble. It was astonishing. The blood and the severed bits of flesh were gone, vanished, as were the implements of torture. The High Father was leaving his mark in this den of evil. The thought of it warmed his heart.

Stiger turned back to the two officers. They were still kneeling, gazing upon him with reverence. An uneasy feeling came across Stiger. He may be a champion, but that did not mean he was a paladin or a priest.

"Will you both kindly get up?" Stiger said, feeling uncomfortable. "I take salutes, not bending of the knee. Such displays are reserved for our emperor and our god."

Both centurions stood, their expressions awed and reverent.

Stiger turned to look first at Father Thomas and then at Therik. The two were fast asleep. His gaze settled on Therik. The king could never go home or return to his people. Castor had already seen to that. Stiger felt a responsibility for Therik's welfare.

"Have the cohorts assemble for march. We've done enough destruction for the day," Stiger said to Sabinus. "We are returning to Vrell immediately."

"Yes, sir," Sabinus said. "What of the prisoners? Are they still to be put to death?"

Stiger had forgotten them. He felt terrible about what he'd done and regretted his actions. He had destroyed their homes and livelihood. They were not his enemy. The innocent often suffered the most in war. Still, that did not excuse his actions or make things right. In truth, he knew for the people of this valley he never could make amends. But there was one thing he could do, and that was spare their lives.

"No," Stiger said. "They are to be set free, unharmed."

"Yes, sir," Sabinus said. "It will be done."

"Prestus," Stiger said, "get a team down here to haul both of them out. They should sleep for some time. I want to be clear. The orc is to be treated with complete respect. Is that understood? He is a king, my guest, and most definitely not a prisoner."

"Yes, sir," Prestus said. "I will see that litters are made. No harm will come to him, sir."

Stiger paused and glanced around the room before returning his gaze to Sabinus.

"Before we depart this valley," Stiger said, "I want the entrance to this space filled in."

"Yes, sir," Sabinus said. "There is plenty of rubble up there to get the job done."

"Very good," Stiger said, and stepped by them. He moved out into the hallway and came to a halt. Something wasn't quite right. The legionary stationed by the stairs appeared shaken. There was an odd smell on the air. Stiger glanced around.

The statue of Castor had melted. It was now a black, smoking puddle that with every heartbeat seemed to be shrinking. The broom that had been propped up by the wall was now sinking into the black pool, as if being eaten alive. It hissed as it was slowly consumed. Stiger watched as the puddle grew smaller.

"The statue, sir," the legionary stammered and pointed. "It just melted. I saw it happen."

"Yes," Stiger said. "The High Father paid this place a visit."

"He did?"

Stiger nodded. "Do not go near that puddle."

"Sir," the legionary said, "all I want to do is get out of this cursed place."

"That makes two of us, son," Stiger said and patted the legionary on the shoulder. Turning away, he made his way up the stairs. When he emerged outside, he saw that the sun was coming up. He stopped and glanced back down the stairs. They had clearly been down there for hours. To Stiger it had been a blink of an eye.

Two sentries stood before the entrance. They snapped to attention.

Stiger looked around at the ruins of the temple and the razed town. He had made a mistake here and felt terrible about that. Now, he had to live with the consequences.

Stiger's attention was drawn by a bark. Dog raced up excitedly. He jumped up, placing his great big paws over Stiger's shoulders, almost as if the beast intended to hug him. The animal's momentum and weight nearly knocked Stiger over. He let out a laugh as Dog's long red tongue began excitedly licking his face.

Chapter Twenty-Nine

"Good morning, sir," Venthus said cheerfully, opening the tent flap. He carried a small portable lantern, which he set on a small table next to Stiger's bed. "You asked to be woken before dawn."

Stiger sat up on his cot, the blanket falling to his waist. The tent was chilly with night air. The brazier in the center of the tent had long since gone out. It had provided more smoke than heat and had not been very helpful at combating the cold. The thick woolen blanket had done more.

Stiger stretched and rubbed the sleep from his eyes. Pulling the blanket aside, he swung his legs off the cot. The rich rug beneath his feet felt good. Stiger stretched his arms again. Dog, who had been curled up in the corner of the tent, raised his head. He looked around before apparently deciding nothing interesting was going on. Dog lowered his head and closed his eyes.

"How long have I been asleep?" Stiger rubbed the back of his neck. He felt more tired than when he had gone to bed. The day after the raid into Forkham, he had marched the legion north all the way across the valley to the position Salt was busy preparing. They had arrived late the night before and made a fortified encampment just beyond the ridgeline, where Stiger's defenses had been laid out by the engineers and were starting to take shape. The demands of command had kept him up later than most.

"Around four hours, master," Venthus said, busying himself by lighting the lamp attached to the tent's main pole, "and, might I say, you needed the rest. Since you've been back you have been pushing yourself too hard."

Stiger reached over to the table next to his bed and grabbed the pitcher and empty jar. He poured some wine. He swished the wine around in the jar several times and then took a healthy swig, washing the sour taste from his mouth.

"You have not been yourself, master," Venthus said, "not yourself at all."

"I haven't?" Stiger was suddenly on guard. He placed the wine jar back on the table.

Venthus stepped back from the lamp, which now burned brightly in the dim tent. He fed it more wick. The light from the lamp rapidly grew and filled the tent with a yellowed, cheery glow.

"No, master," Venthus said, moving over and tying back the flap of the tent. It was still dark outside, though the sky had begun to lighten some. "Before you left for Forkham Valley you seemed rather upset, which, I might add, is understandable, given all that has happened to Vrell."

Stiger relaxed a little. This man was Delvaris's personal slave and had likely been his servant for years. He out of anyone would know Delvaris the best. Stiger understood; he would have to be on his guard.

"I've laid out a fresh tunic for you." Venthus pointed toward a table.

Stiger looked and saw the neatly folded tunic. Boots rested before the table. They had been cleaned of the mud and dirt that had coated them.

"I am afraid your armor will not be ready today," Venthus said.

"Oh?"

"Unfortunately, it is needing a lot of attention," Venthus continued. "It is in a very sad state."

"We had some difficult days," Stiger said, "and it got a little spirited with the orcs on our way back from the summit."

"Hmmm," the slave said, "so I had heard."

Stiger yawned.

"Both the leather master and the armorer have been working on it all night. I was told many of the leather fittings and straps need replacing. The leather master seems to think the straps were aged, almost as if old leather had been used when it was last repaired, which was just before we left the capital." Venthus shook his head in dismay. "It's very strange. I made sure to use the best leather master available."

"It must have been the air under the mountain," Stiger said, understanding that was not the cause at all. Stiger had gotten the armor from Delvaris's tomb, over three hundred years after the man had died. The leather straps and fittings should have rotted away. Instead, they had been well preserved. Stiger wondered if magic had something to do with it. Prior to traveling back to this time, he had used the armor hard.

Venthus gave a shrug and turned to face Stiger. "Do you wish assistance dressing?"

"No," Stiger said. "I will manage this morning."

"Shall I bring your morning coffee?" Venthus asked. "Or would you like it in the command tent?"

"Coffee?" Stiger's head came up eagerly. "I could use some good coffee. Now would be fine."

"Very good, master," Venthus said and ducked out of the tent.

Stiger stood, stripped off his tunic, and donned the fresh one. It smelled clean and freshly laundered. He glanced around the tent. When he had arrived last night, he had been beat and turned in as soon as he had been able. He had not given the tent more than a cursory once over.

There were three trunks, two large and one smaller that was about half the size of the others. A small camp table functioned as a desk. It had been placed in the center of the tent. A writing set along with parchment had been set neatly on the table.

Stiger stepped over to the nearest trunk and opened it. It was filled with folded clothing, including several pairs of boots and sandals. He closed it and moved on to the next. It contained more clothing, including socks, gloves, and spare equipment. All of the clothing was cut from the finest material. The third chest, the smallest, held documents, a number of scrolls, and books among an assortment of other personal items.

A folded piece of velum lay atop. Stiger opened it and found a painted portrait of a young woman. Was this Delvaris's wife? She was exceptionally pretty, with humorous eyes and long brown hair. Stiger had a sudden flash of Sarai's hair. The wrenching sense of loss overcame him with shocking abruptness. He took a deep breath and slowly let it out. He folded the portrait carefully back up and set it aside.

Stiger picked up one of the scrolls, opening it.

Scara's History of the Legion.

It surprised Stiger that Delvaris had a copy of such a rare text. Stiger had once owned a copy himself, but it sadly had been lost, along with his tent, to the Rivan. All of his personal possessions had been taken by the enemy. The gods only knew where they were now.

Closing the scroll and tying the string securely, he put it back in the trunk and picked up a second scroll. This one proved to be a history, too. Another scroll caught his eye. It had the imperial seal. Stiger pulled it out and carried it over to the desk. Sitting down on the stool, he opened it.

There were two scrolls inside. One was a duplicate of the orders from Emperor Atticus. Stiger had seen these before. His own copy had been taken from him when he had come through the Gate. He peered more closely at the orders. Was this actually the same copy? Stiger had folded his own copy so that it fit better in his cloak. This one appeared much newer and without the fold. Could this be the copy Garrack would give him in the future? The more Stiger thought on it, the more he suspected it was.

The other scroll was from Delvaris and one he had not seen before. It was written in a smooth, clear script.

If you are reading this, then I am most probably dead. We don't know each other, though I would have very much enjoyed the pleasure of meeting you. I understand you will be a descendent of mine, a man out of his own time. How I know this, I am unable to share, and even if I wished, I could not.

Stiger leaned back on the stool and held the letter closer to the light.

It comforts me somewhat to know you are a relative and also an accomplished soldier. The emperor has appointed you to command of the Thirteenth. It is my honor, pleasure, and duty to pass on the responsibility for my legion. These are good boys, nearly all of them veterans. Tribune Arvus, Camp Prefect Oney, and Centurion Sabinus are some of the finest fighting officers I have had the pleasure to command. I know they will serve you well. The emperor sent his best soldiers south. We marched with the intention to honor the Compact. I am led to believe you will know of the Compact Emperor Karus entered into with the dwarves.

Stiger paused. Without fully understanding, he had restored the Compact himself, rekindling the alliance. At the time, it seemed the right thing to do, and everything he had learned since had only reinforced his decision as the correct one. He continued reading.

With the exception of a handful, knowledge of the Compact has been suppressed. Those few count themselves guardians of the empire. There is nothing more important than the Compact, for through this alliance we protect not only this world, but our empire.

I leave you Venthus. He has been my constant companion since my early twenties. Twice I have attempted to reward his service by offering him his manumission. Each time, he has refused. He has known no other life, other than that of a slave. It could be Venthus may fear living as a freedman and the uncertainty that might bring. I honestly do not know.

I have always done my best to treat him well. He has repaid me through loyalty and his service to my family. I humbly ask that you care for him and, if able, provide him a comfortable retirement, for he is dear to me.

Venthus also has skills you may one day find of value. I will leave him to explain further.

Before leaving Mal'Zeel, I made arrangements for my wife and children to be well cared for. If the opportunity presents itself, I would ask you to anonymously look in on them. They, the empire, and the future are why I willingly choose to sacrifice everything. I wish you good fortune, for I suspect you will need it.

The letter finished with Delvaris's wax seal. Stiger recognized his ancestor's crest.

Stiger blew out a long breath and set the letter down on the desk, lost in thought. This was not the first time he had wondered how Delvaris had known of his coming. There was still so much he did not understand. Someone had clearly prepared the way for his arrival, assembling allies and a small imperial army for him. Who, and why had they done it?

Stiger decided to share the letter with Father Thomas. Perhaps the paladin would have some further insight. That, unfortunately, would have to wait. Father Thomas, along with Therik, was still sleeping off the healing.

"Your coffee, sir," Venthus said, stepping back into the tent. The slave put a clay mug down on the desk, next to the letter. Stiger almost moved to cover it up, but then decided not to, as it would draw unwanted attention. He casually leaned forward toward the mug, which steamed in the chill morning air. The fragrance of the coffee was rich and inviting. Stiger picked the mug up and sniffed at it.

"Will there be anything else?"

"No," Stiger said. "Ah ... yes ... have the clerks arrived at headquarters yet?"

"I believe some of them have, master," Venthus said. "I saw a light burning when I passed. Shall I send for one of them?"

"No," Stiger said. "I will walk over shortly."

Venthus glanced down at the desk and became perfectly still. His gaze slowly traveled back up to Stiger, his hand going to his mouth.

Silence grew in the tent.

"I see," Venthus said as he peered intently into Stiger's face. "You look and sound just like him, but there was something off about you. I thought you a little distant after your return. I figured it was just me. After all, you had been away traveling with the thane for so long."

"You know the contents of this letter?"

"I do," Venthus said without hesitation, his eyes on Stiger.

"How?"

"The legate shared it with me," Venthus said. "He made me swear to keep the contents in confidence. I have and will continue to do so."

"Then I am him," Stiger said, tapping the scrolls. "The one both of these were meant for."

A look of immense sadness came over the slave. His shoulders slumped and he half turned away, gazing at Dog, who was still curled up in the corner. Dog's head came up and he stared at Venthus.

"My master is dead." Whether Venthus said that to himself or the animal was unclear.

Dog gave a sad whine.

"He was killed before I could save him." Stiger paused, feeling the other's grief. His own was so fresh, Stiger felt his eyes become moist. "I am sorry for your loss."

Tears brimmed in the slave's eyes. Venthus averted his gaze a moment, wiping them away. "I feared when he went with the thane and did not immediately return, the unthinkable had happened. However, the tribune kept receiving regular dispatches and communications from the legate, so I was unsure."

"Arvus and Sabinus knew but told no one else. I assume they were responsible for the fictitious dispatches."

"So, it was a ruse." Venthus's face hardened. He wiped at his eyes.

"I must know your intentions," Stiger said.

Venthus did not immediately reply. The slave's eyes searched Stiger's face.

"Your intentions?" Stiger prompted.

"I will serve, as I served him, faithfully. He asked that I do so. To honor his memory, I shall."

Stiger stood, pushing the stool back with his foot. He stepped around the desk and offered his hand.

"I am Bennulius Stiger, direct blood relative and descendent of the man you served. I would take it as a personal honor to enter you into my service. That is, unless you prefer your freedom, which I shall immediately grant. In such an event, I will do what I can to make you comfortable."

Venthus drew himself up and sounded somewhat indignant. "I said I would serve you, and that is what I intend to do. What shall I call you, master?"

"My friends call me Ben. For now," Stiger said, "call me as you would your late master. Much counts on what is going to occur in the next few days. The men must not know there has been a change, at least not yet."

"That is what I will do, until you instruct otherwise," Venthus said.

"Thank you."

"Is there anything you require, master?"

"No," Stiger said, "and thank you for your discretion."

"Think nothing of it." Venthus gave a bow and ducked out of the tent.

Stiger stared at the tent entrance for a time, thinking. Who had known in advance he would be traveling back in time? Certainly not Thoggle or Sian Tane. Had either known, Stiger felt sure Delvaris would still live. They would not have allowed the minion to kill the legate. He wanted answers, but just as he was starting to think he understood, the puzzle became more complex.

The smell of the fresh coffee drew his attention. He took a sip, savoring the warmth and taste. The coffee had been sweetened with sugar and it was to his liking. This was, he realized, something else he shared with his ancestor.

Stiger put the two scrolls away, along with the picture of the woman, and shut the trunk. He then pulled on his boots and, carrying the mug of coffee, made for the tent entrance.

"Dog," Stiger said. "Are you coming?"

The animal stood, thoroughly shook himself, and followed Stiger out of the tent.

A guard detail was posted outside. None of the guard's positions was closer than ten feet from the canvas walls. This was designed to give the legate some privacy. The legate's tent stood alone amongst the encampment. The nearest tent in the headquarters compound was twenty yards away. In the predawn darkness, the sentries snapped to attention. Ignoring them, Stiger started for the headquarters tent and his office, to his left.

As he walked, he sipped at the hot coffee. Two sentries stood before the entrance to headquarters. Both snapped to attention. Nepturus and another clerk were already at work. They were at their tables, styluses in hand. Both stood to attention, expressing no surprise at Stiger's early arrival.

"Good morning, sir," Nepturus said.

"Good morning," Stiger replied and stopped before the entrance to his office. "I would like to review the strength totals for each cohort. Do you have that available?"

It was time to learn about the legion he had been given.

"I have our strength totals as of yesterday, sir," Nepturus said. "I will bring them in shortly. Once we have today's count, I will give you them as well."

The legion was still sleeping. Soon they would be rousted. Then the morning routine would begin, which included a thorough count of effectives.

"Very good," Stiger said and stepped into the adjoining tent that was his office. Dog lingered behind, sniffing hopefully at Nepturus's hands.

Using steel and flint, Stiger lit a lamp on his table. It provided some light, but not nearly as much as Stiger would've wanted. Nepturus entered, carrying several wax tablets. He laid them down on Stiger's table.

"This also just arrived." Nepturus handed over a scroll. It had an unfamiliar purple wax seal. "A dwarf delivered it."

Stiger turned the scroll over in his hands. It was some sort of parchment, heavier than vellum. He broke open the seal and saw it was from Brogan. Thankfully the dispatch had been written in common, for Stiger did not read the dwarven language. He could only speak it.

"Can you bring me a candle?" Even with the lamp, the light in the tent was dim.

"Yes, sir," the clerk said and stepped back out into the outer office. He returned a moment later with a lit tallow candle in a black iron holder. As he walked, he shielded the flame with his hand. He set it down on the table. "Is there anything else, sir?"

"No," Stiger said, and with that, the clerk returned to his table in the outer office.

Dog trotted in a few moments later and went to the corner. He walked around in a circle several times before settling down and going to sleep.

Stiger quickly read the dispatch from Brogan. A company of dwarves from the Grata'Jalor garrison would be joining them before day's end. From the dispatch he learned Brogan was expected to arrive with more than ten thousand dwarves within the next five days. Another ten thousand would follow soon after.

Stiger rolled up the dispatch and tapped it against his chin. There had been no sign of the orcs so far, but that did not mean anything. If they were coming from Berke'Tah, Theo had assured him it would be several days before they arrived.

Stiger set aside Brogan's dispatch. He would answer it later. He began studying the strength totals. By his calculation, the Thirteenth legion was overstrength, with more than seven thousand legionaries. That was unusual, even for legions in Delvaris's time.

Seven auxiliary cohorts had been attached to the legion. There were now really only six. One had been effectively destroyed and one of the legion's cohorts had been severely mauled. Of the six remaining auxiliary cohorts, these were also overstrength. Two of the cohorts were cavalry, with eight hundred horses between them. It was an exceptionally powerful force. One of the auxiliary cohorts was an artillery cohort and the other three were light infantry, each with nearly twelve hundred men, instead of the normal four hundred eighty. Two of the light infantry cohorts included an archery component, together numbering nearly five hundred archers and slingers. Stiger shook his head in amazement. He had at his command almost twelve thousand men. His own private little army.

He noticed the camp followers were tabulated. There were over thirteen thousand. These included craftsmen, traders, prostitutes, and the unofficial families of the men. There would be women and children amongst them.

The tally also included the legion's current supply situation. The legion had marched south with a huge train of wagons and mules. The quartermaster estimated their food supply would last another five months. That estimate was based upon their current stores, which included food caches seized from the Tervay. The legion had also purchased a large quantity of wine, grain, and oats from the residents of the valley.

"Excuse me, sir?" Nepturus was back.

"Yes," Stiger said. "What is it?"

"Centurion Nantus of Second Cohort is here, sir," Nepturus said. "He has requested a few moments of your time. If you are busy, I can find time for him later in the day."

"Send him in," Stiger said.

Nepturus stepped back into the outer office.

"You may go in, centurion," Nepturus said.

Nantus was an older man, nearing retirement age. Then again, Salt was well beyond his retirement. As long as he could march and was willing, Nantus would be permitted to serve. The centurion's armor was flawlessly maintained. He had the telltale scars along his muscular forearms that spoke of a lifetime of training and fighting. Nantus snapped stiffly to attention and offered a crisp salute. His gaze was fixed upon an imaginary spot just above Stiger's head.

"It's a little early, isn't it?" Stiger asked. "The sun isn't even up yet."

"I heard you started early today, sir," Nantus said in a raspy voice. It was almost as if he had ruined it by screaming orders over his long years of service. "I thought I might try my luck before the line begins and I need to make an appointment."

Stiger understood with certainty there would be a line of officers intending to see him on a wide range of issues this morning. Add to that the defensive preparations and there was a lot that needed doing, which would require decisions to be made. Without a senior tribune, much of the duties tasked to a legion's second in command would fall on Stiger's or Salt's shoulders.

"Well," Stiger said, "congratulations, you are the first of the day. What is it that you want, centurion?"

"I understand, sir, you promoted Mectillius to centurion."

Stiger immediately understood the issue. It had been Second Cohort's Fifth Century that had provided his escort to the summit. Likely there were more senior men within the cohort that had anticipated moving into the next available slot for centurion. Salt had as much said so. Nantus probably had someone in mind for the post, and it clearly rankled the man enough to come see the legate and delicately bitch about it, without actually complaining.

"Yes, I did," Stiger said, deciding to not make it easy for the man.

"Well, sir," Nantus said, "there is a slight problem."

"I don't see that there is," Stiger said. "Would you kindly educate me?"

Despite those dangerous words, Nantus pushed on.

"Mectillius is not very good with his letters, sir," Nantus said, his gaze still fixed at an imaginary point above Stiger's head.

"Well," Stiger said, "that is a bit of a problem, isn't it? To be promoted to the centurion, one needs to be able to adequately read, write, and do numbers. Without such skills, the highest one can go is the rank of optio. Is that what you're getting at?"

"Yes, sir," Nantus said, "that is the problem. I am pleased you see it as such."

"Well," Stiger said, making a snap decision. He liked Mectillius, and for some reason Nantus had rubbed Stiger the wrong way. Stiger had never much liked his decisions being questioned or second guessed by subordinates. "I see it as your problem, not mine."

"My problem?" It was the first time that the centurion exhibited any emotion other than a stiff professionalism. "How is it my problem, sir?"

Stiger stood and picked up his coffee. He took a sip as he eyed the centurion.

"You have sixty days to rectify Mectillius's deficiency," Stiger said.

"I'm afraid I don't understand, sir?"

"It's really very simple, centurion," Stiger said. "You and your other officers from second cohort will spend time each day instructing Mectillius on reading, writing, and arithmetic. At the end of that time, I expect Mectillius to be able to function as any other centurion in this legion. Unless, of course, you feel I made a mistake in promoting him from optio to centurion?"

"Um, no, sir," Nantus said hastily. "You did not make a mistake, sir."

Stiger took a deliberately slow sip of his coffee, his eyes on the centurion. He realized that in the future he would have to be more careful with his promotions, to avoid issues like this. Gods, he hated camp politics.

"Let me be clear," Stiger said, "when I say 'expect,' I mean it to happen. I will not tolerate failure. Is that understood?"

Nantus's mouth fell open as his eyes moved from the imaginary spot to lock with Stiger's gaze. He snapped his mouth shut. The centurion's face turned red.

"I asked you a question, centurion," Stiger said, hardening his voice. "Is that understood?"

"It is, sir," Nantus said. "In sixty days Mectillius will be able to read and write adequately."

"Excellent. Is there anything else you wish to discuss?"

"No, sir."

"Dismissed," Stiger said. The centurion snapped back to attention and saluted. He spun on his heel and stalked out of the office. Stiger watched him go. He was not about to deny Mectillius his chance without good cause, nor would he allow the rank to be snatched away. It would be cruel and unfair.

Stiger sat back down and returned to his strength totals.

"Excuse me, sir?"

Stiger looked up to find his senior clerk had returned.

"Setinnunus, chief of the engineers, is here to see you, sir," Nepturus said.

Stiger rather suspected the rest of his day would be very busy, and with all that needed doing in the construction of the defenses, he figured this was only the beginning. He now had an army at his disposal. He had to prepare them for what was coming.

"Would you care to see him before or after we go through the list of appointments I've made for you this morning?"

"Send him in," Stiger said. "I will see him first. Then we can go over your list."

Chapter Thirty

Placing both hands on the top of the barricade, Stiger looked out on the ridgeline or, more correctly, on his newly constructed wall. The smell of fresh dirt was strong. This was the second time he had fortified this small ridge. He hoped it would be the last. Around him, thousands of men toiled at the backbreaking work. They had been at it for four days, and what had been accomplished was quite impressive.

Sabinus, Salt, and the last of the junior tribunes, Severus Milanus Varenus, had joined him for a planned meeting. He had just finished a tour of the defenses, his second for the day, and was extremely satisfied with the progress of the defensive works. The position had become quite strong.

A gentle gust of wind blew around them. Stiger turned his gaze outward as Salt was running through the list of things that would be wrapped up in the next few hours.

"I expect," Salt continued, "for the remainder of the bolt throwers to be assembled and in place by sundown. Also, the movement of missiles should be completed within the hour…"

The river below glittered almost blindingly, reflecting the sunlight. Without a single cloud to be seen, the sky was incredibly blue. It was, for lack of a better word, a perfect day. Perhaps it was a little crisp, but it beat the rain that had moved in and out the night before last.

Fishhook-like in shape, the ridgeline he had selected for his battlefield bent outward at the middle and gradually ran back on the flanks, almost to the water's edge in either direction. The natural feature created a sort of a half-bowl shape in the center, backed up by the mud-colored river, which was running high and fast due to the recent heavy rains. Debris, limbs, trunks, and occasionally an entire tree flowed downriver, moving by at a speed that was surprisingly fast. The stone bridge, with a long, single arch spanning the river, was the only way within view to cross.

As Salt continued to run through his punch list of work needing to be completed, Stiger's eyes fell on the ends of his line, first to his left and then to his right. Both flanks ran right up to the water. He had directed the ends of the line to be more heavily fortified and anchored. He could not allow his flanks, a natural weak point at the water's edge, to be overcome by the enemy. If that happened, it meant disaster, for the entire defensive line could be rolled up. As such, the flanks had their own more enhanced defensive works, which not only boasted a higher rampart but also spread outward along the river's edge, running for one hundred yards away from the bridge. If any of the enemy managed to work their way along the banks in an attempt to outflank the line, they would not have much room to maneuver and would find themselves caught between an earthen wall and the water. Swords and spears would jab down at them, not to mention arrows raining death.

Stiger's eyes ran over the main defensive position, a fortified line that traveled across the entire summit of the ridge. A trench seven feet deep had been dug just before the summit. Using the dirt from the excavated trench, a six-foot-high berm had been constructed atop the ridge and packed down. Parties of woodcutters had been dispatched to the nearby forest and returned with logs for a defensive barricade, which was now mostly complete. The logs had been set on their sides, one atop another. Thick vertical supports had been planted into the dirt and held the logs firmly in place. The barricade added another four feet to Stiger's wall.

Smaller trees had also been harvested. These were shaped into stakes, which were mounted before the defensive wall and barricade. There were so many, the sight of them reminded Stiger of a porcupine's quills. Numerous stakes had also been placed inside the trench. These were sharpened to vicious, unforgiving points.

Beneath the defensive works and beyond the trench, the men were digging thousands of holes, large enough for a foot. In the holes, smaller stakes were placed and then covered over with grass and leaves. There were also plans to sow the entire bowl with caltrops. The legion had a large supply of these, and Stiger intended to use all of them.

One of the supply wagons, pulled by two mules, worked its way slowly over the bridge. It had been used to haul food supplies out of the valley for the refugees and was now returning. Salt and Sabinus had wanted the bridge demolished. Stiger had overruled them, for he badly desired the orcs to attack him here at this spot. He was creating the perfect killing ground. He knew they would come. The minion had to, if it wanted to kill him. All this before him was just a prelude to the real battle, the one between the High Father's champion and Castor's minion. Should he fail, the World Gate and the future would be Castor's.

The more he thought on it, the more his confidence in their success lessened to a strong hope. That worried him. Before Stiger had traveled back in time, the Sabinus from the future had told him Delvaris fought a battle here on this spot. Well, Delvaris was dead and Stiger had taken his place. The future had changed and events were no longer moving along as they had. Still, they were close enough. Stiger knew his enemy was coming, and to get at him, they would have to come here to this spot—where he had staked everything. He hoped he had made the correct decision.

The last time he had fought here, Stiger had not had sufficient men to man the entire line in a manner to his liking. This time he did. In fact, he had more than he expected. Still, he knew there was the very strong chance he would be outnumbered.

Behind his growing defensive works, Stiger had placed his artillery. Really, it had been Salt and the engineers who had selected the positions. Stiger had reviewed their plans, found them more than acceptable, and simply given his approval.

At his command, he had twenty large ballistae, thirty smaller pieces, and forty bolt throwers. Each ballista had its own position and had been carefully prepared, in that the ground had been leveled and packed down. A defensive berm had been raised around each machine to protect them and the crew should the enemy also bring artillery. Stone balls had been tidily stacked next to each machine.

Covered platforms had been constructed specifically for the bolt throwers. Really, the platforms were small towers that had been set just behind the defensive line. Each platform rose ten feet above the top of the barricade, giving the machines the elevation to fire down into the bowl below.

Looking over the artillery in their positions, Stiger knew he had an impressive amount of firepower at his disposal. A few of the smaller pieces were still being assembled, but pretty much all of it was ready to go. He had seen large-scale barrages before, but never in such a confined position. It would be interesting to see how the artillery crews performed and what effect they had upon the enemy.

Stiger had decided to hold the meeting here along the wall, specifically to get himself out of the headquarters tent and away from the continual interruptions that plagued him. Later in the day, Stiger intended to meet with all of his senior officers to review progress and finalize defensive plans, including unit dispositions. This was simply a prelude, to help him get his thoughts together.

Severus shifted his feet as he listened to Salt's report. He was a young man of no more than seventeen. Despite having begun his own service at such a youthful age, Stiger could not help but look at the tribune as no more than a boy. It was unfair really, but that was just how it was. Both Severus and Sabinus held tablets and had been taking notes of Stiger's decisions about the defensive preparations. Upon return to headquarters, both would pass those decisions onto the clerks, who would cut the orders and see they were distributed to the appropriate officers.

Salt cleared his throat rather loudly. Stiger looked over and silently rebuked himself for allowing his mind to wander. He returned his attention back to the camp prefect, who had been giving a detailed report of his activities.

"Now that we have the barricade in place," Salt continued, "I've given orders for the encampment's walls to be worked on. It's time we strengthened that position as well. I think it would be nice to have a proper wall should we have need of it."

Stiger turned his gaze to the legion's fortified encampment a quarter mile behind the line. The defenses were not as strong as the previous encampment. They included a single, shallow trench, a six-foot turf wall, and staked barricade. As per standard practice, the legion had carried the stakes from their previous encampment.

"Good," Stiger said, in agreement with Salt's decision. The legion spent its nights inside the encampment, tucked in nicely. Stiger had been surprised by the enemy before and was in no mood for taking chances. He fully intended to allow Salt to expand the encampment's defenses. "What of arrow production? I understand from the reports I read this morning more than half of our supply was consumed during the action at our previous encampment."

"Before we marched," Sabinus said, "we were able to recover around five thousand arrows that can be reused." Sabinus paused to offer a shrug. "That still leaves us short, sir."

"To address the issue, I have at least a hundred men working on it, sir," Salt said. "Not only are we repurposing what we managed to recover, but we're also producing additional arrows." Salt paused and a scowl slipped onto his face. "Now, javelins are a different matter, sir. We only have seven thousand on hand. As you are aware, they are a more difficult weapon to repair and manufacture. We've got men working on those we retrieved, along with the blacksmiths. However, in the short term it will not be enough to make a significant difference. We will just have to make do, sir."

Stiger understood, and though far from desirable, on balance he was more than satisfied with their progress on the arrow front. He turned back to Sabinus.

"Do you have an update on the evacuation of the valley?"

"I do, sir," Sabinus said. "Most of the civilians have been evacuated and are thankfully on the other side of Castle Vrell. I don't have a precise count yet on their numbers. It is more of an estimate at this point and I'm not ready to share that either. We do have a few holdouts who refused to leave, but not many. As expected, with the refugees' help we are having no difficulties extending the camp on the edge of the Sentinel Forest. By tomorrow they should have a solid wall and trench for protection."

"And supply?" Stiger asked. "We need to feed them."

"As they moved through Castle Vrell," Sabinus said, "I had a team take inventory of the food stores brought with them and those we helped to haul out. Our quartermaster was also able to have his boys scavenge a good bit. Employing our wagon train helped things along.

"Keep in mind," Sabinus continued as he glanced down at his tablet, "we only have a rough estimate for numbers evacuated. It was easier to tally supplies than people. I feel confident in reporting there should be enough food stores to last them for three weeks, maybe a little more ... perhaps a little less."

"I think that should be sufficient," Stiger said, turning his gaze back to the river and looking to the south as if searching for the enemy, who had not yet entered the valley. "Whatever happens here will be over long before they can run out."

"We also managed to scrape together five hundred short swords from our depot," Salt added, "along with all of our spare shields. I don't remember the exact number, but it was around one hundred in total."

"How many men do we have with the refugees?"

"Fifth Century, sir," Sabinus said. "As you know, they are understrength. Mectillius can help to provide security and a little training to show the refugees what end of the sword use. Prefect Brayus of the Sixth Gaemelian acknowledged his orders and will be returning today. They are expected to arrive this evening. As instructed, he will leave two hundred men at the camp to help augment its defense."

"That's not a whole lot," Stiger said, feeling unhappy about not being able to provide more for the defense of the followers and valley refugees.

"Keep in mind, sir," Sabinus said, "our count does not include able-bodied men and dwarves, most of whom are part of community militias. My understanding is most arrived armed. If I had to make a guess, and not counting the men we are leaving, there are likely more than two thousand armed men and dwarves on hand. I've asked Mectillius for a more detailed tally."

"The garrison in Castle Vrell also has over a thousand warriors," Salt said. "I exchanged messages with the dwarven commander, a fellow named Voran. He promised to send aid if called upon."

Stiger nodded, somewhat satisfied. It was at least one less headache he had to worry about.

"Who will be in overall command of the camp's defense?" Stiger wanted to be certain it was Mectillius. As a legionary centurion, he would be considered senior over any auxiliary officer. Stiger knew that Salt wasn't happy with the man's promotion. He did not want any petty games going on to slight the newly promoted centurion.

"That would be Mectillius," Sabinus said.

"It should be good experience for him," Salt said.

Stiger gave a satisfied nod. Salt had apparently accepted Stiger's decision, with no reservations or hard feelings. The legate had made a decision; he had accepted it and moved on. This was as it should be, but Stiger knew camp politics could be an ugly thing. Salt was a professional officer and Stiger was becoming impressed with his camp prefect as a man who only wanted to do his duty to the best of his ability.

"He's a steady man." Stiger's mind returned to the Vrell Valley. "And what of our cavalry?"

"As ordered, the bulk of our mounted soldiers returned this morning," Sabinus said. "What we have left out there are primarily scouts, maybe one hundred horses in total."

Stiger gave another satisfied nod. The cavalry had been tasked with riding throughout the valley, encouraging people to leave and helping where they could. Now that most of the civilians had been evacuated, it made no sense to keep them out. He had pulled them in so they could rest their horses before the coming action.

"Our scouts," Stiger asked, "have they reported anything?"

"Nothing as of yet, sir," Sabinus said. "There has been no sign of the enemy."

There was a long moment of silence. Salt and Sabinus shared a glance.

"Are you sure the orcs are coming, sir?" Salt asked. Doubt laced his tone. "They took a beating when they came against us. And with what we did to their town and temple … well, it should be clear enough we are not to be taken lightly."

"I have no doubts," Stiger said. "The raid on Vrell was only a prelude. The intelligence we have from the dwarves confirms this. Make no mistake, they are coming with an army, not only for the valley, but also for Old City. We are honor-bound by treaty to help the dwarves defend both, which, as I explained, is why we are here."

"Ah, yes, sir," Salt said, with a slight scowl. "Right now we are the only ones on the field. You say we are allies and I know the dwarves say they are coming, but all I see is our ass hanging out of the toga."

Stiger had to chuckle on that one.

"Right," Stiger said. "Brogan's coming with his army. It is as simple as that. Now, what else do you have for me?"

The tough old veteran looked down at his sandaled feet a moment before glancing back up. "Sir, we are putting all of our efforts here at this ridge. I am concerned about the other two crossings along the river to our east and west."

"What of them?" Stiger asked.

"They have minimal defenses, and compared to this, the fortifications we've constructed are laughable. I would expect the enemy to march up to the river, take one look at the strength of our position, and then begin looking for alternate places to cross. Our scouts have scoured the river and the two most likely places to cross are at those two secondary crossings."

"If I recall correctly, the bridges at either crossing have been demolished," Stiger said.

"They have," Salt said, "just as you ordered, sir. Both were brought down two days ago."

"Well, orcs don't swim," Stiger said simply.

"And if they come with their own bridging equipment," Salt said, "or perhaps even boats?"

"You do have a point," Stiger said. "We will need to patrol the river. It would be unfortunate—perhaps even catastrophic—should the enemy make a crossing and we prove ignorant of it. Severus, please make a note of it. When we return to headquarters, remind me to cut orders to that effect. I want several squadrons of cavalry put on it."

"Yes, sir," Severus said, writing on his wax tablet with a well-used stylus.

"Excuse me sir," a legionary said, having come up to them. He gave a salute.

"What is it?" Stiger almost gave an unhappy sigh but refrained. It was inevitable that someone would come looking for him with an urgent issue.

"Your presence is requested back at headquarters, sir," the legionary said. "A delegation of dwarves has arrived."

"Very good," Stiger said, becoming interested. He wondered what news the dwarves brought. "Please advise Nepturus I will be along presently."

"Yes, sir." The legionary gave a crisp salute, turned on his heel, and left.

"Sir," Salt said, "my professional recommendation is to fortify the secondary crossings as well. We need to build up their defenses." Salt pointed at the river with a hand. "Yes, the bridges have been pulled down. The officers who examined those crossings reported that, even without the bridges, the depth of the river is shallow enough that it is quite possible to wade across. The recent rains raised the river a good bit. I sent a team there to examine if wading is still possible. They reported, with the river up, that wading is out. However, we have to consider a drop in the water level a distinct possibility over the next few days."

"It's that shallow?" Stiger asked, surprised. The river looked deeper and wider than it had in the future. It was fed from numerous streams coming out of the mountains. There was a good chance it would continue to remain high for a few days. At least he hoped so.

"Yes, sir," Salt said. "Once the water level drops, we could have a problem."

"Another point for you, Salt," Stiger conceded as he briefly thought it through. "I believe the enemy's main effort will be here, owing to our leaving the bridge intact. My concern with adding to the defense of the other crossings is that any such effort would tie up significant numbers of our men that I feel will be needed here. It also diminishes our available reserves. If the enemy manages to ford the river at a different location, we could have a problem, along with units that potentially become cut off and isolated. I would much rather place a smaller blocking force at those points and keep our reserves mobile. It would give us the ability to respond in force should the enemy attempt a crossing somewhere else."

Salt was silent a long moment, clearly considering Stiger's words some.

"Sir," Salt finally said. "I agree mobile reserves will be necessary. However, I still strongly recommend we strengthen the defenses at the secondary crossings. They are far enough away that, should the enemy force one of them, they could be across in strength before we could properly respond, mobile reserves or no."

Stiger turned back to the river, rubbing his jaw. He did not like the idea of dispersing his combat power. He glanced back at the prefect. Maybe Salt was onto something.

"What are your thoughts?" Stiger asked Sabinus.

"I agree with Salt, sir," Sabinus said without any hesitation.

"All right," Stiger said, won over. "Salt, you've made a compelling argument. We will strengthen the defenses at both crossings. I believe an auxiliary cohort each should be enough to reinforce the legionary cohorts we already have in position. It is enough force that, should the enemy attempt a crossing at either ford, they should be able to hold long enough for reinforcements to arrive. In addition, we can have them expand the fixed defenses at each crossing. Do you think that sufficient?"

"With the cavalry operating on this side of the river being our eyes and ears," Salt said, "I do, sir."

"It's decided then," Stiger said. "I am leaning toward sending the Sixth Gaemelian, since they are already out and can move straight to one of the crossings." Stiger paused.

"Sabinus, when we return to headquarters, I want to review strength totals for the auxiliaries and decide which other cohort to dispatch. Might as well get both cohorts in position and at work as soon as possible."

"Yes, sir," Sabinus responded.

"Speaking of forcing a crossing." Stiger turned back to Sabinus. "How is construction of our own bridging equipment coming? When the time comes, I want to have the option of forcing my own crossing."

"We now have pontoons for two bridges, sir," Sabinus said. "The work's been completed ahead of schedule."

"Excellent." Stiger was very pleased. Then a thought occurred to him. "I would appreciate your thoughts. Do either of you think it will be problematic bridging the river at its current height?"

Salt turned to regard the water, as did Sabinus.

"It could prove a little tricky," Salt said, "but in a pinch I think we could do it, unless, of course, we get additional rain and the river swells more."

"It's not the water level that presents the difficulty, sir," Sabinus said, "but the debris in the river. If there is a lot of it, like there is now, we could have problems. Teams would need to be in place to guide the debris around the pontoons and downriver."

"I see," Stiger said. "Thank you, gentlemen, for your assessment."

Stiger turned toward headquarters. He knew they likely had more to discuss, but the dwarves were waiting.

"Make sure those pontoons are hidden and out of sight from the other side of the river," Stiger said. "I don't want our enemy to see them."

"We have them loaded onto our wagons," Sabinus said, "and they are out of view. Once you decide you wish to cross, sir, they will be ready to move. Obviously, setting up a bridge will take several hours."

"I understand," Stiger said. "Let's go see this delegation from Brogan."

They made their way along the defensive line, heading in the direction of headquarters. They were forced to weave their way around and through work parties busy packing down the dirt of the rampart or setting the last few stakes of the barricade.

Like the encampment, headquarters was a series of large tents, the sides of which had been rolled up to allow in light and fresh air. Stiger had placed headquarters just behind the center mark of the defensive works. It was the beating heart of their defensive preparations.

Since they were in the field and expecting hostile action, the guard had been doubled. Amidst the sea of activity that rushed around the tents, the guard stood like a series of rocks, standing firm against the waves. They made sure to funnel those coming and going through a central entry point, delineated by a rope fence that stretched clear around the tents.

Couriers could be seen coming and going from the administrative tent. A horse park, which consisted of several lines of orderly stakes, had been set up to tether the dispatch riders' horses. There were more than a dozen horses picketed in the park. The dispatch riders would be waiting in the headquarters compound.

Working their way down the rampart, Stiger saw one of the guards leading three dwarven ponies to the park, with the clear intention to secure them. A few feet beyond him, a dispatch rider finished untying his own horse and mounted up. The messenger touched his heels to his horse and trotted off toward the east.

As he came nearer, Stiger's gaze fell upon his senior engineers, who were gathered around a table under a tent that had been set aside for their use. They were looking down at a map. Setinnunus, chief of his engineers, was pointing something out to the others. Setinnunus was a small man, filled with seemingly boundless energy for his job. All of the engineers had proven quite skilled. Stiger was extremely pleased with their efforts and professionalism.

The sentries snapped to attention as Stiger and his two senior officers arrived. A dispatch rider who was leaving the administrative tent stepped aside and drew himself to attention. With Salt and Sabinus following, Stiger stepped by them and into headquarters.

Ahead, Stiger saw three dwarves waiting for him. They wore armor and were clearly warriors, sporting the green cloaks he recognized as associated with the Rock Breakers Clan. The leader's cloak was made from better material than the other two, who appeared to be much younger. Their beards were shorter and they had a youthful vigor about them.

All of the legionaries in the tent ceased what they were doing and stood to attention at Stiger's approach. Holding a green-dyed horsehair-crested helmet under an arm, the leader turned. From his bearing, Stiger got the impression he had been waiting impatiently for Stiger's arrival.

"As you were," Stiger called. He did not want to stop the legion's work. There was still much to be done.

"I am Thigra, Chieftain of the Rock Breakers," the dwarf said in good common before Stiger could say anything. The dwarf's manner was brusque, almost to the point of rudeness, which only reinforced Stiger's impression. "You are Delvaris."

It had not been a question.

"I am," Stiger said.

Thigra appeared to be in his middling years. He had long blond hair that had been tied back into a ponytail. The dwarf's hair was just beginning to gray, and his beard, like many of the other dwarves Stiger had seen, was tightly braided. It reached down his chest to his navel. His face appeared to be chiseled from rough stone and spoke of a difficult life. His eyes were blue, hard, and piercing as he gazed upon Stiger. Thigra held himself erect like one accustomed to a position of unquestioned authority. He struck Stiger as a dwarf not to be trifled with.

"Thane Brogan sent me on ahead," Thigra said. Stiger thought he detected a hint of distaste in his manner.

"May I introduce my senior officers?" Stiger turned slightly. "Camp Prefect Oney and Centurion Sabinus."

Thigra inclined his head slightly in acknowledgment but said nothing of greeting himself. Instead, he turned to the two other dwarves with him.

"This is my firstborn son, Holdgren, and my second born, Bereg," Thigra said. His gaze lingered on his sons with obvious pride before turning back to face Stiger. His expression hardened once again. "They are young, but there is no better place to prove oneself than on the battlefield."

"We are honored to have you join us," Stiger said.

"We, too, are honored to fight"—Thigra paused a heartbeat and then added carefully—"alongside our human allies. Together we shall earn much legend."

Holdgren snorted, which elicited an unhappy look from his father.

Stiger suppressed his irritation. He needed the dwarves, and the last thing he wanted was to get off on the wrong foot. It was clear they did not appreciate having to associate with humans.

"I thought I would ride ahead and prepare for my warband's arrival," Thigra said.

Stiger perked up at that news.

"When do you expect they will march in?" Stiger asked.

"They are likely four hours behind us. We would have been here yesterday but were delayed." Thigra clenched a fist briefly and then opened it. He let out a heavy breath. "On my thane's request, I stopped to gather up much of the garrison from Old City and Grata'Jalor. It took more time than expected. With them, I have more than two thousand warriors."

"That is the best news I've heard all day," Stiger said, feeling a vast relief wash over him that the first of the dwarves would soon arrive.

"I thought perhaps you might be pleased," Thigra said simply.

"You humans dig trenches and build up walls to hide behind," Holdgren said, with a clear look of disdain thrown to Stiger. "There is not much legend in fighting behind walls. You must meet the enemy shield to shield to know your true worth."

Surprised, Stiger turned his gaze upon Holdgren. He was about to respond when Sabinus beat him to the punch.

"Is that why you dwarves built Grata'Kor and Grata'Jalor?"

The dwarves stiffened.

"I knew another dwarf who thought as you do," Sabinus continued, his disdain dripping with acid as he spoke. "It cost Taithun not only his life, but many others, dwarves and humans alike." Sabinus pointed a finger at Holdgren. "Let me set you straight, son. There is no glory in war, only duty, your comrades, and death. When you grow older, if you survive that long, you will know the truth behind my words. It is kill or be killed and that's it."

Holdgren's eyes went wide in shock and he glanced over to his father. The tent was suddenly quiet.

"That's enough, Sabinus," Stiger said, though he very much approved of the centurion's words.

Thigra's eyes had snapped to the centurion. After a moment's hesitation, he glanced over at his son and then back to Stiger. He barked out a forced laugh. "The ignorance of youth, eh?"

"What other news do you bring?" Stiger asked, eager to steer the conversation away from rocky ground. Thigra seemed grateful for the opportunity to speak about something else, for he jumped on it, even as he shot a glare back at his son.

"Chovhog," Thigra said, "chieftain of the Forge Clan, should arrive in a day or two with another thousand warriors. He brings with him his finest company, the Black Hammers. We are lucky they will be with us, for they are an experienced and professional company. After that, we are on our own until my thane arrives with the army."

"Do you have any idea on when that might be?"

"Last word I heard this morning as we rode through Old City was that Brogan is three or four days away," Thigra said with a shrug. "He could be closer. He is coming with warbands from the Steel Hands, Stouthearts, Stonebreakers, Hammer Fisted, and the Bloody Axe. Due to supply, he too was delayed. This region is quite distant for many of the clans. As such, supply has proven a difficult foe to conquer. But with any luck, there will be no more delays, and rest of the clans should be with us soon after Brogan."

Stiger felt a chill. The Hammer Fisted Clan was coming. They had betrayed Brogan's son, Braddock. Hrove, their chieftain, had attempted to kill Braddock and, in a way, was partly to blame for Stiger's current predicament. He took a breath and reminded himself that the betrayal had happened three hundred years into the future. Hrove might not yet have even been born.

"Let us hope the orcs wait until your entire army gets here," Salt said, speaking up when Stiger said nothing.

"That is unlikely," Thigra said. "Our sources inform us, despite having only assembled two-thirds of the tribes, Therik has managed to put together a considerable host and is now on the move. Like us, food is his problem. Unlike us, the orcs have no supply system set up. They only have enough to feed themselves for a week, perhaps more. Hence the raid on the valley. Therik seeks to extend their supplies as much as possible before he strikes."

Stiger knew that wasn't the complete reason for the raid. It had been to provoke him to follow through on destroying the temple. But he remained silent on that point and also on the orc king, who was even now in their encampment. He needed to explain Therik to both Brogan and Thigra in a way that would smooth things over. He wasn't yet sure how to do that. He was hoping Father Thomas, when he awoke, could help him, for Stiger had pledged revenge with Brogan against Therik for something the orc king had not done.

"Any idea on their numbers?" Salt asked.

"We believe somewhere around fifty thousand," Thigra said. "Our informers and spies are not quite sure, but that seems to be the common number they agree on."

"Fifty thousand?" Salt said, aghast. The camp prefect looked over at Stiger, his concern plain. "Sir, with all we have on hand, it is unlikely we will be able to hold against such numbers, even with the strength of this position."

"We will hold as long as we are able," Stiger said. "Reinforcements are on their way."

"We're still gonna be outnumbered," Salt said.

Whenever was he not? Stiger thought to himself.

"That is why we have been busy constructing the best possible defensive position," Stiger said. "There is a lot of killing that needs to be done, and we are the ones to do it."

"Yes, sir," Salt said. It was clear he was far from convinced, but he picked up on Stiger's hint and fell silent.

"As planned, if needed we will fall back to the mountain." Stiger gestured at the dwarves with a hand. "They have a fortress more formidable than Castle Vrell. It will allow us to hold for some time." Stiger looked over at Thigra. "Isn't that correct?"

"It is," Thigra said. "My thane instructed that in such an eventuality, the mountain is to be opened to you and your people. By the grace of Thulla, we shall not need to do so."

"Thulla?" Sabinus asked.

"The god most of our people worship," Holdgren said with a distasteful look thrown toward the centurion, as if the man were an ignorant barbarian. "He is of the High Father's alignment. I would have thought you would have known that."

Stiger flashed a warning look to Sabinus, who gave a curt nod of understanding to stand down. Clearly this alliance with the dwarves was going to prove difficult.

"Severus," Stiger said, turning toward the tribune. "Would you kindly check with the clerks and find a suitable location for Thigra's warband to camp, preferably next to our fortified encampment?"

"I will, sir," Severus said and stepped off toward the clerks.

"I would be honored if you would dine with me and my senior officers this evening," Stiger said to Thigra. "Your sons are invited, of course, as are any officers you deem worthy."

"That would be acceptable," Thigra said. "First I would like a tour of the defenses you have constructed. As we came down from Old City, from above your fortifications appear quite extensive." He shot a heated glance at his firstborn. "I think it would be educational for my boys to learn how the empire's legions fight."

"I would be pleased to give you a…"

Stiger trailed off as Thigra stiffened, staring past Stiger with wide eyes. They narrowed and the dwarf grew red in the face.

"What is he doing here?" Thigra seemed to bite out the words.

Stiger turned to see Father Thomas, Theo, and Therik approaching the tent. He felt a sudden headache coming on. Their timing could not have been worse. All of the legionaries nearby had turned their heads at the sight of the orc. Father Thomas did not move with his former grace but seemed to hobble along, a result of joints sore with age. Therik had slowed his pace to walk at the paladin's side.

"He," Stiger said firmly, "is with us."

"That—" Thigra jabbed a stubby index finger toward Therik, voice shaking with rage "—is the enemy's king."

All activity in the large tent ceased with those words. Father Thomas stumbled to a stop, a look of sudden concern washing over his face as he took in the dwarves.

"Thigra," Therik said as he and the paladin entered the administrative tent, "is good to see you, too."

"He tried to murder our thane." Thigra drew his sword and turned on Stiger. "How can you allow that piece of filth to walk about your camp unfettered and without a guard? You pledged the blood vengeance to our thane. This is an outrage!"

Two of the headquarters guard entered the tent and moved forward toward the dwarves, drawing their short swords as they advanced. Stiger held up his hand to stop them.

"I not try to kill Brogan," Therik said, firmly stopping several feet from the enraged dwarf.

From out of nowhere came a deep menacing growl. Dog appeared at Stiger's side, his teeth bared at Thigra and his head lowered, ears back. The animal moved to interpose himself between his master and the dwarf. Thigra's eyes fell upon Dog and his rage wavered. Stiger saw it in the dwarf's eyes.

"Perhaps," Stiger said in a loud voice before things could spin out of control, "you will allow me and the paladin here to explain."

"Yes," Father Thomas rasped, "an explanation is in order."

"Thigra," Theo said, "you are going to want to listen."

Growl deepening and becoming more guttural, Dog advanced on the dwarf.

Eyes still on Dog, Thigra lowered his sword before sheathing it.

"Dog," Stiger called, "down."

The growling ceased, and Dog came to a stop but remained standing between Stiger and Thigra. The menace in the animal's posture was plain for all to see.

"This had best be good," Thigra said, eyes going from Dog to Stiger.

"Oh," Stiger said, "it is."

Chapter Thirty-One

Stiger stepped out into the darkness from the officer's mess, which had been commandeered for dining with the dwarves. To combat the cold, the sides of the tent had been lowered. The press of bodies had created a warm fug within. He left the sounds of boisterous laughter, the telling of tall tales, and inebriated merriment behind. Heated wine had been liberally poured, and the results had been predictable.

Once outside, Stiger stopped and glanced back into the tent through the open entrance flap. He did not much feel like celebrating Thigra's warband joining the legion. His heart still ached with Sarai's loss. Then there was the coming battle. He could not count on it going down like the future Sabinus had related to him. But at the same time, Stiger felt trapped. He knew Delvaris had fought a battle in this place. It was a naturally strong position. The river and the lack of any other easy crossing made it the perfect chokepoint. More concerning to him was that the minion knew all this as well. What surprises would the minion have for him?

A chill breeze blew by, ruffling the tent behind him. By the humidity, Stiger judged that there would be rain by morning. A storm might even be on the wind.

How could he beat the creature without sharing Delvaris's fate?

That question lay heavily upon his mind. Stiger wished he had some tobacco. He had always found a good pipe relaxing. When he returned to his tent this evening, he would ask Venthus if he could scrounge some up.

Stiger scanned the semi-darkness of the encampment before him. Torches had been secured to poles at the corner of each street to provide some light amongst the hundreds of tents. Campfires by the dozens lit up the darkened camp just ahead, casting wild, shifting shadows as the flames jumped and danced about. There were many thousands of campfires throughout the encampment. Stiger could see their combined orange glow reflected on the low-hanging clouds above.

"I see you no wish to drink."

Stiger turned to see Therik standing a few feet to his left. He had seen Therik leave a short while before but thought he had retired for the evening. Stiger suspected Therik had been waiting for him. The orc took a step nearer.

"I don't feel like drinking," Stiger said. "I have much on my mind."

"Burden of leader is something few know, and even fewer understand," Therik said.

Stiger did not immediately reply. "I don't think I've ever heard truer words."

"Is good you convinced Thigra I had no part to kill Brogan," Therik said. "I would have killed Thigra had it come to blows and then would be no fixing things."

In the torchlight, Stiger looked carefully at Therik. The orc had not intended the words as bravado. He simply meant them.

"Having a paladin vouch for you is no small thing," Stiger said.

"I don't usually listen to priests, but your paladin is different," Therik said. "Something about him speaks of trust and honesty."

Stiger reflected on what had occurred in the administrative tent. Theo had also spoken passionately on Therik's behalf. Thigra had given Theo's words just as much credence as he had those of Father Thomas. Either Thigra already knew of Theo's new appointment as Brogan's advisor or Theo had always been a close fixture to the thane. Stiger suspected the latter. His friend was most definitely more than he let on.

"You should have let me die," Therik said, breaking the silence that had grown between them. "Tell me. Why you bring me back from death's mistress? Why save me?"

"Do I need a reason?" Stiger turned his gaze out to the darkness as, armor chinking, a file of men on patrol marched close by. The men's gazes were upon Therik as they passed.

"Eyes front," the optio in command of the patrol snapped at his men. "Show some bloody respect."

The optio offered Stiger a salute and then they were past, moving up the street. A few moments later the patrol turned onto a side street and were lost from view.

"I need your reason," Therik said, crossing his large muscular arms.

"Why?" Stiger asked him. "Does it matter?"

Therik's eyes glittered against the torchlight as they gazed at one another.

"I wanted much for my kingdom. I was honored, respected. Children looked up to me. They wanted to be me." Therik fell briefly silent. When he next spoke, it was barely a whisper. "I am without people. I can never go home. You should have let me die." Therik's tone lost the whisper and became firm. "So, I want to know. Why you want me? Explain. I need to know."

Stiger realized he should have expected this from Therik, but he had not given it any thought. There had simply been too much to do and not enough time for anything else, let alone consider what should be done with the deposed king. Therik had clearly been giving it some thought himself.

"I am not perfect," Stiger said, carefully picking his words. "I made mistakes—the razing of the temple, for example. I thought by saving you I would do a small right, after doing so much wrong."

Therik straightened up. He held Stiger's gaze a long moment, then exhaled and seemed to relax, his look softening. A moment later he glanced away, looking off into the night.

"And if I am another?"

"Then I will have to live with it, as I do with all of the other mistakes I've made," Stiger said. "Besides, Castor thought to make an example of you. I was unwilling to let him do that. You deserve better."

"Do I?" Therik asked in a tone that was somewhat strangled. "You not only one with mistakes. I turned from Castor. It cost me all. Perhaps I should have had more faith."

Behind them in the tent, there was an outburst of uproarious laughter. Stiger glanced back through the entrance. He saw Thigra and Theo along with a number of legion officers laughing as Salt offered up a toast. Thigra pounded his palm on the table, shaking the cups and jars.

"You gave me life," Therik said, "but living with failure is not so easy."

"I've learned living is hard," Stiger said, his thoughts returning to Sarai. What would he give to see her again? What would he trade to smell the fragrance of her hair?

Or the touch of her skin on his? The brush of her lips? But that was not meant to be. Stiger turned to fully face Therik.

"Who's to say you failed? The book of your life is not fully written. Neither is mine," Stiger said.

"What are you saying?"

"I think it is what we make of ourselves and how we affect others that matters in the end. In a way, you can say life is the journey, not the destination."

Therik reached up a hand and ran a thumb along his left tusk.

"You sound like priest," Therik said.

"I took part of that from scripture," Stiger admitted and then quoted the line from the High Father's Holy Book. He had been thinking on it a lot since Father Thomas had helped him beat back Rarokan. "Life is the journey; death is the destination."

Therik gave a grunt.

"I helped give you your life back. What you do with the extra time is your business." Stiger paused briefly. "There is a place for you here. That is, should you wish it, of course."

"With you humans? Serving in your legion?" Therik shot him a dubious expression.

"No," Stiger said. "The legion is not the place for you."

"Then where?"

"At my side," Stiger said, once again feeling a deep responsibility for the deposed king. Despite their species being alien to one another, Stiger felt an odd kinship with Therik. The more he thought on it, the more it seemed like the correct decision. Therik needed a purpose and a place in this world. "I would welcome your help, whether it be your counsel, sword, or both. The choice is up to you."

Therik's eyes widened slightly and then narrowed, as if suspicious of Stiger's offer.

"And if I choose to walk through the gates and out into the night?" Therik asked. "What then?"

"Then I shall order the gates opened, and provide you with several days' rations, a cloak, and a sword. I meant what I said."

"Do you still mean to kill the minion?" Therik asked.

"Yes," Stiger said.

"Good," Therik said, disgust creeping into his tone. "My son handed me over to priests. They gave me to Castor's servant."

Stiger looked over sharply at the orc. "It was the minion that tortured you?"

Therik gave a nod. "It told me to give you a message."

"Oh?" Stiger did not like the sound of that.

"It is coming for you," Therik said simply.

"I had no doubt," Stiger said grimly, "for should it not, I would come for it."

"It told me it would meet you here at stone bridge." Therik paused and cocked his head to the side. "How did it know you would come here?"

"That does not matter," Stiger said, for he did not wish to explain.

"I doubt that," Therik said.

Stiger suspected there was more, and though he did not wish to hear it, he knew he had to. "What else did it say?"

"That you have seen it kill you."

Stiger felt a chill run down his spine. How had it known the sword had shown him the vision? Had it really been Stiger that Rarokan had shown mortally wounded?

Who was it? Stiger asked Rarokan, turning his thoughts inward.

There was no reply.

Answer me!

Nothing.

"Is true, then?" Therik asked.

"It seeks to get under my skin," Stiger said. "That is all."

Therik gave a nod but looked far from convinced.

"My son," Therik said, "my army, and the priests will come also."

"I hope so," Stiger said. "I want them all to come, for once your army is broken, I will get my chance at the minion. I will end this madness."

"You are not right in head, I think," Therik said, "to want to face the holy warrior of Castor and its strong medicine."

"Perhaps," Stiger said and gazed meaningfully back at Therik. "Look who I consort with."

Therik gave a grunt that was part laugh. He then grew serious and tapped a fist to his chest.

"To face Castor, you show much heart," Therik said. He then pointed a finger at Stiger. "I fight with you to defeat Castor. I kill my son, too. When all is done, I decide what I do."

"Fair enough," Stiger said in agreement.

Without another word, Therik turned and walked off, leaving Stiger staring after him until he rounded a street corner.

In the distance, thunder rumbled. The sky flickered with lightning. It followed up a few heartbeats later with a deeper and longer rumble. There would be a storm tonight. Dog padded up to him, emerging like a wraith from out of the shadows.

"Hello there," Stiger said, suspecting the animal had been watching him and Therik converse. Could it really understand what he said?

Dog sat down and looked up at him, tongue hanging stupidly out of the side of his mouth. His tail gave a single wag in the dirt.

"Care for a stroll around camp?" Stiger asked. "I have a lot on my mind."

Dog stood and wagged his tail energetically.

"Let's get to it, then."

Stiger set off, slowly walking through the large encampment. Years ago, he had taken to walking at night when problems had plagued him. It helped to lessen the tension and stress. Walking with Dog was itself soothing. There was something about that animal's companionship that just helped. Perhaps it was knowing Dog was there, a constant companion that never judged.

"Whichever god sent you," Stiger said to the animal as they turned onto a street lined with communal tents from First Cohort, "I am grateful."

Lifting a leg to urinate on a tent's guide rope, Dog ignored him. Stiger kept walking. A moment later, Dog caught up, falling in at his side like a good soldier. The animal sniffed the ground as they continued their walk through the heavily shadowed camp.

There were few legionaries up and about at this late hour. Those he did see were gathered around campfires, enjoying their wine ration, talking, or taking a turn at dice. The rest were asleep, for the morrow promised another day of hard labor, beginning at sunup and ceasing only when the sun dipped beneath the mountains.

Stiger passed close to a fire where ten men had gathered for warmth and light. They made to stand, scrambling hastily to their feet.

"Keep your seats," Stiger said, waving them back down, and entered their circle. He smelled the tobacco before he saw that one of the men was smoking a pipe. It flared in the semi-darkness as he took a hearty pull, sucking in the smoke.

Stiger stepped closer to the fire and warmed his hands. Dog sat down at his side.

"May I have a pull?" Stiger asked, looking over at the man.

"Of course, sir." The legionary handed the pipe over to another man, who gave it to Stiger. "It's not as fine as you're likely used to, but it's tobacco."

Stiger took a long pull on the pipe, savoring the warmth and taste. He handed the pipe back to the man and blew out a long stream of smoke. He almost sighed with pleasure.

"Thank you," Stiger said. "It's been far too long since I enjoyed a good pipe."

"My pleasure, sir."

Stiger noticed several jars of wine sitting in the dirt. A few lay on their sides, clearly empty. The men were issued a daily ration and had clearly been sharing. It was a common practice. Stiger could almost sense the weary exhaustion around the fire.

"After a long day of hard work, there's nothing finer than a jar of wine, a good pipe, a warm fire, and the company of one's comrades," Stiger said.

"You can say that again, sir," the man with the pipe said with a chuckle. The others joined in.

"I am surprised you boys aren't asleep yet," Stiger said.

"We will be soon enough, sir," the same legionary said. He was an older man, nearing retirement age. "Is it true, sir?"

"Is what true?"

"About you and that paladin…" The man then hesitated, as if he abruptly realized he had become perhaps too presumptuous. Stiger noticed several of those around the fire lean forward eagerly or became more attentive. He could well guess what was coming.

"About me and the paladin doing what?" Stiger prompted when the man did not speak further. He wanted to hear what rumor was making its way around camp. "It's all right. Ask your question."

"Performing a miracle and healing that orc king?" The man's gaze was intense, hopeful even. "One of my mates heard Centurion Prestus talking about it, sir. But you knows how things get in camp with tales. They grow in the telling."

Stiger thought on it for a moment before he replied. Belief in the gods was strong amongst the legions. In a profession where death and maiming was a distinct possibility, the men tended to be devout believers, worshiping either one or multiple deities. It always paid to offer up the regular sacrifices to Fortuna. At least, one hoped it did, for she could be a fickle god. It did not do to neglect the gods by avoiding services or failing to offer appropriate sacrifices. Legionaries were also seriously superstitious. A good commander recognized this, and Stiger was about to play on it now.

"What's your name?"

"Mictenus, sir," the man said. "Been marching under the eagles for twenty-four years, sir."

"That's a good long time."

"The legion's been a fine home for me, sir," Mictenus said. "It will be a sad day when I muster out and settle down in a veterans' colony."

Stiger understood the sentiment. It was not uncommon for veterans to enlist for an additional five years of service when their initial stint came to an end.

"It's true," Stiger said, deciding the man deserved some truth. Glancing around the fire, he realized they all needed truth. That said, he planned to use it to his advantage. "What you heard is accurate," Stiger continued. "Castor's servants tortured Therik terribly for seeking peace. When we found him, he was on the verge of death, his shade beckoning from the other side." Stiger paused, thinking back on what he had seen in that temple, recalling how they had found Therik. He blinked, bringing himself back to the present, and noticed the men were hanging on his every word. That was what he wanted. "With the great god's blessing, Father Thomas healed Therik, King of the Orcs. I was there."

"And you helped, sir?" Another legionary asked, this one much younger than Mictenus.

"I did," Stiger said.

"You are gods blessed?" Another man asked.

One of the logs on the fire cracked loudly. It sounded like an arrow punching into chest armor. Everyone around the fire started, including Stiger. He chuckled, and grins were passed around.

"Are you gods blessed, sir?" the same man asked again.

"I have been told that I am," Stiger said. "The paladin feels so, too."

"Then we're a doing the High Father's work?" Mictenus said proudly, glancing around at his mates. "It is as I told you, boys. By just being here and fighting these orcs, we're doing the good lord's work."

"You and everyone else in this encampment are doing the High Father's work," Stiger said, knowing what he said here would soon be spread across the entire camp. "As your centurions have likely told you, the legion is here to honor a longstanding treaty with the dwarves. You are here for more than just that. We fight for the High Father, but when it comes to blades and shields... as always, we will be fighting for each other."

"That's the way things just are, sir," Mictenus said. "When the first sword or spear comes at you, all thoughts of the cause go away."

"This time, I am afraid it must be more than that," Stiger said. "We fight to save the empire. The treaty with the dwarves is called the Compact. Our alliance, though long forgotten by most in the empire, was forged in the time of Karus." Stiger heard several of the men whisper the first emperor's name in near reverence. "We're in Vrell to keep up the empire's end of the bargain. The dwarves have called and we have answered." That last bit wasn't strictly true, but it was what they needed to hear, and more importantly, it was one of the rumors floating around camp. "Our alliance protects something of incredible importance. I can't tell you what it is, but know the priests of Castor want it badly and an army is coming to get it." Stiger paused briefly to let that sink in. "So, we all are fighting evil, each in his own way. If it wins, the next battle will be for Mal'Zeel and our families back home." Stiger fell silent and made a point to look around the fire, meeting gazes. "Help me keep it from coming to that."

No one moved. The silence around the campfire grew.

"I want you to tell everyone that," Stiger added.

"You are the champion spoken of in scripture?" a veteran to his left asked. "The High Father's champion, as Centurion Prestus said?"

Stiger was unfamiliar with the particular section of scripture the man was referring to. The empire honored many gods under the High Father's banner, and each sect had its own holy book or books.

"The Delphenic Scrolls, sir," the man prompted.

"I've not read them," Stiger admitted, familiar with the name but not the contents. They related to the god Saturn and something about the empire's future. He would have to correct that oversight. Perhaps Father Thomas would know something more?

"An oracle wrote them," the man added.

Stiger became still. He wondered if this oracle was the same one the dwarves referred to, for Braddock had mentioned her to him. Stiger sucked in a breath and glanced around the fire.

"I am the High Father's champion."

No one said anything. All eyes were upon him. The experience made him slightly uncomfortable.

"Thank you for sharing your pipe," Stiger said to Mictenus.

Stiger turned to leave.

"Thank you, sir, for telling us how it is," Mictenus said, and they all stood respectfully. "We will do our duty for you and the gods. We won't let down the empire none."

"I expect not." Stiger gave a nod and then stepped off into the darkness. "Dog, come."

A flash of distant lighting lit up the sky. Thunder rumbled a few heartbeats later.

Stiger spent the next hour walking the camp, lost in his thoughts. He refrained from visiting any more campfires. When he had had enough and felt sleep beckoning, he made his way to his tent. Someone was waiting for him a few steps from his guard detail. The two guards snapped to attention.

"Menos," Stiger said, surprised to see the caretaker.

"Legate," came the soft reply.

Dog ran to Menos, tail wagging.

"It is nice to see you too," Menos said and patted the animal's head with affection. The caretaker looked pointedly at the two guards.

"Let us speak inside." Stiger held an arm toward his tent.

Pulling the flap aside, Menos stepped inside, closely followed by Dog.

"While he is in there with me, I am to be disturbed by no one," Stiger said to the guards. "Not even my servant. Is that understood?"

"Yes, sir," one of the men said.

Stiger brushed by them and let the flap fall back in place. A lamp had been left burning. It provided dim but serviceable light. Dog went to his customary corner and lay down, almost immediately going to sleep.

Menos was looking curiously around the tent, seeming to marvel at the most mundane of things.

"Why have you come?" Stiger asked when Menos had said nothing. The caretaker seemed wholly absorbed in the inspection of the interior of the tent.

"You took my advice," Menos said, studying the lamp hanging from the support pole. He poked at it with a finger. "I felt you wage your battle as you beat Rarokan back, as I knew you could."

"Father Thomas helped," Stiger said. Somehow, he was not surprised Menos knew about it. "I would not have been able to win without his assistance."

"I know, the paladin told me," Menos said and looked over at him. "You are in a war for your mind and body. You won the first battle. Rest assured, there will be another. The next time, Rarokan won't make it so easy for you."

"As always, you are just full of good news," Stiger said.

"You amuse me, human," Menos said, without any hint of mirth. "No one has dared speak to me as you do for thousands of years, perhaps even tens of thousands. In a way, I find that refreshing."

"And I thought elves were long-lived," Stiger said, in awe of the creature standing inside his tent.

"Noctalum are unique amongst the races," Menos said. "We have a greater measure of the divine spark within us. That is both a blessing and a curse."

"In that there are times you must watch what you love pass on?" Stiger asked.

Menos was silent a long moment as he contemplated Stiger.

"Yes, that is correct. With the passage of time, everything changes. In this way, my mate and I have suffered more than you can imagine." Menos paused and closed his eyes briefly. When he opened them, his silver-eyed gaze seemed to pierce Stiger's soul. There was a sadness there that Stiger had not noticed earlier. "No, that is not correct. I sense from your aura that perhaps you can conceive such suffering. You have my sympathies on the passing of your mate."

Stiger sensed that Menos was being entirely sincere. Like an unexpected visitor, the grief threatened to bubble up again as the sympathy from the caretaker struck home. With effort, Stiger forced it back down.

"Thank you," Stiger said, his throat catching slightly. Then what Menos said a few moments before registered. "The divine spark you spoke of, the one in your life force, is greater, and therefore your lifespan is greater. That is your curse. Is that correct?"

"Rarokan has been revealing things he should not," Menos said, cocking his head to the side in a way no human neck could bend. "Such knowledge should not be shared lightly."

"He did not tell me this," Stiger said. "There are barriers between his mind and my own. What he tells me, I have learned, I cannot trust."

"Then how do you know of such things?" Menos asked curiously.

"During the struggle against Rarokan, his mind was completely focused on Father Thomas and the High Father. The barriers came down and I saw much I had not understood."

"You could read his thoughts?" Menos asked, taking an excited step nearer. He pointed a long finger at Stiger. "You had a glimpse into the mind of a High Master?"

Stiger gave a nod.

"Such a thing has never happened before," Menos said. "You are a lucky man, for there is great knowledge locked away within such a mind, much of it forbidden. Then again, you may be just as unlucky."

Menos spared Stiger a short look before turning away and stepping over to his camp table. He ran a long, delicate finger across its surface before looking back to Stiger.

"The High Masters are the true disciples of their gods," Menos answered. "There is always one per god, no more, no less. These wizards wield nearly unimaginable power and, as I have already told you, move almost freely through space and time with very few restrictions. Rarokan was one of these disciples, a fallen one, if you will. Their power is so great you might even call them demigods, for they and they alone do the direct bidding of their masters, orchestrating and masterminding events on our plane of existence." Menos gave a short pause. "Pray you never meet Castor's High Master of Scarlet. She is death incarnate. It is a good thing her attention is on more important worlds than ours."

Stiger was chilled by the thought of such an evil wizard.

"Now," Menos said, picking up a silver stylus from the desk and examining it. A moment later, he returned it to the desk. "Tell me what you know of the spark."

"I understand it allows the gods to have influence in our world," Stiger said. "It is in both my life force and my soul. It gives me the ability to use *will*, though I am not fully sure how it all works."

"That is an interesting way to look at it," Menos said. "Your understanding of the spark is limited. It is more than you think." Menos gestured a hand at him. "You are graced by it and have free will. I speak not of holy power, but of free choice. The gods only have as much influence as we give them. The same, in a way, goes for Rarokan. That is why he has become so dangerous. He chose against his god."

"Father Thomas has begun teaching me how to withstand the assaults," Stiger said. "I had my first lesson this evening before our feast with the dwarves."

"By training your mind?"

"Yes," Stiger said. "In a way, it is like Eli's lessons to feel the forest."

"He is an elf?"

"Yes," Stiger admitted. "I consider him my closest friend."

"You keep interesting company," Menos said. "How did the paladin's lesson go?"

"Not well," Stiger admitted. "I was never able to feel the forest either."

Menos gave a laugh. "It takes more than one lesson to master the power of the mind."

"Father Thomas told me the same," Stiger said. "Though in this case, I think the sooner I learn the better."

"It is good you do not know more of the spark from Rarokan or how to wield his powers," Menos said, "for if you did, I might have had to kill you."

"What?" Stiger took a step back, suddenly wary. His hand almost went for his sword, but he restrained himself. "Why?"

Menos offered him a thin-lipped smile.

Stiger crossed his arms. "I grow tired of half-answers."

"Very well," Menos said. "Having unrestricted access to Rarokan's knowledge and the ability to use *will* is a dangerous combination. You are the High Father's champion and you can use *will*, but there are limits. Be careful your ambition does not rise to match Rarokan's."

Stiger gave that some thought before replying.

"He wants to become a god," Stiger said. "If he succeeds, he would be more terrible than Castor. I cannot allow him to win, either."

The answer seemed to please the caretaker.

"Agreed. When this madness ends, and the minion is no more, come to me. I will instruct you in the use of your mind. Between the paladin and myself, we should be able to train you in the skills needed to protect yourself from him."

Stiger was surprised by the offer.

"I will take you up on that," Stiger said, "provided we are around. There are a lot of orcs coming."

"There are worse things than orcs," Menos said, with a disturbing, mirthless chuckle. "The Horde is coming. Castor's servant brings mountain trolls, goblins, and wyrms. This world has never seen the Horde, but it is about to, and soon." Menos paused briefly. "There are other places on Istros that harbor populations of the lesser races. Should our enemy succeed here, those isolated pockets of orcs and goblins will rally to the Horde's banner, and with them darkness shall descend upon this world."

"Great," Stiger said. "You just keep bringing good news, don't you?"

The tent lit up with the flash of lightning. Thunder rumbled loudly, seemingly almost on top of them.

Menos gave a laugh that sounded forced. "I am beginning to like you, human. I truly am. Don't ruin the affection I feel toward you."

"What is a wyrm?"

"It is what your people call a lesser dragon," Menos said, "and the elves call a Minor Drak."

"A dragon like you?" Stiger was dismayed by this. He had seen what Menos in his true form was capable of doing.

"They are nothing like me or my kind," Menos said with savage heat boiling his tone. "They are smaller, for one thing. Wyrms don't have the same level of intelligence we have. They are a mere shadow of us. You might even consider them stupid, as they take direction easily from their keepers." Menos grew grave. "That aside, wyrms are very dangerous."

"I don't know how we can fight dragons, lesser or not."

"You cannot," Menos said. "Well, you can try and perhaps you may triumph against one, but not four. No, my mate and I will have to help you. When they come, we shall be there."

"What about the Gate?" Stiger asked. "Who will protect the World Gate? Who will guard it?"

"No one," Menos said simply. "In a way, the World Gate is now useless to both sides. Thoggle agrees with me on this. The minion cannot open the Gate without a wizard's assistance, and none on this world are, at the moment, powerful enough to lend their *will* to the effort."

Menos walked to the entrance of the tent. A hand reached toward the flap and then stopped. He turned back, silver eyes glittering in the lamplight.

"The minion has grown powerful and it comes for you. By killing you, the High Father's champion, Castor wins everything on this world. Should that happen, the future will be a dark one, for all peoples on Istros. We must defeat it, which means you and the paladin must face the creature directly. For only because of you, with your sword"—Menos's eyes drifted down toward Rarokan in its scabbard at Stiger's side, before returning to lock gazes with him—"do we stand a chance to beat it. Everything comes down to this battle."

"But even if I succeed," Stiger said, "it is my understanding the real task set for me is in the future, the time I come from. How will I return?"

"Thoggle and I have determined we may have the means to return you to your time and without using the Gate, which we have both determined we are unable to manipulate."

Stiger suddenly felt a surge of hope, something he had not had for a long time. Despite his grief for Sarai, there was suddenly light at the end of the tunnel. He would be able to return to his time, where he belonged. All he had to do was defeat another of Castor's minions. If it were only as easy as it sounded.

"So you can get me back to my time?"

"We might be able to." Menos gave an unhappy nod. "The price for that will be high. Thoggle has insisted I allow my memory to be altered when we return you to your time."

"I see," Stiger said.

"No, you only think you understand," Menos said.

"Then tell me," Stiger said with frustration. "Tell me what I don't understand. I am tired of not knowing what I need to."

Menos gave a chuckle. This time the amusement leaked through. A thin, frail smile formed on his perfect face.

"When the time comes, my mate and I will handle the wyrms. You must hold the Horde until Brogan's army can arrive. Or, at the very least, allow the thane's army to get near enough to make a difference. That will be your chance, for the minion will become desperate and will likely come directly for you, gambling everything. That is your time, your chance."

"I will do it," Stiger said. "I will face the minion."

"Then we have an understanding," Menos said. "Make sure you defeat it."

With that, Menos turned in a swirl of robes and left the tent.

Stiger sat down on his cot and ran a hand through his hair. It never got any easier. A short time before, he had been tired. Now, he knew sleep would not come easy.

"Excuse me, sir." Venthus entered the tent. "Can I get you anything before you turn in?"

"Wine would be good, preferably heated," Stiger said, "and tobacco if you can manage to scrounge some up."

"I think I can find some, sir." Venthus left him.

Stiger removed his boots and placed them to the side. He was about to lie down on his cot when one of the guards poked his head inside the tent.

"Messenger here for you, sir," the man said.

"Send him in," Stiger said.

A dusty and weary-looking auxiliary cavalryman entered, bearing a dispatch. He saluted and then handed it over to Stiger.

Stiger tore it open. It had been written by the prefect in command of the legion's cavalry contingent. Prefect Hux reported a small column of orcs, seven hundred in total, had made their way down into the valley. They had begun building a camp by the ruins of Riverton. He reported their camp had a defensive berm and an outer trench. Hux expected this to be a prelude of what was to come. He stated his intention to keep an eye out and would send word should more orcs enter Vrell or the enemy begin moving in the legion's direction.

"Did you ride straight here?" Stiger asked, looking up.

"I did, sir," the auxiliary said, his tone weary.

"Find my chief clerk, Nepturus. My guards can tell you how to find him. He will get you some food and a place for you to bed down for the night. In the morning, you can carry my response back to your prefect."

"Thank you, sir." The auxiliary saluted and left.

"And so," Stiger said, "the final act begins."

Chapter Thirty-Two

Gaze fixed upon the enemy across the river, Stiger rested both hands on the wooden railing. He was standing upon a raised platform that had been constructed right behind the centermost part of his defensive line. Its sole purpose was observation—to give him a clear and unobstructed view of the battlefield. Stiger gazed out across the river at the enemy vanguard. Father Thomas was to his left and Therik to his right. Theo stood next to Therik. Tribune Severus was a couple steps behind on the back end of the platform, conversing pleasantly with Prefect Barunus, the legion's commander of artillery. Everyone but Therik and Theo wore their armor. They only had on their tunics.

For over a day, the enemy had poured out of the mountains and into the southern end of the valley. There they had massed, constructing a large encampment near Riverton. Stiger's scouts had kept an eye upon them the entire time. When the stream of arriving formations ceased coming down from the mountains, they had broken camp and begun a slow, almost leisurely march north. From the reports he had received, it became apparent the enemy numbered more than sixty thousand.

Interestingly, they had no cavalry to screen their advance. When he had received word the enemy was on the move, Stiger had put out the legion's cavalry with specific instructions on how to operate. Hux and his boys had shadowed the enemy, harassing and striking at foraging parties and scouts whenever the opportunity presented itself. They had ridden down hundreds of the enemy.

Prefect Hux had even sent back a prize for the legate, a finely crafted short sword. Hux had taken the weapon in personal combat, after having ambushed a party of scouts. He suspected the enemy leader had been an orc of some standing. The sword's grip had been inlaid with silver.

The enemy's march north had taken more than a day, which had allowed Stiger to further improve his position and make it that much more difficult to overcome. The men had worked at the defenses until the enemy had come in sight around four hours ago.

The first enemy formation marched through Bridgetown in a neat column, emerging into view and moving up the road toward the bridge. Each subsequent formation, as it arrived, neatly peeled off to take what appeared to be assigned positions around two hundred paces from the water's edge. Once in position, the enemy stood silently in their ranks, watching the legion's side of the river. Stiger knew this was designed to intimidate.

What Stiger thought was alarming was the sheer size of the enemy host. Though the army was still arriving, it spread outward from the bridge on both sides of the river and had begun to stack up. The enemy army arranged itself block by block in long horizontal columns with a space of thirty yards between columns. With three columns already in place, Stiger estimated there were close to twenty thousand currently deployed on the field, just one third of the enemy's reported strength. What would the entire sixty thousand look like? That, Stiger decided, would be intimidating.

This was technically his second large-scale battle where he was in command, and his first as legate of a full legion. That said, Stiger had never had so many men under his command, and his responsibilities had multiplied exponentially. Leading up to the enemy's arrival, there had been so many decisions to be made that it got Stiger wondering how General Treim ever managed to get things done. When he had left the North, Treim commanded four legions and their auxiliaries, a force nearly the size of the enemy army that faced him now.

Stiger used his past experiences and gut feelings as a compass. He had made decisions he hoped were the correct ones, for if they weren't, men would die. That was a heavy responsibility, one he took seriously.

"Plans are good," Stiger said to himself, "but once the fighting starts, it takes on a life of its own."

"What?" Theo asked.

"Just thinking out loud." Stiger had not meant to be overheard.

"Is true," Therik said. "What you said. You can make plans, but once fighting starts, a good leader be, how you say… moveable?"

"Adaptable?" Theo asked.

"Yes," Therik said. "That is word."

Stiger turned his thoughts inward and closed his eyes, bowing his head slightly.

High Father, lend me your strength over the coming hours, for they shall likely be difficult and desperate. Help me in this fight and lead me to victory. Spare as many of these fine men as possible.

Stiger made sure to commend his spirit over to the great god's keeping. Prayer complete, he opened his eyes, just as another enemy formation came into view, marching to join those already formed up.

To Stiger's trained eye, his enemy appeared highly organized and disciplined. That seriously worried him. They were also uniformly equipped and they moved in a manner that spoke of repeated drill and practice. The enemy host was nowhere near the chaotic mob he had become accustomed to facing. Across the way, Stiger understood he was looking upon a professional force, one to be taken very seriously.

There were formations of heavy and light infantry. Stiger studied the heavy infantry carefully. Those would be the most dangerous units on the field. They were equipped with chest armor, helmets, large rounded shields, medium spears, and swords. The medium spears appeared to be not only for jabbing, but throwing as well. From this distance, he could not tell the type of sword they were equipped with, but that hardly mattered at the moment. They would learn soon enough.

Stiger was also able to make out different races. He could see what he took to be two goblin formations, numbering around two hundred each. They were shorter in stature than the orcs in the neighboring formations, standing about the height of an average man. Their skin was a bright greenish color. He could not make out much more of their features.

"Are those trolls?" Stiger asked Therik and pointed. There was a small formation of fifty of the creatures. They towered over the orcs and were heavily armored, wearing not only chest armor, but greaves as well. They appeared to be somewhere around twelve feet tall. Their formation was much looser than the others and they looked to have orc minders.

"Mountain trolls," Therik nodded. "Very nasty and difficult to kill."

The king was right. Stiger could not imagine having to face off against such a creature. It would surely be a terrifying experience.

"Use bolt throwers," Therik said, pointing toward the nearest tower. "Shoot bolts at them to kill. Not even a troll can stop one. It should kill him good."

The suggestion was a good one. Stiger made a note to speak to Barunus about that. He continued studying the enemy. His eyes found a formation of humans, light infantry off to the left side of the enemy host.

"Theltra." Therik pointed as a new formation arrived.

These were armed and lightly equipped like those they had fought in the tunnels. They marched forward, standards fluttering in the breeze.

"Zealots," Therik spat, "all of them. They sacrifice themselves for Castor. You make sure you watch during fight. No telling what they do."

"I will," Stiger said, filing that away for later. He would have to alert his senior centurions to watch for the fanatics.

"I did this," Therik said, a note of pride in his voice. He pounded a fist to his chest. "I did this. Me. No one else."

"What do you mean?" Stiger turned to him.

"They look like your legion, no?" Therik said. "They fight in order, with control."

"You mean they are disciplined?" Stiger said. "They fight together and not by themselves, as individual warriors? Is that it?"

"Disciplined, is that the word?" Therik asked curiously. He tried the word again, rolling it over his tongue. "Disciplined."

"Yes," Stiger said sourly. "You gave them discipline."

Therik beamed with pride. "It took lots of training and work to do this."

"Thank you for that," Stiger said. He found it more than a little ironic that the individual responsible for the professional army facing off against him was now at his side.

Therik apparently thought Stiger's words extremely funny and boomed out a laugh.

"You do realize my job is to kill them," Stiger said, "to destroy what you've built?"

"You try," Therik said and then smiled broadly, showing off his tusks. "I help you, if you give me sword." He gave a shrug. "Yes and no, is some sad."

"Why did you build this army?" Father Thomas asked, curiously glancing over. "I take it you meant at some point to war against the dwarves and strike at Vrell?"

"No," Therik said firmly and in a tone that sounded slightly offended. "I meant no war. Only small part of it is mine, perhaps thirty thousand. They disciplined. Others are levies and poor warriors. I keep word to Brogan. I have honor." He paused, as if searching for the right words. "I made army to give my chieftains something to think on before challenging me to be king."

"I see," Father Thomas said, sounding dubious. "You built an army to give your own people second thoughts?"

"Also," Therik added, "goblins are trouble. They difficult to put down when rise up. Having army was good way to frighten, them knowing I had a bigger stick. I only had to make example once, not twice." He boomed out a laugh. "Then no more trouble from goblins. They follow Therik after."

Therik paused and heaved a great sigh. "Then there are *gnomes.*" He said the word with an utter loathing and disgust that Stiger found surprising.

"What about them?" Stiger asked.

"There be concern gnomes ignore Brogan and come for us," Therik said. "Is why I prepared army also. My people liked that. Gnomes are no good. They no like money or peace. They sneaky, underhanded fighters who dream on nothing but killing orcs."

"You don't much like gnomes I take it?" Stiger glanced over, interested to hear more on the orc side.

"Gnomes are little shits," Theo said. Stiger noticed that Theo was paying close attention to what Therik said.

"They hate us. We hate them," Therik said, as if it were that simple. "In past they kill many orcs and we kill many gnomes."

"Why?" Stiger asked.

"Because, that is how it has always been," Therik said and then became contemplative. "I think we once worship same god. Not sure. I do know gnomes were part of Horde. My people forget reason it all start. Maybe gnomes too? Now, like the dwarves, gnomes worship Thulla, god of fire and metalworking. So perhaps it is change of god which started long-running hate."

Stiger gave a nod, thinking on what he knew of the dwarves, gnomes, and orcs. The explanation kind of made sense. A lot of hate and suffering had been sparked by differences in one's choice of god. The truth of that was arraying itself before him across the river.

Stiger shifted his gaze from Therik to study his defensive line. He had ordered only half of the cohorts to the wall. The other half had been stood down and were resting. There was no point in deploying his entire force until the enemy did something that indicated they planned an immediate assault.

Stiger's gaze swept his line on the right side and followed it down to the water. He saw a dwarven standard planted on the rampart next to those of a legionary cohort. Thigra's warband had been split and positioned with the legionaries holding the flanks of the line along the river's edge. The chieftain of the Rock Breakers had welcomed the opportunity to join the defenders along the legion's flanks.

"He hopes to gain much legend," Theo said, clearly seeing the direction of Stiger's gaze and guessing at his thoughts.

"Are you referring to Thigra?"

"That is why he took you up on your offer to help hold both flanks," Theo said. "Thigra's great-grandfather, Torga, was a mighty warrior. General Torga is a legend amongst my people and is reputed to have fought with your Karus. You could almost say Thigra has been living in Torga's shadow his entire life."

"Do I need to worry about him doing something stupid?"

"I don't think so," Theo said. "Thigra is a strict follower of the Way. He will do his duty and so will those of his warband. They are solid and proven warriors. No, Thigra is pragmatic, even though he dreams big."

"Proven warriors?" Stiger asked. "Like Taithun and his company?"

"Nothing like him or his dvergr," Theo said, speaking with conviction. "You can rely on Thigra. Trust me on that."

After the initial hostility, Thigra had warmed up to Stiger and the other officers. Stiger had supposed the feast and extended drinking session with the legion's senior officer corps had something to do with it. Perhaps, after what Stiger had just learned, Thigra had been appeased by his key position in the impending battle. He and his warriors would have to hold at all costs. Stiger had inadvertently placed his trust in the chieftain of the Rock Breakers. If what Theo had said was true of Thigra's warband, then Stiger's flanks were more secure for it.

Sabinus climbed up the ladder to the platform. First Cohort held the centermost portion of the line and was arrayed just below them. The legion's eagle had been placed with them in a place of honor for all to see. The gold glittered brilliantly in the sun. The centurion's expression was grim as he came up to the railing, his hobnailed sandals clunking off the thin floorboards. He stepped up next to Father Thomas and looked outward.

"I wish you had let me destroy that bridge," Sabinus said, leaning forward to glance past Father Thomas and over to Stiger. "There are a lot of them over there."

"We've been over this. We have to give them an opportunity to cross," Stiger said. "I've told you, orcs don't much like water. I want to give them an easy way across the river and right into our killing ground."

"Is true," Therik said. "My people don't swim well. Add armor, we too heavy and sink to bottom."

Sabinus gave a nod and turned his gaze back outward.

"Well," Sabinus said, "I'd not attack this position if I had a choice."

"My army attack," Therik said and held both hands outward to encompass the entire defensive line. "My son see this as challenge. He come, and good chance he will win. My army strong and *disciplined.* They come and keep coming."

"We might have a few surprises for them," Stiger said.

"If you look, just behind their line, they've started digging in, sir," Sabinus pointed. "One of my boys spotted them at it a short while ago. I'm not sure exactly what they are doing."

Stiger looked and, sure enough, the enemy was digging in. Stiger counted twelve large formations that made up the first column of the enemy line. Just behind that column and before the next were teams of orcs digging in. They did not appear to be beginning a defensive line, but instead a prepared position. Stiger ran his eyes along the gap and spotted more than a dozen places that teams were busily breaking ground, shoveling away.

What were they up to?

Stiger snapped his fingers as it hit him. He turned to Therik. "You've got artillery too?"

"Not big ones like you have," Therik said, gesturing at the nearest machine. "But we have rock throwers. Our skill at tossing rocks is not great."

Father Thomas stepped back from the railing. The paladin appeared abruptly troubled. His gaze darted out toward the enemy, eyes searching the field across the way. Stiger was about to ask him what was wrong when the paladin spoke.

"I believe I shall take a tour of the line. I think the men might appreciate a kind word and blessing."

Stiger gave a nod, wondering what was bothering him. Had he sensed the minion? Was it that close? The thought of the creature chilled him to the bone. Father Thomas left them, climbing down the ladder.

Stiger turned his gaze back to the growing enemy host. The more he studied the army across the river, the more he understood that exceptionally difficult hours lay ahead. His greatest challenge was before him. There was absolutely no doubt about that.

"My people are putting on a show for you," Therik said. "A big show. Is meant to scare."

Stiger agreed with that assessment. Glancing down at his defensive line below, he knew the effect it was likely having on the legionaries. Though they would man the line and do their duty, he felt he needed to give them something.

Perhaps a little motivational backbone for what would be coming. A speech wouldn't do, as there were too many to speak to and not enough time, but something just as visible.

"I can put on a show, too," Stiger said to Therik before turning. "Prefect Barunus, would you care to join me?"

The prefect stepped over. "How can I help you, sir?"

Barunus was a short man, and young for his post. He was in his early twenties. He had a slight accent that marked him as a foreigner. He had a confident and educated air about him. He also appeared quite cultured, and perhaps a little too refined for a life in the legion. Stiger idly wondered what had brought him to serve the empire.

"The enemy are digging emplacements for their own artillery," Stiger said and pointed.

"Yes, sir," Barunus said with an air that reeked of indifference. "I had noticed."

"You did?" Stiger was surprised by that. He was even more surprised the prefect had not cared to share that information.

"Judging by the size of the enemy host," Barunus said, "it is only natural for them to have artillery, sir."

Stiger's gaze flicked back to the enemy. The prefect had him there. Stiger knew he should have expected Therik's army to have artillery. What else did they have?

"Do you think you can hit the other side of the river?" Stiger asked. He knew the prefect's artillery could strike at the enemy but had put it forward as a question. Stiger did not know Barunus all that well and wanted to see how the man reacted.

"With ease, sir," Barunus replied confidently, turning his gaze upon the enemy. "Would you prefer me to pound their line?" He then pointed out two of the points where the enemy were digging to emplace their own artillery.

"Or would you like the positions they are preparing to be hammered?"

"Let's hit their infantry first," Stiger said. "I would like to boost morale and strike first blood. Later, after they've moved up their artillery and you have something to shoot at, then you can go after their machines."

"You going to attack?" Therik seemed aghast. "Without talking first?"

Stiger blinked as he turned his gaze on the orc. He had not expected this to be a problem.

"I see no need to talk. We all know what's about to happen."

"It no seem right," Therik protested. "No honor, yes?"

"You mean it's not honorable?" Theo asked, sounding amused.

"Yes," Therik said with a bob of his large head. "Not honorable."

"He thinks you are not honorable," Theo said with a smirk thrown at Stiger. "I would have called you disagreeable, but that's just me talking."

Stiger ignored Theo.

"After what Castor and your son did to you, you want to go down there and parley?" Stiger said.

"It is right to talk first. But truthfully," Therik said, "I don't want to go near minion. I do want show them I live." A nasty undertone crept into his voice. "Scare them even more, I think. Some of tribal chiefs have second thoughts about backing my son. And minion worry about how I healed. Yes, I might like that."

Stiger considered Therik for a long moment before speaking. The king did have a point. Perhaps he could use Therik at some point to damage the enemy's confidence.

"There are times for honor. This isn't one of those times. We're gonna let our artillery do the talking for us." Stiger turned to his artillery commander. "Any questions?"

"No, sir," Barunus said, calmly. "With your permission, I will hold back our bolt throwers and the smaller machines to conserve our supply of missiles and lightweight rounds. They will be more effective when the enemy moves for the bridge and comes closer."

Stiger gave a nod of acceptance. "Fire when you are ready."

"With pleasure, sir," Barunus said.

The prefect offered Stiger a salute and then moved off, climbing down the platform. Salt made his way up the ladder a few moments later and pulled himself up onto the platform. Climbing with armor on was not as easy as it appeared.

"I hear we are giving them a bit of a welcoming reception, sir," Salt said and gestured back the way he came. "I do think our prefect of artillery has a little spring in his step."

They both turned and glanced back. Barunus was striding rapidly across the field behind the line toward his command post. Now that Salt mentioned it, Stiger thought the artillery commander did indeed have a spring to his step. He was more eager than he had let on.

"He plays it cool as ice, sir," Salt said, "but really Barunus's just like a little child with a new toy. He can't wait to use his artillery, especially since there was no opportunity to employ those large stone throwers against the Tervay."

"I think you are right," Stiger said.

"If he wasn't so damnably good at his work, sir," Salt said, "you'd have never offered him command of the artillery."

"True," Stiger said, though it had been Delvaris who had hired him. Stiger felt a bit of discomfort at misleading the camp prefect, for he liked Salt. He was a damn fine soldier.

They watched as Barunus stepped by his command post and made his way over to his own platform. It was a four-story wooden tower with a flat platform on top and no safety railing. Barunus rapidly climbed up. A team of signalers waited at the top.

Stiger turned back to the enemy across the river. "We're about to begin thinning their numbers."

"With what the cavalry reported," Salt said, "I don't believe we will thin them all that much."

"Sadly, you are likely correct," Stiger said. "However, it has been my experience that friendly artillery fire dropping stones on the enemy does wonders for morale."

"I quite agree with that statement, sir," Salt said, looking across the river. "Friendly artillery is always a legionary's best friend, unless, of course, they are accidentally dropping stone on your head."

Stiger had been under friendly fire himself and knew exactly what the camp prefect meant. Salt's eyes narrowed as he scanned the far bank and the assembled formations.

"I don't see any bridging equipment." Salt shot a look to Therik. "Do you have that capability?"

"We do," Therik said. "It may not have been brought up yet, or"—Therik gave a shrug—"it may be elsewhere."

Stiger felt a prickle of concern at that.

"Do you believe your people will use it?" Sabinus asked. "I know I would."

"As would I," Stiger said, now feeling Salt's concerns on the subject were dead on. Stiger had reinforced the units holding the two secondary crossings and considerably built up their defenses. Still, the thought of the enemy forcing a crossing concerned him greatly. Stiger studied the river. The water was still high, kept unnaturally so by the recent rains, but Stiger had learned where there was the will, there was most certainly a way.

"Salt," Stiger said, "would you kindly see to it that our patrols along the river between us and the other crossings are doubled. I don't want any surprises."

"I will, sir," Salt said. "I will make sure it is done immediately."

The prefect offered a salute before climbing down off the platform.

"I don't see any priests," Stiger said.

"They're out there with their athames and will show themselves when they are ready," Therik said.

"Athame?" Sabinus asked. "What is that?"

"Sacrificial knife," Therik said, without glancing over. "If you don't go along with priesthood, you might be unlucky enough to find yourself under a priest's athame."

Stiger suppressed a shudder. He had seen such a sacrificial rite. He had no desire to see another.

"Do you think they will come at us today?" Sabinus asked Therik. "It's late afternoon and will be dark soon."

"Our eyes are better than yours at night. My people strike when it is dark."

"Are you sure?" Sabinus asked. "Night actions can be tricky. All kinds of things can go wrong."

"Therik's right," Theo said. "Orcs and goblins much prefer to fight at night, when it is darkest."

There was a deep thud behind them, followed by a whistling almost directly overhead. Stiger spotted the projectile traveling upward in an arc. He tracked the progress of the ball as it sailed towards the enemy, the white of the stone shining in the fading sunlight as it climbed up into the sky.

It flew true and slammed down hard amongst a light infantry formation.

The impact kicked a large spray of dirt up into the air. For several heartbeats the shower of dirt obscured any damage done. When it subsided, it became clear the first ball had been very effective. It had carved out a good-sized gap in the formation, with more than a dozen orcs dead and injured.

The legionaries manning the defensive line gave a cheer at the sight.

"I hope they got my message," Stiger said to himself.

The enemy across the way roared back their rage.

"They got it," Therik said.

Stiger turned to look on his artillery. With the exception of the one machine that had fired, the rest of the crews were standing by. Their machines had already been loaded and stood ready. An officer at each machine was looking intently back toward Barunus's platform. They were waiting for the signal to unleash their deadly barrage.

Barunus was standing upon his platform, with both hands clasped behind his back. He appeared as calm as could be. The prefect turned to a legionary who had been standing next to him and said something. The legionary began waving a checkered white flag, followed by a yellow one.

Almost instantly, and in near unison, the remainder of the large ballistae, nineteen in total, released. The air was filled with screaming and whistling balls.

The sound the balls made was generated by drilling a small hole through each. As the shot traveled at high velocity through the air, it whistled or screamed depending upon the type of hole. Having been on the receiving end of such fire, Stiger knew the sound was downright terrifying.

He turned to see the results of the barrage. Two balls fell short and impacted the river, throwing up geysers of water. Several balls sailed beyond the enemy's main line, impacting harmlessly between formations. Most sailed true. Deep thuds could be heard as the balls smacked home. Wherever they hit, they wreaked a terrible carnage amongst the orderly formations of the enemy infantry.

Stiger was very pleased with what he had just seen. Barunus's artillery crews were well-drilled and appeared highly proficient in their craft. He turned his gaze back to the machines. The crews had not waited to see the damage they had wrought but had immediately and hurriedly set about arming their stone throwers for a second volley. Legionaries all along the line cheered wildly.

Stiger returned his gaze to the enemy's line. He wondered how they would handle a continued artillery barrage. Would they break and fall back in a mad dash? It was certain to be a test of their discipline. He watched and waited to see what they would do.

Several horns sounded from across the river. The enemy infantry exposed to the artillery closed up their ranks, and the wounded were dragged through the ranks and to the rear.

"My orcs stand firm," Therik said with pride and then he sobered. "My son sends you his own message by that."

"I got it," Stiger said, and in truth he did. The enemy was quite determined. "However, I intend to continue sending mine."

"He eventually pull back," Therik said. "But for now, he stands firm. I taught him too well."

Stiger glanced over at Therik. "It does not bother you that we kill your kind?"

"No," Therik said, and then gave a shrug. "Not at all. They share blood with me, but I no longer their kind. When it comes to sword, I hope to kill many." Therik flexed a large hand, as if he were gripping a hilt. "You give me sword. I show you and them how a true king fights, eh?"

Two thuds behind them announced the launching of the next wave of ball. The rest of the machines followed just heartbeats later as the crews raced against one another to see who could fire the fastest. The air was once again filled with whistling ball. The second wave was just as effective as the first.

Stiger grew silent. Over the next hour, he observed the enemy. After the first few volleys of heavy artillery, the enemy commander, likely Therik's son, ordered a tactical withdrawal. The formations pulled back in good order to a point just beyond the range of Barunus's artillery. The prefect had called a halt just as soon as it became clear that he could do no more damage to the infantry.

The enemy's artillery positions were now exposed and out in the open. The orcs brought up twelve medium-sized ballistae. They had positioned them behind the fresh earthworks, which were still being worked on as the enemy machines were being assembled and readied to fire.

Barunus begun to fire onto these positions, focusing more on the precision of his strikes rather than rate of fire. After each machine fired, measurements were taken and aim methodically adjusted. Already, his crews had scored two direct hits, effectively knocking both enemy machines out before they could even be fully assembled. The shot had hit with shocking force, splintering beams and snapping ropes. The result had been catastrophic for the crews working on the machines. They were cut down by a shower of splinters or torsion beams and bars giving way and snapping about with frightful force.

Stiger stepped to the back of the platform after a third machine had been hit and thoroughly wrecked. He looked down on Severus.

"Sir?"

"Send Prefect Barunus my compliments. I am well pleased with the accuracy and proficiency of his barrage," Stiger said. "Kindly ask him to pass that onto his crews."

"Yes, sir," Severus said and stepped over to speak with a messenger as Stiger returned to his position on the platform.

Eventually the enemy managed to fire back, but not before Barunus had knocked out three more machines. The return fire was slow and inaccurate, most often hitting the dirt wall below the barricade. Only one enemy shot had made it over the wall, where it had injured a horse. A couple shots had come Stiger's way, clearly aimed at the tower. Both had fallen short, impacting the wall below. Stiger stood exposed, bold, and unafraid, for he knew the men were watching. He was the example. He was their strength.

As the afternoon wore on and the artillery duel continued, the enemy host grew in size and arrayed itself for the legionaries to see. It was a sobering sight. He thought of what Sabinus had told him of future events. Stiger knew with a certainty the enemy would have a surprise or two for him. But what would that be?

Stiger caught a glimpse of Father Thomas in the distance on the left flank. The paladin wore his armor. It glittered under the waning sunlight. He was walking the line and giving his blessing, leading a prayer when requested, sometimes even stopping for group prayers. Stiger appreciated the paladin's efforts, for the men needed every boost they could get right now. Morale was a tenuous thing, and the waiting before an enemy assault was the worst.

Sabinus had excused himself and climbed down to check in with his men. That left Stiger with Therik and Theo. There was no talking, for nothing need be said. All three of them knew what lay in store.

The sound of galloping hooves drew Stiger's attention. He saw a cavalry trooper charging up to the platform. The trooper pulled back on the reins and slid off his horse. He made for Severus, who had taken to standing by the ladder below to handle the messengers as they came in.

A few moments later Severus climbed up. "Sir, it seems enemy scouts have been spotted moving along the river to the west, around two miles from here and near the crossing, sir."

Stiger gave a nod and dismissed the tribune. It was far from unexpected. Were he in the enemy's position, he would have dispatched scouts as well, searching for a suitable crossing with the intention of flanking the fortifications.

"This," Theo said, gesturing expansively both arms, "is something I had hoped I'd never see."

"I did not want to see it either," Therik said, somewhat wistfully.

That statement drew both Theo and Stiger's attention.

"Really?" Theo turned a skeptical look upon the orc. "I find that hard to believe."

"You do?"

"Of course," Theo said. "You worked to change your people, and part of that is the reformed army before us. Are you seriously trying to tell me you never wanted to see it assembled and in the field?"

"Not here," Therik said, "and not from other side."

"Now that," Theo said, "makes more sense."

Another rider galloped up a short while later. Severus climbed the ladder and handed the dispatch to Stiger.

"Sir," Severus said. "Orcs have been spotted at the east crossing."

"Thank you," Stiger said, glancing down at the contents of the dispatch. From it, he learned the enemy appeared to be studying the depth of the river. That certainly was not good news.

"Do you have patrols beyond the two crossings?" Theo asked, looking over.

"We do," Stiger confirmed. "Any attempt at fording the river should be spotted long before they can make it across."

"Even at night?" Therik asked.

"Hopefully," Stiger said and then felt himself scowl at the orc. He might have to increase the number of his cavalry patrols, just to be certain.

Another rider trotted up. This one was a dwarf on a mountain pony. He did not wear armor but only a simple gray tunic with a purple cloak to indicate he was in the service of the thane. Severus made his way down the ladder and over to the dwarf and took a dispatch from him. They exchanged a few words and parted. The dwarf mounted back up and rode off.

"Sir," Severus said, returning. He handed the dispatch over.

"I can't read this," Stiger said in disgust after opening it and handed it over to Theo. "It's in dwarven."

The dwarf scanned the contents, frowned, and then folded the dispatch and put it in his tunic pocket.

"It was addressed to me," Theo said.

"Well?" Stiger looked over. "What did it say?"

"My cousin is delayed," Theo said unhappily. "Goblins have entered Old City through some of the lower mines and tunnels. Though much of Brogan's army is near enough to reach us in a few hours, he has been forced to push them back. They are threatening the civilians living in the city." Theo let out an unhappy breath. "The rest of the Grata'Jalor garrison is not coming either. Brogan has made the decision to leave them in place to guard our rear, which, on reflection, I think is a jolly good idea." He looked meaningfully over at Stiger. "I don't think we want this line being flanked."

"So," Stiger said, "the enemy is already behind us? Worse, they are in the city we may have to fall back on should things go to shit? Do I have that right?"

"Not quite. Where the goblins are is in the lower reaches of Old City," Theo said. "That's nowhere near the gate to the mountain or Grata'Jalor. They would have to get through the citadel to truly flank us. So, I think we are safe." Theo gestured out at the enemy across the river. "Relatively speaking."

Stiger still did not like it, especially considering Brogan was concerned enough to leave the garrison in place at the citadel. It spoke of the incursion being more serious than Theo let on.

"How long 'til we get reinforcement, then?"

"Tomorrow at the earliest," Theo said, taking a further look at the scroll. "Brogan does not feel it will take long to force the goblins back out of Old City. Apparently, he's already made good progress of it."

Stiger let out a long, slow breath. His gaze traveled back across the river. The enemy had struck in Old City to keep the dwarves from the fight. He was sure of it, and he was on his own for the foreseeable future.

"We will just have to hold, then," Stiger said.

There was a loud *crack* from behind, which caused them all to jump. Stiger turned to see Thoggle had suddenly appeared upon the platform. The purple crystal on the wizard's staff was throbbing brilliantly. It rapidly faded away to a dull, ugly purple.

Thoggle's eyes fell upon Therik. "A week ago, I would not have foreseen you standing here in such august company."

Stiger wondered if the wizard had meant that as a joke. If he did, it fell flat, for no one laughed.

"I am pleased you have decided to join our cause," Thoggle said when Therik failed to respond. The orc's jaw was hanging open slightly.

"You are the wizard they speak of?" Therik jerked a thumb at Stiger and Theo.

"I am," Thoggle said, "and you are King Therik."

"King of nothing," Therik replied. "Now, I am just Therik."

"We shall see." Thoggle stumped his way painfully up to the railing, where he came to a stop next to Stiger. Leaning heavily on his staff, the wizard was silent for a long time as he surveyed the enemy. Stiger thought he detected the wizard's shoulders slump slightly. But the day's light was waning fast and he could not be sure.

"If you are wondering," Thoggle finally said, "Castor's minion is over there, just a short way off, as are his priests with power and the *will* to use it."

"Are you here to help?" Stiger asked, wondering if the wizard would do nothing, like Ogg, as the orcs came against their lines. He recalled his conversation with Thoggle about the wizard using proxies. "Or just talk?"

"I am here to fight." Thoggle shot Stiger an irritated look. Clearly Thoggle did not enjoy being challenged. "And if I am any judge, you are going to need my help, too."

"Do they have any wizards over there?" Stiger asked.

"No," Thoggle said. "They do not."

"Are you certain?" Theo asked, shooting a sidelong glance over at Thoggle. "I had heard of an orc wizard a few years back."

"More than certain," Thoggle said grimly, "for I just killed her."

"You slew Atella of the Red?" Therik asked, eyes widening. He took a step back from Thoggle, clearly alarmed.

"Yes," Thoggle said and pursed his lips. "That evil witch is finally dead, and it wasn't as difficult as I expected it to be."

"So, they only have Castor's minion and priests now. That's a tiny mercy," Stiger said, thinking on the wizard he and his men had encountered in the Sentinel Forest. Eli had managed to kill him before he could wreak catastrophic damage amongst Stiger's men. It had been a desperate moment, and seeing what the wizard had done in just a short span of time, Stiger was grateful Thoggle had dealt with his counterpart on the other side.

A shout of alarm went up from the left side of the line. Stiger's head snapped around. Several men were pointing behind them, up toward Thane's Mountain. They were looking skyward. More men turned to look. Shouts of alarm and panic quickly filled the air.

A moment later, an earsplitting roar ripped across the air.

Stiger almost smiled.

As promised, Menos had arrived as Sian Tane. The great black dragon let loose another roar of rage so loud that Stiger thought the platform vibrated slightly. The dragon, high over their lines, circled once before swinging around and extending his great wings outward, dumping speed and altitude.

Like a great big bird, the dragon gracefully descended, landing several hundred yards behind the legion's defensive line. The ground shook as the dragon claws touched down. Flapping his wings and standing upon his hind legs,

Menos extended his long neck up into the air and let loose a great gout of flame, lighting up the dimming sky and the growing gloom of evening.

Another more distant roar cut across the air from behind the lines in the direction of Thane's Mountain. Though Stiger could not see her, Currose was out there.

"Is that one of the guardians of the Gate?" Theo asked after a long moment of silence.

"It is," Stiger said. "I was told Sian Tane and Currose would be coming to the party."

"The dragon talks too much," Thoggle said in a grumpy tone. "He should not visit with you and meddle."

"I never thought to ever see them out of Grata'Jalor," Theo said in a whisper.

Stiger glanced over at Therik and saw a stricken look on his face. The orc had one hand on the platform's railing to steady himself. It was clear he, too, had not expected a dragon.

"Do you think they got this message?" Stiger asked Therik.

The orc king gave an uncertain nod but said nothing, as if at a loss for words.

Stiger turned his gaze to the orc lines across the river to see how they had reacted to the dragon. In the waning light he couldn't see much, but the lines seemed to have remained solidly in place.

Oddly, Stiger heard cries of alarm and panic close by. He turned and swept his gaze upon his own lines. Men were screaming and yelling. Some had drifted off the line, running or walking down the smooth slope of the rampart. One went running full tilt off toward the tree line a quarter mile away. Others milled about in small groups or individually, staring at the dragon in shock.

Fear gripped Stiger's heart in a rigid fist. He moved over to the back of the platform.

"Severus," Stiger shouted down at the tribune, who was staring dumfounded at the dragon.

The tribune did not respond.

"Severus," Stiger shouted, throwing his parade-ground voice into it.

The tribune shook himself and tore his gaze from the dragon. He looked up at Stiger, a sheepish expression on his young face.

"Quickly," Stiger yelled down, "get word to the officers of every cohort. The dragon is on our side! Send all riders to spread the word. We need to keep order and the men on the lines. Got that?"

"Yes, sir," Severus said.

"Good lad," Stiger said. "Now get on it!"

The tribune ran for the dispatch riders.

"And have the call to reform sounded," Stiger shouted as an afterthought.

"Yes, sir!" Severus yelled back as he ran toward the picket line.

Moments later, riders went galloping off along the lines. Stiger watched the dispatch riders go, shouting as they rode along the lines. He hoped it was enough to hold the men in place, for they faced disaster if a general panic took hold.

A horn blew the call to reform, then again. Within moments, the nearest centurions were shouting orders at their men. Years of discipline that had literally been beaten into the men took hold. Instinctively, they began to respond to their officers. Stiger watched with growing relief as order was restored and the iron discipline of the legion was reasserted. Realizing the danger had passed, Stiger puffed out his cheeks.

"Perhaps," Theo said, "you should have alerted your officers first that a dragon was coming? And maybe me, too? I almost shat myself from fear."

Chapter Thirty-Three

The moon was high overhead, shining its bright light down upon the battlefield. On his platform, Stiger stood rooted in place, silently watching the scene unfold below him. His hands held the railing tightly in a white-knuckled grip. Therik stood next to him on the left, as did Theo on the right. Thoggle, on the other side of Theo, was there watching as well.

Trumpets blared. Thousands of the enemy, carrying hundreds of scaling ladders, made their way across the bridge at a run. Screaming battle cries, they poured out into the bowl below the ridge and began to make their way up toward the trench and defensive wall. The legion's fifty pieces of ballista released, balls whistling overhead and hammering down on the enemy. Each impact thudded into the ground, throwing up a shower of dirt, killing and maiming indiscriminately.

The forty throwers, snug in their covered towers, began cracking away, discharging their powerful bolts into the masses of the enemy. Disregarding armor as if it were parchment, the large iron-tipped bolts punched into bodies, sometimes passing clean through. The deadly bolts had been known to rip off arms, legs, and heads. Stiger had even seen bolts go clean through one enemy and kill the next right behind. The force of the tension-powered bolts was tremendous.

Despite the deadly barrage, the orcs came on, pushing steadily forward. The thousands of concealed foot-sized holes, each with a sharpened stake, had crippled dozens before the orcs realized there was peril underfoot. Still they came, creeping forward and watching where they placed their feet. As they moved up the slopes toward the trench and wall, a rain of arrows from the auxiliaries arced up into the darkness and fell downward. The arrow storm became a near continual shower that rained down ten yards before the trench.

Stiger thought it a wonder any survived the deadly hail and marveled as the enemy continued to push forward. A massed javelin toss aimed for those about to climb into the trench flew out from behind the barricade. The clatter of the metal-headed shower of heavy missiles momentarily overrode all other sound. Orcs fell by the hundreds and still, like an advancing tide, they swept forward, climbing down into the trench.

This wasn't war, Stiger thought, watching the enemy's valiant thrust forward. It was a waste of fine soldiers, nothing short of murder.

The thought of an enemy commander so willing to callously throw away the lives of such well-trained and disciplined soldiers, even if they were orcs, angered Stiger. It surprised him that he held a measure of sympathy for Castor's followers. He suppressed that feeling. He had a job to do.

As those first into the bowl neared the trench and defensive wall, the next formation crossed the bridge. They had to climb and clamber over the bodies of those who had fallen as they began their advance up the slopes. They had to discover for themselves the peril of the crippling concealed foot-sized holes. All the while, the legion's artillery hammered down in a pounding rain of merciless death.

By the time good numbers of the enemy had started to climb down into the trench, Stiger estimated there were more than a thousand orc casualties on the field. The stakes that waited at the bottom of the V-shaped trench took even more lives.

So steep were the walls of the trench, orcs slipped and fell into it and were impaled, the sharpened stakes punching clean through armor and unarmored body parts with uncaring purpose. Others were eager to keep moving forward to get under the shelter of the base of the legion's defensive wall. They shoved those before them, throwing them into the trench, and then clambered down and onto the bodies of wounded and dead. They trampled those unfortunates, in some cases most likely driving the stakes of the impaled deeper.

Stiger's hands gripped the railing so hard his fingers hurt. In moments, the trench was a seething mass of the enemy. Then the first few began climbing out and working their way forward. They huddled under the lee of the wall and must have felt relief at beating the odds and finally reaching safety. Any sense of security was only temporary, and terribly misleading.

From above, legionaries began dropping rocks down on the heads of the enemy sheltering just below. Those that, in the chaos and scramble of the advance, had managed to retain their shields held them over their heads for protection. It wasn't much, as the rocks were in some cases thirty pounds or more. More damaging was the heated sand the legionaries shoveled over and onto the enemy below. Then came buckets of boiling water. The water splashed down, not only scalding exposed skin, but also running under armor and burning away the flesh there. The screams of agony sounded animal-like to Stiger.

It was awful, almost painful to watch, but absolutely necessary. This was war in all its wretched magnificence. When those uninitiated to the horror thought on battles, they never saw this brutal butchery.

Under the light of the full moon, Stiger watched as ladder teams worked their way forward, all the while under an unrelenting barrage. A ladder carrier would drop or release his hold as he tripped, was struck by a missile, or injured in some other way. The heavy ladder would topple to the ground and then inevitably be picked up as another orc lent a hand. The team would continue working its way ever forward through the storm.

Stiger could not help but admire the enemy's courage and resolve. It was an impressive spirit of determination that drove them forward. He also felt a little guilt, since he had helped provide them their motivation with the razing of the temple and town in Forkham.

Stiger glanced back behind his defensive line. The archers were lined up in spaced formations of twenty and broken up along the length of the ridge. Fires had been lit next to each formation. This provided additional light to see what they were doing. Each archer had dozens of arrows stuck in the ground before him.

An archer simply needed to reach down for a fresh missile, aim, and then loose. The legion's archers were firing behind the line with no direct line of sight on the enemy. Their indirect fire was guided by spotting officers positioned on the wall, who, by holding up flags at a certain angle, provided them the elevation at which to loose. Though it would have been preferable to give the archers direct line of sight, Stiger could not afford to, as space along the barricade was needed for his heavy infantry, who were even now preparing to receive the main assault.

Stiger's gaze shifted back to the wall as the first of the ladders went up. It was immediately pushed off and back even before the enemy could begin climbing. Additional ladders crashed against the barricade, and the real assault began. The legionaries fought back, using shield, short sword, spear, and sometimes fists.

The number of scaling ladders being thrown up against the wall went from dozens to hundreds in just a few heartbeats. The fight for the wall was just as brutal and ugly as the advance up the ridge. Stiger watched as a legionary reached over the barricade and stabbed at an orc who was first up a ladder. The legionary's short sword took the orc in the neck. At the same time, two legionaries on either side of the first managed with their shields to push the ladder back and off the wall. Three other orcs were on it, clinging tightly to the rungs as the ladder crashed down into the trench.

Stiger's eyes were drawn to another ladder. An orc holding onto the top of the ladder with his left hand swung a sword one-handed with his right. He slashed it out in wide arcs at a legionary directly behind the barricade. The man easily blocked the clumsy strikes with his shield. Another legionary to the man's left leaned out over the barricade and punched the iron tip of his javelin into the orc's exposed armpit. The creature howled in agony and fell from the ladder, taking the two orcs below him to the ground.

Everywhere Stiger looked, it was the same. The legion was having no problem holding the line and keeping the orcs from gaining purchase anywhere along the wall. The enemy was paying a terrible price for the assault.

Stiger let go a breath he had not realized he was holding and he released the railing. His fingers ached terribly and he flexed them. He had been so focused on the action, he had not noticed the overwhelming noise from the battle. It seemed to crash home as it beat down on the senses. The great cacophony was almost a physical force hammering at his ears in a great jumble of sound.

Turning around, Stiger swung his gaze around to look behind him. Maddeningly, Sian Tane remained where he had landed and was doing nothing to help. The dragon's head was up. His gaze was on the fighting, head swaying back and forth as he looked about.

Currose had not yet shown herself, but Stiger had heard her distant calls before the fighting had begun. Where was she? He also had no idea where Father Thomas had gone. It was possible the paladin was with the surgeons, preparing to care for the wounded. The battle so far was being fought on a mundane level. The orc priests had not yet put in an appearance, nor had the wyrms.

How long would that last?

Shifting his gaze back to the fight below, Stiger wondered what he was missing. To this point, the battle had gone as expected. Surely the minion did not wish it to go that way. Or did it? Rarokan had shown him the vision of Delvaris dying on a battlefield, mortally wounded by Castor's servant. If events played out the same way, Stiger would die in Delvaris's stead on the following day. Castor would win. At some point, somewhere, he knew he must face the minion. Would it be as he had seen in the vision?

The thought of the upcoming confrontation gnawed at him. How could he beat the creature and still survive?

Watching the fighting drag violently on, Stiger felt like a helpless bystander. Plans had been made and were now being executed. For the time being, as the legate he had nothing to do other than observe. It was frustrating, for he wanted to do something, anything. That was the terrible temptation, to interfere or micromanage. It was only with great effort he managed to refrain from doing so, for that was something that could and had led inexperienced leaders to their ruin. Stiger understood he had to let the officers of the legion do their jobs.

Stiger was reminded of his father telling him this in his lectures about leadership. Stiger had been but a youth and had not fully understood. Now, to his chagrin, he did. The elder Stiger, one of the most successful generals the empire had ever seen, had known what he was talking about.

Stiger pushed thoughts of his father away as Salt climbed up to the platform. When it became clear the enemy was preparing an assault, Stiger had sent the camp prefect to eyeball and tour the entire line. Salt's expression was hard, his lips pressed into a thin line.

"Thoughts?" Stiger asked as Salt stepped up next to him, taking a spot between Therik and Stiger.

"What did you say?" Salt said in a raised voice back and cupped a hand to his ear, just behind the cheek plate on his helmet.

"What are your thoughts?" Stiger had to speak up to be heard over the battle raging just below them.

Stiger looked beyond the fighting. Across the river, enemy formations were stacked up and waiting in line for their turn to cross the bridge. The size of the enemy army made it a frightening scene.

"Not too bad, sir. Not too bad at all," Salt said loudly back at him. The camp prefect's face became grim as he leaned forward over the railing and looked directly down into the bowl. He pulled himself back and brought his head near Stiger. "If I was the general across the way, I'd pull back. We're savaging them something terrible. You are to be commended, sir. Your decision to fight here was spot on. That bridge is a natural chokepoint, and the ridgeline hems the bastards in so that only a few thousand can enter the valley at a time. This is some of the finest slaughter I've ever seen."

Stiger gave a nod. The only time he himself had ever seen a worse slaughter was when an entire enemy army had broken on the field of battle and the might of two legions ran them down in a matter of an hour.

"All that aside," Salt said, "they can afford to throw away a few thousand to wear us down."

"Any suggestions?" Stiger asked, doing his very best to keep the unease from his voice, for Salt was dead on.

"If this goes on without letup, we will ultimately have a problem," Salt said. "We may want to consider swapping out entire cohorts sooner rather than later, as we had planned. That way, we can give our boys a bit of rest. Shorter intervals on the wall, sir, might help us to extend the combat effectiveness of our boys. If we do that and keep murdering them the way we are, they are bound to call off their assault to regroup."

"See that it is done," Stiger said, hoping the camp prefect was correct in his assessment on the enemy potentially calling off their assault to regroup. "When the time comes, you choose when and which cohorts need a break."

"I will, sir," Salt said.

Stiger's gaze turned back to the fighting. For a time they were silent, then Stiger looked over at Salt.

"I hate this," Stiger said. "I really hate it."

"I would expect nothing less, sir," Salt said, returning Stiger's gaze. "Watching others do the fighting and dying is always difficult. If it didn't bother you, I'd be a little worried for our chances."

An enemy ball impacted the barricade a few yards to the right. The ball smashed through the topmost log, sending a shower of large splinters out in a deadly spray that took down four legionaries. Thankfully, at that point on the wall there were no scaling ladders. The injured legionaries were dragged off the line to a point where they could be cared for. Men from the second rank moved into the vacant positions, careful to keep their shields up.

"It's our job to watch for problems that need fixing, sir," Salt said, having also witnessed what had just occurred. "It's their job to take what the enemy throws at them."

Stiger gave a nod, but his attention was drawn to Thoggle. The wizard's gaze was fixed upon the far bank. He was absently tapping his staff upon the platform. Stiger patted Salt on the shoulder and moved by Theo, stepping over to the wizard, who shot him a questioning look.

"What do you think the minion and priests are waiting for?" Stiger asked, raising his voice over the noise.

"I don't know," the wizard admitted. "They are just across the river. I find their inaction troubling."

It is waiting for you to become vulnerable, Rarokan hissed. *Tell Thoggle that. He will understand.*

Stiger felt a chill run down his spine. Rarokan had not spoken for some time. He had thought that odd, especially with the prospect of fighting close at hand.

Tell him, Rarokan insisted. *He will understand.*

"Rarokan believes the minion is waiting for me," Stiger said, and then added, "to become vulnerable."

Thoggle became very still. He ceased the tapping of his staff.

"Why let all this play out?" Stiger asked, pressing. "It could have come for me anytime when I was at the farm. Why go to all this effort and trouble?"

"At the farm, you were not as vulnerable as you think," Thoggle said. "I would have known immediately, should a priest with the ability to use *will* or the minion itself have entered the valley. The same goes for Sian Tane and Currose. Our enemy knows it would have had to go through us to get to you."

Stiger had not known that, but something still bugged him about Thoggle's answer. "They got to Sarai and slaughtered all of Aleric's boys."

"That was different," Thoggle said.

"How so?"

"I am sorry to tell you this, but had you been there at the farm when the raid occurred, it is very likely things would have turned out different."

"What are you saying?" Stiger asked. An image flashed across Stiger's mind of Sarai's wrapped body lying in the freshly dug grave. The hurt returned.

"Rarokan would have done anything to keep you alive. You are the one destined to wield him. Without you, his ambitions and plans would crumble to dust and ash. He would have thrown his considerable *will* into keeping you alive. Yes, things would have been very different."

The hurt at losing Sarai was strong, and Thoggle had just admitted he was to blame. He had not even apologized for it. It was Thoggle who had set him on the path to the summit. It was this wizard standing before him who had sent him away from the farm. Stiger felt the rage stir within his breast.

He could sense the hate, anger, and loathing kindling. Rarokan did nothing to fan the flames. It was almost as if the ancient wizard was sitting back and watching with amusement. Stiger's hand almost went for his sword.

Then Stiger drew a breath, knowing he needed to calm down. There must be some sort of an explanation, and he wanted to hear it. With effort, he clamped down on the rage before it could become more. He blew out the breath.

"Good," Thoggle said, eyeing him with a pleased expression. "Very good. Gaining control of your emotions is the key to success. Keep that always in mind and there will be hope for you as you struggle against Rarokan."

Stiger almost snapped back at the wizard, then realized Thoggle was right. He had always prided himself by remaining in control, no matter how difficult the circumstances.

"Why send me to the summit? We almost died, all of us, including your thane."

"But you didn't," Thoggle said, then heaved a heavy sigh. "There were no indications our enemy planned anything untoward. Garand Kos was far enough away that we thought it relatively safe. Had Jorthan not died, I would have known immediately of the danger and come."

The wizard fell silent for a heartbeat and took a step closer.

"I am not infallible. I am truly sorry for your loss."

Stiger read sincerity in his eyes.

"No one is infallible," Stiger said. "Look what I did to Forkham Valley."

Thoggle said nothing but gave a nod.

"The summit turned out to be a complete waste of time, energy, and lives," Stiger said, glancing back out on the battle raging below the platform. "This is all that came of it."

"Are you so certain?"

Stiger looked over at the wizard in question. Thoggle glanced over at Therik meaningfully. The orc's entire attention was focused on the battle. He was so absorbed, he did not move a muscle.

"Look what we gained by sending you to that summit," Thoggle said.

"We got one orc."

"Yes," Thoggle said and turned back to him. "But what an orc you got, and who is to say what will come of it? I believe the High Father chose to accept and save him. Is that not correct?"

Stiger glanced over at Therik and then returned his gaze to Thoggle, giving a nod.

"Well then," Thoggle said, "who is to say the summit was a waste of time and effort?"

Stiger felt himself scowl, the skin on his scarred cheek pulling tight as he glanced from the wizard to Therik. He decided to change the subject to one that was more pressing.

"Why is Sian Tane just sitting there, doing nothing?" Stiger asked.

Thoggle turned slightly to look at the dragon. "Sian Tane is waiting, as am I. Your legion is dealing quite well with the mundane forces of Castor. Father Thomas, Sian Tane, and I are waiting for those with *will* to act. Well, Sian Tane and his mate are really holding off until the wyrms make their move. When they do, both dragons will need all of their strength, knowledge, and *will* to defeat them. No matter how the noctalum look down upon their cousins and despise them, wyrms are very dangerous."

"They're out there?" Stiger asked, looking off into the darkness beyond the river. "The wyrms?"

"Oh yes," Thoggle said. "Four of the vile beasts, and somewhere close. I am able to feel their presence, as I am sure Sian Tane and Currose can. Such a conflict between dragons has not been seen since they first came to Istros from Tannis. Of the noctalum, Sian Tane and Currose are the last of their kind on this world. You might call the noctalum remnants from the Age of the Gods, powerful relics themselves. The lesser dragons, such as the wyrms, came after."

With fresh understanding, Stiger's gaze flicked back to the dragon.

"The minion has assembled this Horde and put all of Castor's assets in play, gambling everything"—Thoggle gestured out into the bowl and beyond using his staff—"to occupy and possibly eliminate those who protect you from powers you have only begun to comprehend. When you are isolated and at your most vulnerable, then and only then will the minion dare to make its move. Do you understand why I am telling you this?"

"I do," Stiger said. "I had suspected as much. I must face the minion, Castor's champion."

"You will face it. Don't doubt that," Thoggle said. "Sian Tane, Currose, Father Thomas, and I will fight, even at the cost of our lives, to give you the best opportunity for success at striking the creature down. Unlike the minion you faced in Grata'Kor, this one has had time to develop. It has grown much more powerful. Do not underestimate it."

Stiger did not like the sound of that.

"So," Stiger said, "it all comes down to that."

"It does. At this time, killing the minion is all that matters." Thoggle paused and tapped Stiger's chest with the crystal of his staff. It flared slightly with the touch. "Though you might not believe it, this is your time."

"My time," Stiger said, considering the wizard's words. A thought occurred to him. "If the minion seeks to kill me, why go to all the trouble to repeat much of what it knows happened in Delvaris's time? Why even bother striking here, at the bridge? Why not somewhere else? Why not change the dynamic, as it seeks to change future events?"

"That is a very good question," Thoggle said with a slow nod. "Changing the dynamic, as you say, would potentially be very dangerous for it."

"How so?"

"We think it seeks to change your history in small ways," Thoggle said. "If it changed major events that had already occurred, it might eliminate itself from the time stream, thereby harming Castor's chances at success."

"But it already changed things in a big way," Stiger said, "by killing Delvaris."

"Did it?"

"What do you mean?"

"With you here," Thoggle said, "assuming Delvaris's place, time travels and flows much as it did. Should the creature kill you in this time period, as it initially killed Delvaris"—Thoggle held up a finger and wagged it—"not in the way it did at the World Gate, but on the battlefield as Rarokan showed you, it gets what it wants: victory. Should such an event occur, there will be no champion for the High Father in the future. This would in turn leave the followers of the High Father's alignment fragmented and leaderless. The alignment Castor serves quite possibly wins at that point, though another would surely challenge him."

Stiger brought a hand up to his chin as he considered the wizard's words.

"But how could it know I would take Delvaris's place?" Stiger said. "It seems killing Delvaris right off could have potentially done what you said and caused itself to be eliminated from the time stream."

"That is another good question," Thoggle said. "Unfortunately, I do not know the answer. It could be killing Delvaris was unintentional. The legate could simply have gotten in the way when the minion came through the Gate and sought escape. It might not even have known who he was. There were others present who survived the experience." Thoggle shifted his staff from one hand to another.

"Who's to say whether it was intentional or not? Yet it does bring up some troubling questions. Delvaris had the sword and Rarokan certainly did nothing to save him or, for that matter, even try. Why?"

Stiger did not have an answer. Had Rarokan known he, Stiger, was coming? He had not thought of it before, but there were now two swords in this time period. Were there two versions of Rarokan here in this time as well? Did the minion have the other? Could it wield it?

It could, Rarokan said, *which would be a disaster.*

"What happened to Delvaris's sword?" Stiger asked. "I've got mine, which I came through the Gate with, but where is the other? The one Delvaris himself wielded."

"I have it hidden," Thoggle said, "somewhere safe. It is in a place the minion shall never find."

Stiger felt vast relief at that.

"What I've told you is only a supposition of how we think time works," Thoggle said with a sudden shrug of his shoulders. "There is a countervailing theory of something we call the multi-verse. It is rather complicated. I shall keep it incredibly simple. Even if you succeed and put things in this time on their rightful path, the future could possibly be a different reality than the one you knew. By traveling into our time, you might have stepped into another reality, one of many. If this theory is true, everything can be changed, the future completely rewritten."

"What?" Stiger asked, incredibly alarmed at such a prospect. "How can that be?"

"I only said it was possibility, a theory," Thoggle said. "Truly, it is one possibility among many. The truth is we don't know and neither does the minion. That is why it is doing its best to keep events close to how it knows or understands they played out."

"Rarokan," Stiger said, thinking things through.

Thoggle raised an eyebrow in question, clearly not quite sure where he was going.

"As a High Master, as a disciple of his god," Stiger said, recalling his conversation with Menos and what he had learned about the wizard imprisoned within the sword, "he traveled through time and space. Of anyone, he would surely know the answer to this question of how time will be affected."

"That is very likely," Thoggle said. "We had considered having you ask him. However, we suspected he would refuse to answer or, worse, if he did, what you would get would not be the truth. Working toward a goal based upon such a falsehood or twisted fiction could potentially have given him another opportunity to manipulate not only you, but events in the time stream. We were unwilling to take that risk."

Thoggle speaks truth, Rarokan said, sounding sullen. *I would have likely used you to my advantage.*

So, you know how the time stream will play out?

I do, Rarokan said. *When I was free, I walked not only the worlds but the flows of time as well. I shall not tell what you wish to know.*

Whyever not?

It is dangerous knowledge, Rarokan said. *And, sadly, I am prohibited by the gods from revealing what I know concerning the flows. It is one of the commandments the High Masters cannot break, even if we wished.*

How many commandments are there? Stiger asked.

Just four.

And attempting to become a god is not one of the four commandments? Stiger asked.

Surprisingly, no, Rarokan said and gave a laugh. *If I had succeeded, I would not have been the first.*

"What does he say?" Thoggle asked.

Stiger blinked, snapping back to the present.

"He claims he cannot tell me," Stiger said. "That it is one of four commandments the gods placed upon the High Masters."

"It is as I thought," Thoggle said and then offered a grim smile. "There is one thing you will know that others will not."

"What's that?"

"If you beat the minion and are able to return you to the future," Thoggle said, "you will have an inkling on how time actually flows, multi-verse or not."

Tell Thoggle something for me, Rarokan said. *Tell my old apprentice, in this supposition he is correct.*

Stiger's eyes narrowed as he looked on Thoggle. Had Thoggle really been Rarokan's apprentice?

One of many, Rarokan said. *Before my imprisonment, I was the head of my order, the master of all that walked the Blue Path.*

"Rarokan asked me to pass on that you are right," Stiger said.

Thoggle's face broke into a grin.

"He also called you his apprentice," Stiger said.

The grin slipped from Thoggle's face. It was all the confirmation Stiger needed.

"Salt." Stiger spun around and hollered so that the camp prefect could hear him. He needed to think on what he'd just been told. "I am going for a walk along the line."

"It will do the men good to see you out and about, sir."

"Want company?" Theo asked, stepping nearer. The dwarf had been close enough to hear much of their conversation over noise of the fighting. Stiger was certain the others had not been able to overhear. Theo's eyes looked concerned, something Stiger thoroughly felt.

Stiger gave a nod and made his way to the ladder. Dog was waiting for him below. The animal looked far from calm and was pacing back and forth. When his feet touched the ground, Dog stopped and padded up to him. He patted the animal on the head and received a lick on the hand for his efforts. Theo jumped from the last rung to the dirt.

Stiger made first for Sabinus, since his cohort was the nearest and holding the center of the line with First Cohort. Sabinus was speaking with another centurion as they approached. At the sight of Stiger coming his way, Sabinus said something that was clearly an order. The centurion shot a glance over at Stiger, gave a nod, and stepped away.

"Sir," Sabinus shouted as Stiger and Theo made their way through the loose ranks of waiting men. Their eyes fell upon Stiger as he passed. Their faces were grim, but he also sensed determination there and that pleased him. As anticipated, word had spread about the miracle of healing Therik and also Stiger being the High Father's champion. He noticed more than a few who made the High Father's sign of faith. That made him somewhat uncomfortable, but their belief in him was necessary. He would use it to get them through the hours ahead.

"How are you holding up?" Stiger shouted back. The noise of the fight was much louder than it had been a few yards behind the line and above it on the platform.

"We're doing just fine, sir," Sabinus said. "Just fine. My boys are sticking it to them something good. The defenses we constructed are strong, which is a great advantage." He gestured out at the enemy. "They are determined, but we can and will hold, sir."

"Very good," Stiger said. "Let me know if you need anything."

"I will, sir," Sabinus said.

"Good man." Stiger patted the centurion on the shoulder. He stepped away, moving on to Second Cohort.

They found Centurion Nantus pacing behind the first rank, which was manning the wall. Four ranks of men stood just behind the first, with men from the second rank occasionally stepping forward to help by jabbing over a shoulder or shield with a javelin or to replace an injured man.

"Keep your bloody shields up," Nantus was shouting as he moved back and forth. The centurion's manner was confident but at the same time irritated as he paced behind his men, calling out encouragements. It was clear he wanted his men more afraid of him than the enemy. "Remember your training! Use your shields to hammer at them. Come on there! Put your back into it."

Nantus suddenly charged forward to the wall, where three legionaries were struggling to force a ladder back and off the wall. Two orcs had climbed up to the top of the ladder, each with a sword. One-handed, they were poking back at the legionaries, who were having difficulty defending themselves as they shoved at the heavy ladder. The orcs, for their part, were trying to clamber over the wall, and the heads of those below poked up over the barricade for a look.

Nantus pulled out his sword and lunged over the heads of his men, plunging the sword into an orc's neck. The creature stiffened and dropped its sword. It fell back off the ladder.

Another legionary from the second rank stepped forward and stabbed the last orc in the arm. As the legionary was preparing to jab again, the orc, sensing his helpless position, leapt off the ladder into the darkness and was lost from view.

"Excellent work!" Nantus roared. "Now push!"

Together, the legionaries pushed the ladder off the wall before those just below managed to climb higher. The ladder tottered for a moment in space and then fell backwards. Nantus patted one of the men on the back.

The centurion stepped back, looked to the left and then right. He pointed at a man with his sword who clearly had just been hit on the head by something. The legionary had removed his helmet and was holding the side of his head with one hand. "Help that man back!"

Men from the second rank rushed forward to assist.

Nantus saw Stiger approach and stepped back from the line. He pulled a rag from a pocket in his tunic and began wiping the blood from his sword.

"How is it going here?" Stiger asked, having to shout. The enemy was having difficulty not only reaching the top of the barricade but gaining any sort of purchase. Still, it was good to ask, for the centurion might have concerns that Stiger needed to hear. By posing it as a question, he was giving the junior officer an opportunity to speak up.

"My boys are holding, sir," Nantus shouted back into Stiger's ear. "We're really giving it to them."

"Keep it up," Stiger said. "We can't let them over the wall."

"They won't get over, sir," Nantus said. "Don't you worry about us none."

"I am counting on that," Stiger said. "Carry on, centurion."

"Aye, sir," Nantus said.

Stiger glanced around once more at Nantus's men fighting along the line. He noticed the men from the subsequent ranks waiting to move forward had their eyes on him. Salt was right, it was good for them to see their legate out and about. He moved off.

They encountered the same confidence and professionalism with each stop. Stiger saw nothing wrong or needing adjustment. The centurions of the Thirteenth Legion were all veterans with years of experience behind them. They knew their job and understood what needed doing.

"You humans are tenacious fighters," Theo said, after their fifth stop. They were behind the right side of the line, standing a handful of yards behind the last rank of legionaries. "I had heard of your legions. I've read the histories of the time before our peoples came to this world, but I'd never have believed had I not seen this with my own eyes."

"This is simply fighting behind a defensive line," Stiger said. "It is necessary because of the size of the enemy army. However, you should see us in the field against a comparable force, where we can maneuver. There, out in the open, we can be just as frightening, if not more so."

Theo looked over at him, clearly wondering if Stiger was exaggerating.

"The legions are designed to be mobile for attack," Stiger said, "but at the same time they are just as good dug in and on the defensive. These"—Stiger held out his arms to encompass the legion—"are the best heavy infantry this world has ever seen. They are professional soldiers. They continually train, drill, and work for times like this. Life is not easy for these men. They are exercised hard and kept on a very short leash. Discipline is rigid almost to the point of inflexibility. When placed in the shit, where others break and run, these boys stand firm. They push back, for they are accustomed to victory and can't conceive of defeat. I count myself lucky just to have the honor to serve alongside them." He paused, looking around at the legionaries holding the line. "This is my home. I am meant to be with the legions."

Theo gave a slow nod as he glanced around. He was clearly seeing the legionaries for the first time as the professional fighting force they were.

"What do you think about what Thoggle said?" Stiger asked.

Theo seemed surprised by the question and sudden change of subject. He hesitated before replying.

"I am just a simple soldier," Theo said, "appointed advisor to the thane by an accident of birth and the ability to match Brogan drink for drink. Well, almost drink for drink. Don't tell him, but I think he's the better drinker."

"We both know you are more than a simple soldier," Stiger said, "as you've always been."

Theo eyed him for several heartbeats and then gave a half shrug.

"I suspected you would figure it out at some point," Theo said. "Honestly, it took you long enough. I am Brogan's spymaster, one of the few the thane trusts implicitly, which is why he sent me to get to know you."

"To spy on me?" Stiger asked. "Or to learn if he could work with me?"

"At first, to see if he could use you," Theo said. "Now, I think, after Garand Kos, he looks on you differently."

"As?"

"If not an equal," Theo said, "then an ally."

Stiger thought on that for a moment. It did not surprise him, not at all. It seemed everyone wanted to use him. He regarded Theo, a dwarf he personally liked.

"I've come to consider you a friend," Stiger said.

"I don't have very many friends," Theo said, with a funny look that bespoke sadness mixed with an uncaring indifference. "Most of my people view me as an ass kisser, a cousin of the thane only eager to partake in Brogan's largess and wealth. They know not my true role."

"Thigra knows," Stiger said, "doesn't he?"

"He does," Theo said and then hesitated. "I also consider you a friend. Be warned, my duty to my thane transcends friendships."

"I understand," Stiger said. "Now, about Thoggle?"

"You're in an unenviable position," Theo said.

"I was hoping for more than that," Stiger said.

"Concerning the minion, I think the wizard is right. The creature is too afraid to make big changes that will affect the future. But if I were it, I'd try to cheat a little to win, like the ambush at Garand Kos. That caught everyone by surprise."

"What about the part with Delvaris's death?"

"From what I understand, the World Gate activated unexpectedly, while Brogan was giving a tour to the legate," Theo said. "It is possible Delvaris was simply in the way when the minion wanted out. Some would think a pissed-off dragon is motivation to leave in a hurry."

"But?" Stiger prompted, sensing more from Theo.

"It was great timing by the minion."

"Which means you don't think it was a coincidence?"

Theo shook his head.

"Neither do I," Stiger said. "Not at all."

"Somehow," Theo said, "it knew you would take Delvaris's place."

"That is my thinking as well," Stiger said. "I just don't know how."

"That doesn't really matter at the moment," Theo said. "What does is the here and now. You need to focus your thoughts on this battle and winning it. Judging by the minion's actions to date, I would expect more than just a frontal assault on your defenses." Theo looked back on the line. "This may all be a sideshow to fix our attention."

"I agree," Stiger said, looking over the backside of the defensive line. "I just wish I knew what the creature is planning."

He started walking again and Theo fell in at his side. It was time to see the next cohort.

"Dog, come."

An hour later, they were back at the platform. Stiger found Therik seething when he climbed up.

"They waste lives needlessly," Therik shouted, looking Stiger's way and throwing a hand out to point across the river. "This position is too strong. Why do they do it? Why waste lives of my people?"

"Because Castor doesn't care," Thoggle said. "Your warriors' lives matter little, other than as tools to be used and discarded. You should know this."

"What do you mean he doesn't care?" Therik asked, clearly distressed despite his words earlier to the contrary. "They are his people, too."

Salt and Theo stepped nearer, listening to the conversation.

"The objective is not taking this ridge," Thoggle said.

"Then what is?" Therik asked.

Thoggle turned and looked meaningfully to Stiger.

"I don't understand," Therik said.

Thoggle waved a hand at Stiger.

A brief tingling ran through him, almost as if Stiger had touched the hilt of the sword. But this was different. It happened so fast, he wondered if he had imagined it.

The effect it had on Therik was profound. The orc took a step back and pointed a finger at Stiger.

"Who are you?" Therik asked and then turned to Thoggle. "How did you do that?"

"I am Bennulius Stiger, and the wizard concealed my true features."

"You are not Delvaris," Therik said.

"No," Thoggle said. "He is not. Delvaris died months ago. The minion killed him. Stiger is the High Father's champion, and that is why the minion is here." Thoggle stopped and waved his staff around the battlefield. "All of this is just so that he and minion can face off against one another to decide matters between gods."

Therik looked from Thoggle to Stiger, clearly wanting to disbelieve.

"It is all true," Stiger said. "And it is one heck of a story. I promise, when this is all done, to tell you everything."

Therik glanced over at Theo, who was looking at them with a smirk.

"You knew?" Therik asked.

"Of course," Theo answered. "There is a larger game at play."

"I meant what I said, there is a place for you here at my side." Stiger glanced over to his left, noticing Salt, who appeared wholly unsurprised by the wizard's revelation.

"You knew, too?" Stiger asked the camp prefect, surprised.

"I did," Salt said. "Arvus informed me after he went to see you at the farm."

"And you said nothing?"

"I saw no need, sir, as I had already seen the emperor's letter. Legate Delvaris shared it with me himself." The camp prefect stepped closer and offered a hand. "It is a pleasure to meet you, Legate Stiger."

"The pleasure is mine," Stiger said, taking the hand and shaking it warmly.

"I think it time to put you back," Thoggle said, "before someone other than our small circle here sees you."

The wizard waved a hand at Stiger. He felt the tingling again.

"He looks same," Therik said.

"Once you've seen his true form," Thoggle said, "the web I spun no longer works."

An enemy ball whistled by the platform, missing by mere feet. It impacted the ground harmlessly behind them.

Stiger put Therik from his mind and turned back to look on the battlefield. Under the pale moonlight, the enemy down in the bowl looked like a mass of bugs surging forward toward the trench and wall. The trench had nearly been filled in by bodies as far as he could see. The orcs could walk across the trench now. They stood, almost in line, waiting for a chance at a ladder. Some of the bodies under their feet moved with life.

The artillery, along with the archers, were still hammering the bowl, which was chock full of the enemy. Many of the enemy's heavy infantry had resorted to holding their shields above their heads in groups to protect themselves against the rain of missiles. That only partially worked against the arrow barrage, since their rounded shields did not interlock well. The shields were nothing against the power of the bolt throwers, which punched right through to strike those sheltering beneath. The shields were also useless against ballista balls.

The enemy had suffered several thousand casualties, and still they came on. Stiger's gaze traveled toward the bridge. Formations were stacked up behind it, waiting their turn to move over it and join the battle. Across the way,, Stiger could see thousands of campfires twinkling against the darkness.

He glanced up at the moon as a cloud slid across it. The battlefield darkened just a little. Stiger remembered what Therik had said about his people seeing better at night. The clear skies might soon pass to overcast. That would limit visibility. He knew he had to begin thinking about changing the dynamic. It was time to start preparing for his flanking movement, knowing it would take hours alone to bridge the river. He turned to Thoggle.

"It is time to end this. To do that, I need Brogan's army. I understand they are not far away in Old City dealing with a goblin incursion. Can you hurry the thane along? Is there anything you could do on that front? The real battle is here."

"I would need to leave and, yes, there is likely something I can do." Thoggle glanced out at the enemy's campfires. "Be certain on this, for once I go, I will be unable to return for several hours. Our enemy will sense my absence. They may have been holding back because I am present."

"We are slaughtering them here." Stiger walked up to the railing. Thoggle followed him, painfully stumping after. "While we kill them by the bushel, my men are taking casualties. As my men begin to tire, those casualties will continue to mount over the next few hours. We can easily hold until morning and beyond. However, to do what needs to be done, to break them and bring the minion to battle, I need Brogan's army. If he delays too long, my men will become blown and will be unable to go over to the attack when the time comes. We need his army here, sooner rather than later."

"Very well," Thoggle said. "I will see if I can get his army here by morning. I wish you good fortune."

He tapped his staff on the wood planking. It flashed a bright light that was immediately followed by a loud *CRACK*.

Thoggle was gone.

"Send for Centurion Sabinus," Stiger said to Salt. "I have a job for him."

Chapter Thirty-Four

Stiger looked up from the map he had been studying. There was a small crowd gathered around the table in the command tent to study the map. Salt, Hux, Thigra, and Theo were present. Therik, on Stiger's invitation, had joined them as well and hulked over everyone. The fighting along the defensive line could be heard in the background. It was a constant reminder that every moment Stiger remained here was one he was not supervising the battle.

The administrative tent stood just a few feet away. It buzzed with increased activity as messengers came and went. Stiger glanced over and saw both Sabinus and Setinnunus working their way toward his command tent.

Two guards stood before the entrance. They snapped to attention as the senior officers stepped by them and into the tent. Sabinus and Setinnunus moved up to the table. They both stiffened to attention.

"Now that we are all here, we can begin." Stiger turned to Sabinus and Setinnunus. "Give me an update on your progress."

"As ordered," Setinnunus began, "the bridging equipment has been loaded onto the wagons. The teams have been hitched and driven out of the encampment. Both bridges and the boats are good to move out on your orders. I've also personally ridden down to the river and checked the water's height and flow. Forcing a crossing will prove a challenge, but not an insurmountable one. My engineers stand ready to get the job done, sir."

Stiger gave a satisfied nod, well pleased with his chief engineer. Delvaris had clearly assembled the best of the best for his legion. He looked to Sabinus for his report.

"I have a day's pre-cooked rations for five thousand men loaded onto a mule train," Sabinus said. "If I had another hour, I could double that."

"I am afraid we can't spare an hour," Stiger said and turned to his camp prefect. "Salt, would you see that additional rations follow after them?"

"I will, sir," Salt said. "Say another day's rations for five thousand? Or would you prefer more? We've got plenty of salt pork."

Stiger gave it some thought. The force he was planning on detaching would be on their own for more than a day. This would include the dwarves, which was why Thigra had been asked to join the meeting. Speed and maximizing his available manpower was all that mattered at the moment. The sad truth was that in a few hours' time there would likely be fewer mouths to feed, and those rations for five thousand would stretch a little.

"I think another five thousand will be sufficient," Stiger said. "At the moment, I don't want to pull more of our reserves off of the line than we already have to help move supplies. If needed, we can always forward additional rations later."

"I concur, sir," Salt said.

Stiger motioned at the table for everyone to draw closer. He had outlined his plan an hour before to those gathered around the table and asked them to think on it. He had called them back together, for it was time to begin the final review and discuss any potential challenges or obstacles. Stiger was conflicted about this plan of action, as it was nearly the same one Delvaris had pursued. This meant there was a strong chance the minion would know what he intended. Still, Stiger had considered his options and felt it was the only path open to him if he had a hope of seizing the initiative.

"Excuse me, sir," Nepturus said, stepping into the tent holding a dispatch. "I apologize for interrupting. Another dwarven messenger has arrived. He said he was instructed to wait for a response."

Stiger motioned with his hand for the dispatch. Nepturus stepped over to him. Stiger took the letter and opened it.

"It's in dwarven." Stiger handed it over to Theo. "Do you think you could ask your people to write in common?"

Theo ignored Stiger's comment and read the dispatch. "It seems my cousin has sent part of his army on ahead. Two warbands should be here within the hour. They have exited the mountain's gate." Theo paused and looked up at Stiger. "Both warbands were dispatched earlier this afternoon."

Which meant, Stiger realized, they had marched before Thoggle had even left. Still, it was welcome news.

"Does it say how many warriors Brogan has sent?" Thigra asked.

"Around six thousand," Theo said. He looked over at Stiger. "Chovhog of the Forge Clan who we were already expecting, is leading them and sent this messenger on ahead of his arrival."

"That's perfect," Stiger said, doing the math in his head. He would add them to his flanking expedition.

"Chovhog wants a report on the conditions here," Theo added. "He is asking to know just how bad things are."

"That sounds like Chovhog," Thigra said. "He probably believes he is coming to our rescue."

Stiger looked over at his clerk, who had remained. "Nepturus, I will have a response for the messenger shortly."

"Yes, sir," Nepturus said and withdrew.

"Six thousand warriors will do nicely," Stiger said. "Okay, I would like to get things moving. Let's review the plan one last time."

"There is no need," Thigra said as a hand idly stroked the braids of his beard. "I have already considered *your* plan. My warriors will not participate. We shall remain deployed on the line, as we currently are."

"What?" Salt asked. "Explain yourself, dwarf."

"I refuse to serve under a human commander," Thigra said.

"Excuse me?" Stiger leaned forward, placing his palms down on the table. "I was under the impression we were allies?"

"That is true," Thigra said, "but that doesn't mean you command me or my warriors. Brogan has my allegiance. I go where he orders me. I do what he says. The only way I would consider joining this *expedition* of yours"—Thigra gave him a thin-lipped smile—"is if I am placed in command."

Stiger felt his anger mount. They were in a difficult position here, and just yards away men were fighting for their lives. Thigra was wasting Stiger's time with pointless games. It took some effort to tamp down on the anger that started to course through his veins.

"I would appreciate your support in this, Thigra," Stiger said. "I am asking for your assistance. By withholding your two thousand warriors, you threaten the success of our flanking movement."

"I thought I just made this obvious," Thigra said and crossed his arms over his long beard. The thin-lipped smile remained in place. "The only way you get my support is by placing me in command. You can always write Brogan. If he agrees … well, then I will do as he commands."

"There is no time for that," Salt fairly roared at the dwarf. It turned heads in the administrative tent.

Stiger ground his teeth. This was maddening. There was absolutely no way he could consider placing Thigra in command of the entire expedition. He didn't know the dwarf's capabilities as a leader. Stiger needed someone he could rely upon, like Sabinus, to carry it through. Would Chovhog prove just as intractable?

Stiger rubbed his jaw as he considered the smug-looking chieftain of the Rock Breakers. Cleary Thigra felt he had Stiger between two fires with no way out.

"About that, Thigra …" Theo pulled a folded piece of parchment out from a pocket in his cloak. "Perhaps you might consider reading this, eh?"

There was a mischievous twinkle to Theo's eye as he handed it over to the chieftain, whose smile slipped from his face as he unfolded the parchment. He cast the spymaster a suspicious look. As he began reading, his eyebrows drew together and a scowl formed. He looked up once more at Theo and then over at Stiger before he returned to the parchment. After another moment, he tossed it down on the table. Stiger recognized Brogan's seal at the bottom.

Thigra shot a hate-filled look at Theo.

"It seems," Thigra said to Stiger, barely concealed rage in his voice, "my thane has seen fit to place me and my warband under your command. I will do as you want."

Theo winked at Stiger before reaching forward to retrieve the parchment. The spymaster carefully folded it up and returned it to his cloak pocket.

"Well," Stiger said, eyeing Theo a moment. Theo was one sly bastard. "Now that we have settled questions on the chain of command, let's review the plan. By my calculation, with Thigra's boys, the additional two warbands, First Cohort, our cavalry wing, and the two cohorts already in position at the crossing, we will have a force of more than eleven thousand with which to flank the enemy. More importantly, courtesy of Setinnunus, we have two pontoon bridges ready for deployment to make this happen." Stiger paused and turned to his chief engineer. "How many boats, again?"

"We've constructed forty flat-bottomed boats, sir," Setinnunus said. "As we prepare to deploy the bridges, the boats will allow us to establish a bridgehead on the other side." Setinnunus paused and looked over at Hux. "We constructed the boats with the cavalry in mind; they are more flat-bottomed barges than anything else. We should be able to easily move several squadrons across to scout beyond the bridgehead"—he shifted his gaze to Sabinus—"followed by infantry, of course."

"I like that a lot," Hux said. "It's been terribly boring sitting back and cooling our heels while the rest of the legion gets in on the action."

"Excellent, Setinnunus," Stiger said and then turned to his senior centurion. It was time to reinforce Sabinus's authority over the expedition. "Sabinus, you have overall command of the expedition." He paused a moment and glanced over at Thigra. The chieftain looked supremely chafed and offended.

"Thigra," Stiger said, "I would take it as a personal honor if you will act as Sabinus's second-in-command. Theo has spoken highly of your steady nature and the quality of your warband. If our alliance is to have any chance of succeeding, there will be times when humans command and others when dwarves command."

Thigra appeared genuinely surprised by the offer. His eyes flicked to Theo, who gave an almost imperceptible nod. Had Stiger not been watching, he might have missed it.

"Will Chovhog supersede me?" Thigra asked Theo. "He no doubt will want to."

"I would assume not," Theo said. "Chovhog would be under you. Is that not correct, Legate?"

"That's correct," Stiger said. "You will retain your position as Sabinus's second."

"Then, I heartily accept," Thigra said with broad-toothed smile and looked over at Sabinus. "We will kill many of the enemy and gain much legend."

"We will," Sabinus confirmed.

"Right, let's get back to it." Stiger pointed down toward the map. He traced a finger along the river. "Taking both bridges and the boats, you will march upriver to this crossing point here, to the demolished wooden bridge. Once there, you are to bridge the river. Use the boats to get as many over to the other side as possible to better secure the bridgehead. This would, of course, include parts of the cavalry." Stiger paused to look up at Sabinus and Thigra. "My recommendation is to continue to use the boats even after the bridges have been put up. The goal is to make your crossing as rapidly as possible. Speed is the key. The quicker you are, the better your chances of slipping across the river undetected."

"Yes sir," Sabinus said.

"You all are aware Thoggle left to hurry Brogan. I am hoping by the time you complete the bridges, which will take several hours, the rest of Brogan's army should begin arriving." Stiger paused and looked over at Setinnunus. "I don't wish to put words in your mouth. How long do you feel it will take you to deploy both bridges?"

"Six to seven hours, sir," Setinnunus said. "We will strive to do it quicker, but I cannot promise anything."

"Okay," Stiger said, looking between Sabinus and Thigra. "I intend for Brogan to cross with you. If things go poorly for us here, I may change my mind, but I think it unlikely. We are holding firm. That said, whether Brogan is with you or not, you are to get across and proceed with all possible haste toward the enemy's position on the other side of the river. You are to advance to contact and strike the enemy on the flank as hard as you can."

"Sir," Sabinus said. "If Brogan is not with us by the time we move, we are sure to be badly outnumbered as we advance on the enemy's main body."

Stiger did not immediately reply as he considered how best to respond.

"That's a risk we have to take." Stiger understood full well the men and dwarves of the expedition would be the ones taking the risk. "I have good reason to believe Brogan will be there with you. Besides, you will have one major advantage over the enemy." Stiger turned his gaze to Hux. "Isn't that right, Prefect?"

"It is, sir," Hux said. "Nearly eight hundred mounted is a powerful striking force."

"In mountains," Therik said, "is all up and down. Nowhere good for horse soldiers in mountains."

"You mean it's no good for cavalry in the rugged mountains of your lands?" Theo asked the orc.

"Yes," Therik said. "My people no believe in mounted soldiers. We have no need."

"We're not in your mountains," Hux said. "I shall do my very best to educate the enemy as to their lack of foresight."

Therik's look became hard as he gazed at the prefect.

"With any luck," Stiger said, "your appearance on the enemy's flank will come as a complete shock. If I had to make a guess, I'd say Therik's people are not prepared to face cavalry on the field of battle." Stiger paused and turned to Therik. "Is that right?"

"Yes." Therik's gaze was still on Hux, who returned the orc's gaze with one of equanimity.

"That means their tactics are likely woefully inadequate for coping with a large mounted force," Stiger said, "which should help your chances dramatically."

"That is not a surety," Thigra said. "This entire expedition smacks of desperation. We're slaughtering them well enough here. We should continue to do so, not split our force. With Brogan on the way, it makes it less likely the enemy can overcome the defenses."

"Thigra," Theo said in warning.

Stiger held up a hand to stop his friend. He could not tell them that he already knew Delvaris launched just such an expedition, catching the enemy by surprise. Instead, he would have to use an alternative argument.

"Nothing in war is certain," Stiger said. "Thoggle went to speed along Brogan. We don't know if he will be successful or that the thane's army will arrive in time to make a difference. We have been hoping for a pause in the fighting to allow us a respite, but there hasn't been one. Despite horrific losses, the enemy shows no signs of letting up. Even if they do pause to regroup, they will just come again and again."

"They will," Therik confirmed. "They look to wear you down, and they have not even sent in their trolls. When that happens, things will get difficult."

"It is as Therik said. Eventually our boys will tire," Stiger said. "I need not tell you what will happen. This is why we need to seize the initiative. To even begin to do that, it will take hours of preparation, perhaps as many as seven or eight before you can fully cross, march, and come in contact with the enemy. With a bit of fortune, Brogan's army will arrive in time to reinforce you. If Brogan hasn't made it by the time you are ready to march downriver, then so be it."

"I see, sir," Sabinus said. "What you ask will be very risky, even with the cavalry. We already know the enemy has scouts on the other side of the river."

"Those scouts appear to have only been interested at looking for suitable crossings. None have been spotted at this crossing for some hours," Stiger said and picked up a dispatch from the table. "I had the opposite bank of the crossing scouted. Our scouts could find no sign of the enemy within a two-mile radius. Hopefully, this means we can catch them by surprise. Once you have established your bridgehead, push the cavalry and foot patrols outward to keep the enemy's eyes off the crossing. If your presence is detected, you don't want them knowing your true strength."

"Without Brogan's army," Sabinus said, "once we march, we may find ourselves in trouble and unable to return."

"I understand," Stiger said and truly he did. If it all went badly he would be sending more than eleven thousand souls to their deaths. "However, by the time you effect your crossing, the sun will be well up. You will have our entire wing of cavalry at your disposal to screen your advance. The enemy should not be able to sneak up on you, and if they maneuver to attack, you will have an early warning. As I said, I am hoping Brogan will arrive in time to join you also." Stiger paused. "In such an eventuality, Brogan shall assume command of the expedition."

"I understand, sir," Sabinus said. "Do I have permission to withdraw if I need to?"

"You do," Stiger said. "I will leave it up to you. If you are discovered and the enemy maneuvers against you, you may fall back. However, I am counting on this flanking movement helping to shift the initiative to our side. With a little bit of fortune and speed on your part, you will cause a general panic and potentially force the enemy to withdraw from this side of the river. When that happens, we shall go over to the attack, force our way down into the bowl and over the bridge to join you."

"How will we get word to you when we are in position to attack?" Thigra asked. "Sending a rider back to the bridges and then on to you will take too much time."

"We will position a team on the riverbank, a thousand yards upriver from our defensive line," Salt said. "Send a squadron of cavalry to make contact. They can shout anything that needs to be conveyed across the water."

"That will work," Hux said. "I will detach a squadron just for that purpose. One other thing, sir?"

Stiger nodded for the cavalry prefect to continue.

"I am concerned about taking all of the cavalry with me," Hux said. "You will still need the river patrolled in the event the enemy attempts a crossing of their own."

Stiger looked to Sabinus for his opinion.

"I'd like as many as I can get, sir," Sabinus said. "The more men we have in the saddle, the better our chances."

Stiger turned to Salt for his opinion.

"I'd feel more comfortable with the patrols continuing, sir," Salt said. "However, the flanking expedition will, I think when the time comes, have a greater need for every available trooper."

Stiger did not like the idea of paring down the patrols along the river, especially now that he knew the enemy had the capability to bridge. He weighed the risks for another moment as everyone in the tent had their eyes upon him.

"Perhaps we retain three squadrons?" Stiger suggested, for he agreed with Salt and Sabinus. "One for messaging and two for patrols."

"We can also send out foot patrols, sir," Salt said. "It would dilute our reserve a bit, but having extra eyes are better than none."

"This is a risk we will just have to take," Stiger said. "Hux, leave behind the three squadrons. Take everything else with you."

"Yes, sir."

"Thank you, sir," Sabinus said with evident relief at getting the majority of Hux's cavalry.

"Brogan and I planned this flanking movement out in advance." Stiger looked at each one in turn around the table. "The thane and I have been trading messages for the past few days, discussing strategy. When we settled upon this plan, it was one of the reasons we left the stone bridge in place. We both feel that sending a flanking force out, around, and behind our enemy is our best option for successfully breaking the enemy." Stiger paused and looked directly at Sabinus. "Get across the river and hit the enemy hard. When it is time, we will fight our way across that stone bridge out there and join you both across the river."

"I look forward to it, sir," Sabinus said.

"Any additional questions?" Stiger asked.

"No, sir," Sabinus said.

"Sabinus, pull your cohort off the line," Stiger said. "Seventh Cohort will be taking your place. I sent Severus with orders for them to move into position and prepare to relieve you."

"Yes, sir," Sabinus said.

"What about my boys?" Thigra asked. "Who will take their place along the line?"

"I've split one of the reserve cohorts," Stiger said. "They should be in position and waiting." Stiger took a look around. "Are there any other questions? Any additional thoughts?"

No one spoke up.

"See you on the other side of the river," Stiger said and held out his hand.

"I will be there, sir," Sabinus said and shook.

"Make sure you keep me apprised of your progress. Don't leave me in the dark."

"We will, sir," Sabinus said.

"I will see you too," Stiger said to Thigra and held out a hand.

"Count on it," Thigra said and shook.

With that, Sabinus and Thigra left the tent. Looking like an overeager schoolboy, Setinnunus followed behind them. It was not often that a legion's chief engineer got to bridge a river during a major battle *and* do it under a time crunch.

"I should like to go with them," Theo said.

Stiger looked over at the dwarf and raised an eyebrow, surprised.

"I think it's time I fought with my brothers," Theo said. "I'm not much for standing on the sidelines while others fight for me. Besides, I will have a good story to tell my son when he is old enough to understand."

"Is that really the entire reason?" Stiger asked. Theo seemed a little over melodramatic.

"No." Theo sounded amused. "You are getting to know me only too well."

"The real reason?" Stiger asked.

"Chovhog is known for his difficult manner. He will not be pleased to be placed under the command of a human and even less pleased to find Thigra over him. I will smooth things out for your Centurion Sabinus so that there are no problems prior to Brogan arriving with the bulk of his army."

"Now that makes more sense," Stiger said and flashed a grin at Theo. "I appreciate your efforts."

"Oh, and no need to write a letter to Chovhog," Theo said. "I will act as your messenger. Also, before I leave, I will write to Brogan, asking him to begin using common for his dispatches, as I will be unavailable to translate. Can you see to it the message is delivered to the mountain?"

Stiger gave a nod.

The orc king looked as if he wanted to say something. Therik shifted slightly.

"Don't tell me you want to go too?" Stiger asked.

"No," Therik said. "I will be staying with you."

"Then what is it?" Stiger asked.

"I've never seen a dragon," Therik said. "So far dragon boring. I stay. I wait for him to do something."

Stiger glanced over at Therik and wondered on the orc's sanity.

"Unbelievable." Theo shook his head. "Your people are being slaughtered out there and all you can think of is seeing the dragon doing something?"

"It is difficult to watch, but they turn back on me," Therik said. "I get revenge for that. But I want to see dragon do something."

"I think I will see Nepturus," Theo said, "and get that message to Brogan written."

Theo ducked out of the tent.

Stiger turned to Salt. "Any thoughts?"

"Besides our allies being difficult to work with and full of themselves?" Salt asked.

"Besides that," Stiger said.

"Only that it will be very dangerous for the flanking force, but you already know that, sir. Are you sure this is the best way?"

"No," Stiger admitted, "but I have reason to believe it will succeed."

"Reason being a view of our time from the future?"

"Yes," Stiger said. "The only problem is the minion knows Delvaris did this as well."

"Explain what you say," Therik demanded. "How you and it know of such things?"

"The minion and I both came from the future," Stiger said.

"What?" Therik narrowed his eyes.

"I will explain later," Stiger said, "but just trust me for now."

"I trust," Therik said. "You explain later."

Salt returned to the matter at hand. "Then, if the creature knows... well, that makes this move much more dangerous."

"I know, but I just don't see any other way to break the enemy army and bring the minion to a fight," Stiger said unhappily. "Do you?"

Salt shook his head. "If we do as Thigra suggested, hold the line, and play it conservatively, everything hinges on Brogan. If he doesn't arrive in a timely manner, our boys will wear down and we will be evicted from this defensive position. At that point, we have two choices. Fall back on either our fortified encampment or the dwarven mountain, then wait for Brogan to come save us. I am not sure what kind of shape the legion would be in at that point, sir."

"Agreed," Stiger said, not wanting to think on such an eventuality. It was rare for a legion to be beaten, but it had happened before.

"Sabinus will have the advantage of his cavalry operating over open ground," Salt added. "That alone increases his chances for success. Hux is one of the best cavalry officers I've ever known. Delvaris would not have given him the job of commanding the cavalry wing had the man not proven himself. Yes, I think this plan has a chance for success, sir." Salt rested a hand on the hilt of his sword. "If it fails, with the cavalry as a screening force, Sabinus should be able to retreat back to the bridges. I would think he would be able to cross over to our side, destroying the bridges behind him. If that happens, we end up back where we started, with us on one side of the river and the enemy on the other."

"My thoughts exactly," Stiger said. "Now, I've been away from the battle for too long. I want to get back to the observation platform."

Stiger left the command tent and passed through the administrative tent. Theo was writing at a desk, Nepturus hovering over his shoulder. Severus was just returning as Stiger stepped back out into the night with Therik and Salt.

"Sir," Severus said, spotting them and stepping over. "As instructed, I waited until the Seventh was in position. They stand ready to relieve the First."

"Thank you," Stiger said and started to step by the youth. "See Nepturus and tell him I will be on my platform."

"Sir, I have a request?"

"Yes?" Stiger turned back.

"I would like to go with First Cohort," Severus said. "I want in on the fighting before it is over. I don't much like being an errand boy."

Stiger regarded the tribune for a long moment. He considered telling him flat out no, but then recalled he himself had led a legionary company, the Seventh, at nearly this boy's age.

"Very well," Stiger said, feeling a bit of regret at giving in. "Attach yourself to Sabinus, as his aide. But first tell Nepturus where I will be."

"Thank you, sir," Severus said with evident excitement, "and I will, sir."

"Just make sure you come back alive," Stiger said. "I have nearly run out of tribunes, and without you, I will have to start using Dog to run errands."

"I will, sir," Severus said.

Stiger nodded and the youth stepped off.

"That's not the place for him, sir," Salt said. "His eagerness for action could very well get him killed."

"We were both that age once," Stiger said. "You know how it is, eager to be at it before you realize just how terrible war really is."

"I don't think I can remember that far back," Salt said, glancing after Severus.

"He is young warrior," Therik said. "Is good he goes to fight and blood himself."

"As long as the blood doesn't come at the cost of his life," Stiger said.

He was about to turn for his platform when his eyes fell upon the medical compound, which was a series of six tents just beyond headquarters. A legionary was helping a wounded comrade up to the compound. The injured man was limping badly. Outside the tents, the wounded had been laid out on the grass in neat rows. Medical orderlies moved amongst them. As he watched, two orderlies lifted a man on a stretcher and carried him into a tent, where the surgeons likely waited.

Nepturus had tracked down Father Thomas. Stiger had learned the paladin was in with the surgeons, doing what he could to help. The paladin's medical skills, beyond those divine ones he wielded on the High Father's behalf, were on a level equal those of a typical legion surgeon. Stiger felt no need to call the paladin to his side. He had a feeling that when it was time, Father Thomas would be there.

"Any idea on casualties?" Stiger asked Salt.

"Last I heard," Salt said, "and this was an hour ago, somewhere north of four hundred all told. No real breakdown yet. The cost's likely higher by now."

Stiger gave a slow nod. Four hundred was such a large number. The number of casualties was sure to grow. Stiger considered visiting the wounded, but then disregarded the idea. There would be time for that later.

That was, if he survived his coming encounter with the minion.

Instead, Stiger made his way back to the platform and climbed back up. Salt and Therik followed him up the ladder. Resting his hands upon the railing, Stiger turned his attention back to the fight, carefully studying what he saw. The clouds above had thickened and the moonlight had diminished. From what he could see, it looked much as it had when he left. The artillery continued to fire and the bolt throwers cracked away. Balls screamed by overhead, and the archers continued to rain death on those near the trench.

Like an immoveable steel wall, the legion held the line, keeping the enemy from climbing over the barricade. The position that had been constructed here was unyielding, and it clearly showed in the terrible toll they were wreaking on the enemy.

"How many casualties do you think they've suffered?" Stiger asked Salt.

"If I had to guess, sir," Salt said, his eyes sweeping the bowl, "somewhere around eleven thousand, perhaps even twelve. It's hard to tell exactly. They've packed themselves in tight down there."

"And we just sent a similar number on a flanking movement," Stiger said.

"Exactly, sir," Salt said.

"How can your people keep coming?" Stiger asked, turning to Therik. "They go to certain death."

"They throw themselves on your swords," Therik said, sounding thoroughly disgusted. "My people go to everlasting life for Castor."

Therik spat over the side of the platform.

"This is all about belief," Salt said, shaking his head

"That and rage," Stiger said.

At a fundamental level, Stiger had always known it came down to belief. He and his side followed the High Father's teachings. The orcs followed Castor. It all boiled down to faith and who would hold the key to the future of this world each side called home. It was why they were here, on this battlefield, willingly slaughtering each other. Stiger eyed Therik and wondered what it would have been like to live in peace with such a race. Was it even possible?

Below them, the change out of First Cohort had begun. Sabinus's cohort had been arranged into four ranks, with the front rank engaged and holding the line. Those not directly locked in fighting stepped back and away as Seventh Cohort moved up and took their place. When everything was ready, and the men of the Seventh were in position, a whistle was blown and those holding the line stepped rapidly back. Seventh Cohort stepped forward and into their places. It was efficiently done, and Stiger was pleased to see it handled so well. There was very little disruption.

Only one orc had managed to get halfway over the wall before receiving several jabs from swords and being bashed backward by a shield. The ladder was pushed back off the wall a moment later.

Without any real delay, Sabinus had First Cohort form up for march, which Stiger supposed surprised the men and likely pissed them off. They would've thought they had been pulled off the line for a breather. Instead, Stiger was sending the legion's best cohort into mortal danger worse than what they had just endured. Though Stiger couldn't hear it over the sound of the fighting, the order was given to march.

Sabinus turned, looked up at Stiger, and gave him a crisp salute. Stiger returned the salute. Sabinus spun on his heel and began marching with his men.

Had he made the right decision? In five hours it would be sunrise. Stiger watched First Cohort march off into the night. He had a terrible feeling he hadn't.

CHAPTER THIRTY-FIVE

"Sir." A legionary, having climbed up to the platform, saluted. The first hints of the sky lightening were behind him. "This just came into headquarters. Nepturus said you would want to see it straight away."

Stiger took the dispatch, opened it, and scanned the contents.

"Sabinus and Setinnunus have made good time of it," Stiger said to Salt. Therik looked over curiously. "One bridge has been deployed and they have begun their crossing. At the time of writing this, Sabinus estimates he has forty percent of his force across. The other bridge should be in place within a couple of hours."

"That is impressive," Salt said. "Any sign of the enemy?"

"Sabinus says there is no sign of them. He believes the enemy to be ignorant of our crossing the river," Stiger said.

Sabinus had also thanked him for sending along Theo. Apparently, there was very little love lost between Thigra and Chovhog. Theo had worked to keep their mutual animosity for each other in check and both chieftains apart.

"Thank you," Stiger said to the legionary and handed back the dispatch. "I will not have a reply."

The legionary saluted again and climbed back down the ladder.

Stiger turned back to the fighting. The intensity of the enemy's assault had lessened over the last hour. The orcs seemed to be making less of an effort.

"They are getting tired, sir," Salt said. He did not even have to shout to be heard. This told Stiger much about the intensity of the fighting across the entire line, the ends of which were lost in the gloom of night. "They may be compelled to call off their assault soon just to regroup."

Stiger agreed. A number of the enemy below were drawing back and away from the walls. They were losing their will to fight, which was a good thing, for the men on the line needed a break. Stiger had no illusions about the rest of the enemy army, which was fresh and rested. Most of it had not yet become engaged. The enemy had plenty of reserves.

"They send more," Therik said. "When they come next, they no fool around. They send best warriors. You see trolls, too."

"Great," Stiger said.

"Excuse me, sir."

Another legionary had climbed up. He saluted and held out a dispatch. Stiger took and opened it. He recognized Brogan's seal. Thankfully it was written in common. They had traded several messages within the past few hours as Brogan's army left the mountain.

"Brogan's army is almost to the crossing," Stiger said. "At the time this was written, he was a mile away, which means he's already likely there."

"That's right good news, sir," Salt said. "Best news I've heard all night."

"Brogan's army is fourteen thousand strong," Stiger said as he continued reading. Stiger's last dispatch to the thane had requested the dwarven army's strength. "He was forced to leave two thousand warriors in Old City to protect the civilians. It seemed the goblins attacked the dwarven population, causing a great loss of life."

Stiger handed the dispatch over to Salt. The old soldier's eyes were not as good as Stiger's, and in the dim light he had to hold it close to even read it. After he had scanned the contents, Salt handed the dispatch back to Stiger.

"Even with the reduction in numbers, it's still good news, sir," Salt said. "Brogan brings fourteen thousand more than we had. That brings the strength of the flanking column up dramatically."

"It does," Stiger said and turned to the legionary. "Thank you. Tell Nepturus I shall have a reply shortly."

The legionary saluted and left.

Stiger glanced up. The sky had become overcast, with the moon only occasionally visible through a cloud. It was possible another storm was on the way. Stiger hoped that was not the case, for it would mean combat operations would become more difficult and time-consuming, especially in light of his flanking movement.

The sky had begun to lighten slightly, but due to the cloud cover, the ground was still shrouded in near darkness, lit only by dim moonlight. Across the river, the fires from the enemy's camp glittered back at him like a star-filled night.

Even though the flanking movement would soon number twenty-five thousand, they would still be outnumbered. Worse, the minion likely knew what Stiger intended. If so, why had there been no scouts along the river near where Sabinus had set up his bridges? That really bothered him.

What was he missing?

Stiger felt a vibration through his boots. He looked over at Salt and their eyes met in question. The platform trembled, and then shook. Stiger reached for the railing to keep himself upright.

"Look," Salt shouted, pointing behind them.

Stiger turned.

Sian Tane had stood, wings extending outward. The dragon, jaws bared, took a couple of menacing steps forward toward them. The tower shook with each massive footfall. The dragon's gaze was fixed upward at the sky.

Just then, a flash of bluish light from above lit up the entire field. It was almost like a lightning bolt had slashed across the sky, but somehow Stiger understood it wasn't. He looked up and blinked. The moon's outline could just be seen behind a cloud. A large, dark shape emerged from the cloud, streaking downward toward the battlefield.

It was hard to make out its form, but Stiger knew what it was. A cry from the creature above confirmed it. Then he saw another emerge from the cloud, just behind the first, and his heart clenched in fear. They were diving toward his line. The second screamed an animal cry of rage.

"Great gods," Salt breathed.

The wyrms had arrived. There was absolutely nothing Stiger could do about it. There had been no warning, nor was there any order he could give that could stop what was to happen as the two wyrms dove down towards the battlefield.

All fighting had ceased, as every eye looked skyward. There was yet another cry. This one was much louder and deeper, and sounded, at least to Stiger's ears, more ferocious. The cloud before the moon seemed almost to part as a truly massive shape plunged down through it and toward the two wyrms, both of which were much smaller. It was Currose, and she had a tremendous speed advantage over the two wyrms.

Like a great bird of prey, she extended her talons to strike and closed on the rearmost wyrm. The smaller dragon attempted to turn, but it was too late. The two forms merged, and then a terrible, agonized screech filled the air as they collided. Stiger could almost imagine Currose's talons sinking in as she struck the wyrm, powerful claws plunging through skin and muscle, forming a death grip on the smaller dragon.

The stricken wyrm snaked its head around and blew a stream of fire on Currose. The noctalum's head shot forward through the flame and her jaws clamped down on the wyrm's neck, just beneath the head. The fire immediately ceased. The wyrm twisted in Currose's grip and managed to free itself from her jaws, but not her talons. Ripping and tearing at each other with their talons and teeth, both dragons began to tumble in a death dance, twisting in the air as they hurtled straight down toward the ground.

A dark shape flashed overhead, causing Stiger, Salt, and Therik to duck. It was accompanied by the beat of massive, leathery wings. A blast of wind knocked Stiger backwards onto the railing of the platform. A massive black tail the width of a hundred-year-old oak tree snaked after, coming within three feet of the tower. Sian Tane gave his wings an enormous beat just above the defensive line, knocking men flat. The gust of wind threw orcs off their scaling ladders and to the ground. Sian Tane beat at the air again, arcing upward towards the other wyrm.

The wyrm, traveling downward at a fast clip and apparently seeing the noctalum coming for it, had a change of heart. It abruptly banked away to the south, flapping its wings rapidly to gain speed and altitude before the noctalum could catch up.

There was a tremendous thud from behind the tower as something massive hit the ground hard. The tower swayed dangerously with the impact. Stiger held onto the railing for dear life, and for a moment thought it might go over. Then the swaying stopped.

He looked around.

Several hundred yards behind them, something had crashed down in the forest. He knew it must have been the two dragons. Yet even with the dim moonlight, he couldn't see much, for it was concealed by the trees. Silence settled across the battlefield, almost as if orc and human alike held their collective breaths.

A tree snapped and another crashed to the ground as something in the trees moved, shifting about. One of the dragons roared. The other replied in a high-pitched screech. The sickening sounds of ripping and tearing could be heard. A titanic struggle, hidden by the trees, was underway. The ground shook violently. Trees snapped and crashed to the ground. There were screams, cries, grunts, and what sounded like the snapping of jaws.

A gout of dragon flame illuminated a large form as it set more than a dozen trees on fire. Another blast of flames set more afire. The flames lit up the struggle between the wyrm and dragon. It was a ferocious fight, with no thought toward mercy or quarter. They clawed at one another, biting, tearing, and ripping. There was a brilliant flash of light, like lightning, a deafening scream of rage followed by another longer jet of flame. This was followed by another flash, this time of greenish light. There was a concussive *boom*.

The tower shook again as something heavy fell to the ground. Then there was silence. Amidst the burning trees, Stiger saw movement, but no more fighting.

Who had won?

Currose reared up, stretching out her wings and extending her head toward the sky. The great dragon roared what sounded to Stiger like exultation at her victory and kill. It was awesome, terrible, deafening, and frightening all at the same time.

You have been blessed this day, puny mortals. You have witnessed the might of the noctalum, a powerful voice said, and Stiger realized it was in his head. Currose was speaking to them all. *The filthy wyrm is dead.*

She roared again, then leapt up into the air, wings beating with incredible force. With a series of great flaps, she began to circle, gaining altitude. Currose climbed higher and higher with each flap of her massive wings. Stiger could see large droplets of blood fall from her body as she clawed her way up into the sky.

In the distance, to the south, there was another roar. Stiger had forgotten about Sian Tane. He must still be chasing the other wyrm. Every eye along the field was fixated on Currose as she climbed higher. She extended her wings outward, catching a draft of air and holding it. She seemed to hang in space for a long moment, before banking and diving for the ground. Picking up speed, she flew just above the trees of the burning forest before turning south.

Stiger felt a terrible gnawing fear overcome him. The dragon skimmed the ground, closing the distance toward the tower with frightful speed. The fear was awful. It drove him to his knees, and he had to hold onto one of the supports of the platform to keep himself upright. Out of his peripheral vision, Stiger saw that Therik and Salt were similarly affected.

All Stiger wanted to do was press himself to the platform floor and find a place to hide. He even considered throwing himself to the ground in search of safety. It was shameful, he knew, but his mind wasn't being rational. Then the dragon shot by the tower, so close he felt the wind of her passage. There was an explosion of flame and heat, then suddenly the fear was gone.

Stiger shakily stood up. Illuminated by fire from below, the dragon began flapping her wings, beating at the air again, gaining altitude as she flew over the river. In her wake, hundreds of orcs burned in the bowl. They were being consumed alive by the dragon fire, which was an odd bluish color. Stiger could feel the intense heat radiate at him. Everyone on the battlefield had been stunned into immovable shock.

A flash of green light arced up toward Currose from across the river as she flew over the far bank and the enemy's camp. It was a mere dart of green light and it missed, disappearing into the clouds. Another flash reached up from the same spot and struck her. Briefly the dragon was surrounded by a greenish tinge of fire, illuminating the noctalum against the night sky. It dissipated rapidly. She continued to beat her wings, perhaps a little quicker than before, gaining even more altitude.

Another dart of light shot up at her. She banked to the left and it missed. Stiger realized Castor's priests were attacking the noctalum. Currose responded with a roiling fireball of her own, which streaked toward the ground with frightful rapidity. It exploded on the spot where the darts had emanated. The sound of the explosion reached them a moment later as a deep *crump*.

There were no more darts of greenish light after that. Currose flew higher, traveling south after her mate Sian Tane. Then, she was into the clouds and lost from sight.

The dragon fire in the bowl continued to burn. The shrieks of the dead and dying filled the air, but beyond that, utter silence reigned across the battlefield. Everyone was stunned by what they had just witnessed.

"Show's over! Push those bloody ladders off the wall," a lone voice rang out from below. It shattered the massed silence. "You're all standing around with your cocks in your hands, you dumb bastards. Now do as I bloody say, or so help me, I will start handing out charges! Who wants punishment detail?"

The call was picked up by other centurions along the line, and within moments the air was filled with shouts and orders from both sides. A horn across the river sounded. Another joined it. To Stiger, it didn't sound like a horn call to retreat, but to advance. And that was just what the orcs did, throwing themselves once again into the effort to overcome the fortified line—but, Stiger thought, with less gusto.

Regardless, the fight was back on.

Stiger shot a glance over at Therik. The orc gripped the railing tightly, his gaze fixed upon the south, where Currose had disappeared into the clouds.

"Well," Salt said to the orc, "you wanted to see the dragon do something. Now you have. What do you think?"

"Is not something you see every day," Therik said.

"You can say that again," the prefect said, gazing over into the bowl at the orcs who had been killed by dragon fire. Their bodies still burned as the dragon fire consumed itself. The stench of burned flesh was nearly overpowering. "I wish the dragon had done more before flying off."

"She goes to help her mate," Stiger said.

"The enemy is here, sir," Salt said. "The dragon could have burned a few more before leaving. It would have been nice to even the odds a little more."

"Wyrms," Stiger said to himself, wondering where the other two wyrms were. Thoggle had told him there were four, and yet only two had shown themselves.

"What?" Salt looked over at him in confusion.

Stiger realized he was missing something.

"What did you say a moment ago?" Stiger asked, a thought hitting him.

"I was saying that the fight was here, sir," Salt said. "The dragon could have done more."

A cold feeling stole over Stiger. He turned his gaze across the river toward the enemy's staging positions. He could see thousands of campfires twinkling in the distance, but not the enemy themselves. He tried to recall if he had seen any of the enemy across the way as the fireball had hit the ground. Oddly, the fire had immediately extinguished itself upon contact.

The gloom of the night had begun to give way a little. Stiger wondered if the sword could lighten things up for him to see a bit more. His hand slid to the sword. The familiar tingle ran up his arm. He could not see the enemy army. All he saw were the fires, which he had seen before. Everything else had lightened considerably. He could see down into the bowl and across the river like it was daylight, but as his eyes traveled farther toward the enemy camp, all that was visible were the fires. Something was amiss.

The priests conceal something, Rarokan said.

"I've been a fool," Stiger said.

"What?" Salt stepped nearer, as did Therik.

"Across the river," Stiger said, "much of their army is gone."

"But I can see their fires," Salt said, "and they are still before us, with another formation coming across the bridge now, sir."

Stiger looked down into the bowl. It was packed with orcs, almost shoulder to shoulder. Another fresh formation of orcs was indeed marching its way across the bridge. Despite that, Stiger knew he was right. Only a few thousand had been left to fix his attention. The minion had made its move, and that was different than how Stiger knew this battle had played out.

"My people are not dumb animals," Therik said, which only confirmed Stiger's supposition.

"Apparently, not," Stiger said. He began pacing the small platform, thinking furiously. He was sure the enemy army had come across the river. But why had he not received any word from the scouts? After several moments, he stopped and looked to Therik and Salt.

"I am certain the enemy has bridged the river themselves. They are somewhere downriver, either crossing or already crossed," Stiger said. "Had they been upriver, the messenger from Sabinus would have spotted them."

"Are you sure, sir?" Salt sounded doubtful. "I would think we would have gotten some word of that if it had occurred. We have scouts out downriver."

"I am certain," Stiger said, now wishing he had kept more of his cavalry back for patrols. "This is the situation as I see it and our options. Much of Sabinus's force is already across. Brogan is likely at the crossing and waiting to go over. We can disengage here and pull back to the mountain. The only problem with that is it would potentially allow for Brogan's army and our boys to be cut off and isolated." Stiger pointed out into the bowl. "With much of their army gone and somewhere downriver, we could go over to the attack, push into the bowl, and destroy the forces before us, then turn to face whatever is coming."

"Attack, sir?" Salt asked, sounding extremely skeptical.

"Yes," Stiger said. "I would like your thoughts."

"Sir," Salt said, "we don't even have confirmation that the enemy crossed yet."

"I know," Stiger said. "I am certain it will come shortly. I would like your thoughts for when it does."

"Pulling back to mountain is mistake," Therik said.

"He's right," Salt said and took a moment to gather his thoughts. "If what you say is true, sir, we've already split our army and put ourselves at great risk. It will take time to get the flanking expedition back to our side of the river. Should we retreat to the mountain, Brogan and Sabinus would surely be left hanging out in the open and cut off. They would be destroyed. Attacking out into the bowl is also a mistake. If we did, and succeeded, our boys would be blown and in poor shape for a second fight. We could also find ourselves in a bad position when the enemy arrives."

"Go on," Stiger said. So far, he agreed with everything Salt had said.

"There is another possibility, though," Salt continued. "We could pull back to our fortified encampment, recall Brogan and Sabinus. It will take them several hours to get Sabinus's men back to our side and organized. Repositioning an army and moving it about takes time. The flanking expedition is nearly twenty-five thousand strong. We have almost ten thousand here. There is a good chance the enemy does not know Brogan is close, nor that we've detached a force. We allow the enemy to attack us, and when their attention is completely fixed on the encampment, Brogan can strike."

"There won't be time to bring the artillery with us," Stiger said, considering the idea. It had merit. The enemy likely thought Brogan was still in Old City. There would not have been time for them to learn otherwise. The more he thought on it, the more he liked the idea. "We would only have the walls of the encampment for defense."

"The walls of the encampment are good," Salt said. "They are shorter in length than the line we currently occupy. We will be able to better concentrate our defense, which will make it easier to withstand an assault by a superior force."

"I like that idea. All of our supplies are here," Stiger said. "If we pull back to the mountain, we give that up to the enemy, and we know they only have enough food to last them a week, maybe a little longer. That would allow the enemy to extend their operations for months and then they could take their time at doing whatever they wish."

"Another option is to go join Brogan's army and meet the enemy on an open field of battle," Salt said. "But that would mean giving up the supplies."

"If we do that," Stiger said. "We might get cut off from the mountain ourselves with no supply."

Stiger did not much like the idea of giving up their supplies. The encampment was a quarter mile to the rear, at the edge of the forest, which was on fire. It sat along the road that led to the entrance to the mountain. The more Stiger thought on that idea, the more he liked it. The tricky part would be disengaging here.

"What do you think?" Stiger asked Therik.

"Me?" Therik asked. "You want opinion?"

"Yes," Stiger said.

"I like his idea," Therik pointed to Salt. "I think it work. Walls of encampment strong enough to hold for some hours. No way minion or priests know yet Brogan's army close. He surprise and ambush and then we attack. You give me sword and I help."

"How many men do you think we will need to hold the line?" Stiger asked Salt. "We will have to leave a force here to hold for a time, at least long enough to get the bulk of the legion on the way to the encampment."

Salt rested his hands upon the railing and studied the action below. He was silent for a several heartbeats.

"At least the first rank of each cohort," Salt said. "It will be tricky to pull off, sir. They will need to disengage from the line and come together at a common point before withdrawing. That way it makes it less likely one portion of the line doesn't get isolated and cut off. And if it does, we can go to their aid as a cohesive force."

"That makes sense," Stiger said. "Once the enemy gains the wall, the rear guard will need to move quickly. How difficult that movement will be is a question ultimately left up to our enemy. Once over the barricade, the quicker the enemy becomes organized, the harder it will be on our rearguard."

"That is true, sir," Salt said. "As I said, it will be tricky."

"What do you think?" Stiger asked Therik.

Therik held his hands up as if to say he did not know. But then apparently reconsidered. "They below are tired and be slow to follow. But I think they also be careful. You hurt them good. They might think trap. You not have as difficult a time as you think."

"Let us hope it is so," Stiger said.

A rider galloped up to the platform and Stiger knew the man brought with him his confirmation. The man slid from his horse and didn't even bother to tether it. He climbed up the ladder. The cavalry trooper offered a salute.

"Sir," the auxiliary said. He was breathing heavily and had a slightly wild look to his eyes. "The enemy is crossing in strength downriver. They struck with dragons, sir. Most of the boys there were burned. Those that weren't, ran. I've never seen anything like it, sir. There was nothing we could do. How do you fight a dragon?"

Stiger closed his eyes. He felt his stomach sink at hearing what the wyrms had done to his defending cohorts. The two that had occupied Sian Tane and Currose had been an intentional distraction. Stiger suspected the noctalum had known of the wyrms proximity and been waiting for them to make their move, hence Currose appearing just above the two wyrms as they began their dive on the line. It had left the crossing unprotected and vulnerable. Stiger felt guilty for sending good men to their deaths. He took a calming breath and opened his eyes. He had to focus on the job at hand. "How many are crossing, do you know?"

"Thousands, sir," the trooper said, "and there is nothing to stop them, sir. They are using boats to cross, a lot of boats."

"How long ago was this?"

"Half an hour," he said. "I rode hard as I could, sir."

"Thank you," Stiger said. "Report to Nepturus at headquarters. We will use you as a dispatcher until you are able to rejoin your squadron."

"Sir." The trooper swallowed, his throat catching. "I have no squadron. They were all killed. I was the only one to win through, and that was by riding into the forest and… and hiding, sir."

Stiger gave an unhappy nod as he thought on what was coming for them. He could not blame the man for hiding after enduring a dragon attack. He was grateful he had simply made it through to report.

"The dragons," Stiger said, "are they still at the crossing?"

"No, sir," the man said. "When I ducked into the forest, they flew off to the south and back over the river. I watched them go, sir."

"You've done good, son," Salt said. "Now report to headquarters and make sure you eat something after you do. We will find a place for you. I promise. Dismissed."

"Yes, sir." The man saluted and then climbed down the ladder.

"It's settled, then. We pull back to the encampment," Stiger said. "Salt, I think it will take the enemy some time to become organized and begin marching our way. It's, what, two miles to the crossing?"

"That sounds about right, sir," Salt said.

"Very good," Stiger said. "I want scouts sent downriver, so we know how far off they are and when they march. I will call a meeting of all senior officers at headquarters. We need to begin preparing to fall back on the encampment, and I want it done in good order. You will personally lead the rearguard."

"Yes, sir. I will get right on it." Salt made his way down and off the platform. "I will see you back at headquarters shortly, sir."

"What if wyrms come?" Therik asked.

"Let's hope our dragons are not too far away," Stiger said as he pulled out a dispatch pad and wrote out two notes, one to Sabinus and the other to Brogan. He spent more time with Brogan's, outlining his thoughts. Then he signed each and added "confirmation requested."

He made his way down the ladder and jogged over to headquarters, his armor chinking with each footfall. Therik followed him. The guards snapped to attention as Stiger moved by them. Nepturus shooed a messenger away and stood to attention.

"Make sure these get out right away," Stiger said and handed over the messages. "This one to Brogan and this one to Sabinus. It is imperative they get these messages as soon as possible. Understand me?"

"Yes, sir," Nepturus said. He jogged toward the dispatch riders.

"You," Stiger said, pointing at one of the other clerks. "I want all senior officers here yesterday. Also, advise the surgeons they will need to move the wounded back to the encampment immediately. We will be giving up the defensive line to the enemy, and soon. Got that?"

"Yes, sir." The clerk ran out toward the dispatch riders.

"It will be interesting to see if we survive to next day," Therik said, as all eyes in the tent fell on him. "I think it will prove test of which god is stronger."

"Much comes down to this," Stiger agreed.

"Can I have sword now?" Therik held out hand. "You will need it soon."

"You," Stiger said to one of the guards. "There is a sword in my office, leaning against one of the trunks. It has silver inlaid on the hilt. Give it to Therik."

"Yes, sir," the guard said and ducked into the command tent. He returned a moment later, Dog following him out. He handed the sword to Therik.

Dog padded up to Stiger and sat down by his side. Stiger absently patted the animal on his head.

"I know this sword," Therik announced as he tested its weight and balance. "It belonged to one of my chieftains, Toraki."

"Is that a problem?" Stiger asked.

"Not at all," Therik said. "I never liked him anyway."

Chapter Thirty-Six

Stiger stood just to the side of the encampment's main gate as the last of the legion's cohorts marched through. The men were tired and worn but also relieved to be entering the safety of the encampment's walls. He noticed their eyes on him as they moved past. In them he saw hope and the confidence he would get them through the coming ordeal.

An officer marching by with his men offered a salute. Stiger gave the centurion a nod and then turned his gaze outward toward the rearguard two hundred yards away. Leading the mixed bag of legionaries from almost every cohort in the legion, Salt stood just behind the formation. These men had been the last to hold the defensive wall. Formed up into two hasty ranks, they fell back in good order.

Stiger did his best to be patient as he watched Salt maneuver his formation steadily backward, slowly closing the distance to the encampment. Beyond the rearguard, back along the defensive line the legion held and defended throughout the night, the artillery burned. Black, greasy smoke billowed upward into the dawning sky. The towers that had housed the legion's bolt throwers had also been fired. Stiger had made certain before pulling off the line that all of the artillery was destroyed. He had even detailed an officer and century of men to make sure the job had been done correctly. He did not want to see his own machines turned against him. It was a regrettable loss in equipment, but there'd simply been no choice.

Glancing upward, Stiger figured the plumes of smoke could be seen across much of the valley. Definitely Brogan and Sabinus would be able to see them. At least, he hoped so. He had staked everything on Brogan and Sabinus.

Stiger's eyes slid back to the rearguard. To their front was a growing mass of orcs. Falling back one step at a time, the front rank of the legionaries kept their shields pointed outward toward the enemy. Swords were held at the ready.

Once the wall had been given up, the enemy tentatively began climbing over the barricade and past the burning towers. Stiger estimated there were now more than a thousand enemy over the defensive wall. Most were simply shadowing the rearguard, but a good number appeared to be poking around the abandoned defensive positions. They were most probably searching for loot. That suited Stiger just fine, for he wanted to get all of the men safely into the encampment.

So far, the enemy to Salt's front seemed to have no interest in challenging the rearguard. With no apparent leadership, the enemy that had made it over the barricade so far were completely disorganized. Stiger figured this was likely the only reason they had not already attacked. He wondered how long it would take before someone with authority asserted any serious control.

Father Thomas, with Dog at his side, stepped from the encampment and up to Stiger. It was the first time Stiger had seen the paladin since the fighting had begun. Stiger glanced over and offered a nod. Father Thomas was certainly no longer the middle-aged warrior priest who had accompanied him through the Gate. Stiger was again startled by the paladin's appearance. He appeared old and extremely weary to Stiger's eyes, nothing like the man he had known.

Placing his hands on his hips, Father Thomas took in the scene before him.

"Out of the fire and into the encampment?" Father Thomas said, in a sort of half jest. When it did not elicit the reaction he had anticipated, the paladin grew serious. "How long before the rest of the enemy army gets here?"

"Soon enough," Stiger said.

"So soon you felt the near immediate need to give up your defensive works and retire to the protection of the encampment," Father Thomas said. It wasn't a question, but a statement.

"For once," Stiger said, acutely feeling the frustration of the situation, "I wish things would go our way. Is that honestly too much to ask?"

"Huh," Father Thomas grunted.

"Fortuna always seems to load the dice against me." Stiger slapped a palm against his thigh. "The enemy caught me with just one boot on. Why didn't I see it? This is certainly not how we know it went down with Delvaris."

"I would think you of all people would know better than to expect everything to go as anticipated."

Stiger held the paladin's gaze a long moment and then gave a slow nod before turning his gaze back to the rearguard. It was a lesson he already knew.

"In war," Stiger said, feeling a little chastened, "nothing ever goes as planned."

"Exactly," Father Thomas said and then looked behind them at the encampment. "This is quite a risk you are taking by moving the legion here."

"You think we should have pulled back to the mountain?" Stiger asked, surprised but interested to hear the paladin's opinion. "Or perhaps meet the enemy out in the open?"

"I don't rightly know," Father Thomas said. "War is your battlefield. Mine tends to be more spiritual in nature. Thoggle is not here. Neither are the dragons. An enemy army is on our doorstep, and with them will come priests with *will* and the minion. I would like our odds better were they with us, for everything is now on the table, as a gambler might say."

Stiger keenly felt the paladin's concern. He had wagered it all with just one throw of the dice, and Stiger did not like gambling. He much preferred to stack the odds in his favor whenever possible. He turned his gaze back to the rearguard, which was now fifty yards away. The enemy had continued to follow and closed the distance to the rearguard, coming within ten yards of Salt's shield wall. Stiger sensed the enemy were collectively working themselves up to something. Salt must have suspected the same.

"Halt," Salt shouted. The formation ground to a stop. "Tighten up. Ready shields… shields up!"

The shields came together with a solid-sounding *thunk.* The enemy stumbled to an uncertain stop.

"We're gonna give them a gentle push with our shields and a poke from our swords," Salt shouted. "Got that, boys?"

"HAAAH!" the men shouted in unison.

"Prepare to advance," Salt shouted, his head swiveling first to the left and then right. "Advaance!"

"HAAAH! HAAAH! HAAAH!"

The formation moved forward toward the enemy at a slow, measured step. One of the legionaries began beating the inside of his shield with his sword. It was a steady, rhythmic thunk. The entire formation picked it up. The steady thunking beat was an intimidating and ominous sound. Almost immediately, the enemy began backpedaling. The legion had already shown them how efficient it was at killing, and none seemed very eager to test the armored slaying machine advancing steadily at them.

"Halt," Salt called after twenty paces, when it became clear he would not be bringing the enemy to battle. His demonstration had had an expected result. The enemy backed up another twenty-five paces and then also stopped. The camp prefect held his formation in place for a count of thirty and then gave the order to begin stepping backward again.

This time, the enemy did not move to pursue.

"That seems to have gotten their attention," Father Thomas said.

"It did," Stiger said, still thinking on what the paladin had just said about Thoggle and the dragons not being with them. He turned to the paladin. "Yes, I gambled. We're on our own for a bit and will just have to make do. Brogan and Sabinus are out there. I am sure of it. Thoggle is likely with them too, which I think is why he has not returned. I sent messengers before we quit the line, giving them my intentions and expectations."

"Have you received word back yet?" the paladin asked.

"He has not," Therik said.

Stiger glanced over. He had not heard the orc join them.

"There hasn't been enough time for word to get to them and back," Stiger said, though privately he was worried. He had hoped to have received something before giving up the defensive line along the ridge, but time had not been on his side. The scouts reported the van of the enemy column already in march and Stiger had felt compelled to quit his line before he had wanted to.

"I came down from wall to show you something," Therik said and pointed.

In the distance, Stiger could see what appeared to be a dust cloud. He knew without a doubt what it was. There was a dirt road that ran along the water's edge to the downriver crossing.

The main body of the enemy army was approaching, and they were kicking up an awful lot of dust.

The last of the scouts had come in a short while before and reported the main body was a little over a mile away. Enemy skirmishers were closer. The dust only confirmed those reports. Stiger's unease increased tenfold.

Had he made the wrong decision by bringing the legion to the encampment?

He could have brought them to the mountain and held there like he had done in his own time. Stiger shook his head. He was convinced that would have been the wrong decision. They would have been terribly outnumbered, with the only option being to retreat into the mountain and close the gate behind them. Brogan and Sabinus would be left to fend for themselves against a force more than double their number. With Stiger's way, his small army was still in the field, and there was the chance that Brogan and Sabinus could achieve surprise. At least, he hoped so.

He glanced around, looking up at the fortifications of the encampment. The gate and dirt rampart rose some twenty feet above them. Stiger ran his eyes along the walls of the fort. They appeared solid. He, Father Thomas, and Therik were standing just beyond the outer trench, which was some ten feet deep. The walls of the trench were very steep with sharpened stakes at the bottom. A series of wood planks bridged the trench. It was all fairly standard for an encampment, but at the moment Stiger suddenly wished he had thought to add further to the defenses. A second trench would have been nice.

On this side of the fort, facing southward, was open ground that looked toward the ridge. On the opposite side of the fort and out of view lay thick green forest, part of which continued to burn. Though flames could no longer be seen, smoke from a sullen, steady burn drifted up and out of the trees.

Stiger hoped that the walls were enough to hold back the enemy, at least long enough for Brogan and Sabinus to arrive. The lack of a messenger returning worried him something fierce. He truly had no idea where the flanking expedition was or if they were even on their way yet. It was even possible Brogan and Sabinus had run into trouble themselves.

By his side, as if sensing his thoughts, Dog growled.

"Easy boy." Stiger laid a hand on the animal's head and absently patted him.

Stiger turned his gaze back to Salt. The rearguard was almost to them. As he approached to within ten feet of the trench, the camp prefect ordered a halt and dressed his lines. The orcs facing them had not advanced any farther.

One rank at a time, Salt sent his legionaries back and into the fort. Like the others who had passed earlier, these men were clearly weary and tired. They were also relieved to have made it to the safety of the encampment walls. He could see it in their eyes and manner.

"Nicely done, boys," Salt's voice boomed out. "Nicely done."

Stiger rubbed at his eyes, which were dry and scratchy from lack of sleep. He badly needed sleep, but knew none would be forthcoming. Such was the way when in the field and facing the enemy. Sleep was always a commodity in short supply.

Salt came up to Stiger. Above them, manning the walls, were more than one hundred legionaries, armed with the last of the javelins. They stood ready for a toss, a fact that the enemy seemed to be aware of. The enemy made no move to venture closer but simply watched, standing just out of range.

"Are the last of the scouts in?" Salt asked.

Stiger had his eyes on the enemy. He did not like what he saw. Though they came no closer, it was plain to him they had not lost their will to fight. They shouted taunts in their own language at the retreating legionaries and made rude gestures. Once someone came along and got them organized, those words and gestures would all be translated into physical violence.

"Sir?" Salt asked.

"What did you say?" Stiger looked over.

"Before we seal the gate, I want to be sure the last of the scouts are in. I don't want to leave anyone out with this lot."

"They're in," Stiger confirmed. "We've also had some of the survivors from the cohorts positioned at the crossing downriver come in as well. From what they reported, I am guessing near forty thousand will be here soon, not counting those right before us."

The last of the rearguard made their way past. Only a century of picked men Salt had held back remained. They formed a double-ranked line just before the officers and the wood-planked bridge. The centurion in command of the century glanced over at Salt with a questioning look, clearly wondering what the holdup was.

"Sir," Salt said, turning to Stiger and giving him a meaningful look. "Would the legate kindly enter the fort? That way, the rest of us can get behind those fine-looking walls."

He gave a nod and—along with Father Thomas, Therik, and Dog—made his way over the trench and through the gate.

"All right," Salt shouted. "Bring it on inside, boys."

The legionaries did not need any further encouragement. They jogged into the encampment. The last of them, with Salt overseeing, drew in the planks. The heavy gate was closed shortly after. It banged shut with a deep thud. Several men manhandled the heavy locking bar in place. Stiger watched for a moment as the work at sealing the gate was completed. He then made his way up to the wall, with Father Thomas and Therik following after. The men manning the wall moved aside for them to pass.

Stiger placed both hands on the top of the barricade and scanned the scene before him. Nothing outside the encampment had changed. The enemy was just beyond missile range. They milled about, either hurling insults at the legionaries or talking amongst themselves. A few spotted Therik and pointed excitedly. Stiger could sense outrage stirring amongst them.

Therik ignored his own people. He was scanning the mass of enemy as if looking for someone or something.

"Well, sir," Salt said, joining them a short time later, "we're tucked nicely inside, and the barbarians are locked outside."

"That we are," Stiger said, turning to the camp prefect. Salt had proven he was worth his weight in gold and Stiger felt lucky to have him as his second in command. He felt a mutual respect growing between them. "Good job on getting the rearguard inside without incident."

"Thank you, sir," Salt said. "For a moment there, I thought we might have to fight for it."

"It's a good thing you didn't have to," Stiger said. "It might have proved a little tricky when it came time to disengage."

"That it would, sir. I have no doubt about that."

"We will have a senior officers meeting shortly," Stiger said. "Prior to your making it back, I called for a meeting and sent messengers out to the senior centurions. They are to see their cohorts settled first. I've also given orders for the men be fed and watered."

Salt looked around. "Is that coffee I smell?"

A line had formed behind the back of a small cart a few yards behind the gate. Several men were distributing steaming mugs of black liquid poured from large jars.

"I had the cooks make some coffee as well," Stiger said as he stifled a yawn. "Figured after the night we just endured, the men could use it."

"I could use it," Salt said. "And by your looks, so can you, sir."

Stiger absently nodded as his eyes searched out the approaching dust cloud. "We have a short breather, it seems."

"Yes, sir," Salt said, following Stiger's gaze. "It certainly appears that way."

The first of the enemy's fresh formations came into view. They marched in an organized column four across. Stiger could see a team of enemy officers who had positioned themselves so that each newly arrived formation had to pass by them. With arm gestures and sometimes an escort, they guided the formations to where they were to be deployed around the encampment. Those enemy who had climbed up the bowl and come over the wall were also organized.

The sky had brightened, and the sun peeked over the mountains. The overcast clouds had given way to a clear blue sky.

"My son," Therik said, placing both large hands on the top of the barricade. Therik's voice shook with rage. "I kill him for dishonor me."

Stiger followed the king's gaze and saw an overly large orc with a personal guard had stopped to speak with the group of enemy officers. The guard formed a protective ring around Therik's son.

"And here I thought I had a complicated relationship with my father," Stiger said to himself as he glanced back over at Therik.

"Sir," a legionary said, having come up, "the officers are ready for you."

Stiger looked around and saw that just down the rampart, his senior officers had assembled. He had asked that the meeting be held near the wall and not at headquarters. He wanted to be close to the wall should something happen.

"I will be back shortly," Stiger told Father Thomas and Therik.

Father Thomas gave a nod. Therik's gaze remained fixed upon his son.

With Salt following, Stiger made his way down to the officers. They had to step around a line of men. Several lines had formed, as four cook wagons had been rolled up. Precooked rations were being quickly distributed to tired and hungry men.

As Stiger joined them, he noted the officers' haggard looks and drawn expressions. The fight through the night had taken its toll upon them. He was also pleased to see grim determination. These men were the toughest of the tough. They would be the first to set the example for their men and last to quit. These officers were not promoted to senior centurion without having seen hard action and repeatedly proving themselves over a lifetime of service.

Stiger made a show of studying the sky.

"Gentlemen," Stiger said, bringing his gaze back down to the men gathered around him in a half circle. A few glanced upward. "I thought perhaps last night when it clouded over we might have some rain. I am pleased to report Fortuna has once again come to our aid. It looks like it will be a real beauty of a day, perfect for a fight. Yes, that fateful goddess has delivered once again with no inclement weather to slow our enemy down."

That drew out a few laughs. Stiger sensed a lightening of the mood. They needed to see him in control and confident of the legion's current circumstance and position. Once a leader lost his head, everything was over. Stiger had seen it happen.

"I want to congratulate you," Stiger said, becoming serious. "You fought your men well. I could not have asked for more or been prouder. We killed many of the enemy. Unfortunately, the job's only half done. We have more to kill." Stiger paused and sucked in a breath, thinking on what he wanted to say next.

"As you are no doubt aware, we will shortly be surrounded. We can't change that, and I won't lie to you. You deserve the truth. The enemy surprised us with their crossing of the river. Worse, our turning movement is now badly out of position." Several of the officers shared concerned looks. "That said, this is where we want to be. Our allies, the dwarves, have come with an army. They are out there, along with the flanking expedition dispatched last night. I recalled them both before we gave up the defensive line."

Stiger paused to allow that to sink in before continuing.

"So, the short of it is we have a force of over twenty-five thousand, including all of our cavalry outside the walls," Stiger said. "I believe the enemy to be ignorant of their presence. Once we are attacked—and make no mistake, we will be—the enemy's attention will become wholly fixed upon us. That is when our boys will strike." Stiger noticed several nods. "Their appearance should come as a rude surprise. The hard part will be holding the walls long enough for the dwarves and our boys to get into position to strike. So, that is what we must do. We hold and bleed the enemy something good for their troubles. Are there any questions so far?"

"Yes, sir," a centurion said. "Will the dragons be coming back to help?"

Stiger knew that word had likely gotten around about what had happened to the cohorts at the crossing. The man was really asking what happened if the enemy's dragons came back.

"For those who have not heard," Stiger said, deciding complete honesty was in order on this subject, "wyrms—those are smaller dragons. Well, two of them attacked the defensive cohorts at the crossing downriver. I understand it wasn't pretty. Both cohorts, for all intents and purposes, have ceased to exist as cohesive fighting formations." That got everyone's attention, with men stiffening or straightening up. "As of now, we don't know how many survived. I suspect very few made it." The officers shifted uncomfortably at that bit of news. "I don't know where our two dragons are, but they are undoubtedly in the area. They came to stop the wyrms from attacking us and did so last night. You saw what they can do. I am certain they are out there hunting the enemy's dragons. I tell you this so that you and your men will not worry about the wyrms. We can't afford to. Focus on your job, which is holding the walls. Now, are there any other questions?"

"Sir," said Prefect Tennelus. He was in command of the auxiliary cohort of archers. "My archers are out of arrows and the slingers have expended their supply of lead shot. We're down to just plain stones now."

"Your men did good work. We shall use your archers in reserve," Stiger said. The archers were issued with short swords and shields as part of their standard issue, but also only light leather armor. They would be a last-resort reserve.

"Yes, sir."

Salt spoke up. "How would you like the legion's cohorts distributed on the walls, sir?"

Stiger gave it a moment's thought.

"Second Cohort will hold the north wall." He pointed. "Fourth the east wall. Sixth on the south wall, and Eighth will hold the west. The rest and our auxiliaries will act as our reserves. Salt will see to the dispositions of the reserves. Any questions on that?"

There were none.

"Very good," Stiger said. "Soon as we break, make sure you move your cohorts to the appropriate position. I would like a head count from every cohort."

Stiger made a point of meeting the gazes of each officer. "There are some difficult hours ahead for us. The enemy has priests with occult powers. You can't begin to imagine what they are capable of doing. We have a paladin of the High Father to help counter that threat. No matter how bad things get, no matter how strange, we must hold the walls. If at any point our defense cracks, we will all be doomed. Make sure your men understand that. From this point on, there is no escape, but of our own making. We must hold. We have relief on the way, and once they hit the enemy, we, too, will attack. When it comes, make sure you are ready for that order. I expect you to do your duty and will tolerate nothing short of that."

Stiger paused briefly.

"Get your cohorts in position. After I've seen your strength totals, we will have another meeting in about an hour to further review dispositions to see if any changes need to be made," Stiger said. "That is all. Dismissed."

The officers broke up, heading for their respective cohorts.

"That was a little cheery," Salt said.

"It was necessary," Stiger said. "Salt, when the time comes and the enemy attacks, I will handle the east and south wall. You take the north and west."

"Got it," Salt said.

"Good," Stiger said and yawned. "After you position the reserves, how about we get some coffee and then take a stroll around the encampment? I think it would be good to be seen by the men."

"Coffee sounds lovely, sir. A morning walk would be nice, too," Salt said enthusiastically. "Very kind of you to ask."

Chapter Thirty-Seven

The enemy was working their way through a series of what seemed to be organized chants. Stiger could not understand what was said, as it was in orcish, but he had to admit the chanting was unnerving. It reminded him of the massed chants the crowds made during gladiatorial games.

The sun was up, high overhead. It was just past noon and the air was becoming unseasonably warm. A gentle breeze occasionally blew down from the mountains and helped to relieve the growing heat of the day. Wearing armor and standing under the sun, men began to cook as they waited for the enemy to begin their assault.

Stiger stood with Therik on the corner of the south wall. He felt uncomfortably hot in his armor. His helmet had become loose. He adjusted it, untying the straps and then refastening it. Sweat trickled down his forehead and into his eyes. He wiped it away.

He looked out at the scene before him. It was not one to build confidence. The encampment was thoroughly surrounded. From his current position, Stiger could see a good portion of the enemy host. Hundreds of enemy companies were to his front, formed up and chanting away. Stiger had started counting standards but had given up. There were simply too many. A short while before, he had made a point to walk completely around the walls of the encampment to see the enemy's host in its entirety. The size of the enemy's army was overwhelming.

"So, this is the Horde," Stiger said.

"It is," Therik said.

The working estimate of the enemy's strength had been woefully inadequate. He figured there were at least seventy thousand fresh warriors now deployed around the encampment. These had not yet seen action. More concerning to Stiger were the enemy formations that were still arriving and marching onto the field. Stiger had spotted half a dozen orc priests moving amongst them, busy conducting what appeared to be religious services and offering blessings.

For several hours, enemy axe parties had been heard in the forest. The fire had mostly gone out. Thin wisps of smoke rose from amongst the trees, a reminder of the battle fought between dragons. The axe parties had since fallen silent.

The enemy had been busy making battering rams for the gates and additional ladders to scale the walls. The rams had been placed out in the open for the defenders to see. Large bundles of sticks had also been stacked to the front of the formations. These, Stiger understood, would be used to fill the trenches so the enemy could cross to assault the walls. Oddly, there were battering rams positioned at only three of the encampment's four gates. There was no ram at the encampment's main gate. Stiger wondered why. Surely, with the enemy's numbers, they would assault all of the walls and gates simultaneously?

Stiger placed a hand upon the barricade. The wood was rough and had not been smoothed. He picked free a large splinter and then tossed it over the edge. He was still plagued with doubts about his decision to hole up in the encampment. Having seen the true size of the enemy's host, those concerns had only become magnified. Even having a force outside the walls numbering around twenty-five thousand, Stiger was beginning to doubt whether Brogan and Sabinus could successfully surprise and roll up the enemy. The move into the encampment was looking more like a last stand.

Should he have withdrawn to the mountain?

No, came the reply from Rarokan. *You belong here. The minion is here. I sense it close by, waiting for its opportunity to strike.*

Stiger stilled, as a sudden fear came over him.

Are you going to try to take control again? Stiger asked. *During the fight that's coming?*

Perhaps, one day, Rarokan said, *but not now. Too much is at stake. When the time comes I shall lend you my* will. *I shall seek to take nothing more in return.*

Stiger sensed Rarokan was being truthful. Still, he was not sure he could trust the wizard. But he knew he had no choice.

You don't have a choice, Rarokan said, *for our enemy is getting ready to strike.*

Stiger thought on that for a minute. He and Rarokan needed an understanding if they were going to work together, for that was what Stiger desired. He needed the wizard's help if he was to succeed.

You will take no more souls, Stiger said. *You can keep the life force spark, but not the soul spark. I will not be a party to that.*

I do what I wish, Rarokan said, sounding amused. *I will take what I want.*

You will not, Stiger said.

What can you do to stop me?

Stiger thought about that for a long moment and then almost grinned.

How deep do you think the water is at Bowman's pond? Stiger asked Rarokan.

There was no reply.

I went swimming there once. You may recall, for I brought you with me.

Again, there was no reply.

Really, I trekked up there to bathe after working at repairing the fencing of the pasture. It was an exceptionally hot day. Sarai thought I smelled just plain awful. She wouldn't let me in the house. She gave me some soap and sent me off.

Stiger paused, thinking back on Sarai and that day. That night when he had returned was the first time they had made love. He pushed the memory aside and continued with Rarokan.

It was quite refreshing, but I was surprised that as I got toward the middle of the pond, the water became deep. My feet couldn't even touch the bottom. So, I think it's really simple. Unless you agree to my terms, after this fight I will take a hike back up to the pond and drop you in. With any luck you might never be found.

You wouldn't dare. You need me.

Stiger thought he sensed doubt.

Do I? Stiger asked. *I am the High Father's champion. Do I really need you after we get rid of the minion?*

Rarokan did not immediately reply.

There was a rippling of the enemy's ranks to the front of the fort. A priest holding a wooden staff stepped through the press. With him was a tall, powerful orc Stiger recognized as Therik's son.

The king sucked in his breath.

Stiger studied Therik's son. He was tall, and very muscular. He had donned a purple cloak that hung over the back of his plate armor. He moved with a natural confidence and authority, much like Therik had when Stiger had first met him at Garand Kos.

"What's your son's name?" Stiger asked.

"Hommand," Therik said. "That is Cetrite, High Priest of Castor. He was a nobody before the minion arrived."

Stiger shifted his gaze to the High Priest. Cetrite wore a long black robe that was covered in arcane symbols. The priest's robe was hooded and he had drawn it up so that his heavily tattooed face could barely be seen. A powerful hand gripped the wooden staff.

Hommand spotted his father standing amongst the legionaries on the wall and simply pointed at him. Therik did not move.

Cetrite said something to Hommand. The two of them were standing before a formation of five hundred orcs, who were drawn up in neat, orderly ranks. They both turned to look at the formation. Hommand said something to the warriors.

The formation gave a cheer filled with enthusiasm. The cheering was picked up by the rest of the enemy host. It seemed to last for a long time. Therik's son, clearly enjoying the moment, held up his arms. The enemy cheered louder.

"Too bad he's not in spear range," Stiger said.

"He is for me." Therik grabbed a javelin from the nearest legionary. He drew back, aimed, and threw in one smooth motion, grunting as he did it. The javelin flew up into the air and slammed down bare inches from its intended target.

"That was a good toss," the legionary said to Therik.

"Not good enough," Therik replied.

Hommand turned. With the cheering, he had not heard the javelin land. He pulled the javelin out of the ground, made a show of examining it. He felt the weapon's point as he gazed back on his father. He broke the weapon upon a knee and then turned his back to Therik. All the while, the mad cheering continued, though boos could be heard, with many of the enemy to their front pointing at Therik in apparent outrage.

Answer me now, Stiger said, returning to his conversation with Rarokan. *Agree, or you can go for a swim when this is all done.*

I agree.

Stiger thought the answer came a little too quickly.

"Give me another." Therik held out his hand for a javelin from the next legionary. "I spit him good this time."

A screech from above dragged their attention upward. A dark blue-colored dragon, much smaller than the noctalum, was descending with frightening speed, talons extended. With the clear sky, where it had come from Stiger did not know. It was a shock. The dragon struck the gate with a tremendous crash. The ground shook with the violence of the crushing impact. Men were knocked from their feet. Stiger went to his knees, catching himself with a hand on the barricade. He felt the heat before he saw it. The dragon shot a blast of fire along the wall, burning men just feet from him.

The dragon roared. Stiger felt a terrible fear steal over him. He huddled against the barricade, crying out in panic. His eyes were on the fearsome creature as it began moving into the fort, climbing over the ruins of the gate.

Draw me, Rarokan said. *It is using its* will *to frighten you.*

Stiger wanted nothing more than to run. The fear increased. He went to all fours and hid his face in the dirt of the rampart.

Draw me, Rarokan insisted.

Stiger could not move.

Touch the hilt.

"No," Stiger cried.

Do it now! Rarokan shouted. *It will push back the fear.*

Stiger's muscles at first didn't want to cooperate, but his mind desperately wanted the fear to end. He reached for the sword. It was a struggle just to move his arm and overcome the paralyzing fear. Finally, his finger brushed the hilt. A surge of energy flowed into Stiger and, with it, the fear retreated. It was still there, but was not as strong as before, no longer debilitating.

Pulling himself to his feet, Stiger was at a loss for what to do. Men just feet away were engulfed in flame, writhing away on the ground. Those who were not touched by the fire were overwhelmed by fear. So too was Therik, who was curled up and hiding behind a discarded shield.

The wall on the other side of the shattered gate exploded in fire as the dragon let loose another spray of death. Men burned, screaming in agony before their lungs burned too. Then they writhed in unspeakable torment before expiring.

Stiger looked on the dragon. It was huge. Not quite as large as the noctalum, but it was still damn big. There was something magnificent about the fearsome creature. The dragon was a dark blue color, almost to the point of black. Its eyes were a reddish color.

The wyrm was moving through the gate and into the encampment. The dragon reared up and Stiger got a good look at its back, which was covered by thick, armored scales. The dragon blew out a jet of fire into the encampment. The fire sprayed outward at least sixty feet, setting men and tents on fire. It burned those crippled by fear and helpless.

The sight of good men being killed in such a way infuriated Stiger. But he still did not know what to do.

Attack it, Rarokan yelled in his mind. *You must hurry.*

Stiger drew the sword; the familiar tingle was instead a surge of incredible power that made his hair stand on end. The tiredness from lack of sleep vanished in an instant.

Stiger felt time slow to a crawl, even as the sword exploded into blue flame that licked at the air.

How do I kill it? Stiger asked. The dragon seemed to be moving in slow motion. Fighting it seemed an impossible task.

Stiger saw Dog confronting the dragon, teeth bared. The dragon hesitated and actually took a step back. Then it roared at Dog.

Stick it now, Rarokan shouted at him. *Quickly, before it attacks the guardian or becomes aware of us.*

Stiger understood. Shoving cowering men aside, he ran along the wall toward the destroyed gate and dragon. He ran through dragon fire, which had mostly burned itself out. He felt the intense heat on the air and through his boots. The dirt had been turned to a glassy crust and crunched with every footfall.

The dragon had stopped moving deeper into the encampment, its attention now on Dog. It was so large that, though the head and neck were inside of the encampment, its back legs and tail were still at the gate. Stiger ran for all he was worth. He came to the edge, where the shattered gate had been, and launched himself into the air, leaping for the dragon's back. As Stiger was in midair, the dragon blew out another gout of flame, this blast aiming for Dog.

The dragon never saw Stiger coming. He landed hard on its back. The wind was driven from his lungs as he drove the sword down deeply into the blue armored hide.

The sword slid in with only a little resistance. The force of the landing helped to drive the sword deeper. The hilt of the sword exploded with heat as the dragon screamed in rage, then what sounded like sudden fear and panic.

Stiger tried to let go as pain from the sword surged up into his body, but he couldn't. He could feel Rarokan eagerly draining the life force out of the fearsome creature, even as it struggled to fight back against the wizard. The dragon tried to shake him off, bucking like a horse. Its exertions carried it farther into the fort. Stiger held onto the sword as the dragon sought to dislodge him. The sword was in deep, and even if Stiger had wanted to, he could not have let go. His hand seemed cemented to the sword.

The dragon snaked its head around, jaws opening for him. Stiger saw rows of serrated teeth that were nearly as tall as a man come nearer.

Stiger screamed as the sword's power slammed into him. The surge of energy increased to a tidal wave as Rarokan took the last of the creature's life force in one great rush. Stiger's vision went white. Every inch of his skin seemed to be on fire. Had the dragon breathed fire on him? The dragon screamed again, somewhat feeble this time. Then the wyrm's legs gave out, and everything went still.

Stiger blinked, his vision returning as the rush of power faded. The dragon was dead. He struggled to get air back into his lungs. Everything around him had gone completely still. He was finally able to suck in a breath.

Stiger still gripped the sword, which was embedded almost up to the hilt into the dragon's back. It throbbed with power in his hand.

He glanced down at the wyrm. It was still and lifeless, covered in armored, fishlike scales that reflected the sunlight slightly with a metallic blue tinge. The dragon's wings were drawn up to its body. The neck snaked outward in the dirt. The red eyes were closed, never to open again, and a long, thick, pink tongue hung limply out of a mouth filled with wicked-looking teeth. Oddly, Stiger felt regret at killing such a magnificent beast. He pulled the sword free and stood tall on the fearsome creature's back. The weapon burned with an intense blue flame. Stiger breathed in, feeling more alive than he had ever felt.

Yes, Rarokan said. *Finally…I have regained a measure of myself and my* will… *You are much* more *than you were, more than you were ever meant to be.*

You took its soul, Stiger accused, becoming angry.

No, Rarokan said, and Stiger sensed truth in the words. *I wanted to. I only took its life force, which is more than enough. You now have the power to face Castor's servant and withstand its considerable* will.

Satisfied, Stiger climbed down off the dragon and glanced around. Everything had gone silent. He could not see Dog. He desperately hoped the animal was okay. All eyes in the encampment were upon him. It was clear they were stunned by what they had just witnessed. Stiger felt dazed himself. He turned around in a complete circle and came to a stop. The dragon's long tail stretched out through the ruined gate.

He saw Cetrite had moved up near the encampment's entrance, just fifteen yards from Stiger. Hommand was with him. Stiger's gaze met Cetrite's. The orc priest stretched forth his staff. Black lightning arced out toward him. Without even thinking about it, Stiger held up the sword. The black, spidery lightning struck it with a flash, crackling and snapping with the impact upon the glowing blade. Then it was gone.

The priest's eyes narrowed and it took a step back, pulling Hommand with it.

The legionaries gave a hearty cheer.

"Delvaris…Delvaris…Delvaris," they shouted.

The priest said something to Therik's son, who turned, drew his sword, and shouted to an orc just behind him with a horn. The horn call was a long, steady blast. There was a moment of silence. The enemy host gave a great shout and surged toward the trench that surrounded the encampment. Hundreds of the enemy carrying the bundles of sticks moved forward and tossed them into the trench.

The assault was on.

Stiger's eyes swung around the gap in their wall where the gate had been. The wall to his right still burned with dragon fire. The bodies of burned legionaries littered the wall and the slope leading down into the encampment. It was a horrific sight. He put it from his mind.

"I need a line!" Stiger shouted at a group of legionaries from the reserve who were milling about just yards away. He pointed with his sword toward the gap. "I need a line, now!"

Stiger glanced around. Orcs were throwing bundles of sticks into the trench every few feet to form bridges from where the enemy would make their assault on the walls. They had only moments to get a shield wall set or all would be lost.

"You heard the legate," a centurion amongst them roared, shoving and pushing men forward toward the gate. "Get moving."

The first orc made it through the trench, pulling himself up and out. Stiger strode forward, passing over the ruined gate to confront it. The creature spotted Stiger, bared its tusks, and swung a hammer at him. Stiger ducked and stuck it with his sword, which punched right through the chest armor like a heated knife in butter. There was a sizzling sound. The hilt of the sword, already hot in Stiger's hand, grew warmer. The orc's eyes glazed over and it fell back, dead. Another orc climbed over the bundles of sticks that had been tossed in and leveled a sword at Stiger, but it did not move forward to strike. Others orcs began climbing up out of the trench or over the bundles of sticks.

Stiger moved forward to attack before they could come together against him. The first orc he attacked seemed slow as it moved its sword to block his strike. Stiger knocked the creature's blade aside and jabbed it through the neck. The creature fell back into the trench, knocking another who was climbing out backward and down onto the sharpened stakes below. Stiger jabbed another right behind it as it too was climbing out. All it took was a nick on the arm and death was immediate. As Stiger fought onward, the sword's flame grew in brilliance with every life taken.

More orcs climbed out of the trench, and soon their numbers became too great. Stiger rapidly found himself giving up space so they couldn't surround him. The fighting was becoming hotter by the moment. He struggled to kill and keep the enemy away from him. A sword snuck through his defense and smacked down painfully on his shoulder armor, almost knocking him off balance.

Staggering, Stiger retreated a couple steps as a hammer swung out into the space where he had been. Then, Dog was there, jumping on the back of a warrior who had thought to strike from the side. The animal ripped and tore at the orc's shoulder, taking him to the ground. Therik was beside him, roaring and hurling oaths in his own language as he fought using the sword Stiger had given him and wearing only a simple tunic.

The king slashed open the neck of his opponent. Therik pounded his chest and let out an animal-like roar before engaging another of the enemy. Out of the corner of his eye, Stiger saw Father Thomas wading into the fight, his beautifully crafted saber flashing brilliantly in the sunlight. Though old beyond his years, the paladin moved with the grace of a dancer.

Stiger lost track of time. He had no idea how long they fought, taking orc after orc. His focus became single-minded. The rage the sword had fed him was absent, and in its place there was a terrible determination to kill all before him. He had to buy enough time so that a defensive line could be formed before the gate.

Something hit Stiger hard on the back and knocked him to the ground. He lost his grip on the sword and it went flying. Dazed, Stiger rolled onto his side. As he did, a large foot slammed down into the ground where his head had been a moment before. Stiger looked up at a massive armored thing standing above him with a large spear in hand. The thing struck down for his chest. He rolled again. The iron spearhead hammered into the ground next to him.

Stiger pulled his dagger and scrambled backwards. He was able to get back to his feet and came to a crouch.

The creature looked much like an orc but was far larger, at least twelve feet tall and without the tusks. Its skin was green, but unlike an orc, it was very hairy, almost as if it were covered in fur. It was also very muscular and powerfully strong. He found himself facing a mountain troll.

Its eyes fell on the dagger in Stiger's hand. A leering smile broke out on its ugly face. The creature showed him yellowed and rotten teeth as it lumbered forward.

Stiger looked around for his sword and saw it behind the troll. There were no other weapons within easy reach.

"Okay, big boy," Stiger said to it, studying the troll carefully so that he could better understand his opponent's weaknesses. The creature wore plate armor over a thick brown woolen tunic. The armor covered both its chest and back. It also wore greaves, which protected its shins, and vambraces for the forearms. "Shall we dance?" Stiger asked it, flashing the troll a smile of his own.

The troll seemed to get his meaning, for it charged, lumbering forward. Stiger stood his ground as it came nearer. He could feel the heavy footfalls of the troll through his boots. The troll swung the end of the spear like a club, aiming for his chest. Stiger ducked and dove to his left, rolling in the dirt as the spear swung harmlessly overhead and coming right back up to his feet. It was a neat trick Sergeant Tiro had taught him years ago.

The troll's momentum had carried it past Stiger. Before it could turn around, he lunged after it, driving the dagger into the back of the troll's unprotected knee. The troll screamed as the blade went in and staggered a step. It whipped the spear back and around to get at Stiger.

Stiger gave the dagger a vicious twist and felt the blade cut through tendon before dodging backward and away. The troll, limping badly, turned around. There was murder in its eyes. Stiger took a couple of steps backward then, with a flick of his wrist, reversed his hold from the hilt to the blade. Before the troll understood what he was doing, Stiger threw the dagger with a smooth, practiced motion. The dagger landed spot on with a sickening, meaty thwack and imbedded itself dead center in the troll's throat.

Surprise mixed with pain registered in the troll's beady eyes. It dropped the spear and reached up, feeling the hilt of the dagger. It drew the blade out and then looked at it as green blood flowed freely from the wound and down its chest armor. The troll opened its mouth and a thick stream of blood flowed out. It began to choke. The troll released the knife, tottered a moment, and then fell forward to the ground. Its legs twitched.

The fighting was still going on around Stiger. He reached down and picked up his sword. As he did, an orc rushed him. Stiger brought his sword up and blocked the strike, turning it aside. The tip of the orc's blade scraped across Stiger's chest armor. Then they crashed together and went down in a tumble as the orc's momentum carried it forward.

Stiger almost lost his grip on his sword as the orc landed atop his sword arm. With his free hand, he punched the creature in the face again and again until it moved to get away from him and the repeated blows. Suddenly free, Stiger got back to his feet and made to lunge for the orc, who had pulled himself up to his knees. Someone grabbed him from behind, roughly dragging him backward. Stiger saw the green arms of an orc wrapped tightly about his chest and fought back, trying to swing his sword at the creature.

"Stop," the orc shouted in his ear. "It is Therik."

Stiger relaxed and allowed Therik to continue to drag him back and through a line of legionaries who had placed their shields to the front. Therik released him and stepped back. Stiger blinked, regaining his senses. The intense single-minded focus was gone and with it came a severe tiredness that threatened to buckle his knees. The sword had dimmed, too. Stiger saw Dog still out beyond the line. The animal knocked an orc down and neatly ripped open its throat.

"Dog," Stiger shouted. "Come."

Dog turned and immediately bounded back toward him. The legionaries of the line opened their shields so the animal could get through. Stiger, Therik, and Dog moved back through four ranks and found themselves standing before the body of the dragon. The tail trailed backward through the line and beyond the gate. Father Thomas joined them a moment later.

"You crazy." Therik grinned and pointed his sword at the dragon's body. The king was breathing heavily from the exertion of the fight. So too were they all. "Taking on wyrm by self...I never have thought it. Then you take troll." He pounded Stiger on the back. "I like you."

Stiger glanced around as the sound of the assault on the fortified encampment slammed home. He could see the tops of scaling ladders land. There had been no opportunity to remove the dead on the south wall. Those sent to secure the south wall fought amid the burned and charred remains of those who had died to dragon fire.

Stiger turned his gaze around, looking over all four walls. The scene was the same. Legionaries fought using their shields and the barricade for cover. They jabbed and poked with their swords at orcs who made it to the top of the barricade, even as they struggled to throw the ladders back off the wall.

A cry from a dragon caught Stiger's attention. His heart dropped at the sound of it. The fighting everywhere paused. All eyes turned skyward.

A wyrm dove toward the ground less than a quarter mile away, its wings tucked back and flying at great speed. It was heading south and away from the battle. Close behind it were the two noctalum. They were gaining on the smaller dragon. It was a very satisfying sight. Stiger hoped they caught the dread creature, for he did not want to face any more wyrms.

Stiger made for the south wall and climbed to the top, near the ruined gate. He had to step over several bodies. The stench of burned flesh was nauseating. At the top, he found there were no scaling ladders within ten yards. He glanced over the side, looking down at the enemy. They had bridged the trench in several places and thrown up ladders against the walls. Additional ladders were being worked across the trench. Stiger studied the walls for a long moment. The legion was holding.

A solid-sounding *thud* from one of the other gates told Stiger the enemy had begun to use their battering rams. His gaze went back to the breached gate. An entire cohort stood firm before it, shields to the front. The enemy pressed against the shield wall, beating away with swords and hammers. Short swords regularly darted out at them, taking a terrible toll.

Stiger's gaze went to the enemy beyond the walls. Most were still in the formations they had arrived in. They stood in well-organized ranks and watched the assault unfolding before them. With the breach in the walls and the enemy's great numbers, Stiger understood the defense of the encampment was ultimately doomed. The question was, how long could they hold? And how long 'til Brogan and Sabinus arrived? If they arrived.

Stiger heard something. It was a low humming sound that grew to a loud crescendo, almost drowning out the sound of the fight. He had never heard anything like it. He moved along the wall behind the defenders toward where he thought the sound was coming from. Therik followed and together they worked their way farther along the wall, just behind those fighting to keep the enemy from climbing over.

Stiger came to the corner of the wall and looked over toward the forest. The sound of the humming had intensified. It seemed to vibrate the air and made the hair on his arms stand on end.

What magic was this?

"What's making that racket?" Salt asked. The camp prefect had come to investigate himself.

"I don't know." Stiger studied the enemy along the wall at this spot. A hundred yards of open ground lay between them and the edge of the forest. Stumps from hundreds of trees bore mute evidence of the forest being cut back by the legion. These unfortunate trees had been used in the construction of the encampment. Entire formations with hundreds of orcs were waiting their turn for the ladders amongst the sea of stumps.

Stiger's eyes fell upon the nearest. The orcs seemed unsettled by the humming and it showed with their assault along this wall. The intensity of the attack died off. The formation incredibly disintegrated before his eyes as the orcs broke ranks, at least five hundred of them. They began moving hurriedly away from the forest side of the encampment.

"Gnomes," Therik breathed.

Stiger glanced over at Therik and saw his eyes wide with the horror.

The humming sound increased.

Stiger saw movement amongst the trees. The first few gnomes emerged. Hundreds came into view and then thousands. Dozens of gnomes rode on the backs of large dogs and moved in concert, much like a cavalry squadron. Stiger realized after a moment that they weren't riding dogs, but wolves. They carried spears the size of a javelin.

The gnomes continued to hum as even more of their kind stepped from the cover of the trees. One gnome walked forward and out into the field of tree stumps that had moments before been occupied by orcs. The gnome climbed up on an unusually large stump. He wore a chest plate that was painted black.

Now that Stiger noticed it, he saw many of the gnomes wore similar armor. The gnomes had painted their armor in many different colors. Blue, green, yellow, red, and orange were just some of the colors. The army of thousands of diminutive figures in their brightly painted armor under a bright sun was a rainbow of color. But there was only one in black. Stiger suspected it was Cragg.

The gnome stood for several heartbeats and looked upon the orcs streaming away from his army. He slowly pulled forth his sword, looked back upon his people, and then pointed it at the enemy. The gnomes exploded forward, rushing toward the retreating orcs.

Stiger shook his head. He had expected Brogan and Sabinus to relieve them, but certainly not the gnomes. There were tens of thousands of the tiny creatures. They swarmed out of the forest, charging forward and after the retreating orcs. Upon reaching the enemy, the gnomes tore into the orcs. Entire formations that had not yet broken now fell apart. Others, showing more discipline, turned to face the unexpected assault and attempted to withstand the tide of diminutive rage.

Still the gnomes came, emerging from the forest in a great wave. They screamed their high-pitched voices hoarse, while at the same time many hummed their unsettling war cry. Stiger found it hard to look away. The violence of the assault was incredible—astonishing, even.

A series of horns rang out from the east. Stiger turned his head to look. He had to move back to the south wall to see what was going on. When he got there, he saw Brogan's army lined up in battle formation, company upon company stacked up in neat, organized blocks. Standards fluttered in the early afternoon air as the dwarven army advanced.

Stiger could just hear their heavy footfalls as thousands of dwarves marched forward in perfect step. With them, Stiger saw the standard of First Century. To the side of Brogan's battle line, Hux's cavalry maneuvered. Their wicked-looking lance tips glittered in the sunlight. The cavalry had formed a double line and were wheeling about for a charge at the enemy's flank.

The relief Stiger felt was intense. He closed his eyes and offered up a prayer of thanks to the High Father for their deliverance, for the enemy was now caught between two armies, one gnomish and the other dwarven and human.

There was a deep *boom*, as if a lightning bolt had struck close by. Stiger's eyes snapped open. Another *boom* followed, more ominous than the first.

The minion, along with Cetrite the priest and Hommand, stood with half a dozen orc priests just before the gate. The defensive line blocking the way into the encampment had fallen back, leaving several dead in their wake.

Stiger had difficulty focusing on the minion's features, as it was terribly twisted. But it was more than just that. What he was sure had once been human was now bent and misshapen, warped by an evil that was almost beyond comprehension. A shadow surrounded it, as if even the sunlight shied away.

The minion wore a black robe, which was in tatters. The skin that was visible had turned a purplish black and appeared to be rotting off the bone. With each shambling and shuffling step it took, the ground smoked.

This was his enemy.

The minion, facing complete defeat, had become desperate enough to gamble all on a final battle. Stiger knew they had both gambled all. He understood the time had come for the confrontation he had been dreading—Delvaris's fate.

"This is my time," Stiger said to himself, vividly recalling what Thoggle had once told him.

Up until this moment, he had thought it Delvaris's time, but that wasn't right. He was the High Father's champion, and this moment was why he was here. He had been so concerned about the future, he'd lost sight of the here and now. The time period did not matter one bit. All that did was the task ahead of him.

"Where are you going?" Therik asked.

"Sir?" Salt said, concern plain in his voice.

Stiger ignored them. He made his way rapidly down from the wall. As the minion advanced into the fort, the legionaries backed away from the hideous monstrosity. Cetrite sent forth a bolt of black lightning, which crackled with energy and struck several legionaries, felling them instantly.

Stiger pushed his way through the men.

"Sir," Centurion Nantus called. "You can't go out there!"

Stiger ignored him too. He pushed past more men and through the defensive shields, until he stood between the men and minion. His rage had returned at the sight of Castor's servant and the orc priest casually killing his legionaries. His hand rested on the hilt of his sword. Rarokan fed him anger, rage, and hate. With it all flowed power. It coursed through his veins. He willingly accepted and embraced all of it.

Stiger drew Rarokan. The blade flamed with brilliance. Dog padded up to his side, head lowered, teeth bared and growling deeply. Father Thomas made his way through the line as well. Therik joined him a moment later. Together they faced Therik's son, Castor's monstrosity, and the priests.

A bubble formed around the two sides. The legionaries behind had drawn back. Those enemy just outside the gate who could see what was happening had also stopped to watch.

"It all comes down to this," the minion hissed at Stiger in common, black spittle dripping to the ground, where it smoked in the dirt. Despite the warmth of the day, Stiger felt a chill emanating from the creature. Beyond them he could hear the sounds of fighting. The dwarven horns sounded again.

"I'm surprised you finally found the courage to face me," Stiger said. "You've lost here. Your army is crumbling around you. It's over."

"You might think that," the minion said. "We both know you've seen what is to come."

"I have," Stiger said and then gave a slow smile. "We also both know time can be altered. Things can be changed. The outcome you seek is far from certain."

Stiger thought he detected a hint of uncertainty in the creature's eyes.

"All I need to do is kill you and my lord wins," the minion hissed.

"Sometimes it's easier to say you're gonna do something than actually do it," Stiger said.

The minion held out a horribly twisted and disfigured hand. A black obsidian sword materialized from thin air into the hand. The blade appeared to absorb light. Black fire licked along the edges of the midnight sword.

"You should never have followed me back," the minion said. "You should have remained in your own time, on your own plane."

"That is where you are wrong," Stiger said to it. So deformed was the creature's face, he was having difficulty keeping his focus on its features. In fact, he wanted nothing more than to look away. He resisted the urge. "This is my time, not yours."

The minion, though a horribly twisted and unnatural thing, moved with lightning quickness. It rushed at Stiger, lunging forward. Stiger brought his sword up just in time and blocked the strike. The two swords rang with the impact, blue and black sparks cascading through the air.

The minion took a shuffling step back.

Crack!

Thoggle was suddenly there, several feet to Stiger's left. The crystal at the top of the wizard's staff flared with light. He held it forth and Stiger felt a surge of energy from Thoggle.

The earth lifted up in big, solid chunks behind Cetrite. The wizard pointed his staff at one of the orc priests and the chunks flew right at the orc. Having no chance to react, the priest was hammered down into the ground with a sickening crunch.

There was a moment of stunned silence. Then Cetrite struck at Father Thomas. The paladin responded. Black lightning met white in a fearsome exchange that caused the air to hiss and pop with intensity. Two of the orc priests threw out their hands and green bolts of light shot at Thoggle. The wizard raised his staff in warding and the bolts were deflected away, one shooting past Stiger. He heard it impact the men behind him with a *pop* that was followed by a scream of pure agony.

Out of the corner of his eye, Stiger had a flash of Therik advancing. Sword drawn, he went for his son. Dog exploded forward, jumping on a priest, taking him to the ground.

Then the minion attacked. Stiger barely managed to block the next blow. He lost track of what was happening around him, focusing solely upon the creature of evil.

Rarokan fed him energy. He felt powerfully strong and impossibly quick. Stiger punched his sword forward. The strike was fast. The minion barely managed to avoid the blade. It skittered back a couple of steps, then lunged, striking out toward Stiger's midriff. He swung downward to block. Their two swords connected in a shower of sparks. Rarokan's energy waned a little. Grunting, Stiger drove the tip of the minion's blade into the ground, where it hissed and smoked. The minion swung a fist toward Stiger's face. He ducked, taking a step backwards and out of the way.

They stared at each other a heartbeat. Then the minion thrust a hand out and tendrils of inky blackness shot forth through the air toward him. Stiger felt a massive upwelling of power from Rarokan as the wizard attacked. The sword flashed so brightly, Stiger was forced to look away. A concussive blast followed as the minion's magic met Rarokan's.

Stiger looked back as soon as the flash faded. The minion had retreated several steps. There was a smoking gash in its chest, at least three inches long. No blood issued forth, as the skin appeared cauterized. The creature's eyes narrowed as its free hand gingerly touched the wound.

"So be it, champion," the minion hissed, malice and hate dripping over every word. "Sword against sword it is."

It shuffled forward.

Crouched and ready, Stiger advanced to meet it. The minion attacked again. They traded a series of strikes and counterstrikes, the minion moving faster and faster with every lunge and jab. Stiger began having difficulty blocking the blows. He found himself on the defensive and giving ground. There was no chance to consider attacking. Sweat beaded his brow as he worked desperately to keep the minion's blade out of reach, which kept coming closer and closer with every attack and lunge.

Stiger stumbled on a body of a legionary, and as he did, his defense faltered. One strike slipped through, and with it he felt an intense pain in his side. The tip of the midnight sword cut right through his armor like it was parchment.

Stiger cried out as the minion took a step backward. What remained of its tortured face split into a wide, hideous grin.

No, no, noooo! Rarokan screamed in what sounded like mounting panic. Stiger felt a resurgence of strength from the wizard, even as he staggered back a step, hand going for his side where the midnight blade had pierced his armor. Stiger blinked rapidly, his vision swimming.

Rarokan fed him even more strength. Stiger sensed desperation from the wizard and understood from it the wound was mortal. He could feel Castor sucking his life force from him with each passing breath.

Stiger's blood flowed thickly through his fingers and splashed out onto the ground. Each breath was an agony. The blue fire that had licked from his sword had gone out. It no longer even glowed. The minion, grinning at him, took a shuffling step backward.

"I win," the minion hissed. "My master wins."

The rage within Stiger swelled.

"Rarokan," Stiger said aloud, struggling to get the words out despite the terrible pain he felt. Each breath was becoming a painful struggle. "I give you permission to take not only this creature's life force, but its soul as well."

Agreed.

The twisted smile slipped from the minion's face. Stiger got the impression the minion had heard Rarokan speak. He brought his sword up, which exploded once again into a brilliant blue flame. At the same time, Stiger felt his strength waning. It was becoming difficult to hold his sword up. He needed to end this now.

The minion, with grim determination, began to close the distance between them once again, clearly intent upon finishing him.

Stiger advanced to meet it, but his strength gave out in a rush and he collapsed to a knee. Stiger struck the tip of his sword into the ground just to keep himself upright. The minion laughed, a terrible hacking sound, as it raised its sword for the final blow. The creature held the sword high but hesitated, savoring the moment of its triumph over the High Father's champion.

Coming out of nowhere, Dog jumped on the minion's back, snarling madly. The animal ripped and tore at the minion with its teeth. Knocked off balance by the large animal, the minion staggered several steps. It hissed angrily as Dog continued to bite and tear.

The creature reached an arm back and bent it around at an unnatural angle. It gripped Dog's neck. There was a flash of green light and Dog was tossed several feet before crashing to the ground and tumbling limply until stopped by the dragon's tail.

Dog did not get up.

Stiger's heart almost stopped at the sight of Dog lying there lifeless. He felt a resurgence of rage and hate as his gaze returned to the minion. This creature was responsible for the death of Sarai, and now his dog. It had caused untold suffering in Vrell. There would be more suffering and death were it not stopped, here and now.

With the last vestiges of his strength, Stiger stood. The minion was distracted, and still looking at Dog. Black blood ran down its back and to the dirt, where it steamed and hissed. Stiger got the feeling Dog had hurt it badly.

Never one to pass up an opportunity, Stiger attacked. He swung his sword, hammering the minion's midnight blade away in a powerful blow. Rarokan flashed brilliantly and the minion's sword shattered into smoke. The creature looked around, shock and astonishment in its eyes. Screaming his rage born out of loss and suffering, Stiger brought his sword up and jabbed, the blade sliding into the minion's twisted breast.

Their eyes met and Stiger saw fear reflected back at him. It lasted but a moment. The minion opened its mouth and what came out sounded like thousands of tormented souls crying out from the great beyond. The cold sensation intensified. The minion took a shuffling step backward and off the sword. Then, with a thunderclap, it collapsed in on itself. It was gone, as if it had never existed. Rarokan had taken both its life force and soul.

He had won.

Stiger swayed slightly, feeling the rage and anger leaving him in a rush. He looked around and saw the paladin's sword neatly cleave Cetrite's head from its shoulders. Dog lay crumpled upon the ground a few feet away, still and unmoving.

Therik battled his son, trading blow for blow. Hommand was giving ground and looking desperate.

Thoggle gripped the last of the priests by the front of the tunic, holding the orc up in the air, its feet kicking desperately. White fire coursed up the wizard's arm and into the priest. The priest's eyes emitted a matching white light, as did its mouth, which opened in a silent scream. Stiger even thought he saw light come out from the priest's ears. The orc went limp, and as it did, the light died. Thoggle tossed the priest aside as a child might discard an old doll.

Stiger fell to his knees. He shivered, feeling the warmth begin to leave his body.

He had lost. The High Father had lost.

On his knees, Stiger blinked as his vision swam badly. It cleared in time for him to witness Therik backhand his son with a powerful blow. Hommand dropped his guard, and as he did, Therik drove his sword deep into his son's stomach. The orc king reached forward with his free hand and pulled Hommand closer, so that their faces almost touched. Therik spat in Hommand's face and then pushed him roughly off his sword, allowing the usurper to fall to the ground.

Therik stood over his son, who raised a pleading hand to his father. A look of disgust twisted Therik's face. He drove his sword downward, viciously punching it through the chest armor and into the heart. Hommand stiffened. The king released the hilt and stepped back, a look of satisfaction on his face as Hommand's eyes rolled back and he went still.

The minion had been defeated, and so had Castor's high priest. As his strength continued to drain from his body, Stiger felt a great chill. He understood he had failed, but at the same time he was looking forward to joining Sarai in the great beyond. He welcomed it.

No! Rarokan screamed in his mind. *Fight Castor's touch! Fight it!*

Stiger could not see how he could win this final battle. He felt a last reserve of energy flood into him from Rarokan. It wasn't enough. He collapsed to the ground, looking up at the sky and thinking the blue was particularly striking. He had never seen such a beautiful sky.

Closing his eyes, and prepared to cross over, he let go. As he did so, he felt a hand upon his forehead and warmth flood into him, but it was too late. He had already surrendered to death and could see Sarai waving to him from across the great river. He felt intense longing at the sight of her and a peaceful joy that they would soon be reunited. The boatman waited to ferry him across. All he needed was some coin.

Chapter Thirty-Eight

His eyes fluttered open. Stiger did not know where he was. It took him a moment to realize he was staring at the top of a tent. He coughed, his mouth tasting incredibly dry and foul. He felt like he had not moved in over a month. All of his limbs were stiff and his joints ached.

"You are awake."

Stiger turned his head. It required some effort to see Venthus moving to his side. He tried to speak and it came out as a feeble croak.

Venthus helped Stiger to sit up. The slave handed him a mug of wine, which Stiger greedily gulped down. He coughed as some of it went down the wrong pipe. Venthus took the mug away when it was empty.

Feeling a little better, Stiger glanced around his tent. A lamp hanging from the central pole had been lit. Stiger realized it was dark out. Night had fallen.

"How long?" Stiger managed and then cleared his throat before trying again. "How long have I been out?"

"A week, master," Venthus said.

Memory of the battle and fight with the minion flooded back in a rush. Stiger remembered dying. Alarmed, he felt for the wound the minion had inflicted upon him and at first could not find it. He lifted up his tunic to see. There was a small pink scar where the blade had pierced him. It was only a thin line, about an inch and a half in length.

Stiger traced his finger over the line. It hurt slightly as he touched it. He had been so sure the wound was mortal.

Stiger looked up at Venthus. "How did I survive?"

"That," said another voice, "is something I can answer for you."

Stiger turned his gaze toward the entrance. Thoggle stumped painfully into the tent.

"You may leave us," the wizard told the slave.

Venthus glanced at Stiger in question.

"I assure you, he will be quite all right with me," Thoggle said. "He and I have matters to discuss that are best spoken of in private."

Stiger nodded to Venthus.

"You must be hungry," Venthus said. "I will return with some stew, master."

Stiger had not realized how hungry he was. His stomach rumbled at the thought of food.

"I am ravenous," Stiger said. "Some stew would be wonderful."

Venthus bowed and stepped out of the tent.

Stiger felt incredibly weak. He was having difficulty just remaining in a sitting position. It took a surprising amount of effort to remain upright. He placed his hand down on the cot to better support himself.

"Your slave is extremely devoted to you," Thoggle said, glancing after Venthus. "He has not left your side since you were brought in here."

"He belonged to Delvaris," Stiger said. "I kind of inherited him."

"He strikes me as more than just a simple slave," Thoggle said. "It would do well for you to keep an eye upon him."

"What happened?" Stiger asked. He had thoroughly tired of games. "The legion, is she safe?"

"You defeated the minion," Thoggle said, coming closer to the cot. The wizard leaned heavily upon his staff. "Well, you and Rarokan beat it."

"And then what?" He had been out of action for a week. He desperately wanted to know what had occurred.

"We won." Thoggle took a seat on a stool by his bedside. "After the minion, their High Priest, and Therik's son fell, the orc army collapsed and fled soon after. It also helped they were being squeezed between two armies, one of which was gnomish. A few thousand of their more devout warriors made a stand near the northern end of the valley the next day and a second battle was fought. The man you call Salt led the legion quite well, I might add. The enemy was broken completely." Thoggle gave an amused grunt. "The gnomes are busy hunting down the survivors in the mountains. The end result is the orcs will squabble amongst themselves for years to come, tribe fighting tribe for dominance. Brogan will, of course, continue his games and add to their divisiveness. All in all, I think things turned out very well for us."

Stiger felt tremendous relief. It was like a weight had been lifted from his shoulders. The legion was safe, and the valley too. Sarai would be pleased with him. She had given him a precious gift, and that had been her love. She had made him want to be a better man, and he felt, in a way, that he was.

He had a recollection of her waving to him from across the river. She was holding hands with her daughter. Sarai's husband stood right behind her, a comforting hand on her shoulder. She seemed happy and smiled before turning away and disappearing to a place he couldn't follow. That last bit wasn't quite right. She had gone somewhere he couldn't yet go.

Stiger was comforted in knowing she wouldn't be alone, that she was with her family. And in a way, Stiger was with his—the legion. She would not be waiting for him. That much was clear.

"What of the future?" Stiger asked. "Everything will be as it should?"

"From what you told me when you first arrived in our time period, the final battle did not go down exactly as it had in your future, but I think it close enough to have set things nearly right. Well, I hope so at any rate."

Stiger gave a weary nod. He felt himself growing tired. Sleep beckoned like a long-lost friend.

"How did I survive?" Stiger asked, once again touching the scar. "That was a mortal wound. I felt Castor draining my life force."

Thoggle hesitated.

"Father Thomas healed me, didn't he?"

The wizard gave a nod, but something about his manner alarmed Stiger.

"Tell me," Stiger insisted.

"You were struck by a night blade," Thoggle said. "It is a dreadful weapon, almost as fearsome as Rarokan. To heal you from its grip—and one is never ever really healed from such a weapon—Father Thomas gave up his own life in favor of yours."

"No," Stiger whispered. He fell back onto his cot. "No, no, no! I was ready to die, to join Sarai. I saw her from across the river. I was so close. Why would he do that?"

"You cannot be permitted such an escape," Thoggle said. "You are the High Father's champion, the key instrument to our future. What Father Thomas did was noble. Be grateful for his sacrifice. Make sure you do not squander his gift."

Stiger placed a hand upon his forehead, devastated that the paladin had given up his own life so that he may yet live. His would be another shade that haunted Stiger's lonely nights.

Stiger cleared his throat.

"What of Dog?"

"No one has seen him since the battle," Thoggle said. "The last I saw him was after the minion struck him with a killing spell. Later, when there was time, I went looking for his corpse and found … well, nothing."

Stiger closed his eyes, feeling sick to his stomach as the grief at the passing of both Father Thomas and Dog threatened to overwhelm him. He focused on calming himself, slowly breathing in and out. When he opened his eyes next, he discovered he had fallen asleep. Thoggle was gone. Therik was sitting on a stool by his side, and the sun was up. He could see it shining through the tent. The orc helped him sit up.

"I am surprised you are still here," Stiger said.

"Why?"

"Don't you want to claim your kingdom?"

"There is no go back," Therik said. "I fought with you, and no more follow Castor. My people no take me. They see what I do."

"I'm sorry you can't go home."

"I not sorry," Therik said and pointed at Stiger. "You dragon and troll killer. Interesting things happen by you. I stay and see more, yes?"

"I have an elf friend who thinks as you do."

"I stay, yes?" Therik asked insistently. "As you offered?"

"Yes," Stiger said. "You can stay. I could always use another …" He paused, not quite believing what he was about to say, "friend."

"Hah!" Therik clapped his hands together, a smile breaking out. "Wizard says if I stay with you, more fighting coming. You give me sword. Now you must give armor. We kill many together. We make legend they sing of. You and I fight as friends, yes?"

Stiger felt himself become amused at Therik's genuine enthusiasm. Stiger felt that, in a way, he and Therik were kindred spirits.

"Yes," Stiger said, "my friend. We will fight together, and I promise I will get you some armor. Though I suspect the legion's armorer will have to make it from scratch."

Therik gave a pleased nod and then sobered.

"Don't forget, one day, as promised, I kill you."

"You can certainly try," Stiger said.

Therik bared his tusks at him in a grin.

Stiger noticed a cold bowl of stew had been set out on his camp table. He motioned for it. Therik handed it over to him. Stiger ate greedily. Though they said little after that, Therik remained with Stiger for a while. Venthus eventually shooed him out.

Belly full, a terrible tiredness stole over Stiger. He lay back down on his cot and went to sleep.

Chapter Thirty-Nine

Stiger knelt down at Sarai's grave under the apple tree, feeling a deep sense of loss. Oddly, someone had planted white flowers around the grave. They were like nothing he had ever seen, and very similar to roses but without the thorns. The scent of the flowers reminded Stiger of the rosewater Sarai had been fond of using on her hair.

Stiger wondered who had done it. He figured a neighbor had likely planted them. It was an act of kindness, and for that he was grateful. He thought Sarai would have appreciated the gesture.

He wished things had been different, but there was no changing that now. He was the High Father's champion and had work to do. He must go on. With such understanding came the sad realization that those around him might suffer for who he was. He felt bitter about that but knew in war there were no rules. He had no illusions he was fighting a war, one of the gods' own making.

Sarai had shown him something he had never before known. For that, he was grateful. Stiger took a deep, unhappy breath.

She had deserved better.

"High Father," Stiger prayed, bowing his head, "I ask that you take care of this woman, and her family."

Stiger sat down, leaning his back against the tree. He remained for a time, allowing the afternoon to wear on, then finally stood. This was his final goodbye. He would never return to this place.

It had been a week since he had woken from his wound and subsequent healing. He gazed around the ruined farm. The bodies of the dwarves and orcs had been removed. The orcs had been buried in a mass grave. The dwarves had cared for their dead, including Captain Aleric, according to their custom.

Stiger made his way over to the woodpile that he had labored at for so long. He picked up the rusted axe, which had been where he'd left it, embedded in the chopping stump. He turned the axe over a few times and then, with a dull thud, returned it to the stump.

Sabinus, along with a squadron of auxiliary troopers, had dismounted and tethered their horses. They waited a few yards away. The men talked amongst themselves or threw dice to kill time. Though there were no more orcs in the valley, Stiger was the legate. Everywhere he went, an escort would go with him, especially now that the officers and men of the legion knew his real identity.

He had told them all who he was and why he had pretended to be Delvaris. He had also shared the emperor's letter. Salt and Sabinus both had wholeheartedly supported his decision. Stiger had expected rejection or perhaps even outrage at the deception. Instead, the men had responded with devotion and—more surprising—loyalty mixed with sadness at the news of Delvaris's passing.

It had moved Stiger greatly but at the same time concerned him. They had witnessed him slay a dragon and kill a creature of an evil god in single combat. He had almost died for his troubles. In a way, they viewed him as a holy representative of their god and, though true, it made Stiger more than a little uncomfortable. He was just a man like any other, flawed and imperfect, with more than his fair share of regrets.

Sabinus and the escort respectfully gave him space as he worked his way around the farm. After a time, Stiger found himself in the barn. The walnuts he had harvested lay scattered across the floor. He grabbed one of the nets that had been thrown down on the floor and began gathering the nuts up. He tossed them into the net. These he had harvested with his own two hands. It was one last reminder of his time with Sarai, and for some reason he felt he could not leave them behind. He tied the net closed in a loose knot and slung it over a shoulder.

Stepping back out of the barn, he came to a stop. Dog waited just a few feet away. The animal's tongue hung out of his mouth, making the hairy beast look a little crazy. They stared at one another for a prolonged moment, Stiger's memories flashing back to more peaceful times at the farm. The memories were so vivid, he felt tears prick at his eyes.

Then the moment broke and Dog bounded up to him in greeting and jumped up, throwing his large paws onto Stiger's shoulders and licking his face vigorously. So enthusiastic was the greeting and tail wagging that Stiger was almost bowled over. He hugged the big animal's neck.

"All right, all right," Stiger said, laughing, "I'll admit it, I'm happy to see you too, boy."

"That's quite touching, don't you think?"

Stiger eased Dog down and saw both Menos and Thoggle standing just a few feet away. Thoggle had spoken.

Dog padded up to Menos and received a pat on the head, along with a thin-lipped smile.

"Your guardian has returned," Thoggle said, regarding the animal that was happily accepting a scratching on the neck from the noctalum. One of Dog's rear legs began to work as if he were scratching himself. "I am thinking this is a good sign."

"You plan on sending me back," Stiger said. "Is that why you are here?"

"To be exact, we plan on returning you to your time," Thoggle said.

"And I know how you're going to do it, too," Stiger said.

"You do?" Menos said, raising an eyebrow.

"See?" Thoggle said with a grin. "I told you he wasn't as stupid as he looks."

"Thanks," Stiger said. The wizard seemed more relaxed than Stiger had seen ever him. So, too, did the noctalum. They were almost friendly.

"Has Rarokan said anything?" Thoggle asked.

"No," Stiger said with a glance down at the sword. "Since I woke up, he hasn't said a word. I can't even sense his presence. I am starting to wonder if he's dead."

"Dead," Thoggle repeated with a look at Stiger's sword. "In an attempt to save you from Castor's touch, it's possible he gave you everything, including his own soul spark. Doubtful, but possible."

"Rarokan only cares for himself. He would do no such thing," Menos said.

Thoggle gave a shrug.

"He will take instruction from me to discipline his mind," Menos said, taking his hand from Dog and pointing a delicate finger at Stiger. "He will do it. That is non-negotiable, wizard."

Thoggle turned back to Stiger. "Yes, you will."

"You won't hear me argue," Stiger said, holding up his hands. "If he's still in there, I'd rather be safe than sorry."

"There is hope for him," Menos said. "You may be correct about this human not being as stupid as he looks."

"Did you both come here to insult me?"

"Partly," Thoggle said. "But really we came to speak with you about your future, and I mean that quite literally."

"Are you certain the future will be the same?" Stiger asked. "Events did not unfold as they should have, or as I understood them to have. The minion cheated, so I did also by sending Sabinus and Brogan to the upriver crossing. That was opposite from what I know happened." Stiger paused a moment, thinking it through. "In hindsight, I guess it was a good thing I chose to cheat too."

"You did?" Menos asked with what Stiger took to be mild surprise, mixed in with a hint of irritation. "I take back what I just said about you not being stupid."

Thoggle shot the noctalum an unhappy look and then turned back to Stiger.

"As you are aware, we don't fully understand how time works," Thoggle said. "We do believe there are a set of rules by which the gods abide. Whether that is mandatory or by mutual agreement, we simply do not know. We know for certain little things can be changed, but not important events."

"Had Castor succeeded in killing you in our time period," Menos added, "we think there would've been profound consequences. That would have been a serious event modification. The war amongst the gods would have, in all likelihood, escalated as other gods moved to bend the same rules to gain advantage over the others. Chaos would have followed."

"So ... you think these rules are most likely adhered to by mutual consent of all the gods?" Stiger asked. "As opposed to being mandatory rules that cannot be broken?"

"We believe it to be that way," Thoggle confirmed. "But again, we do not know. You must understand, this is only supposition"

"In answer to your original question, when you return we don't know what you will face," Menos said. "We hope it will be the time stream you left behind, albeit with very minor changes. In truth, it could be another reality, ours and not the one you came from. Again, we are unsure. We do know that once you return, as the High Father's champion there are other alignments that will seek to stop you. We both agree your greatest trials are to come."

"Fantastic," Stiger said. "You both are rays of sunshine. Do you ever bring good news?"

"We tell you how we see it," Thoggle said.

Stiger rubbed the back of his neck and glanced down at his feet. A moment later, he looked back up at them.

"Well, then," Stiger said. "I've been thinking about going back, and I have some ideas I would like you both to consider."

"About that," Thoggle said. "Before we go further, you should know it will take us time to prepare for your return."

"How much time?" Stiger asked.

"We think two to three years, maybe more," Thoggle answered. "I need to store up the necessary *will*." Thoggle paused and held his thumb and index finger slightly apart from one another. "And ... there are a few *tiny* things you and Brogan must do first."

Stiger looked from wizard to noctalum and back again, suddenly wary.

"I am not going to like this, am I?"

"Probably not," the noctalum said. "It starts with the elves."

"You must get something for us," Thoggle said.

"Let me guess," Stiger said, "the elves will not want to part with it?"

"I may have to once again revise my opinion of your intelligence level," Menos said.

"Great," Stiger said and shook his head, wondering what madness they wanted him to undertake. "Just bloody great."

Epilogue

(The Present)

Braddock, thane of the dwarves, looked upon the hole in the air between the two crystal pillars. It was black, ominous, and appeared bottomless. The Gate room throbbed with power, so much so it made the hairs on his arms and the back of his neck stand on end. The minion had stepped through the hole just moments before, escaping through the portal to the past.

"I will go also," Braddock said to Stiger and Father Thomas, the words escaping his mouth before his brain could catch up. He stepped forward.

"No," Ogg said forcefully before being consumed by a wracking cough. "You must not. Only the two of them go back."

"You've known this?" Braddock asked, becoming irritated with the wizard.

"From the moment my master took me on as an apprentice," the wizard said. "I have been preparing for this my entire life."

"Thoggle knew also?" Braddock asked, stunned by the magnitude of what had been concealed from him. He was the thane. They should have told him.

"Thoggle waits on the other side," Ogg told him, coughing. Blood flecked his lips, which twisted into a sneer. "As does Brogan, your father."

"My father," Braddock said, gazing toward the portal with an intense longing. Gods, he missed his father. What he would not give to see him again, to speak with him just one more time. He almost took a step forward toward the portal.

"You must remain," Ogg implored him. "Stiger must go. It is his destiny, his fate. He is the Tiger that the Oracle has spoken of."

"The Tiger's Fate?" Braddock whispered, his mind racing as he thought back on the oracle's writings. If what Ogg said was true, Stiger's future held a potential fate that was worse than death. "No..."

"Now you understand, Braddock," Ogg said. "The sword has always been meant for him, forged for his hand alone. He was not simply the restorer of the Compact, but also the direct instrument of prophecy, an important game piece of the gods."

"I..." Braddock turned to Stiger, completely shaken to his core. He was at a loss for words. He took a breath and settled for truth. "At first, I thought I would dislike you, but I've since learned you are a man of great legend. For that, you have my respect. Upon my personal legend, I will be here when you return through the World Gate. I will wait for you."

"The sword," Stiger asked, looking over at the wizard. "What of it?"

"You must master it... before it masters you," Ogg said, and broke into a coughing fit, which wracked his body terribly. The wizard sucked in a ragged breath and almost fell to his knees. "I cannot hold the Gate open for much longer... You have to go!"

Braddock watched as Stiger held the wizard's gaze for a moment more then moved toward the Gate. He shared a glance with Father Thomas. Stiger regarded the hole for several heartbeats, then took a deep breath, as if about to jump into a pond. He stepped through, vanishing in an instant, as if he'd never been. Father Thomas followed and vanished a moment later.

It had happened so fast that Braddock blinked in shock, then started as thunderclap snapped loudly about the Gate room.

"Ogg! What have you done?" Braddock demanded, staring at the World Gate in horror. The portal had closed and everything had gone silent.

"Only what was necessary," the wizard replied, straightening up.

Ogg had aged years in mere moments. Had Braddock not witnessed it, he would have thought it impossible.

"You promised you would hold open the World Gate," Braddock said.

"I did nothing of the sort," Ogg snapped.

"You lied." Braddock took a step backward. He had never known Ogg to deliberately lie. "You are truly without honor."

"I never lied," Ogg said, his lip twisting with a sneer. "I told them both that as long as there is a wizard of great power holding the Gate open, travel between both sides is possible. I never promised to bring them back."

Braddock looked at Ogg, not quite believing what he was hearing. Without Stiger, the Oracle's prophecy could not be completed. They were all doomed.

"Braddock, it had to be done. Sending them back was the only way."

"How does that help us?" Braddock demanded.

"Look around." Ogg gestured about them. Braddock looked, and could now see beyond the columns. Where before there had been fire and smoke, now only a haze of smoke remained. The scene about the Gate room was one of complete desolation. It had been fairly wrecked. Braddock was relieved to see that Currose was stirring and showing signs life. The great dragon had survived her encounter with the minion, and a wizard. Of her mate, nothing could be seen. Braddock wondered where he was.

"Legate Stiger and Father Thomas set things right," Ogg said, flashing Braddock a tired smile. The wizard seemed pleased with himself. "They succeeded."

"And died!" Braddock raged at the wizard. "You sent them back to die."

"I sent them back to set things right," Ogg countered, "which they did. Dying was only a natural end to a means."

"You dare jest at a time like this? Who will make the choice?" Braddock pressed, becoming angry. "Who will choose when it is time?"

"Someone will," Ogg said in a tired tone of indifference. "Someone always does."

"The Oracle said—"

"That is but one interpretation."

"One interpretation," Braddock said, feeling sick. "Or just yours?"

"Does it really matter at this point?" Ogg asked him wearily. "I was doing as I had to. There was never any other choice to be made. Thoggle knew this when he set me down this torturous path."

A clash of steel drew their attention toward the stairs and platform, which led back up to Grata'Jalor. Braddock was surprised that the balcony had remained intact. The sound of fighting intensified and drew nearer.

"I am too weak to fight." Ogg gripped the staff tightly. "All of my energy is spent. I have none left. Your sword may be required, My Thane."

Braddock hefted the sword that was still in his hand. Hrove's warriors held Grata'Jalor. What a fool he had been to trust Hrove with such a critical task. It had nearly cost them everything. Braddock would call him to account. Such a betrayal could not be forgiven, and the payment for Hrove's actions deserved to be remembered for an age. As the fighting grew closer, Braddock resolved to make an example of Hrove that future generations would have difficulty forgetting.

Ogg and Braddock waited. The dragon roused herself, but it was clear she was in no condition to put up much of a fight. Dark reddish blood flowed freely from numerous wounds, pooling in the dust and around the debris. She looked at them rather blearily, and then up toward the balcony, from which an intense struggle could be heard. Screams, shouts, orders, and oaths echoed down to them from the passageway.

The fight abruptly ended, punctuated by an agonized scream. This was followed by several indecipherable shouts and the pounding of many feet. Human legionaries burst onto the balcony, followed closely by Naggock, commander of Braddock's bodyguard.

Intensely relieved, Braddock let his sword fall, point resting upon the stone floor. The dragon allowed her head drop. It landed with a solid thud that he felt through his boots.

"My Thane," Naggock greeted from above before starting down the stairs. "I am relieved you live."

"No more than I," Braddock said.

Several more shouts and orders could be heard beyond the balcony. Sabinus and Eli emerged into the gate room. They stopped briefly to survey the scene below and then made their way down the stairs and warily passed the wounded dragon.

"Tell me, what is going on out there?" Braddock asked Naggock.

"It seems with the gates to the mountain closed, Hrove never expected to have to defend Grata'Jalor," Naggock said. "The majority of his warriors appear to be in Old City." A look of concern passed over Naggock's face. He lowered his voice. "We think they have attacked the human refugees from the valley."

"Gods." Braddock did not like the sound of that. If Hrove's warriors slaughtered the humans, it would make relations going forward very difficult. "We will need to bring the army into the mountain and make sure we can save as many as possible."

"We think the other dragon is in Old City, too," Naggock continued.

"My mate is in Old City," Currose told them, without bothering to lift her head. Her weak voice trembled. "I have let him know the World Gate is safe. He has told me what is left of Hrove's warband is fleeing the city."

"They are fleeing your mate, then," Braddock said.

"No," Currose answered, "they are not."

Sabinus glanced around. "Where is the legate?"

Braddock looked over at Ogg before turning back to the centurion. "He has gone through the World Gate, back in time, to set things right."

"I see," Sabinus said and smiled oddly, sheathing his sword. "I can't tell you how very pleased I am to hear that."

Braddock could not understand the centurion's reaction. "I am afraid he is not coming back."

Eli looked with sad eyes upon the World Gate.

"You knew his fate," Ogg accused, catching the elf's look. "Do not deny it."

"I will not," Eli replied with sadness. "Ben Stiger was a good friend. I have always known he would go without me into the past."

"Who will make the choice?" Braddock asked again. "He who is spoken of by the oracle is gone. Who will make the choice that must be made?"

"I will," a voice rang out from the balcony above.

Braddock knew that voice. He looked up and blinked. It could not be true.

"It is my fate, and my responsibility to make that choice. I will accept none other in my place."

Braddock looked over to Ogg, who appeared just as stunned. The wizard's mouth hung open in astonishment.

Impossibly, it was Stiger.

The legate walked calmly down the stairs and over to them. The largest dog Braddock had ever seen followed him down the stairs. The dragon picked her head up off of the floor and regarded the legate. He nodded respectfully as he passed. The dog padded up to the dragon and their muzzles briefly touched and then parted. It was almost as if the two knew each other. Braddock shook his head and turned his gaze back to Stiger.

The legate looked different than when Braddock had last seen him, just moments ago. The hair around his temples had grayed slightly, and his face looked older, more lined. Humans aged much quicker than dvergr, but even this seemed excessive. Braddock had no doubt this was the same man who had stepped through the World Gate, it was just that he was somehow older. There was also a tinge of sadness about him.

"How?" Ogg breathed with a glance back at the World Gate. Then his eyes widened, and he began a low, harsh cackle, which turned into a deep belly laugh. Tears streamed from his eyes. "Thoggle, you old fixer… only you would pull one over on me like this… only you."

"What do you mean?" Braddock demanded of Ogg. "You just told me he died in the past. Here he is, alive and well. Explain yourself."

"The Tomb of the Thirteenth," Ogg said. "Thoggle preserved the legate in stasis, just as he did First Cohort." Ogg paused and turned to Stiger. "Garrack probably woke you when he did Sabinus. You stayed hidden so that you would not affect the flow of the time stream."

"It is true," Stiger said to Braddock in the language of the dvergr. He was fluent in it, with just a touch of an accent. "Though it has only been minutes for you, I've not seen you in years. You should know I counted your father a very good friend. I hope you and I will one day grow as close."

"My father?" Braddock asked in his own language.

"Brogan, Theo, and I spent many nights seeing who could out-drink the others. I am not ashamed to admit I often lost."

"Theo?" Braddock asked, confused.

"Theogdin," Stiger said.

"Garrack's father," Braddock said with a nod, suddenly feeling the pain of the loss of his closest friend. "He was my father's spymaster."

"And a good friend," Stiger said.

Braddock looked closer at the legate. Stiger had aged, but it was still the same man, just older and wiser. He was a man of two worlds now, Braddock thought, both the past and present. It was really remarkable.

"Your father gave me this," Stiger said, pulling a scroll from a pocket in his cloak. He handed it over. Braddock's hand trembled as he took it. "It is a letter from father to son. He asked that you open it in private. I believe it to be thoroughly personal."

Braddock looked down at the scroll and felt a moistness in his eyes he was oddly not ashamed of. He nodded thankfully and tucked it away in a pocket. Later, when he had time and some privacy, he would open it.

Stiger turned to Eli. There was a moment of silence as they regarded one another.

"I know why you chose me all those years ago," Stiger said, switching back to common.

"One day, I knew you would," Eli said, "though I never expected you to become a friend."

"I know. It is good to see you again," Stiger said and stepped forward to hug his friend. They slapped each other upon the back.

"You have returned," Eli said simply as they broke apart. "That is all that matters and what I had hoped for."

"Yes," Stiger said.

"How long has it been?" Eli asked, raising an eyebrow.

"A little over five years," Stiger said, "give or take a month."

Eli gave a nod.

Stiger turned to Sabinus with a warm smile. "And you, it must have been torture not saying anything to me."

"Yes, sir," Sabinus said with a broad smile. "It was, but I knew what was at stake. It was some of the men that had the hardest time of it. Welcome back, sir."

"Very good." Stiger clapped the centurion fondly on the shoulder.

"Where is Father Thomas?" Braddock asked. The effect of that question on Stiger was profound. A look of deep sadness and loss crossed his face.

"Father Thomas will not be joining us." The legate turned to Ogg. "How long do we have until the planes align?"

"Around twenty-four months," Ogg answered, to which Stiger nodded.

There were some raised voices coming from above. Several legionaries appeared on the platform, along with an armed orc in legionary officer armor. Braddock grew angry at the sight of the creature.

"What is the meaning of this?" Braddock demanded Stiger.

"Oh, him?" Stiger looked over and jerked a thumb at the orc. "He's with me, and we have a present for you."

The dragon eyed the orc but did nothing other than watch. Braddock noticed the orc was carrying a gagged and bound dvergr down the stairs. The orc was holding the dvergr with one arm around the midriff as if he were a giant doll.

"Therik," Sabinus said as the orc stepped by the centurion. "Good to see you again."

The orc nodded and then tossed the bound dvergr down in front of Braddock, where he landed hard on his stomach and released an *umff.* Therik kicked the dvergr and then used his foot to roll him over on his back.

"Thane Braddock," Stiger said, "I present you with Hrove, chieftain of the Hammer Fisted Clan. He is your prisoner now. You may do with him as you wish."

Braddock glanced down. Hrove looked to have been thoroughly beaten. Braddock looked back up at Stiger in question.

"How?"

"My legionaries are cleaning out Old City of Hrove's filth," Stiger said. "I knew you would want to get your hands on him, so we made sure to take this traitorous bastard alive."

"Your legionaries were outside the mountain," Braddock said, confused. "They wouldn't have had time to get to Old City."

"Not those legionaries," Stiger said and then grinned. "I brought much of the Thirteenth back with me. I have eight thousand men cleaning out Old City." Stiger glanced down at Hrove. "The bastard intended on massacring the refugees. They didn't expect to find us waiting for them. His warriors never had a chance."

Braddock looked down at Hrove. The chieftain's eyes locked fearfully on his thane. Braddock felt himself smile. He knelt down beside Hrove. The chieftain trembled.

"We're gonna have some fun together, I think," Braddock said and patted Hrove gently on the chest. "Yes, it's gonna be a scream."

Hrove tried to say something but the gag prevented it.

"Save your breath," Braddock said, patting Hrove once again on the chest again. "You will need it, especially with all you have to answer for."

He stood and turned to Stiger.

"Thank you, for this little present," Braddock said. "I can't tell you how much it means to me."

"I thought you would approve," Stiger said and then turned to the orc. "Braddock, may I introduce Therik, a former king and a follower of the High Father."

Braddock turned his gaze upon the orc and then what Stiger had said hit home. This orc followed the High Father and not Castor. It was shocking, for he had never heard of such a thing happening. Therik offered Braddock a nod, which he returned.

“I knew Brogan,” Therik said. “He good dwarf. Strong drinker.” Therik tapped his chest armor. “I better.”

“Right,” Stiger said and glanced around the Gate Room. “I am going to leave you with Hrove and get back to my men to help them clean up the city.” He paused and turned back to Braddock. “We still have the Cyphan to deal with, and they have an army. Then we have to get the Key from the emperor, hopefully before the enemy can. I am afraid he is in danger. So, lots to do, you see.”

“The Key?” Braddock asked with a frown. “You don’t mean to open the World Gate, do you?”

“I want the Key in my possession,” Stiger said, “so someone else cannot make that choice for me.”

Stiger turned away, with Therik following, and started for the stairs. He stopped on the first step and turned back.

“Sabinus, Eli, you both are with me.” Stiger started up the stairs. “Dog, come.”

End of Book 4

A Note from the Author

I want to thank you for reading *The Tiger's Time.* I sincerely hope you enjoyed it. Stiger's journey will continue in *The Tiger's Wrath,* out in 2019! Writing a book like this takes a tremendous amount of time, effort, and energy. A review would be awesome and greatly appreciated.

Important: If you have not yet given my other series—Tales of the Seventh or The Karus Saga—a shot, I strongly recommend you do. All three series are linked and set in the same universe. There are hints, clues, and Easter Eggs sprinkled throughout the series.

The Series:

There are three series to consider. I began telling Stiger and Eli's story in the middle years... starting with Stiger's Tigers, published in 2015. *Stiger's Tigers* is a great place to start reading. It was the first work I published and is a grand fantasy epic.

Stiger, Tales of the Seventh, covers Stiger's early years. It begins with Stiger's first military appointment as a wet-behind-the-ears lieutenant serving in Seventh Company during the very beginning of the war against the Rivan on the frontier. This series sees Stiger cut his teeth and develop into the hard charging leader that fans have grown to love. It also introduces Eli and covers many of their early adventures. These tales should in no way spoil your experience with *Stiger's Tigers.* In fact, I believe they will only enhance it.

The Karus Saga is a whole new adventure set in the same universe ... many years before Stiger was even born. This series tells how Roman legionaries made their way to the world of Istros and the founding of the empire. It is set amidst a war of the gods and is full of action, intrigue, adventure, and mystery.

Give them a shot and hit me up on Facebook to let me know what you think!

Best regards and again thank you for reading!

Marc

Join Marc's Newsletter

Stay up to date! Care to be notified when the next book is released and receive updates from the author? Join the mailing list! You can find it on Marc's website:

http://www.MAEnovels.com
Facebook: Marc Edelheit Author
https://www.facebook.com/MAENovels/

Made in the USA
Monee, IL
21 August 2021

76228652R00444